Imhotep

JERRY DUBS

Copy editing by Ted Palik

teddpal@hotmail.com

Cover design by Kyle Mohler

kcmohlerdesign@gmail.com

Cover photograph by Jerry Dubs

ISBN-13: 9781519070289

FOR DEB

Thank you for taking this adventure with me.

CONTENTS

ACKNOWLEDGEMENTS

Originally self-published as an ebook, "Imhotep" quickly began to generate reviews. Many were encouraging. Many suggested improvements. Some were rather critical. Some pointed out errors. Considering each of them important, I re-wrote passages, I deleted sections, I corrected errors. What you hold now is the result of several years of collaboration. Thank you to the hundreds and hundreds of readers who offered their praise, encouragement, criticism and observations.

IN THE TWO LANDS

KING DJOSER - Ruler of The Two Lands (also called Kemet)

Hesire - King Djoser's personal physician

Imhotep - Royal architect, adviser and physician

Inetkawes - King Djoser's wife

Kanakht - Vizier to King Djoser and to Djoser's father, King Khasekhemwy

Sekhmire - Commander of the palace guard

Sati - His wife

Siptah - His son

Prince Teti - Son of King Djoser, Prince of The Two Lands

His personal guards:

Bata, Meryptah (brother of Meryt at Iunu), **Nesi** (brother of Makare at Khmunu), and **Rensi**

AT IUNU, TEMPLE OF RE

Hetephernebti - Sister of King Djoser, and High Priestess to the sun god Re

Meryt - Wbt-priestess in Temple of Re

AT KHMUNU

Makare - Commander of guards at Khmunu, brother of Nesi

Nimaasted - Priest of Thoth at Khmunu

Tama - "Voice of Truth" for the goddess Ma'at

Samut - Messenger in service of Tama

Waja-Hur - High Priest of Thoth, scribe of the company of gods

AT SAQQARA and INEB-HEDJ

Paneb - Chief artist at the necropolis of Saqqara

    Ahmes - His adopted son

    Dedi - His oldest daughter

    Hapu - His youngest daughter

Jarha - A friend of Paneb

Takhaaenbbastet - Paneb's wife

AT TO-SHE and KOM OMBO, TEMPLES OF SOBEK

Djefi - First Prophet of the crocodile god Sobek

Bakr - a guard at the Temple of Sobek

Dagi - A boatman for High Priest Djefi

Karem - A boatman for Djefi

    Kem - Karem's wife

    Kiya - Karem's daughter

Neswy - Yunet's uncle

Pahket - Servant girl

Sesostris - Priest of Sobek and stepfather to Djefi

Siamun - Commander of the guards at the Temple of Sobek

Yunet - Chantress at the Temple of Sobek, sister of Djefi, former wife of Siamun

AT ABU, TEMPLE OF KHNUM

Rudamon - Physician at the Temple of Khnum

Sennufer - Priest of Khnum at Abu, father of Sekhmire

PROLOGUE

Waja-Hur, Reckoner of Times and Seasons, was confused.

Holding a charcoal drawing stick in his hand, he stood halfway down the tomb's unfinished hallway. He wiped his hand against his white linen kilt, leaving behind a black smudge.

His frail body quivered slightly as he stretched himself to examine the hieroglyphs drawn along the top edge of the wall. His own hand had drawn them, he was sure. He was, after all, Scribe of the Company of Gods, high priest for the god Thoth. He had been drawing hieroglyphs all of his life. He recognized his work.

But the hieroglyphs were wrong.

Where he had meant to draw the symbol for eternity, he had instead drawn the hieroglyphs for a hundred lifetimes.

Waja-Hur shook his head.

A hundred lifetimes was a long time, a very long time. One lifetime was proving to be too long and wearisome for him. There was no one left alive from his youth. His children had grown old and passed on. Their children were growing old now, and still he lingered in The Two Lands, a tired old man ready to make the final journey to Khert-Neter.

He sighed.

A hundred more lifetimes would be enough for him, but the Book of the Dead called for eternity, and Kanakht, vizier to King Djoser, ruler of The Two Lands, deserved nothing less.

The inscription over the false door must invite Kanakht to pass through it to The Fields of Reeds for eternity, not for a hundred lifetimes. As they were drawn now, the symbols created a doorway that would open after the passage of five thousand years.

What had he been thinking?

He picked up a rag to wipe away the incorrect symbols.

Down the long hallway, at the entrance to the tomb, the boy who was holding the reflecting disk sneezed. The polished brass plate the boy was holding jiggled, making the sunlight that angled into the tomb swirl.

Waja-Hur gave a small gasp at the illusion of motion. Putting his hand on the wall to steady himself, he dropped the rag. As he bent to pick up the dirty cloth, he felt a wave of dizziness, as if he were spinning like a dancer at one of Re's festivals.

Squatting, he leaned against the wall and waited for the feeling to pass. These moments of unease had started several floods ago. At first he had thought they were harbingers of his own passage to The Fields of Reeds, like ibises flying before the great flood, but they had proven to be merely another annoyance, another burden added to the weight of his long life.

Breathing slowly and deeply, he waited for the world to stop spinning around him. Then he stood, charcoal-smudged cloth in hand, and tried to remember what he had been doing. It had seemed important, but now it was gone.

Shaking his head in frustration, he turned to walk toward light.

DISAPPEARANCE AT SAQQARA

Tim Hope abandoned his fight against the sand.

It coated his sandals and feet; it had worked its way into his backpack. It was in his hair and in the webs between his fingers. Sitting with his back propped against the remains of a wall that once had formed the southern border of King Djoser's funerary complex, Tim was surrounded by Egypt's desert sand.

He put his pencil down and rubbed his hands together, trying to brush away the gritty sand.

A series of shadows crossed over him as a khaki-dressed guide led a ragged line of tourists past him. Their legs moved awkwardly as they took exaggerated high steps to keep sand from trickling into their shoes.

Tim watched them pass and then turned his attention back to the notebook propped against his knees. He added finishing lines to a pencil sketch of his bare feet, crossed at the ankles, sandals dangling loose. In the background of his drawing, desert dunes stretched off to a cloudless western horizon. Off to the east, behind his feet, the rough, pitted blocks of the Step Pyramid rose, angling off the edge of his paper.

In the top left corner of the drawing he wrote, "Addy, There's sand between my toes, under my fingernails and in my hair. I hate it. I hate the way it finds its way into every piece of clothing. I hate how dirty it is. I hate how gritty it feels."

He reread the words he had written to his fiancée. He thought about erasing the angry words and replacing them with something more upbeat, but it was hot, he was tired, and he missed her terribly. The sand was annoying, but he knew that his anger was really aimed at Addy's absence.

"That's Djoser's Step Pyramid off to my right. It's less impressive than it should be because there's nothing here to compare it to. I know it's huge, but not compared to the sky and the endless desert. And all this . . ." he paused, searching for the right adjective, then gave up and wrote simply "sand."

He closed the journal and held it off his lap so he could stretch one leg and then the other. The tourists had gathered around the base of the pyramid. The interior of the ancient tomb was no longer open to the public, so they listened to a description of passageways, chambers and shafts that lay beneath King Djoser's burial monument. When he finished his memorized recitation, the guide directed them around to the north side of the pyramid to see a statue of the long-dead king.

As the tourists shuffled away, three of them hesitated, then turned and walked quickly in Tim's direction. The shortest of them, an Arab wearing a blue-and-white-striped galabia, led the way. The other two appeared to be an American couple.

She wore blue jeans and a white T-shirt with a picture of Sylvester the Cat. Instead of the leather sandals most natives wore, she wore hiking shoes. Thin, with red hair beneath a straw hat, she had a complexion that the Egyptian sun, even now, at the end of winter, could burn through in an hour. Tim hoped she was wearing a heavy sun block.

The man wore sunglasses and a Boston Red Sox baseball cap, a loud Hawaiian shirt with large flowers, khaki shorts and black and red high-top sneakers. Tall and powerfully built, he walked with the loose, graceful gait of an athlete.

As they passed by him, Tim saw that the woman was frowning. Her eyes darted from the guide to her friend and then to the uneven sand. She seemed worried and upset, as if she didn't want to be here. Something about her – her size, her demeanor or perhaps just her frown – made Tim worry about her.

The man was smiling around a large wad of gum, which he chewed energetically. He paused every few steps to scan the tomb site. During one pause, he raised his sunglasses and, looking straight at Tim, winked and then, with long easy strides, he caught up with the guide and the woman.

They seemed an unlikely couple.

Addy and I probably seemed like an odd couple, Tim thought.

Addy was tall and slender with blonde hair, usually pulled back in a tight pony tail. Her eyes were bright and questioning. Tim was short and dark skinned with curly black hair. He had a sleepy look that made people think he was too relaxed, perhaps even a little slow.

We probably looked like strangers, he thought, thrown together by chance.

The guide led the Americans past Tim to a small, mud-brick guardhouse that stood over the entrance to the Tomb of Kanakht. Tim knew that, like the Step Pyramid, the tomb was closed to the public; he had tried to talk his way past the guard just an hour ago.

As they got closer to the tomb, the guide called out a greeting in Arabic. He and the tourists waited by the gate. The guard, who had been resting in the shade behind the building, walked slowly around the corner, wiping sand from his hands onto his uniform pants.

The guard and the guide spoke quietly. American dollars changed hands. The guard opened the iron gate, and the guide and the couple disappeared inside the dark doorway.

As soon as they were out of sight, the guard shut the gate and returned to the shady side of the building.

Tim had heard that you could gain entrance to a "closed" tomb with the right bribe. His problem was that he didn't know how large the bribe had to be to work. Addy just would have confronted the guard and demanded to know how much money he wanted. Tim thought that such a direct approach wouldn't work here in Egypt where train schedules were viewed as gentle suggestions and prices were hints written in chalk.

When he had talked with the guard earlier Tim hadn't raised the subject of a bribe. He thought there had to be an etiquette about it, but it wasn't covered in any of the guidebooks he'd read. At least now he knew that American dollars, not Egyptian pounds, were the correct currency.

Tim opened his journal and pulled out a sketch he had made of the layout of the Saqqara complex.

The small pyramid of Unis, not much more than a crumbling mound of limestone blocks, lay behind him and off to his left, just beyond the southern wall. He had passed it on his way in to the courtyard of the Step Pyramid. To the north was the Serdab, a small chamber in which the only known statue of Djoser had been found.

That's where the rest of the tourists probably are, he thought.

They would be taking turns peering through a small spy-hole in the enclosure to look at the statue. The real statue was in Cairo; the face that stared back at the tourists was a reproduction.

He had seen the Serdab earlier that day when he was making his sketch of the grounds. Now he was waiting until the tourist buses departed so that he could spend uninterrupted time sketching the long-dead king. He had dismissed the cab that had brought him the fourteen miles from Cairo to Saqqara. If he couldn't catch a ride with a late-arriving tourist, he would walk the short distance into Memphis and find a ride there.

Tim got to his feet and stretched. Opening his backpack, he put his notebook map away, took a drink from one of the water bottles in his pack and then swung the pack onto his shoulder. Just then the guard reappeared from behind the building and shouted through the iron gate at the entrance of Kanakht's tomb.

Pulling the gate open, the guard leaned into the doorway as if listening to someone. He jerked back as the guide rushed out of the tomb.

Outside the doorway, the guide stopped and looked around. His eyes swept the area, resting for a moment on Tim. Turning back to the guard, he waved his arms as he talked. He pointed at the open doorway and moved closer to the guard, talking and shaking his head in disbelief at the guard's shrugs of denial.

When he shook an accusing finger too close to the guard's face, the guard pushed him away.

Surprised, the guide staggered backward, swinging his arms to keep his balance. He caught himself and then leaned forward to rush back at the guard, but stopped when he saw that the guard had drawn a billy club from his belt and was waiting with it cocked in his hand.

Drawing himself up to the little height that he had, the guide extended his arms toward the guard, his hands unclenched, apologizing. The guard shook his head and waved the billy club, shooing him away.

The guide walked off, glaring back over his shoulder at the guard. After a few steps he stopped and, changing direction, approached Tim, who was still standing by the wall.

"Excuse me, 'cusez-moi. English, Français?" he asked.

"English," Tim said. Although he knew some Arabic, he thought the guide's English would probably be better.

"A mistake," the guide said, indicating the guard with a slight tilt of his head.

Tim waited.

"You saw us into the tomb, yes?"

Tim nodded. "Yes."

"Where did they go?"

"I'm sorry?" Tim said.

"The man, the woman. The tall man, the woman with the hair red. You saw them. Where they went? Which way?"

"I didn't see them come out."

The guide looked ready to lose his temper, but he forced a smile. "You didn't see? No? You are playing funny with the policeman?" He nodded again at the guard.

Tim shook his head. He hadn't been watching the tomb, but he was sure that he would have seen the couple leave.

"No," he said. "No joke, no funny. I'm sorry, I didn't see them come up. I think they are still in there."

"No, no, not there." The guide dismissed the idea. "You are a mistake. They came up."

Tim almost smiled at the guide's English, but he saw that beneath his bluster the man was worried; he hated to see tourists and their American dollars disappear.

Tim held up his hand. "Honest. I did not see them come up. And anyhow, where would they have gone? The bus is still here." He pointed to the parking lot. He saw that a taxi cab was sitting beside the bus. He hadn't noticed it before, but his back had been to the lot.

"Yes, where?" the guide said. Then he suddenly whirled in a circle, as if expecting the couple to be sneaking up behind him. "Always the funny. Here … not here."

"Maybe they are in the taxi," Tim suggested.

The guide shook his head. "My taxi." He pulled keys from the pocket of his robe and dangled them in front of Tim. The guide bounced from one foot to the other, thinking. Then he said, "You tell them Hamzah gone without them. They walk to Mena House. Very funny. Yes."

The guide walked to his cab, his head turning to look around the complex, expecting the Americans to suddenly reappear. Tim looked over at the Tomb of Kanakht. The guard was watching him.

Tim shifted the weight of the backpack and then looked back up at the guard, who continued to watch him. Then he remembered the worried look on the woman's face and a sense of unease stole over him.

Something happened down there, he thought to himself. Something happened and the guide and guard are trying to cover it up. Their shoving match was just a distraction staged for me.

He stood there for a moment wrestling with his conscience and then he heard Addy's voice telling him what to do. Reluctantly, he approached the guard.

"I didn't see them come up either," Tim said as he approached the guard.

"No English."

Earlier he and the guard had talked in English for fifteen minutes. Tim wondered if he laughed now and made a joke of the guard's stiff response, would the guard relax and laugh with him? But the man's face was pinched and angry.

"Right," Tim said under his breath as he tried to compose his thoughts in Arabic.

"No English," the guard repeated.

Tim switched to Arabic: "I didn't see them go."

"Closed to public," the guard answered in English.

Tim stayed with Arabic. "The man and woman didn't come out. Are they there?" he pointed to the tomb entrance. "Should we see?"

"No one there. Closed to public."

Tim shook his head. "They went in. Not come out," he said in Arabic. He felt like he was negotiating the price of a counterfeit tomb relic.

"No one there. Closed to public." The guard's hand played with the billy club. He blinked and his right leg started to bounce.

"We should see," Tim insisted.

The guard shook his head. "No one there."

"Can we see?"

"No one there. Closed to public."

Off to his right, Tim heard voices as the group of tourists, finished staring at Djoser's statue, emerged from behind the Step Pyramid and began walking toward him headed for the Pyramid of Unis. He watched them high-step carefully through the sand. Then he looked down at the sand by the entrance to the Tomb of Kanakht. It was filled with footprints leading into the tomb.

The guard followed Tim's gaze and saw the footsteps. He scuffed at the sand, wiping out the prints, and then stood in front of the gate, his arms folded across his chest.

"Closed to public."

Tim and the guard stared at each other for a moment, and then Tim shook his head and looked out to the parking lot.

Hamzah and the taxi were gone.

It's possible, Tim thought, that the couple came out of the tomb while the guard was around back. I had my head down writing in my journal. They could have slipped past me and went to hide in the back of the cab. Maybe they are heading back to Cairo with Hamzah now. He remembered the playful smile on the American's face. Perhaps he had planned to play a joke. Or maybe the girl felt ill and they had gone to the taxi for her to rest.

Or they could have crossed over to the colonnade, walked back to the Step Pyramid and could be wandering around the northern courtyard. But they might still be in the Tomb of Kanakht. But why?

Tim didn't think the Americans were hurt, he couldn't imagine the little guide being able to overpower the big American. Still.

He looked around for another official, but didn't expect to see one. The antiquities department was understaffed and the idea of guarding a huge mound of stones that had been around for thousands of years was a low priority.

Back home Tim would have called 9-1-1 and let the police sort it out. He hadn't bothered to bring his cell phone on the trip. Even if he had it, he had no idea who he would call, perhaps the embassy.

And tell them what?

Following the ruins of the colonnade that ran along the eastern edge of the complex, Tim walked away from the Tomb of Kanakht and the angry guard. He reached the northern end of the pathway and scanned the area for the Americans.

The Step Pyramid now lay between him and the Tomb of Kanakht. He walked across the courtyard toward the pyramid, unsure of what to do.

He stopped by a large rectangular hole dug into the sand. A path, wide enough for three people to walk side-by-side, led from the edge of the hole down a gentle sandy slope and into a dark tunnel that angled toward the pyramid. Tim knew that it led to a central subterranean shaft, which in turn led down to the granite-plugged vault where Djoser's mummy had once rested.

The tunnel was big enough to hide the two tourists.

He took a few steps into the tunnel and then forced a cough; he didn't want to interrupt the couple if they had found a hiding place for a more personal reason.

As he stepped into the tunnel and out of the sunshine, the contrast between the bright sand outside and the shadows took his sight away. He pinched his eyes shut, hurrying his pupils to dilate. Then he took only a few more steps before the tunnel ended at an iron gate.

No one else was in the tunnel.

He pushed on the gate, expecting it to be locked. It was.

But there is no guard, he realized. So why is a guard assigned to a small, nearly unknown tomb out in the open while the antiquities department trusted an unattended gate at the end of a dark tunnel to keep tourists out of the Step Pyramid?

Tim pressed his face between the bars of the iron gate, but the darkness inside the tomb was too complete.

"Hello! Anyone in there?" he called. He pulled on the gate. There was no give to it, as if it were not just locked shut, but welded in place.

He called again, expecting at least a hollow echo of his voice to come back to him from the ancient room that lay out of sight.

"Anyone? Hello!" he shouted louder.

The reality of the tomb suddenly struck him: its age, how it had been carved from the desert rock by hundreds of men using primitive tools, how a flesh-and-blood king with the power of life and death over an ancient kingdom had been entombed here amid chanting and incense and songs and prayers.

He closed his eyes and imagined the tomb lit by torches. He pictured the rough, granite walls alive with shadows cast by a procession of priests in sheer white linen robes led by Anubis, jackal god of the underworld, and Thoth, ibis-headed scribe of the gods, and the goddesses Ma'at and Hathor. He imagined the sounds of keening mourners, the hollow rattling of sacred sistrums, the shuffling of pall bearers carrying the royal mummy prepared for an eternal life of joy in Khert-Neter, the Field of Reeds. He could almost smell the sharp tang of incense spread to sanctify the chamber, the perfumes of the men and women of the king's court, the dryness of the desert.

With his face pressed against the iron bars, Tim waited for the vision to fade, for the echo of his calls to answer him. But the air in the granite chamber, compressed by the weight of thousands of stones and the stillness of thousands of years, seemed too dense for his words to penetrate.

"Or there's no one here," he said to himself, shaking off the vision.

He walked back up the slope to the surface and was surprised to see that the afternoon had given way to dusk. A tour bus engine started in the distance and he realized that unless he ran through the courtyard and waved the bus to a stop, he would have to make the hike to Memphis or spend a night sleeping by the tomb.

Unless I catch a ride with my buddy, the guard, he thought.

Suddenly he understood why a guard had been assigned to an insignificant tomb that few tourists knew existed: because the lock on the tomb gate was broken.

Until the lock was repaired, a bureaucrat in the department of antiquities could assign someone — a friend or a cousin or a nephew — to guard the tomb. The guard would accept bribes to permit guides to get their guests into the "secret" tomb. The guide would earn a hefty tip from the impressed tourist. The guard would split the bribe with the bureaucrat and so three families would have additional income, all from one broken lock.

Which meant that if he waited until the guard left for the night, Tim could enter the Tomb of Kanakht, satisfy himself that the Americans really had sneaked out of the tomb and, more importantly, spend hours sketching tomb drawings undisturbed by other tourists.

He went back down the sandy tunnel to the Step Pyramid gate. Shrouded by the darkness, he removed his backpack and sat against the cool granite stone to wait for night to fall.

This is the kind of thing Addy would have done, he thought as the dusky light soaked into the sand. Before Addy, he never would have broken rules by staying somewhere after closing. He never would have considered sneaking into a tomb that wasn't open to the public. He would have returned to his hotel and called the embassy. Let them handle it.

"Where's the fun in that?" Addy would have said.

He could almost hear her voice. He missed her more than he ever imagined he could.

They had been planning this trip to Egypt for more than a year. They had researched all of the archaeological sites, studied Egyptian history and bought a language course to teach themselves Arabic, laughing over whose accent was worse.

She had bought a large National Geographic map of Egypt, which they had hung on a wall in their small apartment. As they had decided which sites to visit, they had pinned notes to the map. They had used red yarn to track their travel plans, even bringing the yarn into Cairo, their starting point, from off the map.

An orange pin marked Cairo. "Four days" was underlined on the note the pin held. Beneath the heading they had listed: Giza: Khufu, Khafre and Menkaure; Bazaar: cartouche necklace saying 'life and love;' an ankh; Alabaster mosque.

Abu Simbel, Aswan and Kom Ombo were marked with yellow pins, signifying day trips.

The longest notes, held by red pins, had been stuck on the map at Saqqara and Luxor. They had planned to stay a week at each of the sites, plenty of time for him to sketch the pyramids of the Old Kingdom at Saqqara and the temples of the New Kingdom built at Luxor. It would have given Addy time to talk with camel drivers, laborers, farmers, shop clerks and policemen.

They had planned to create a book of Tim's pencil sketches, capturing the ancient feel of the country, and intimate profiles Addy would write about the 'real people' of the country, not the leaders and the fads.

They had limited themselves to three weeks, because that was all their credit cards could absorb.

Tim had agreed to the trip to satisfy her; he would have been happy to simply hide in their apartment during their vacation and sketch and make love to her.

"That's a typical weekend, Tim," she had told him. "We need an adventure. You need an adventure. We'll remember this all of our lives."

He leaned back against the tunnel wall, closed his eyes, and cried.

INTO THE TOMB OF KANAKHT

The night was darker than he had expected.

Tim swung his backpack off his shoulder and set it on the ground by the tunnel entrance. Using his flashlight, he searched through his backpack for extra batteries. He put the spares in his pants pocket, flicked off the flashlight and pulled the backpack onto his shoulders.

There were no electric lights at Saqqara. A crescent moon hung low in the sky casting indistinct shadows that stretched from low standing walls, half-rebuilt pillars and mounds of debris from recent excavations. Tim squinted at the Step Pyramid and it seemed to magically disappear, its existence marked only by the absence of stars where its form pushed into the night. He opened his eyes wide and allowed the grainy texture of the exterior to take form, giving the pyramid substance again.

It was a trick of the light. Tim loved it because it gave shape and form to the darkness.

He walked to the Serdab. Through the small opening he saw the shadowy face of Djoser, dead five thousand years, staring back at him through the darkness. He reached through the opening to touch the statue and suddenly imagined the king's stone arm coming to life and grabbing his wrist in its dead grasp.

He yanked his arm quickly out of the hole, breathing deeply through the unexpected rush of adrenaline.

His arm was intact, untouched by the inanimate stone. He laughed at his panic. Still he was cautious as he put his hand back into the hole and traced the contours of the king's face with his fingers.

The cheekbones were higher and broader than in portraits of kings from later dynasties, especially the religious rebel Ahkenaten. Djoser wore a ceremonial beard, a long and narrow goatee. His ears were pushed forward by the royal nemes head cloth that covered a thick traditional wig. His eyes, even in this reproduction, were empty sockets, the crystals stolen long, long ago and left out of this reproduction.

He pulled his arm out and looked through the opening again, recalling what he remembered about Djoser.

He had been the first Egyptian king to claim that he was divine, giving himself the royal name of Horus Netjerikhet: "Divine of Body." He had been king during a disastrous seven-year famine when the Nile had failed to flood its banks and leave behind the rich soil carried down from central Africa that the ancient Egyptian farmers depended on. And despite his royalty and power, Djoser's memory had almost been overshadowed by his physician and architect, the famous Imhotep.

Tim sat back on his haunches and stared at the Serdab and beyond it at Imhotep's most famous work, the Step Pyramid.

It had been built five thousand years ago.

Easy to say, so hard to grasp, Tim thought.

My grandfather's father fought in World War I, just a hundred years ago, but that's so distant in the past that it might as well have been fought by Roman legions. No one alive now actually remembers it. In another hundred years it will be as distant to people living then as the Civil War is to me, he thought. And in nine hundred years, it will be as distant as "Beowulf" or the crusades is now.

Another thousand years and I'm back to Christ, back before the Dark Ages, before the plague, before people understood that the planets circled the sun. The world was small and flat.

And I'm not even halfway to Djoser and Imhotep.

He stood, grabbed his backpack and headed around the pyramid for the southern wall where the Tomb of Kanakht was waiting, had been waiting for five thousand years.

The area was deserted; the parking lot dark and empty. No one was standing guard at the tomb. Tim put his hand on the iron bar of the gate and pulled. It swung open easily. He nodded to himself. He had been right about the broken lock.

Stepping past the gate, he stopped for a moment listening and calming himself.

He clicked on the flashlight.

He was standing on an iron grate. Two steps ahead, it disappeared. Tim took one step and looked down. An open, narrow staircase spiraled underground. There was no banister, just a central post or newel to provide a handhold. He grabbed the newel and began his descent. The iron lattice work of the staircase steps scattered the flashlight's beam into pale shards of light that were quickly eaten by the heavy darkness.

I should have counted the steps, he thought after what seemed a full minute of climbing down the narrow stairs. When he paused to shine the flashlight around him, he saw that he was near three pale beige walls. The entrance above him was beyond the reach of his flashlight's beam. A few more steps brought the sand-covered floor into view.

He stepped off the staircase and bent down to look closely at the floor. There were smudged footprints, but the sand was too loose to hold anything well defined.

Two of the walls of the chamber were painted with scenes typical of tombs for high officials. One held a mural of men hunting hippos from a reed boat, the other showed Kanakht and his wife seated before an array of naked dancers at a banquet. The scenes were not completed, Tim realized. In some areas the painting gave way to line sketches as if the artist had not had time to finish the work. Apparently Kanakht had died before the tomb was complete.

Other than the stairwell there was only one exit from the chamber. Walking toward it, Tim played his flashlight on the floor, watching the smudged footprints. The lintel of the doorway smacked hard against the top of his head. He stepped back and brought his free hand to his scalp to check for bleeding. Although he was not tall for a modern American, he was about half an inch taller than the mourners for whom the doorway had been built.

Tim rubbed his forehead and thought about the tall tourist. His head would almost have touched the low ceiling.

The next chamber also was empty. Unfinished murals edged the top of the walls; the ceiling was painted dark blue with stars. A sketch showed that the sky goddess Nut was to be painted supporting the ceiling. In the corners of the room sat round spotlights, placed there when the tomb had been open to tourists.

Tim entered the next chamber, careful to duck as he passed through the doorway.

A huge granite sarcophagus lid, much larger than Tim remembered from other tombs, took up the center of the room. Tim moved the flashlight's beam around the walls, which were more fully decorated than the previous chambers. Diagonally from him, there was another opening, a hole more than a doorway; probably the entrance robbers had used thousands of years ago. It wasn't surprising, almost all the tombs had been raided. That was why King Tutankhamun's tomb was so unusual; ancient thieves had overlooked it and the treasures buried with the boy-king had been found intact.

The sarcophagus lid had been raised and then swung to the side to allow the modern grave robbers, calling themselves archaeologists, to remove the body. The lid was raised about a foot above the floor, balanced on two rough stones under opposing corners. Tim could see that the bottom half of the stone coffin, sunken into the floor, held an opening shaped to receive a mummy. He knelt to look more closely, to be sure that it didn't hold the two American tourists.

It was empty.

He stood and started to walk around the sarcophagus toward the other doorway. His face became entangled in a spider's web and as he brought his hands up to wipe away the threads, he stepped backward. Instead of solid floor, his foot found emptiness where the sarcophagus lid had been swung aside. Falling backward into the void, his foot dropped to the bottom of the lower stone coffin, throwing him off balance. He lurched forward in panic, and his kneecap hit the edge of the stone opening.

He yelped and spread his hands to catch his fall. The flashlight clattered across the tomb floor. Misjudging the angle of the sarcophagus lid, he hit his shoulder against the stone. He twisted away from the pain and found himself falling.

When he stopped moving, he slowly flexed his left arm and reached across his body to rub his right shoulder and arm. Nothing seemed broken. He sat up in the darkness and hit his head hard against the sarcophagus lid.

"Jesus Christ," he swore as he realized that he was now lying in the mummy-shaped opening where Kanakht's body had once lain. Above him the massive stone lid was supported only by two, uneven corner props. He waited silently, listening for a grinding sound that would precede the falling of the lid, sealing him in the granite coffin.

He heard his heart beat, he heard air pass in and out of his lungs, but there was no sound from the stones.

A dim glow from the edge of the opening told him that his flashlight was still working. Gingerly he reached up and touched the stone lid. His other arm found the edge of the opening and he rolled gently toward it. He pulled himself through it and stood up.

The low light from the flashlight cast an ominous shadow from the sarcophagus lid against the wall. Tim pictured its crushing weight falling back into place, trapping him beneath it. His legs suddenly felt rubbery and he sat on the tomb floor, his back against the wall, his eyes on the lid and the narrow opening through which he had fallen.

The flashlight lay just beyond his reach, its yellow light aimed at the stone crypt. He rolled on his side and reached out for it. When he picked it up the beam went off. He shook it. The light came back on and then flickered away leaving him sitting in complete darkness.

Forcing himself to stay calm, Tim unscrewed the flashlight lens and checked the bulb. It seemed to be seated firmly in the socket. He pushed the power button forward. Nothing happened. Shifting to his left, he reached into his pocket and removed the fresh batteries. He unscrewed the bottom of the flashlight and carefully slid the batteries out onto his lap. Then he put the fresh ones in, tightened the bottom and tried the light.

Nothing.

He decided that a contact inside the flashlight body must have snapped during the fall. It was damage he couldn't repair.

He put the flashlight and the old batteries in his backpack. In the front pocket of the pack he had stored a handful of wooden matches. He pulled them out now, put them in his pants pocket, saving one, which he ignited.

Getting to his feet he walked to the doorway. Before he passed through it, he glanced across the room at the hole he had seen earlier.

"Anybody over there?" he shouted.

The match burned close to his fingers. He shook it and dropped it. He pulled out another match. There were five remaining. He lit the match and walked quickly toward the damaged door, his free hand shielding the small flame from the air created by his movements. He swept the opening at the doorway with his hand to clear away cobwebs, but the area already was clear.

He pushed the match through the doorway and leaned in behind it.

"Hello?"

There was no answer. He saw an empty hallway that ran as far as the light from his match reached. The match burned low and he dropped it. The falling, failing flame briefly illuminated footprints in the sand beyond the opening.

The Americans could have hidden behind this wall, he thought, and waited until the guide had left. They could have emerged while I was on the other side of the pyramid complex. Or maybe they had left while I was looking at the map. Either way, they aren't here now.

He lit another match and then followed it back around the sarcophagus and through the doorway. It took one more match to reach the winding stairs. He climbed in darkness, both hands on the center post, his feet feeling their way up the steps.

Outside the tomb, he turned and pushed the gate shut.

The site was still deserted; the moon still lay just above the horizon.

Back at the tunnel by the Step Pyramid, Tim used another match to find a smooth resting spot, and then he laid his head on his backpack and tried to sleep.

He thought of the granite lid that could have fallen back in place and sealed him in the tomb. He doubted if his screams would have been heard by anyone unless they were in that room.

He had never felt so scared or so alive.

EMPTY ROOM AT THE MENA HOUSE

He'd never felt this gritty.

Sand coated his clothes, it caked his skin. He felt as if he'd bathed in it and gargled with it.

In life before Egypt, Tim washed his hands whenever he passed a spigot. Eating hot wings required rolls of wet paper towels. Ice cream was never allowed to drip from a cone in his hands. His shirts were unwrinkled and always tucked in his pants.

Now he felt as if he'd slept in a cat litter box. And he had no idea how, in the middle of the desert, he was going to get rid of that feeling.

Dawn had arrived at Saqqara; the tourists had not. Tim staggered out of the tunnel and found a secluded spot to shake the sand from his clothes. He stripped down to his boxer briefs and shook each article of clothing before putting it back on.

It didn't help.

Surrendering to the grit, he walked to the parking lot and waited for the first tourist to arrive in a cab. He would either pay the driver to take him back to Cairo while the fare toured the site or he'd wait until the tourist was ready to return and try to talk him into letting him ride along.

It was late-morning when he got back to his room at the New Palace Hotel, a small hotel near the Egyptian Museum. His room didn't have a bathroom, but the community shower down the hall was not in use.

Two hours later he was showered, shaved and almost sand free.

Before washing, he had emptied his backpack and wiped everything clean of sand. He'd taken the backpack outside, turned it inside out and beaten it with a broom.

Now he sat on his bed, journal on his lap, and sketched from memory the shadowy sarcophagus in Kanakht's tomb. In the background he drew the hole in the broken wall that he hadn't explored because his flashlight had broken.

He looked at the drawing and wondered about the American couple.

He should have gone into that hidden hallway. Now he wasn't sure if it ended after a few feet or if it continued into another chamber. He really wasn't positive that the Americans had not been down there.

Falling in the sarcophagus had scared him and he'd panicked. When he'd emerged from the tomb, he'd still had three unused matches. He should have used them to go into that dark hallway and make sure that it was empty, that two bodies weren't lying there.

The guard at Kanakht's tomb had seemed sure that the couple had left the tomb, but Tim knew that he hadn't seen them leave. And the guard had been around the back of the building so he wouldn't have seen someone depart. Although Tim had been looking at his map, he believed that he would have sensed movement if the couple had come out of the tomb.

They could still be there, he thought.

Hamzah, the guide, had seemed sure they weren't in the tomb. But Tim wondered now if the concern on Hamzah's face had been over losing the income or if it had been fear that something bad had happened to the tourists.

Something in the tomb? Like what - a mummy come to life? A secret passage? Another vertical shaft that they could have fallen down?

Hamzah had mentioned the Mena House.

Even though they were off in the distance, the three great pyramids at Giza towered over the Mena House Oberoi. Tim stood in the hotel's circular driveway looking at the monuments, hazy in the distance, partially hidden by date palm trees planted around the sprawling resort on the western edge of Cairo.

There wasn't much traffic moving in the early afternoon. He looked for Hamzah and his taxi, but didn't really expect to see him. The taxi-driver guides would have found their customers early in the day and would be busy until dusk.

A short, broad staircase, flanked by twin archways reaching three stories high, led to the lobby. A couple stood by one of the stone arches, watching Tim as he approached.

The man wore a red plaid, flannel jacket, a bulky camera bag slung over his shoulder. She had bushy black hair and was wearing a knitted wool sweater. Tim thought someone should tell them they were in the middle of a desert.

They looked anxious, as if they were waiting for someone who was running late.

"Hi," Tim said.

They turned in unison. She smiled automatically, he looked puzzled.

"You folks staying here?" Tim asked.

She looked at her companion and he nodded.

"I don't want to hold you up, but I was wondering if you could help me."

The man in the flannel jacket looked out over the driveway that circled through the courtyard, then turned back to Tim.

"If we can," he said. "We just got here a few days ago and everything we'd planned has gone wrong. We're supposed to be getting a ride to the airport, but our ride isn't here. The guy at the desk doesn't seem too worried about the ride being late." He nodded toward the lobby doors.

Tim shrugged. "Egyptian time. Everything moves slower and happens whenever it happens. Did you try slipping him some money? I've been told that can speed things up."

They looked at each other. Then the man said, "We had a bad experience with that on the train from Alexandria."

"Sorry," Tim said, "It's really hard to get used to the way things work over here. It's like they just let things happen instead of trying to make them happen on time. But things somehow seem to work out."

The woman nodded and looked hopeful.

"Yeah," the man said. "You're probably right. We've been a little tense. I'm Jerry," he said, offering his hand.

"Deb," she said, offering hers.

"Tim." He took their hands in turn. "Look, I ran into an American couple yesterday and took some pictures for them down at the Step Pyramid, but I lost the note with their names and room number on it. He was tall, had a Boston baseball cap. She was thin, red hair?"

They both nodded.

"We saw them yesterday morning," Jerry said. "He looks a lot like a friend of ours, an overenthusiastic practical joker. That's why I remembered them. Didn't talk to them, though. Sorry."

"But they are staying here, I didn't get that part messed up, did I?" Tim asked.

"They were eating breakfast here when we saw them," Jerry said.

Deb nodded. "I saw them by the pool the day before. I remember worrying about her getting too much of this sun. She was really pale, not bad or unhealthy or anything, just, you know she's a redhead. I think they were staying in the same guesthouse that we're in," she said more to Jerry than to Tim.

"Guesthouse?"

"Yeah," Jerry said. "There are two guesthouses, well, three if you count the rooms by the pool. There's the Palace Wing and the Garden Wing. That's where people stay, not here in the main building. We just came over here to call the taxi company. Again. Each guesthouse has its own desk and mail. We're in that one, the Garden Wing," he said, pointing to a three-story building across the landscaped courtyard.

"The Garden Wing. Well, thanks, you two," Tim said. "Hope everything works out for you."

"Thanks," Jerry said, but he didn't sound optimistic.

"Diane," Deb said suddenly. "I think I heard him call her Diane."

"Diane," Tim repeated.

"Yes," Deb said. "Or maybe Diana."

Tim waited expectantly to see if she would remember more. She looked up at him and shrugged. "I didn't hear her say much. She seemed shy."

Jerry looked amazed. "I didn't even see them," he said.

"No, you were reading and then you fell asleep."

"I didn't fall asleep, I was just resting my eyes."

"We fly twelve hours so he can take a nap," she told Tim, her voice light and teasing.

Jerry adjusted the strap of the camera bag. "Well," he started to say, and then smiled at her. "Well, it was a really good nap. Worth the flight."

A gleaming white taxicab pulled into the driveway.

"That your ride?" Tim asked.

"It is now," Jerry said, adjusting the weight of the camera bag. "Let's go, Deb. I don't want to give the driver a chance to get out of the car."

"Good luck," she said to Tim as they hurried away.

"Thanks," he called after them. He started to walk to the guesthouse and then had an idea. He went inside to find a gift shop. A few minutes later he walked across the courtyard to the guesthouse where the Americans were staying.

The entrance led to a security desk where an extremely fat clerk stood in front of a wall of wooden, pigeon-hole mail boxes, each identified with a number engraved on a brass tag. The clerk held a yellowed handkerchief in his right hand, which he used to mop sweat from his face. He looked tired and hot and bored.

"Hi," Tim said.

"Hello, sir." The clerk's voice was low and gravelly. "Room number?" he asked, turning to get a key.

"I'm not a guest," Tim said.

The clerk frowned and said, "You'll need to go to the main building, sir. Only guests are permitted entrance."

"OK, I just want to leave a message for some friends," Tim said.

"Their names?"

"Hers is Diane or Diana."

"Last name?"

Tim shook his head. The clerk seemed to shudder. Then he asked, "Room number?"

Tim shook his head again.

The clerk nodded to himself and pursed his lips. He placed his hands on the counter and leaned forward slightly. He talked to Tim slowly. "You don't know your friends' names or their room number? You can see, sir, how that might present a difficulty in leaving a message for them." He mopped his face and looked at Tim expectantly.

"He's a very tall American and she has red hair. When I saw them yesterday she was wearing a straw hat and he was wearing a baseball cap. Boston Red Sox." Tim patted his head for emphasis.

The clerk nodded, processing the information. "I am a graduate of the American University here in Cairo. I have many, many American friends. I understand the concept of a baseball cap. I even know about the Boston Red Sox and their accursed sale of the Baby Ruth. More to the point, I know which couple you mean. But, sir, the question remains, what are their names?"

Tim pulled a folded twenty-dollar bill from his pocket. He reached across the counter and gave it to the clerk.

"I was hoping you could help me with their names," he said.

The clerk eyed the money but didn't reach for it.

"I am not a camel driver," he said and mopped his forehead.

Tim wasn't sure if the amount of money he had offered was too small, if his technique was wrong or if the clerk was bartering for a larger bribe. He leaned closer to read the clerk's nametag.

"Hasa?"

"Yes, my name is Hasa."

"Hasa, I'm sorry if I offended you. See, I met this couple at the Step Pyramid yesterday. They asked me to take some pictures of them. We were supposed to meet for breakfast this morning, but I missed them. But I met this other couple, out by the courtyard, and they said they had seen my friends and thought they were staying in this guesthouse."

The clerk studied Tim. "So you are a photographer. You take photographs of tourists for money?"

"No, no. I'm not a photographer."

"You took their photographs?"

"Yes. Look, they're Americans. I'm an American. They said they'd forgotten their camera yesterday. It was a favor." Tim surprised himself with the ease of the lies.

"Perhaps if you showed me the pictures I could be sure that I'm thinking of the right guests," Hasa said, holding out his hand.

"I don't have the photos."

Hasa looked suspicious. "Yet you were going to give them the pictures this morning, yes?"

"No, see, the pictures are on my laptop. I don't carry that with me. We were supposed to meet this morning and take some more shots over by the Giza pyramids. They said they'd be here for a couple more days."

Hasa shook his head. The movement freed a rivulet of sweat, which rolled down his cheek. He corralled it with his handkerchief.

"Look," Tim said. "How about if I leave a note and you can give it to them. OK? That way you haven't disrupted their privacy and they can decide if they want the pictures they asked me to take.

"You know, Hasa, I wish I did have my laptop with me to show you the pictures because they were really good. In one picture they were standing at the base of the Step Pyramid, her arm around his waist, his over her shoulders. The sun was low enough that their faces weren't shaded by their hats and they had the sweetest smiles." As he talked, he took from his backpack a pencil and an oversized postcard he had bought a few minutes ago in the gift shop and started to write a note.

"In another picture, they are walking away from the camera, from me, up through the colonnade at the edge of the southern courtyard. Long shadows from the late afternoon sun cross the ground behind them."

Hasa looked at him suspiciously and Tim wondered if he had blathered too much.

He finished the note and gave it to Hasa. The folded twenty was beneath the postcard.

"Thank you, Hasa," Tim said.

Hasa looked at the twenty and nodded at Tim. "I don't think I believe you, Mr. Hope," he said, reading the note. "But I will keep your money and I will give them the message and let them decide."

Tim was sweating almost as much as Hasa by the time he left the guesthouse. Dark circles had spread under the arms of the gray T-shirt he was wearing.

Now I know why I don't tell lies more often, he thought.

He went into the resort's lobby and hurried across it to the Sultan Bar. The western wall of the bar was open, strands of wooden beads hung from the ceiling, twenty feet above him. Tim could see the gardens that surrounded the resort and, rising up beyond the shrubs and trees, the gray triangle of the Great Pyramid of Khufu.

A few Egyptians sat in the low green chairs that were clustered around the small round tables in the bar. The bartender, wearing a red vest, leaned against the polished bar formed in the shape of an octagon. Tim pulled out one of the chairs by the low bar and ordered a Stella beer.

The bartender was much friendlier than Hasa had been. It didn't take Tim long to find out that the desk clerks came to work early in the morning. A second shift started in less than half an hour, at three o'clock.

Beginning to feel like a detective, Tim asked the bartender if he knew the tall American and the woman with red hair. He wondered what Addy would think of him asking questions of strangers and telling lies to desk clerks.

"I see them every night," the bartender told him. "He is a great lover of our beer. She likes any drink with fruit. Fruit and little umbrellas. She likes the umbrellas."

"Last night? They were here last night?"

The bartender nodded. "Sure, sure, every night."

Tim felt disappointed. If they had been here last night, while he was fumbling around in Kanakht's Tomb, then he was wasting his time because they were safe. And he'd wasted twenty dollars on Hasa.

My adventure is over, he thought.

"No," the bartender continued, laughing, "That's not right. They weren't here last night. Last night we had the singing contest. The karaoke. I was wanting to see him singing. He is so funny. All the time funny. But he didn't sing. I would have remembered."

Tim waited until he was sure Hasa would have left his post before he returned to the guesthouse.

The late shift clerk was an elderly man, his short, curly hair thinning and gray. He looked up and smiled as Tim approached the desk.

Tim saw that the oversized postcard that he had given Hasa was sticking out of one of the slots.

"Oh, great, I got mail," he said, pointing to the postcard.

The clerk turned to look where Tim was pointing. He retrieved the card and gave it to Tim. In precise block letters Hasa had printed on the card "Mr. Brian Aldwin or Ms. Diane Maclaine, Room 324."

"Thanks," Tim said. "Say, Diane has our keys. Could you give me a key? It's Room 324."

The clerk looked puzzled. Displaying the postcard, Tim pointed to the room number that Hasa had written on it. Then he patted his pockets and shrugged.

The old man smiled and nodded. He reached in the cubbyhole and picked up a duplicate key for the room and gave it to Tim.

"I'll bring it right back," Tim said as he took the key.

Tim hurried up the stairwell heading for the third floor.

He knocked on the door of the room. When there was no answer he steadied his right hand with his left and slid the key in the lock.

He pushed open the door and stepped inside. Shaking with nervousness, he stood listening for a minute before turning on the room lights. He had no idea what he would do if Brian and Diane were there taking a nap. He could try to explain why he was there, but he wasn't sure what he would do if they decided he was just trying to steal from their room. Remembering Brian's size, Tim was sure he didn't want to frighten them.

However, the room was empty.

He chained the door behind him and then walked over to a sliding door that opened onto a small balcony. It was too far to jump to the ground, but if someone tried to open the room door, Tim might be able to swing over the side and then drop onto the balcony below him.

He hoped he wouldn't need to.

There were two single beds in the room. Both were made, but Tim had no idea when the maid would have straightened the room, so it was possible that they could have been slept in last night and made this morning. A wooden bench with a back sat against the wall at the foot of the bed nearest the door. Tim lifted its hinged seat. The compartment beneath it was empty.

A small table and two chairs were tucked into an alcove by the balcony door. A guidebook to Saqqara was on the table, along with computer printouts listing all the casinos in Cairo.

There were no used towels in the bathroom. In the closet, Tim found clothes in a hotel dry cleaner bag. The receipt on the bag showed it had been returned two days ago. The waste cans were empty. There were no signs that anyone had been in the room that day.

A dark green, paisley print suitcase lay on a metal stand by the closet. Inside he found a paper envelope tucked in the lid's cloth pocket. It held two tickets for an Air Egypt flight from Cairo to Aswan. The flight was for six p.m. today.

Tim looked at the digital clock by the bed. It was after four; the flight was scheduled to leave in less than two hours.

He put the tickets back and closed the suitcase.

If I was going to be on a flight in less than two hours I'd already be at the airport, he thought.

He unchained the door and, after listening for footsteps, opened it slowly and stepped outside. He shut the door slowly and quietly and then turned to walk toward the stairs. After he passed a few rooms, he stopped and turned back to make sure no one was following him. He bent over as if to tie his shoe, realized that he was wearing sandals, and laughed to himself.

Some detective, he thought.

No one was behind him in the hallway. He went back down the stairs and returned the key to the silent clerk, who gave Tim a friendly smile.

In the hotel courtyard he found a bench that gave him a view of the pyramids framed by a nearby cluster of date palms. He shrugged out of his backpack, removed his sketchbook and sat on the bench.

As he sketched, he watched the driveway, hoping for a car to arrive with Brian and Diane. When the shadows on the angled sides of the pyramid began to shift, Tim decided to check the room again. It was almost seven o'clock.

He went into the main lobby and asked the desk clerk to ring Brian Aldwin in Room 324. After letting the phone ring for a full minute, the clerk shrugged and told Tim that no one was answering. Perhaps he would like to leave a message?

"I'm supposed to take them to the airport," Tim said. "They haven't checked out and gone with someone else, have they?"

The clerk checked the register.

"No, they are still with us. Perhaps you have the wrong time, or perhaps they are running late."

Tim nodded. "Well, I'll sit outside for a couple minutes, but if they're much later, they'll miss their plane. Thanks for checking."

He walked to the guesthouse and got the room key from the silent clerk. There was no answer to his knock, so he entered the room again, calling their names. Still no answer.

If they haven't checked out, then the hotel safe will still have their passports, and they aren't going anywhere without those, he thought.

Suddenly he was sure something had happened to them.

There was no telephone directory in the room so Tim called the reservation desk and asked for the number of the American embassy.

"Is there a problem, sir?"

"No," Tim said. "My sister was going to leave a message for me there, since I wasn't sure about my travel plans."

"Embassy of the United States," a woman's voice said a minute later.

Tim didn't know whom to ask for.

"Hello," she said.

"Hi. I'm an American citizen." *That sounded pretty lame,* he thought. "I'm not sure who to ask for."

"What is the nature of your business? Have you lost your passport? Have you violated an Egyptian law? Are you experiencing a health problem? Do you have information or know of someone who may have information about security matters?"

She walked through the list mechanically.

"No, none of those. I think two people are missing."

"Just a moment, sir. I'll transfer you to security."

The line went dead and Tim thought the connection had been broken. Then there was a series of clicks and a man's tired voice said, "Jim Kamin, security."

"Mr. Kamin?"

"Yes."

"I think two Americans are missing."

"Missing? And you are?"

"I'm Tim Hope."

"United States citizen?"

"Well, yes."

"Is that Tim for Timothy?"

"What? Yes, Timothy. Look, I'm not sure . . . ”

"Mr. Hope, now you say some people are missing. Did you see them taken? Have they been harmed? Why do you think they're missing?"

"They're not here."

"And 'here' is?"

"In their room."

"And where might that be?"

"Wait. Here's what happened," Tim said. "I saw them go into a tomb yesterday and then their guide came out but they didn't. I mean, I don't think they did, at least I didn't see them and I don't think there's another exit from the tomb. At least I didn't see one, although there was this other doorway and I didn't check where it went. But that doesn't matter. Anyhow, I checked at their hotel room today and their stuff is here and they had tickets for a flight to Aswan tonight, but the tickets are still here. So, I think something happened to them in the tomb."

"Did you say bomb? I didn't hear about any bombing," Kamin said.

"Bombing? No, there wasn't any bombing I didn't say anything about a bombing."

"Then why do you think something happened to them in the bomb?"

"No, I said 'tomb.' Something happened to them in the tomb. When I went in they weren't there. Now they aren't here and they didn't take the tickets with them. They missed their flight."

"Was there a shooting? Because I didn't hear about any shootings."

"No, there was no shooting, no bombing. They just didn't come out of the tomb and they aren't in their room."

"And you are?"

"Are what?"

"In their room."

"Yes," Tim said, stifling a frustrated sigh. "Their suitcases are here, their tickets, their clothes."

"You had a key to their room?"

"Look. I just want to report these people missing. Perhaps the embassy could send someone to check out the tomb where I saw them."

"Look, Mr. Hope. People miss flights all the time. Tourists get sidetracked and change plans all the time. If you have any evidence other than unused tickets, tell me. Otherwise, I think we should just wait a few days and see if they turn up. If they don't, then we'll contact the Egyptian authorities."

"What if they're hurt?"

"Well you said there wasn't any bombing or shooting. And I have to tell you that, relatively speaking, Egypt is a fairly safe place for tourists. Not like Miami or New York."

"So, we just wait?"

"Yes. Now if you would like to tell me exactly where you are."

Tim hated telephones. He couldn't recall a single telephone call he had ever made to someone in authority or to a business that turned out the way he wanted.

He remembered learning that ninety percent of communication was non-verbal: crossed arms, shrugs, hand gestures, smiles, frowns, winks, scowls, a raised eyebrow. The telephone line, a lifeless strand of metal carrying a monochromatic wave of electrons, stripped away color and life. It was hard enough to communicate in person with someone you knew. To make sense to a stranger with such a handicap was impossible.

He closed his eyes and pictured Addy leaning forward to whisper to him, her mouth opening softly, her lower lip a glistening, inviting crescent, the upper lip slightly drawn up, the juncture of the soft red lip and her pale skin sharply, achingly, beautifully defined. He could feel her breath, its gentle sweetness brushing against his cheek as she exhaled.

The air, caressed by her mouth and tongue, became alive. It lapped against his ears, entered him and warmed him as sunshine warmed his skin.

"Mr. Hope? You still there?"

Tim hung up the telephone.

"Addy," he said softly. "I have to help them. I can't ignore them. I can't make a phone call and pretend I've done everything I should.

"You know that, Addy. You know that."

A SECRET ENTRANCE

Tim spent the night in Brian and Diane's room, hoping that they would come back and prove they were not missing, and worrying that they would come back and find him trespassing in their room.

While he waited, he read the Saqqara guidebook they had left on the table, hoping to find information about the Tomb of Kanakht. He imagined secret passages and deadly open shafts. Although the location was marked on the map with a small black square, the book never mentioned Kanakht's tomb.

Saqqara had been the official cemetery for Memphis five thousand years ago. The necropolis lay in the desert beyond the reach of the Nile. Memphis, called Ineb-Hedj or "The White Wall" in ancient times, had been a fortified city built along the river.

During the thousands of years since they had been built, the temples had fallen and the pyramids had been partly buried by sand; but closer to the Nile, the homes, shops, schools and markets of the people who lived in Memphis had been completely washed away by the relentless annual floods. Although some of the stone monuments at Saqqara had been quarried for later buildings, and others had been vandalized, much of the ancient burial ground survived.

Nothing was left of Memphis.

The Step Pyramid, the largest tomb at Saqqara, was closed to the public, as were the five other large pyramids that stood outside the main complex. Throughout Egypt there were fewer and fewer tombs open to the public. The collective moisture exhaled by thousands and thousands of tourists had been proven to be more dangerous to wall paintings than tomb robbers.

But tourists were still allowed to wander the open courtyards; to pass by the resurrected walls of the colonnade; to walk through the massive geometric entrance to the pyramid courtyard; to sit in the heb sed court, where King Djoser had been re-crowned; to gaze up at the cobra-headed frieze along the Southern Tomb and at the papyrus-capped pillars of the Northern Court.

The burial complex was huge, far beyond the scale of monuments even imagined today. And the temples and carvings, colonnades and statues, all of that work, that vision and beauty had been built to surround and showcase the enormous Step Pyramid, the jewel of Djoser's eternal resting place. It rose from the surrounding desert as if it had always been there and would remain there always. Weathered by sand and wind, crumbling from age, the ruins were more imposing, more awe-inspiring than any pristine reconstruction could have been.

Tim imagined the workers, their wives and children, the priests, the dancers and musicians, the soldiers and members of the royal court all standing before the completed structure and sharing a single thought: that they, the people of Egypt, had built this. Their imagination and vision, their strong backs and skilled hands, their precise measurements and understanding had brought this form into existence.

The Step Pyramid is actually a tower built with a series of stone squares, or mastabas, set atop each other, each one smaller. The diminishing size of the stacked mastabas gives the pyramid its pointed shape through a series of steps, unlike the more famous pyramids of Giza which had a smooth, slanted alabaster veneer encasing the stepped exterior.

The square base of the pyramid is about two hundred feet long on each side and twenty-six feet high. The six steps of the pyramid raise its peak almost two hundred feet above the desert. The entire structure is a headstone for the burial chambers, which are underground.

A main shaft descends a hundred feet into the desert to Djoser's burial chamber. From that central shaft a network of tunnels branches away, leading to rooms where goods were stored for the king's afterlife. Eleven more shafts, just east of the main tunnel, lead to additional burial chambers, possibly intended for Djoser's wives and daughters.

Tim put the guidebook aside. As the evening wore on, he grew drowsy but, afraid of being caught sleeping like Goldilocks if Brian and Diane came home late, he made coffee using the small coffee pot in the bathroom.

He poured himself the last cup and sat at the room's desk with his journal.

"Addy," he wrote, "I'm hiding in a room at the Mena House waiting for people I've never met. Their names are Brian and Diane and I'm afraid something happened to them, I saw them go into the Tomb of Kanakht near the Step Pyramid. I didn't see them come out – although it's possible that they did and I missed them – but they haven't been seen at the hotel since then.

"If they haven't returned by morning, I'm going to go to Saqqara and go back inside the tomb and search it more thoroughly. There was a hallway that I didn't go in the first time I searched because my flashlight broke. I bought some candles so I don't have to worry about another flashlight incident.

"I called the embassy earlier, but they want to wait a few more days.

"I picture Brian and Diane at the bottom of some burial shaft deep under the desert, weak and hungry, unable to escape, calling for help, waiting for someone to hear them. If I don't find them tomorrow, I'll check the hotel room again and then go to the embassy in person.

"I'll make sure, somehow, that they'll take over and search for them.

"At least I'll have done everything I can.

"I love you. Always."

He closed the journal and turned in his seat to look out the window. The room faced east, so he saw the glow of lights from Cairo and the occasional bouncing lights of a car arriving at the Mena House or heading back to the city. A set of headlights approached from his right, growing larger, then, as they passed they seemed to recede, not toward Cairo, but into the past.

Susan's cell phone had rung at the very minute she was parking her car at the TGIF restaurant that night six months ago.

She had reached for the cell phone while getting out of the car and so forgot to pull the keys from the ignition. As the locked door had swung shut, she had realized what she had done and had said "Shit!" to Addy who had been on the other end of the phone call.

"I just locked myself out of the car."

"Did you ever join Triple-A?" Addy had asked; knowing the answer her best friend would give.

"God, you can be such an M-O-M," Susan had said and Addy had laughed. Tim had heard that laugh as he sat with Addy in their apartment.

"What happened?" he had asked.

"Susan locked herself out of the car. Can you believe it? She hasn't done that for more than a week," Addy had told him, careful not to cover the mouthpiece so Susan could hear her.

"It's your fault," Susan had told Addy. "You called right when I was getting out of the car."

"Oh, my," Addy had apologized. "Can't have you doing two things at once. Thank God you weren't chewing gum, too, there could have been injuries."

"You are such a ... sweet friend," Susan had said.

"Where are you?" Addy had asked with exaggerated exasperation.

"TGIF."

"I'll bring the spare keys over, but you can never call me MOM again," Addy said, smiling into the phone, her eyes sparkling.

"OK," Susan had answered. "How about if I call you a mother?"

"I'll take you over," Tim had said, bending to pull on his sneakers.

"Don't be silly. It's just across the river. I'll be back in an hour, longer if she buys me a drink," Addy had said, leaning over to kiss him goodbye. She had missed slightly and kissed the corner of his mouth.

So casual, so careless, it had been one toss-away kiss among the thousands they had shared. Nothing about it said that it was the last one.

Tim fell asleep in the chair, Addy in his dreams, Brian and Diane on his mind.

He awoke befuddled and stiff. The room was dark and quiet. The clock by the bed read four thirty. He went into the bathroom and washed his face, looking up to see himself staring back from the mirror, sleepy and confused. Was he trying to find Brian and Diane because he'd lost Addy? Was he trying to help them because no one had helped her?

It didn't matter. He would search the tomb and help them if they were there, report them missing if they weren't, because they weren't coming back to the hotel room where their tickets, luggage and passports were waiting.

The old clerk was asleep on a chair behind the counter. Tim slipped past him and into the courtyard. The warm Egyptian air was heavy with the weight of the darkness, filled with a promise of mystery.

Off to the west, the pyramids were hidden by the night. Tim turned slowly. The trees behind him, along the edge of the Mena House courtyard, were shadows etched against the eastern sky where night was beginning to lose its grip.

As he looked into the fading darkness, the opening words of "The Rubaiyat" came to him.

"Awake! For morning in the bowl of night
Has flung the stone that puts the stars to flight;
And lo! The hunter of the East has caught
The Sultan's turret in a noose of light."

Catching the scent of jasmine as he turned back toward the main house, Tim suddenly realized how far he had traveled from his home and his family, from his past.

He walked quickly across the deserted courtyard.

When he stepped through the lobby doors, he came to a halt.

A sand-colored tile floor stretched out before him. A red-jacketed clerk holding a water can turned slowly away from a wildly colorful bouquet of flowers held by a polished brass pot, which sat atop a carved wooden stand at the center of a magnificent oriental rug.

The boundaries of the lobby were marked by carved wooden columns fronted by small palm trees planted in more polished brass pots. The beige plaster ceiling was almost hidden by angled wooden beams woven together like window tracery to form an arabesque pattern. In the middle of the lobby, a large Islamic lamp hung from a coffered ceiling, four of its wooden panels inset with octangular carvings.

It was a scene from a dream, an oriental palace brought to life.

Last night, nervous about breaking into Brian and Diane's room, he had walked through the lobby to the bar without even noticing it. Now it looked magical and mysterious.

Tim saw the desk clerk watching him and realized that aside from the clerk and the man who was watering the plants, he was the only person in the lobby. He walked over to the clerk and tried his Arabic, "Sabah el-kheir."

The clerk smiled. "Good morning to you, sir," he answered, recognizing Tim's accent and telling Tim that he could speak English.

"I couldn't sleep," Tim said. "I'm going to Saqqara this morning and I'm kind of keyed up. Is there anyplace I can get some breakfast this early?"

The clerk nodded and pointed off to a red-carpeted stairway to the left of the reception desk. "Al Shams is always open," he said.

"Shukran," Tim said.

The clerk smiled. "You're welcome, sir," he answered.

Tim looked around the deserted lobby. "When do the taxi drivers start to arrive?"

"Usually after breakfast, sir, in ... " he looked at a clock behind the counter, "three hours, perhaps."

"None earlier?"

"No, but I know a driver I could call. He could be here by the time you finish your breakfast. Would you like me to retain him for you?"

"Yes," Tim said. "Please. Thank you. Ana mamnoon."

The clerk nodded. "It is nothing, sir. Enjoy your breakfast."

When Tim returned to the lobby, the clerk raised his hand and waved to him.

"Na'am," Tim said as he reached the counter.

The clerk nodded toward the doorway where a sleepy-eyed, young Egyptian stood, his hands stiffly at his sides.

"His name is Musa. He is a very good driver. And he is my sister's husband's brother. He will treat you very well."

"Musa?"

"Yes, Musa." The clerk looked at Tim expectantly and Tim realized he was expecting a tip. He held out a five-pound note and raised his eyebrows in question.

The clerk took the money smoothly. "Bissalama," he said.

Tim shook his head. "I'm sorry, I don't know that word."

"It means 'have a safe journey.' "

The predawn light fell on an empty parking lot of Saqqara. On the twenty-minute ride, Tim had decided to take Musa with him into the tomb; he would be another set of hands to help carry Brian and Diane if they were down there and needed help.

As they walked from the unlit parking lot, headlights appeared on the road from Cairo. For a frightened moment Tim thought that a police car had followed him, but then he realized that he was being paranoid. No one knew he was planning to illegally enter a closed tomb.

He and Musa passed through the door at the entrance wall and entered the southern courtyard. Behind them, Tim heard the slam of a car door.

"Hello! Marhaba! Bonjour!" a voice called from the parking lot.

Tim walked on, ignoring it. Musa, walking beside him, said, "It is the guardian of the antiquities. We did not purchase tickets."

Tim shook his head. He saw the tomb of Kanakht just ahead and didn't want a guard to tell him it was off limits again.

"We couldn't, Musa. They weren't at the ticket booth."

"No," Musa said. "We are not to be here without them. Without paying the fee."

Tim kept walking. "Well, we're already in here. We'll pay them on the way out."

Musa stopped. "No, I am sorry. We must pay them first. If they are not here, we do not pay them. But now that they are here we must pay them. I must not have the guardian of the antiquities angry. We must go back and pay them."

"Hello, please! Min fadlak! Bonjour!" the voice called again.

Tim was a few steps past Musa, just a short distance from the tomb. He turned to the young driver. Tim understood that Musa made his living bringing tourists to the sites, he needed the "guardians of the tomb" to remain his friends.

"OK, I'll wait here." He took three twenty-dollar bills from his jacket and gave the money to Musa. "Here, you buy the tickets, pay the guardians of the tomb, whatever. Is this enough?"

Musa looked at the money, more than triple the admission fee. It was true what his brother's wife had said about the Americans, they were wealthy beyond belief. He nodded, took the money and left Tim standing alone by the Tomb of Kanakht.

As soon as Musa passed through the entrance door, Tim turned and walked as fast as he could through the loose sand. He opened the gate to the Tomb of Kanakht and stepped onto the iron grating. He turned and smoothed out the sand under the gate. Then he gripped the newel of the spiral staircase and started climbing down into the tomb.

Once his head was below ground level, he turned on his flashlight.

He quickly stepped down a half dozen steps and then stopped to listen. There were no sounds from outside. He took six more steps and then stopped. Once he was farther down the staircase, he moved without stopping until he had reached the bottom of the stairs where he turned off his flashlight and listened again.

It will take Musa and the guard some time to search the above-ground complex before they even think of me being in this tomb, he thought.

After his breathing had slowed from the nervous descent and he still hadn't heard any sounds from above, he turned on the flashlight and looked carefully around the chamber. Hunters on a reed boat still had their spears raised over a roaring hippopotamus on one wall. On another wall, a banquet was in progress. Dancing girls arched backward, their hair hanging to the floor. Kanakht and his wife sat side-by-side holding cups in their hands into which a servant girl poured wine. To the left, a table held loaves of bread, roasted geese and ducks, baskets of grapes and plates of lentils and chickpeas. Beneath it stood jars of beer.

Some of the outlined figures had not been painted. The other two walls were bare; the tomb had not been finished. Tim played the light slowly over the walls, looking for cracks or any straight lines that would indicate a man-made opening. He moved the light over the floor looking for soft spots or signs of an opening to a shaft.

Finished in the first chamber, Tim remembered to stoop below the lintel when he walked through the doorway to the next chamber. The decorations here were more formal, stylized paintings of gods and goddesses. Again the paintings were unfinished. And again there were no obvious openings.

He lay on the floor and used his light to scan across the flat surface. He saw footprints in the dust, no doubt some of them from his visit two nights ago. Seized by an idea, he stood close to the wall and tried to look at the surface from a low angle, hoping to highlight handprints, although what that might tell him, he didn't know.

"Hello, Mr. Tim," Musa's voice echoed through the outer chamber. It sounded distant. Musa was still above ground.

Tim pushed away from the wall, his heart racing.

He walked quickly through the chamber to the doorway that led to the main burial room with the stone sarcophagus. Inside he stooped close to the floor and shined the light around the line where the wall and floor met.

"Mr. Tim, Mr. Tim," Musa called from above.

Tim froze as he heard two sets of footsteps on the iron staircase.

He abandoned his search in the tomb chamber and hurried to the broken wall.

Leaning into the opening, he looked across the broken stones to the floor inside. As he did, he heard Musa and the guide reach the bottom of the staircase. They were arguing in Arabic, but they were talking quickly, the words a steady stream that Tim couldn't understand.

In the passageway he saw ridges of sand that could be footprints.

He stepped across the fallen stones, careful not to trip.

"Hello, Mr. Tim."

The acoustics in the tomb made the voice sound as if Musa was at Tim's shoulder. Tim jerked around, expecting to see the driver standing there. The chamber was empty, but he saw light shining through the doorway on the other side of the sarcophagus.

He walked down the hidden passageway. He moved the light around the ceiling, down the walls and across the floor. The hallway continued five feet more and then stopped. No one was here and there were no hiding places, no open holes, no bodies, no other exits.

He stooped to give himself a low-angled view of the floor. The sand was rippled on the floor at his feet and down the passage for another step or two. After that it was smooth and undisturbed.

Tim heard Musa and the guard talking, they sounded closer.

He wondered if they could see his light glimmering from this hidden passageway.

He followed the disturbed sand to the wall and looked closely, placing his cheek against the wall and shining the light across the wall instead of directly at it. Just beyond where the footsteps stopped there was a line running up the wall, not exactly a crack, but a straight ridge.

Tim stood in front of the wall where the sand was most uneven. He stooped and looked at the floor. The sand was scraped away in an arc, as if someone had taken a wide broom and swept it away from the wall in a half circle.

"Hello, Mr. Tim," Musa called. They were in the tomb chamber, just on the other side of the wall behind him. He looked desperately at the wall, sure that it held some secret.

He turned off his flashlight so that Musa and the guard wouldn't see the light. He stood unmoving, willing them to walk away.

A soft light from the burial chamber filtered through the hole in the wall behind him. The deflected light showed shadows that Tim's harsh direct light had not. Two handprints were on the wall, just above his head. He leaned forward and reached up to the prints, placing his hands against the wall.

He pressed against the wall and waited. Nothing happened.

"Mr. Tim, Mr. Tim."

The voice was just on the other side of the wall, the lights bobbing closer.

Tim twisted to look at the opening, shifting his weight against the wall, and it moved, quietly pivoting to create a doorway.

Part of the beam from Musa's light flashed through the hole three feet from Tim.

Tim slipped through the open doorway. On the other side he pressed against the extended edge of the stone door and it silently swung shut. He leaned against the stone and listened for Musa's voice, but the tomb was silent.

DJEFI, FIRST PROPHET OF SOBEK

Ahmes couldn't stop talking and Paneb, who usually had to remind himself to be patient with his adopted son, was as excited as the eight-year-old boy was.

Earlier, in the pre-dawn darkness when they had started walking from their home in Ineb-Hedj, the boy had been quiet, still sleepy. Now, with Re's sacred barge having emerged from its nightly journey through Khert-Neter, there was light for their walk through the narrow wadi to the entrance of the vizier's tomb in Saqqara. Ahmes skipped eagerly through the sand, sometimes walking backwards through the shallow gully so he could watch his adored stepfather as they talked about the gods who had arrived two days ago.

Ahmes was naked, his head shaved except for a side lock of hair, knotted near the scalp above his ear and hanging loose to his neck.

Paneb, whose head was shaved smooth, wore only a short linen kilt, which he would remove when they reached the tomb and he started working. He wore the shendyt to please his wife, Takhaaenbbastet, who had made the bleached white kilt herself and who thought he should wear it as a sign of his rank. She said that only common workers went about without a kilt.

Although he was chief artist at Saqqara, known even to Netjerikhet Djoser, King of the Two Lands, Paneb knew who was chief of his household. So if Taki wanted him to wear a shendyt, then he would. It was a small matter and it gave her joy. But he knew better than to make it dirty.

"The netjer was so tall, Father. Have you ever seen anyone so tall? And so strong?" Ahmes stopped his prancing long enough to mimic a spear toss.

Paneb shook his head. He had done a lot of head shaking in the two days since the gods had walked out of the tomb, the god smiling, the goddess squinting in the light, her skin so pale you could see through it.

That day had promised to be exciting enough.

Paneb and Ahmes were to escort Djefi, high priest of Sobek, the crocodile god, to inspect Kanakht's tomb in Saqqara.

Kanakht, overseer of the Two Lands and adviser to King Djoser, had instructed Paneb to paint scenes in the tomb entrance showing himself with the crocodile god. And now Djefi was arriving at Ineb-Hedj to approve Paneb's sketches.

Paneb and Ahmes had watched Djefi's boat approach the pier used by officials of The Two Lands. There was a mast in the center of the boat, but no sail was unfurled. Paneb explained to Ahmes that sails were used when traveling up the River Iteru, because the winds blew that way, always against the current of the river. On trips down river, the flow of the River Iteru and oars provided the speed.

The cedar wood boat slid silently along the wooden pier. Water dripped from the glistening oars as the ten rowers pulled them up onto the boat. One of the boatmen jumped off to secure the vessel.

The messenger who arranged the visit had told Paneb to prepare a sedan chair for Djefi and to have four strong men to carry it. He had emphasized the word strong.

The carriers stood beside Paneb and Ahmes waiting to see how heavy their burden would be today.

With the boat tied off at prow and stern, a crewman placed a wide gangplank from the boat to the dock. Two young men steadied an immensely fat man dressed in a white robe with a leopard skin, the sign of a priest, draped over his wide, round shoulders, as he stepped onto the plank. Paneb saw that the plank was wide enough for the escorts to stay beside the priest as he stepped awkwardly from the bobbing boat.

From his right, Paneb heard one of the chair carriers sigh at the sight of the heavy priest and another wondered aloud if his pole was strong enough. "That's what your wife wonders every night, isn't it, eh, Marhu?" another carrier asked. The others laughed quietly.

Paneb pretended he hadn't heard them.

Paneb had never met Djefi, but he had heard about him. Although high priest, Djefi was young enough to be mistaken for an acolyte. But he was said to be as savage as the crocodile god he worshiped. There were rumors of accidents that happened to those who stood in his way, including his step-father who had been high priest before him.

It was hard to reconcile that fearsome reputation with the man who was already sweating and panting after walking from the boat to the sedan chair. Wobbling flesh hung from his arms. Three layers of chins rolled back from his flushed face and buried a silver strand that held an amulet around his neck. Folds of fat pushed against the front of his linen robe. Even though his eyes were heavily lined with green kohl, they looked small, pushed back into his heavy cheeks.

The young bodyguards lowered him into the chair. Then they ran back to the boat and retrieved short ceremonial spears.

Djefi sat breathing heavily and looking around as if he was confused.

Paneb went to the sedan and knelt so he would not be looking down at Djefi when he talked to him. "First Prophet of the Great Netjer Sobek, I am Paneb, chief artist of Saqqara."

Djefi's head turned slowly to him. He held a linen cloth in his left hand and dabbed at his face with it as he studied Paneb for a full minute.

When he spoke, his voice was high pitched and squeaky, as if a small boy was being held captive inside his great quivering bulk. "Good for you, Paneb. Why am I still sitting beside this boiling river when I have tomb scrawlings to inspect?"

"Forgive me, First Prophet," Paneb said. He stood and backed away from the sedan chair and nodded to the carriers.

Paneb and Ahmes walked quickly to the street to lead the way for the carriers. They waited until the young guards returned to the sedan. Then the carriers silently counted together before hoisting Djefi off the ground and then, after another count, smoothly up to their shoulders.

The guards took their positions in front of the sedan and the procession moved into the shady streets of Ineb-Hedj.

In a few minutes they reached the edge of the city and passed beyond the white walls that gave it its name. They walked briskly through the green fields that surrounded the city and then, abruptly, the desert began.

Paneb could see that Ahmes was trying hard to maintain decorum, but the boy's eyes were full of questions. The carriers started to breathe deeper and louder as they carried Djefi through the soft sand. One of them broke wind loudly and Ahmes almost laughed out loud, but a stern look from Paneb stopped him.

The priest had covered his face with the sweaty linen cloth.

As they neared the tomb, the wadi narrowed at a sharp bend and there was no room for the sedan to be carried safely through the rock-strewn gully. The carriers stopped and waited for instructions.

"Are we there?" Djefi asked, raising the damp cloth from his face.

Paneb returned to the sedan.

"No, First Prophet. But the wadi is too narrow for the men to carry you farther. The tomb is just ahead, around this narrow bend."

"Am I to walk?"

"It is just a few paces."

"Why hasn't the path been widened? Do you expect King Djoser to soil his feet if he visits Kanakht's eternal home?"

Paneb wasn't sure how to respond. He was chief artist, responsible for the tomb drawings and paintings, not the engineer who directed the digging of the tomb.

"Kanakht, you will pay for this," Djefi said quietly, his eyes raised in the distance as he thought of the absent vizier. Then he turned his attention to the carriers. "Am I supposed to leap from the sedan? Lower me!" he commanded in his high-pitched voice.

Once the sedan was lowered, the bodyguards hurried to his side and pulled him to his feet.

He shook them away and looked crossly around the wadi. "Well?" he asked.

Paneb bowed and turned to lead the priest to the tomb.

Djefi was panting heavily before they got through the narrow section of the gully. To Paneb he looked like any other overly successful merchant, but only a man who would happily cheat you in a trade, not a man who would happily feed you to a crocodile.

Djefi's two bodyguards carried their short spears casually by their sides. Aside from the remote threat of a jackal or a desert lion attacking there was little to fear in Kemet. There was no civil unrest and the borders of Kemet had been secured by Kha-sekhemwy, father of Netjerikhet Djoser, King of the Two Lands.

Djefi was too busy panting to complain as they walked to the tomb. Paneb thought the priest seemed distracted and withdrawn. The guards walked a few steps behind Djefi, talking quietly to each other.

The wadi twisted left and ended against a sand bank where a limestone outcropping marked the edge of a high table. A tunnel had been dug into the stone. It angled down for a few paces and then leveled out, moving deep under the stone, which rose higher in the distance to form a plateau.

Paneb stopped by a wooden frame his workers had erected outside the tomb. The top of the frame held palm branches, creating a shaded rest area. Three rough wooden stools were half buried in the sand under the canopy.

Paneb moved the stools to the side to make room for Djefi to stand in the shade. Then he gave two, slightly concave, polished brass disks to Ahmes. The boy hurried off to position the mirrors outside the tunnel entrance to reflect sunlight inside. As Ahmes carried the reflectors to the tunnel, Paneb turned to Djefi to explain what he would see inside the tomb.

But before he began to speak, he heard Ahmes shout in alarm.

"Father, someone is in the tomb!" the boy called as he ran through the sand to Paneb's side.

Djefi looked curiously at the tomb entrance. The guards looked more attentive, but not alarmed. The tomb was empty; there was nothing to steal. More than likely, someone had used the tunnel as a shelter for the night.

Paneb was responsible for the tomb until it was given over to Kanakht, and so he touched Ahmes' shoulder and said, "Wait here, son."

He glanced at Djefi to see if the priest was angry, but it seemed that Djefi was still preoccupied by whatever had been on his mind earlier. His guards raised their eyebrows in question. Paneb smiled back reassuringly and turned to walk to the tomb.

Before he had taken a step, they emerged.

The god was tall, taller even than Nubian slaves Paneb had seen two years ago when the priest of Khmunu had brought the black giants with him on his way to Iunu for Re's festival. The goddess had hair the color of a dying fire. Her skin was as white as Taki's linen.

The god's torso was painted with bright yellow and red flowers. His feet were red and black. She wore straw matted on her head like an inverted bird's nest. Her legs were covered with blue cloth and a large cat was painted on her white chest.

Whatever had been on Djefi's mind earlier vanished when he saw them.

His hands on his hips, Brian stood at the tunnel's exit twisting his shoulders to loosen them after walking hunched over through the low passage. Diane held a hand up to the brim of her straw hat, shielding her eyes as she looked at the men a few yards away.

"Brian, who are those people?"

He stopped twisting and started to roll his tight shoulders. "Don't know, babe. Welcoming committee? Tour guides? Farmers? Ticket takers? Somebody selling souvenirs?"

She shook her head. "I don't think so, Brian. Two of them have spears."

"Huh," he grunted. "Maybe they're javelins and it's some kind of track meet. Maybe I could get in it. I used to be pretty good with the discus."

She looked at him sharply. Even after a year with him, she still got quickly annoyed when he made jokes at inappropriate moments, and being confronted by armed savages was an inappropriate time for humor.

"Let's go back inside and go back to the hotel. We have a flight to catch tonight. We shouldn't have sneaked away from the cab driver. Let's go back," she said.

Brian dropped his chin toward his left shoulder, making the vertebrae crackle. "No," he half grunted, "It was a Frisbee. I was good with the Frisbee. The discus wasn't as much fun. Too much spinning before you throw it. Although getting dizzy was fun." He dropped his head the other way and more vertebrae popped. "Ahhh, that feels good."

"Brian," Diane said quietly, talking out of the side of her mouth.

Djefi's bodyguards started to edge forward in front of the priest, but he extended his arms to keep them behind him. He took a step forward leaving the shade of the canopy and bowed his head slightly, keeping his eyes on the two gods.

"Welcome, eternal netjrew," Djefi said. "I am Djefi, priest of Sobek, son of Seth, father of the Nile, honored by all in The Two Lands."

Startled to be addressed, Diane looked up and frowned. She didn't understand a word the man had said.

Djefi wondered if he had been wrong to speak first and welcome the gods. *But it would have been more wrong to stand silently and not make them welcome,* he thought.

Djefi's movement had brought him out of the shade. He was backlit by the afternoon sun. "Brian, I can see right through his robe, or whatever. The fat man is practically naked."

"Yep," Brian answered. "But he's overdressed compared to the naked spear dudes. This must be, like, the World Naked Olympics. You think?"

Brian turned back to Djefi and raised his right hand, the fingers splayed into a "V" like Spock in the 'Star Trek' movies. He couldn't remember the Vulcan greeting, so he said, "Whatever."

Djefi copied the gesture and mimicked the sound in his squeaky voice.

A wide smile broke over Brian's face. "You guys forget to get dressed this morning?"

Djefi studied them for a moment and then reached a decision.

He didn't know where they had come from, or if they really were gods. Whatever or whoever they were, they were different and unusual. It was a time of change and unrest in Kemet and perhaps they were a gift from the gods, tools for him to use in the plans he was making with Waja-Hur and Kanakht. He needed to understand how to use this gift. He needed time.

He waved one of the guards to his side and whispered to him. The guard bowed and then turned away and began to jog back down the wadi toward Ineb-Hedj.

"Eternal netjrew, I will have you escorted to To-She, home of Sobek."

Brian and Diane looked at him blankly.

Without turning away from the gods, Djefi called Paneb to him.

"I have sent for camels for our guests," Djefi said.

"Yes, First Prophet of Sobek," Paneb answered, bowing to Djefi.

"Perhaps it would be easier for them to understand us if we were to draw pictures, as we do on the tomb walls," Djefi said.

"You wish for ink and papyrus, First Prophet?"

Although he kept his expression composed, muscles in Djefi's jaw clenched and unclenched. "No, Paneb. You are the artist. Draw a camel in the sand for the guests," he said quietly.

Paneb nodded. He looked around for something to use to draw in the sand. He saw the stools and thought of breaking them apart. Then he saw the guard, standing apart from them, watching.

He walked quickly to the guard and borrowed his short spear.

"Brian, what's going on?"

"Don't know, babe. I think the one naked guy ran off to get something and Boss Hogg here is trying to tell us something, but it sounds like he's got a mouth full of consonants. He needs to buy a vowel, know what I mean?"

Paneb approached the gods walking slowly, the point of the spear at the ground. He didn't want them to think he was attacking them. He didn't want to find out what a god would do if he felt threatened.

Kneeling in the sand, Paneb used the shaft of the spear to smooth an expanse of sand. Then, standing, he used the point of the spear to gracefully draw the profile of a camel. He looked at the god and then drew a figure wearing a cap and sitting atop the camel.

"Looks like we're going for a ride, babe."

"No, we're going back to the hotel," Diane answered.

"Aw, we flew across the entire Atlantic Ocean to get here. Let's loosen up and have a little fun. We miss the flight to Luxor, big deal. It's not like the temples down there are going anywhere. They'll be there tomorrow. Let's see what old Boss Hogg has in mind. I don't know where we are, but I'll bet there aren't many other tourists here."

"And that's a good thing?" Diane asked.

Instead of answering, Brian walked up to Paneb and held out his hand for the spear. Paneb was afraid of offending him, but didn't want to upset Djefi either. He stole a glance at the priest, but got no sign from him.

Paneb offered the spear to the god and backed away, still bowing.

Brian walked carefully around the camel sketch and cleared a small space by the head of the figure riding the camel. He stuck his tongue out as he concentrated on drawing. When he finished he stepped back so everyone could see his work.

Djefi stepped closer. The guard walked over beside the priest to see the god's work. Ahmes, overcoming his fear, sidled up beside his father. Djefi looked puzzled at the drawing. Paneb was amused, but kept his expression serious. The guard waited to see what the others would do. Ahmes, without thinking, laughed and clapped his hands.

Brian turned to the boy and gave him a broad smile and a thumbs up. "One thousand points for the naked, bald kid. Come on, folks, lighten up," he said to the adults. "It's a smiley face."

Brian carried the spear to the guard. He tugged gently on his arm and said, "Come on."

He led the guard a few paces down the wadi, away from the others. The guard looked excited and worried.

Once they were a safe distance from the others, Brian drew back, raised his forward leg and in a blur of motion stepped forward and smoothly threw the weapon at the bank of the wadi, grunting as he released it. The spear buried itself halfway into the sand.

Swinging his throwing arm in a circle, Brian walked to the spear. He pulled it out and gave it to the guard, motioning for him to throw it next. The guard stepped toward the bank and threw the spear. The tip entered the sand and the spear wobbled and then fell over.

Brian retrieved it and walked back to the guard.

Then he held the spear aloft again and moved his arm through the throwing motion, snapping his wrist forward as his arm extended. "Here, try again, naked spear-chucker dude. Snap the wrist." Brian demonstrated the motion with his empty hand.

The guard nodded and tried another throw, snapping his wrist as he released the spear. It hit the sand and the tip disappeared far enough to support the weight of the shaft.

Brian clapped loudly, startling the guard, who was looking proudly at the spear.

"Alright," Brian cheered the guard, "yes, yes, yes! Now," he said, slapping the guard on the back, "We get your hips into the throw, maybe a big old Luis Tiant leg kick and you'll be the envy of all the naked spear-chucking dudes."

Djefi called the guard to him and spoke quietly.

The guard immediately ran over, pulled the spear out of the sand and walked down the wadi to watch for the other guard.

"Uh-oh, looks like Boss Hogg is upset," Brian said to Diane.

"Brian!" she scolded, but her lips played into a smile.

Brian turned to Djefi. "OK, Boss, where to?"

Djefi stared at the huge god, his face tight with the effort to control his anger at being addressed so casually. He had no idea what the god had said, but he understood the tone. *Even a god, if this man is a god, should show respect to a priest of Sobek,* he thought.

"I am Djefi, First Prophet of Sobek, Netjer of Iteru, Father of the Waters," he said, placing a fist against his chest.

Brian nodded. He pointed to the priest and said, "You, Djefi." Then he patted his chest and said. "Me, Tarzan."

"Tarzan," Djefi repeated.

"Naw, I'm pulling your leg." Brian laughed and shook his head. He patted his chest again. "Brian."

"Brian," Djefi said in the same quiet, menacing voice Paneb had heard earlier.

The artist looked at the powerful, playful god and the short, terrifying priest and wondered which would survive.

The first guard returned riding one camel and leading two others. He reined the camel to a stop and leaned forward and talked to it. The camel lowered itself to a kneeling position. The guard swung a leg over the camel's small hump and slid down to the sand. Then he went to each of the other camels and ordered them to kneel.

Brian walked over to the camels, the first guard trailing after him. He turned back to the tomb and called, "Come on, Diane. It's camel time."

Circling carefully away from the camels' faces, he approached one of them from the side. "You got any double humpers? I was kind of expecting to sit down between the humps, you know?"

The guard smiled at him.

"No saddles, huh?"

Another smile.

Diane joined him.

"We are supposed to ride these? I hope they have liability insurance," she said.

Brian patted the dusty side of the camel. "Look, the hump isn't that big, I mean, it's not pointy or anything. I'm sure they wouldn't let us on these if it wasn't safe. Adventure, babe, adventure. Think of the stories we'll have when we get back home."

The first guard came over and stood close to Brian, his back to Djefi.

He placed his open palm against his chest and quietly said, "Bakr."

Brian repeated the guard's name. Then he took the guard's right wrist and pulled his arm toward him. Reaching with his right hand, Brian clasped the guard's hand in a handshake, their palms pressed together, thumbs interlocked and fingers pointed up.

The guard looked up at the large god, his eyes glowing with excitement. "Brian," he said softly.

"Yep," Brian said, squeezing the guard's hand and then releasing him. "Now, let's ride us some camels."

He turned and lifted Diane by the waist, easily swinging her atop the kneeling camel. Then he walked to a second camel and mounted it. "Yo, Bakr, you coming?"

The guard looked to Djefi who nodded his head curtly. Bakr mounted the third camel and shouted "Hup." The three camels rose ungainly.

"Whoa!" Brian laughed, almost pitching forward from the camel.

Diane held the reins tightly, her body tense.

Bakr turned his camel and climbed out of the wadi. Brian's and Diane's camels followed, swaying from side to side, heading away from Ineb-Hedj, across the desert to the oasis of To-She.

As soon as the three were out of sight, Djefi took Paneb and Ahmes aside. He told Paneb not to tell anyone about the gods. "Sobek wishes to speak with them … alone."

Although he didn't understand why Djefi was being secretive, Paneb nodded his head.

Djefi reached out and patted Ahmes' head. The movement seemed unnatural and, although Paneb flinched, he felt a flicker of pride that Ahmes did not offend the priest by moving away from him, possibly because the boy's attention was still rooted on the strangely dressed gods.

"Understand, Chief Artist, Sobek does not want you to speak of these netjrew," Djefi's boyish voice took on a hard edge. "There should not be even rumors of them. No one is to know of them. Understand?"

Paneb nodded again, unable to meet Djefi's eyes.

"You do not want to anger Sobek." Djefi's voice grew even higher pitched. "Sometimes, in his rage, Sobek takes children."

Djefi's sweaty hand rested for a moment on Ahmes' head. His face was bland as he watched Paneb to be sure the artist understood. "Sometimes, he takes children," the priest repeated.

Paneb could not speak. He looked at Djefi. The priest's dark eyes stared back unblinking. Then the priest frowned down at Ahmes, turned away and waved the remaining guard to his side. The guard helped Djefi walk away, back toward the sedan chair to return to Ineb-Hedj.

Paneb stood staring after them, his stomach a knot of fear.

"Are they truly netjrew, father? Did they come from Khert-Neter?" Ahmes whispered.

Paneb looked sadly at his son. "We cannot speak of this," he said.

"Not to Mother?"

"No, Ahmes, not to anyone."

"Because Sobek will take me? I am the 'children' the First Prophet meant?"

Paneb's eyes filled with tears. He wiped them away with the back of his arm.

"Yes, Ahmes. But, we won't let that happen. There is a proverb from before my father's time. It says, 'People bring about their own undoing through their tongues.' Our tongues will not bring about our undoing, Ahmes. We will honor Djefi's demand. I do not understand why he wants it so, but he does. So, my son, we will talk no more of the netjrew."

"But we can when we are alone, can't we?"

Paneb shook his head. "No, Ahmes, not even then." He saw the disappointment in his son's eyes. "Except when we are here and there are no workmen with us. Only then."

Ahmes looked at the tomb entrance, his eyes still seeing the gods who had emerged from the dark opening.

"Father, did you see how strong his arms were? Did you see how he threw the spear?" Ahmes threw a pretend spear, mimicking the god's motion and swagger.

Paneb reached down and stroked his son's smooth head.

"Yes, Ahmes, he was the tallest and strongest netjer I have ever seen."

Paneb and Ahmes entered the tomb to search for the entrance the gods had used to journey from Khert-Neter, but they found only what they expected – walls and rock.

Later, instead of returning home, Paneb decided to spend the night at the tomb with Ahmes, hoping to exhaust the topic of gods and spears by letting him talk and ask his questions. Paneb thought it would be easier for them to keep the secret if Ahmes had a chance to ask all of the questions he could find.

The next day they worked alone in the tomb and Ahmes remained full of questions.

Was the goddess Bastet? And shouldn't her head have been a cat's head like all the statues? Why did she have red hair? Which god was he? Was he a god from some other land? Could a god even be "hesy" – from outside Kemet? What was outside Kemet? Did anyone go there? Did they have different gods? I wouldn't want to share our gods, would you? If a god could come here from Khert-Neter, could we go to Khert-Neter and then return? Would we see our ancestors there?

By the evening of the second day Ahmes at last grew quiet. Although Paneb welcomed relief from the constant questions, he wondered what the reflectiveness meant.

Now as they approached the tomb on the third day since the gods' arrival, Ahmes had grown more interested in repeating what he had seen, as if planting the memories so that one day he would be able to tell his children about the time gods had walked out of a tomb.

It was too early for Paneb to breathe a sigh of relief, the threat Djefi had made still clutched at his heart whenever he thought of the fat priest, but, at last, he felt that it might be possible that they could keep the secret.

He wondered how much longer they would need to. Eventually, he reasoned, the gods would leave Sobek to visit other gods at their temples.

Paneb and Ahmes sat on stools under the palm shelter. Paneb had removed his kilt and hung it from the canopy.

A sack with rolls of papyrus lay in the sand at their feet. Ahmes looked at the rolls and, realizing what they were, tried to sit quietly and erect, like an adult.

"You've guessed, haven't you?" Paneb asked.

Ahmes nodded. "You'll let me draw today."

Paneb reached into the sack and pulled out a papyrus.

"Thoth?" Ahmes asked, remembering which god his father had been drawing the day before.

Paneb shook his head. "Yes and no."

"No, Father, not baboons," Ahmes slid off his stool and squatted over the sand, his arms touching the ground like a baboon, which often represented the god Thoth. He grunted like a baboon as he reached one arm high in the air and scratched his armpit with the other.

"Wait, don't move," Paneb said suddenly. "That is a perfect pose, let me sketch it." Then he smiled and Ahmes started to laugh, happy to have been tricked by his father.

A noise from the tomb stopped their laughter.

Ahmes looked anxiously at his father.

Paneb reached into the bag and pulled from it a stone mallet.

He stood slowly, Ahmes moved closer to him. Together they watched the tomb entrance where a shadow had separated itself from the background and a figure stepped out into the morning sunlight.

Ahmes gasped and Paneb raised the mallet.

Seeing the fear in their faces and the stone hammer in the man's hand, Tim Hope raised both his hands to show that he was unarmed. In his best Arabic he said the first thing that seemed helpful: "I come in peace."

LOST CITY OF INEB-HEDJ

Horus swept in from the west, riding updrafts rising from the hot desert sand. The hawk was watching the man and boy in the wadi when it saw a shadow move at the bottom of the sandstone outcropping. Tucking its wings, it dove closer and saw that it was another man. Calling out once in a raspy cry, the hawk spread its wings and veered away toward the river leaving the desert necropolis behind.

Tim had an unsettling premonition that something fundamental was about to change.

Earlier, after the wall had slid back into place inside the tomb, he had waited a few minutes to be sure the taxi driver and guard had not found a way to follow him. Then he had pulled the plastic toothpick from his Swiss army knife and wedged it into the nearly invisible crack at the top of the section of wall that had opened for him.

It had taken only a minute to see that Brian and Diane were not in this section of the tomb. During that time, Tim had felt a strange lightness settle over him as if the air were richer and cleaner.

The hallway he had found himself in was different from the other parts of the tomb.

Although most of the paintings were unfinished, the outlines were cleaner and stronger. The scenes that were painted seemed artificially bright and vivid, as if they had been painted yesterday. They looked as if paint would come away on his fingers if he touched them.

And the floor here was clean, as if it were swept on a regular basis.

He had followed the corridor toward the morning light and stepped outside the tomb to see a naked man with a stone hammer standing under a small palm-topped canopy made of four poles stuck into the sand. Near him, a boy crouched by some papyrus rolls; one of them was unfurled showing a baboon. The sky above them and the desert beyond them was vast and empty.

Tim's appearance at the tomb entrance had startled Paneb and Ahmes into stillness as they waited to see what the strange god would do. Ahmes lowered his arm from his baboon pose and waited by his father whose fingers tightened on the handle of his stone mallet.

They had watched the flight of Horus as the sacred hawk approached and then called to the god outside the tomb. Now the god spoke to them.

"Sabah el-kheir," Tim spoke slowly in Arabic and then in English, "Good morning."

For Paneb, the appearance of another god from this tomb was more than he could absorb. He dropped his stone mallet and stood unmoving, his eyes wide and fearful.

Tim wondered how bad his Arabic was. Had he mistakenly said something threatening?

"Do you speak English? Parlez-vous Français?"

"Father," Ahmes said quietly. "Is he another netjer?"

Paneb nodded his head and whispered back, "Did you not see Netjer Horus welcome him?"

Tim shrugged out of his backpack and swung it in front of him. Squatting, he dug through a pocket until he found his Arabic-English phrasebook.

Paneb took a hesitant step toward Tim.

"Welcome, Eternal Netjer," he said, remembering how Djefi had addressed the gods. "I am Paneb, chief artist of the necropolis of Saqqara. This is my son, Ahmes."

Ahmes stepped up beside Paneb, beaming with joy that his father had thought to introduce him to a god.

Tim looked up from his book. Whatever language they were speaking, it was unlike anything he had heard. He knew that there were dozens of dialects of Chinese, but he thought that Arabic was pretty standard.

Saqqara? Had the man said 'Saqqara?'

He tucked the phrase book back into a pocket.

Standing, he opened his arms and looked left and right to show that he was taking in the entire area. "Saqqara," he said.

The man and boy both nodded vigorously.

Tim took his bearings from the sun and then pointed east toward the river and Memphis.

"Memphis."

The man and boy looked at each other. The man shook his head and said, "Ineb-Hedj."

The limestone wall into which the tomb entrance was cut blocked Tim's view of the plateau behind him. He waved his hands toward the monuments that he knew sat atop the plateau.

"Step Pyramid. Bent Pyramid. Any of this ring a bell?" he said, smiling in frustration. "King Djoser?"

"Netjerierkhet Djoser," Paneb said quietly, unconsciously nodding his head

Tim pointed to the tomb behind him. "The tomb of Kanakht?"

The artist nodded and repeated Kanakht's name.

"OK," Tim said to himself, "We've got the nouns down."

He worried that Memphis didn't seem familiar to them and their nudity bothered him, but they seemed comfortable, like a nudist family.

He picked up his backpack and walked over to them.

"I'm Tim," he said, extending his right hand.

The man looked curiously at Tim's outstretched hand.

Ahmes, who had seen Brian shake hands with the bodyguard Bakr, understood what Tim wanted to do. He stepped forward and took Tim's hand. "I am Ahmes, son of Paneb," he said.

Paneb's knees suddenly felt weak. What was his son doing, touching a god? But the god seemed pleased and was gripping Ahmes' hand firmly.

"Pleased to meet you, Ahmes," Tim said, repeating the sounds that he hoped were the boy's name.

Paneb hesitantly reached out to the god with his hand. Tim released Ahmes and took Paneb's hand.

"I'm Tim," he repeated to the artist, emphasizing his name.

"Tim," Paneb said, marveling at the soft, warm touch of the god's skin. He had feared that the god's touch would have been burning, or perhaps as cold and hard as stone.

Ahmes spoke for his awe-struck father. "Paneb," he said gesturing at his father.

"Paneb. All right, then," Tim said, careful to keep his voice cheerful. "We've got the introductions out of the way, and I know you don't understand a word I'm saying, but I want to find out where Brian and Diane went."

Ahmes caught the name of the god 'Brian.' He looked at his father and pointed across the desert to the path Bakr had taken when he led Brian and Diane to the oasis of To-She. "Brian," he said.

"You understand me? That's great!" Tim said. "Now, it was two days ago, right? Did they say where they were going? Were they, oh, I don't know, lost, confused, injured?"

Ahmes and Paneb waited for the god to say another word that they could understand.

"You have no idea what I'm saying do you? You just pointed over that way and said 'Brian' because 'Brian' means desert or something else that's over there."

Tim scratched his head, trying to think of a way to communicate.

Ahmes saw his frustration. He ran back to the shelter and took a long-handled brush from the bag. Kneeling on the sand by Tim's feet he drew a smiley face. "Brian," he said, pointing to it.

Tim looked at the round face and wondered if 'Brian' meant happy. But why did they point across the desert when they heard 'Brian' if the word meant happy?

Paneb, shaken out of his daze by his son's fearlessness, finally moved. He touched Ahmes' shoulder and gestured for the brush. Then he cleared a space on the sand and re-created his drawing of Brian wearing his baseball cap and riding a camel.

"Of course," Tim said, looking at the cleanly drawn profiles. "You're the guy who's re-creating those tomb drawings. You're an artist."

He held out his hand for the brush and then, copying Paneb's flat style, drew a second camel with a woman on it, her head covered with the straw hat he remembered her wearing.

Paneb and Ahmes nodded their heads eagerly. Tim pointed at the drawing of the woman and said, "Diane." Then he pointed to the man and said, "Brian."

Then he pointed off across the desert and shrugged, hoping they would name a town he recognized.

"To-She," Paneb said.

Tim dug out his map of Egypt and spread it on the desert floor. Paneb stood, looking over his shoulder; Ahmes sat beside him, his eyes bright with excitement as he looked at the colors and shapes on the map.

Tracing the blue wavering line that ran down the center of the map, Tim looked at Ahmes and said, "The Nile River."

When he got no response, Tim dug through his backpack and pulled out a plastic bottle of water. He splashed some on his hand and then pointed again to the river. "The Nile," he repeated.

Paneb understood and spoke first. "Iteru," he said.

"Iteru?" Tim said. He looked at Paneb and Ahmes. How could they live along the Nile and know it by another name?

Suddenly his fearful premonition returned.

Leaving his backpack behind, he ran to the edge of the wadi and scrambled up its loose sand. He reached the top of the steep bank and looked toward the tomb, expecting to see the top of the Step Pyramid rising above the plateau.

Impossibly, he saw nothing but sky.

He kicked off his sandals and ran across the desert, climbing the slight rise to the plateau's top. He came to the desert highland where half an hour earlier he had arrived with Musa, where he had walked through the reconstructed entrance-way and entered the small building that housed the plateau entrance to Kanakht's tomb. Now the colonnades and the walls, the cars and the parking lot, the temple pillars and the huge pyramids themselves were gone.

He stopped, breathless from exertion and panic.

Standing there shaking and wobbly, he stared across the flat expanse. Its emptiness was broken only by a few low mastabas. Two nights ago he stood here and squinted at the Step Pyramid, making its form seem to disappear in the darkness. But even as a dark shadow, the pyramid had been massive and eternal.

Now it wasn't here.

He slowly turned, taking in the ancient burial ground's spacious emptiness. And then, continuing to turn, he saw in the distance the green of the Nile's valley, richer and darker and fuller than he remembered it. And along the river, rising from its banks he saw a city of mud brick homes surrounded by a thick white wall: The long-dead city that Tim knew as Memphis, the city that Paneb and Ahmes had called Ineb-Hedj.

He didn't know how long he stood there, his mind struggling to make sense of what he wasn't seeing.

The last time this plateau had been empty was five thousand years ago, before the Step Pyramid had been built. He thought of the sweep of days, the billions of lives that had not yet been lived, the dreams not yet dreamt.

The faces of his friends, his dead parents, of Addy, swept past him. Here in this incredibly distant past none of them had been born. And none of them had died. They each had lived, or would live, in a sliver of time that was yet to come.

He looked west, into the desert, into the land the ancient Egyptians called Deshret, the red land. He pictured the thousands of miles that stretched out before him from this spot, out across the rest of Africa, across the Atlantic Ocean to his home, to the dark street where he had lost Addy. But all he saw was endless sand and air shimmering above it as it gave up its heat.

The emptiness of the space between this place and his home, the incomprehensible length of time between this now and the now when he had held Addy overwhelmed him with sadness. In all this space and time, there would be only a few years when she would live. Those years were far in the future from this moment, and, for Addy, they had already ended.

He realized that it didn't matter to him where or when he lived in the long sweep of time if it couldn't be with Addy, and she had been taken from him.

Standing alone, five thousand years from his life and from Addy, he realized that until now he never had really understood that he would never see her again. Their time together had come and gone. It had ended. Forever.

He shouted her name, a long, strangled cry of pain and loss.

Over and over again he cried out her name.

The atmosphere is a closed environment. He had read that with every deep breath, a person inhales molecules of air that had been breathed out by Julius Caesar as he lay dying on the steps of the Roman Capitol.

And so Tim filled the air with Addy's name. Ages from now when she would be born and they would meet and love, their every breath would be filled with his love for her and with his pain at his loss.

He shouted and screamed and cried until he sank to the barren desert floor, drawing ragged, sobbing breaths.

"What should we do, father?" Ahmes said.

From the wadi they could hear the god screaming over and over again, the sounds filled with pain and rage.

Paneb was almost thirty years old. He had stood close enough to touch King Djoser. He had seen the beautiful priestess Hetephernebti. He had watched the river flood and wash into the streets of Ineb-Hedj.

He had seen the priestess of Isis re-enact the goddess' grief and tears when her husband Osiris was torn apart by the evil god Seth. He had heard songs about her great lamentations when she found that her child, the great god Horus, had been poisoned by his evil uncle.

Her grief must have sounded like the cries that came now from the plateau above them.

He stood with Ahmes and rested his hand on his son's shoulder, feeling the small muscles and bones and fragile life beneath his hand.

"The netjrew have greater lives, Ahmes. They see the dawning of a thousand years, they know joys we cannot imagine. When you rise so high above, then, Ahmes, when you fall your pain must be so much greater.

"I don't know why this netjer is in such pain. I don't know how we can help him. But if he asks us, we must do whatever we can," Paneb said.

"Do you think someone has died?" Ahmes asked.

"We all enter Khert-Neter, Ahmes. It is passing to a better world. No, I think this netjer has lost something that is now beyond his reach."

"Isn't there anything we can do?"

Paneb nodded. "Yes, Ahmes. I have an idea."

Feeling a presence, Tim turned to see Paneb standing by the path that led from the wadi to the edge of the plateau.

His pain remained a sore knot in his heart, but his anger was exhausted, emptied into desert sky. He felt immensely lost and isolated but at the same time immensely free and unburdened. Addy was gone, but she was gone from the other time. As long as he was here he could think of Addy as a dream that was yet to happen.

Tim got to his feet. He knew his face was streaked with tears, but he didn't want to run his sand-covered hands against his skin. He walked to Paneb, who watched him with undisguised friendliness and compassion.

Tim wanted to try to smile, but knew it would seem false.

He sighed deeply, collecting himself.

Brian and Diane. They were the reason he had come here, wherever and whenever 'here' was. He would find them and help them return to their world. Their world. Part of his mind wondered if he even wanted it to be his world anymore.

"Paneb," he said, his voice hoarse. "Brian and Diane?"

Paneb pointed away from the river, off to the southwest and said "Brian, Diane, To-She."

They returned to the wadi. Tim's backpack was where he had left it, the map on the ground beside it, four small piles of sand holding down its corners.

If I am in ancient Egypt, Tim realized, then there won't be any interpreters for my English. My smatterings of Arabic won't be understood. I know some of the ancient names of people and places, but nothing of the everyday words.

He crossed his arms, studied the map for a minute and then looked off into the distance.

He had no idea if this was a hostile place, who he could go to for help, how he would travel. Were Brian and Diane in danger? Did they even understand where they were?

He saw that Paneb and Ahmes were waiting for his attention. Ahmes was standing near the shelter, almost bouncing from one foot to the other, a hopeful smile on his face. Tim saw that the sand by the boy was filled with drawings.

The hair on Tim's arms stood up as he looked at the drawings. They were drawn exactly in the style of the tomb murals. Using symbols, they told a story.

WELCOMING A GOD

The sand drawings reminded Tim of the symbols engraved on the Pioneer 10 probe launched into space in the 1970s.

The spacecraft passed by Mars, swung beyond it to Jupiter and then slipped past the giant planet into the dark void. It was the first man-made object to leave the solar system, so scientists mounted a plaque on the craft in case aliens corralled the tiny ship as it hurtled past them.

The plaque showed a line etching of a naked man and woman standing in front of a silhouette of the spacecraft. The man's right hand was raised in greeting. A diagram of a hydrogen atom, its wavelength meant to establish scale, and a series of converging lines were designed to help the aliens figure out where our sun is located. A schematic drawing of the solar system's planets, with a binary code showing their relative distances, pinpointed the origin of the space probe.

The idea had been to find a way to communicate basic information to an alien life form.

Paneb had taken the same approach.

Brian and Diane, drawn in profile, were holding hands. He had a baseball cap on his head and a short spear in his free hand. A small cat was at her feet. Tim puzzled over that for a minute until he remembered the Sylvester the Cat shirt she had been wearing.

They were facing a fat man who welcomed them with two hands turned palm up and extended. A crocodile-headed man stood behind the fat man. At his feet stood two small men, each armed with a short spear. Beside them was a long, thin four-legged animal with a curved snout like an aardvark.

A vertical line separated the first group from the next drawings.

In the next series of drawings, the baseball cap, the cat and a spear were drawn above a camel standing in profile. A boat with a curved prow and stern held a crocodile and spear. Three circles followed and then the baseball cap, spear and cat were drawn beside a palm tree. Two more circles separated them from the boat at a palm tree.

A lake was drawn beside the palm tree. A man with a crocodile head stood beside the tree.

As Tim looked at the last drawing, the feeling of sandy grittiness on his hands and face grew too annoying. He turned and walked to his backpack where he dug around until he found a pack of wet wipes. He pulled one out and carefully cleaned around his eyes and then his mouth. Conserving the small wipe, he folded it carefully and then cleaned between his fingers and in the small crevices of skin under the joints of his fingers.

Finished, he looked at the neatly folded square, incrusted with sand, and wondered if he could somehow clean it and remoisten it. If he was interpreting the drawing correctly, then Brian and Diane were three days away by camel. That put a lot of sand between them and him.

He shook the tissue and tucked it in a corner pocket of the backpack.

When he returned to the drawings, Ahmes and Paneb were standing in different spots.

"OK," Tim said. "Let's give those nouns a workout." He smiled at Ahmes, who smiled shyly in return and then looked away.

Walking to the first drawings, Tim pointed at Brian and Diane and said their names.

Paneb nodded.

Pointing at the fat man, Tim said "To-She."

Paneb shook his head and ran lightly to the last set of drawings. He motioned in a circle that included the lake, palm tree and the god Sobek. "To-She," he said. Then he returned to the fat man and said, "Djefi."

"Got it," Tim said. "To-She is the place, Djefi is the fat man. Djefi greets Brian and Diane and then they go off on a camel. The little guys must be soldiers." Tim remembered that in tomb paintings, secondary characters, no matter how large in life, were drawn at a smaller scale to signify their relative insignificance.

"Wait a minute, the dog thing is gone. Where's the dog thing?" he asked, pointing at a smooth spot by Djefi where the strange creature with the curved snout had been sketched in the sand.

Paneb ignored his question. Instead he walked over to the first set of drawings and began to explain in Egyptian. "The two netjrew were greeted by Djefi, First Prophet of Sobek, and his bodyguards. A guard took Brian and Diane by camel. Djefi left by boat. It will take Brian and Diane three days to travel by camel to To-She. Djefi will get there two days later on his boat."

Picking out the names in Paneb's speech, Tim found that the sound of the language was becoming less grating. Although it was tempting to try to teach Ahmes and Paneb English, he realized that unless one of them was with him constantly to serve as an interpreter, he would need to learn ancient Egyptian.

He wasn't sure what had happened with the dog figure, perhaps it had been a mistake they had corrected, but Ahmes had seemed embarrassed about something. Either they had decided not to tell him something or else they were trying to hint at something.

Tim put the question aside. He was in a foreign land and a foreign time. He needed friends, so instead of interrogating Paneb, Tim clapped his hands softly and looked at the tomb artist with a smile.

"Thank you, Paneb," he said, giving a slight bow.

Turning to his backpack, Tim pulled out a bag with a large sweet cinnamon roll he had taken from the restaurant after breakfast. He carried it to Paneb and Ahmes. He tore off part of it and offered it to Ahmes, who started to reach for it and then stopped himself, looking to Paneb to get his father's permission.

Paneb nodded and Ahmes took the piece of roll. Tim tore away another piece and offered it to Paneb, who took it gravely as if receiving a communion wafer. Tim said, "To friends," and bit into the sweet pastry.

When Addy's friends were setting Tim up on the blind date where he met her, they had described her as intelligent, driven, analytical and organized. They had meant it as a compliment. Her personality was so forceful that they had forgotten to mention how beautiful she was. Tim had assumed that she would fall into the "nice personality" category of the other blind dates his friends had arranged.

They had met for an afternoon walk in a park, a cup of coffee afterward. Her blond hair was pulled back in a ponytail. A few delicate wisps of hair had escaped and floated at the nape of her neck. When Tim first saw her, the sun was behind her and she seemed to glow with its energy and light.

While they exchanged half-embarrassed greetings, his eyes kept drifting to her neck where those wisps of hair and the smooth curve of her neck looked so exposed and innocent. He had to consciously keep himself from reaching out and touching her.

Later, over coffee, as he looked at her green eyes, so alive and full of interest, he blurted out that he thought she was beautiful.

"I know," she answered, smiling into her coffee cup.

He was taken aback by her confidence and smugness. His face showed it and she laughed, a series of light musical notes that he wanted to hear over and over again.

"No, no, I don't know that I'm beautiful. Well, maybe," she grinned at him. "But I know you think so."

She sipped her coffee, her eyes on him, deciding how open she should be.

"Tim," she said, setting down her cup and reaching over to place her hand over his. Her touch thrilled him and he wanted to turn over her hand and trace its contours with his fingertips.

"Tim, you should never, ever play poker. Your face doesn't hide anything. When we were in the park, I would have run away from you if my friends hadn't told me, over and over, that you're not really a pervert."

She laughed again at his confused expression.

"Oh my god. You are going to be so much fun."

He knew he was blushing now. Her words suggested that they would see each other again.

"Here," she tugged at his hand and placed it on her neck; at the very spot he had stared at earlier.

He felt the tender thickness of the hair as it emerged from her skin and then how it grew softer and willowy until it seemed to merge with the air. He brushed her skin gently, realizing how thin the boundary was between her body and his, how the surfaces of their skins, sliding softly along each other, were really no boundary at all.

"My god, that's electric," she said leaning her neck into his hand.

Reluctantly he slid his hand away. "They told you I'm not a pervert?" he asked. "How did that come up?"

She laughed again. "They were telling me that you're an artist and then, Jeanne, I think it was, said, 'Oh yeah, don't worry if he really, really looks at you. He's not a pervert.' "

"Thanks, Jeanne," Tim said.

"They all really like you, Tim. And they were right."

"I'm not a pervert?"

"I don't know, yet," she said, grinning. "I mean you do really study things. You know you felt the texture of the napkin when we sat down, don't you? And when we got our coffee, you held the cup up to your face, closed your eyes and took a long, slow breath of its aroma. When people come in, you don't just glance at them, you really look at them as if you're trying to memorize them.

"And, to be honest, I kind of like the way you look at me. It's not exactly naked hunger, but it's certainly intense. You seem able to control yourself in public, although I'm not sure I will be able to the way you just touched me."

"Will be able?"

"Yes," she said. "I think you're about to ask me out on a real date."

Tim realized as he chewed the cinnamon roll that it was a little easier to think of her now. The love he would always feel for her seemed to be pushing at the pain that had overwhelmed him earlier up on the plateau.

For the first time, he thought it might be possible one day to remember her without pain.

The sweet taste of the roll was something Ahmes had never imagined. What other things did the gods have that he had never imagined?

This god seemed very different from the two who had arrived earlier. *But then people are different,* he thought, *the gods would be different, too.* He had always pictured them in a vague way as strong, powerful, fearless; as hard as the stone in the tombs.

But this god looked and felt like any other person. He did seem different when he looked at things because he seemed to drink them in and to see past them. And at other times, like now, he seemed to have left his body. Perhaps his body was here in Kemet and at the same time his ka was in Khert-Neter.

It must be very strange to be a god, Ahmes thought. He took the last bite of the sweet roll. *Strange and very nice.*

Paneb kept stealing glances at Tim.

He had seen Hetephernebti, priestess of Re, several times. She was happy and smiling, often stopping to talk with people as she walked through the streets of Iunu where the great temple of Re stood. He had seen the stern-looking Waja-Hur, priest of Thoth, several times here at the tomb when he came to draw hieroglyphs from the Book of the Dead. He was ancient, and although unbent by the years he carried, he had seemed weary and almost angry.

This god was as different from Brian and Diane as Hetephernebti was from Waja-Hur, or from Djefi.

The male gods surprised Paneb with their energy. *But then gods must be so full of life, it would be hard to contain it in a body,* he thought. Although Brian had been larger and stronger, this god, with his intensity and quietness seemed more powerful. There was something about his face, an openness and honesty, that made Paneb want to help and protect him.

As if he could help and protect a god.

Ahh, what will Taki think?

She was so attentive to the things that their family needed to survive from day to day - cooking, fetching water, making linen to barter at the market for food, shaving their heads, caring for them every day.

She had little time for the gods, except, of course for Ptah and Bes. But all the women wore amulets of Bes to help with childbirth and to keep snakes out of the home.

He felt sad some times, worried that Taki was so involved in living this life, that she never got a glimpse of what their eternal life would be like.

When he took priests to see his tomb paintings of the gods, Paneb would watch their reactions. Sometimes as they studied the drawings, Paneb would see their eyes focus beyond the tomb walls, and he knew that his art had opened a window for the priests to see into Khert-Neter. They would stand a little straighter, their voices would grow softer, even their movements would become more graceful.

Paneb was inspired by those moments, by the proof that his work was pleasing to the priests and so, perhaps, to the gods. He wished he could share that feeling with Taki, so she could understand his love of the tombs and his eagerness to stand in the dimly lit underground chambers painting and communing with the gods, especially Ptah, the god who guided his hand.

But then sometimes, when Taki was teaching their daughters to cook or to weave linen and Paneb saw Taki's concentration reflected in the faces of his beloved daughters, he knew that they also communed with the gods.

She should meet this god, he decided. It was a gift he could give her.

Tim shook himself free from his reverie and looked across the desert as if finding himself here for the first time.

He couldn't walk across the desert, hoping to survive for three or four days, hoping to accidentally stumble across To-She. For the moment, Brian and Diane were beyond his reach. He needed transportation; he needed a better way to communicate than scratching in the sand. He needed a plan.

He stood, careful to keep his damp fingers from touching the sand.

He picked up the long brush Paneb had used to draw in the sand. Ahmes hurried to his side to clear away a space in the sand.

Tim drew a box with a doorway. He pointed to it and looked at Ahmes, who said 'hewet.'

Pointing to the house again, Tim said, "Hewet of Paneb and Ahmes." Then he placed his hand against his chest and said his name. Ahmes' mouth gaped open in surprise. He turned to Paneb.

"Father, he wants to come to our house!"

"Yes, Ahmes, I think so," Paneb agreed, wondering if the god had read his mind.

Tim continued to draw, making a circle to represent the sun and then a dashed line to show it moving across the sky and setting.

Paneb nodded. "At night. I think, Ahmes," he said, recalling Djefi's orders to be silent, "that the netjrew like to be secretive."

"That's why we never see them, isn't it?" Ahmes said.

When dusk came, Paneb sent Ahmes ahead to make sure that no one was along the path to Ineb-Hedj and to tell his mother that she should prepare for a guest.

They had spent the afternoon teaching the god their language. They took turns drawing in the sand and saying the words to match the pictures. At other times they had acted out ideas, pretending to eat, drink, sleep and ride camels. The god was shy at first, depending on Ahmes and Paneb to decide which words to teach. But when they ran out of ideas, unsure what he wanted to learn, the god pulled an object out of the sack he carried.

He lifted part of it and showed Paneb and Ahmes that it was filled with pages of papyrus only smoother and whiter.

The god drew pictures on the pages and asked Ahmes and Paneb to describe them.

One picture showed two men fighting. Another showed a crocodile attacking a man. Others were less exciting: a boat, a man walking across the desert, the sun rising and setting. He drew a snake, a scorpion, a fire, and a water pot. His drawings were quick and accurate and Paneb, remembering how the god Brian had thrown the spear so deeply into the sand, wondered if there was anything the gods could not do.

It was dark as Paneb and Tim approached the outskirts of Ineb-Hedj. They were greeted by Ahmes who was out of breath after running from their house back to the edge of town.

"Mother wouldn't let me go because I wouldn't tell her who the guest was," he said. "I told her it was someone you met at the tomb, but I didn't know his name. She asked what he did and if he wore a kilt."

Paneb smiled. "What did you say?"

"I told her it was a surprise."

Paneb nodded. "It will be, it will be."

Tim followed none of the conversation. He knew that the crash course in Egyptian that afternoon was just a start at acclimating his ear to sounds he had never heard before. He hoped that being immersed in the language would make him learn it quickly.

The moon was in its last quarter, however, the stars were bright and it was easy for Tim to follow Paneb through the maze of hard-packed dirt streets of Ineb-Hedj. Mud-brick homes with open doorways and narrow open holes for windows were scattered along the tree-shaded pathways. At some places a group of three or four homes faced each other in a half circle with a rock-lined fire pit in the center of the clearing.

It seemed that Paneb was leading him through back alleys, avoiding areas where Tim heard the sound of people talking. Once they startled a pen of geese and Paneb's pace picked up as the geese began to honk. At one house a young goat tethered to a post cried out as they passed.

Soon they left the crowded area and entered a neighborhood where the pathway was wider and straighter; the houses were larger and set back from the street. Most of them had head-high, mud-brick walls surrounding a small courtyard.

They followed the street into a small cul-de-sac, where a larger house stood beside two smaller homes. The smell of cooking spices and horseradish coming from the larger home reminded Tim that he hadn't eaten since they had shared the cinnamon roll.

They stopped in the dark clearing and Paneb pointed to the small house at their left. "The hewet of Taki's mother," he said. Pointing to the other smaller home, he said, "Hewet of Taki's sister."

As Tim nodded his understanding his stomach growled in hunger.

Paneb smiled at this human-sounding god. "Taki will have prepared food." He started to pray that the food would meet this god's approval, but then wondered to whom he should pray. If the god approved, he approved. He had seemed a very generous god so far. Paneb hoped it would continue.

"I call my wife Taki, but her name is Takhaaenbbastet."

Tim repeated the longer name and Paneb nodded approval.

He pushed open the gateway in the whitewashed wall that enclosed the courtyard and entered, holding the gate open for Tim.

Directly in front of them was a palm-leaf-topped canopy, similar to the one Tim had seen at the tomb, although the poles supporting this frame were sturdier than the ones at the tomb. Beneath the canopy was a pool of water.

Tim saw Paneb glance up at the dark roof of the low house. A narrow staircase followed the left wall to the flat roof. He could see the outline of two arches on the roof and wondered what they were.

Paneb led him around the canopy and past the steps. In the dim light coming from the doorway, Tim could see four columns supporting an overhanging roof that provided shade at the front of the house.

The aroma of garlic and onions mixed with roasted goose grew stronger at the doorstep. Tim wondered if Taki had prepared a special meal because she was expecting a guest or if this was the welcome Paneb received every evening.

"Welcome to my hewet, Netjer Tim," Paneb said, reciting the words as a ritual welcome.

Taki and her oldest daughter had their backs to the doorway when Tim and Paneb entered.

"Beloved sister, this is Neb Tim," he said to his wife using the title 'Lord' with Tim's name.

Taki and her daughter turned to the doorway.

She wore a long, black wig and a white linen dress with a single strap over her right shoulder. Gold bracelets were on her wrist, and an alabaster amulet of Bes, the dwarf god who protected households, dangled from a coarse gold chain around her neck.

Her daughter, nude except for a linen belt that hung around her waist, its ends hanging by her side, stood beside Taki. She looked a year or two older than Ahmes, her body still boyish and un-shaped.

Taki held a platter with a roasted goose on it. Her daughter held a bowl of beans.

They juggled the bowls when they saw Tim, almost dropping the food onto the house's hard-packed dirt floor.

Paneb had seen three gods arrive this week and spent all day with this one. There had been moments when he had forgotten that Tim was a god. He also had gotten used to Tim's strange looks. He hadn't thought of the effect Tim would have on his family.

Paneb, his head shaved, was wearing only the pleated kilt he had put back on before returning to Ineb-Hedj.

Tim was wearing khaki shorts, a white T-shirt with a drawing of Family Guy's Peter Griffin and a safari jacket vest with a dozen pockets and flaps. Although cut short, he had a full head of curly, black hair. And although only average in height for a twenty-first century American, he was half a foot taller than Paneb.

Paneb stepped quickly across the small room and took the roasted goose from Taki and placed it on the low table beside her. His daughter recovered and placed the bowl beside the goose.

Tim promptly forgot the greeting he had memorized, and said in English, "Good evening, Takhaaenbbastet. Thank you for receiving me." He blushed when he realized that it made no difference how polite he was because she wouldn't understand a word he had said. He hoped that his tone and body language would ease her fear.

Before the confusion could begin to clear, Paneb's youngest daughter, Hapu, ran crying into the house. She was followed by Ahmes who held a dead scorpion in his hand.

She held her left arm stiffly in front of her. Even in the dim light from the lamps Taki had lit, Tim could see the red swelling where the scorpion had stung her.

As Taki bent to take her daughter in her arms and comfort her, Paneb ran to the next room and quickly returned with a knife. He went to Hapu and grasped her arm, preparing to cut open the wound.

Without thinking, Tim shouted "Wait!"

He and Addy had taken first aid courses while planning the trip and had studied treatment for problems that they thought were likely in the desert: heat exhaustion, dehydration, and various animal attacks, including the one Tim feared the most - a camel bite. He knew a scorpion sting was painful, but less likely to be fatal than whatever Paneb was going to do with that wicked-looking knife.

Paneb had stopped and was watching Tim, his eyes full of fear.

Tim swung his backpack off his shoulders and squatted beside it. He dug out his first aid kit and opened it. Taking out a pack of instant cold compresses, he squeezed one of the packs to activate it.

Sitting cross-legged on the floor, he motioned for Paneb to bring Hapu to him. The girl, astonished at Tim's appearance, stopped crying when she saw him. With Paneb's gentle urging she approached Tim.

"Name?" he asked Paneb in Egyptian.

"Hapu," Paneb answered softly.

"Hapu," Tim said, reaching out to touch her shoulder. "I know you can't understand me, but neither could my dog when I talked to him and we got along fine. And I promise I won't ask you to roll over or jump through a hoop." He smiled, hoping that his attempt at a calming bedside manner would work.

He felt Paneb and Taki watching him and thought for a second about the knife in Paneb's hand.

He laid the ice pack on his left leg and sat Hapu on his right. Leaning away from her to reach his first aid kit, he tore open a cleansing wipe. He took her injured arm in his hand and gently cleaned the swollen area around the sting mark.

He took a tube of first aid cream and dabbed some on the sting, spreading it softly.

"You're doing great, Hapu. Really brave," he whispered.

He tore a small strip of gauze and folded it to make a bandage, which he placed over the sting. Then he wrapped gauze around it to hold the bandage in place.

"You've probably never felt anything this cold," he told her pointing to the cold compress. He held the ice pack up to her and lifted her hand to it. He nodded encouragement as her hand reached for and then touched the icy pack.

She jerked her hand away and cried, "Mother, mother!"

Taki started to step forward, but hesitated, fearful of this man her husband had addressed as 'lord.' Tim waved her forward and held the pack up to her. She touched it and jerked away as Hapu had done.

Tim held the compress against his forearm. "Nefer," he said, hoping they would understand the word as good instead of beautiful. "Ahhh," he said, hoping it sounded like a sigh of relief and not pain.

He felt Ahmes sidled up beside him. The boy touched the cold compress. Instead of jerking back as Taki and Hapu had, he pretended it felt good. "Ahhh," he said, trying to sound like Tim.

"Here, Hapu, you try it," the boy said.

With her brother holding her hand, Hapu touched the cold compress again.

"Ahhh," Ahmes said.

Hapu giggled and mimicked her brother with a small "ahhh."

Tim slowly moved the compress from his arm to Hapu's.

"Ahhh," he said.

Ahmes put his small hand on the compress and said, "It will help you, Hapu." He leaned forward and whispered to her, "He is Netjer Tim. He's very nice. And he's not scary either."

MEASURING THE BALANCE OF KEMET

Sitting under the canopy of his boat, Djefi's thoughts were as dark as the slow moving water.

He had never seen the River Iteru so low. It had been dropping steadily for seven years, ever since King Djoser had taken the throne and declared himself a living god. There was barely any current to slow Djefi's boat on its upriver voyage to the canal that led to To-She. The trip would be shorter than Djefi expected.

However, with the water so low, the boatmen had to watch for rocks along the riverbed that might scrape the bottom of the boat. Unless they were ignorant sons of dung beetles, Djefi thought angrily, they would have enough sense to avoid collisions, wood-scraping jolts which could shake the boat enough to cause beer to slop out of a golden cup and on to a fine linen robe.

Dagi, who had been piloting the boat when it struck submerged rocks, was now nursing open cuts on his back from the lashing Djefi himself had administered. The boatman would have been beaten longer had Djefi not tired from the heat and exertion after ten lashes. The priest could have ordered another crewman to continue the whipping, but Djefi was too exhausted to even listen to the man's screams.

And now, because of Dagi's carelessness, Djefi, tired and angry, sat in a foul-smelling robe with one less cup of beer available to drink.

But they would be back at To-She tomorrow, thanks be to Sobek!

He would be off this swaying boat and back among the shaded pathways of the oasis that he and Sobek called home.

The two strange gods – if they were gods – would be there by now and Yunet would have met them. Djefi was eager to hear her opinion of them because, even though the chantress lacked the training and delicacy of spirit to be a webt-priest or even a ka-servant, she did have an uncanny ability to see things that fell below Djefi's elevated view.

She would know if this Brian was truly a god and Diane truly a goddess.

He sighed and stared off into the distance.

So much was happening.

Even in To-She, away from the river and isolated from the rumors that ran up and down The Two Lands, Djefi had heard of the unrest caused by the prolonged famine. Kemet was in discord, and now strange gods walk out of Kanakht's tomb.

It was too much to be coincidence; Djefi was sure that their appearance had to be related to the famine and to the plans Kanakht had hinted at when Djefi met him at Khmunu.

What will Yunet think of my meeting with the royal adviser and with Waja-Hur, that shrunken old priest?

Djefi hadn't returned to To-She after the meeting because Kanakht had sent him to inspect the tomb. Did the adviser know the gods would appear? Did he have that kind of power, to make gods appear?

Djefi had so much to discuss with Yunet.

His meeting with Kanakht and Waja-Hur had taken place almost three weeks ago. He had been summoned by Kanakht to travel upriver to Khmunu, where Waja-Hur lived. The ancient priest to the god Thoth seldom traveled anymore.

The trip, which took more than a week in each direction, had disrupted his planning for the festival at To-She, but even a high priest did not refuse an invitation from the man who was second in power only to King Djoser.

Kanakht had arrived from the other direction, following the river down from the town of Waset where King Djoser was holding council with priests of Khonsu, Mut and Amon. The harvest season was approaching and, all along the river, everyone knew how meager the results would be. King Djoser was consulting with the priests in hopes of finding a way to restore balance to Kemet.

"He seeks advice," Kanakht had said and coughed a wheezing laugh.

The three men met in Waja-Hur's private quarters inside the Temple of Thoth. The room stood by itself, away from the dark inner chambers of the small temple. It was little more than a mud-brick shack and as poorly furnished. Niches in the wall were filled with small statues of the gods. There were no windows and only one doorway, through which shadowy light spilled onto the dirt floor.

Waja-Hur, naked except for a thin linen belt, was little more than a shadow himself. He looked as old as the Two Lands. He stood in a corner, barely visible in the dim light, but reeking of the smell of death. He was overseer of the royal mortuaries and, as his own death approached, he spent more and more time in the embalming chambers.

Kanakht was half the age of Waja-Hur but still old enough to be Djefi's father. The royal adviser wore an immaculate white linen robe and a wide, golden pectoral, a symbol of his power. He had served as adviser for King Djoser's father for much of his life and he spoke of the current king with an off-hand familiarity that came from his years in power.

"Djoser didn't seek advice when he decided to call himself 'Divine of Body.' But now, when it is clear the gods are offended by his pretentiousness, now he wants me to find a miracle," Kanakht complained.

"It is too late," Waja-Hur said in a raspy whisper.

Each year, when the sacred white ibises arrived and the star Sopdet followed golden Re into the morning sky, the river rose like a groom's staff on his wedding night. It would empty itself over the land for fourteen days. When it returned to its banks, it left behind the moist, black fertile soil that was the gods' gift to Kemet.

But for seven years the flood had been no more than a trickle from a spent old man. The water barely overflowed the bank and left behind little more than a damp coating.

"The Golden Falcon," Kanakht said, dryly referring to King Djoser by the king's favorite nickname, "isn't flying high now. He knows Kemet cannot survive another year of famine. The granaries are empty and this season's harvest will not fill them. Hunger will creep across the land like jackals from Deshret, stirring up unrest and thoughts of revolt."

Waja-Hur nodded in agreement. "The balance is disturbed," he said in the grating whisper that was all he seemed to be able to manage any more.

Djefi had heard that years and years ago, when Waja-Hur was young, he constantly traveled up and down the river. Whenever he entered a town he would call the villagers together and loudly preach to them for hours, extolling the importance of truth and fairness and balance. Afterward, he would sit and record their names on papyrus rolls, taking as much time as was needed to record the name of every man, woman and child who came before him.

Only royalty and the wealthy could afford embalming to preserve their bodies. For the rest, only their names would survive. Having their names recorded by a priest of the god Thoth was their only path to immortality.

And now, for more than twice the life spans of most of the people who lived in the Two Lands, Waja-Hur had represented Thoth. In his old age, he had come to be regarded by many as the god himself, aging, but apparently immortal.

Although Djefi admired the old man's long dedication to his god, he was glad that age had withered his vocal stamina. Balance and fairness were all well and good, but Djefi was high priest of Sobek, a powerful god of action. Just the idea of listening to the old man's pious prattle made Djefi tired.

And, he thought, looking around the empty room that Waja-Hur called home, I'll probably have to remain standing to do it. Where in Seth's holy name is the furniture? Not even a stool?

"Waja-Hur," Djefi said, "I know that you are tireless in your service to Thoth, but surely even you sit sometimes. Can we not get some chairs, and perhaps a jar of beer?"

"You are not in balance," Waja-Hur answered.

"I would like to be balanced on a chair," Djefi answered in his squeaky voice. "Preferably one with a cushion. Surely ... "

The old man frowned at Djefi, but shuffled slowly to the narrow doorway where he called out in a startlingly loud voice. A boy brought a square stool and, following Waja-Hur's pointed direction, placed it behind Djefi.

The fat priest gratefully sank onto it. The boy turned to leave, but Djefi caught his arm. "A jar of beer. And not the weak temple beer."

Kanakht laughed quietly.

Djefi returned to the conversation. "You say King Djoser seeks advice from priests, but he wants you, his adviser, to find a miracle. Shouldn't he be asking the priests for a miracle and seeking advice from you?"

"And my advice would be for him to perform a miracle. There is nothing I can do to make the water flow. It is in the hands of the gods. And he says he is a god, so ... " Kanakht said.

"The time is not right for miracles," Waja-Hur interrupted. "Balance. There is no balance."

Djefi ignored the old man. "You told the king to perform a miracle? That was your advice?" he asked Kanakht, stunned at the man's daring. Without thinking, he added, "And you are still alive?"

A large shadow moved outside the doorway, larger than one that would be cast by a boy carrying beer. Realizing his vulnerable position, the fat priest broke into a sudden sweat. He had been instructed to leave his bodyguards at his boat. He was here in Waja-Hur's temple, surrounded only by the royal guards who accompanied Kanakht on his travels.

Was the shadow outside cast by a guard, ready to arrest him for treason? He had heard that King Djoser was ever alert to words spoken against the Two Lands. Djefi hoped that what he had just said was not treasonous.

He knew how traitors were treated. He felt his bowels gurgle and had an awful vision of soiling himself in front of these powerful old men. He must be careful not to blurt out anything again.

Kanakht saw Djefi glance at the doorway and the sweat that began to seep through the priest's robe.

"Don't worry, First Prophet, he is one of my guards, loyal to me not to King Djoser," he said. "And to answer your questions, I am not an idiot. I advised him to consult with priests to see what the other gods could do."

Waja-Hur hawked loudly and spit. "Kanakht has always been able to balance his advice."

"I know what you think of politics, old friend," Kanakht said.

"At To-She, politics is practiced with the jaws of a crocodile," Djefi said, his squeaky voice rising higher as he tried to impress the two experienced men. "Where is that boy with my beer?"

Waja-Hur made a soft strangled sound that could have been laughter, but Kanakht nodded his head at Djefi.

"I've heard of the strength of your convictions, First Prophet. We believe in your willingness to protect the Two Lands. We respect Sobek's power and strength. He is a great god, unafraid of action."

The words were spoken as a compliment and Djefi felt that they should have put him at ease, but instead they brought another rush of sweat. Djefi was sure that he was missing something obvious to Kanakht and Waja-Hur.

There is a message under Kanakht's words, Djefi worried.

Waja-Hur broke the silence that followed. "Balance, First Prophet. Gods walk the green lands of Khert-Neter, not the Two Lands. Restore the balance."

Djefi looked from the old priest to Kanakht. He was surprised to see sadness and resignation chase each other quickly across the adviser's face.

Suddenly, Djefi had a frightening thought: Are these two old men plotting to kill King Djoser? Is that how the balance is to be restored? Is Kanakht telling me that they are too weak to do it themselves and that I should do their work for them?

How was he supposed to respond? He was unknown at the royal court and could never denounce Kanakht as a plotter against the king's life. However, his silence now would be interpreted by the men as agreement to their plot.

His stomach felt as if it were full of curdled beer as he realized that he was being brought into a treasonous plot against his will.

Kanakht misunderstood Djefi's confused silence. "Ahh, Djefi. You see the problem. There are hard decisions to be made. Sacrifices are needed for the Two Lands."

Djefi's mind raced. Perhaps they are testing my loyalty. It is possible that Kanakht has been sent by King Djoser to see if I will agree to a revolt. But what if they are sincere and I refuse? Will I live to walk away from this or will the guard who is waiting outside the door take me? If I agree and the coup fails, then the king will have me killed. But if it succeeds, how much will I gain? What would be expected? Surely they don't expect me to actually kill the king myself.

"A lot to think about, eh, Djefi," Kanakht said when the priest remained silent. "We are talking here, alone, just the three of us. We are men of honor who, in this long time of suffering, have the interest of the Two Lands in our hearts. That is all.

"Our duty is to Kemet, Djefi. And, of course, to Thoth," he said, nodding to Waja-Hur who seemed to be holding his breath.

"And to Sobek," he said, nodding to Djefi. "And to King Djoser. Our duty, Djefi, as you well know, is to think about what is best for the Two Lands and to make that happen, no matter how difficult or unusual it might seem."

Djefi opened his mouth to respond, but no sound came out.

"We are men of power and purpose, you and I and my old friend Waja-Hur," Kanakht said intently. "Our words, Djefi, are the breath, the tjaw, from which the Two Lands draws its life. Our ideas and thoughts, First Prophet, are the very soul, the ba, of Kemet.

"You are First Prophet of Sobek, the Rager, whose sweat created the River Iteru, you understand these things. You know that when the Two Lands is threatened, it is we who must defend it. I can only imagine what the great Sobek would do.

"Ah, well, I go on and on, as always, eh, Waja-Hur? And you, Djefi, you have a festival to prepare. I look forward to visiting you at To-She for The Cutting Out of Sobek's Tongue. Unfortunately, King Djoser will not be there. He is preoccupied with the coming flood season. I hope you won't take his absence as a slight against the great god Sobek."

Djefi marveled at how the man could so easily use words to mean what they did not.

"Thank you for meeting with us, Djefi. Your litter is waiting to take you back to your boat," Kanakht said.

Djefi realized that the meeting was abruptly over, that he had been dismissed.

They aren't even interested in my response. Such arrogance! But, he thought, such power and confidence. This is what it is like to live so close to the throne, to be at the very center of power.

The boy reappeared, empty-handed but followed by two sedan carriers. They approached Djefi and each offered him a hand to help him rise from the low stool.

"Balance, First Prophet, balance," Waja-Hur whispered.

Djefi grasped the hands of the carriers to pull himself up.

"I like your ideas, Djefi," Kanakht said. "We will consider your plan carefully."

Djefi realized that although Kanakht's words were said to him, they were intended for the ears of the carriers. With those few words, Kanakht had planted false ideas in the carriers' heads, ideas that could later incriminate Djefi and make him appear to be the author of whatever plot Kanakht and Waja-Hur were scheming if the plan failed.

A cold wave of fear passed through Djefi as he grunted himself to his feet, clenching his ass cheeks to keep from breaking wind, or worse, in front of Kanakht and Waja-Hur.

"Stay the night, Djefi," Kanakht said quietly as the priest reached the doorway. "I'll visit you at your boat in the morning. I need your help at the tomb I am having built at Saqqara. We'll talk again tomorrow."

And so, Djefi, thought, I have been summoned to Khmunu only to be entangled in Kanakht's plot to overthrow Djoser. Well, it is done. Waja-Hur will side with Kanakht if the plot comes to light and I, will be blamed.

Rousing himself from his thoughts, Djefi looked at the passing canal bank to get his bearings. They were passing a sharp turn in the canal, where a crooked tree leaned out over the water. He recognized the spot. They were almost home, almost back at To-She.

THE TEMPLE OF SOBEK AT TO-SHE

"I can't believe I fell off twice and you didn't fall once," Brian said as he and Diane followed Bakr up another dune.

"Don't even talk to me," she answered angrily.

"C'mon, babe, how was I supposed to know we'd be riding camels for three days?"

Diane kept her eyes focused on the short hairy ears that bobbed up and down far in front of her as she swayed sideways on the camel. Three days, and she hated the desert more each day, the stinking, plodding camel more every hour and her former boyfriend more every minute.

In her mind, he had become her 'former' boyfriend the first time he had challenged Bakr to a race and the two of them had disappeared yelling and cheering over a sand dune and she had found herself utterly alone in the middle of the desert.

When they had left the tomb atop the camels, all of her attention had been directed at staying on top of the shifting animal.

She had to admit that it had been sort of fun.

But after she had settled into the swaying motion of the camel, she had started to feel seasick. She had gulped air and fought the queasiness by telling herself they would soon be back at the Mena House bar where she would put any other tourist's story to shame with this adventure.

When she had realized that the camel was going in a straight line and not circling back to the tomb as she had expected it would, she had screamed hysterically at Brian to make the driver turn around.

"I'm not sure we didn't turn around, babe," Brian had said. "No landmarks, and the camels really don't leave much in the way of footprints in the sand. That might be the hill over there that we went over when we left Boss Hogg.

"Anyhow, you gotta admit, babe, this really is cool. I feel like Lawrence of Arabia."

He had taken to camel riding as quickly as he took to every other physical activity. And he and Bakr had already forged the kind of 'jock' bond she had seen Brian make with everyone he met: man, woman or child.

He was in love with action. He didn't care if someone was male or female, black or white, straight or gay. All he cared about was how they 'worked.' She had been worried when she took him for the first time to meet her parents and her grandfather, who was confined to a wheelchair after losing both legs to diabetes.

But Brian and her grandfather had quickly become best friends. Instead of shying away from the man's disability, Brian wanted to know how he did everything, if he felt phantom movement in his lost legs, how he exercised his arms, if he preferred to be pushed or to move himself.

They had talked about things that everyone in her family had been embarrassed to ask, and her grandfather loved him for that acceptance.

But as endearing as he was, it was tiring trying to keep up with him all day, every day. Especially when he was giving all his attention to Bakr and being such a jerk.

"Look, babe," he was saying now, "I know you're mad at me, and I understand that, but I think we're almost at this 'Toasty' place Bakr keeps mentioning."

"He's saying To-She, not 'Toasty' and I went past being mad at you the first time I had to go to the bathroom out in the middle of the desert," Diane said.

"To-She, huh? Well, whatever he's saying, I think we're getting close, 'cause the last time I challenged him to a race, he shook his head and pointed over the next hill ... "

Diane interrupted him. "Dune, they're freakin' sand DUNES, Brian! We're in the middle of the desert and we're going to die."

" ... next hill, dune, whatever," Brian continued. "All I'm saying is, Bakr said 'Toasty.' So I think we're close."

He reined his camel lightly and using his foot, nudged the camel's neck away from Diane.

Bakr was riding ahead of them, so Brian pushed his hips forward on the camel, and said "hup," as Bakr had taught him. The camel broke into a light jog.

He caught Bakr before they crested the dune.

"To-She is just over this dune. We'll soon have cool, fresh water and hot food. I can smell the bread baking and the fish roasting, Brian, can't you?" he said.

Brian understood 'To-She,' 'water,' and 'food,' but the rest was lost to him.

When they camped at night, he had tried to learn the language, just to make conversation because Diane wasn't talking to him anymore. But it was hard. He had never been good with foreign languages, and the words of this one sounded extra harsh to his ears, but Bakr had been patient and now some of the words were starting to sound familiar.

Food and water sounded good to him.

So did 'To-She,' whatever it was.

Although he tried to keep a happy face in front of Diane to keep her spirits up, Brian was worried.

He had tried to check the Internet for baseball news the first evening they were out, but his cell phone wasn't picking up any signal. Not even a roaming signal. That had never happened before.

He had noticed that there had not been any airplanes flying overhead and when he was riding with Bakr, he had tried out every famous name he thought Bakr might know. Not one brought even a glimmer of recognition from Bakr. He hadn't recognized the names of Omar Sharif, or Yasser Arafat, or even Muhammad Ali, which really worried Brian because he had read that everyone, actually everyone on the planet knew Ali's name.

They reached the top of the dune and Brian reined his camel to a stop.

"We're there!" he shouted back at Diane. "We're at Toasty!"

After three days of empty, endless blue skies above him and continuous, identical waves of sand at his feet, Brian thought the jagged green leaves and rough shaggy bark of the palm trees at the oasis were unbelievably beautiful.

"They'd better have a clean bathroom," Diane said when she caught up with him at the top of the dune and could see the oasis.

"Look, babe, I'm sorry I got us into this. But there's bound to be someone here who speaks English and we'll get everything straightened out. You'll be soaking in a hot tub with a cool drink tonight."

Diane looked directly into his face and Brian realized for the first time that she was not just uncomfortable with the heat and the bouncing camel ride, but that she was terrified.

"Brian, look at me. I'm sunburned; my lips are cracked and bleeding. My ass and back hurt from riding this damn camel for three days. I haven't had any real food since we left the hotel three days ago and we have no idea, not even a glimmer of a clue about what's up there. There are slave traders in Africa, Brian. Slave traders! They kidnap women and sell them to oil sheiks!"

"Babe, no, no, that's not going to happen. Bakr here, he's a good guy. He's not some slave trader."

"What about the fat guy? Did you see him, Brian? Did he look like a happy old tour guide to you?"

"It'll be all right, Diane. I promise."

"You promise? You have no idea either, Brian. You can't promise anything. Whatever happens up there is out of our control." She glared at Brian and then kicked her camel to make it trot. "It's every woman for herself now, Brian. You're on your own."

When they reached the shade at the edge of the oasis, Bakr slid off his camel without waiting for it to kneel. Released, the camel wandered off toward the water. Then Bakr helped Diane dismount and then led the couple into the grove of trees.

As they got closer to the lake at the heart of To-She, they heard voices. Bakr motioned for them to wait and he jogged off toward a cluster of mud-brick huts. He returned a minute later with a jar of cool beer and a large round loaf of bread, still warm from the oven. He handed it to Brian and told them to wait a little longer. Then he turned and walked toward a stone building with painted columns that stood away from the huts.

Brian tore off some bread and ate it and then sniffed the beer before taking a deep drink from the jar.

"Hey, babe, this beer is really good. And the bread is still warm." He tore off a chunk and ate it. "Mmmmm, fantastic, come on, have some."

Ignoring him, Diane paced and complained: There was no bar, no hotel, no air conditioning, no roads, no other Americans and no sign of a bathroom or shower.

Brian finished the beer and bread then he stretched and worked out the kinks in his back and legs. He shared her worries, but there was little to be gained by complaining, so he leaned back against a tree and tried to take in everything he could, imagining himself in a baseball dugout studying an opposing team as they warmed up before a game.

Children played by the edge of the lake, splashing water and chasing each other while a few women washed clothes in the water and others sat in the sand working at something in stone bowls and talking. No one seemed in danger or afraid; everyone seemed relaxed and unhurried.

The kids, except for being naked, were pretty much like kids anywhere, he thought. They chased and yelled at each other.

Four older boys were playing a game of catch. Two of them stood apart from each other, each carrying another boy piggyback. The riders threw a ball to each other, trying to toss it just out of reach. Sometimes the standing boys would stumble as they tried to get into position for their rider to catch the ball. Then they would fall laughing to the soft sand. Once in a while after a dropped catch, the riders would slide down and switch partners.

Brian was trying to work out the rules the kids were using, when he saw a woman leave the stone building where Bakr had gone and walk in their direction.

She wore a white linen skirt wrapped around her waist and a wide, beaded necklace that draped over her chest, leaving her small breasts uncovered. Her long black hair was braided, held back with a narrow band decorated with dark red and blue beads. Instead of the heavy swipes of dark blue kohl that Bakr wore under his eyes, she had a thin green line of eye shadow that outlined the top and bottom of her eyes, meeting at the outer edge in a point and extending to form a short line.

She looked a little older than Brian and Diane, but not yet thirty. As she got closer, Brian saw that a long deep scar ran down her right cheek. Even with the scar, Brian thought she was stunningly attractive. Sunlight seemed to dance across her brown skin.

It wasn't until she stopped near them in the shade of the small grove of trees, that Brian noticed the two girls who trailed behind her. The girls were naked except for a narrow belt that hung loosely around their boyish hips. They were as tall as the woman, but younger, their breasts were just beginning to form and they hadn't grown pubic hair.

As soon as he saw them, Brian turned his eyes away, uncomfortable with their nudity. He didn't mind seeing the little kids naked, but these two girls were too close to being women.

"Greetings great Netjrew, welcome to To-She, home of Netjer Sobek. I am Yunet, chantress of the temple of Sobek," the woman said.

Brian understood nothing except 'To-She' but he smiled at her and answered with the welcoming phrase Bakr had taught him. Then he pointed to himself and said "Brian," then at Diane and said her name.

The woman turned to him and nodded as he spoke, but her attention was on Diane. She took a step toward her and slowly raised her hand, as if calming a frightened horse. Diane stood still, her arms crossed protectively, as the woman's hand touched her red hair cautiously. Once she was satisfied that Diane's red hair was not truly on fire, she brushed her fingers through it, almost as if she were petting Diane.

"Netjret Diane," she said softly.

She stepped back slowly and without turning to the girls, she said, "Take these gods to the temple and bathe and anoint them. Bring them to me when they are comforted."

Then she turned and walked back to the stone building.

One of the girls approached Brian and reached for his hand. The other took Diane's hand, and then they led them toward the building where Yunet had gone.

Inside the building, Brian was led through a doorway to his right; Diane was taken to a doorway on the other side.

"I just want you to know, Brian," Diane said as they parted, "whatever happens, I do blame you."

Light filtered softly through palm branches that lay across the wooden beams that crossed the open ceiling of the room where Abana stopped with Diane.

The walls were painted with scenes from the lake outside: on calm water, shallow reed boats carried fishermen who used nets to catch fish that seemed to jump from the water into their boats; flocks of brilliant, white birds flew across the pale blue horizon; ducks swam near the shore where gazelles bent their graceful necks to drink.

Two more girls, a little younger than Abana, were waiting in the large, square room. They stood by a circular stone slab with a hole in its center. Buckets of water sat on the ground beside them.

Abana took Diane's hand and led her to the center of the stone circle. Hesitantly, she touched Diane's shirt and blue jeans. She raised her eyebrows in question.

Taking in the buckets, Diane nodded. "Yeah, I get it."

She sat on the ground to untie and remove her boots. Abana gasped and then clapped her hands sharply, motioning to the younger girls. The girls ran to a corner of the room and came back with a low, wooden chair. Together they offered their hands to Diane and helped her to stand.

Sitting back into the chair, Diane undid her jeans and tugged them off. Then she stood to pull off her T-shirt, which she dropped on the chair. She slipped off her white thong and unclasping her bra, she shrugged out of it, adding it to the pile of clothes on the chair.

Naked, she stepped onto the stone slab and looked expectantly at Abana.

The Egyptian girl was rooted to the ground. She had never seen skin so pale and smooth.

"Quit ogling and let's get on with it," Diane snapped, then she closed her eyes and braced herself.

Abana heard the irritation in the goddess's voice. She bowed and apologized. Of course the goddess would be anxious to be bathed. *She is beautiful beyond words,* Abana thought. *What a blessing to be chosen to serve her.*

At Abana's signal, the girls raised their buckets and slowly poured water over Diane. Abana stepped forward with a linen cloth and gently began to wash the desert's grit from the goddess.

The cool water was refreshing after three days in the desert. After she got over her initial fear and then the awkwardness of being bathed, Diane began to enjoy the soothing attention of the three girls. They washed her slowly, working perfumed soap into a lather and then rinsing her. After a few minutes the younger girls began to sing a soft, lilting melody as they worked. They washed and rinsed her a second time and then gently patted her dry with linen towels.

Abana led Diane to a narrow raised platform that was covered with white linen. Tables on either side of the bed held painted ceramic jars. Abana showed her a small wooden step beside the bed and held her arm as

Diane stepped up and then sat on the bed. Diane noticed a sweet, slightly bitter fragrance hanging in the air.

The two girls walked over and stood on either side of the bed. Abana gently pushed on Diane's shoulders until she lay back, her head resting on a pillow that was nestled in a curved wooden headrest. Once she was settled, the girls began to rub scented oil on her arms, gently massaging her.

She didn't know that she had drifted off to sleep until Abana softly shook her shoulder. The young girl was smiling at her with undisguised affection. Abana signaled for her to roll over onto her stomach so they could complete the massage.

As she rolled over she realized that the tension that had built up during the trek across the sand had been drained away by the massage. She felt relaxed for the first time since she and Brian had left the taxi at the Step Pyramid. It was only three days ago, but it seemed like another lifetime.

As the girls began to rub her back, she sighed deeply.

There is so much to think about, so much to worry about. But it is hard, she thought, as the girls kneaded her shoulders, so hard to concentrate when it feels so good.

Sunlight slipped through the ceiling at a steep angle when Diane awoke. Flickering oil lamps had been lit and Diane thought for a moment that she was alone. Then Abana approached the bed and spoke to her soothingly.

"Thanks," Diane said. "That was great. Now, if we could just call the Mena House and arrange a taxi ride."

Abana smiled at her as the two young girls approached from the shadows where they had been sitting while Diane slept. One of them carried a white linen sheath dress across her extended arms. The other held bleached white sandals, made from twisted reeds. Diane noticed that an ornamental wooden box now sat on the bedside table and the low chair where she had dropped her clothing was empty, and had been moved near the bed.

Abana held out a hand and helped Diane step from the massage table. The girl with the linen sheath stepped up and with Abana's help raised the sheer dress over Diane's head. Diane raised her arms and let the soft linen fall to her shoulders.

The other girl knelt by her feet with the sandals and when Diane was ready, slipped them onto her feet. They led her to the chair where one of the girls stood behind Diane and gathered her hair away from her face.

Abana opened the box of cosmetics. One of the girls took a polished silver mirror from the box as Abana leaned toward Diane to begin applying makeup. She worked carefully and slowly, making up Diane's eyes, plucking hair from her eyebrows, adding lipstick and finally tying her hair back with a colorful linen band.

Satisfied, Abana took the silver mirror from the young girl and handed it to Diane.

Although she was expecting it, Diane still gasped when she looked into the mirror. Staring back at her was a tomb painting come to life – a living Egyptian goddess.

Brian was dressed in a short linen kilt and wore a wide beaded necklace. His eyes were outlined with green kohl and his bare chest glistened with the sheen of massage oil.

He sat on a straight-backed wooden chair by a table that was heaped with dishes of food.

Yunet sat at the end of the table. She wore a linen dress that was gathered just below her breasts. A single, wide strap that held the dress over her left shoulder covered one breast. She was sipping from a silver cup as Diane was led into the room.

Yunet nodded toward a chair across the table from Brian. As Diane approached the chair, she saw that its legs were carved to look like lion's paws.

"Wow, babe, you look like Cleopatra. I'm thinking Russell Crowe for myself, you know from that gladiator movie. No wait, that wasn't Egypt. Maybe Rock from that mummy movie." Brian flexed his biceps and laughed.

At the sight of Brian, the tension flooded back into Diane's body. While she had been with Abana and the two other girls, she had tried to pretend that she was at an Egyptian-themed spa. Although part of her knew that her situation – whatever that was – hadn't changed, she had tricked herself into enjoying the only pleasant experience she had had in days.

Now, seeing Brian dressed like an ancient Egyptian and laughing, oblivious to their danger, her anger at him returned and, as it did, fear rushed in, filling her with a stomach-churning feeling of doom.

"Hey, are you OK, Diane?" Brian asked.

She stumbled as her legs weakened. Yunet, who was nearest to her, stood quickly and put her arms around Diane to steady her. Brian came around the table and put his hand on Diane's shoulder to pull her into his arms, but she turned angrily away from him. Yunet pulled her in closer, holding and comforting her as Diane began to shiver and cry.

Brian reached out to caress her hair.

"Diane, babe, it's OK, really. I just got a bath and a wonderful massage and then Yunet set out this fantastic meal. I mean, it's like a feast. I don't know where we are or who these people are, but they're nice people,

Diane. Really, they're OK. We'll get this all sorted out and get back to our trip. You know we will."

Yunet spoke softly to one of the serving girls. The girl took Brian's arm and tugged him toward the doorway.

"Diane?" he said softly.

She shook her head and cried silently. Brian let himself be led from the room. When he looked back, he saw Yunet stroking Diane's hair and murmuring softly to her.

He asked about Diane the next morning when Pahket, the servant girl who had led him away from Diane and Yunet, came to his small room. When he said Diane's name, Pahket nodded, smiled and said "netjret nefer." So he patted his chest and said "Brian." Pahket nodded again and smiled.

"Brian go to Diane," he said, making the fingers of his right hand walk across the palm of his left.

Pahket nodded vigorously and then took him to breakfast in the same room where he had seen Diane and Yunet the night before. There was no one there, but the table was set with fresh fruit and bread, still warm from the ovens.

After breakfast Pahket accompanied him as he searched through the temple, calling Diane's name at each doorway. Although he had been embarrassed by Pahket's casual nudity when he first saw her in the morning, by midday, after seeing that everyone they encountered wore as little, he stopped thinking about it.

The stone building where he had eaten and slept had only a few enclosed rooms, two small, shaded courtyards with shallow pools of water and a larger courtyard surrounded by walls made from palm tree trunks.

At the larger courtyard, a canal from the lake passed through an opening in the palm trunk wall where it fed a pond that took up almost half the enclosure. A pathway wound around the pond to a stone shrine at the far end of the courtyard.

When Brian started to follow the pathway, Pahket grabbed at his arm and shook her head. He pulled free and walked along the stones with her following cautiously. Halfway around the pond he heard from his left, across the water, a long roar that sounded like a lion trying to gargle.

He stopped and cocked his head, trying to identify the source of the sound.

Pahket pulled at his arm again, tugging him back to the building.

When he turned to look at Pahket, he saw a flash of low movement at the edge of his field of vision. He quickly turned to it. A jolt of disbelief ran through him when he realized that he was watching a crocodile. It had raised itself up on its legs and was running faster than he imagined they could move, headed for the water.

It reached the lake and soundlessly slid into the water, disappearing beneath the surface.

Another roar from the far side of the water brought Brian's attention back to the land. He saw now that the entire lake bank was filled with crocodiles sunning themselves. As he watched, two of them raised up on their legs and bellowed, snapping their jaws challengingly at each other.

He took another look at the small shrine and saw motion along its floor. A crocodile emerged from the shadows carrying the bloody leg of a goat in its mouth.

Brian cupped his hands around his mouth and shouted toward the small building.

"Diane! Diane!"

Pahket tugged once more on his arm, shaking her head.

"OK," he agreed when there was no answering call from the small chapel, "we can go now."

That day and then another passed without Brian catching a glimpse of Diane.

There were no locked doors and, aside from the crocodile courtyard, Pahket didn't try to stop him from going anywhere else in the settlement. He looked throughout the temple and walked through the rambling collection of mud-brick huts.

Most of the huts had only three sides, just enough he saw, to support cross beams that held palm branches atop the roof to keep out the sun. There really wasn't anywhere for someone to hide.

Not that these people try to hide anything, he thought.

All of the children and most of the men were naked; a few men wore the same kind of short kilt that Brian wore. Although some of the women wore kilts like Brian's, most of them wore just a narrow cloth belt with one end hanging down a little from one side.

He tried to remember if he had ever heard of a place like this.

I should have heard about it on the Discovery Channel or something, he thought.

The oasis was much larger than it had looked when he first had seen it as he, Bakr and Diane had crested the last sand dune. The lake was small enough that he could see the opposite shore, but he realized that the flatness of the calm water made the distance seem shorter than it was. He estimated that it would take two or three days to hike around it.

A few small boats were tied to wooden posts by rough docks built along the canal that fed the lake. The boats were made of bundles of waxy reeds lashed together to form a long, thin hull that curved up out of the water at both ends. Another bundle was tied to the center of the boat to help keep the crew dry.

Even simpler reed rafts were pulled up on the bank of the canal. Brian had seen men take these rafts out fishing on the lake. The rafts looked like surfboards, yet the men balanced on them effortlessly.

Brian ached to try one, but he needed some place safe to practice. He didn't want to fall into the same water where those huge crocodiles lived.

On the other side of the village, he had found grape arbors and beyond them orchards of fig and olive trees and gardens with onions, radishes, and cucumbers. There were other plants he'd never seen before and open fields of something he thought was wheat, but it looked shorter and darker than the wheat he remembered from his childhood drives through the farms of southern Pennsylvania.

There were pathways everywhere, too many for Brian to explore each one. First he followed the ones that looked most traveled and then he tried some that looked like they were little used.

A few stopped at the edge of the oasis, ending where the scruffy grass gave way to sand. Brian stood there, peering off into the unending emptiness, wondering why a path to this spot even existed. Others ended with a view toward a rocky area that rose from the desert near the western horizon. There was nothing for comparison, so Brian couldn't tell if the outcropping was a mile away or twenty miles away.

Two of the pathways ended by larger mud-brick homes where Brian and Pahket were greeted warmly and offered food by the families who lived there.

Throughout the two days Brian saw nothing electronic: no televisions, radios, telephones or even light bulbs. Near the end of the second day it struck him that either everyone had perfect vision or no one had good health insurance or – and, this worried him so much that he tried not to think about it – glasses didn't exist.

While he was unsuccessful in finding Diane, the time he spent with Pahket was useful as he began to learn more of the language.

Pahket was an enthusiastic teacher. At first she couldn't understand how Brian could not know the language that everyone in her universe spoke, but once she understood that he didn't know even the simple words for walking or tree or crocodile, she was eager to teach him.

And Brian, who had had trouble remembering the signals his third base coach flashed during baseball games, found that because there was no other way to communicate, his attention was more focused and he began to learn the language quickly.

But when he used his new-found skill to ask Pahket about Diane, she only smiled and said that Diane was with Yunet.

"Where is Yunet?" he asked.

Pahket only smiled and answered with a shrug.

Although he was worried about Diane, there was nothing at To-She that gave any sign that they were in danger; he had been pampered since their arrival.

Each morning Pahket greeted him in his room, bathed him and took him to breakfast. In the middle of the afternoon, when the heat of the desert began to penetrate the shade of the oasis, she led him back to his temple room where she and two servants bathed him again and then massaged him until he fell asleep. During the first massage, Pahket had gently brushed her hand against his penis, which responded by rising to her touch. Embarrassed, Brian had firmly moved her hand away from his groin. She had moved on to his legs, but each day she made the unspoken offer again.

He had continued to turn her away, but as he grew more comfortable with her he wondered how much longer he would refuse. Her nudity no longer surprised him, and he saw that everyone here had a different attitude about sex and was more comfortable with their bodies.

Once while walking by the orchards, they had come across a couple who were energetically and loudly enjoying sex in the shade of a date palm grove.

The man grunted with each insistent thrust and the woman echoed him with a high-pitched squeal. The woman saw Pahket and Brian watching them and responded with a wide smile and a louder squeal, spurring her partner on to a faster rhythm.

Pahket had put one hand over her mouth to stifle a laugh and with the other hand pulled Brian down the path. Away from the noise of the couple's lovemaking, Pahket had taught Brian the words to describe what they had just seen. She had laughed while imitating the man's movements and the woman's high-pitched moan.

Brian was amazed at the comfort Pahket showed about sex, delighted at the humor in her risqué impersonation and he felt an undeniable desire for her, which he had to hide by turning away.

On the morning of the third day, Brian's routine changed.

When Pahket woke him, she brought a change of clothing. The kilt she wrapped around him after his morning bath was so thin it was almost transparent; its linen belt was wider and embroidered with pale blue threads. He had gone barefoot for two days, but now she brought him white sandals.

Instead of the wide swaths of protective dark kohl under his eyes, Pahket carefully painted his eyelids themselves with a lighter, green kohl.

He balked when she began to spread lipstick on him, wiping the red ochre away with the back of his hand. She tried again and he shook his head and put his hand over his mouth.

The two servant girls looked alarmed, but Pahket remained calm.

"You must wear this, Netjer Brian. Djefi has returned and has asked to see you. Please, let me do this."

Reluctantly he removed his hand.

She leaned forward, her expression serious and intent. Brian pursed his lips, trying to provide as large a target as possible. When the servant girls tittered, Pahket turned to scold them, but she caught something in their eyes and turned back in time to see Brian winking at them, his mouth a wide grin.

"I do this for you, Pahket," Brian said in Egyptian when he saw the disappointment in Pahket's eyes. He added in English, "But I shouldn't wear lipstick for ole Boss Hogg, don't want to get him too excited."

Djefi was seated under an awning of palm branches in the large courtyard. Beside him stood a muscled, hard-looking guard Brian had not seen before at To-She. The guard held the shaft of a long spear; its tip rising higher than his head. He was naked except for a dirty linen belt into which he had tucked a long knife with a chipped blade.

Two young boys, one holding a ceramic jar, stood on the other side of Djefi. The boys watched Brian with open curiosity as Pahket led him to the edge of the awning where she stopped and bowed to Djefi.

"Welcome home, First Prophet," she said, her eyes avoiding even a glance at Siamun, the guard who stood beside Djefi. Siamun was a terrifying, impulsive man avoided by all.

Djefi dismissed her with a fluttering wave of his fat hand.

During the journey from Ineb-Hedj to To-She, Djefi had thought a great deal about Brian and Diane, but was unable to decide if they were truly gods appearing in Kemet at this time of unrest or simply very strange outlanders.

It seemed unlikely that it was coincidence that they had appeared at the very moment when Kanakht and Waja-Hur were ensnaring him in their plot to assassinate King Djoser.

He wondered: Have the gods arrived to warn me away from the plot or to help me succeed? Are they a reminder of my divine duties as First Prophet to Sobek, an inspiration to spread Sobek's cult beyond To-She? Or were they called here by Djoser, divine as he claimed and able to summon gods to his aid?

"I hope you'll forgive me if I remain seated, Netjer Brian. It has been a long journey from Ineb-Hedj. The river is so low, as I'm sure you're very aware," Djefi said.

Brian understood some of what Djefi said, but he was more conscious of the setting and body language. Djefi was not the quivering, sweating 'Boss Hogg' Brian had mocked at the tomb of Kanakht. He was relaxed and clearly in charge.

The armed man beside him stood attentively on the balls of his feet, ready to move quickly. When the guard turned his head to look at the two young boys on the other side of Djefi, Brian saw that he was missing his right ear. Jagged scars on his bare chest, were more evidence of a history of knife fights.

"Greetings, Djefi," Brian said in Egyptian, bowing his head in welcome. "I am an honored guest."

"Ahh, he speaks our language now," Djefi said.

"He is learning, First Prophet," Pahket said proudly.

Djefi turned his head toward her, his eyes slowly leaving Brian to rest on Pahket.

"And what else has he been doing?"

"He looks for Netjret Diane constantly. He asks questions."

"About?"

"Everything," Pahket said. "About the lake, about the orchards, about you. Sometimes he says names and asks if I know them. He asks about places I do not know."

Djefi raised his eyebrows.

"New York, Cairo, Iraq, America," she said, repeating the sounds she had memorized from Brian's frequent questioning.

Djefi fluttered his hand again, dismissing the nonsense. Then he asked, "Has he said how to make the river rise?"

She shook her head.

"Has he talked about King Djoser or Vizier Kanakht?"

Pahket shook her head.

"Or Waja-Hur?" Djefi added.

"No, First Prophet."

Djefi turned from her and looked at Brian. He didn't know what to make of this large, pale man – or god – standing patiently before him. His shoulders and arms were larger and stronger looking than anyone Djefi had ever seen. He had seemed insulting and arrogant at Kanakht's tomb, but now he seemed patient and civilized.

Djefi turned back to Pahket. "What do you think about him?"

Pahket was prepared for this question. When Bakr had arrived with Brian and Diane he had told Yunet that Djefi had found two gods at the tomb of Kanakht. Djefi wanted them to be quietly cared for and watched to try to discover why they were here.

When Yunet had decided to take Diane to her home on the far side of the fig orchard, she had told Pahket to stay with Brian. Pahket was instructed to answer Brian's questions and to allow him to go anywhere he wanted, except to Yunet's home. She also was to listen to him and watch him for clues about who he was and why he was here.

"I think he is lost, First Prophet, almost more than lost," Pahket said. "He seems sad at times, confused at others. Everything I show him seems new and different to him."

Djefi squinted at her and looked back at Brian.

"How can a god be 'more than lost'?" he said to himself. He motioned one of the boys forward and took from him the ceramic jar of beer. He drank and belched. The other boy came forward with a linen cloth and dabbed at Djefi's lips.

"So, Pahket, is he a god?"

Pahket looked at the ground, unable to meet Djefi's eyes as she answered. "I do not know, First Prophet, I have never met a god. But he is unlike other men. He is both gentle and powerful. He seems to have boundless energy, but he conserves himself. I am not wise, First Prophet, but he is different than other men, I think."

Brian followed some of the conversation, picking out words here and there. He knew they were talking about him and he was frustrated that he couldn't speak their language enough to ask the many questions that he had.

He had spent three days spinning his wheels. Although Pahket had been kind, she really had not been helpful about answering the only two questions that mattered: 'Where was Diane?' and 'How can we get home?'

Boss Hogg has had time to contact the authorities, to arrange for someone to come and get us. But instead he sits here interrogating Pahket, Brian thought impatiently

Djefi had sunk into a reverie, trying to decide what to do next. He needed to leave To-She to attend a ceremony at Iunu, but he didn't want to leave without resolving the question of who Brian and Diane really were.

Brian surprised him from his thoughts by stepping forward and asking in Egyptian, "Where is Diane?"

"She is my guest," Djefi answered. "She is safe."

"I want to see her," Brian said.

Djefi had met with Yunet before Brian had been brought to him. Yunet had told him that Diane was angry with Brian and that she had obeyed Diane's wishes to be kept away from Brian.

She hadn't told Djefi about the nights when Diane cried herself to sleep and Yunet took her in her arms and held her until the tears stopped. She hadn't told him that she caressed the beautiful goddess' red hair while she slept or that she thrilled to the touch of Diane's delicate arms and legs when she massaged her in the hot afternoons. And she hadn't told him about the flecks of gold she saw in the strange green eyes of the goddess or of the softness of her hands or the curl of her lips when she smiled.

She had told Djefi that Diane was angry with the god Brian and that the goddess – for Yunet was sure that Diane was a goddess – would bring greatness to the god Sobek once she had regained her serenity.

Djefi had heard the unspoken emotion in Yunet's voice, and so had Siamun.

"She wants this 'goddess' because she can't hold a man," Siamun had sneered after Yunet had gone.

Djefi thought there was some truth in what Siamun said, but he also trusted Yunet. If she could calm this strange goddess, then perhaps Djefi could find a way to use her. He hoped that she had come to The Two Lands to aid him in the conspiracy that Kanakht and Waja-Hur were spinning.

"I want to see her," Brian repeated, taking another step toward Djefi. "I want to know where she is."

"She is my guest," Djefi repeated. "As are you. You are both in my safe-keeping."

Brian lapsed into English. "I want to go to the American embassy. I am an American. I have rights. You can't just keep us here. I demand ... " He stopped as Pahket put her hand on his arm and he realized that he had begun to shout.

"Our god grows angry," Djefi said quietly.

Turning to the guard, Djefi spoke in a hushed whisper. "Siamun, I leave in the morning for Iunu. I will take Yunet and the goddess Diane with me. The god Brian will stay here. I don't want him to disrupt my journey or to follow me. So take him into the desert, on one of your hunting trips. Keep him there for a few days so he doesn't see me leaving."

Djefi turned back to Brian and Pahket.

"Pahket, tell him that Siamun will take him hunting in the desert. When they return, he can see the goddess."

She nodded and turned to Brian to explain what Djefi had said in words she knew he would understand, but Djefi interrupted her.

"You can explain later, Pahket, just take him and prepare him for a trip. Tell him I have to, oh, I don't know, just calm him down." He stopped speaking and no one moved for a moment. "Well, you can go now," Djefi squeaked, waving a hand in dismissal.

Pahket reached out a hand to take Brian's arm to lead him to his room.

"I'm not leaving until I see Diane," Brian said, refusing to move.

Djefi ignored him and turned to Siamun, speaking softly so that no one else could hear.

"Take him into the desert. Test him, watch him. I want to know what he truly is. I want ... " Djefi stopped as he saw Siamun tense and reach for his knife.

"I said, I want to see Diane," Brian said louder, pulling his arm away from Pahket's grip. He took a third step toward Djefi. "I want some answers."

Pahket pulled urgently on his arm, her eyes on Siamun who had drawn the knife from his belt.

Brian saw the guard, the knife held casually in his hand, but his eyes alive and eager.

"Now just hold on," Brian said, holding out a placating hand. "I don't want any trouble. No one has to get excited here." He realized he was speaking in English. He wanted to switch to Egyptian, but suddenly he couldn't remember any of the words. He looked at Pahket for help.

She read the confusion in his eyes.

"Brian," she said soothingly, reaching up and turning his head away from the confrontation with Siamun, "Djefi said Diane is safe, and so she is. He has arranged a trip for you. When you return, you will see Diane."

Brian looked back at Siamun. The disfigured guard still held the knife ready and was watching Brian and Pahket closely.

"I could take you," Brian said softly in English. "But then what? I'm still stuck here without Diane and no way to get back to Cairo."

He looked down at Pahket and nodded.

Then he addressed Djefi. "I leave now," he said in Egyptian, the words returning as he calmed. "I see Diane tomorrow."

Djefi smiled sweetly.

"As you wish, honored guest."

JOURNEY TO IUNU

"Tomorrow we leave for Iunu and The Feast of Re in His Barge. I have no idea what that means. Paneb has never been to the town of Iunu or to the celebration, so he can't describe it. But he says that Djefi should be there, so I'm hoping that I'll catch up with Diane and Brian."

Tim put down his pencil and ran a hand over his newly shaved head.

He knew that there would be fewer questions when he traveled with Paneb and his family if he looked like one of them. So this morning he had asked Taki to shave his head. She insisted that he call her by her nickname since the night he had treated Hapu for a scorpion sting. His naturally dark complexion was growing duskier every day and he was dressed like Paneb, wearing a short kilt, although he wore his boxer briefs underneath. He looked like he could be Paneb's cousin, his tall cousin.

With his sketchbook on his lap, he sat cross-legged on the roof of Paneb's home. There was a little shade from the ragged fronds of a palm tree that grew beside the house. The morning sun was starting to push the shade off the roof. When the shade disappeared, the only shelter would be under the overhang that shielded the front porch, but Tim was reluctant to go there because of the flies, drawn there by the lingering aroma of food and, despite frequent baths in the river, the pungent smell of bodies sweating to alleviate the desert heat.

Although much of the heat and smells were vented through the arched openings on the roof that he had wondered about when he first saw Paneb's house, the inside of the home remained heavy and thick.

And so Tim sat on the roof sketching. Paneb and Ahmes were working at Kanakht's tomb. Hapu, the scorpion sting already forgotten, was playing with some friends a few houses away. Taki and her eldest daughter Dedi were at the market picking up food and portable goods to be used to make trades.

As chief artist, Paneb earned a generous allotment of food, salt and precious oils, enough to take care of his family and the two households of in-laws who lived near him.

Taki had taken some of the surplus salt cones and some homemade linens to the market to trade for fruit and dried meat for their trip. She also wanted to get some smaller valuables – gold rings and precious stones – that she could trade for food at Iunu.

Money didn't exist here in the Egypt of King Djoser. Instead of seeing it as an inconvenience, Tim saw the system of bartering as one of the things he liked about this ancient time.

Another was the Egyptian sense of time.

They lived at a slower tempo and if they were aware of time, it was in the sense that its passage formed a hazy backdrop to their life. It was a measure, not a master.

They lived amid an endlessly repeating cycle of days, each one sunny and dry like the day before it. They watched the regular rising and falling of the ceaselessly flowing river, and were surrounded by a desert unchanged by seasons.

They didn't slice time into a series of individual moments and then stitch them back together with anxious anticipation. They didn't keep appointment books to make themselves accountable for each minute. There was neither tick nor tock.

For them, time was the seamless background of a comfortably familiar setting. Marked by the daily journey of the sun god Re arcing through the sky on the celestial river Nun, each day was a repetition of his circular journey, which began with his rebirth each morning.

Re was not expected to arrive at six a.m. or to depart at eight p.m. Instead, his arrival brought the start of the day and his departure ended it. Events defined time, they were not ordered by it.

It was true that Paneb made plans each day, but he did not watch a clock. The tasks he set for himself were completed in the time they demanded, they didn't expand to fill a schedule or contract to squeeze into a slotted time.

Tim, who never wore a wristwatch, thought this view of time seemed more right than the frenetic pace of his world, his time. For him, the slower tempo meant there was more time for each new experience.

He remembered when he and Addy had taken walks she always ended up shifting her weight from one foot to the other, eager to reach their destination but forced to wait as Tim paused to test the rubbery sturdiness of a fan-shaped tree fungus or to sketch the jagged edge of a broken tree stump.

Her mind always had been on the destination, Tim's on the journey.

And what a strange journey I am on, he thought. The wall in the tomb of Kanakht had opened into a world that had existed almost five thousand years before Tim had been born. It was hard to accept or understand.

But he was positive that the Step Pyramid didn't exist in this here and now; he had seen the empty plateau. Paneb had told him that Djoser had been king for seven years now, something he easily remembered because of the lack of flooding and the diminished harvests that followed.

Tim knew about the famine. It was recorded on a famous stele from Sehel Island. The stone inscription had been ordered by Djoser to record his anguish over the pain the long famine caused the people of Kemet and to remind them of how he had ended it through a sacrifice to the ram-headed god Khnum.

There wasn't much else that Tim knew about Djoser's era. The king had lived long before the huge pyramids had been built at Giza and more than a thousand years before King Tut. The only other name Tim recalled from Djoser's era was that of the famous architect Imhotep, but Paneb hadn't heard of him.

When Tim had asked him about Imhotep, the artist had frowned and shrugged. Seeing Tim's disappointment, Paneb tried to cheer him up by telling him about someone famous who would be at the ceremony: the high priestess of Re, a wise and beautiful woman named Hetephernebti.

They began walking to Iunu just after daylight.

Tim, Paneb and his family traveled with a small group of villagers who also had decided to go to the festival. Paneb told Tim the journey would take from three to six days, depending on the heat, on how fast the oldest cared to walk and on how many diversions they encountered.

Tim's modern map was little help, but from Paneb's description of the trip, gathered from neighbors who had been at Iunu before, the temple was not far inside the delta of the Nile, or Iteru, as Paneb called it. Tim estimated the trip was no more than thirty or forty miles, less than an hour's drive in his time.

But by mid-morning he understood why Paneb had allowed so much time for the trip.

At the outskirts of Ineb-Hedj, even before the trip had begun properly, two of the men began a debate about the best place to cross the river. There were many small boats and barges by the city that the younger man, a father traveling with three little children, wanted to use.

The other man, named Jarha, was older and had no children in his group. He argued that the trail was easier to follow on this bank.

"But the boats are here," the young man said. "We should use them."

"No, no, no. There is less shade over there. You'll burn your feet off," Jarha countered.

"It looks fine to me," the father said, shielding his eyes as he looked across the slow moving water.

Jarha shook his head. "Here, sure, it looks fine right here, but, trust me, this side is better once we get away from the city."

"But we need to cross," the young man replied.

"They have boats at Iunu. Do you think there are only boats at Ineb-Hedj? And see, we don't cross the whole river. It splits apart. Iunu is in between. So, if we cross here, we'll have to get back in boats, and barter with the ferrymen again once we're there," Jarha explained.

Jarha's wife joined in the argument now.

"But I think they ask for more at Iunu," she said.

"That doesn't matter," her husband answered. "Either way you have to cross half the river up there."

"Not if we cross it here," the young man said.

"We don't have to cross all of it at Iunu, because it breaks apart," the woman said, talking to her husband. "So it should be closer. But I think the boatmen there are greedy, not like our boatmen."

"Either way," Jarha said, shrugging as if that ended the conversation.

Paneb touched Tim's arm and led him into the shade where the rest of the family was patiently waiting with some friends. While the other two men continued to argue, one of the men in Paneb's group opened a jar of beer and began to pass it around.

"What are they arguing about?" Tim asked Paneb. "I understand that it was about the river, but I didn't understand all of what they said. And why do we wait while they argue? Why don't we move on and let them catch up?"

Paneb scrunched his face and frowned as if Tim's question raised an idea that had never been considered before.

"Why would we want to separate when we could stay together?" Paneb answered.

"Together for safety?" Tim asked.

"Safety? Safe from what?" Paneb said. "No, we want to be together. We're friends, why should we separate?"

"We go faster if we don't wait for them."

Paneb smiled at Tim's foolishness.

"But we're going to the same place."

Tim nodded his understanding. "And no one is in a hurry."

Tim wanted to ask more, but his limited command of the ancient language made it too frustrating, so he accepted a cup of beer and leaned back in the shade feeling very Egyptian.

The villagers walked on in fits and starts. If someone tired, they all stopped and rested, everyone making a show of acting as tired as the one who had stopped.

On the second day one of the men caught sight of a herd of gazelles along the riverbank so they formed a hunting party. Although the travelers waited most of the day for the hunters' empty-handed return, the time wasn't wasted. The older men who had stayed behind took the children fishing, using a wide net, its edges weighted with stones. When the hunters returned, laughing and blaming each other for their futile chase, they found freshly roasted fish and flat emmer wheat bread waiting for them.

They walked in the mornings and again in the evenings, taking long breaks in the afternoons when the day was hottest. During the breaks the children played and swam, the adults sat and talked or napped in the open air under the shade of trees along the riverbank.

They found that Jarha had been right about the trees. Across the river the thin line of growth along the bank quickly gave way to scrubby grass and then bright sand.

On the fourth night they camped along the river overlooking a long, green island. They had walked past several smaller islands near the end of the day's hike. Looking at his map, Tim decided that they were camping where Cairo would eventually lie.

The large island upstream was Roda, where the Meridien Hotel would be built, Tim decided. The longer island to the north, just across from the group's encampment, would eventually hold the Nile Sheraton and the Cairo Tower. On the other bank of the river, the Egyptian Museum would some day display four-thousand-year-old mummies of pharaohs who had not yet ruled the ancient land where Tim found himself. The New Palace Hotel where he had been staying was just a block away from the museum and five thousand years distant.

According to his map, the river, which was growing wider, divided into two main branches just north of the islands. The east branch flowed toward the area where the Suez Canal would be built. The left branch turned northwest, flowing in the general direction of Alexandria.

The next evening they decided to move away from the expanding river to camp.

"The ground is too wet there," Paneb explained as he and Taki pulled dried food from the sling he carried.

"Jarha said there would be crocodiles there. And hippos," Ahmes said excitedly. Hapu's eyes grew wide and Taki protectively put her arm around her young daughter.

"That Jarha," Paneb said, "he tells big stories, Ahmes. Why he once told us he had ridden a hippo that it took him under the river and he saw a whole city of hippos living there, with a king hippo that had a golden necklace."

"Was there a queen?" Hapu asked.

Paneb nodded. "A queen, servant hippos and even dancing hippos."

Taki held her hand over her mouth to hide her laughter.

"Did they sing?" Hapu asked.

Ahmes understood that his father was trying to distract his little sister. "I heard a hippo sing once, Hapu," he said. He arched his arms and blowing out his cheeks he waddled toward his little sister. "He sounded like this, 'Blub, blub, blub, roar, roar,' "

Hapu shrieked in pretend fear and then started to imitate him.

Later, as the children wandered from campfire to campfire, visiting with their friends, Paneb told Tim that they would arrive in Iunu tomorrow.

"Jarha said there is a river crossing just an hour's walk ahead. Iunu is across the river there."

"Jarha?" Tim asked.

Paneb nodded. "He shouldn't have told Ahmes about crocodiles and hippos, but he does know the river." Paneb rubbed his back against the rough trunk of a palm tree. "I'm told that even if you do see them, they usually are far away. But still, we'll watch for them." He paused, his eyes focused on the distance. "It would be exciting to see a hippo. I've drawn them, but always from the drawings of other artists."

Tim nodded, happy to talk with his new friend. Even if he didn't understand every word, he felt the camaraderie in Paneb's voice.

"I draw from others' drawing, too, Paneb. It is better to see the thing. I hope to see a hippo tomorrow. I hope it is far away."

Paneb smiled. "But not too far."

Tim woke before dawn.

He had always been an early riser and now that he went to sleep as night fell, he found himself waking before sunrise.

He left the encampment quietly and headed for the river, following the slight reddish glow that marked the east. Even though the sun was announcing its arrival at the horizon, the sky above remained dark and blazing with stars.

When he got close to the river, he turned left, looking to the north toward Iunu. Even as he looked, he knew there would be no light glow, no indication that a town lay waiting up there in the darkness.

In the thousands of years stretching forward from this night it will only be in the last hundred years that man will conquer night's darkness, he thought. Then, looking at the bright, sparkling jewels of light above him, he sighed. And lose all of this.

The ground grew soft and mushy as he got closer to the river, so he turned to follow the bank northward looking for firmer footing to approach the water for his morning bath.

A slight breeze drifted from the water toward the cooling desert sand. It carried the richness of the river mingled with the exhalations of the palm trees along the riverbank and the scent of the damp earth. Drawing a deep breath, he said to himself, "It smells green and alive."

The sun was over the horizon now. Rose-colored light washed across the sky, filtering down through the leaves of the palm and sycamore trees that lined the riverbank. Short willow trees and papyrus stalks rose along the water's marshy edge, hiding the water.

Walking slowly, crocodiles and hippos in mind, Tim approached a willow that stood on a small mound by the water. He sat by its trunk and opened his sketchbook. He had started to take time each morning to write down what he had seen or learned the previous day.

As he stared out across the water, wondering about what he would see at the festival tomorrow, he noticed movement on a small island a dozen yards off to his left.

A curved boat made of bundles of reeds was pulled out of the water. Standing beside it, in knee-deep water among floating blue water lilies, a naked teenage boy was smearing himself with mud.

With his back to Tim, he stretched out a thin arm and spread the dark river mud across it, carefully working it between his fingers. He had swiped an uneven coat of mud across his shaved head and down his neck.

Tim knew that the Egyptians gave their children adult responsibilities and freedom at an early age. Girls often married at thirteen and had a child a year later. Boys joined in their father's trade before they were ten years old, and usually married by age sixteen.

Even though he no longer wore the side lock of youth, the boy across the water seemed young to be out by himself at this early hour. Tim wondered if he was preparing himself for a hunt, using the mud to hide his scent or as camouflage.

Looking at him with an artist's eye, Tim thought that the boy's back and shoulders were not muscled yet.

The boy bent to pick up another handful of mud and twisted sideways to start spreading it on his back. As he turned he saw Tim, and Tim saw that the boy was clearly a young girl.

Mud was smeared across her small breasts and down her flat belly. Her hands, cupped and filled with mud, were poised by her narrow, boyish hips. She stopped as she saw Tim watching her.

For a moment they looked in each other's eyes. Tim was embarrassed to be caught spying on her; she seemed surprised, but not offended or frightened. Tim turned away first, his eyes stopping on the reed boat by her feet.

"Hello," she called across the narrow watery divide. Her voice was light and cheerful.

Tim wanted to slink away and hide.

She looked down at the mud that was oozing out of her hands and began to smear it across her buttocks and the back of her thighs.

"I must leave," Tim said, as much to himself as to the girl.

She looked up, a smile playing on her mouth. "Where?"

Tim put his sketchbook back into the sling bag and got to his feet. Suddenly his voice felt thick and he didn't trust himself to talk.

"Re has appeared," she said, nodding toward the growing light. "His strength will soon dry this mud and I am not ready."

"Ready?" Tim managed to say, his eyes still averted.

"Yes," she said. "The water is not deep here. Come help me."

Tim looked at the water and then back at the boat. Hesitantly he took a step toward the water.

"Your kilt will get wet," she said.

Tim waded into the water. Mindful of the scolding he would get from Taki, he raised the hem of the kilt above the water level and walked toward the island. As the river bottom sloped up to the island, he let the kilt's hem fall back in place, covering his now wet boxer briefs.

She turned away from Tim, presenting her naked back.

He looked down at his feet and then scooped up a handful of the heavy mud.

"Hurry," she said. "Along the middle." As she spoke she quickly bent down and gathered more mud to cover her other arm.

Tim glanced at her tapering back and quickly put the mud on the areas she had left uncovered. He tried to keep the mud thick between his hands and her tawny skin and his eyes from looking at her mud-caked back.

He was still wiping mud between her delicate shoulder blades when she glanced up at the sky and then darted off through the reeds, skirting the small island. "Bless you," she called as she pushed through the leaves.

Tim sighed in relief that the strange encounter was over and then turning, he stepped on the edge of her reed boat, lost his balance and fell face first into the mud.

THE FEAST OF RE IN HIS BARGE

Unlike Ineb-Hedj, Iunu had no walls around it. A scattering of mud-brick huts marked the outskirts of the town. Jarha led them along a worn, dirt trail that wound past the huts. Soon there were more homes, built closer together. The trail widened and became a street.

The pilgrims had arrived in Iunu.

They followed the street to a large open plaza. In the center of the plaza, atop a low stone mastaba stood a short obelisk covered in electrum, a combination of gold and silver. Hieroglyphic symbols filled its gleaming surface.

"The Radiant One," Jarha said reverently to Tim and Paneb as they looked at the obelisk. It was a four-sided tapering shaft. Tim realized that the Washington Monument from his time was a larger version of it, without the precious metal coating.

Jarha pointed across the plaza to an opening at the end of a covered causeway.

"Re comes out there, floating in his barge. See the canal, there?" Jarha swept his arm across the plaza, following the path of the canal, which led to the central mastaba and then continued past it to a temple entrance at the far end of the plaza.

"Where should we stand?" Paneb asked, looking at the crowd that was milling around the edge of the plaza.

"Close to the beer and food," Jarha said with a laugh. He clapped Paneb on the back. "After an hour or so, it won't matter where we are, we'll be too drunk to see anything anyhow."

It was late afternoon. The festival would begin at dawn tomorrow. In the meantime, Paneb and the other pilgrims were expected to enjoy the hospitality of Re.

Awnings had been raised around the perimeter of the plaza to provide shade for tables filled with food, beer and wine, all provided for the pilgrims by the temple of Re.

The south wall of the courtyard was given over to sellers of souvenirs: gold amulets of Re, small scrolls of papyrus filled with magical hieroglyphs, carvings in cedar wood of the sun god, and bouquets of flowers. Taki and her daughters took their pouch of rings and gemstones to those tables to begin haggling with the sellers.

Tim followed Paneb and Jarha to the food tables. Ahmes tagged along with them, his head swiveling about as he looked at the crowd and took in the noise and commotion. A juggler walked by, tossing five gold-colored balls and chanting, "Praise to you, oh Re, great of power."

A priestess, dressed in an ankle-length gown of the sheerest linen, seemed to float by, the crowd opening a path for her and the two little girls who walked in front of her strewing flower petals on the ground. She was followed by an acrobat who turned somersaults and walked on his hands.

"Father," Ahmes said, tugging at Paneb's arm. "Did you see the priestess?"

Paneb turned to look where his son was pointing.

"You'll see plenty more of them tomorrow," Jarha said.

Paneb and Ahmes looked at the graceful figure as she disappeared in the crowd. Then they looked at each other and smiled.

Even though the pilgrims left their camp outside Iunu before dawn the following day, when they reached the central plaza they found a crowd already gathering. Torches lining the walls of the plaza and the central canal cast flickering light over the sleepy faces of the pilgrims.

In the center of the plaza, the electrum-covered obelisk gathered and reflected light from the torches, gleaming with an otherworldly brightness. Some of the crowd knelt facing the obelisk, reciting prayers to the sun god. Others stood in small groups talking and laughing, a few were already by the beer jars.

Standing by Paneb, Tim searched the crowd for Diane and Brian. He hoped that Brian's height and Diane's red hair would make them easy to spot, even if they were dressed in native kilts as he was.

Paneb noticed Tim scanning the crowd. He pointed toward an open area across the canal from them, near the obelisk where several white-garbed girls stood with palm branches in their hands.

"Djefi will be there," he said.

He shrugged in response to Tim's unspoken question. "I asked Jarha."

Young girls wearing garlands of flowers and the white robes of Re's priestesses began to walk along the walls of the plaza extinguishing the torches. Others smothered the flames of the torches along the canal, leaving lit only the circular stand of torches around the base of the obelisk.

The crowd hushed as the plaza dimmed into near darkness.

"There is Djefi," Paneb said quietly, nudging Tim and pointing across the canal.

An extremely fat man sat on a chair that had been carried out to the canal. Beside him stood a strikingly beautiful Egyptian woman. She wore a white sheath with a single strap over her right shoulder. Pink flowers formed a crown around dark braided hair that fell to her shoulders.

And beside her, holding her hand, was Diane.

She was dressed as an Egyptian with a thin linen dress and white sandals. She wore the same makeup as the woman beside her, but her bright red hair stood out even in the dim morning light.

As Tim wondered how he would make contact with her and where Brian was, a dry rattling sound began to steal across the plaza as two lines of priestesses, twisting sistrums in their hands, appeared at the opening of the canal.

Everyone turned toward the sound, which now was joined by lyrical chanting. The priestesses walked along the canal until they lined the length of it. Then they knelt and continued to softly sing praises to Re. Some of the devout in the crowd joined in the song.

Two men, wearing masks shaped into the head of a ram, complete with curled horns, emerged from the covered causeway, walking in the waist-deep water of the canal. Gold colored ropes draped over their wide shoulders were attached to a barge, which they pulled from the darkness. As the barge came into view, sunlight broke over the horizon lighting the plaza with a rosy glow.

Some of the crowd cheered, others began to sing louder. Tim saw that Taki and Dedi had their eyes closed, their faces turned toward the rising sun as they sang the words of Re's litany. Hapu had been hoisted to her father's shoulders. She was wide-eyed, taking in the spectacle, as was Ahmes, who stood between Tim and Paneb. Even Jarha was quiet, his eyes agleam as he watched the progression.

The barge held three young girls, each with a golden tray heaped with flower petals. They tossed small handfuls of the petals from the barge, some of them landing in the water, others reaching the banks of the canal where young boys and girls darted forward to grab them.

In the center of the barge stood a polished wooden platform supporting a golden statue of Re, seated on a throne, his hands in his lap, a golden disk encircling his ram's head.

Standing behind the god, her hands raised in a protective stance, stood a tall priestess. Her silhouette glowed beneath a transparent pleated gown. As the barge came closer, Tim saw that her skin was covered with powdered gold.

"Hetephernebti," Paneb whispered.

The barge slowly advanced to the central obelisk. Two boys followed the barge, relighting the torches on either side of the canal as Re passed. When the barge reached the central island, the two ram-headed men tied the golden ropes to posts at the base of the obelisk, and then walked to the back of the barge to steady it as Hetephernebti walked from the barge to the obelisk.

Climbing over the low courtyard walls, the sunlight was greeted by clouds of incense that rose from trays carried among the crowd by young acolytes.

Suddenly the background hum of the sistrums stopped and Hetephernebti began to sing in a beautiful, clear soprano voice that floated over the crowd as light and warm as sunlight. Even the beer drinkers stopped and watched as she stood before the sacred ark and sang.

"Homage to thee, O thou who risest in the horizon as Re, thou restest upon law unchangeable and unalterable. Thou passest over the sky, and every face watcheth thee and thy course, for thou hast been hidden from their gaze.

"Thou dost show thyself at dawn and at eventide day by day. The Sektet boat, wherein is the Majesty, goeth forth with light; thy beams are upon all faces; the number of red and yellow rays cannot be known, nor can thy bright beams be told. The lands of the gods, and the lands of Punt must be seen, ere that which is hidden in thee may be measured.

"Alone and by thyself thou dost manifest thyself when thou comest into being above Nut. May I advance, even as thou dost advance; may I never cease to go forward as thou never ceasest to go forward, even though it be for a moment; for with strides thou dost in one little moment pass over the spaces which would need millions and millions of years for men to pass over; this thou doest and then thou dost sink to rest.

"Thou puttest an end to the hours of the night, and thou dost count them, even thou; thou endest them in thine own appointed season, and the earth becometh light. Thou settest thyself therefore before thy handiwork in the likeness of Re when thou risest on the horizon."

There was a moment of solemn quietness and then the young priestesses began to shake their sistrums again and the crowd joined in their chant: "Praise to you, oh Re, great of power."

As the chanting grew in strength, Hetephernebti walked across the surface of the water, leaving the island for the courtyard. As she approached the crowd, the people fell to their knees. Gently she reached down and touched them, raising them back to their feet, all the while softly singing the litany of Re.

To Tim's modern eye she seemed like a combination of a rock star, a supermodel and the pope. When little children clung to her legs, she smiled and stopped, stooping down to kiss them. Young men were torn between desire and reverence; older men smiled as if at a favorite daughter's wedding, tears running from their eyes. Girls in the crowd wanted to grow up to be the beautiful Hetephernebti, women adored her purity, her undisguised gentleness and power.

As she walked the perimeter of the crowd, unhurried and peaceful, but moving steadily, Tim saw men carry baskets from the courtyard entranceways. Some of the baskets were piled with roasted oxen and duck. Other baskets were filled with chickpeas, lettuce, onions and other vegetables, others with heaps of freshly baked bread.

The aroma of the food began to overtake the scent of the incense and as Hetephernebti, her circuit complete, returned to the obelisk, the chanting ended and the crowd grew quiet.

"Welcome to the House of Re," Hetephernebti said.

"Enjoy his blessings!"

As Jarha tugged on Paneb's arm and nodded toward the tables where jars of beer stood waiting, Tim leaned down and quietly asked Ahmes, "Come with me?"

Paneb nodded his approval.

"Take care of him," Paneb said.

Tim and Ahmes looked at each other unsure who was to take care of whom. When they realized that they both had the same question in mind, they began to laugh.

Paneb saw what they were laughing at.

"I was talking to both of you," he said, smiling at the idea of his son taking care of Tim. Although Tim had denied being a god, Paneb saw the way Tim could do anything and the way he understood and looked beyond things. *If he's not a god,* Paneb thought, *he still is more than a man.*

"They make the beer different here. They add fruit to some of it. And they have wine, made from grapes," Jarha said to Paneb as he led him away.

"I know all about wine. I've even drawn nobles drinking it."

"Ahh, but now you can drink it, Paneb. You'll draw it so much better, eh?" Jarha said.

At first Tim and Ahmes just walked among the crowd, taking in the sight of so many people in one place and listening to the varied sounds. Seeing Ahmes' excitement, Tim was reminded his own excitement when his parents had taken him to a small carnival that had set up in his hometown when he was Ahmes' age.

They stopped to watch a juggler tossing small gleaming balls that represented Re. The crowd formed a circle to give him room. As he finished three acrobats somersaulted into the clearing.

When acrobats moved on, Tim leaned down to talk to Ahmes.

"I want to cross the water. Help me find a path."

Ahmes looked at him questioningly. Priests and nobles had their own gathering place, apart from the commoners, on the other side of the canal that divided the courtyard. Each side was supplied with food and drink. There was no reason to cross the canal.

But Tim had seen Hetephernebti on both sides of the water, so he knew that there had to be a dry way across. And that was where Diane was.

As they walked along the canal edge, Tim tried to observe Diane without drawing attention to himself. She seemed to be enjoying herself, drinking wine and allowing the strikingly beautiful woman with the pink flower tiara to feed her fruit and bread from a tray held by a young boy.

She reclined on a low wooden divan, her head resting on the lap of her companion who was idly caressing Diane's bare shoulders. The black woman drank from a golden goblet and occasionally helped Diane raise her head to drink from it also.

They were watching an elderly harpist who was accompanied by two young girls who sang softly while rattling sistrums. From the look on Diane's face, Tim guessed that the heat and wine and soothing music would soon have her asleep.

There was no sign of Brian.

Near the women, the fat priest Djefi sat in a cushioned chair, eating and drinking steadily. A line of boys carried jars of beer and platters of food to him. Although he had an eye on the musicians, Tim thought the priest looked preoccupied by something, casting glances at Diane and then looking off into the distance. Whatever was bothering the priest of Sobek, it didn't seem to interfere with his drinking.

Tim remembered tomb paintings of religious festivals. In addition to the priests and the musicians, the paintings often showed nobles throwing up from drinking so much. It was clear that the party around him was heading in that direction.

"Tim," Ahmes said. "There." The boy nodded toward the island in the center of the canal where the gleaming statue of Re sat on its barge.

At first Tim didn't see what Ahmes meant, then the boy looked pointedly at the edge of the island and Tim saw it: A walkway, submerged just below the water line, led from the island across the canal to the courtyard. The walkway was painted pale blue so that it was almost invisible.

He remembered now how Hetephernebti had seemed to walk across the water at the beginning of the ceremony.

His attention was drawn from the walkway by loud voices just behind him and Ahmes. Two men, fueled by beer and full bellies, were arguing over a small black statue of Horus. Tim couldn't understand their slurred words, but from their tone, he knew where the argument was heading.

The crowd around them began to edge away, forming a circle. The men threw off their kilts and began to circle each other. Instead of trying to stop the fight, the crowd began to cheer them on. The men had no weapons, and judging from their sluggish movements, Tim doubted that they would be able to do each other too much harm.

Ahmes edged closer to the opening of the circle to watch the men. Tim thought to pull him away, but he saw that other young boys were at the front of the crowd, eager to see the excitement.

The men continued to circle, each of them talking loudly. Tim didn't understand them, but assumed it was the same kind of trash talk he would have heard back in the twenty-first century.

Suddenly one of the men rushed the other, his arms wide to grab him. The other man, shorter and stockier, tried to dodge him, but moved too slowly. They collided and fell to the ground. Tim heard the air rush from them as they landed.

There was no movement from the two men for a moment and Tim was surprised to feel disappointment that the fight was already over. Then the stocky man farted loudly, bringing a laugh from the crowd. He pushed up on his skinny opponent and swung a leg up into the air for leverage.

With a loud snort and more breaking of wind, he managed to push the skinny man off to the side and began to swivel slowly around him. The thinner man, his legs spread wide for balance, pushed hard, but was slowly losing the struggle to remain on top.

Now the crowd began to shout at the fighters. The muscles on the heavier man's neck pulled tight as he pushed hard. The thinner man, fighting to keep his vanishing advantage, tried to dig his toes into the hard dirt.

The heavier man grunted and pushed hard, edging sideways in the dirt. The thinner man, pushing down, suddenly found himself staring at the empty ground as the other fighter swiveled on top of him.

The thinner man fell face down in the dust as the stocky man swung on top and straddled him. The winner sat on the other man's bare buttocks and bounced up and down, his arms in the air, and shouted his happiness as he celebrated his victory.

Some in the crowd cheered, others laughed. A few waved their hands in disappointment at the short match and turned to walk away.

The winner struggled to his feet and extended his hand to the loser, helping him up from the ground. Another man stepped out of the crowd with a jar of beer and handed it to the winner, who passed it along to his opponent with a comment that Tim couldn't hear. They both laughed and walked over to where their kilts lay on the ground.

As they walked away Tim thought about a bar fight he had seen while he was in college, six years ago and five thousand years in the future.

There had been so much more anger and frustration in that fight. This had been a wrestling match, intense and strenuous, but the point had been to master someone, not hurt him. The fight he had seen in college had started as an argument over a spilled drink and ended with a man sprawled unconscious in the gravel parking lot behind the bar. The men had started with the same circling and verbal taunting. But instead of wrestling, they had turned their fists on each other.

Tim had stood paralyzed among the small crowd that watched. He had wanted to stop the fight, but both men were larger than he was and he had been afraid that he would become a target. The crowd itself had had a blood fever about it, eager to see serious violence.

Egged on by the crowd, the men had swung white-knuckled fists at each other until one's wild hook caught the other in his throat. The man had clutched his neck and fallen to his knees unable to breathe. The other had circled behind and kicked him in the kidneys, sending him sprawling over the stones. Then he had stood over him and kicked and kicked, lifting the loser's inert body off the ground over and over until the crowd turned away in disgust.

Tim thought about road rage, school shootings, drive-by shootings and other violence from his time when strangers unleashed their anger and pain on people they didn't know.

Are people more violent in my time or are there just better weapons and more opportunities? More tension? More frustration?

He thought about the horrors of the Inquisition and the evolution of torture, the advances in weapons from sharper, harder metals to gunpowder and guns and on to nuclear bombs and chemical warfare. There was a steady increase in the destruction man was willing and able to inflict. But there were advances in medicine and agriculture, too. And a greater awareness of the needs of people throughout the world, and even of the pain suffered by some animals.

The cute ones, he thought.

The advances in the ability to kill are just the normal march of progress that also led to new ways to help and save people. And no doubt, he thought, there are people alive here in the distant past, who would welcome the ability to overcome their enemies more thoroughly.

The pace of life here is slower and people aren't taught to measure their worth by the size of their television screen or their four-wheel-drive. Lives aren't driven by clocks, and multitasking doesn't exist. There's no need for it. Although their lives are simple and they don't have much compared to people from my time, he thought, this life seems like a vacation.

He was left with a central question: Are people less violent here in the past, or are there simply fewer irritations and less need to vent tension and frustration?

He looked around at the crowd with different eyes.

This wasn't a romantic fantasyland that he had wandered into. These were real people, capable of as much love and as much violence as his neighbors back home. They felt hunger, they grew old, and they died, usually in fewer than thirty-five years. They started their adult lives early with marriage, work and childbirth, and while they didn't face the frustrations of corporate America, they were subject to the whims of the king and depended on the annual harvest for survival.

Right now, he knew, the harvest was uncertain.

He didn't know about King Djoser.

TIM AND DIANE

Tim waited all day for the right time to cross the canal, but it never came.

If Brian had been with Diane, he would have gone to the edge of the canal and waved a greeting, calling out in English, as soon as he had seen them. But he was worried about Brian's absence.

Paneb had told him that Djefi was mean and vicious. Was Brian being held hostage? Had he been hurt?

Tim wanted to talk to Diane privately and find out. They could make a plan, meet somewhere, go back to the tomb and return to their lives. At least, they could. Tim wasn't sure if he wanted to return, there was nothing waiting for him in the future but memories.

Djefi, however, was only half the problem. The black woman never left Diane's side, and Diane seemed happy with all the attention. She smiled when the woman caressed her, ate from her hand and snuggled up against her to nap when the afternoon heat started to press against them.

As the early evening light began to lose its strength, the festival caught a second wind.

Many of the pilgrims had taken a nap. They were awake now and ready to be entertained.

The ram-masked men returned, untied the barge and pulled it around the far side of the stone island to continue its trip. The twelve pairs of torches that lined the canal from the central island to the far wall, where the barge would leave, were lit. Hetephernebti returned, accompanied by her coterie of young girls, all dressed in white gowns. Three harp players set up on the far side of the canal by the nobles and a line of priestesses holding sacred sistrums lined the second half of the waterway.

Hetephernebti had washed away her glittering gold covering. Backlit by the setting sun, her elegant form was a dark silhouette sheathed in a translucent gown trimmed with bands of deep gold and dark red. Accompanied by the strumming harps and the dry rattle of the sistrums, she began a song of praise to Re as the ram-masked men began to pull the god and his barge slowly down the canal toward the western exit.

The eastern side of the electrum obelisk was dark now, the torches on that side unlit. The hieroglyphic etchings on the northern and southern sides were caught in shadows cast by the flickering torches. As Tim saw them he felt a disturbing wave of déjà vu and flashed back to the ceremony he had imagined beneath the Step Pyramid.

The uneasy recognition stayed with him, coloring the excitement he felt rising from the crowd as it joined in Hetephernebti's chant. While the eastern edge of the plaza held on to the fading, dusky light, dark shadows fell as a shroud from the western wall that encircled the courtyard. A darker shadow defined the exit through which Re's barge would pass.

Now the priestesses began to extinguish each torch as Re's barge passed and the courtyard grew darker.

Although the crowd continued to chant the praises of Re, Hetephernebti seemed to have sunk into a trance. She stood by the entrance to the tunnel that represented the netherworld, chanting the forms of Re's name to help him on his nighttime journey through Duat: 'He of the West,' 'He Who has Command Over his Cave,' 'He who Renews the Earth,' 'He of the Netherworld.'

Tim saw dark forms emerge from the 'netherworld' entrance, priestesses portraying gods who would accompany Re through the night and help him in his rebirth tomorrow morning.

One figure was a slight girl who held a large ostrich feather, symbol of the goddess Ma'at, Re's closest ally. Another wore a headpiece made of the horns of a cow with a golden disk rising between them, a sign of the goddess Hathor. The goddess Nut, who would swallow Re at night and give birth to him in the morning, waited with them for the arrival of the barge.

Hetephernebti's chanting of Re's names ended and she began to call out magical spells to help the god survive his twelve hours in the land beyond life.

As the priestess extinguished the next to last pair of torches, Tim heard a whispered excitement course through the crowd. Along the shadowy walls walked men carrying bags that seemed alive with movement. Some small children near Tim began to whimper and he saw a gleam of anticipation and fear in the eyes of the adults near him. He looked around for his friends, but could not see them.

Re's barge slid quietly into the dark opening, the last two torches were extinguished and Hetephernebti began to wail in mourning at the god's passing. All around him, women and girls joined in the lamentation. Caught up in the moment, the older men shuffled their feet and wept silently. Young boys, trying to be brave, looked down at the ground but Tim saw their shoulders shudder as they sobbed.

Suddenly the crying was interspersed with shrieks, coming from the edges of the plaza, now dimly lighted by the first of night's stars. Tim saw movement as the pilgrims nearest the walls began to jump and scream.

The frenzied movement rippled across the plaza, preceded by cries and shouts and then Tim saw the reason: swarms of scarab beetles, the symbol of Re's rising and rebirth, had been released from along the walls. The heavy-bodied black beetles scuttled quickly among the pilgrims' bare feet, climbing over them as they skittered across the plaza.

The crowd danced away from the dangerous looking beetles, trying to avoid contact with the sacred symbols. After the first rush of adrenaline, the pilgrims, knowing that the beetles really were harmless, began to laugh and shout exaggerated warnings to each other.

As the scarabs disappeared into the shadows, the pilgrims, murmuring their approval of the ceremony, turned to the food and beer tables that had been refilled.

Tim looked to the western wall where the barge was now out of sight. The torches along the walls and canal were being relit. Tim saw the 'goddesses' at the exit look out over the crowd for a moment before turning to enter the cave of night.

In the flickering light, Tim realized that the girl who was holding the ostrich feather was the same one he had seen smearing the Nile's mud on herself yesterday.

The crowd grew quiet as they finished eating and drinking. Worn from the day's excitement, the children began to gather with their parents, and some families filtered away from the plaza toward their campsites.

On the other side of the canal, where no scarabs had been released, some of the chairs had been replaced by low wooden beds. The nobles and priests, too tired or drunk to return to their rooms, were lounging there, talking and drinking.

Tim saw Djefi's round form slouched in a chair, his feet propped on a footrest. His arms hung limply at his side. His head twitched occasionally as he slept. Diane and the black woman were lying on a palm-frond-filled mat on the ground.

Servants moved among the slumbering nobles and priests, gathering empty ceramic jars and wooden plates.

Paneb and Ahmes approached Tim as he looked across the canal. Paneb was walking stiffly, clearly trying to keep his balance. One hand rested on Ahmes' shoulder as they approached. Tim saw the women waiting near one of the arched openings in the plaza wall.

"We're going back to the camp," Paneb said slowly and carefully.

Tim smiled. Even drunk, Paneb was a considerate host. He shook his head. "Go without me," Tim said. "I will be there soon."

"Do you know the way, Netjer Tim?" Ahmes asked. "I can stay with you."

Tim shook his head. "Go with your father, Ahmes. I can find you," he said.

"Of course he knows the way," Paneb said a little too loudly. "Do you forget who he is?"

"Are you sure?" Ahmes asked Tim.

"Yes, go with your father. I am fine," Tim said.

"If you drink any beer, be careful to look in the jar first. I saw some kids putting some of those nasty dung beetles in some of the jars," Paneb said over his shoulder as Ahmes led him away. "I never heard of such a thing. Such a waste. Why if I had done that … "

His voice trailed into a low murmur. Ahmes looked back once and waved at Tim, who returned the wave.

Once Paneb and Ahmes were outside the plaza, Tim walked casually to the edge of the canal near the island.

Behind him only a few families and stragglers remained, all of them clustered near the food and beer tables. Across the canal, he heard only the deep breath and occasional snort or snore from the nobles.

Looking carefully into the canal, he found the nearly invisible footbridge just below the water's surface. Cautiously he stepped onto it and crossed to the island where he found a similar underwater bridge to the other side of the canal.

Once on the opposite bank, he crouched and waited for a moment to see if there would be any reaction from the group of sleepers. Seeing none, he tip-toed to Diane's small group.

Djefi was snoring heavily; Diane and the black woman were entangled, breathing softly and deeply.

Tim knelt by Diane and touched her shoulder.

"Diane? Don't be startled. Are you alright? Where's Brian?" he whispered.

She opened her eyes and looked at him.

"My name is Tim. I'm from our time. I can help you."

Her gaze was unfocused and Tim wondered if she was too drunk to understand him.

"I saw you and Brian enter the tomb. I followed you. Where's Brian? Is he hurt?"

She shook her head. "Who are you?" she asked sleepily, raising herself up on her elbow.

"My name is Tim," he spoke slowly.

"Don't know any Tims. Sorry," she started to giggle, then suddenly leaned toward him and vomited. Then she sank back on the bed and closed her eyes. As she lay back, Tim saw that the black woman was awake, watching and listening.

He stood slowly to leave and gasped in surprise as the other woman reached across Diane and grabbed his kilt.

"Who are you?" she hissed in Egyptian.

"Who are you?" he answered, straightening up. He tried to sound important and godly, but knew that his voice sounded frightened.

"What do you know of Brian?" the woman asked loudly, her grip tightening on his kilt.

She spoke too quickly and Tim didn't understand the question. He looked down at her hand and said, "No."

She pulled tighter as he backed away. The kilt's waist tore and the linen came loose in her hand. Wearing only his boxer briefs, Tim turned away from her.

"Stop him! Stop the thief!" the woman yelled. Tim saw Djefi stir and other shadows began to move. He ran toward the island, hearing footsteps following him.

Afraid of slipping on the narrow submerged walkway, he ran past it and dove into the water. Staying under it, he swam through the darkness toward the opening in the western wall.

"Where is the thief?" a temple guard asked as he ran up to stand beside Yunet who was by the canal, staring into the water.

"Get me a torch!" she commanded.

"I don't see anyone," the guard said.

"Of course not, it's too dark. He went in there. Get a torch!" She watched the water and looked along both banks of the canal, watching to see where he emerged.

The guard returned with two companions, each of them carrying small torches, their flames wavering uncertainly. There was no movement atop the water or along the canal. To Yunet, who had never heard of someone swimming underwater, the stranger's disappearance was impossible.

"Get more guards, search the plaza."

"What does he look like?" The first guard asked.

She looked at him in disgust. "He'll be the wet one, you idiot. Go!"

Tim stayed under the water as long as he could and then feeling his way along the bank, he rose slowly to the surface, quickly sucked in fresh air and then swam back toward the bottom of the shallow canal.

The water was dark, so he swam along the edge, feeling his way away from the shouting woman. He focused on swimming and staying near the bottom of the canal and tried to push away thoughts of spears slashing through the water or a circle of guards waiting when he broke the surface.

He didn't know how far he had swum, but the water seemed darker now. Bubbles escaped from his mouth as he released the pressure that was growing in his lungs. He hoped they wouldn't be seen on the surface.

He pushed his arms out, pulled back again and knew that he needed to get some air.

Feeling the bank on his right side, he floated upward. He felt his heart beat fast and hard as he broke the surface and drew air deeply into his lungs.

He was inside the exit tunnel. The canal stretched away toward the lighter area outside. He heard the woman still shouting and saw shadows hurrying across the island to the other side of the canal.

He closed his eyes to help them adjust to the darkness.

When he opened them he saw that someone was standing back from the canal in the darker shadows by the tunnel wall.

"I saw you," she said.

Tim stood still, unsure what to say. The canal ran flush against the other side of the tunnel. A narrow footpath ran along the side where he stood. He wondered where it would lead.

"Yesterday, by the river. Early in the morning," she said.

With a start Tim realized who she was.

"Help me," he said quietly. "Help me leave." He looked back out the tunnel and saw torches bobbing closer to the canal entrance.

The girl followed his gaze and saw the guards coming closer. "Give me those," she said, pointing to his boxer briefs.

"What?" Tim said.

"Hurry," she said.

Although Tim didn't know that word, he understood the urgency in her voice and heard the footsteps behind them drawing closer to the canal opening. In the darkness of the tunnel he slid the wet boxer briefs off and handed them to her.

She turned and ran down the path away from the plaza. Tim leaned back against the wall, trying to make himself less visible.

In a few seconds she returned. "Follow me," she said. She reached out her hand and took his. Pulling him gently she led the way down the path and turned into a narrow opening that left the main trail.

"I am Meryt. You talk strangely," she said.

"I am Tim," he said as she led him along a winding garden path to the back of the temple complex.

"What thief? What are you talking about?" Djefi squeaked in his high-pitched voice. He had struggled to his feet, but was not fully awake. He didn't understand what Yunet was talking about and why men were running around the nearly deserted plaza carrying torches. He felt his stomach gurgle as another flush of half-digested food and wine prepared to spew its way out of his stomach.

"Another netjer," Yunet said quietly.

She was speaking slowly, separating her words carefully. She did that sometimes when Djefi made her explain something a second time.

"What do you mean?" he asked, looking around for a serving boy.

"He spoke their language. He mentioned netjer Brian," she said.

Suddenly Djefi fell to his hands and knees and threw up. Yunet turned away. She understood communing with the gods and she enjoyed the feeling of oneness she experienced when she had drunk enough of the sacred wine. But she never threw it up again. One did that only if they continued to drink more than they needed.

But Djefi is a man of excesses, she thought. Like all men.

"Boy!" Djefi shouted weakly.

A servant boy ran to him, sized up his bulk and quickly waved for another boy to join them.

"More wine. And bread. Much more bread! And help me to a chair," Djefi commanded.

Yunet looked around the plaza. The guards had followed the wall around the entire courtyard without finding the intruder. Two had entered the narrow tunnel entrance by the western wall. They hadn't returned yet.

"We were sleeping," Yunet told Djefi, speaking slowly again. "I heard someone approach. He knelt by Diane and talked to her in that strange language they use. She answered him, then she got sick and fell back to sleep. I asked him who he was, but he refused to answer. Then he ran away. I grabbed his kilt, but it came loose."

"Was he big like the other one?" Djefi asked.

She shook her head.

"He looked like an Egyptian. He was dressed like a common worker." She held up the torn kilt. "But he wore something else."

Djefi waved his hand at her comment. He was more interested in what the stranger had said.

"Wake Diane," he said.

Yunet didn't want to disturb the goddess, she was so delicate and innocent lying there as everyone around her shouted and ran. Such serenity and calmness! But she knew that Djefi wouldn't be satisfied until he had asked her about the stranger.

Hetephernebti was sad.

People were so consumed by their fears and ambitions, their desires. They were so busy planning and plotting their lives that they failed to live them. Each waking moment was a gift from Re. His warmth and blessing were given every day to everyone: poor, strong, crippled, farmers, builders, merchants, women, children, young and old.

All he asks in return is for us to live, fully alive and aware. He brings light and life to all. We can surely take his energy and use it to live. It should be so simple, she thought.

Djefi and his small entourage were almost vibrating with anger and distrust. *Just look at him, fat, sweating, angry. How can he live like that?* She wondered.

"A thief in the night. This is not the hospitality one expects," he said sulkily. His tiny voice, so odd for his size, was petulant, like a little boy who has been denied the last sweet cake.

Hetephernebti nodded. "Please find First Prophet Djefi a comfortable seat," she said to a serving girl. She looked at Yunet who stood slightly behind the quivering priest. With her dark flashing eyes and tightly pressed lips, it was obvious to Hetephernebti that it was Yunet who was bringing the charge.

The servant brought a chair for Djefi, who ungainly plopped into it.

"Now, First Prophet, what has the thief taken?"

Djefi squirmed in his seat. He held out a hand to Yunet who put the torn kilt into it.

"He left this behind," he said.

She nodded gravely as if leaving a torn kilt behind were a high offense.

"I hope you were not harmed by the dropping of his kilt," she said.

Djefi stared at her, aware that she was mocking him.

"He didn't leave it, it was taken by force," he said indignantly.

Hetephernebti kept her expression impassive.

"And your guards found this," Djefi held up the still damp boxer-briefs. "He was wearing it. It was found at the pathway that leads to the area where the pilgrims are encamped. I suggest you have the encampment searched."

Hetephernebti shook her head.

"They are my guests. No one was injured. Show me the injury if there was one. If not, then I will not search the pilgrims. The celebration is a time of peace and harmony, not distrust."

"Perhaps in Iunu you don't find it alarming when a stranger attacks a group of sleeping pilgrims, your guests," Djefi said.

"Dear Djefi," she answered. "I am not making light of this. But truly, there was no harm done, except that this man was disrobed unexpectedly. You are intact. I am sorry that your slumbers were interrupted."

"He spoke a foreign tongue," Yunet said.

"Foreign?"

"Unheard of before."

"Why, I wonder, did he approach you?" Hetephernebti looked at Diane, standing just behind Yunet. Djefi had not trusted leaving her unattended.

Hetephernebti knew much more than Djefi suspected she knew, but she wanted to see how the priest would answer, what secrets he was willing to keep.

"It is your temple," Djefi answered. "I don't know why people do things here."

Hetephernebti nodded thoughtfully, trying to show Djefi that she took his fears seriously.

"I'll ask the guards to look for him. I am very sorry your rest was interrupted. I am sure that when I place myself in your hospitality next month, I will be more secure."

Tim's first meeting with Meryt had been entirely by chance.

Shortly after Tim had emerged from the tomb and had begun to live with Paneb's family, Hetephernebti began to hear rumors of a god walking among men in the city of Ineb-Hedj. Although she had stayed in Iunu to prepare for the Feast of Re in his Barge, she had sent two young priests to the city to track down the rumors and the netjer who had chosen to live among them.

The priests sent word to her that they had missed him because the god had departed Ineb-Hedj to travel to Iunu for the feast. So Hetephernebti sent Meryt and two other priestesses out each day to meet pilgrims from Ineb-Hedj and to see if there was a strange god among them.

When Meryt had seen Tim's underclothing as he waded across the river, she had known that he was the stranger. When she heard him speak with his awkward accent, she was sure.

Hetephernebti had asked Meryt to watch the strange god during the festival and to help him with anything he needed. And so Meryt had been watching from the tunnel as Tim stealthily crossed the hidden footbridge to talk with Diane. She had seen him dive into the water and swim to the tunnel entrance and she had planted his boxer-briefs farther up the trail to divert the pursuing guards.

After she and Tim had entered the temple grounds, she had asked how she could help him. He had told her about Diane and Brian, saying that they had come from a distant land. He had said that Djefi had taken Brian and Diane to To-She and that he wanted to find and help them.

When Tim fell asleep, exhausted from the excitement of the day, Meryt had met with Hetephernebti, telling the high priestess what she had seen at the plaza and everything Tim had told her.

Hetephernebti was King Djoser's sister. Although she lacked his ruthlessness, she had his political sense. She knew that although knowledge wasn't always power, it was often the difference between life and death. And so she gathered information, collecting facts and rumors, even keeping track of the travels of other priests and members of Djoser's royal circle.

The long famine that had afflicted the Two Lands since her brother had declared himself divine was not life threatening, even in the worst years there was enough food to survive. But not enough to flourish.

The feast she had just provided had nearly drained her supplies. She and her overseer of the temple granaries knew how depleted the surplus was, but she refused to allow the diminishing stocks to affect her.

Re would provide!

The farmers and the townspeople had food every day. True, the supplies of wheat were diminished and there was less barley for beer, but there were fish in the river and ducks and geese along its banks.

The discontent, Hetephernebti knew, was coming from those closer to Djoser: the priests, the governors of the nomes, even members of her brother's royal court. During times of plenty they lived nearly as well as the king. But now, even though there was less throughout the land, Djoser insisted that the tributes sent to the royal house remain the same. And rightly so, she thought. Were he to expect less it would be an admission that the country was diminished.

However, the governors and mayors, who were closer to the people, received less in taxation and knew that they could not raise taxes without protests from the landowners on whom they depended. And so they were caught in a squeeze: Although they received less from the landowners, Djoser expected them to make their usual contribution to the royal granaries.

There had been more travel along the great river Iteru than usual this season. Priests and officials were visiting each other so often Hetephernebti wondered how they had time to fulfill their duties. She knew that they were not being more sociable; they were comparing notes on the mood of the people, perhaps even plotting.

She knew that Djefi had traveled to Waset at the same time that Kanakht had gone there to visit Waja-Hur. Now Djefi was keeping secrets about two strange visitors, perhaps gods themselves, perhaps assassins from a foreign land, unafraid to plunge a knife into a divine body.

She couldn't interrogate Djefi or those who were with him, but she did have one of the strangers with her now. Was he a god, as some claimed, or something else?

ABANDONED

When he was a child, Brian had believed everyone thought he was stupid.

Always large for his age, he was constantly outgrowing his comfort, consistently clumsy, forever apologizing for knocking something over or breaking something or bumping into someone.

Tired of apologizing, he had withdrawn. It was easier to nod his head and just walk away, listening to the scolding turn into a distant buzz. After his father abandoned the family, Brian tried to do things for his mother, but they always came out wrong. He burned eggs when he tried to make her a birthday breakfast and she had made him eat them while she told him he was "stupid, stupid, stupid." He tried to pry open a stuck window for her and drove his hand through the glass. He quit trying.

His middle school gym teacher was the first to understand.

When Brian couldn't throw a softball as hard or as far as the weakest, scrawniest girl in class, the teacher blew his whistle to quiet Brian's jeering classmates and ordered them to run laps if they had so much energy. Brian had been mortified. He expected to be scolded by the teacher now, asked to explain why he couldn't do something as elementary as throwing a ball.

But the teacher didn't ridicule him. Instead he asked Brian if he would have time to help him coach an elementary-school baseball team.

At first Brian thought it was a joke, some trick to embarrass him further. But the teacher seemed sincere and Brian was so hungry for positive attention that he was willing to risk trusting this stranger.

They met after school and the teacher began by telling Brian that he was going to teach him how to instruct the little kids to throw properly. Brian knew that he was really the one being instructed, but he pretended to go along with the teacher's charade.

Surprisingly, the throwing motion came to him naturally and quickly. His body growth had slowed and suddenly he could control his long arms and legs. His tosses quickly grew stronger and more accurate. They continued to work together and by springtime, the gym teacher told him that he should try out for the baseball team.

The baseball coach and gym teacher were good friends. As he had talked less and less at home and school, Brian had become unconsciously adept at reading body language. Now, as he watched the two men talk, he saw that there was more than friendship between them. Something in the eyes of the baseball coach seemed sad when he talked with the gym teacher; the way he stood near him seemed protective.

Brian made the team and quickly became a power pitcher, called on for the must-win games. The coach stayed late after practices to teach him to hit, and as his batting became more reliable and powerful he became the team's third baseman on days he didn't pitch. The gym teacher came to all the games.

Quiet and modest, Brian was a natural leader, someone who led by example. Knowing what it felt like, he was careful to never mock an infielder who booted a grounder behind him or an outfielder who threw to the wrong base. When he did speak, it was always supportive.

He made his first group of friends and was determined not to lose them.

When the gym teacher died the following fall of leukemia, Brian understood the sadness in the coach's eyes; he had known that his friend was dying. Brian thought about the friendship and loyalty that the coach had shown, allowing his dying friend to live out his days doing as much as he felt he could do, living fully until the end.

Through high school and college Brian grew as a powerful athlete. He was driven, willing to work hard to learn new skills. Because of his size and strength and talent he was always expected to be a leader. He took the role seriously, studying other athletes who were viewed as leaders. He copied the quiet, supportive style of those he admired, avoiding the caustic, screaming styles of others.

And he always found comfort in losing himself in his team.

His team now was a small group of hunters.

The morning after Brian's audience with Djefi, Pahket had awakened him as usual, but she had seemed quieter. He hadn't known enough Egyptian to ask her about her mood, but he had an uneasy feeling that she was doing something against her will.

He had asked about Diane. She had smiled and nodded, but didn't tell him anything.

After they had eaten, she had led him outside where Siamun and three other men, two barely out of their teens and the third, an older man, were waiting. Each of the men had a leather sling over his shoulder and carried a short spear. Siamun also had his knife tucked in his linen belt. A fifth sling had lain on the ground. Brian had pulled it on, surprised by its weight. From the sloshing motion he had known that it contained a skin of water.

"Diane?" he had asked Siamun, who had offered a humorless smile in return.

Brian had turned to Pahket to ask her what to do. Her head had been down, her eyes on the ground.

"Go with him, Netjer Brian. It is the way to see Diane," she had said.

Brian had looked at Siamun and the three other men. He had been sure that they were not taking him to see Diane, but he refused to believe that Pahket would quietly hand him over to an execution squad. Although he didn't like Siamun, he didn't know what choice he had. He didn't plan to fight four armed men.

If Pahket said this was a way for him to see Diane, then he would follow it through. He would see this to the end and somehow find her.

The men had been restless. After Brian had picked up the sling, Siamun spoke in Egyptian, too fast for Brian to follow. Then he had turned and started to walk away, the men following him.

They wound through the village, away from the canal, headed for the orchard. On the other side of the grove, they took an overgrown path that led past a hut Brian hadn't seen before.

They came to the edge of the oasis and kept walking. The trail became less and less distinct as they left the scrub grass at the edge of To-She and entered the desert.

He suspected that Siamun was taking him along trails that normally were not used, following paths that were steep, terrain that was hard to climb. But Brian was used to sports hazing and his twenty-first century diet and conditioning made him stronger and more durable than Siamun and the hunters.

On the third day out, they crept up on a water hole where a small herd of antelope was drinking.

Siamun paired Brian with Neswy, the oldest man of the group who was always lagging behind the others, insulted by Siamun for his weakness. Although Siamun showed the old man no respect, Brian had seen the others lighten Neswy's load when Siamun wasn't looking, even skimping on their water rations, offering some to Neswy.

Siamun placed Brian and Neswy behind a boulder along the trail the antelope had followed to reach the water hole. Siamun and the others would circle around the herd and flush them into the ambush. If the hunt was unsuccessful, it would be because Brian and Neswy had failed. Brian understood that Siamun had put the weakest hunter – Neswy – and the least experienced – himself – in the most critical position.

He was setting them up for failure.

Leaning against the boulder, seeking shade, Neswy looked hopefully at Brian. He held his spear in a hand that Brian saw was quivering, either from fatigue or fear of Siamun.

The other men circled the water hole, moving slowly, testing the still air for any movement. They separated as they went, spacing themselves around the small herd, leaving the area by the trail open.

Neswy gripped and regripped his spear. He peered around the boulder to see the antelopes and then leaned back against the rock, breathing deeply.

Brian approached him, careful to stay low so the antelopes wouldn't see him. When Neswy looked at him, Brian patted his open hand against his chest, and then shook the spear slightly. Neswy looked puzzled.

Brian hit his chest again and mimicked tossing the spear. Then he motioned for Neswy to step aside. Neswy nodded his understanding and moved aside to make room for Brian.

Brian listened for a moment, then slid down onto his belly to peer around the boulder. The antelopes were still drinking. Occasionally one would lift its head, its ears turning to scan for sounds.

He stood in the shadow of the rock and waited for the others to flush the game.

Brian knew it would be very hard to time a throw as the antelopes went streaking and leaping past, so he decided to wait until the antelopes were close and then to step out from behind the rock, shouting to get their attention. He hoped they would attempt to veer away from him, presenting him a larger target with a side view for a frozen moment.

He wished he could talk to Neswy and ask his advice; the older man certainly had a store of experience. It was frustrating to be placed in this situation. He wondered if Neswy felt the same way, if he understood that both of them were being tested.

There was a subtle shifting in the light as the edge of the sun touched the western horizon. With it came shouting as the other three hunters, having crawled as close as they could to the drinking antelopes, rose up and charged toward the watering hole.

Brian listened hard for the sound of the herd clattering his way. Their small hooves made hardly any sound on the soft trail, but he heard the animals snorting as they rushed toward him.

A stillness came over him now, the same focused feeling that enveloped him on those rare days when as a batter Brian could see the pitcher's grip on the baseball as he whipped his arm forward, when he could see the stitching on the ball as it spun toward home plate and he knew, positively knew, that he would swing the bat at the right angle and time and speed to meet the ball squarely.

Nothing else existed.

Brian stepped out from behind the boulder, unafraid and confident.

The antelopes were much larger than he expected, and moving quickly. In his own time, apart from the pace that existed everywhere else in the universe, Brian saw the eyes on the lead antelope widen as it registered his presence. He saw its nostrils flare as it gulped in air. The hairs on its ears waved in the breeze it generated during its long leap.

The antelope's right shoulder twitched as it started to turn in midair, then it shuddered again as the animal twisted back to head directly for Brian.

The others in the herd scattered away, springing off to the north, away from the trail.

The lead animal seemed to float now, its head coming low as it aimed its short spiked horns at Brian. Its front hooves hit the sandy trail, kicking up a spray of dirt and sand. Its front shoulders flexed, the muscles tightening as it launched itself forward. The antelope's back legs hit a fraction of a second later, and, kicking back, added more speed to its movement.

Brian stood his ground, his weight forward on the balls of his feet, his body relaxed, his mind clear as he waited until the antelope was airborne. He could smell the animal now, its earthy, musky scent carrying the heavy sound of its panting.

Suddenly it was on him, its horns so close and clear he could see the twisted pattern of their growth. He moved now, leaning smoothly, his left knee bending as if he were leaning away from an inside fastball.

Gripping his spear with both hands, like a baseball bat, he twisted down and away from the antelope. He swung the spear parallel to the ground, his wrists snapping it forward just before the wooden shaft struck the antelope's oncoming front legs.

The spear shaft shattered. The antelope pitched forward, unable to stop its forward fall.

The world returned to its normal speed.

Brian pushed off with his flexed left leg, propelling himself forward as if moving from a catcher's stance. Dust flew up from the trail as the antelope hit the ground hard, its lungs emptying with a loud grunt.

Neswy charged out from behind the boulder, his spear raised overhead, both hands gripping the shaft as he ran toward the fallen animal. Brian threw himself at the antelope's head, determined to keep it still until Neswy could reach it.

He wrapped his arms around the animal and heard himself whisper quietly to it, as if to a frightened colt. The antelope recovered from its fall and began to kick and twist, trying to escape his grip.

Neswy reached them and pushed his spear into the antelope's ribs, aiming for its heart.

The antelope twisted its head violently and bawled at the pain. Brian held tightly, his face turned toward the antelope's as he kept talking to it. "I'm sorry," he whispered over and over again.

Neswy pulled the spear out and raised it overhead for another thrust. The antelope kicked out with its rear legs and caught Neswy's right knee. Brian heard a brittle crack as the bone shattered, and Neswy screamed out in pain. The antelope continued to twist in Brian's arms; its movements more frantic but less powerful.

Brian released his grip enough to turn his head. Neswy was on the ground, the spear at his side, his hands over his leg. Blood ran down his calf. When he saw Brian looking at him, the old man twisted on the ground, reaching for his spear to pass it to him.

Brian saw Siamun and the others jogging toward them.

The antelope shuddered suddenly and snorted one last time. Blood and mucus ran from its nostrils, its bladder emptied and it lay its head almost gently on the ground.

Brian released the antelope and scrambled to Neswy who was rocking on his side, his bloodied leg stretched out on the ground, the lower half of it cocked at an unnatural angle. He was moaning softly.

Following Sianmun's orders, the hunters gutted and butchered the still warm antelope, wrapping the meat in linen cloths they had brought with them. They put the heavy cuts in the slings to carry back to To-She, setting aside a small portion to roast over their fire that night.

Siamun had glanced at Neswy's injury with a strange, satisfied smile on his dark face, then, dismissing him, had turned his attention to the antelope. He hadn't spoken to Brian.

As the adrenaline high of facing down the antelope dissipated, Brian found himself growing angry at the way Siamun ignored Neswy, and confused by the way Neswy accepted it.

The old man was unable to stand. The antelope's kick had ripped the skin from his knee, tearing away the ligaments and shattering the kneecap. Brian had washed the grit from the wound and made a splint using the shaft of his broken spear, holding it in place with strips torn from his kilt.

Neswy seemed grateful for Brian's help, but said little and, dragging himself away from the campfire, curled into a silent ball.

Brian thought of his useless cell phone, lying somewhere in his room at To-She, its battery exhausted from being turned on and off again as he unsuccessfully tried to find service. He hadn't seen anything resembling a medical facility or a doctor. And, although he hadn't thought the words consciously, he knew that he was some place, perhaps some time far away from everything he knew.

This hunt is like something from the Stone Age, he thought.

He knew Siamun wouldn't help Neswy, and, although the other two hunters seemed less sinister, Brian knew that they wouldn't provide any help unless Siamun ordered it.

When morning came, Siamun and the others slung their heavy bags over their shoulders and prepared to return to To-She. As usual, they ignored Brian.

Still curled into a ball, Neswy lay with his eyes half open. His leg was swollen, the skin red and tender around the now dirty bandage.

Brian was only a little surprised when, after kicking sand over the smoldering campfire, Siamun and the others started to walk away, leaving Neswy behind.

"Stop," he shouted as the three turned to leave.

Siamun turned to look at him.

"Neswy," Brian said, gesturing to the old man.

Siamun shrugged. Then he looked at Neswy, who was dragging himself to the boulder so he could sit up. "Can you walk, old man?"

Neswy continued to drag himself, his eyes pinched shut in pain.

"We take," Brian said, angry that he didn't know enough Egyptian to argue or to call Siamun the names that were racing through his head.

Siamun mimicked Brian's poor Egyptian, "We take." Looking down at Neswy, he said roughly, "Get up."

Neswy shook his head.

"We can't leave him, you don't just leave someone behind," Brian said in English.

Ignoring Brian, Siamun rejoined the other two hunters. "Go," he said when he reached them.

The three of them walked away.

Brian's temper rose. In a baseball game, if one of your teammates got hit by a pitch and charged the mound, you went with him; you didn't leave him hanging out there alone. If someone got spiked at second base, you ran over and helped him, carried him off the field if he needed it.

"Get back here," he shouted at Siamun and the others.

They continued to walk away, ignoring him.

Brian took a few steps toward them. "Siamun, you bastard, get back here! You can't leave him behind," he shouted.

Siamun paused briefly, but didn't turn from his path.

"You son of a bitch! I'm not leaving him behind. You little bastard, you! I'll bring him home and then I'm finding you. I don't care who you are or how many friends you have backing you. I don't care about your little knife. You hear me, you little son of a bitch!"

Brian had never been this angry before.

He wanted to charge after Siamun and break his leg, leave him behind to die in the desert. He knew the others would fight with Siamun, but he didn't care. He was full of anger and confidence. He could take them.

But, even infuriated, he tried to get his anger under control, to harness the energy rather than waste it. He realized that even if he did defeat all three of them, he would still be in the middle of the desert with an injured man, unsure which way to go.

He stood alone, halfway between Neswy and Siamun, his chest heaving, his hands clenched as he watched the three hunters walk away.

Siamun walked with his eyes straight ahead.

He didn't want to admit it, but this "god" impressed him. Brian had easily kept up with them on a journey that even Siamun viewed as a difficult trek across the desert. He had stood unflinching before the horns of a charging antelope and moved with lightning speed to bring it down.

Siamun had watched that with mixed feelings. He had never seen a man put himself directly in the path of a charging antelope. For all their delicate grace and beauty, their incredible speed and sharp horns made the animals dangerous. And, as Neswy had learned, their small, hard hooves were perilous as well.

Up until the last moment when Brian seemed to bend like a tree in a storm, Siamun had thought the outlander would be gored and trampled. But somehow, moving so quickly that it was a blur even in Siamun's memory; Brian had swayed away from the charging animal and then attacked it all at the same time.

Brian had been quiet and unassuming during the trek. The violence Siamun heard now in Brian's voice made him wonder if he truly was a god. And what he would be like in a fight.

If he gets out of the desert alive, we shall see, Siamun thought.

Brian watched them disappear across the sand, noting that they were moving southeast, the sun angled off to their left.

Neswy was propped against the rock, watching Brian.

"Go," the old man said softly, nodding in the direction the other three had gone.

"You have a broken leg, you're not dying. This is ridiculous," Brian said in English.

He knelt by Neswy and asked, "Do you know where To-She?"

Neswy nodded.

"OK," Brian said. He stood and looked toward the water hole. There were short scraggy scrubs, but no trees, nothing that he could use to make a platform to drag Neswy behind him across the desert.

"What would MacGyver do?" he asked himself. "Take an inventory," he answered himself.

He reached down to pat his pockets and felt only the torn linen of the short kilt he wore. Unlike Siamun, he had no knife tucked in its waist. He knew that his sling contained a half-empty bladder of water and some flat bread cakes. Neswy had nothing except the narrow linen belt all the Egyptian men wore.

He picked up his water bag, gauging its weight and looked at Neswy.

At least he's small. Well, Brian thought, everyone here is small. He probably weighs no more than a hundred twenty pounds.

He picked up the water bag and walked to the water hole where he filled it, his mind on the journey ahead, trying to visualize how it could work. He would have the water bag in a sling over his shoulders. Neswy could ride on his back. Brian tried to see the old man there, one leg stiff, pushed out in front of them, unable to grip Brian's waist.

Walking back toward Neswy, he passed the antelope carcass, the bones and entrails lying in the sand, the animal's skin beneath the bloody mess. *Another sling,* he thought, looking at the hide.

He laid the water bag on the sand near Neswy, who was watching him carefully. Returning to the carcass, Brian pulled the hide from under the bloody organs and bones.

The skin had been stripped from the torso and thighs of the antelope, but the lower part of the legs, where there was little meat, was still inside the skin. Brian pictured the hide from the legs tied together to form two straps. The back part of the hide could serve as a sling in which Neswy could sit while Brian carried him.

He dragged the antelope skin down to the water hole and rinsed it clean, rubbing sand into it to help scrape away pieces of flesh that clung to it.

He laid it to dry over the boulder they had hidden behind yesterday, then went back to the pile of offal and picked out a thighbone. Finding a hand-sized rock, he broke the bone, and then sharpened the edge of it against the boulder. Using the pointed bone he scraped along the bony lower legs of the skin and then pried it loose with his fingernails.

As Brian worked on the hide, Neswy staggered up to stand on his good leg. He leaned against the boulder and watched Brian work.

"I am Yunet's uncle," he said.

Brian nodded without looking up.

"Siamun and Yunet were together, you understand?"

Brian stopped now and watched Neswy, focused on what he said, trying to catch enough words to understand.

"They had a fight, she cut off his ear. He would have killed her, but I was there and I stopped him. Well," Neswy looked away, "my brother and I stopped him. My brother died a little later, also while out on a hunting trip with Siamun. Now it is my turn. The other two, they are afraid of Siamun. They aren't bad, just afraid.

"If you go now, you can catch them," Neswy said quietly, nodding in the direction Siamun had gone.

Brian shook his head and returned to his scraping. He hadn't understood everything Neswy had said, but he knew the old man was suggesting that Brian go without him.

That's not going to happen.

"You know where To-She," he said awkwardly. "We go To-She together."

"Three days," Neswy said. He nodded at the water skin. "Little water."

Brian shrugged.

GATHERING AT TO-SHE

Kanakht sat under the white linen awning on his barge, his eyes on the slowly passing riverbank, his mind unfocused, drifting. He picked a spot along the river, a thick stand of papyrus plants, their thick triangular stems rising from the water, taller than a man. As his barge moved downriver headed for To-She, the plants came closer, but his attention drifted and when he looked again, the papyrus was past him.

I'm getting old, he thought.

He tried to refocus, pulling together the threads of his thoughts.

Waja-Hur is fixated on the idea that King Djoser overstepped his bounds when he declared himself a god. He blames the series of meager floods and the resulting famine on Djoser and the unbalance that the king's declaration of godliness has brought to the Two Lands. In Waja-Hur's mind, everything bad that happened in the past seven years is because of Djoser, anything good happens despite the king.

Djefi is full of ambition, for himself and for his god Sobek. Although, without our prompting, the young priest never would have thought of removing Djoser, he will grasp at the plot as a way to advance himself and his crocodile god. Is his ambition strong enough?

Although he needed Waja-Hur for religious legitimacy and Djefi would provide the means and setting for Kanakht's plans, Makare was the key to the plot.

Commander of the small garrison at Khmunu, Makare was ambitious, but cautious. Khmunu was several days downriver from Waset, where Djoser and the court were centered, but Makare still reported directly to Sekhmire, who was head of the royal guard, defender of the House of Horus, and protector of King Djoser himself.

Kanakht assumed that Sekhmire was loyal to Djoser. As much as he disliked the king, Kanakht knew the man was no fool. Djoser would have tested Sekhmire's loyalty and found ways to bind the soldier to him – power, riches, luxury, and women.

But Makare, stationed away from the center of power, hungered for the attention and riches that surrounded the king.

Hoping to drive a wedge between the young soldier and his commander, Kanakht had showered Makare with praise, wondering aloud why Makare wasn't at the royal court. When Makare had pointed out that here at

Khmunu he was in charge of the garrison, even though it was small, Kanakht had agreed.

"And you've done a wonderful job, Makare. You've proven that you are ready for something larger, something more important."

"Did Sekhmire say that?" the young soldier had asked.

"He doesn't need to. Everyone knows it."

"But what would I do in the royal guard? Sekhmire commands it."

Kanakht had agreed, then planted the seed. "Things change, Makare."

After this festival at To-She, Kanakht would visit with Makare again and invite him to serve in his personal guard. He would explain that even if Sekhmire wouldn't promote him, that he, Kanakht, would find a way to help Makare rise to his deserved level.

Kanakht needed him, his strength, and his willingness to kill.

Tim had spent two weeks with Meryt and every day he was surprised and excited by her. He admired her curiosity and enthusiasm, her innocence, her intelligence, her energy and, even though he was reluctant to admit it, her beauty.

His Egyptian had improved immensely. Unlike Paneb and his family, who had used short, simple words and had spoken slowly around Tim, Meryt had refused to baby him. He had learned to pay close attention, and soon her normal conversational speed had become comprehensible. Although he wasn't fluent, he could hold a conversation.

"Did Hetephernebti tell you to teach me your language?" he had asked during one of their early conversations after she had saved him from the guards during the night of the Festival of Re in His Barge.

"How else could we talk to you?"

"What else did she ask you to do?"

"I am to learn everything about you and to tell you everything you want to know."

They were sitting quietly beside each other on the rough wooden deck of Hetephernebti's barge as it floated slowly upriver toward To-She, pushed by the winds that the desert heat drew up river from the Mediterranean Sea, so many miles behind them.

"Hetephernebti heard that you are a god. Are you?" Meryt asked in her direct manner.

"No."

"They say you healed Paneb's daughter with magic."

"It was just, I don't know the words, it was just healing, not magic."

"They say you are an artist," she said, starting to tease him now.

"Yes."

"Draw something."

"What would you like?"

"Draw me."

She stood. As always, she was naked except for her linen belt. She posed in stiff profile her arms outstretched to welcome a guest in the formal style Tim had seen countless times in tombs. He reached over to gather his notebook and pencil from the backpack he had retrieved from Paneb before the kindly tomb artist and his family had left Iunu. When he looked up she had changed position and was standing like a hunter on a boat, an imaginary spear held overhead, her mouth turned down in a serious frown, her dark eyebrows gathered.

He looked down at his notebook to draw a horizon line, trying to refocus his mind to look at her as a model, not as a very young, very beautiful woman whom he was finding more and more attractive and intriguing.

When he looked up, she had dropped to the deck and was sitting cross legged, pretending to be drawing in her own notebook, her face studious, as he supposed his had been. He shook his head, she shook hers, mimicking his movement.

"You have to sit still," he said.

She leaned forward and crawled across the wooden deck to him, suddenly serious.

"Netjer Tim, life is not sitting still. Any artist can draw me sitting still. But that is not life. That is what they paint in tombs. I am not ready for a tomb, am I?" she said as she came closer. "If you are a god, you can draw me moving. That is life."

He looked at the light lying softly across her silky skin which was drawn tight across the smooth muscles of her arms and shoulders as she leaned toward him. He saw open trust in her eyes, a playful tug of a smile on her lips.

"I'm not a god," he answered.

Neswy shook the water skin. Finding it empty, he tossed it aside, throwing off Brian's stride as he carried the old man down another dune.

"Over there," Neswy said, pointing with one arm, the other draped loosely around Brian's neck and chest.

Brian looked where Neswy pointed. In the soft predawn light he saw an odd shape on the horizon, an irregular mound that broke up the flat line of the horizon.

"Those are the rocks you can see from the edge of To-She. Once we get there, it's only a half a day, no more. We're almost home."

Neswy's voice was just a whisper now, but it didn't matter. Despite three days of the man's constant talking, Brian understood little of what he said. He heard "To-She," "sand," and "walk." The rest was just so many harsh whispering sounds, growing weaker each day.

They walked at night. Or rather he walked at night. Neswy rode on Brian's back, sitting in the sling Brian had made from the antelope's hide. The straps, skin from the animal's legs, had grown stiffer and stiffer as they dried. Now they cut into Brian's shoulders, wearing away at his strength.

They had walked just a few hours the first day, trailing Siamun and the other hunters, never actually seeing them, but heading in the same direction. When they had reached some rocks, Neswy had asked Brian to stop and set him down in the little shade the boulders cast.

They had rested there until the sun was almost down, and then resumed the trek, Neswy using the stars to keep them on track. When Brian tired, they stopped, lying in the lee of a large dune, covering themselves with the stiffening hide to shield themselves from the sun.

The second night, Brian thought Neswy would die.

The old man had talked constantly in Brian's ear, nudging him to the right or left if Brian wandered off course. Brian recognized the nonstop chatter as the way Neswy distracted himself from the pain of his shattered knee. As the night wore on, Neswy grew quiet and then started to moan.

When the moaning became constant, Brian stopped.

"Neswy?" he said softly.

Neswy groaned in answer.

Brian looked down at Neswy's right knee. Blood had dried over the open wound. The joint was swollen and his lower leg, although held in the makeshift splint, looked a little twisted. Red streaks ran from the knee up his thigh.

"Stop?" he asked in Egyptian.

"No," Neswy answered. He lifted his head from Brian's shoulder and pointed into the sky. He counted slowly, pointing at a line of three stars. He laid his head back on Brian's shoulder and softly murmured, "home."

Brian studied the sky. He saw the row of brighter stars, the lowest seeming to be the most distant, pointing in the direction he was facing. He looked at the stars surrounding the three, trying to memorize the pattern.

They just looked like a bunch of flickering points.

"Damn you, Siamun. I swear I'll kill you," he said quietly.

Four men were rowing hard, their backs glistening with sweat, as the boat passed Kanakht's barge on the canal that led to To-She.

Awakened from a nap by the sound of the men grunting as the boat splashed by, heading away from To-She, Kanakht caught only a blurry glimpse of the figure who sat in the boat's stern, unprotected from the sun, arms and legs crossed, a dark scowl on his face.

The boat swept by without the man looking up.

In the old days, Kanakht thought, when Djoser's father, King Kha-sekhemwy sat on the throne of the Two Lands, a traveler passing someone along the River Iteru would never have been so rude. News and greetings would have been exchanged, food and drinks offered, and politely refused.

If someone had passed by like this, the king would have sent a fast boat from his armada to bring the offender back and beat sense into him. He would have carried the reminder to be polite on his broken back the rest of his life. Order was maintained under King Kha-sekhemwy, both within the Two Lands and beyond the borders, where the king's armies watched over Kemet.

Kanakht looked across the canal, past the low trees that lined the waterway, off to the golden red desert that lay beyond, that always lay beyond, isolating and protecting the Two Lands.

Things are so different since Kha-sekhemwy has gone on to his life in Khert-Neter, the vizier thought.

At times, Kanakht thought it would be good to give up this burden and to follow King Kha-sekhemwy to the afterworld, to join his ancestors, to awake each morning to music and beautiful women, to never feel tired or sad again.

That time may not be so far off, although Waja-Hur seems to have taken up permanent residence here in the Two Lands, Kanakht thought. But there is so much to do. Not only has Djoser offended the gods bringing year after year of famine to the Two Lands, but he seems ignorant of the very ways of governing Kemet.

Kha-sekhemwy led his armies and kept the land strong. He gave me authority to watch over the land, to manage the buildings and the granaries, to collect the tributes from foreign lands and the taxes from within Kemet.

He trusted me.

But Djoser ignores the health of the land. His army has grown weak. He constantly watches over my shoulder, always asking why this is done and why that is done. Do I need to maintain homes in so many cities? Why do the governors of the twenty nomes write to me instead of to him?

Kanakht sighed deeply, caught himself doing it and scolded himself.

There is no time for weakness. I will be in To-She by evening. I'll meet with Djefi and see what this fat priest has been thinking since we last talked.

Hetephernebti camped just outside To-She, close enough to gather water easily, but far enough from the crocodile-filled lake to feel safe.

A large tent housed the priestess and her attendants. The few others who had accompanied her on the trip upriver from Iunu slept outdoors beneath awnings. Meryt, as a wbt-priest, normally would have stayed in the tent with Hetephernebti, but instead she went with Tim to find a shaded spot for their camp.

He had told her about Diane and Brian, how he had followed them from his country to Saqqara and Ineb-Hedj, where he had learned that they had gone with Djefi to To-She. He told her that they were lost and he had come to help them find their way home.

Now that he was in To-She, he was eager to find them.

"Djefi is angry with you. He is dangerous, Netjer Tim," Meryt said.

Tim nodded, remembering how Yunet had tried to restrain him at Iunu when he spoke with Diane. Meryt had told him that Djefi had demanded that Hetephernebti search the camp for him and how the priest had accused Tim of being a thief.

"I am with you and Hetephernebti," Tim said. "She will protect me."

Meryt shook her head, completely serious for once. "We are in To-She, Netjer Tim. Hetephernebti cannot protect you here. If Djefi finds you and takes you, we can do nothing. Nothing, Netjer Tim, nothing."

Tim was silent for a minute. He knew that Hetephernebti was King Djoser's sister and he had assumed that the relationship would give her some kind of power over Djefi. He knew that they had traveled with a small party, just the priestess, her immediate attendants, a few boatmen, who would double as guards, and himself.

Hetephernebti doesn't need a large guard to protect herself, she is the king's sister, after all, but her power here at To-She will be limited by the small number of guards in her group, he thought. He shook his head. He wasn't used to thinking of life in terms of naked power.

Where's Jim Kamin when I need him? Tim thought, remembering the security official at the American embassy.

He realized Meryt was watching him, waiting for him to decide what he wanted to do. He had no idea what that would be.

"Netjer Tim," she said, "I know people who live here. Let me visit them and find out about Brian and Diane. When we know more, then we can decide how to help them."

He nodded agreement.

She saw him looking at the palm trees and the people walking through the grove headed toward the center of the settlement.

Meryt shook her head. "Please stay here, or visit with Hetephernebti."

"Why?" he asked. "Don't I look like everyone? Don't I talk like everyone?"

She smiled, the expression making her face young again, and Tim wondered how old she was. He hadn't asked her, unsure if women five thousand years ago were as sensitive of their ages as they were in his time.

Her body was slim, her breasts small. He guessed she was no more than sixteen, perhaps as young as thirteen, a thought that made him feel guilty when she flirted with him.

Although he knew that women in ancient Egypt married in their early teens, he couldn't help but think of Jerry Lee Lewis and his twelve-year-old cousin. He knew it was simply a cultural difference that women, and men, married later and later in life as living became more complex.

She seems so mature, so much older, he thought.

And I'm rationalizing.

"No, Netjer Tim, you look and talk like a god. You will fool no one."

"I'm not a god," he said. "A god would not listen to you. But I will."

She reached up and touched him softly on his bare shoulder.

"I will not be long."

She turned and walked toward the village. He watched her, admiring her shape and the way she moved. He realized what he was doing and turned away, embarrassed.

He pulled his backpack from the small pile of possessions they had brought with them. Digging out his notebook, he settled against the palm tree and opened to a blank page.

"Addy, I'm at a place called To-She, where the crocodile god Sobek is worshiped. I'm traveling with a priestess of the god Re. We've come here for some sort of festival, but I'm really here to see if I can finally meet up with Brian and talk to Diane when she's not drunk. Oh, and I'm traveling with a girl who's been helping me. She reminds me of you."

He paused and looked at the last sentence. He had written it without thinking. He wondered if it was true or if he was rationalizing again.

T here was no one at the temple entrance to welcome Hetephernebti.

Never mind, she thought, I can find my way to Djefi's chambers.

She had come alone, walking among the villagers, pausing to talk with some women and their children who were carrying water from the lake to their homes beyond the temple entrance.

Djefi should have had someone at the canal to greet his guests, she thought. The Cutting Out of Sobek's Tongue was the major festival for the crocodile god. But To-She was off the river, away from the mainstream and not as many priests and royal officials would be attending.

Hetephernebti knew that her brother wouldn't be here. He was in the south, meeting with priests near the first cataract where the river narrowed, tumbling against rocks as it pushed its way through the desert into Kemet.

She knew he would be cajoling, flattering and, if necessary, threatening the priests. He would show them that he was concerned about the meager floods, that he was acting to bring the water and its rich black earth to the

Two Lands and that if he failed it was because they had not done enough to persuade their gods to help him.

As long as he enjoyed the loyalty of Sekhmire and the army, he would sit secure on the throne. But if the priests or the governors or dissatisfied officials of the royal court were able to persuade Sekhmire that King Djoser was not a god and that Kemet would prosper without him on the throne, then his life would be in danger.

Ah, Teti, she thought, thinking of him by his childhood nickname, I hope you are as persuasive and commanding as you ever were. I pray that Re looks upon you as a brother and gives you his blessing.

Hetephernebti was mildly surprised to find the hallways of the temple empty. Then she realized that most of the workers would be in the kitchens and bakeries preparing for the beginning of the feast.

She walked unhurriedly down the hallway that led to Djefi's chambers. As she got closer she heard voices. She recognized Djefi's high-pitched voice and the low, stately rumble of Kanakht.

For a moment she thought to wait outside the doorway. *But a priestess of Re does not eavesdrop,* she thought.

She pushed open the wooden door and abruptly the talking stopped.

"I said I was not to be interrupted," Djefi shouted. Then he saw that it was Hetephernebti who had entered the room.

He blanched and stopped talking.

Kanakht, ever the diplomat, came toward her, his arms extended in greeting. "Hetephernebti, blessed of Re," he said.

"Lord Kanakht," she said, embracing him and feeling that his solid frame had grown thinner in the weeks since she had last seen him.

He pulled back and looked into her eyes. She saw the same intelligence and strength there she had seen when she was a little girl and he had been adviser to her father. But there was a tiredness there she had never noticed. He broke eye contact first, nervously glancing at Djefi.

"Greetings, First Prophetess of Re," Djefi said. "We were just talking … "

"About your dear brother," Kanakht interrupted. "I was telling Djefi that King Djoser could not be here and that he sends his apologies. And me," he laughed softly.

"Yes," Djefi agreed.

Hetephernebti looked at Djefi. He touched his forehead with a cloth, sopping up the beads of sweat that had appeared.

Suddenly there was a loud noise from the hallway, a voice shouted something they couldn't understand and there was the unmistakable sound of a body hitting a stone wall. The wooden doors swung open and a huge man wearing a torn kilt, his skin sunburned, his lips bloodied and cracked, pushed through.

"Where is Siamun?" he demanded in a strangely accented voice.

Djefi shrank back from the stranger and glanced around looking for help. Hetephernebti waited calmly, looking from Djefi to the stranger.

The man looked at her, dismissed her with a glance, and did the same with Kanakht.

He started to shout now in a strange tongue, his voice rising louder and angrier. The only word that Hetephernebti could understand was Siamun's name. Then the giant sank to his knees, his eyes rolled up into his head and he fell face forward on the floor.

THE CUTTING OUT OF SOBEK'S TONGUE

Brian woke up angry, confused, and exhausted. He opened his eyes to a dark room with the sound of scuffling footsteps approaching.

He didn't know where he was. The last thing he remembered was pushing into Djefi's chambers, screaming that he wanted to kill Siamun.

The footsteps came closer.

He moved his right arm, making sure it wasn't tied down.

He tried to look in the direction of the sound without moving his head. He didn't want the intruder to know he was awake. He knew it wasn't Pahket, he would have recognized her footsteps. These were softer and more cautious.

Siamun?

When he had first arrived here, Brian had noticed how much brighter the night sky was, seemingly packed stars. At the same time the nights were darker because there were no artificial lights, just torches or campfires.

Apparently there were no windows in this room. Brian couldn't see even the dark outline of whoever was approaching him, even though they were so close now that Brian could hear the person's breathing.

The darkness would be as extreme for the other person, Brian realized.

He sat up quickly and turned, stretching his arms out to grab or stop the attacker. His hands found the intruder's arms, which felt small and only lightly muscled.

It's a woman or a boy.

Holding the person tightly, Brian rolled off the bed, pinning the attacker beneath him.

"Don't hurt me," the intruder said in almost a whisper.

"Did Siamun send you?"

"English."

"I don't care if you're English or French or German."

"Speaking English."

"I am speaking English," Brian answered. "Oh, my God, so are you."

He relaxed his grip and reached out to help the intruder to his feet.

"Are you OK? Who are you?"

"Not so loud, Brian."

"How do you know my name?"

"Shhhh." Tim coughed softly and looked over his shoulder. "If I get caught, they'll, well, I don't know what they'll do."

There was a light scraping sound and a flare of light as Tim lit a match. The two men studied each other in the flickering light. Tim thought that Brian was much more gaunt than the tourist he had watched swagger across the sands at Saqqara. His face was sunburned and his lips scabbed and bloody.

Brian broke the silence.

"You look familiar."

"My name is Tim Hope. I was at the Step Pyramid when you and Diane went into Kanakht's tomb. I followed you and ended up here."

Brian looked worried.

"Where exactly is here?" Brian asked.

"Yeah, it's more of a when than a where," Tim said.

Brian shook his head.

Tim leaned closer. "I don't have a lot of time, Brian. Djefi is looking for me. And there is no one here to help us.

"This is going to sound unbelievable, but when you and Diane went into that tomb and through that opening in the wall, you went into the past, about five thousand years into it. We're in ancient, I mean, really ancient Egypt, back before the pyramids, back before the Sphinx, back before Moses, before King Tut, way back … "

Remembering the hunt and his useless cell phone, Brian nodded his head. It explained everything, but it made no sense at all.

"I was sitting against the wall at Saqqara when you and Diane went into the tomb. You even looked at me and winked."

Brian remembered now, the little guy writing in a notebook.

"When you didn't come out of the tomb, I did some checking around. I found your room at the Mena House and waited there, but you never came back. I got in the tomb and followed you here. I've been trying to find you for a couple weeks now. I saw Diane last week, but she was too drunk to talk. I'm not sure I can get close enough to talk to her here, she's always with some woman."

"Probably Yunet," Brian said.

"So, we have to figure out how to talk to her and then sneak back to Saqqara. Then we can get back into the tomb and back to our time," Tim said.

Brian realized that, now that the adrenaline rush had worn off, he was almost too weak to stand. The last day in the desert had drained him, leaving him exhausted and shaking. The only thing that had driven him on had been his desire to find and strangle Siamun.

"I don't understand," he said.

Tim nodded. "I don't either. I have no idea how to explain it. All I can say is that we're here, in this *now* and the only thing I can think of is to get back to the tomb and try to open the wall the other way."

"No," Brian said. "I don't understand about Diane. I don't understand what you said either, but I don't know what's going on with Diane. She got really pissed at me when we were riding camels out in the desert on the way here. Then when we got here, she just ignored me. I haven't talked to her; I haven't even seen her. Now you say you saw her and she was drunk?"

Tim glanced at the doorway.

"I shouldn't stay here much longer. Look, I have a friend, her name is Meryt. I'll ask her to figure out how we can talk again and how to get a message to you. Meanwhile, try to talk to Diane, tell her what I told you about where we are, I mean in the past. If you can figure out how to get away from here, we'll get to Ineb-Hedj, that's the town near the tomb we came through, and then we'll get back to our time."

"Djefi isn't a problem, but Siamun is," Brian said.

"You said his name before. Who is Siamun?"

"He's like Djefi's enforcer. He's a heartless bastard. He left me and an old man out in the desert to die. The old man had a broken leg," Brian said.

"I heard a little about what happened. Neswy is telling people that you have the strength of a god, that you carried him through the desert without feeling the heat, that you brought down a charging antelope with the wave of your hand."

"I felt the heat. Believe me. Is Neswy OK?" Brian asked.

"I guess. He's certainly able to talk."

Brian nodded. "Good."

Tim shook his hand as the match burned close to his fingers. The small flame went out leaving them again in total darkness.

"Look, I really have to go, Brian. Somebody will talk to you and set up a time for us to meet again, maybe in two days after this ceremony is over. Meanwhile, try to talk to Diane, OK?"

Brian nodded. "Yeah, I'll try to find her, maybe Pahket will help me. I don't know. I don't know."

Tim reached over and gripped Brian's shoulder.

"We'll get out of this. Djefi may be a bad guy, but I've made some friends. We'll be OK."

"Tim, right?"

"Yeah."

"Thanks, Tim. I just need a little rest and I'll be ready. You're right, we'll be OK."

Tim stayed in Hetephernebti's camp the next day, passing the time restlessly, waiting for Meryt to return, and hoping for news about Diane or Brian.

In the middle of the afternoon he saw some people run past the camp toward the village. There was a sense of excitement in the air. Tim wanted to follow, to find out what was happening, but now that he had made contact with Brian he felt a responsibility toward him and Diane. He didn't want to make things difficult for them by being caught by this Siamun.

When Meryt returned she was bubbling with excitement.

"Perhaps you are not a netjer," she teased, "but Brian must be."

"What happened?"

"You know that he saved the old man, well, now he has saved a child."

The story of Brian's heroic rescue of Neswy had continued to spread through the village, gaining more details with each retelling. Brian now had the power to chase away enemies by merely staring at them, the ability to fly across impassable dunes and the courage to stare down desert lions.

"They say that he arrived with Neswy on his back and waited patiently for the villagers to help him. Then, although he could hardly stand, he began to run so fast, faster than anyone had ever seen anyone run. They say Sobek was calling him to the temple. But now, after today, they think he is a god, greater than Sobek," Meryt said.

"What happened?"

"He was standing by the lake, under a tree. It's a place they say he often stands, just looking over the water. Some children were playing near the water. Suddenly a crocodile, some say it was Sobek himself, others say that no, it was just a crocodile, but even so.

"The crocodile stood up on its legs. When they do that, Tim, they can run very fast. It started to run at one little girl, her name is Kiya. Brian saw this, but even as fast as he can run, he could not get to Kiya before the crocodile.

"Then he raised his arm over his head, swung it forward and at the crocodile, so fast, his arm was a blur. This is what people say, Netjer Tim.

"Suddenly the crocodile stopped. It plopped on its belly. Oomph! And it didn't move. Kiya's mother ran up and picked up the little girl. Brian went back to looking over the lake.

"How could he do this, Netjer Tim, if he is not a god? He just points at things and they stop? How? Can you do this, also?"

Tim shook his head. He had suspected when he first saw Brian from the way that he carried himself that he was an athlete. He could be a baseball pitcher. If he could throw a rock a hundred miles an hour, it could stun a crocodile. *That would explain it, but still,* Tim thought, *that was an incredible throw.* He found himself feeling proud of Brian.

If the people think he's a god, it might give him some protection from Siamun.

"**W**hen evil Seth defeated Osiris, he cut the god into pieces and scattered them across the Two Lands. Isis, the beautiful wife of Osiris, was beyond despair but she was also devoted beyond understanding. She refused to believe that her immortal love was lost. She traveled for many years, gathering together the pieces of her beloved.

"She found all the parts of Osiris that his evil uncle had spread across the world. Well, not all the parts. She could not find his tongue.

"She searched, Netjer Tim, she searched everywhere. How can you not know this story?

"Seeing the great devotion of the beautiful Isis and seeing that she was beginning to fear that she would never find all of her beloved, a hippopotamus told her what had happened.

"Sobek, who has a great appetite and will eat everything that comes before him, had swallowed the tongue of Osiris by accident. He would never have done it on purpose, what god would? But he had, and now he feared what Isis would do. And well he should.

"Do you know what happened, Netjer Tim? I think you do. I think you just want to hear the story from my beautiful lips? Are my lips not beautiful? Yes?

"Isis stalked Sobek. She was fearless and she was powerful.

"She caught him and she pried open his massive, toothy jaws and she forced him to disgorge the tongue of her beloved. Now Isis had recovered all of her husband. But what of Sobek, that great, sullen god? He had known of the pain Isis felt. He had known she was searching for the tongue that he had swallowed. And he had kept it secret.

"And so Isis had her revenge. She cut the tongue from Sobek."

Tim and Meryt were alone, sitting in the shade of the orchard, away from Hetephernebti's encampment and away from the villagers at To-She. It was the day after Brian's miraculous rescue of the child and they had gone there to be alone to talk about how he would meet again with Brian and to find out what Meryt had learned about Diane.

She had taken his hand as she led him along a worn path and then off onto a winding trail that ended at the edge of the orchard. Tim had carried a small sack that held some bread and a jar of beer. They were sitting on the soft grass, the jar of beer beside them, the sack curled open to show some of the bread cakes.

"So Djefi will cut out the tongue of a crocodile tomorrow?" he asked.

"No, Netjer Tim," she shook her head and rested a small hand on his leg. "That is what happened before the ceremony. I mean, no one cuts out a crocodile's tongue. They may have done that long ago, but now we don't do that. We celebrate what happened after the cutting out of Sobek's tongue."

They were both aware of her hand on his leg. She moved her fingers slowly, touching the smoothness of the skin beneath her hand. He reached down and casually took her hand in his, removing it from his thigh.

"So what does happen?" he asked through a suddenly thick throat.

"Well, Sobek became very upset. He had lost his tongue after all. And he likes to eat more than anything. He grew quiet and sulky, not like Sobek at all. He didn't bellow and thrash in the water, he didn't mount the young maiden crocodiles and ride them, he didn't chase the young males away from his lake. He just floated in the dirty water near the edge of the lake and brooded.

"Then a young crocodile was chosen to help Sobek. He was sent to find the Master of Flavors. They thought that if something so tasty and appetizing could be brought to Sobek, perhaps his tongue would regrow and he would once again be the great and powerful god Sobek.

"Oh," she jerked her hand away from his and covered her mouth, "I forgot part. They couldn't sew Sobek's old tongue back on because Isis had ground it into little pieces. She is a very beautiful goddess and very devoted to Osiris, but very vengeful."

Meryt stretched and then smoothly twisted to lie on her back, resting her head on Tim's lap. She looked up at him and smiled.

"So the Master of Flavors rode on the back of the young crocodile and came to the place where Sobek was. He brought with him a bag filled with the freshest herbs and the most unusual and tasty spices.

"He used coriander and mint and sesame and parsley to flavor a roasted leg of lamb. The aroma from the meat was so strong and so delicious that Sobek's eyes began to water, perhaps in regret, perhaps in longing. But the magic of the food was so great that his tongue began to grow back. Who could resist such a treat?

"Then the Master of Flavors prepared a sea bass and then a pigeon. Each of them were flavored exactly how they should be flavored. You will see tomorrow. And with each bite, with each inhalation of the fragrance of the food, Sobek's tongue grew and grew."

She nestled her head against his lap and reached up with a slim arm to touch his face.

"Why do you not desire me, Netjer Tim? Am I displeasing to you?"

Tim shook his head, unable to speak. He put a hand on her bare shoulder, careful to avoid brushing against her breasts. He softly squeezed her shoulder and then helped her to sit up.

"Meryt," he said softly, "you are very beautiful, very pleasing."

"Oh," she said. "You look so sad, Netjer Tim. I have upset you." She started to rise.

Quickly he reached out and held her wrist. "No, stay, Meryt. You haven't upset me. You have been only good to me."

She settled back in the grass beside him and looked at him expectantly

"Are you like Isis? Are you devoted to some goddess?"

He looked away and felt his eyes brim with tears. Suddenly he found himself crying, quietly and fully.

Meryt slid close to him and put her arms around him, drawing him to her to comfort him.

After a few moments, he sighed deeply and using the heels of his hands, wiped his eyes dry.

"A long time ago, there was a woman named Addy." He felt strange saying her name aloud to another woman, as if the words he was about to say would form an epilogue to the love he and Addy had created.

"We were together for only a little while, but we believed that it was just the beginning of a long life together. Our lives were stretched out before us and we knew that wherever we went, whatever we did, we would have each other. And then, she died."

"Could you not bring her back, Netjer Tim, like Osiris and Isis?"

He shook his head. Meryt was so innocent and trusting, so filled with the beliefs of her time. It was part of why he cared for her so much.

"There was an accident. I wasn't there. Other people were there, but they didn't help. They didn't even call for help, they just turned away, afraid to get involved." As he spoke, he remembered the weeks after her death as he badgered the police for information and recklessly haunted the place she had died.

The highway exit Addy normally took to get to the restaurant where her friend was stranded was closed by an overturned tractor-trailer. So she entered the city a few blocks away, driving through a part of town she normally would have avoided.

A week earlier in that neighborhood a fourteen-year-old boy who called himself Master Nation had decided to increase his profits by heavily cutting some coke he was selling. Word got around that his product didn't deliver. His dealer immediately knew what had happened. Deciding that his reputation had been damaged, he told Master Nation to give up the extra profit he had made. The boy had refused.

Addy was sitting in her car at a stop light when the dealer drove by and emptied the clip of an automatic pistol at Master Nation before speeding away. The boy managed to get off one shot in return before he fell. That bullet hit Addy in the shoulder and ripped through the subclavian artery, a medical term Tim never would forget.

She went into shock.

There were people on the street and in the houses who had seen or heard the shooting, but no one came near her car. All it would have taken, he learned later, was for one person to push against the spurting wound, one person willing to reach through the shattered window.

She had quietly bled to death, growing colder and weaker with each beat of her heart.

"She died alone, away from me," he told Meryt. "I couldn't help her and now," he drew in a deep breath, "she is gone from my life forever."

He was relieved that Meryt didn't say anything in response. She accepted his pain and his loss without trying to minimize it. After a moment, he sat up, pulling himself away from her. She looked at him, her expression a mixture of sadness and love.

Opening his arms, he drew her to him and held her, his arms around her smooth, soft back, her arms encircling and embracing him.

"They think he's a god," Kanakht told Djefi. "Who is he? Where did he come from? What is he? Why wasn't I told about him?"

Djefi squirmed in his chair. He wasn't used to being spoken to in such a direct, threatening manner. This was To-She, he was supposed to be in charge here. But Kanakht was vizier, second only to King Djoser, so Djefi tried to compose himself. He knew that his voice would be squeaky if he didn't calm himself before he spoke.

Kanakht hadn't been at Iunu, so he hadn't seen Diane. Djefi didn't know if he should keep her presence a secret; he didn't even know why he wanted to, only that he had found in the past that it was good to know things that others didn't.

"We haven't talked since he arrived," Djefi offered.

"No, Djefi, we talked just yesterday," Kanakht said.

"But Hetephernebti arrived and then he broke into the chamber."

"Yes, Djefi, I was there," Kanakht said. He was suddenly tired, tired of the energy it took to deal with Djefi without losing his temper, tired of the traveling he knew was ahead to keep his plan moving toward its fulfillment.

"I found him in the desert a few weeks ago. He didn't speak our language and seemed confused. I brought him back here and gave him shelter. Siamun took him hunting and they got separated. I thought he was lost in the desert until he arrived yesterday." Djefi was gaining strength now, bolstered by the logic of his half-truths.

"I didn't see any reason to trouble you about a lost stranger," the priest added.

Kanakht paced slowly in front of Djefi. He knew the priest was hiding something, everyone always did. He tried to decide if it mattered, if investigating this Brian was worth the effort.

Not today, he thought

"First prophet, you and I and Waja-Hur, we each have a role, a destiny. The fate of the Two Lands is something we cannot leave to chance. You understand, don't you?"

Djefi nodded his head slightly. *It would be unseemly to act too eager,* he thought.

"Yes," Kanakht continued. "As you know, King Djoser has been preoccupied with his self-elevation to godliness. However, you will be dedicating a new temple at Kom Ombo. That is close enough to Waset that Djoser must attend. I'll make sure of it. It would be too great an affront if he didn't.

"Now, First Prophet, I wonder how the mighty Sobek, Rager of the River, will treat a man who is pretending to be a god. Because, Djefi, this is the heart of the matter. Djoser has offended the gods. We know this because the gods have not sent the great flood ever since Djoser declared himself to be one of them.

"I am just a man, you are just a man. We know that. We know that we will enjoy eternal life in Khert-Neter. But now, Djefi, now we are just men, mortal men. So is Djoser, despite his pronouncements.

"So, how will Sobek welcome this impostor?" Kanakt asked.

Djefi shook his head without thinking.

"No, Djefi." Kanakht came closer, so close that Djefi could smell the onions the vizier had eaten at breakfast. "That will not be good enough, Djefi. Not good enough," he hissed. "We will not let events rule us, Djefi. We will rule them.

"The Two Lands are not held together by chance. We are not playing games, Djefi," he rounded on the priest. "Djoser will be at your dedication. You have an opportunity to let Sobek show the Two Lands what the gods think of Djoser's posing. You will not let it pass."

If you want Djoser dead, just kill him, Djefi thought. *But Djoser will have bodyguards, of course. Does Kanakht expect the crocodile to attack and devour the king on the spot? How am I supposed to make that happen?* Djefi's mind was spinning.

He wanted to talk to Yunet. They had talked a little on the trip to Iunu, but she had been preoccupied with Diane, assuring Djefi that even if the red-haired woman wasn't a goddess she was something so unusual that she had to be protected.

Now that he thought of it, Yunet had warned him about Brian. She had said Diane was afraid of him, that he was dangerous.

I shouldn't have sent Siamun to Kom Ombo, Djefi thought. He had needed someone to make sure the temple grounds would be prepared for the dedication and no one motivated people like Siamun, so Djefi had sent him south to oversee the work.

He wondered suddenly if he should tell Kanakht about the other stranger, the one who had approached Diane at Iunu. *But no,* he caught himself. *If I do that, then I have to tell him about Diane and then explain why I didn't mention her before.*

He sighed. So much to remember.

"You can sigh all you want, Djefi, but there is work to be done. After Djoser is gone and balance is restored to Kemet, then there will be time to return to the rhythms of the Two Lands. Everything will return to normal. But first, Djefi, first there is work to be done."

"Yes," Djefi answered.

"Now, this Brian. Get rid of him. Taking him into the desert didn't kill him. Find some other way. I don't like strangers in the Two Lands and I especially don't like strangers here during this time of unrest."

"I don't have anyone ... I have sent Siamun to Kom Ombo … I don't know … " Djefi stammered.

Kanakht turned to walk away.

"Take him to Khmunu, to Waja-Hur. There are plenty of men there who are not afraid to kill a stranger, or a god. Waja-Hur's embalmers will be happy to have this Brian as a new specimen," he said over his shoulder. Then he stopped. "Yes, take him to Khmunu. You and I and Waja-Hur should all talk together. You'll have time to think about our conversation, to divine what Sobek will do at Kom Ombo. Yes, Djefi. Come to Khmunu."

Brian emerged from the night shadows.

Tim and Meryt were awake waiting for him. The rest of To-She slept and snored, bellies filled with food from the day's feast and the many jars of beer that accompanied it.

"She's asleep, drunk. Just like she must have been at that other party," Brian said as he squatted beside them in Hetephernebti's encampment.

"Did you talk to her?" Tim asked.

Brian nodded.

"Just for a little, before Yunet took her away. She said she's not going anywhere with me. I didn't tell her about you. I don't trust her. I'm positive she tells everything to Yunet, and Pahket said that Yunet and Djefi are close. So," he shrugged.

Tim and Brian looked at each other, each hoping that the other would have an idea.

"Did he say anything about going to Khmunu?" Meryt asked.

Tim shook his head.

"What did she say?" Brian asked.

"She asked if you said anything about a place called Khmunu."

"Hetephernebti said Djefi was going to Khmunu and then on to Kom Ombo," Meryt continued. "She said he was taking several boats. He usually takes only one. I think he is planning to take Diane and Brian."

"Did anyone say anything about you going someplace with Djefi?" Tim asked Brian.

Brian shook his head.

"You understand her," Brian said, nodding at Meryt.

"It's been a few weeks, so, yeah, I'm understanding more and more. But it's hard," Tim said.

Brian shook his head. "That old man, I carried him on my back for three days and he talked the whole time, well, except for when he passed out or fell asleep. I have no idea what he was talking about. Pahket taught me some, but she talks real slow for me."

"You know, Brian, people think you're a god or something. First you saved Neswy and then that little girl from the crocodile."

Brian shrugged. "I was lucky. I mean, it wasn't a real long throw and the thing wasn't moving that fast. I just had this rock in my hand, and, well ... " He looked away. "Nolan Ryan would have killed it. I just stunned it."

Tim reached out and patted Brian's shoulder. "You're a hero to these people. Really. Look, I don't know what to do about Diane. Do you think she really wants to stay here? I mean, you and I could head back to that tomb ourselves, if you think that's what she wants."

Brian shook his head. "No. She's pissed off at me, but she can't want to stay here. She'd miss her friends, her credit cards, her family. I don't think she realizes what's going on, or else she's given up hope because she doesn't think I can help her. I don't know."

"We're planning to leave here tomorrow," Tim said. "Meryt said Hetephernebti is going to a town called Waset, to meet King Djoser. Then everyone is going to Kom Ombo. Djefi is building a temple there. So he'll be there for sure. He's been taking Yunet and Diane with him everywhere he goes, so they'll be there. Meryt said that he's taking several boats, so you'll probably be going too."

They were both quiet again, thinking of what it meant.

"Either you and I leave now, without Diane," Tim said, "and you don't want to do that, and neither do I, or else we follow Diane and try to persuade her to come with us. She's bound to come to her senses soon."

Brian rolled his neck, cracking the vertebrae. He hunched his shoulders, stretching and twisting.

"You OK?" Tim asked.

"Yeah," Brian sighed. "I just hate this. I got us into this, all of us because you followed me and Diane. Now I can't get us out. I can't kidnap Diane and carry her off. So, yeah, I'll stay close to her. Maybe

Pahket can teach me more of their language so I can talk to Yunet or something. But I'll stay close to Diane."

"And keep an eye out for us," Tim said. "We'll be leaving before you, so when I get to these towns I'll find a place where we can get together. If worse comes to worse, Brian, I'll meet King Djoser. Meryt thinks he'll help us, then it won't matter what Djefi or Yunet want. So, a couple weeks, everything will be worked out."

Pahket was proud of Brian.

Wherever they walked in To-She, people stopped and stared at them. Many of the women in the village would stop what they were doing to approach Brian to thank him for saving little Kiya. They knew the price of bringing an infant into the world and how hard it was to see a child through its early years.

Two days after Brian had saved the little girl, her father had brought Brian a kilt, its hem decorated with small green crocodiles.

"For you, Netjer Brian," he said, offering the neatly folded kilt with both hands. His wife stood quietly behind him, holding Kiya's hand.

Brian took the kilt and, unfolding it, held it to his waist.

The family stood nervously, waiting for his reaction.

"It's perfect," he said, in English. They recognized his tone, but not the words. Without thinking, Brian loosened the strip that held the plain kilt he was wearing, and let it fall to the ground. Then he wrapped the new kilt around his waist.

"Good," he said in Egyptian, looking down at the kilt as he tied its strap around his waist. "Very good. Thank you."

He reached out a hand to the father. The man looked at him as Bakr had weeks ago at Saqqara. Brian took the man's hand and taught him how to shake hands. "What's your name?" he asked in Egyptian.

"Karem," the man answered.

Brian smiled widely. "Finally, a name I can recognize. KA-REEM," he said in English, pronouncing the name loudly and distinctly as if he were a radio announcer at a basketball game. He laughed and said the name again.

The family laughed hesitantly, unsure why this god was laughing.

Brian clapped the father gently on the back and thanked him again. Then he knelt by Kiya.

"You're a pretty little thing," he said in English. "But you got to learn to watch out for stuff. Here's what I do. You have to pay attention to things, right? But you can't focus on one thing too much. It's like this."

He brought his hands up to the side of his face and curled the fingers to form a tunnel to look through. Kiya copied his motion. He nodded his head to show she was doing the right thing. While she looked through the small window of her hands, Brian slowly reached around out of her field of vision. Clapping his outstretched fingers against his thumb to imitate a crocodile's mouth, he tickled her side.

She dropped her hands and laughed.

"See, you can't get tunnel vision," Brian said.

He put his hands up and stared at her, nodding permission. She reached over and he pretended to be surprised.

When she put her hands up to take her turn he shook his head and gently pushed her hands down. "No, don't limit your view. You got to see everything."

Then in Egyptian he said, "Be watchful." He looked over his shoulder at Pahket, to check if he had said the words correctly.

She nodded her approval, her eyes brimming with happy tears.

Later that day, as they walked alone in the green fields beyond the orchard, Pahket told him that they would be going with Djefi to visit a priest at a town called Khmunu.

"Diane is going?" he asked.

Pahket nodded.

"Same boat?" he asked.

"I don't know Netjer Brian, but at night we will leave the boat, so you can be with her then."

There was something in her voice that caught his attention. He knew that even when he understood the individual words she said that he sometimes missed all of her meaning. He looked at her now and thought he caught a hint of sadness in her eyes.

Meryt lay curled on the deck of Hetephernebti's boat, gripping her stomach, her face tight with pain.

She had stayed away from Tim the previous day, telling him that she did not feel well. She hadn't seemed concerned and when he saw her wearing a kilt he had assumed that she was menstruating.

He knew that the way women were treated during their monthly cycle varied among ancient societies. He had no idea how the ancient Egyptians dealt with it. So he spent the day with his note pad, sketching the river scenery and constructing future conversations with Diane, trying to find the right tone of persuasion or sternness. He realized that he didn't know her well enough to guess at her responses, but he wanted to be prepared.

Now when he saw Meryt in pain, he ran to her and knelt by her side.

With her eyes shut tight she didn't realize that he was there.

He laid his hand against her forehead. It was burning hot.

She opened her eyes at his touch.

"Netjer Tim, you must stay away."

He smiled at her. "Do you think I will get what you have?" he asked gently, brushing her forehead softly.

She nodded.

A shadow appeared over them.

"She has the wasting disease," Hetephernebti said. "And yes, Netjer Tim, you will catch it. Come with me." She turned and walked toward the canopy that covered the deck at the stern of the boat.

"I'll be right back, Meryt," Tim said, touching her frail arm.

"We will arrive at Khmunu tonight," Hetephernebti said. "We will put her ashore there. Waja-Hur will watch over her ending days."

Tim was stunned, hoping that he misunderstood her.

"I am very sorry, Netjer Tim. Meryt is so young and it seems so unfair. You have grown close, haven't you?"

"No, wait," he said. "What do you mean, her ending days?"

"She has the wasting illness," she said, her voice resigned and sad.

"I don't understand."

"She cannot eat or drink, it gives her pain," Hetephernebti said with a sigh. "When she empties herself there is blood. We cannot help her. The disease passes quickly from one person to another. I have seen entire families brought down with it. It is so very sad. The children and the elderly always die. Meryt is not a child anymore, but she has little strength."

"We can't just let her die," Tim protested.

Hetephernebti smiled sadly. "We cannot help her, Netjer Tim. There is nothing to do. At Khmunu I will put her in Waja-Hur's care. She will be made comfortable and when her ka passes to Khert-Neter, he will prepare her body for the journey also."

Tim heard her, but his mind was elsewhere. He imagined Addy dying alone in her car while strangers stood by watching. If he turned his head just a few degrees he would see Meryt lying alone in her pain, drifting toward death, but alive. Still alive and in need.

Even if he couldn't save her, he could stay with her, hold her and comfort her. He realized with a hot rush that his feelings for her had grown much stronger than he had admitted to himself.

He looked up and saw that Hetephernebti was watching him, her eyes searching his face, trying to understand what he was thinking and feeling. Somehow he didn't feel it was an intrusion, but rather that she was trying to find out what he really wanted and how she could help him.

"I cannot leave her, Hetephernebti."

"You will catch the illness. You are strong. It is possible you will recover. And it is possible that you will not."

He nodded slowly, his thoughts within. He didn't believe in fate. He didn't believe that the tractor-trailer had overturned so that Addy would take a different exit and find herself in a dangerous neighborhood. He didn't believe that she had died so he would find himself here alone and he didn't believe that the one person he had grown to care about had become deathly ill so that he would die here, five thousand years before his time.

He believed that the chaotic path he had followed simply led to this situation and he would deal with it, and then continue to follow that path wherever in the unknown future it would lead. He believed in himself and that he would never leave someone in need.

He looked at Hetephernebti's kind face, saw the warmth and concern there, but shook his head slightly. "I cannot leave her."

KING DJOSER IN THE GARDEN OF MA'AT

"**S**o, dear sister, I have heard exciting news from your distant province. I hear that gods are walking the Two Lands in Iunu."

King Djoser and Hetephernebti were walking hand in hand through a small garden near the Temple of Ma'at in Khmunu. Although they were alone, his personal guards patrolled the perimeter of the grounds.

"Yes, brother. It seems living gods are walking throughout Kemet," she answered softly.

Although Djoser's face showed no anger, Hetephernebti felt his grip tighten on her hand. She knew the royal blood they shared did not protect her from her brother. His power over the people of Kemet was absolute; they lived, married and died by his leave. If she had ever shown the slightest desire for the throne, he would kill her without a glimmer of remorse.

But she had never married, so there was no ambitious spouse to look upon Djoser as an obstacle to power. Her religious devotion to Re was known throughout the Two Lands. She suspected that she was the one person in Kemet who would speak honestly to her brother. She knew he valued that truthfulness, even if it meant that she sometimes reminded him of her disapproval of his self-proclaimed divinity.

"Tell me about them."

"Well, first of all, I'm not sure that they," she emphasized the word, a small atonement to her brother, "are gods. Djefi has been hiding two of them, or trying to. But Djefi is so inept ... "

"But dangerous," Djoser interrupted. "There are stories. Djefi's tiny voice and unbecoming size make him seem a fool. I fear that beneath all that hulk and pomposity there is very little. He is just an empty shell, but all the more dangerous because he is constantly striving to prove that he is more than he knows he is."

Hetephernebti nodded in agreement. Her brother had an uncanny ability to see into a person's very ka and to understand what they would do before they did. She wondered what he saw in her and realized that whatever it was, it allowed her to stay alive and to be his confidant.

"He sent the one called Brian into the desert with that soulless animal Siamun. Something happened out there and one of the hunters was injured. Siamun left the crippled hunter and Brian without food or water to die in the desert, three days out of To-She. Brian staggered into To-She just before the start of the festival, carrying the crippled man, alive, on his back. Then the next day he saved a child from a crocodile. The people at To-She are ready to worship him instead of Sobek."

"Then Brian had better watch his back," Djoser said.

"There is a woman. Her name is Diane. Djefi actually brought her to Iunu, but he kept her secluded. I don't know anymore about her except that she is constantly watched over by a woman Djefi trusts," Hetephernebti continued.

"And your personal god?"

Hetephernebti stopped walking and turned to face her brother-king. "My personal god is Re, dear brother. I love and respect all the gods. All of them," she said, looking into his eyes. "But I am, first, last and always, a servant of Re."

Djoser leaned forward and kissed her cheek.

"Re is fortunate to have such a servant. Tell me about Tim."

She was not surprised that he knew Tim's name.

"He says he is not a god," she said.

"Do you believe him?"

Hetephernebti considered this longer than he expected. It was a question she had been unable to answer for herself. His unexpected devotion to Meryt – he was secluded with her even now, exposing himself to the wasting disease without any sign of fear or regret – made her think it was possible he was divine. He was rumored to have saved Paneb's daughter from a scorpion sting and Meryt had reported how he had disappeared from Djefi's camp in Iunu, knifing without sound into the canal's water and swimming beneath it like Sobek.

"He has powers that are unusual. Sometimes when I watch him, I think he is looking at things beyond what I can see. Yet he seems to be flesh and blood. I think he would shed his body as any of us would. I have seen pain in his eyes and I have seen love, the kind of love I see in the face of Re when I chant his thousand names."

As ever, Djoser cut to the heart of the matter. "Should I fear these 'gods,' dear sister?"

It was another question she had considered during the trip upriver. It certainly was strange that the three had appeared now, just before the flooding of the river Iteru, and just as whispers of a plot against Djoser were appearing. Gods or not, were these three strangers a threat to Djoser and to the Two Lands?

"I believe Tim comes in peace. I think Brian is a force that Djefi should fear. I do not understand Diane. Not yet. I think, dear brother, that there are others, closer at hand, that deserve your attention more."

Now he stopped.

He was aware of the travels of everyone up and down the great river. His spies had already reported much of what Hetephernebti told him about Brian and Tim and Diane. He knew what Hetephernebti was about to tell him, but he wanted confirmation of his suspicions. The discontent in the Two Lands was something he allowed to ferment, watching to see who would be drawn to it and who would defend him. It was easier to deal with one's enemies when one knew who they were.

He was relieved that Hetephernebti wanted to talk about it. Her willingness was proof again that his trust in her was justified, that she was not part of the plot.

"Ah, you speak of Kanakht," he said.

She nodded, relieved that he had raised the vizier's name first. "Yes, and others. He spent time alone with Djefi at To-She and he plans to meet with Waja-Hur in a few days."

"Tell me more, dear sister."

There will be a time, Kanakht thought, not too long from now, when I won't have to make excuses to do whatever I want.

He was waiting for Makare in the small room that served as headquarters for the garrison at Khmunu. As was his custom, Kanakht had arrived early for his meeting. He never allowed a meeting to start without him or, more importantly, give the people at a meeting the opportunity to talk about him before he arrived.

He had told Djoser that he needed to meet privately with Makare to probe the depth of the guards' loyalty here in Khmunu. He had explained to Djoser that he needed to meet the young guard without Sekhmire, commander of the royal guard, so that Makare would speak more freely.

Kanakht frowned to himself. He planned to use Makare as the human knife who would cut down the upstart Djoser. Sekhmire would execute Makare if he ever suspected the young soldier was thinking about harming the king.

Yes, we need to meet privately, Kanakht thought grimly.

It was the famine that had led Kanakht to question Djoser's fitness to rule the Two Lands. The river Iteru had always flooded. Every year. Without fail. But after Djoser declared himself the living incarnation of Horus, the river receded, withdrawing its blessing.

Priests throughout Kemet looked at each other knowingly, but no one spoke the words. Still they formed in Kanakht's mind.

Djoser has angered the gods. He has led the country away from ma'at.

Kanakht knew that Djoser would not, could not retract his claim to divinity. Faced with a choice between his personal loyalty to the royal house and his love of the Two Lands, Kanakht made an uneasy decision: Djoser had to die.

However, open rebellion was impossible. And so Kanakht had recruited quietly, forming alliances in the dark, away from Waset, hidden from Djoser's watchful spies.

He told Djoser that he was investigating the rumors of unrest, gauging the allegiance of the guards, sounding out the trustworthiness of the priesthood beyond the immediate area of Waset, where Djoser had taken up residence.

The investigation gave Kanakht excuse to travel as he did, to meet with those he needed to see. Those meetings would be seen as his devoted attempt to thwart an uprising, not to lead it. At least he hoped so. There were times when he talked with Djoser that he thought he saw a glint of suspicion in the king's eyes. But then what king was ever not so?

I'll certainly be suspicious, he thought.

He wondered if the effort to gain the throne and the energy it would take to keep the double crown on his head would be worth it. At times the eternal rest and comfort of Khert-Neter seemed more and more attractive.

There were so many threads to hold in his hand.

As he waited on Makare, he wondered if the soldier's older brother, Nesi, was having any success upriver at the first cataract. King Djoser's son, Teti, was there trying to find a practical way to ensure a good flood: clearing boulders or digging canals. Nesi was part of Teti's bodyguard, but his allegiance was to Kanakht. It was bought with gold and maintained by the beautiful young servant girl whom Kanakht had given him. Nesi was supposed to help Teti have a fatal accident, ending the line of succession so that there would be no blood relative to contest Kanakht's claim.

Still in his teens, Prince Teti was given to the bold games of the young. The river at the cataract was treacherous. It had been Kanakht's idea, carefully planted so that Nesi thought it was his, to help Teti meet his death in the river. With the churning water, the boulders and Teti's reputation for carelessness, there was a reasonable chance that Teti's death would be accepted as an accident.

Now he needed to bring Makare more fully into the plot to assassinate the king.

While Kanakht was meeting with Makare, word of Prince Teti's accident reached King Djoser.

He and Hetephernebti were still walking in the Garden of Ma'at, the conversation moving from matters of state to family news. A shout from his guard alerted him. He turned and saw a messenger running toward him, one of the royal guards at his side.

Djoser accepted the news of Teti's accident calmly, until the messenger had left.

Hetephernebti placed a hand on his arm. "I will go with you, brother."

His face was composed, but she saw a hard glint in his eyes. "Kanakht is behind this. At night sometimes I wonder about my father's death, if it was Kanakht and not General Babaef who had ordered the attack. I wonder if Kanakht meant to take the throne then, but Nebka proved stronger than Kanakht expected. I kept him close so that I could better keep watch on him.

"Now I wonder if I have been too kind. If Teti …" he let the thought hang unfinished.

"The messenger said he was injured, not dead," she said.

Djoser turned to her, his voice icy. "He is injured now. But if this was not an accident, then whoever had their hand in it has a weakened target."

They had reached the edge of the garden where they were joined by his guards. He motioned for one of them to approach.

"Send this message to Abu, to Waset, to wherever Teti is in his travels. Tell his guards that if any more harm comes to him, they will all die, their families will die, their homes will be burned, their bodies will be fed to jackals."

The guard turned to run off to send the message.

"Wait," Djoser said. "Send the message yourself, do not trust it with anyone. And then follow the birds by boat as quickly as you can." He gave a curt nod and the guard turned and ran toward the docks.

When Djoser traveled, he took with him pens of homing pigeons trained to return to Waset, carrying messages to officials there. The birds were not used often; the pace of life in Kemet seldom required urgent communication, unless there was a war or a threat of invasion. The country's desert border and powerful reputation made invasion unlikely.

Now his guard would release several birds to Waset, sending only one was unreliable because hawks often took the pigeons. From Waset, more birds would be released, carrying Djoser's message south to Abu where Teti had been hurt and also to Kom Ombo and Edfu, cities that lay along the river between Abu and Waset.

"Yes, come with me, Nebti," Djoser said using his sister's childhood nickname. "We have more to talk about. I need your eyes and ears, and honest heart to watch over Kemet."

She nodded. "I will be what you need, brother," she said. "I must see to Tim and then I will meet you at your barge."

He had already turned to walk away, his guards closing in around him.

"Hurry, Nebti. We leave for Waset immediately."

Tim held Meryt's head in his lap. A half-empty bowl of barley broth was on the floor beside him. His right hand held a damp cloth he had used to wash her face, trying to comfort her and lower her temperature.

He felt the presence in the door before the shadow fell across him.

"I must leave, Tim. There has been an accident with King Djoser's son. I will leave a boat and an attendant here to bring you to Waset when Meryt … no longer needs your attention," Hetephernebti said.

Tim nodded his understanding. "Can you ask Waja-Hur to stay away? He frightens Meryt."

He looked drawn and tired, sitting on the floor in the shadows, his kilt dirty, his head covered in rough stubble. Meryt was pale and drawn, but still alive, much to Hetephernebti's surprise. In fact, although the hut was in darkness, Hetephernebti thought that Meryt looked less pale than she had before and it seemed to her that the lines that had formed around Meryt's eyes had loosened their grip.

Hetephernebti had often seen that in the dying. As their body gave up its struggle, they appeared to reach a peace with themselves.

"I will speak with him, but he is Thoth and I cannot command him."

"Thank you. We should be able to follow you in two or three days," Tim said, turning his attention back to Meryt.

Hetephernebti raised her eyebrows, but didn't question him.

"What happened to King Djoser's son?" Tim asked.

"Teti was with his companions at the first cataract, trying to find a way to help the river flood. They were exploring rocks in the river and he fell. Or was pushed. One of his guards is being held until King Djoser can speak with him. Teti is being taken to Waset so the king's physician can attend him."

Tim looked past Hetephernebti, past the doorway, his eyes unfocused as he tried to recall everything he could about Djoser.

"I don't remember anything about Teti, but I'm sure that Djoser will be fine. And this famine will end soon."

Hetephernebti felt a chill run through her as she listened to his casual prophecy. After a moment she nodded toward Meryt, her eyebrows raised in silent question.

Tim shrugged lightly. "I don't know, but I will try everything I can."

He had decided that Meryt was suffering from dysentery, a disease that was common in refugee camps during his time. Part of the diagnosis was based on what he recalled from the research he and Addy had done before the trip. Part was pure hope, based on what he thought he could treat.

The illness was caused by bacteria. It was spread through poor hygiene. The severe dehydration it caused made it dangerous, often fatal among the young and the elderly.

He had chlorine tablets to purify water for her so she wouldn't be exposed to more bacteria. He had a small bottle of antibiotics that would overwhelm the infection-causing bacteria. He had some salt tablets that would help her retain water and some aspirin for her fever.

He hoped that he had guessed right.

Meryt had been unconscious most of the first day they had been ashore and Tim couldn't figure out how to get any of the antibiotics into her system.

When she woke toward evening he made her swallow a penicillin tablet and drink some water in which he had cooked a little barley. The next morning her fever seemed worse. He crushed another penicillin tablet and dissolved it in a small cup of boiled water. Sip by sip he got her to drink the water, but then she threw up, crying her apologies as she retched.

Later that day she seemed almost normal, but very tired and without appetite. At his insistence she drank some young wine that had not fermented and took another penicillin tablet. Tim spent the night lying beside her, checking her shallow breathing, fearful that it would stop and that he wouldn't have any idea what to do.

Knowing he would be of no help to her if he got sick, he took care to wash his hands thoroughly and to keep his food at the other side of the small hut.

Today she had seemed more alert at times, but extremely tired. Although the diarrhea had passed, he suspected that was because she had been unable to eat. She had taken two more doses of the penicillin and a few aspirin, but she had eaten very little and drank virtually nothing.

Was she improving? Would she live? Tim didn't know.

He brushed Meryt's head gently and looked up at Hetephernebti.

"I just don't know," he repeated, his voice soft and worried.

Hetephernebti paused a moment, then turned and was gone.

"What don't you know?" Meryt whispered weakly, her eyes still shut. "I thought you knew everything."

Tim put down the damp cloth and caressed her cheek with his hand.

"I know you should eat more soup," he said.

She tried to smile. "Can I have a drink?"

Tim smiled back at her.

It was the first time she had asked for anything.

THE EMBALMERS OF THOTH

The wounds on Dagi's back were pale, red grooves. The whip lines had scabbed over and healed, leaving pink flesh behind. In a few months the marks from the lashing Djefi had given him would be completely healed, but the humiliation and resentment would never go away.

No longer a pilot, he knelt on the boat's wooden deck and pulled an oar, one of eight rowers who fought against the current of the slow moving river as Djefi's three boats angled toward the village of Khmunu.

The waterfront there was empty except for a few small fishing boats.

King Djoser and his small armada had departed a week earlier, sails unfurled and rowers pulling hard for Waset so the king could be with his injured son. Five days later the last of Hetephernebti's boats had followed upriver, carrying Tim and Meryt, who was still weak but past the worst of her illness.

Kanakht also had left Khmunu, summoned by King Djoser to follow him to Waset.

Kanakht's meeting with Makare had been more successful than he could have hoped. The young soldier was filled with dreams of commanding an army and was willing to do whatever Kanakht asked him to do. However, the news from Abu was not good: the assassination attempt on Djoser's son Teti had been unsuccessful.

Kanakht hoped that the attack looked like an accident. He had little faith that Nesi could be trusted to stay silent for long if Djoser's torturers interrogated him. If Nesi had been arrested, then Kanakht would need to oversee the interrogation himself. His presence would remind Nesi that Kanakht's name could not be mentioned. If it looked as if Nesi were weakening, then Kanakht would have the torturers push hard enough to kill the young guard before any secrets were divulged.

This can be managed, Kanakht had told himself as his boat's small sail filled with wind and he began the journey to Waset.

Arriving after everyone in the royal party had left, Djefi was surprised to see the waterfront so deserted. He had expected Kanakht's boat to be there. *After all,* he thought, *the vizier had all but ordered me to come to Khmunu.*

As soon as his boat slid near the bank, Djefi sent a runner into Khmunu to find a sedan chair so he could be carried to Waja-Hur's room. The old priest would know where Kanakht had gone.

"**W**hat do you mean he's come and gone? He told me to come here. We're supposed to meet, to talk about this thing," Djefi knew his voice had risen to a squeaky pitch and he felt his face flushing. He looked around Waja-Hur's dark room.

Why doesn't Waja-Hur have any furniture in this filthy little chamber?

Waja-Hur blinked his eyes and stared again at the angry fat man standing just inside his doorway. The man wore good robes and he had been brought here on a sedan. He had greeted Waja-Hur by name, but the aged priest had no idea who this fat man was.

His old friend Kanakht had been here. Was it yesterday? No, last week. It didn't matter. Time had shifted in the Two Lands. The colors had faded from today, but the past was bright.

When he had walked the temple this morning all the wbt-priests were strangers to him, yet they had greeted him by name. The altar that he always had used had been moved to a new room that had never been there before, or had it? It had seemed eerily familiar.

A young boy had approached him to drape the leopard skin robe over his shoulders and Waja-Hur had said, "Where is ... " and then had stopped, unable to remember the name of the boy who performed this service.

Only Thoth, the Reckoner of Times and Seasons, the One who Measured out the Heavens and Planned the Earth, the Master of Balance, remained the same.

Even Kanakht had seemed strange when they had met, talking of the king, but calling him by the wrong name. When Waja-Hur had corrected him, saying, "I think you mean King Kha-Sekhemwy, old friend," Kanakht had looked at Waja-Hur with concern and confusion.

Balance, Waja-Hur thought, the balance has shifted and people, places, even the land itself has moved. Only the gods remain steadfast.

He closed his eyes for a moment remembering his youth. All the faces and names, the colors and smells were there. He could almost feel the sunshine on his shoulders, so broad and strong, so different from the thin, tired back he carried now.

"Waja-Hur, where did Kanakht go? Is he coming back here?"

He opened his eyes; the fat priest was still here. He did look familiar, but Waja-Hur could not remember why.

"Yes," he said finally. "He was here, but he left."

Djefi shifted his weight. "You said that. Is Kanakht coming back?"

Waja-Hur shrugged, then he remembered something, a snatch of conversation. "He said that someone named Teti has been hurt, yes. A boy."

"Prince Teti? King Djoser's son?"

Waja-Hur was confused. He remembered Djoser as a little boy, trailing along, so straight-backed and proud behind his father, King Kha-Sekhemwy. Could he be old enough to have sired a son? Then Waja-Hur had a flash of the boy grown to manhood and wearing the double crown of the Two Lands.

Is it a vision from Thoth, a glimpse into the future, or a memory that somehow has escaped me?

Djefi was so frustrated that he wanted to scream. Kanakht was gone. Djoser had been here and departed, apparently because of something that happened to Teti. *Is Kanakht plotting with others also? Does he have plans within his plans? What else is he scheming that I don't know about?*

Djefi found a soothing tone to talk to Waja-Hur. "Did Kanakht mention Brian? Did he say anything about him, ah, visiting the mortuary?"

Waja-Hur stared at Djefi in confusion. Then his glance traveled past the fat priest to a shadow that appeared in the doorway.

"First Prophet Djefi, I am Nimaasted, Thoth's servant. I am sorry I was not here to greet you."

Djefi turned, startled at the man's sudden appearance.

"Good evening, Waja-Hur," Nimaasted said. "Kanakht asked me to entertain First Prophet Djefi when he arrived. May I take him with me? You'll be able to visit with him tonight at the ceremony with Ma'at."

"Kanakht spoke with you? He left instructions?" Djefi asked.

Nimaasted took Djefi's elbow and steered him to the doorway. "Yes, he left instructions about Brian and he asked me to offer you his apologies. He was commanded to leave by Djoser himself," he said softly. "Please come with me and I will tell you everything. I have a comfortable chair and refreshments waiting. I am not quite as devout as Waja-Hur."

Turning back to the old priest, Nimaasted said, "Thank you, High Priest. I will send someone with your evening meal and to bring you to the ceremony."

"What has happened to him?" Djefi asked as he struggled into the sedan chair.

Nimaasted looked sadly toward the darkened doorway of Waja-Hur's room. "He is communing more with the gods than with us lately."

Brian looked over his shoulder at the three small boats. The dusky red western sky silhouetted their thin masts. On the far bank of the river, a cluster of palm trees edged along the water, backlit by the setting sun. Beyond them the land rose slightly before leveling off and turning dry as the narrow strip of fertile land gave way to dry sand.

He admired action: the grace of a gymnast, the power of a racehorse, the guts and desperation of a boxer, but there was something so serene and foreign in the view he saw here that he felt an unexpected swelling in his chest and he sighed deeply.

Watching him, Pahket caught the melancholy of his expression, but misunderstood it. Earlier she had seen Brian talking with Diane, using their private language, their voices quiet. It seemed to her that Brian had been pleading, the tone of his voice urgent. Diane hadn't said much in return. Her arms had been crossed and she seldom looked into Brian's face as he talked.

Now Diane had walked ahead with Yunet, following Djefi's sedan chair toward the Temple of Ma'at. All of the attendants and boatmen were following, Brian and Pahket among them.

When Djefi had returned from his visit to the temples this afternoon, he had called Brian to his boat and told him that they all were going to attend a ceremony at the Temple of Ma'at. Tomorrow, Djefi had told Brian, he would be given a boat and would be free to return to his country, to visit other temples, to go where he wanted. He was, of course, welcome to remain a guest of Sobek.

Brian had asked if Diane could go with him.

I have no power over her. She is a guest and may do as she likes, Djefi had answered.

Then Brian had talked with Diane and his happiness at Djefi's news had crashed head on against her cold anger at him.

"What will you do, Netjer Brian?" Pahket had asked him later. "Are you leaving Kemet?"

He had shrugged and given her a small smile. "I have to find someone, Pahket. He is here, or at a town called Waset. Tomorrow I will look for him. Can you come with me?"

"I will ask," she had answered, her heart swelling with happiness.

Now they were walking with the boatmen up the small incline that led away from the water toward the temple complex.

Pahket had never been away from To-She before. She found the trip, the excitement of seeing new places, even the motion of the river, which was so different from the sluggish canal at To-She, almost overwhelming. Change, she found, was disturbing.

Even the land here was different. The soil was sandier and there were fewer trees and less grass along the river. The buildings were more scorched by the sun. The path they were following into the temple complex was hard packed and hurt her bare feet.

The path soon turned into a broad avenue. A few of the torches that lined it had been lit as the evening faded. When they reached the Temple of Ma'at, Pahket was mildly disappointed because the complex looked smaller than the temple at To-She.

But as they came closer, she saw that it was more finely made. There were no visible seams in the stone columns and the painted symbols and hieroglyphs were bright and beautifully drawn.

She stopped at the doorway to admire a painting of the goddess Ma'at. She was a beautiful woman dressed in a sheer linen robe, a purple belt gathering the transparent material at the waist, its loose ends falling to her knees. Her black hair was trimmed with golden beads and a narrow gold headband secured a white ostrich feather that rose high above her head.

It was this feather, the symbol of truth and order, which a person's heart was weighed against when he died. If the heart was free of sins and as light as the feather, then the owner was maa-kheru – true of word – and was admitted to the green fields of Khert-Neter. If the heart weighed down its side of the scale, it was fed to Ammut, a demon with a crocodile's head, the front half of her body that of a lion's, the rear half that of a hippopotamus. If Ammut ate the heart, the owner experienced the death of oblivion and was no more.

Wavering torches lit the way as they walked through the temple, emerging at the far end into an amphitheater bordered by a reflecting pool.

Djefi's sedan had been brought to the front row and he was being helped onto a stone bench covered with pillows. Pahket saw Diane and Yunet sitting on a bench near him. A tall man in priestly robes was bent toward them, speaking. When the man straightened, he scanned the amphitheater, stopping when he was looking directly at Brian. He bent down again to speak to Diane and Yunet, and then he turned away to walk up the steps toward Brian and Pahket.

"I am Nimaasted, servant of Thoth," he said, stopping in front of Brian and bowing his head lightly. "You are Brian?"

Brian nodded in return.

"Djefi said you are his guest. Welcome to the Temple of Ma'at."

"Thank you," Brian answered.

Nimaasted nodded once more and then was gone.

Two rows behind Brian and Pahket, the boatmen sat together. Dagi and Karem had watched Nimaasted approach and speak to Brian.

"Who was that?" Dagi asked.

Karem shook his head.

Dagi turned to the other boatmen. "Anybody know who that was?"

"That was, ahh, I can't remember his name, but I remember his look, he's the overseer of the embalmers," one of the boatmen answered. "He came to our boat a couple of years back when one of the rowers stood up, shouted his mother's name and fell over dead. Remember that? We had just made a run up from Waset, following the current. We weren't working all that hard."

"I remember that," another said. "It was hot that day."

"Not that hot," the first man answered.

"Hot enough," the other countered.

There was a murmuring along the row as the other boatmen began to recall the death.

"Aren't the embalmers under Thoth," Dagi asked Karem, "not Ma'at?"

Karem thought for a moment. "Or Anubis," he answered.

"Anubis doesn't have a temple here," Dagi said.

"I don't know," Karem said.

"Either way," Dagi said, "it isn't Ma'at. Ma'at doesn't have embalmers."

Karem looked at his friend.

"We need to watch Brian," Dagi said. "I don't trust Djefi. He sent him into the desert with Siamun and now he's being friendly? And an embalmer is stopping to talk to him?"

"I'm not on the same boat," Karem said.

Dagi nodded. "That's strange, too. You should be. I think Djefi moved you to a different boat because Brian saved your little Kiya."

Karem nodded, then he said, "I don't understand."

"Djefi knows Brian saved Kiya, so he knows that you'll help Brian in return, see? So he separates you. But there's no reason for him to do that unless he's planning something."

Karem shook his head. "Look, I don't like Djefi either, but I think you're still angry because ..." he left the sentence unfinished.

Dagi looked at his friend. "Keep an eye on Brian. I'll do the same."

Pahket had explained the idea of ma'at to Brian, both the ideal and the goddess who represented it, so he was prepared to follow the enactment of the weighing of the heart. He wasn't prepared for Tama, the woman who was high priestess for the goddess Ma'at.

Tama had been high priestess of Ma'at for most of her thirty-one years. She had entered temple life as a child, given up by her family to live with the aged woman who was high priestess of Ma'at at the time. Chosen for her beauty and intelligence, Tama had been trained to observe the truth, to see past appearances and to accept what she saw, whether she agreed with it or not.

That vision of the world granted her a serenity that was reflected in her calm features.

The influence of the nearby Temple of Thoth and Waja-Hur's constant reminder that balance was important had played a part in her life, too. She interpreted balance as a middle path to be followed in all things: diet, exercise, speech, study, sleep, even worship of the gods.

Brian didn't see all this when she emerged from the darkness to play her part in the ritual re-enactment of the weighing of the king's heart.

He saw a supremely confident woman, whose assurance was reflected in her strong, melodic voice. He saw a radiantly beautiful woman, whose diet and exercise kept her body remarkably fit and strong, even for a culture in which hard work was a daily part of life. He saw a woman whose flashing eyes and ready smile revealed an intelligence and acceptance that drew admirers.

The ceremony passed, but he saw only Tama. At some point a bent old man was led to her, accompanied by a boy carrying a large scale. The man carried papyrus and ink to record the results of the weighing of the heart. But all Brian saw was Tama, stepping forward and extending her hand to welcome and help the old man.

A king appeared, escorted by a woman wearing the long horns of a cow. The king said, "I have done ma'at," repeating the phrase three times. Brian heard only the delicate rustle of Tama's sheer robe as she bent to take the king's heart from the golden bowl he carried.

As Brian watched the ritual, Pahket stole anxious glances at him. She saw where his eyes were directed, she saw him mouth the words that Tama spoke and she knew that this god had found his heart's desire.

From the shadows of the amphitheater, Nimaasted also watched. He saw the naked hunger in Brian's face as he watched Tama, and Nimaasted knew how he would lure Brian away from the safety of the boat.

Brian was surprised by his attraction to Tama.

He returned to the boat in silence. Pahket gave up talking to him the third time he responded to her by saying "uh-huh."

He thought about Diane and her refusal to go anywhere with him, ever again. He knew that he hadn't approached her correctly, angered by her obvious irritation toward him. He wondered if Tim was also here in Khmunu and how he would find him.

But mostly he thought of Tama.

Part of him wanted to get to know her better, to see if she could possibly be everything he imagined. Part of him knew that was impossible. He wanted to carry the memory of what he had seen and imagined with him forever, but he wanted to test that memory against reality so he wouldn't be living in a fantasy world.

He fell asleep, whispering her name to himself over and over again, like a schoolboy.

He woke to the smiling face of Nimaasted hovering over him.

"Tama," Nimaasted said gently, as if reading Brian's mind. He held the white ostrich feather in his hand. "The priestess wishes to see you."

"What? Why?" Brian woke slowly.

Nimaasted shrugged.

"You can ask her. Come, do not keep her waiting."

He stood and extended his hand to Brian.

Around them the boatmen slept, some snoring, others moaning and turning on the rough wooden deck. Pahket, having left Brian to himself when they reached the boat, was sleeping under the canopy in the stern, a spot she and Brian usually shared.

Brian quietly followed Nimaasted from the boat, both of them unaware that one of the boatmen was watching.

Dagi waited until Brian and Nimaasted were halfway up the sloping bank before he rose and crept across the deck. He slid quietly into the water so that he wouldn't present a silhouette against the night sky if someone was watching.

Once on land, he jogged cautiously up the slope. Brian and Nimaasted were just cresting the small incline. Dagi watched them enter the town. Quickly he followed.

Dagi expected that Siamun would be lurking in the shadows to ambush Brian, to send him to the death that Brian had escaped in the desert. Although he was afraid of Siamun, Dagi's hatred for Djefi ran deep enough to overcome his fear of the priest's thug.

He didn't know Brian, but he knew that Brian had saved Yunet's uncle from a slow death in the desert and that he had saved his best friend's daughter from the jaws of a crocodile.

And so he followed Brian and Nimaasted, angry and fearful at the same time. He tried to stay far enough behind them that they wouldn't hear his footsteps, but close enough that he could follow whatever turns they made and get to Brian in time to help him, if he needed help.

He thought he saw them slow their pace after a few blocks and so he tucked himself behind a tree in case they turned to look back up the street. The sound of muffled footsteps emerged from the alley just beyond the tree where Dagi was hiding.

He waited for two heartbeats, and then peeked around the tree. Three men were walking quickly and silently toward Nimaasted and Brian. Dagi started walking as fast as he could while staying quiet. As he passed the next intersection, he saw a fist-sized stone on the ground. Stooping, he picked it up.

The three men were less than a block away from Brian when they broke into a run, still trying to be quiet.

Dagi started to run and shouted out a warning at the same time.

Brian stopped and looked back toward the shout. He saw three men running at him. One of the attackers, looking over his own shoulder, saw Dagi running toward them. He turned toward the boatman.

Although his attention was drawn to the men who were running up the street, Brian stayed mindful of Nimaasted. When he saw the priest reach under his robe, Brian leaned quickly into him and pushed against his chest, hooking his foot behind Nimaasted's ankle. He saw a flash of a knife blade as the priest fell backward drawing his hand from out of his robe to catch his fall.

Brian turned to the other three men. He saw that one of them had turned and was running away from Brian toward the man who had called out a warning. He couldn't see the man's face, but from the size of his muscled shoulders, Brian guessed it was one of the boatmen.

Before he thought it through, Brian began running toward the two attackers who had continued toward him. He knew that he could outrun them and escape, but he couldn't leave the boatman behind to face the attackers after the boatman had risked his own safety to warn Brian.

He guessed that they would have knives, but he had his speed, his size and his strength.

The two men slowed as they saw Brian come toward them. Brian didn't hesitate. He picked the man on his right and charged into him as hard as he could, lowering his shoulder as if barreling into a catcher at home plate.

He felt a sharp pain in his side, but heard the man gasp as his lungs emptied from the collision. Brian felt the crunch of bone as his shoulder slammed into the man's ribs.

Running past the fallen man, Brian headed for the third attacker who was holding a knife extended as he circled the boatman. When the attacker turned his head at the sound of Brian's approaching footsteps, the boatman saw his opportunity and swung a muscled arm at the man's head.

The assailant tried to turn away from the blow, but Brian heard the rock in the boatman's hand crack against the attacker's head. The man staggered and looked up, blood streaming down his face, just as Brian ran past him, his strong right arm outstretched to clothes-line him. He caught the man's exposed neck with his forearm, knocking him off his feet.

The attacker flew backwards and hit the ground hard, gurgling as he collapsed, clutching his throat.

The boatman shouted "Get down!" and Brian dropped to his hands and knees as Dagi threw the rock past him. The third assailant was only a few steps away, his knife raised overhead as he charged at Brian. The attacker dodged the rock, swerving quickly to his right away from Brian.

The change in direction gave Brian time to come out of his crouch. He squared off to face the assailant who had regained his balance and was crouching to attack. Dagi picked up the knife from the fallen man and stepped up beside Brian. The attacker looked from the knife in Dagi's hand to the sheer size of Brian.

He turned and ran.

Brian looked up the street to where Nimaasted had fallen and saw that the priest also had disappeared into the night. The man whose ribs Brian had cracked was on his feet, limping away from them.

Dagi knelt by the other man, whose face was turning white as he gasped and held his battered throat.

"Who sent you?" Dagi asked.

The man shook his head, his eyes wide as he struggled to breathe.

"Djefi?"

The man looked confused by the name.

Brian heard a noise and looked up the street. He thought he saw movement in the doorway of one of the homes. When he looked back down he saw Dagi drawing his knife across the man's throat.

"No!" he shouted, but it was too late.

Dagi stood, leaving the knife on the ground.

"He tried to kill you," Dagi said. He pointed to Brian's side where a slow stream of blood fell from a cut near his hip.

"You can't come back to the boat," Dagi said. "I know that Djefi is behind this, even if that dung beetle wasn't hired by him."

Brian was thinking the same thing. Hearing noise from up the street now, he drew Dagi into the alley. "Go back to the boat. Protect Diane," he said.

Dagi nodded and turned to leave.

Brian reached out a huge hand and gripped the boatman's scarred shoulder. "Thank you. You saved my life," he said.

Dagi gripped Brian's strong arm and they looked in each other's eyes. Then the boatman turned and, staying in the shadows, ran toward the river.

Brian watched him until he was out of sight. Then he looked down at the pain in his side. The wound was a slice, just across his hipbone on his right side.

He took a deep breath and then exhaled slowly through his nose.

Nimaasted would come back with more guards. The attacker who had run away would return, angry and determined. Brian didn't know anyone in Khmunu, he was injured and, if Dagi was right, Djefi was trying to have him killed.

Everyone he knew was either on Djefi's boats or back at To-She.

Except Tim.

And he had no idea where Tim had gone.

He heard footsteps on the hard-packed path and saw light bouncing off the mud walls of the homes as torches were carried down the street.

Brian glanced back at the body on the ground and then turning, he ran into the darkness.

Khmunu was a small village spread along the river's east bank. There was a marketplace, a few bakeries and a densely packed residential area that thinned quickly as it spread from the market.

The Temple of Thoth, with its own workshops, bakery, brewery and storage rooms, lay away from the river at the eastern edge of town. The embalming mortuaries were across the river, for it was only in the western land that bodies could properly be purified.

The Temple of Ma'at had been built on the southern end of town closer to the river so that a canal could be dug to feed the pond beside the temple's amphitheater.

Running blindly down a dark alley, Brian turned right at the second intersection and, slowing to an easy jog, headed toward the river. When he and Nimaasted had walked into town from the boats, Brian had been thinking only of meeting Tama. Now he realized he had no idea how far they had walked before he had been ambushed.

He tried to remember the earlier walk when he and Pahket had made the trip to the Temple of Ma'at. As far as he could recall, they had left the boat, walked straight away from the river and then turned right on a broad avenue that had been lined with torches.

He slowed, listening for the sound of pursuers. Now he could hear the river up ahead in the darkness lapping gently against Djefi's three boats. He hoped Dagi had gotten back on his boat without being seen.

Turning south, Brian followed the river, leaving Khmunu behind him as he looked for the canal that would lead to the amphitheater and the Temple of Ma'at.

At the canal, he turned to follow its flow to the Temple of Ma'at, unsure of what he would do next.

Crouching in the darkness by the western wall of the temple complex, he saw torches moving in the darkness, their light scraping against the rough stone of the temple walls. He moved down the sloping canal bank. Looking for escape, he saw a narrow opening built into the temple wall to allow the canal to enter the complex.

He heard voices carrying down from the temple entrance, but couldn't make out the words. It didn't matter; he probably wouldn't understand them anyhow. The torches stopped bobbing as the men formed a circle by the temple entrance.

Peeking over the canal's edge Brian saw a small group of men, their dark brown chests gleaming in the yellow light. They waited outside the temple entrance while one of them entered.

When he emerged, with Tama by his side, Brian saw that it was Nimaasted. Brian watched them talk and then Tama gestured for the men to enter the temple.

They're searching for me, he thought.

He sat on the slanted canal bank and watched as the men entered the temple. After the last torch had disappeared, Brian continued to stare in that direction, his eyes slowly adjusting to the darkness while his mind adjusted to his situation.

Baseball had always provided Brian with a way to deal with life. He worked hard, prepared and trained. He was part of a team. He never gave up. *The game isn't over until the fat lady sings,* he thought.

Absentmindedly he pulled a blade of rough grass and twirled the narrow leaf in his fingers.

There aren't any chalk lines, no rules, no umpires, no playing field here, he realized. At the end of the game, he wouldn't shake hands with his opponents, clap their backs, and say 'good game.'

Men had attacked him. One had been killed and now they were looking for him. He knew that Tim had told him the truth about their situation: there was no American embassy to rescue him.

He had no idea what kind of police system they had here, if courts even existed. Were there jails?

If he was caught by Nimaasted would there be a trial or would they just cut his head off right there on the spot? He remembered Siamun's brutal laugh when he had turned his back and left Brian and Neswy to die in the desert.

"Damn it," he said softly to himself.

I didn't do anything, just defended myself. That's the truth. But who do I tell?

The thought tickled his memory and he recalled what Pahket had said: Ma'at stands for truth.

He couldn't throw himself on Djefi's mercy, or Nimaasted's either. He didn't see any way he could survive alone without eventually being caught. The only other person in authority was Tama, priestess of Ma'at, priestess of Truth.

The night grew lighter as the men emerged from the temple. He watched as they broke into three groups. Most of them stayed by the temple entrance, two turned and started to follow the temple wall away from him. Two more turned his way.

He looked at the temple wall, the solid stone reaching over his head. He looked down the canal back to the river. He could follow that and stay on the run. He looked back at the temple walls. He would be safe in there, it already had been searched.

The canal.

The searchers were close enough now that he could hear them talking.

He slid down the bank. The canal was chest deep. He walked down it, his feet sinking into the soft mud that lined its bottom. At the wall, he reached under the water, checking to see if there were bars or some other obstacle. Feeling nothing there, he took a deep breath of air, ducked under the dark water and pushed through the opening under the wall.

THE TRUTH FINDS BRIAN

Brian dreamed that he was playing baseball.

A jet flew far overhead, its white contrail and distant roar comfortingly familiar. He was on the pitcher's mound, cloying brown dirt beneath his feet. Stretching away from his golden island was a carpet of grass so vivid and green it hurt his eyes. The white lines connecting the bases were so fresh he could see each particle of flaky chalk.

His eyes swept the stands, filled with kids and their parents, teenagers talking and animated, middle-aged men and old-timers, nodding knowingly at each other's comments. Their bright shirts and bare, waving arms were a colorful blur as they talked, pointed or reached for a beer passed hand-by-hand across the row, waiting for the game to begin.

He leaned forward as his catcher flashed a sign at him, two gnarled fingers calling for a curve ball. The batter spit into the dirt. The stream of saliva moved in slow motion, splattering and splashing in the dirt, raising a miniature dust storm just outside the batter's box.

In his dream, Brian straightened up, felt the taut leather of the ball in his hand, its raised stitching brushing along the edge of his index finger. As he peered at the catcher's glove, he could smell the freshly cut grass and feel the sun soak through his uniform and warm his muscles. The batter stopped waving his bat, poised now, wrists cocked and ready to swing. The infielders stopped their chattering and shuffling. They leaned forward on the balls of their feet and locked their eyes on home plate. The crowd stopped moving, held its collective breath in anticipation.

The world was a frozen, golden moment poised to unleash energy and action, balanced just on the lip of expectation.

He smiled and moaned.

"When did you find him?" Tama asked the young attendant.

"Just a few minutes ago, Voice of Truth."

"Do you know who he is?"

The young girl shook her head.

"I will see to him, Nany. Please don't speak of him to others until I see you again."

The attendant nodded her head and backed out of the doorway of the small storage room where she had gone to get a jar of oil to replenish the temple lamps.

"Nany," Tama called, "don't forget your oil, dear."

The girl came back into the room embarrassed by her forgetfulness. She picked up the ceramic jar and turned to leave. Tama reached out and brushed her fingertips across the girl's shaved head.

"Thank you, Nany," she said as the girl walked out into the hallway.

Tama stretched, extending her arms as high as she could, raising herself on her toes. She breathed in deeply and then exhaled slowly through her mouth as she lowered her arms and came back down onto her heels.

It was early morning.

Nany had come to her while Tama was in the midst of the slow stretching movements she practiced each morning before she meditated. Tama knew the little girl would not have interrupted her without good reason. After the excitement of the previous night, Tama was expecting more unrest until the disturbance was resolved.

In her mind she pictured a heavy stone dropped from high into the still water of a pond. The stone was the killing last night. The violent splash of the water was the frantic, urgent search that had brought Nimaasted to the temple door demanding to search the grounds.

The ripples from the splash would continue moving, spreading beyond the immediate moment, rebounding on themselves until the killing was understood, the murderer caught and punished. Even then, the murdered man's family would continue to suffer his loss, as would his friends. The friends and family of the murderer would suffer in a different way, tainted by his guilt. Everyone affected by the killing would be changed, some would become more angry and driven by their pain would say or do harmful things to each other. The ripples would continue far longer than most people realized.

And here, at her feet, sleeping soundly with a smile on his lips was the man – or god – who called himself Brian. He was the one Nimaasted had insisted was a murderer, a dangerous, evil demon even more fearful than Ammut, eater of hearts.

True, his arms were fearfully muscled, his legs looked immense and powerful. He was huge, much larger than anyone Tama had seen before in the Two Lands. But his face seemed so happy and peaceful. She wondered what he dreamed. Was it a beautiful woman? A banquet and jars of beer? The feeling of power as he killed someone?

Those were the things that drove men, she knew: sex, possessions, and power. To many men, and to many women, there was little else.

She wondered: What drives this man-god?

She squatted beside Brian. She was wearing only a short kilt. Her necklaces and bracelets were on a stand by her bed, as was the long, black wig she wore in public. Her shaved head was lightly beaded with perspiration from her exercise. She was well aware that she hadn't bathed yet. She could smell her own musky fragrance, as well as a heavier smell that came from Brian.

"Good morning," she said, watching his eye lids. She saw movement behind them, the kind of restless wanderings that showed someone was dreaming. Slowly she reached out to nudge his arm and bring him awake.

Brian sat up, jerking his arm away from the unexpected touch.

In the split second between wakefulness and the moment when he opened his eyes, Brian saw again the man's throat, red and gurgling after Dagi had drawn the knife across it. A wave of panic swept over him, rekindling the fear he had felt the previous night when he had stood in the shoulder-deep canal and decided that his only chance to escape the searchers was to dive into the black water.

Lurching backward now, he slid across the ground floor, instinctively drawing his knees up to his chest as he opened his eyes.

"Not the dreams of the innocent," Tama said to herself.

Brian raised an arm to shield his eyes from the light that streamed in the doorway behind the person who was kneeling in front of him. He guessed from the shape that it was a woman, but he couldn't see her shadowed face.

"You are Brian?" she asked.

"Yes," he answered, his throat rasping.

"Did you kill that poor man last night?"

Brian shook his head. "No," he answered. "The man attacked me. Three men attacked me. And the priest Nimaasted. He was with them."

Tama studied his face. She had never talked with him before and she knew nothing about him. Was he a practiced liar? Would his face show the truth behind his words? She didn't know.

At least he isn't pretending to not know about the killing, she thought.

"Who did kill him?"

Now Brian paused. He couldn't name Dagi. The boatman had saved his life.

Sitting in the darkness of the temple storage room last night, Brian had tried to understand what had happened. He couldn't think of any reason for three armed men, four if he counted the priest Nimaasted, to try to kill him. It had to be Djefi's idea. That was what Dagi had suggested when he told Brian it was not safe to return to the boat.

Brian knew that Djefi disliked him. Djefi had hidden Diane from him. Djefi had sent him into the desert with Siamun. And now Djefi had sent assassins to kill him. The only reason Brian had come up with for Djefi's murderous hatred was that, in some way, Djefi viewed him as a threat.

He had fantasized last night about getting revenge against Djefi. He had pictured himself as the movie character Jason Bourne, somehow possessing incredible fighting skills and using them to capture Djefi. But he knew that all he really wanted was to return home, to be with his friends, to play another game of baseball.

He shook his head now. "I don't know,' he said, looking at the ground.

Tama knew he was lying. He had thought, decided he would not tell her and now was looking at the ground instead of meeting her eyes. God or man, he was easy for her to read.

She knew that she should send for Nimaasted, but she also knew that truth would not be served that way. Nimaasted had pretended to be full of righteous anger last night, insisting that something evil was afoot. But she had seen anger in his eyes, not fear. He had been lying to her also.

Now the key to last night's killing was sitting in a storage room here in her temple.

She wondered if he was just part of the broader mystery.

Hetephernebti had spoken of it last week when they had met: Kanakht had held secret meetings with Waja-Hur and journeyed all the way to To-She to meet with Djefi. Hetephernebti was sure that the three men were plotting to kill King Djoser. However, the three commanded no military might and had only a handful of personal guards.

What is their plan?

Tama looked at Brian, sitting quietly on the floor. He didn't seem dangerous. He hadn't tried to escape or to attack her.

He knows what happened last night. Could he be the key to help unlock the greater mystery?

She knelt and sat back against the wall, her legs folded to the side, wondering what to do.

As she turned so that the light wasn't directly behind her anymore, Brian realized who she was. "Ma'at!" he said.

"I am high priestess for Ma'at, Voice of Truth" she said. "My name is Tama."

He remembered seeing her talk with Nimaasted last night, allowing him into the temple to search for him. Had she already sent someone to fetch Nimaasted and his guards? Was he about to be arrested?

His plan last night had been to escape the men who were hunting him by hiding in a place they already had searched. He had hoped to figure out the next step this morning.

He saw that Tama was alone. No armed guards were standing by to take him. He could overpower her and run away, but where? He decided to trust her.

"Help me," he said.

Tama studied him as she thought. Hetephernebti had told her about Tim, how he had chosen to stay with Meryt in the final days of the wasting disease. Miraculously, Meryt had recovered and had left with Tim just a few days ago.

Hetephernebti also had told Tama about the other strangers, Brian and Diane. They had arrived in the Two Lands a few days before Tim had. She said that Tim had come to the Two Lands in search of them. Tim had told Hetephernebti that Brian and Diane were lost and needed his help.

"Stand," she told Brian.

She motioned for him to turn. There was a streak of red on his kilt by his right hip. She thought at first that it was proof that he had cut the man last night, the dying man's blood spurting onto Brian's kilt. But then she saw that there was a fresh wound on his hip above the red stain. The blood was his own!

So Nimaasted lied when he said that the man who was attacked had been unarmed, she thought.

She glanced around the room. There was no weapon here.

She closed her eyes and tried to picture what had happened, weighing Nimaasted's words against the wound in Brian's side and Hetephernebti's warning that Nimaasted's master, Waja-Hur, was involved in a plot.

"I didn't do anything wrong," Brian said earnestly, interrupting her thoughts. "Please help me."

If he is a god, she thought, then he doesn't need my help so by asking for it he is testing me.

If he is only human then either he killed the man last night or he has been falsely accused. If he killed the man, then he could easily kill me and he has no need of my help. If he has been falsely accused, then he would fear Nimaasted and fear being caught.

Tama turned the questions over in her mind. They formed a logic puzzle, a delicious mystery, something she enjoyed solving, although she realized that in this case, her pleasure was coming at a terrible expense. A man had been killed, and the man who stood before her had been accused of the crime.

If only I truly had the power to weigh a man's heart and see if he has followed ma'at, she thought. But I have only my eyes, my ears and my heart.

Smoothly she came to her feet. Brian watched her, filled with excitement at finding her and hoping that she would believe him and help him.

"Stay here," she said, watching to make sure he understood.

Brian nodded and sat back on the floor. He had nowhere to run, no one else who could help him. He would trust in Ma'at.

She turned right outside the storage room, heading back to her chambers to prepare for the day and to give thought to the puzzle of Brian.

She stopped at the next hallway and looked back to be sure he had stayed in the storage room.

The hallway was empty.

During their meeting a few days ago, she and Hetephernebti had agreed that she would journey across land to Waset, traveling not as Tama, high priestess of the goddess Ma'at, but as Tama, a widowed woman traveling to visit her family. She would listen to the workers she met, to the other travelers in the Two Lands, to the talk in the rest houses and markets along the road.

Hetephernebti had told Tama that she suspected Djefi, Kanakht and Waja-Hur were plotting to overthrow King Djoser. Hetephernebti would protect her brother, helping him in any way she could. Tama knew this. And so the priestess of Re was traveling with her brother-king telling him what she knew, advising him and helping him to understand and anticipate whatever attack Kanakht was plotting.

Tama would travel beside the river, listening to the murmurs and rumors, evaluating the mood of the people, taking the pulse of the Two Lands, searching for the truth.

Hetephernebti asked Tama to meet her in Waset where Hetephernebti hoped to hear that Djoser still had the love and support of the people.

Tama wasn't as optimistic as Hetephernebti. Even in Khmunu she had heard whispers that Djoser had offended the gods by declaring himself one of them. She realized that Waja-Hur was mumbling those very thoughts to anyone who would listen, which was why she needed to travel outside Khmunu and listen to people not poisoned by the thoughts of the bitter priest.

"There was another," Nimaasted said to Djefi.

Djefi sat beneath the canopy on his boat. He had sent all of the crew onshore to gather provisions for the long trip upriver to Kom Ombo. He wanted to rise from his chair and strangle the unapologetic priest. *If Siamun were here …* he left the thought unfinished.

"You had three embalmers. How could they not take this one man?" Djefi asked, trying to keep his voice calm. "Did you not understand Kanakht's orders?"

Nimaasted paced in front of Djefi. Kanakht had promised Nimaasted that he would be the one selected to take Waja-Hur's place when the aged priest journeyed on to Khert-Neter, a trip that looked more and more imminent every day. Old Waja-Hur frequently failed to recognize anyone, even Nimaasted, who had served him for ten years.

The old man forgets to eat sometimes. Soon we will feed him by hand, or allow him to die, Nimaasted thought.

Kanakht had told Nimaasted that an evil man was traveling with Djefi, a man whose very existence was an affront to the gods, a man who was a threat to the balance of the Two Lands that Waja-Hur held so dear.

The vizier's speech, and there had been much, much more to it, had no more substance than the hot winds that blew in from the desert; Nimaasted recognized lies and misdirection. But he also understood the unspoken promise in Kanakht's words, a promise of power in return for this killing.

But Kanakht had not explained how huge the man would be, or that another god would come to his rescue. Once Nimaasted had seen Brian's size, he had recruited three embalmers, men who were comfortable with death, men who would not be afraid to kill another.

The embalmers were to come upon Nimaasted and Brian suddenly in the night, to surround them and show that resistance was useless. Then they would take Brian across the river, bound and helpless. Once on the west bank, they would kill him, in whatever fashion they chose.

But someone had materialized in the night and shouted an alarm. Brian had reacted more quickly than Nimaasted thought possible for a human, first shoving him effortlessly to the ground, then running as fast as Horus flies to strike one embalmer, using his shoulder, like the god Apis, the bull, crushing the man to the ground. Then down the dark street to kill the third embalmer and off into the night, vanishing like a spirit.

After Hetephernebti's visit last week, Nimaasted had heard rumors that strange gods were walking the Two Lands. Was Brian one of them? Was the strange shadow who appeared to help him another? Was the stranger the same one who had stayed with Hetephernebti's ill wbt-priestess? Had he somehow returned to help his fellow god? How else could one explain Brian's escape and his disappearance?

"Usually when I ask a question, Nimaasted, I get an answer. Did you not understand Kanakht's orders?"

Waja-Hur is old and growing senile, Nimaasted thought, but he is still a hundred times more priestly than this fat, sweating pig who sits in front of me, demanding answers.

"First Prophet Djefi," Nimaasted said, controlling his anger, "Kanakht neglected to mention that this man was a god or that another god would come to help him. I cannot battle gods."

"What gods?"

"I have heard the rumors, First Prophet. Strange gods are in Kemet. If you had seen this Brian last night ... No one but a god could move as he did, could have the power he has. No one but a god could know our plan when no one knew it but you, Kanakht and myself. No one but a god could materialize in the street in the middle of the night and shout a warning to this Brian."

Djefi's voice rose to an hysterical squeak. "No, Nimaasted, no. You are making things up to explain your failure! We ask you to do something and you failed. There is no more to it than that."

Nimaasted was seized with a nearly overwhelming desire to rush at the fat priest and push him off his chair and into the river. Instead, he clenched his fists and breathed deeply. He had risen to his position by solving problems, not creating new ones.

"As you say, First Prophet. Yet we have searched all of Khmunu and Brian is not in the town. We have searched every home, every hut, even the temples, yes, even the Temple of Ma'at. Brian is not to be found, neither is his accomplice."

"He must be here. You must search again," Djefi insisted.

As Djefi spoke, a boatman appeared at the edge of the bank carrying a sack. Behind him more of the boatmen appeared, returning from the markets of Khmunu.

"I leave shortly," Djefi said. "Send word to Kanakht when you've found and disposed of this Brian."

Nimaasted bowed his head and withdrew. His appearance was one of acceptance and humility, but in his mind he wondered: If I find this Brian, should I apologize and seek to align myself with the powerful god instead of this fat, quivering priest?

"What do you call your language?" Tama asked Brian.

"English."

"Teach me," she said. "You may be a god, you may not. But I cannot know your thoughts if you must talk in my language. So, if I am to know the truth, I must learn your language."

Brian wondered what she saw in his eyes as he stared at her, unable to look at anything else, wishing he could spend days simply admiring her.

She was so beautiful and graceful, so alive and honest in her movements. Everything she did, walking, sitting, speaking, it all had an economy and a purity that reminded him of what he loved about sports. He thought of video clips of Joe DiMaggio playing the outfield, so graceful and effortless.

It was late afternoon and they were in her chambers. He had been taken to a secluded part of the pond and allowed to bathe. His kilt had been washed and returned to him. As each hour passed, he grew more optimistic that she would help him, that she believed he was innocent.

Tama walked to a window and beckoned Brian to her. She pointed to the sun as it floated just above the western horizon. She turned to him.

He could smell the perfumes and oils she had used. He fought to keep his eyes from drifting from her face, so perfect in its proportions, so open and honest, to her bare shoulders.

She saw his struggle. Raising her hand, she turned his head firmly toward the window and pointed to the setting sun again.

"Sun," he said in English.

"Sun," she repeated.

Then she waved to the sky, pale blue and empty.

"Sky," he said.

"Sky," she repeated. "Sun, sky."

She turned to him and studied him. "Netjer?" she asked.

It was a word he had heard often from Pahket. "God?" he repeated in English. He shook his head. "No, not god."

It was the answer she hoped for. Turning away from him she walked to the doorway where an attendant waited.

"We will be leaving at sunset. Please have the donkeys ready by the south gate. And spread the word that I will be in seclusion with Ma'at. My trip is to be a secret."

The attendant nodded and left quietly.

"So, Brian," she said, approaching him, "we will take a trip together. Hopefully we will discover the truth about Kemet. And the truth about you."

PRINCE TETI

Hesire was an old man who hoped to grow older.

But as the doctor looked at Prince Teti's blackening fingers and thought of the news he would have to give King Djoser, he wondered if he would live to see tomorrow.

Prince Teti's left forearm had been badly broken, the jagged end of the bone ripping through the flesh and skin when the prince had fallen from a boulder in the river near Abu. The doctor at Abu, a man named Rudamon, whom Hesire had trained himself, had set the arm and encased it in a cast made of palm leaf fiber lint and tree bark. Rudamon had used mud from the River Iteru to pack the ragged gash where the bone had protruded through Prince Teti's arm.

Hesire had not removed the cast when Prince Teti had arrived in Waset; he wanted to allow the river's mud to do its work healing the wound. Besides, the only true way to know if the bone had been set properly was to do it yourself, to feel the bones fall snugly together. Hesire trusted that Rudamon had done that. Unwrapping the cast now would serve no purpose, except to cause the prince pain.

But Prince Teti's fingers had started to turn black, not the dark red and purple from a fall, but something more sinister.

Hesire would watch for red streaks to appear above the cast on Prince Teti's forearm. If the streaks appeared and grew, then the arm would have to be removed.

Hesire was not optimistic. The darkening fingers were a bad sign.

It was this news that Hesire feared to bring to King Djoser.

A prince with one arm was not a prince, he was a cripple. A king needed strength, but even more so, he needed to project strength.

In a letter Rudamon sent to Hesire, he had described the injury and his treatment.

Unsure who would read the letter before it reached the hands of the royal physician, Rudamon had been careful in his description of the injury and its cause. He had been told that Prince Teti had fallen from a boulder in a rocky stretch of the river near Abu. The prince's guards had been with him. The prince had lost consciousness. One guard said the prince's head had been underwater, another said it had not.

The rumor that had reached Hesire's ears was that a guard named Bata had been found holding Prince Teti's head under the water at the base of the rock. At least that was what Rensi, the guard who found them, claimed. Bata denied it, saying that he was supporting the unconscious prince, waiting for help.

The lack of detail in Rudamon's terse description made Hesire wonder if there was something more to the accident. Rudamon's caution itself was a clue that he suspected the injuries had not been accidental and that he didn't fully believe the allegations made by the guard Rensi.

Hesire decided to keep his comments to King Djoser focused on Prince Teti's injury and treatment. There were others, Sekhmire, for example, whose duty it was to protect the king and his family.

As far as healing the prince, there was little more Hesire could do, except wait. He could offer King Djoser no assurance that the bone would knit back together, or that it would heal straight if it did.

Prince Teti was fifteen years old, strong and sturdy like his father, who had great strength in his hands and powerful legs. King Djoser could lead a march from sunrise to sunset as he had many times under his father's militant rule. True, the king was shorter than some men and not as fleet as others. But his stamina, Hesire shook his head, his stamina and strength of will were amazing.

Apparently Prince Teti had inherited his father's iron will.

According to the letter from Rudamon, Prince Teti had bitten completely through a leather strap while Rudamon had pushed the bone back into place, but he had not uttered a single cry.

"Aside from the arm, are there other injuries?" Hesire asked, standing before the seated prince, his brief examination of the arm complete.

Prince Teti took his time responding. He had the same unhurried disposition as his father, thinking carefully before speaking. Hesire wondered idly if it was a trait that was carried in the royal blood or if the prince was unconsciously emulating his father.

"There was a bump at the base of my head, in the back near my neck. But it has disappeared. And there is a cut on my back."

The physician looked at the prince's back. The cut started below the shoulder blade, a dark, scabbed gash with a wide bruise at the bottom. The gash narrowed as it climbed up his back.

"Where was the bump, Prince Teti?"

He reached behind his head and pointed to a spot at the base of his skull. Hesire saw that the line of the cut pointed directly to the spot Prince Teti was touching.

"**C**ome, sister, walk with me," King Djoser said to Hetephernebti, repeating the words he always used when he wanted to confer privately with the only remaining family member from his childhood.

Kanakht rose to accompany them.

"Kanakht," Djoser said, "Please send a message to Abu. I want the guard Bata held until I have a chance to talk with him myself. No one is to help him or harm him. I want him worried, as he should be, but unharmed."

Kanakht looked from Djoser to Hetephernebti, but their faces betrayed nothing. He bowed his head and withdrew.

Djoser took his sister's hand and led her to the doorway that opened to his personal garden behind his palace at Waset.

They walked to a stone bench set beside a small pool in the center of the garden. The shrubbery around the water was cut low, giving Djoser a place to talk, free of fear that anyone was lurking nearby spying on him. Sekhmire, commander of his personal guard, stood by the doorway, his back discreetly turned to the garden.

Hesire had left immediately after giving his medical report to the king, obviously relieved that he had been allowed to leave unharmed after telling the king that his son might lose an arm.

Hetephernebti waited in silence as her brother digested the awful news. She knew he would speak only when his thoughts were in order.

His face was calm, his lips set in a gentle smile, but she saw that his eyes were unfocused. He was looking within.

Leaning down, he swept his hand through the water in the pool. Still turned away from Hetephernebti he spoke so softly that she wasn't sure if he was addressing her or just allowing his thoughts to take form in the shade of the garden.

"Water, fire, air. What thought do they give to their actions?"

Djoser brought his wet hand to his face. He tasted the water, careful as always to not disturb the subtle makeup he wore.

"The river rises, Nebti, or it doesn't. It floods, washing away houses, or it ignores the Two Lands and denies us the rich earth from Kush. It simply acts, regardless of the consequences. The wind carries the scent of the lotus blossoms to us, or it grabs fistfuls of sand and hurls it in our eyes. Thought? I don't think so.

"The fire bakes our bread, roasts our oxen, nourishing us, or it destroys, remember the fire in Tahta last year?"

She nodded.

"An untended cooking fire, its embers not as cold as the owner thought, stirred back to life at night and spread. How many homes were burned, how many families lamented their losses that season?" he said.

"Am I a god, Nebti, or am I not a god? Is the river a river only when it brings us riches? Is the wind the wind only when it carries a pleasing fragrance? Am I a god only when the land and people flourish, only when I do what others think is right?"

She saw that although his voice remained calm, his fists were clenched.

"Does the river consider its actions? No, Nebti, it acts as a river acts. So with the wind, so with fire. They are and they act. No more than that! If I act as I act, it is all I can do."

She laid her hand on his arm, caressing the smooth skin.

"The gods did not harm Teti because ... " she began.

"This is not about Teti," he said, cutting her off. "Kemet deserves a god to rule it. The people need more than a man as leader. Why does a man follow another man? Fear, rewards, love? Can fear not be overcome, cannot greater rewards be offered, cannot even love change to hate? Only to a god are we steadfast. You to Re, Waja-Hur to Thoth. Your devotion does not waver.

"But can a god permit his son to be attacked? Yes, Nebti, I know that Teti did not fall from a rock. My son would never fall from a rock. That is why that guard will be kept alive. I will find the truth. But will the people continue to regard me as a god if I allow my son to suffer? Can a god have a crippled son? No, Nebti, I think not. I will have a son who is sound in all respects, or I will have no son."

Hetephernebti couldn't stop a small gasp. Djoser chose to ignore it.

She stroked his arm again, absently comforting him as she thought.

"Dear brother," she said. "I have told you about the strangers."

He looked at her, his eyes searching hers, an unspoken question there.

"The one who was with me, he has healing powers, remember? One of my attendants had the wasting illness. He healed her. He healed a little girl of a scorpion sting."

She felt the muscles of his arm tighten beneath her hand.

"He will be here tonight," she said.

Tim was standing by the prow of the boat as it docked at Waset. Meryt stood by his side, supported by his arm around her small waist. As they walked off the narrow gangplank, he walked ahead of her, reaching back to hold her hand. When she entwined her fingers in his, he responded with a gentle squeeze.

During the trip upriver from Khmunu, he had continued to boil water before permitting her to drink it. He had prepared her meals himself, not trusting the hygiene of others. Her sense of humor returned first, followed by her inquisitiveness and then, at last, her energy.

As she stepped on land, she felt as if the journey from Khmunu had taken her not only from illness to health, but also from childhood to womanhood. She and Tim were not lovers, but she knew that they would be, if only he would allow it.

The early days of her illness were lost to her in a hot haze of fever and pain. Her first memory of her new life – that was how she viewed her miraculous recovery – was of Tim. She had awakened before dawn, thirsty and free of the stomach pains that had felt as if Sobek was gnawing on her belly. Her head was in his lap as he sat, leaning against the mud brick wall of the small hut they were using. He was asleep. Although his face was drawn from worry, a small smile rested on his lips.

She had reached up a weak hand and traced the curve of his lips, feeling the raspy scratch of the stubble of his beard that had grown overnight. As her fingertip had moved slowly across his lips, he unconsciously had kissed it, so loving and gentle, even in his sleep.

She had brought her hand down to her mouth and kissed the same spot on her fingertip.

A guard was waiting for them on the riverbank.

"Come with me," he said, turning and leading them to a broad avenue that led inward to the town.

They arrived at a wide doorway in a smoothly plastered whitewashed wall. Guards stood by twin pillars embedded by the doorway.

"Where are we?" Tim asked Meryt.

"I've never been to Waset," she said.

The guard paused by the doorway.

"High Priestess Hetephernebti is with King Djoser, they want to see you," he said. He stood aside and motioned for them to enter the building.

Tim's mouth went dry and he felt his heart begin to race. King Djoser! A few weeks ago, in the dead of night at Saqqara, he had slowly pushed his hand through the opening in the wall of the Serdab and traced the contours of the stone bust of the king's face, a statue of a man who had been dead five thousand years. Now Tim was about to meet him.

"Say 'Life, prosperity, health,' when we meet him," Meryt said.

"Really?"

"Tim, I have never met the king, but everyone knows how you greet him. After that ..." she shrugged her small shoulders.

King Djoser was seated on a golden throne on a slightly raised dais. He wore a white linen kilt. A broad jeweled pectoral covered most of his chest. In his right hand he held a flail, royal symbol of power.

Hetephernebti stood behind him on his left, an older man in immaculate white robes stood at Djoser's right hand.

"Life, prosperity, health!" Meryt said when she and Tim had come to a stop. Tim echoed her words, happily surprised to hear his voice match Meryt's sincere tone.

Djoser nodded in response.

"I am pleased to see you well, Meryt," Hetephernebti said.

"Thank you, High Priestess," Meryt said. "And you are well, I hope."

Hetephernebti smiled at the girl's question, how like her to make innocent conversation even in the presence of the king.

"They say you are a god," King Djoser said, ignoring the exchange between the two women.

"I have heard some people say that," Tim answered, glancing at Meryt. "But I am just a man, King Djoser."

"Life, health, prosperity!" Meryt added automatically, nudging Tim.

"Life, health, prosperity," Tim said quickly.

Kanakht leaned toward King Djoser and spoke softly. The king listened to his adviser and then said, "You healed the girl of the wasting disease. What heka did you use?"

Tim shook his head. "It was not magic, King Djoser."

"Life, health, prosperity!" Meryt said again after the king's name was mentioned.

King Djoser smiled at her. "Little bird, I have heard your sweet song. You do not need to sing every time my name is mentioned."

Returning his calm gaze to Tim, he said, "Not magic?"

"Where I come from," Tim said, choosing his words carefully, "we have a different way of treating some illnesses. It worked with Meryt. I was …" he started to say lucky, then changed his mind, "I was blessed by the gods."

"And you healed a girl who was stung by a scorpion?" Djoser asked.

Tim looked to Hetephernebti, whose face remained friendly, but otherwise unreadable.

"It was a small thing," Tim said.

King Djoser nodded his head and then stared off in the distance for a moment. "I have a task for you, man who is blessed by the gods," he said. He raised his hand toward a darkened corner of the room where a figure stood in the shadows.

Prince Teti came forward, holding his broken left arm stiffly at his side. He stopped at the foot of his father's throne and stood there facing him, his back turned toward Tim.

King Djoser leaned forward and spoke to his son. Sitting back in his throne, he looked down at Tim. "This is my son, Prince Teti. Heal him."

Tim wanted to throw up. He didn't know why his hands weren't shaking, because his stomach was quivering in fear.

He, Meryt and Prince Teti were in a small chamber off the throne room. The young prince was standing stiffly, watching them, as was a guard who stood by the doorway. Tim heard the sound of footsteps receding as the king, Hetephernebti and the king's adviser left the throne room.

"Meryt, I need my bag," he said, referring to his backpack, which he had left on the boat.

"I will get it," she said.

"Hurry," Tim said as she turned toward the door.

"Who are you?" Prince Teti asked after Meryt had gone.

Tim didn't know how Prince Teti had been injured. He saw that Prince Teti's left arm was bandaged, but Tim had no idea what had happened or when it had happened. The boy was standing straight; his chest pushed forward, his chin held high. Although he seemed composed, Tim saw that Prince Teti's right hand was balled into a fist, the fingers on his other hand were splayed open, as if trying to escape from pain.

"My name is Tim," he said.

"I mean, are you a physician, a priest or a god?" Prince Teti said.

Tim thought before responding.

He had always believed that he could draw, but he had never realized the importance of that confidence until he had met students in his college classes who didn't have his assurance. Their lines were hesitant, their vision small.

Eventually he had come to see that self-confidence was often as responsible for success as was talent. In some cases more responsible. He hoped this would be one of them.

In the back of his mind he wondered what would happen to him if he failed to heal the prince, or, worse, if he somehow harmed him. He caught those thoughts, recognized them and tried to forget them until later.

He tried to smile comfortingly. "I do not have a title, Prince Teti. I am just someone who wants to help you. I have some medicines that may help. I don't know about ..." He was saved from admitting his ignorance by the sound of footsteps behind him.

Hesire, the physician, had entered the room. He walked quickly to them, his eyes darting from Tim to Teti as he approached, looking to see what had been done.

"Prince Teti," he said. "I came as soon as your father told me that he had asked another," he looked at Tim, evaluating what he saw, "another physician to look at your injuries."

"Thank you," Tim and Prince Teti said at the same time.

Hesire drew himself up and addressed Tim formally. "I have been instructed to assist you," he said.

Tim tried to imagine that conversation: He wondered if Hesire had tried to persuade King Djoser that he needed to be present to prevent Tim from damaging Prince Teti or if Djoser had ordered Hesire to keep an eye on him.

Either way, he was grateful. And worried.

"I am sorry if my manner is strange," Tim said to Prince Teti. "First, can you tell me how you were injured?"

Prince Teti looked at Hesire, who nodded approval. "I fell onto rocks in the river at Abu."

"His back was also injured, as was his neck," Hesire added.

Prince Teti turned his back to show Tim the wound. Tim recognized the red swelling around the cut as an infection. He made a mental note to give Prince Teti some antibiotics.

Tim turned to Hesire.

"Did you treat his arm?"

"No," Hesire answered. "Rudamon, a physician at Abu set the broken bone which had pushed through the skin."

Without thinking, Tim glanced at Prince Teti, who was managing to keep an impassive face. Whatever the boy thought of his father ordering him to see a stranger, he wasn't showing any anger or concern.

"Prince Teti," Tim said, "I am sure that you have been treated properly. But your father asked me to look at your injury, so we shall. Hesire," he said, turning to the physician, "your hands are more practiced than mine. I need your help. Please. I have some medicines from my distant land that may help Prince Teti. But I need your skillful hands and eyes to help me."

Hesire was surprised by Tim's request. When King Djoser had told him that he had ordered another physician to examine Prince Teti, Hesire had assumed that he was being punished for delivering the bad news about Prince Teti's injury. He had expected the new physician to attempt to blame him for anything that went wrong.

Instead, this stranger was openly asking his help in front of Prince Teti.

As he nodded his agreement, they heard light footsteps approaching. Looking to the sound they saw Meryt returning with Tim's canvas backpack.

Tim took the backpack from her and set it on the floor near him. Then he turned to Prince Teti.

"May I see your arm?" he asked.

Prince Teti extended the arm.

The fingers were swollen and dark, the forearm was pushing tight against the palm-bark at both edges of the cast. Tim wondered if he should press against the injury as he had seen doctors do on television shows, but he had no idea what that would tell him.

He tried to break the problem into small parts.

It's swollen, probably from an infection, he thought. The swelling has trapped blood from the wound in Teti's hand. *R-I-C-E,* he thought, repeating the first aid mantra of treatment for most injuries: Rest, Ice, Compression, Elevation.

He touched Hesire's shoulder and motioned for him to step a few paces away from Prince Teti.

"The blackness in his fingers ..." Tim began.

"Yes," Hesire nodded, "It is a bad sign. That is why I told King Djoser that the arm may need to be removed."

Tim froze. Did King Djoser expect him to amputate his son's arm?

"Of course, King Djoser does not want that to happen, which is why, I believe, he asked you to look at Prince Teti," Hesire said.

Tim tried to put the thought of amputating an arm out of his mind. *I'm starting to get a lot of things I have to remember to forget,* he thought.

"I think the blackness in the fingers is blood turned black," Tim said.

"Do you think we need to drain them?" Hesire asked.

Tim thought of Paneb and how he had grabbed a knife to treat his daughter's scorpion sting. "No, I think we can remove the blackness without a knife," he said to Hesire.

"In my country," he continued "we think it is very important to keep the wound clean. So, would you please unwrap the cast? We can check the setting of the bone and inspect the wound."

Hesire nodded and turned to Prince Teti.

As Hesire cut off the cast, Tim dug through his backpack. He had gauze, antibiotic pills and antibiotic cream, and a white padded splint. He also had some Ibuprofen that would reduce the swelling and ease Prince Teti's pain. After the arm was recast, Tim would ask Prince Teti to carry it in a sling to keep it elevated.

"Meryt," he said, "I need a length of linen, as long as you are tall."

She leaned forward and whispered to him, "I know that you can help him, Tim. You must know that, too." Then she turned and left the room.

When Tim turned back to look at Teti, he almost passed out from the sight of the unwrapped arm.

It was grotesquely swollen, the entire forearm was smeared with dried blood and mud and the wound where the bone had pierced the skin was a pus-filled bubble. Quickly he turned to his backpack and knelt over it, as if searching for something. He waited for the blood to return to his head and the wave of nausea to pass.

He thought of how he dealt with seeing Meryt's beautiful naked body every day: He tried to picture her as a model in a drawing class, and focused on the lines and contours. Although it was working less and less with her as he came to care for her, he hoped the method would help him through this examination.

He composed his face before rising to face Prince Teti and Hesire.

Forcing himself to look at the arm, he tried to analyze what he saw, to think about what caused it and what he could do. As he did, a wave of calm entered him.

Lightly he touched Prince Teti's arm, his fingers almost floating over the dried mud caked there.

"Hesire, is there water here, and a cloth?" Tim asked.

The physician motioned toward a table that stood beside a chair behind Prince Teti.

Tim realized that his fears had narrowed his vision and he hadn't truly seen the room. He gestured to Prince Teti to sit on the chair. Standing beside the chair, he held the arm gently. Moistening the cloth, Tim began to clean the dirt from the wound. He let the water do the work of softening the mud, waiting until it was easy to pat away.

As he worked he focused on the warmth of Teti's arm, flush from the blood that was pooled there. He felt the smooth young skin stretched tight beneath the swollen wound.

Once the mud and blood were cleaned away, Tim wrapped his hand around Prince Teti's forearm and held it, asking the prince to relax his arm's weight into Tim's hands. With his other hand under the arm, nearer the elbow, Tim slowly pressed his forefinger against the bone. He closed his eyes, focusing his attention on the solid feel of Teti's radius bone. He allowed the other fingers of his hand to follow the swell of the muscles.

Slowly he moved his hand down Teti's wrist toward the injury, his finger following the firm line of the bone. As he neared the point of the fracture, he felt Prince Teti stiffen. The flesh around the injury was swollen, but Tim was able to trace the line of the bone.

"I'm sorry if this hurts," he said as he heard Prince Teti draw a deep breath.

Slowly, Tim squeezed the forearm around the wound, breaking the thin scab that was holding in the pus that had accumulated there. He gently cleaned it away with the damp cloth.

Meryt had returned and was quietly waiting, holding a roll of linen.

"Hesire," Tim said, "please hold Prince Teti's arm for me."

Tim went to the backpack and retrieved the tube of antibiotic cream and the roll of gauze.

As Hesire held the arm, Tim packed the wound with the cream, thankful that it did not need stitches, and then wrapped gauze around it. He placed the splint under the bone and wrapped more gauze around it to hold it in place.

Measuring off a length of linen, he tied a sling around the prince's shoulder to support the broken arm.

Finished with the arm, Tim picked up the pill bottles.

Shaking two antibiotics and then some Ibuprofen into his hand, he asked Meryt to get a cup of water for Prince Teti. He gave Teti the pills and asked the prince to swallow them.

While Prince Teti took the last of the pills, Tim washed and dried his hands with the leftover linen.

"Prince Teti," he said. "Please keep your arm in the sling, even as you sleep." Taking the cup, Tim filled it with water and held it over the water bowl. "Your arm is swollen with blood. If you keep your arm raised, then," he began to pour the water back into the bowl, "the blood will slowly flow down and away from your arm. Like this.

"The medicine I put on your arm will help it to heal. Tomorrow or the next day, your arm will return to normal size. Then we must cover it with a hard covering, like Hesire had on before. Please, Prince Teti, please be careful until then."

Prince Teti nodded his understanding.

"Will I be a cripple? Will I lose my arm?" he asked.

"I do not think so," Tim answered. "The treatment Hesire gave you saved it. This will help you grow strong faster."

Prince Teti nodded once more and walked from the room.

Suddenly Tim was exhausted, but he knew there was more he needed to do.

"Thank you, Hesire. You did save his arm. I could not have helped him without you."

Hesire didn't know how to answer. He knew that he had done little except stand by. He wasn't sure what Tim had done, except to remove the healing mud and replace it with something else. The pills he had fed Prince Teti, were they heka? He didn't know.

Had Tim told Prince Teti that Hesire had saved the arm in case the treatment didn't work? Tim's voice and actions seemed true, but Hesire's mind was still filled with questions.

He wanted to believe in this stranger, this man who said he wasn't a god. He really did.

Tim picked up his backpack and held out his hand to Meryt. As they walked to the doorway, he leaned to her and whispered, "I've never been so afraid."

"You are a great doctor, Tim. You saved my life," she said. "You will heal Prince Teti."

IMHOTEP ARRIVES

Long after Meryt, who was still weak from her illness, fell asleep that night, Tim sat beside a flickering lamp in their chamber wide awake and marveling over the day he had just experienced.

He had met King Djoser!

The last time he had stayed awake this long – the night in Diane and Brian's room at the Mena House – seemed as if it had taken place in another lifetime, to a different person. He had spent much of that night reading about Saqqara, the Step Pyramid, King Djoser, and the land he had ruled almost five thousand years ago.

And now Tim had met him.

Although Djoser ruled in the Third Dynasty, well into the recorded history of ancient Egypt, he was the earliest Egyptian king whose name Tim recognized. From his reading that night at the Mena House, Tim knew that an earlier king named Narmer had united Upper and Lower Egypt to form the Two Lands. But it was Djoser, who ruled five hundred years after Narmer, who was better remembered, immortalized by his stone tomb, the Step Pyramid. The great pyramids of Giza were modeled after it. Imhotep, architect of the Step Pyramid, was perhaps even more famous than King Djoser.

Where is Imhotep? Tim wondered. He had assumed that the famous Egyptian who was architect, physician, and adviser to the king would be standing beside King Djoser in the throne room, as Kanakht had been. But he was not, and Tim had not even heard Imhotep's name mentioned. He made a mental note to ask Meryt about the missing Imhotep.

Tim stretched and looked down at his sketchbook. He had begun to draw Meryt, nude as always, sleeping peacefully on her side, her back to him. The dim light of the room shrouded her in shadows, softening her small form, making her look even younger than she was.

He knew that thinking of her as a child was a cultural bias. In this time and place, a girl of thirteen was a woman, not a child. But every time he fantasized about kissing or touching Meryt, something he caught himself doing more often as they spent more and more time together, he felt a twinge of conscience and then a flush of guilt. In his old world she would be a girl, and it would be wrong for him to think of her the way he was now, or even to look at her as he was now as she slept.

The lamp's light gave her dark skin a soft sheen, its shadowy glow gently washing over the smooth muscles of her back. His eyes followed the curve of her body's profile, from her delicate shoulder down the slender line to her waist over the angled rise of her narrow hips, across the lithe contour of her backside to the tapering length of her thighs.

A year is simply how long it takes the earth to swing around the sun, Tim thought. Does it really matter how many times that has happened since Meryt's birth? Is the movement of the planets and stars a more relevant way of measuring her maturity than looking into her eyes? Is counting the number of days and nights that have passed since her birth more meaningful than her touch and her smile?

He looked down at his sketchbook. With his pencil, little more than a stub now, he drew the curve of her hips sweeping inward to her narrow waist. Her arm rested on her side, her elbow bent slightly as her forearm draped away from him into the shadows toward the wall.

Lightly he outlined the soft rise of her back as it widened to her shoulder. He regripped his pencil to shade in the shadowed curve that led to her spine. He followed the smooth shadow toward her lower back.

He could go to her now, unwrap the linen belt that held his kilt in place and curl up beside her. She would sense his presence, know it was him, and push against him. She would roll over and open her arms to welcome him and pull him closer.

If I touched her, caressed her shoulders, felt the smooth skin of her arms, the delicate strength of her fingers, would it be wrong? If I had been born in this time and place, I wouldn't think about it. I would be as free to love her, as she feels free to be with me.

There was a rolled cotton sheet at the foot of the small bed. Setting aside his sketchbook, Tim stood and walked to the bed, unavoidably aware that he had become aroused. He picked up the sheet and shook it open. Gently he placed it across her bare form, covering her to her waist. He leaned over her and tenderly stroked her cheek.

"I'm sorry, Meryt," he whispered. Bending closer, he kissed her forehead and then, turning, he walked back to his chair to wait out the night.

It was midmorning when Tim and Meryt were called to the royal chambers.

Tim had fallen asleep in the chair. He woke to the touch of Meryt's hand sliding across his stubble-filled skull.

"You need to shave before we meet with Prince Teti again," she said. As he opned his eyes, a dream disappeared. Its substance already lost, only a warm feeling remaining. He leaned forward to hide the excitement he felt beneath his kilt, wondering if Meryt had noticed.

"I've sent for a barber. He should be here soon," Meryt said, turning her back and walking to a table that held a tray of bread and fruit.

Tim tasted his morning breath. "I should bathe," he said.

"After the barber," Meryt said over her shoulder. "There will be time."

Prince Teti and Hesire were waiting in the royal chambers.

The prince wore a half smile as he fought to keep his regal demeanor. Hesire was almost bouncing on the balls of his feet.

Tim and Meryt stopped a few feet away from the prince, but Hesire waved them forward.

"Come closer, closer and look. Your heka is very strong, the swelling is almost gone."

Tim lowered his backpack to the floor and approached the prince.

"Good morning, Prince Teti," he said.

"Good morning, Netjer Tim," Teti answered, apparently deciding that Tim was indeed a god.

Tim decided not to argue with his patient.

He touched Prince Teti's side and extended his other arm toward a window. "Come with me to the light, Prince Teti."

He was relieved to see that the simple first aid and the power of modern antibiotics had worked their 'magic' over night. The prince's fingers were almost normal size and the blackness had begun to fade to a normal looking bruise. Tim decided to leave the wrap in place and put a hard cast around the broken bone.

"I stayed awake through the night, holding my arm so," Prince Teti said, raising the fist of his injured arm to his shoulder.

"You have a strong mind, Prince Teti," Tim said.

"I do what needs to be done."

Tim waved Meryt closer. "I'm sorry, Meryt, but could you please find me another length of linen and some wheat flour? Oh, and a bowl of water."

Hesire stopped her with a gesture. "No, Netjer Tim," he said. "Your hemet does not need to run errands." He clapped his hands and two servant boys ran into the room. He bent to them and gave them orders. They ran quickly back out the door.

Meryt stood silently, her eyes on Tim, who allowed the moment to pass. He knew that hemet meant woman and that Hesire had just suggested that Meryt was more than just Tim's medical assistant. Hemet also could mean wife.

"Your hemet is beautiful," Prince Teti said so quietly that only Tim could hear.

Although they could have been a simple compliment, but Tim heard much more in Prince Teti's four words. The way he said 'hemet' made Tim think that the prince understood that Hesire had overstated the relationship between Tim and Meryt. The prince's eyes as he looked at him told Tim that Prince Teti really did believe that Meryt was beautiful and that he saw her as a woman, not a little girl.

"Yes," Tim said, as much to himself as to Prince Teti. "Yes, she is."

When the boys returned with the supplies, Tim asked Hesire and Meryt to help him with the cast.

They mixed the flour and water to make a soupy paste. Then they tore the linen into foot-long lengths and soaked them in the flour mixture. Tim's idea, remembering craft projects from grade school, was to create a cast from paper mache.

Once the linen was soaked, he wrapped the damp strips around Prince Teti's arm to create a cast. When he finished, Tim tied a sling to support Prince Teti's arm.

"Once this is dry," he told Prince Teti, "it will be hard as wood. But if it gets wet again, then it will grow soft and be useless."

"How long?"

"Ah ..." Tim didn't know how long a broken bone took to heal. He turned to Hesire. "How long do you think it will take to heal?"

"Forty days," Hesire answered easily, happy to be asked his opinion in front of the prince. "Prince Teti is young and strong. Forty days, no more!"

Tim nodded and said, "Forty days, Prince Teti. But I would like to see you again tomorrow."

Prince Teti nodded. "It will be so, Netjer Tim."

"Oh, wait," Tim said as Prince Teti turned to leave. He dug into his first aid kit and pulled out the antibiotics and Ibuprofen. "Please swallow these again," he said, giving some pills to the prince.

After Prince Teti had gone, Tim turned to Hesire.

"Thank you, Hesire. We must watch the prince's hand. If it swells again, then the cast is too tight and the injury is, uh," he didn't know of a word for infected, "unwell."

Hesire nodded.

"The heka that you gave him. Can you tell me what it is?"

Tim thought about the idea of germs and bacteria and viruses. How could he explain that to Hesire? He took the old man's wrist and found his pulse, then turned his wrist over to allow Hesire to find his.

"Yes, yes," Hesire said, "The voice of the heart. We know of it."

"The voice of the heart," Tim said, picking up on Hesire's term, "carries blood throughout the body."

Hesire nodded. "Yes, yes."

He probably thinks I'm a simpleton, or else talking down to him, Tim thought.

"The blood gives the body strength. The heka, the medicine, I gave Prince Teti will make his blood stronger."

"Will it help a man who is not ill?" Hesire asked, a soft urgency in his voice.

"I don't understand."

Hesire sighed softly. "I have a friend, an old friend. I've heard that he is not well, that his thoughts leave him and he knows not where he is. Otherwise he remains strong and active, for a man of his age, that is."

Tim shook his head. "No, Hesire. Where I come from some people have the same illness. There is nothing we can do except watch over them. I am sorry."

Hesire had expected that answer. He nodded knowingly. "My friend has lived a long life, soon he will be happy once more with the body of his youth in Khert-Neter."

The next morning Tim and Meryt were called again to the royal chambers to see Hesire and Prince Teti.

The cast had dried and felt solid. The prince's fingers looked healthier, and Prince Teti was in an even brighter mood.

"The feeling has returned to my hand," he said, wiggling his fingers.

"You heal fast," Tim said, returning Prince Teti's arm to the sling. "You might be healed in only thirty-eight days," he said with a grin.

"You make light of this?" Prince Teti asked. His voice was suddenly tinged with anger and hurt.

Taken aback by the prince's tone, Tim was reminded that he was dealing with royalty, with someone who expected to be taken seriously at all times, someone whose word meant life or death.

Hesire moved toward them to intervene, his mouth open as he tried to find words to calm Prince Teti.

Tim had a fleeting thought about royal inbreeding and mental instability, then realized that despite Prince Teti's view of himself, he was still a fifteen-year-old boy who was in pain and who had thought for several days that his arm would be cut off.

He put a hand gently on Prince Teti's shoulder and looked directly into the prince's eyes. "Yes, Prince Teti, I make light of this. Not of your pain, but of the injury. You are strong and can laugh at this broken arm. It will heal and be stronger than ever. Your will is stronger than this injury. And laughter, Prince Teti, is a strong medicine. With it you show the gods that you are at ease, that you are unafraid. It makes your body stronger and keeps your spirit light."

Hesire and Meryt stood motionless, waiting to see Teti's reaction.

"Are you unafraid?" Prince Teti asked, his tone one of curiosity, not menace.

"I was afraid, Prince Teti. All of my life I was afraid," Tim said.

He thought of the needless worries from his past – finding the right clothes for a party, auditioning for school plays, anxiously showing his first drawings to a friend, being late for an appointment, getting into the right school, mispronouncing a word when ordering at a restaurant – all of these fears that had seemed so real and large at the time. Now he saw that they had been meaningless. The energy he had wasted, the hesitation he had felt, all so unnecessary.

Tim turned to his backpack and dug inside the front pouch. Finding what he wanted, he reached for Prince Teti's cast. With a few, sure strokes he drew on the cast a vulture's spread wings, the ancient symbol that was often drawn around the king, to show divine protection.

"When I was younger, I was afraid of shadows. There," he said, capping the black marker, "your arm is protected twice."

Prince Teti looked at the drawing and smiled. "And now?" he asked.

"Strange things have happened to me, Prince Teti," Tim answered. "I have felt fear when there was no need. Fear deserted me when it should have warned me. I think I have lost my respect for fear."

As he spoke, Tim was unaware of what he was saying until the words came out, and hearing them, he felt a weight lift from his heart, a lightening of his spirit that reminded him of the buoyant mood that had come over him when he first had emerged from Kanakht's tomb and breathed the air of ancient Egypt.

The room itself seemed to grow brighter. Tim was suddenly aware of Meryt's gaze. He knew without turning to her that she was watching him, seeing him with a heart filled with love. He felt Hesire's concerns: for Prince Teti's health, for his unnamed friend's wanderings into dementia, for his own aging body, for the Two Lands. He saw the pride and confidence in Prince Teti's eyes.

Although he knew that the life and energy he felt now were confined to a stone chamber that would be reduced to crumbling dust by the time he would be born, he understood that each passing moment was real and important even though it arrived and departed in the blink of an eye. He suddenly realized that he needed to touch each moment, to let each passing second fill his life, expanding and rising.

Without thinking he slowly reached out his hand and tenderly caressed Prince Teti's shaved head, feeling the smoothness of the oil with which the prince had been anointed that morning, sensing the slight brush of the nubs of his hair, the underlying firmness of his skull, aware somehow of the dreams and hopes of the fifteen-year-old man-boy.

Hesire and Meryt stood transfixed. Aside from King Djoser, no one would ever think to touch the prince in such an intimate way.

Prince Teti stood unflinching, his eyes on Tim's face. He saw that Tim's eyes were looking past him, seeing something in another realm. He felt an energy and warmth in Tim's touch and he believed that this living god was transferring to him a touch of his immortality.

"All will be well, Prince Teti," Tim said. "All is well."

As his hand slid from Prince Teti's smooth head to his shoulder, Tim was suddenly struck with a thought.

He turned the prince so that his back was to the light. Then Tim traced the line of the wound on Prince Teti's back, up to the base of the boy's skull where the bump had been.

"Prince Teti," Tim said. "Tell me again about your injury. You said you fell. Where were you?"

"In the river, at Abu."

"No, I mean tell me where you were standing."

Prince Teti looked puzzled.

"Were you between some rocks, in an area where the water runs fast, near the shore?"

"I was standing atop a boulder, to get a view of the river."

Tim stretched an arm out at waist height. "This high?"

Prince Teti laughed. "No, Netjer Tim, a boulder." He reached his good hand over his head. "A little higher than this."

Tim thought for a moment. "How many companions were with you?"

"Three."

"Where were they?"

Prince Teti squinted his eyes as he thought back to the river. He looked at Tim, realizing what he was asking. "Yes, Netjer Tim. Nesi was behind me. He had given me his shoulder to help scale the rock. Bata was in front of me, below in the river. Rensi was on the riverbank. He is afraid of water, well actually the mud and stones at the bottom of the water."

"And you fell forward, didn't you?" Tim asked.

Prince Teti reached around to touch the wound on his back. "Nesi," he whispered.

Tim shrugged. "I don't know, Prince Teti. It seems strange that you would have a cut on your back if you fell forward. If someone threw a rock at you, then it could cut your back as it did and hit the back of your head where the bump was. It fits."

"Why?" Prince Teti said, more to himself than to Tim.

Prince Teti was seated by his father that evening when Tim was ushered into the throne room. Kanakht stood to their right. Hetephernebti stood behind Prince Teti, her hand resting on his shoulder, her fingers idly playing with the linen strap that was his sling.

Tim and Meryt stopped a few feet from the throne and bowed their heads. When King Djoser motioned him forward, Tim glanced at Hetephernebti, but her face held only the official smile she reserved for state events.

Meryt nudged him softly and he stepped forward, uncertain about the protocol.

"We are grateful for your help," King Djoser said as Tim stopped in front of him.

He raised his left hand showing Tim a flat ceramic object that was shaped like a large keyhole. Two thick beaded strands were attached to it. Each of them ended in a mass of smaller threads filled with tiny beads. The throng of threads looped together to form a necklace.

Tim hesitated, unsure what to do.

"Come forward, Netjer Tim," Prince Teti said, seeing Tim's uncertainty.

Tim stepped closer to King Djoser, whose raised throne kept the king above him.

It struck Tim that King Djoser was, in a way, the most beautiful person he had ever seen. It wasn't so much the arrangement or proportions of his face although the wide pronounced cheekbones and strong nose complemented each other perfectly. There was an undisguised intelligence in his dark, deep-set eyes and a calmness about his mouth, the full lips forming a gentle smile. He gave the impression of someone who has found an inner calm and wishes only to help everyone around him.

King Djoser stood, and bending forward, draped the object he was holding around Tim's neck. Tim felt the large ceramic counterbalance come to rest between his shoulder blades. The wide array of tiny beaded strands formed a necklace that fit snugly around his throat.

Reaching up, he slid his fingertips across the small beads, enjoying the smooth, rhythmic feel of the small bumps.

King Djoser turned his head slightly toward Hetephernebti. "He needs a new name, dear sister, a name from the Two Lands. What was it you said about him?"

"His healing?"

"Yes, but there was something else. Ah yes, that you think he came in peace."

Hetephernebti nodded, not surprised that her brother remembered her exact words.

"Welcome to Kemet, 'He Who Comes in Peace.' We present you with this holy menat of the goddess Hathor as a token of our gratitude," King Djoser said formally to Tim.

The weight of the menat's counterbalance pulled the polished strands of beads against Tim's neck as he felt himself float away from his body.

In his mind's eye he rose into a high corner of the stone room and looked down at the assemblage. King Djoser sat on a high-backed wooden chair; its surface gleaming with an overlay of gold. He wore a pleated kilt, its hem embroidered with dark brown designs. In his left hand he held a nekhekh, the short handled flail that symbolized his power. A shepherd's staff, another symbol of his office, leaned against the back of the chair. He was not wearing a wig today; his wide, full skull seemed to glow in the chamber's light. A wide, beaded pectoral swept across his bare chest in a colorful arc as it stretched from shoulder to shoulder.

Hetephernebti, her slim dark body a shadow beneath her transparent white robe, stood beside him. Black hair from her wig hung in straight woven strands to her shoulders. Kanakht, erect, but fighting against the stoop of age, stood on the other side of the king. He wore a heavier robe. His hands were clenched in fists by his side.

Young Prince Teti sat in a lower chair beside his father and in front of his aunt. He wore only a short kilt. A white slash of linen – his broken arm's sling – crossed his bare chest to his shoulder.

And standing in front of them, Tim saw himself as they did: a moderately tall, thin man, a light patina of oil on his shaved head softly reflecting the torch light. Hanging between his shoulder blades was an ancient pendant, larger than a man's open hand, its surface carved with the protective image of a vulture wearing a headdress and holding a royal flail. From this distance and angle Tim saw that his shaved head looked a little large for his slight shoulders, and his hands, although relaxed, seemed poised and confident.

With a tingling glow of recognition and satisfaction, Tim realized that he looked exactly like the ancient statue of the man who carried the name King Djoser had just spoken, the name that translated as 'He Who Comes in Peace,' the name Tim had just wondered about a day earlier: Imhotep.

His consciousness seemed to expand, growing as it had the other morning after he had examined Prince Teti. He saw the people of Kemet walking their fields, bringing in the meager harvest, he saw the reed fishing boats bobbing in the river's sluggish current, he felt the clouds of dust that rose from the donkeys as they carried bundles of papyrus from the river, or sacks of wheat from the granaries. He could smell the dryness of the land, he could hear the murmurs of the families as they gathered for their evening meal and spoke their misgivings.

He was filled with the mood of the Two Lands, its resignation to the destiny delivered by the gods, its underlying contentment to be living by the flowing source of life, its busyness in the day-to-day gathering of food, weaving of cloth, baking of bread, brewing of beer, building of huts, quarrying of stone.

His heart was filled with the ache King Djoser felt for the hunger of the Two Lands, the desire the king felt for the riches of a heavy harvest and for the gold and precious stones from the land of Kush and for the tall, straight cedar wood from the land of Retenu. He saw a vision of the land as it would be in the years long after King Djoser's reign: the serene Sphinx rising from the plateau near Giza, the forest of pillars in the temples at Karnak, the sandstone beauty of the mortuary temple of Queen Hatshepsut, the hidden riches in the Valley of Kings.

In a spiraling swirl, his thoughts and imaginings swept through the Two Lands, following the river back to Waset, back to King Djoser's sprawling palace grounds, back to this small stone chamber where he knew that he had been transformed into the man who would forever be remembered as Imhotep.

AN OFFERING TO KHNUM

Kanakht wondered why blood wasn't dripping from his tightly clenched fists.

He had gotten word from Nimaasted this morning that the outlander Brian had somehow escaped the assassins at Khmunu. *It was impossible,* he silently fumed. One man against three assassins and Nimaasted, although the priest really couldn't be counted on for much. And then Nimaasted claimed that a god had materialized in the middle of the night, shouted a warning to Brian and then killed one of the attackers.

If Nimaasted was correct, then the god who had miraculously materialized at Khmunu and thwarted his plans was standing right here in front of him, wearing a sacred menat draped in place by King Djoser's own hands. And he – Kanakht, vizier to the king, second in power only to the throne – he was standing beside King Djoser, his face set in a practiced mask, smiling falsely while the blood pounded through his brain and a humming sound from inside his own head filled his ears with such a noise that it almost drowned out King Djoser's voice.

"Imhotep," the king repeated. "Yes, the name suits you."

"I am honored, King Djoser," Tim answered, bowing his head.

"I have been traveling the river from Iunu up to Abu, Imhotep. I have talked with priests and prophets. I have met with seers and fortunetellers. I have looked for magic and miracles. Akhet, the season of the inundation, is drawing near. I have sacrificed to Hapi, Lord of the Fishes and Birds of the Marshes. I have called on him to bring the great waters and the silt to feed my people.

"Has he heard? Will he come?" King Djoser asked the questions softly.

Tim wasn't sure if King Djoser expected him to answer, or if the king was thinking aloud. His confusion vanished when the king turned his wide head directly toward him and waited.

The night he had met King Djoser, after he had tamped down his desire for Meryt, Tim had sat awake trying to recall everything he had read about the ancient king.

There were two memorable events during the reign of King Djoser: the building of the Step Pyramid at Saqqara and the seven-year famine. From what Meryt and Paneb had told Tim, the famine was now in its seventh year. If the histories of the five-thousand-years-ago period were accurate, then the flood would return to its full strength this year, bringing the rich soil from inner Africa to the sandy riverbanks of the Nile.

The Step Pyramid was remembered because its ancient stones still rose from the plateau at Saqqara. The famine and its length were mentioned in ancient texts, but more visibly, the events were commemorated on a stone monument or stele that described a dream King Djoser had. On the stele he had recorded his anguish over the hunger in Kemet and how the gods spoke to him, telling him that they would relieve the famine. The god who spoke to King Djoser, Tim remembered, was Khnum, the ram-headed god.

"King Djoser," Tim answered trying to recall the words that had been carved on the stele, "Hapi will come. The river will swell, the plants will flourish, bending under their fruit, everything will be brought forth."

King Djoser stared at him, the confident smile unchanging, assessing his words. Tim realized that the king must be surrounded by people who constantly gave him the answers he wanted to hear – or that they wanted him to hear. He wondered how a ruler could ever get honest advice.

"King Djoser," he began again, hesitantly, hoping that he remembered correctly. "There is more."

The king gave an almost imperceptible nod of his head.

"There is a temple at Abu."

"To Khnum," King Djoser answered.

"Yes. Make a gift of land to the temple. Enrich it. Khnum will welcome the gift. He will embrace you. He will come to you in a dream, King Djoser, and put your heart at ease."

The walls of the chamber turned black, curved and began to move toward each other. As they grew closer, all Kanakht could see was a pinpoint of light centered around the face of the man-god Imhotep.

It was a struggle for Kanakht to stay upright and to keep this mask of unconcern on his face. As if from a great distance, he heard King Djoser's low voice, but the words were indistinct. It didn't matter. He had heard enough.

Where did this Imhotep come from?

How could he know what he knew?

For a moment Kanakht had thought that the significance of Imhotep's suggestion would be lost on King Djoser, but he knew that he was grasping at straws. King Djoser was not the warrior his father had been, but he was ten times the politician. He knew the birth names of every official and every priest. He knew the names of all their wives and children. He understood every family connection in the Two Lands.

The high priest at the temple of Khnum was Sennufer, an unassuming, pious man, perfectly suited for a small temple at the far reaches of Kemet. By itself an offering of land to him would be harmless.

But such an offering would bind the holy man more closely to the throne. More importantly, it would inspire more loyalty in the priest's son, and that son was Sekhmire, commander of King Djoser's personal guard.

Assuming that the commander would remain steadfast to King Djoser, Kanakht had not even considered bringing Sekhmire into his plot to kill the king. Instead, Kanakht had recruited Makare in Khmunu and Makare's brother Nesi, one of Prince Teti's guards. Kanakht expected that after King Djoser and Teti were killed, Sekhmire would be realistic, realize that the power had shifted and understand that it was in his best interest to align himself with Kanakht as the vizier took over the throne.

But if Sekhmire felt too much loyalty to the dead king, it was possible he would seek revenge for King Djoser. And it was possible that his increased loyalty would lead to heightened vigilance and the plot would be uncovered. Who knew what rumors were leaking from Makare's mouth or – Kanakht almost passed out at the thought – from the fat lips of the priest Djefi?

Well, Kanakht thought, steeling himself, I knew there were risks. If this Imhotep was not part of my original calculations, then I must change my calculations. Djefi will be here soon. I'll push him, frighten him. When I'm finished he'll know that this is no game we are playing.

Kemet itself depends on us.

It was with little gestures that Sekhmire was bound to King Djoser: the way the king extended his hand seeking Sekhmire's help as he disembarked from the royal barge; how the king turned his back to no one but Sekhmire, showing his complete trust; how he listened without interruption to Sekhmire's reports, acknowledging the commander's authority over the security of the Two Lands.

Sekhmire was well paid. His spacious home had a beautiful garden and a pond. His wife was supplied with enough servants to make her life agreeable and pleasant. He never wanted for oils or meat or bread.

His life was good. Respect, authority, love, and comfort were his.

When he first heard news that Makare, his commander at Khmunu had met privately with Kanakht, he had taken no action, but remembered the incident. Then word had reached him that Makare had begun to visit a letter-writing scribe to draft private messages rather than using the scribe who was attached to the compound at Khmunu. Sekhmire had hoped that Makare was simply writing love letters to a mistress, but he kept a closer watch on the commander in distant Khmunu.

Then the priest Djefi had suddenly become active, leaving his desert oasis and visiting Waja-Hur, of all people, at the same time Kanakht was there. Makare had been at the meeting also.

While Sekhmire focused on the travels of Kanakht and the suspicious activity of Makare, Prince Teti was injured at the other end of the country. Sekhmire hoped it was an accident, but in his heart, he suspected that it was something sinister.

One of Prince Teti's guards, Bata, had been accused of trying to drown the prince, and so Sekhmire had ordered him arrested. But Sekhmire knew it was no coincidence that Makare's brother Nesi was with the prince when the 'accident' happened.

Sekhmire had dreaded the conversation he knew he needed to have with King Djoser and so he had steeled himself the morning after Prince Teti's fall when King Djoser had summoned him for a private audience.

"Tell me what you know," King Djoser had commanded in his quiet way.

Sekhmire had. He told the king about the travels of Kanakht, the sudden activity of Djefi, the private letters that Makare was having written.

"I did not think of Makare's brother Nesi, King Djoser," he admitted.

"He was brought to your attention by Kanakht, wasn't he?" King Djoser had asked, knowing the answer.

Sekhmire had nodded.

"Who is watching Makare?" the king had asked.

"A man named Ankhu," Sekhmire had said. "He is a member of Makare's guard and my wife's cousin."

"And Nesi?"

"I am not having him watched right now, King Djoser."

"He is Makare's brother?" the king had asked.

Sekhmire had wondered how King Djoser kept track of the relationships of an insignificant guard. He knew that the king had other sources of information, but still he was amazed at the king's wide knowledge.

"Nesi and the other guard, a man named Rensi, returned here with Prince Teti. They are away from the palace visiting their families. The third guard, Bata, is under arrest at Abu. I have assigned two of my men, Katep and Bai, to accompany Prince Teti while he is with us."

Djoser waited patiently. Sekhmire reviewed his answer, knowing that something was missing, something that the king wanted to hear.

"Nesi is Makare's brother, your lord, yes."

"And you suspect Makare and Kanakht are plotting against me?"

Sekhmire closed his eyes, ashamed of his failure. It was so obvious to him now.

"I will have Nesi arrested immediately," Sekhmire said.

Afraid of the king's anger and embarrassed by his failure to anticipate Nesi's action, Sekhmire was stunned when King Djoser spoke gently, with approval.

"You have done well, Sekhmire, anticipating my desire as always. Do not arrest Nesi. Instead, we will watch him and see who meets with him. The same with Kanakht and this priest Djefi. See who they meet, watch where they travel. It is better, Sekhmire, to have a known enemy, than to be surprised. We will let them plot and see who else is drawn to them."

Sekhmire had nodded his understanding, amazed again at King Djoser's knowledge and planning.

King Djoser stood, indicating that the interview was over. He stepped to Sekhmire and placed a hand on the commander's arm. His face lit up as he smiled, the troubles of a brewing revolt forgotten for the moment. "What of your son, Sekhmire? Tell me, do you still plan to turn little Siptah into a warrior like yourself?"

And now Sekhmire had learned that King Djoser was about to honor the god Khnum with a grant of land. His father's temple would grow in importance.

He stood outside the royal chambers and breathed deeply, his heart filled with love for King Djoser. He would never let anyone harm the king.

A cluster of blue water lilies floated along the edge of the small pond in the walled garden. Tim leaned against the rough trunk of a carob tree. Meryt sat along the edge of the pond, her legs half immersed in the water.

His backpack with his sketchbook and first aid kit lay untouched on the grass beside him.

Meryt had led him to the garden after his audience with King Djoser. She had sensed that he needed a quiet place to think and to digest what had happened. She had given him the time and space, sitting quietly, enjoying the shade and solitude. Her mind also was filled with questions, but she saw that Tim, or Imhotep as King Djoser had renamed him, had questions he needed to answer for himself.

And so she waited, content to be with him but growing eager to resolve the questions about them, about his feelings for her. He was so different from her brother and from the boys she had known growing up. He was hesitant about some things, yet direct and confident about others. She sensed that he wanted to be with her, but he never approached her and she wasn't sure what he would do if she approached him. He enjoyed touching stones, trees, leaves, and fabric, everything they encountered, but he stayed his hand from touching her. He looked at her hungrily at times, but never gave voice to his desire.

Just this morning she had seen him stirring, strong and ready beneath his kilt when he awoke, but he had hidden it, denying his desire.

So unlike a man – or a god, she thought.

Meryt leaned forward and looked at her reflection in the still water of the pond. One eye looked back at her, the other, as it did sometimes, drifted away. The cast eye had been the sign that the gods favored her.

Her parents had decided to find a way to bring her to Hetephernebti's attention even when she was a baby. When Meryt was five years old, Hetephernebti passed by her while she was standing at the front of a crowd at a festival. The priestess had stopped to touch her, as she often did with children. Seeing Meryt's wandering eye, Hetephernebti had paused a little longer and spoke with Meryt.

Pleased with the intelligence in the answers the little girl gave, Hetephernebti had sought Meryt's parents and offered to bring Meryt to the Temple of Re for training. For Meryt's parents, it was the answer to years of prayer, for Meryt it was natural progression. Her earliest memories were of her mother telling her that she was special and that the gods would seek her service.

She had lived at the Temple of Re for eight years now. The rhythms of the festivals, the words of the sacred hymns, the lightness of the anointing oils and the acrid sweetness of incense were part of her. Hetephernebti had come to depend on Meryt, and Meryt, in return, gave the priestess her love and loyalty.

But the years of familiarity with the god Re and his loving priestess had brought a curious growth in Meryt's heart.

Hetephernebti spoke of Re's blessing, of his desire that people should enjoy their lives, that they should live fully aware of everything around them. Meryt had taken Hetephernebti's words to heart.

When the hawk-god Horus flew overhead, she not only saw him, she also heard the sound of his wings as he climbed higher in the sky. When the god dove through the air, she imagined how the wind must feel as he cut through it.

The water from Iteru was not just a rippling brown surface. It was something to be touched and tasted. She had slapped her hands hard and flat against its surface, feeling the unseen strength of the water, she had thrown handfuls of it into the air and felt it rain down on her in light splashes.

Even the warm fingers of Re were subject to her wondering mind. She felt the difference in heat from morning to midday and into the dusk. She coated herself with the river's wet mud and allowed Re to bake it, the sun's strength tightening the mud, turning it into crumbling dust.

Surrounded by a world that delighted and fascinated her with its sound and colors, its touch and tastes, Meryt began to understand the relationships between the heat and the wind, currents of the river and the rhythms of the land. She felt herself to be an extension of the Two Lands, as much a part of Kemet as the trees and the sand and the gods themselves.

And she began to wonder if the gods gave rise to the land or if the land and the longing hearts of the people of Kemet brought the gods into existence. When she held her extended fingers to shield her eyes so she could look at the sun, she saw a fiery disk, not a god. Watching the flight of a hawk, she was mesmerized by the beauty of its movement, but she saw a bird, not a god.

Hippos, crocodiles, ibises, jackals: all were gods and all, in Meryt's eyes, were deserving of her wonder, but no more than the workings of her fingers, the flights of her dreams, the scratchy bark of the date palm tree, the earthy aroma of baking bread, the sweet juiciness of a fig.

She lived in a land of miracles and wonders. If the hawk was a god, then so was the sparrow. If the sun was a god, then why not the stars? If King Djoser was a god, then why not Hetephernebti? Why not Tim, and why not her mother, her father, even herself?

Tim looked across the garden, his eyes unseeing, his mind focusing on his breathing. He felt the moist garden air move through his nostrils, swell against the back of his throat and draw down into his lungs as he pushed his belly out lightly.

He concentrated on the temperature of the air, picturing it as a healthy blue as it entered him and a darker shade as he expelled it, taking with it his anxiety and confusion. What was left was calmness, not an answer yet, but a placidity that would allow him to slowly re-enter his consciousness through the smells, sounds and sights that surrounded him. He would allow his sensations to unfold, embracing his environment and bringing an openness that would allow him to re-center himself.

Although he had never taken lessons in meditation, he had searched for ways to settle himself as an experiment, looking for new ways to experience his sensations.

In his mind's eye he pictured his breath, but his concentration wavered.

His awareness bounced in splintered thoughts from the living face of King Djoser, to the three syllables of the name Imhotep, to the harsh shadows that marked the angry face of Kanakht, to the strange out-of-the-body experience he had undergone in the king's chamber.

He closed his eyes to block the distraction of the colors of the garden and the lithe form of Meryt sitting by the pond. He heard the slight rustle of the leaves of the tree above him, the liquid murmur of the water where Meryt stirred the pond with her smooth, brown legs.

He wanted to fall backward on the ground, raise his arms to the sky and split open, freeing his spirit to fly across this strange land.

Refocusing part of his mind on his breathing, he allowed his thoughts to stream undirected, overwhelming and exhausting themselves until finally his attention turned wholly back to his breathing. One … two … three breaths without thought. He felt the slow, rhythmic throb of his heartbeat. Moving outward, he sensed warmth on his left arm, unprotected from the sun by the uneven shade of the small carob tree. He opened his eyes, his mind still and clear.

Meryt's narrow back was turned to him, her head bent slightly as she looked down at the water of the pond. The soft curve of her right breast came into view as she reached down to trail her fingers through the water.

She felt him watching and turned her head, her shoulder swiveling around toward him. The sunlight highlighted the fragile line of her collarbone and swept across the smooth skin of her chest. He saw the darker circles at the tips of her small breasts, the small, raised nipples. Her skin was drawn tight against her ribs as she twisted in place to look at him. The tender curve of her lower stomach arced downward toward soft, dark tufts of hair, just hidden by her slender legs.

A flush of desire swept through him. Looking up at her face, he saw that she was watching his eyes, had seen where he looked. She was waiting: open, willing, and patient.

For the first time he was not embarrassed by his desire. Here, now, this time and place, it felt right and natural. He had changed from Tim, lost and wandering, to Imhotep, as much a part of this ancient land as the carob tree behind him or the warm desert air that carried the lotus blossom's fragrance.

He stood, his eyes never leaving her face. She turned away from the pond and stood also, her arms at her side brushing against the narrow linen belt she wore around her naked waist. Slowly he stepped toward her, certain of his desire, feeling that he had been reborn when King Djoser renamed him, that he was truly a part of this ancient land now and that touching her and holding her was exactly what he was meant to do.

When she was within reach, he lifted a hand to her face and brushed his thumb tenderly across her cheek. Her eyes were bright with happiness, a smile played on her lips. He put his hands on her shoulders, slid his fingers down her arms and took her hands, interlocking his fingers with hers.

Bending his head down to hers, he lightly kissed her forehead and her temples. She turned her face up to his and their mouths met. As they kissed, he felt her press closer to him, her bare skin touching him softly, then pressing harder, generating heat, making him feel reborn and alive.

She broke away from their kiss and holding his hand, led him through the garden; down the hallway of the palace to the room they shared. At the entrance, they hesitated as they heard a sound within.

Hetephernebti was standing inside. On the bed lay new linen kilts.

"Good afternoon, dear Meryt, Lord Imhotep," she said, her voice and ever-present smile not betraying her happiness at seeing them flushed with desire for each other. She had noticed their mutual attraction when she first saw them together. Through the weeks she had avoided asking Meryt about it, but it had been obvious to her that the fondness the two felt for each other had been growing.

She felt guilty that she was interrupting them now, but there was nothing she could do.

"King Djoser has sent you new clothing and has invited you to accompany him on his trip to Abu to survey the island and banks of the river for an appropriate gift for the Temple of Khnum."

"Thank you, High Priestess," Tim answered, aware that his voice was husky with desire. "When will we be leaving?"

Hetephernebti frowned a little as she looked to Meryt.

"I am sorry, little sister," she began, then seeing Meryt's stunned face, she added quickly, "no, no, you are going also. I am sorry for the timing." She turned back to Tim. "When my brother is seized with an idea, he acts. I am to bring you to King Djoser now. His barge is waiting. I am sorry, but we leave now."

AMBUSH IN TAHTA

Brian saw the two men waiting to ambush them.

He was walking between the two donkeys, holding the short ropes that looped around their necks. Tama rode on the donkey to his right, her body rocking lightly with the donkey's plodding gait.

The donkey to Brian's left carried their supplies: flat round loaves of bread, skins filled with water, a fresh robe and ostrich feather for Tama to wear once they reached Waset, and trade goods: rolls of linen, small ceramic bottles, some filled with cooking oils others with massage oils, cones of salt and a few pieces of jewelry.

They had left the town of Tahta on the west bank of the river an hour ago and were following the road south toward Waset. They had crossed the River Iteru as soon as they left Khmunu, boarding their skittish donkeys onto a wooden raft that was poled across the slow-moving river. The ferryman, recognizing Tama, refused her offering of a small bottle of perfumed oil until she explained that it was for his wife and daughters to enjoy.

The men Brian saw now were hiding behind a cluster of three palm trees up along the sandy road. Tall date palms, shorter carob trees and thorny acacia trees lined the road. Greener sycamore trees grew closer to the riverbank. All of the trees were dusty, their leaves curled up as evening fell.

Brian had watched the men move from tree to tree, trying to find a hiding place closer to the road. One of them carried a short, thick club, the other might have had a knife, Brian wasn't sure; unpolished stone didn't glitter like a metal knife would.

"I see them, Brian."

Tama's voice was calm and even.

It was always calm and even, he'd learned.

"I won't let them hurt you," he said, trying to match her calm voice.

"I know," she answered.

They had been traveling for five days, following the river upstream; slowly heading south to Waset where Tama planned to meet Hetephernebti, and where Brian hoped to find Tim.

Their destination lay another nine days ahead.

Travel was at a slow walking pace. Although Tama sometimes rode one of the donkeys, Brian always walked, happy for the exercise. They rested when they were hungry, tired or sleepy. They stopped and talked at each small village, some as small as three or four mud huts grouped around a stone circle that marked a common cooking fire.

There was no wealth here.

The men and children wore no clothing, some of the women wore a short kilt, others just a rough linen belt. Their hands were callused and dirty; their skin was weathered by the sun and the sand.

Their expressions when they saw Brian and Tama approaching were eager with anticipation of news.

By the second encounter, Brian began to understand: He was traveling among the people of a stone-age culture. Although the great river united them, making long-distance travel feasible, most of the population worked, loved, gave birth to their children and died within sight of the mud hut in which they had been born.

Brian soon realized that Tama saw the world differently than he did. Although they shared the same sense of observation and evaluation that he used when he played baseball, she extended it to everything and she didn't draw the conclusions he naturally made.

In high school Brian had been stronger, faster and simply more athletic than most of the other players. As the competition evened out in college, he had learned that he couldn't just hope that he could throw faster than a batter could swing. He had learned that on some days his fastball wasn't fast enough so he had to depend more on a curveball or placement of a change-up, tantalizingly just out of reach. If he saw that the outfielders were shading to left field, he couldn't hope that he could pull the ball past them, he had to shorten his swing and punch the ball the other way.

He had learned to observe himself and other athletes honestly and to use his knowledge to give him an edge, or in those rare cases where the others were simply better than he was, he learned to play his hardest and to graciously acknowledge defeat.

There was always tomorrow and another game, another chance.

Tama had the same honest way of viewing everything, but she didn't filter the world through her expectations.

When Brian saw a man running or throwing he evaluated the man's speed and strength and compared it to his, determining whether he could beat him. Tama made no comparisons, instead accepting each man's speed or strength as an expression of the man. For Tama, faster or stronger didn't mean 'better.' It just meant faster or stronger. She didn't hope that on another day he would be faster or slower, she accepted what he was when she saw him and refused to extend the observation to 'what might be' or 'what could be.'

While one sunset could be redder than another, or filtered through a distant haze of clouds, it didn't make it more 'beautiful' to Tama.

An ox was different from a donkey, not better. It might be stronger for plowing but it wasn't as suited for riding. How could one view one as better than the other? A hawk had more speed and was more deadly than a goose, but a goose could feed a hungry family. Which was better?

When Brian had come to understand her views, his first thought was that she wouldn't be much fun at a sports bar arguing whether Willie Mays was better than Joe DiMaggio, or settling the dispute over whether Muhammad Ali was truly 'The Greatest.'

He tried to see what the world would look like through her eyes. But he had spent too many years watching television advertisements, answering which was his favorite color, his favorite zodiac sign or baseball player or ice cream flavor or hair color. Was he a leg man or a breast man? Blondes or brunettes? Yankees or Red Sox?

As they learned each other's languages better, Brian found that Tama's way of viewing the world went far beyond her reluctance to draw conclusions or comparisons. Counting, organizing, and grouping were concepts she disliked. He sometimes caught a glimpse of the depth of her views, but never fully understood them.

"Tree," she repeated in English one day as they rested in the shade of a grove of date palm trees.

Brian nodded. "Tree," he said, touching the trunk. Then he repeated the word in Egyptian.

"Yes," Tama said. "But this," she knocked her fist against the trunk of the tree, "this is not a tree. 'Tree' is the word we use, but this," she knocked on it again, "this is real, Brian, not just the wind and the sounds we use to name it, not just the picture we have in our heads. Do you see there is a difference between our name for something and the thing?"

Brian nodded, although he wasn't sure why this was important.

"The words, Brian, they separate us from the world. When we name something we think we understand it. But the words divide us from what is real. 'Tree' is not real. This," she touched the tree again, "this is real."

The sun was down and only a leftover reddish glow seeped out of the western sky.

As Tama and Brian neared the palm grove two men separated themselves from the trees and blocked the narrow dusty trail.

"What's in the packs?" asked the taller man, who was holding the club. Brian saw that the 'knife' in the other man's hand was just a short, pointed stick, sharp enough to stab with, but not edged for slicing.

"Greetings," Tama said, ignoring the question. She slid from the donkey on Brian's side. "Don't hurt them," she whispered from behind him.

She opened the sack on the near side of the donkey. "I'll show you," she said louder to the two men.

Brian felt her push some linen into the waist of his kilt at the small of his back. "Keep your front to them," she whispered.

She slid between Brian and the pack donkey, taking the lead rope from Brian. She walked up the path where the two men waited, pulling the donkey behind her.

Brian tensed as he saw shadows move ahead of them in the grove; there were more than just the two men in front of him. He knew he could rush the two men on the road and knock them down before they could do any harm. The taller man barely came up to Brian's shoulders and they both looked weak and undernourished. But he didn't know how many more were lurking in the shadows.

He looked from the grove to Tama who had stopped just in front of the men.

"Here," she said. "There is some bread and some salt cones, some linen, which your wife might like, and some oils. The plain bottles are cooking oils, the others are oils for your skin. In the small roll of linen there are a few pieces of silver jewelry."

Brian couldn't believe that she was telling them about the jewelry, but he trusted her. She had much more knowledge of the people.

As the taller man approached the donkey, Tama dropped the rope and stepped back to give him room. He dug into the pack, lifting a roll of linen out into the fading light. He pushed it back into the bag and dug around for a moment before bringing out a ceramic oil bottle. Pulling out the stopper, he sniffed at the oil. He returned the bottle to the sack and bent over to pick up the rope, his back to Brian and Tama.

As if she knew what Brian was thinking, Tama held her right hand behind her back, motioning for Brian to stay where he was.

"We'll be taking this and the donkeys, too," the man said.

Tama nodded as if he had made a reasonable request.

"I understand," she said. "Will you leave us a skin of water? The road is long and dry."

The man started to walk away with the donkey. "The river is right over there. There's plenty of water there," he said without turning back to look at Tama and Brian. "Go get the other donkey," he said to his partner.

The small man walked cautiously toward Brian, his fist tight around the short wooden knife. Brian let go of the rope as the man got nearer, careful to keep his back turned away from him.

When he got closer, Brian could see that the man was young, no more than fifteen, possibly the taller man's son. He looked frightened, but whether it was of Brian or the taller bandit, Brian couldn't tell.

When the boy hesitated to lean down to pick up the rope, Brian thought of what Tama had said. He smiled at the boy and said, "I won't hurt you."

Brian saw that the boy was shaking as he picked up the rope and turned to leave. The donkey balked at moving, so Brian reached out and swatted it lightly. It lurched forward.

As the boy led the donkey past Tama, the priestess touched his arm lightly and whispered, "I'm sorry."

The boy ducked his head low, as if avoiding a striking hand, and led the donkey to the older man. Darkness fell as they disappeared into the shadowy trees.

"There were others in the trees," Brian said to Tama as he joined her on the path.

She nodded. "I saw them."

"I would have fought them. All of them."

Tama studied him for a moment. "You would have won," she said. Then she added, "Do you know who they were?"

Brian was puzzled by the question. He didn't know anybody here in ancient Egypt. "No," he answered.

"I think they were the rest of his family. They must be very needy."

"How can you know that?"

"If the people hiding in the trees had been other bandits they would have come out into the open. A show of force would be more effective. If they were not other bandits, then they were either friends or family of the bandits or else they were strangers. If they were strangers, then they would have helped us, or at least come out to see what was going on. And it would be very unusual for all of these people to just happen to be at the same place at the same time.

"So," she continued, "the people in the trees had to know the two men who were on the road, but they couldn't have been accomplices. They must have been children, wives and perhaps a grandparent or two. I'm sure you would have defeated them."

Brian looked down at the road, embarrassed. "I'm sorry," he said. "I didn't figure that out. I wouldn't hit children or women."

Caught up in understanding the encounter, Tama had spoken without thinking of Brian's feelings. She heard the hurt in his voice and saw his shoulders slump. She didn't understand why Brian depended so much on her approval, but she knew that he did. He was so strong, so physically imposing and secure in his strength and his movements, yet he seemed fragile at times.

She touched his shoulder with her fingertips and felt the muscles twitch as he looked up at her suddenly.

"I know you wouldn't hurt them, Brian. I was just stating a fact. I know you would defend me. I thank you. Your bravery gives me strength. And we will need your bravery yet tonight."

He looked up at her, questioning. He felt her hand still on his shoulder and hoped that she was leaving it there because she enjoyed the feel of his skin as much as he enjoyed her touch.

"When I saw the man's crude club and the boy's little knife I knew we weren't in danger. You could easily have subdued them. Then I saw the fear in the boy's face and the desperation in the man's. So I decided to offer them our goods. They must be facing hard times to attempt to rob us. True, I am only a woman, but you are a most imposing man.

"But then he got arrogant and greedy. Instead of accepting a gift, he decided to take everything, including our water skins, even after I asked if we could keep one. So now we must find them and get everything back."

"How?" he asked.

"Turn around," she answered.

There was a three-quarter moon and Tama wanted them to be less visible, so instead of wearing the linen robe she had hidden in Brian's waistband, she carried it. He had removed his white kilt and was carrying it coiled in a tight roll.

They walked along the road, listening for sounds of the family.

Brian was worried that the bandits would get away but Tama reassured him that they would be eager to eat the bread they had taken. She thought they would move away from the road and set up a camp for the night.

Soon they saw a small campfire off in the trees, away from the river. Tama and Brian found a grassy spot to wait. "I want to let them eat first," she said.

After they settled, Brian thought about the bandits. "Does this happen often?" he asked.

She shrugged and then realized that the movement was barely visible in the dark. "I don't know," she said.

"At Khmunu there is very little crime. Sometimes men will get angry with each other and there is a fight. A man and wife may argue or fight. But why would you take something from someone? I understand if it is food and you are hungry. But if you take clothing or jewelry and wear it, everyone would see it. And a donkey? No, never."

"It must be different out here," he said.

She thought for a moment and then laughed. "I was going to say that it could not be different, but then, we have no donkeys, do we?"

They were quiet for a little while.

Brian thought about the encounter on the roadway and how Tama, wearing only a narrow belt and reed sandals had walked unafraid toward an armed man. He thought about how the blood had pounded through his veins as he watched her and worried for her. For a little while, when the man with the club had walked toward her, Brian had been torn between running forward to protect her and following her request to stay where he was. If the man had started to raise his club, Brian would have been there in five hurried strides. When he would have reached the man, Brian knew he would have been out of control.

Tama thought about the unexpected pleasure she had taken in touching Brian's shoulder and how his statement that he wouldn't hurt children or women had affected her. And, always honest with herself, she admitted that knowing he was behind her had given her more courage to face the men than she would have had if she had been alone. He seemed solid and reliable, and, strangely, more interested in helping her than in trying to prove himself innocent of the killing at Khmunu.

"It is different in my country," Brian said, breaking the stillness. "In my country people are in love with things – with clothing and jewelry and ..." he thought of huge, gas-guzzling SUVs, two-hundred-dollar sneakers, big screen televisions and everything else that made modern Americans so obsessed with material wealth. "And other things. They would take things they do not need, just to have them," he continued.

"I think people in my country are more violent. They kill each other all the time. Husbands kill their wives, strangers kill each other, and children even kill their parents."

Tama waited to be sure he was finished speaking.

"Are they angry with each other? So angry that they want to kill? I don't understand."

Brian scooted closer to her. "It is very easy to kill someone in my country. We have," he didn't know the word for weapons, "we have sticks that can kill from far away, just by pointing them. We have things that fly and can drop fire on towns and kill everyone there. We have many, many more people and they live very close to each other. Some of them work very hard and have very little. It makes them angry."

"Do they have food? Do they have wheat and salt and oil?"

"Tama, there is so much more to have in my country. And everyone wants everything. When they see that other people have things that they want themselves, sometimes they become crazy. They think the world isn't fair and that they have to take what they want to make it fair."

"Isn't there enough for everyone?"

"I don't know," he sighed. "Some countries are very, very poor. They may not have enough, I don't know. My country is very wealthy, but people don't want to share. No, that's not right. We just believe that if someone wants something they should work to get it."

"That seems fair," she said.

"Yes, but, somehow things have gotten messed up. I read that ..." he began.

"You can read?" she interrupted him. "You are a priest?"

"No, most people can read in my country. Where was I?"

"Working to get things."

"No, that wasn't it. Oh, somehow just a few people own almost everything and they don't want to share. And if one of the people who doesn't have anything gets lucky and becomes one of the people who has everything then they won't share."

Suddenly Brian felt very sad. Tama saw his eyes and read his heart. At times he reminded her of Waja-Hur before his illness. The priest was beloved by the people because he felt their fears. He sincerely tried to help them reach Khert-Neter. Brian seemed to be filled with the same desire to help others and the ability to feel their pain.

Brian sounded unhappy with his own country, and lost here in hers. Yet he continued to try to help others. She had heard the stories about his heroics at To-She and she had seen his concern for others with her own eyes. She didn't believe that he was a god, but she thought that he had a god-like depth to him, that his heart was as light as Ma'at's feather, despite the pain he felt for others.

"Why are you here?" she asked, reaching up and stroking his cheek.

Brian moved his face against her hand. He knew that if he looked at her and saw desire in her eyes that he would be overwhelmed with his desire for her. But he was afraid he would see pity in her eyes instead.

"I don't know, Tama. I didn't try to come here.

"I don't really know where here is. I mean, when Diane and I came out of the tomb I didn't know anything was different. Then after we got to To-She I knew something really weird had happened, but I didn't know what to do. I was scared, really scared, but I tried not to show it."

He looked at her and shrugged. "It doesn't do any good to worry, you just do your best and figure things out. Then Tim found us and explained what had happened and how we could get away. But then Diane wouldn't talk to me.

"And then I helped Neswy and that little girl and I started to feel like I was brought here for a reason, that there was some kind of purpose for it. But I really don't believe in that stuff. Sorry, I know you're a priestess, but I never really got into religion. So this whole "here for a reason" doesn't feel right. I'm just trying to figure things out and do the right thing."

Tama looked at his face. His eyes stared into the distance as he fought against the loneliness she heard in his voice. She saw him as a powerful natural force, a vortex of compassion and strength, absorbing others' pain and offering comfort without expectations. She was drawn to his strength and now, as she saw his unease, she wanted to comfort him, to offer, if not her strength, then at least relief from his anxiety.

"What is the right thing, Brian?" she asked, caressing his shaved head and the back of his neck.

He reached up and grabbed her wrist, gently, but firmly.

"Tama," he said in a rough whisper, "I know that it is different here and if I was normal, I'd be jumping at every chance. I think you are incredibly beautiful. But ..." he stopped speaking as she placed a finger on his lips.

"Words," she said, shaking her head. "They are powerful, Brian. They bring our thoughts to life, but sometimes they keep us from what is real."

She leaned close and replaced her finger with her lips, inhaling his breath as she kissed him.

Her hand slid down his chest.

He reached for her, but she already was moving, straddling him as he sat on the grass. For a delicious moment he felt her hover over him and then she moved closer.

Pulling back from their kiss, she looked at him, her eyes seeking his. She saw his uncertainty give way to hunger and desire. In her eyes, he saw eagerness and playfulness.

Sitting on the grass, Brian reached back with one arm to steady himself as they moved to her rhythm. He pressed his other hand against her back feeling the muscles tighten as they made love.

He found himself laughing with her, finding a joy in their lovemaking that removed him from time. There was her touch, her smell, the taste of her mouth and there was nothing else.

ON THE ROAD TO WASET

A rustling noise woke Brian from a deep, exhausted sleep.

The night air seemed to absorb the faint moonlight that filtered through the palm fronds. He heard the soft sound again, coming from his left. He sat up and, turning to his left, he saw a glowing shape approaching through the bushes.

He rubbed his eyes and the shape took form as the goddess Ma'at dressed in a pure white linen robe that reached to her ankles. Black hair fell to her shoulders in braided plaits and an ostrich feather, the symbol of truth, rose over her head.

"The children have fallen asleep. It is time," Ma'at said in the calm voice he recognized as Tama's.

He had no idea what she was talking about.

She held out her hand. "Ma'at will visit them and reclaim the donkeys. Come with me, but stay in the shadows beyond their fire. Don't worry," she said, "if I need help, I will signal you. Come, before the adults fall asleep."

He stood and realized his kilt had come off sometime during their lovemaking.

"Over there," she said smiling.

He found it on the grass behind him and wrapped it around his waist.

He realized that he hadn't spoken to her since they had been together. Then, remembering her words from earlier in the night, he decided that their actions had spoken more than any words would.

He nodded his understanding and walked over to her. She turned to leave and then suddenly turned back to him and reaching up, cupped his face with both hands. She studied his face, trying to read his mood, to understand his silence. He smiled at her and opened his mouth to thank her, and then catching himself again, he simply smiled and turning his head, lightly kissed the palm of her hand.

Tama's speculation about the attackers proved eerily accurate.

Light from the small campfire showed three small shapes curled together just at the edge of the circle of flickering flames. An elderly man sat near them, propped against a tree, his head turned to the side, his mouth open as he snored. The larger man, the one who had robbed them, sat cross-legged by the fire, an empty water skin by his side. The boy who had been with him was across the fire sitting beside his mother who was examining a roll of linen. Ceramic jars from the packs sat by her side.

Tama stopped by the edge of the camp and motioned for Brian to wait there. Then she walked into the open area. As she moved, she seemed to transform. Always graceful, she seemed now to float rather than walk. Her shoulders were drawn back more; her arms stayed straighter, her wrists were bent slightly, opening her palms in front of her.

The woman saw her first. Her fingers, busy examining the threading of the linen, stopped moving. Her face froze in astonishment. Her husband, seeing his wife's expression, followed her eyes. He stood clumsily and unconsciously wiped his hands on his dirty thighs.

He started to speak, but Tama raised a hand, stopping him.

"Have you done ma'at?" she asked, evoking the ritual question that was asked during the weighing of the heart, when ma'at meant to live an honest life without lying, cheating, or harming anyone.

Knowing the answer, the woman looked at her husband and wondered if Anubis himself would burst into the small clearing and use his jackal's fangs to rip her husband's heavy heart from his chest.

"Have you done ma'at?" Tama repeated, her tone quiet but insistent.

The man looked at the ground, fearful, knowing that if he lied to the goddess he would die the final death and never see Khert-Neter.

"A woman was walking on the road with her servant when they were accosted by two men," Tama said, as if telling a fairy tale. "Seeing their great need, the woman offered them food and oils and water, fine linen and gold. Her words were sweet and filled with love. The great god Thoth heard them and recorded them."

The woman started to cry quietly. Her son reached out a hand to comfort her. The father's face grew hard and Brian, watching from the shadows, wondered if the man's guilt would lead him to violence.

"Good man," Tama said, her voice softer now. "Kemet needs balance. Those with wealth and food must share with those who have none. The gods provide enough for all. I know that hunger and need are hard taskmasters. They darken thoughts and sway the heart. They can lead a man beyond ma'at.

"Tell me your story that I might weigh your words."

The man looked up now and Brian saw that the anger and fear in his eyes had given way to sadness.

"We live in Edfu, Voice of Truth."

"That is many days from here," Tama said.

The man nodded. "My fields are far from the river's bank and the ground was not flooded last year. I worked the land but the ground was

225

barren. Only weak shoots arose, too small to grow, even though I prayed to the gods and made offerings," he said, accusation seeping into his voice.

"When Shemu began, there was nothing for me to harvest. I heard from boatmen that downriver there were fields too full to harvest, that if I traveled there I could find work and be able to feed my family.

"And so we gathered all we had and took to the road, looking for those fields."

"The governor of your nome, did he not provide food and salt for you?" Tama asked.

"Ha! He only takes. He sends his men. They count each grain of wheat, each fig and cucumber and take their share. But no, Voice of Truth, he does not give back."

"Are his granaries empty?"

The man shrugged. "I do not know. I only know that there is no food for me and my family there. But there have been no rich fields here either. We have walked many days. At each village I offer to work. We find a generous soul here and there who gives us bread, but I have not found any work."

"Are there others like you?" she asked.

The man looked confused.

"Others who walk the land looking for food," she explained.

The woman spoke up now. "My husband is a good man, Voice of Truth. He works hard and provides for us. He is a good father. What would you have a man do?"

Tama turned to the woman. "A man must care for his family, yes. But he must keep balance. Stealing everything from another is not made right just because you have nothing. Look to your heart. You know this is true.

"Again," she repeated, turning back to the man, "are there others who walk the land in hunger?"

"I have seen a few others, Voice of Truth, but it is hard to wander without knowing what you will find. The boatman was mistaken; the harvest has been small all along the river. We are going home.

"What you said is true," he admitted. "I took too much from the traveler. I was wrong."

Tama waited for a moment to allow the man to think that she was weighing his words. She knew that he was telling the truth; she had anticipated the story he would tell. She and Brian had encountered other wandering families, all of them following rumors of heavy harvests, all of them disappointed and tired.

"Your words bring you back to the path of ma'at," she said solemnly. "But truth in words alone is not enough."

"I would return the goods, if I could," the man said quickly.

"In the morning the woman's servant will come to you. Keep one of the donkeys to help you with your travels. The servant will divide the goods, taking what he needs and leaving some with you. Balance will be restored and Ma'at will be served.

"I will go to your governor and soften his heart. The granaries will be opened at Edfu when you return."

"As you say, Voice of Truth," the man said.

"Thank you," his wife added.

Tama turned and walked into the darkness.

"**C**an you really get the governor to release grain?" Brian asked.

Tama was walking beside him. They had one donkey; its packs lighter now. Brian had gone to the campsite early in the morning and, as Tama predicted, the stranger offered Brian both donkeys and all the goods.

Brian had left most of the bread, one of the two water skins, a few rolls of linen, a salt cone and two small pieces of jewelry with the family. In the morning light, the father had looked even smaller and less imposing than he had the previous evening.

He had started to apologize, but Brian had shaken his head.

"Balance has been restored," Brian had said, repeating the ritual phrase Tama had instructed him to use.

He had seen the boy watching him. Dropping the donkey's lead rope, Brian had walked to the boy and laid a large hand on his shoulder. "You are brave," he had said, saying the words Tama had given him. "You father is a good man. Follow him."

Then he had gathered the donkey's rope and left the small clearing.

Tama nodded in answer to Brian's question.

"The governor will release grain. It is his duty to care for the people. I will speak with Hetephernebti and King Djoser if needed. The people must be fed."

They walked in silence for a few minutes.

Brian stole glances at Tama. She had removed her linen robe and was dressed as a commoner, dark kohl at her eyes and wearing only a linen belt. But when he looked at her, he realized that he was looking not at her small, soft breasts or the curve of her hips, but at her face and eyes. He knew her body and he wanted it, but it was her ideas and view of the world that fascinated him most.

"Last night …," he began.

"Yes?" she answered, expecting him to be like other men and ask about their lovemaking – to ask her to explain her motives, to evaluate his performance, to promise another opportunity.

"... When you went to that family. It looked like you changed. Your voice was different, you walked differently."

She smiled in relief, happy that her initial view of Brian had been correct. Although his physical size and power were unusual, his true strength lay in his heart.

"That has always happened," she said. "When I wear the robes of Ma'at I feel her spirit come over me. It may be an illusion," she added, "it may be real. I do not think that the difference matters. Whether the presence comes from Ma'at herself or from within me, the feeling is the same. Do you understand?"

"I think so. I read stories about guys being traded to the New York Yankees. They say when you put on their uniform, you feel like a Yankee, that you actually become a better player."

Tama stopped walking. Brian stopped also and looked at her. Her face was scrunched up and serious.

"Brian," she said, laying her hand on his arm. "I didn't understand anything you said. You talked in your tongue and the words were strange. I am sorry. But I think I felt your understanding."

Brian started to laugh. He was in a foreign land, thousands of years in the past, walking along with a donkey and a beautiful naked woman talking about the New York Yankees, the one team in baseball he despised. He was trying harder than ever before in his life to understand another person's mind but he was talking in a language she didn't understand.

And he was happier and more content than he had ever been. Everything around him was strange and different and he had never felt more at home.

He stepped forward and, still laughing, he put his hands under Tama's arms and picked her up. He lifted her high off the ground. Laying her hands atop his strong arms, she joined in his laughter.

Pulling her close, he held her, careful to not squeeze too hard. She wrapped her arms around his neck and clung to him, both of them shaking and laughing.

"You hesitated to speak last night," Tama said later while they walked along the road. "After we were together and before I visited the family."

Brian nodded. "You said that words sometimes get in the way."

The trees along the road opened to a grassy clearing. Brian walked beside Tama as she led the donkey toward the river. When they reached the riverbank, Brian lifted the sacks from the donkey so the animal could drink freely.

Tama pulled the last of the bread from a sack and breaking it in two, offered half to Brian. She held the dry bread in her hand and walked toward the river. Brian waited by the sacks. He had gotten used to her moods during their trip and recognized that there were times when she wanted to be alone.

He sat on the grass and watched the donkey back awkwardly from the water's edge, its front hooves covered in mud. Tama stood upstream from the donkey, her back to Brian as she watched the river and ate.

It was early afternoon, too early to make camp. The next village, a town called Sohag, was just an hour's walk away. They planned to trade some linen or jewelry for food there and rest a few days. Tama said it was the halfway point in their walk to Waset.

When he was a child, Brian had learned to escape from the shouting of his mother by shutting down his thinking and focusing on whatever he saw: the grain of wood on the paneling inside the trailer home; the way fibers in their worn carpet wove in and out of each other, twisting and knotting; the worn fabric on their sofa and how the colored threads came together to make rectangular patterns.

He learned to study with his eyes, allowing his mind to narrow to the visual world and ignore the sounds of anger and poverty.

When Tama said that words sometimes get in the way of reality, he thought he understood, but he would have said it differently. He thought words warped reality, scraping the joy from it, twisting it so hard that the happiness bled from it like water from a dirty dishrag.

He looked at her now, standing naked by the water. He saw her brown tapering legs, the tight, round curve of her bottom leading to the smooth, muscled lines of her back. Beyond, the sky was a pale blue, the far bank a sandy brown with a scattering of trees, their long ragged leaves arching into the sky.

He saw the colors and contour, but didn't give them names. He could smell the river, a rich, organic mixture of water, plants, and fish, its aroma a combination of watery clarity and loamy fecundity. The grass, the donkey, the trees, and the wind blowing in from the desert all colored the air around him, making it seem alive. He contributed to it, too, his salty perspiration mixing with the oil Tama had given him to protect his skin.

Finishing his bread, he walked over to the donkey, which was grazing along the water's edge. It ignored him as he rubbed the coarse hair along its neck, moving away from him, searching for taller grass.

Brian unbelted his kilt and draped it over a small bush.

The river was low, the bare bank curving down steeply to it. The brown water rippled around unseen rocks, catching on reeds near the bank. Stepping carefully in the slippery mud, he entered the water, feeling the soft river bottom squish beneath his toes.

He walked toward the center until the water reached his waist, then leaning forward he dove under and swam, pulling himself along with long, strong strokes. After a while he turned and floated on his back, drawing himself against the slow moving current, then rolling over, he swam toward shore.

Tama was standing in the water near the shore. Although she bathed in the river, she was not a swimmer. She watched Brian as he swam toward her. When the water was shallow enough he stood and walked to her.

"Take me out there," she said, pointing toward the middle of the river and walking toward him.

"Sure," he answered in English.

"Sure," she echoed, trying out the sound of the word.

Taking her hand, he led her into the water, sweeping his free arm under her legs to carry her when the water came up to her waist. She wrapped her arms around his neck and looked around her at the rising water as he walked toward the river's center. Her eyes were wide with excitement. The water rose to his chest now. Her face would be under the water if she tried to stand.

"Hold on," he said. He pushed her around to his back. He felt her breasts press against him and her legs wrap around his waist as she settled in, her arms a little tighter now around his neck.

"Ready?" he asked.

"Yes."

He leaned forward and dove under the water, pushing them deeper and deeper. Then he arched his back and curved toward the bank, rising to the surface.

When his head cleared the water he heard her laughing and sputtering.

"More," she said, wrapping her legs tighter around him.

Taking a deep breath, he dove under again.

He carried her through the water and under it, swimming until his shoulders started to tire, and then he headed for land. She stayed on his back until they reached the steep, slippery bank, then she slid off so he could pull himself up. Then he reached down to help her to shore.

Once they were both on land, Brian lay on his back on the grass, looking up at the empty sky, enjoying the rush of air as he breathed deeply, the languid feel of his arms and legs, tired from the exercise. He saw Tama's head as she bent down to sit beside him.

She put her hands under his wet head and, crossing her legs, laid his head on her lap.

"Thank you," she said, her voice a little higher and breathless. "I felt like a hawk soaring through the air, effortless and weightless."

Brian smiled. He rolled his head, settling his weight in her lap.

She brushed her hand along his lips, across his cheek and then followed his jaw to his chin. She cupped it briefly and then caressed beneath his chin and along his throat.

"I must learn that," she said, as much to herself as to Brian. "Can you teach me?" she asked. "Is it very hard?"

He shook his head. "No, it's easy. You just have to be careful when you start. The only thing with rivers is the rocks. And I guess crocodiles here. I didn't think about that," he said. "But the ocean, that's more dangerous because of the waves and undertow and sharks."

His head bobbed as she laughed quietly.

"What?" he said.

"More words I do not know."

"I'm sorry," he said.

"No, no," Tama said. "I love the sound and the look on your face when you talk in your language. I must learn it better."

He closed his eyes and focused on her touch as she caressed his shoulders and chest.

"I do believe that words sometimes keep us from what is real," she said. "But now I must learn new words to understand you better. They have two faces."

Brian stretched his arms above his head. One hand found one of her feet, which he held, his thumb massaging her. The other hand found the smooth muscle of her lower back. He let his arm lower until his hand cupped the side of her hip. He kneaded the flesh softly, enjoying the feel of the skin and muscle beneath his hand.

"When the words come from within, when you are freeing an idea, then the words are powerful. They give life to the thought. They can ignite a fire in another person's mind. Waja-Hur could do that when he was young. His voice was rich and strong; the words that he said were powerful seeds. They could bring the very gods to life," she said.

"Other times, words hide life, or make it pale and meaningless.

"When I say river from now on, it will be a rich, powerful word. I will remember today and the feeling of floating and swimming. But when I say it to another person, they may only hear the flat ribbon of brown that wanders through the Two Lands."

She looked down at Brian, his eyes closed, his face muscles relaxed.

"It made you very tired," she said.

He nodded.

"I will let you sleep."

He shook his head and raised his face to kiss her.

"It is like dying," she said afterward, "or what I hope dying will be like."

"What do you mean?" Brian asked. He leaned down and kissed the top of her head. They were lying beneath a palm tree, their legs intertwined, their heartbeats still slowing from their lovemaking.

"My thoughts are slowly erased, I don't see the trees, I don't hear the birds or feel the sun, all of my attention goes to my skin and then within. The energy draws into a little ball and then it explodes and I am nothing but joy. That is the death. Then I begin to come alive again, slowly, but with a feeling of happiness that overwhelms all else. That is the rebirth in Khert-Neter."

"That sounds good," Brian said, "But what if all that happens when we die is that we're dead? I mean, how do we know what happens? Why would we even think that something happens after we're dead?"

Tama lifted her head to look up at his face.

"I know," she said. "That is a hard thing for me. I have been trained to look for the truth, to use my eyes and ears and touch and heart, but also to test what I see and hear and feel and think. If it is not true, then it is not true, no matter how much I wish it to be true.

"But I cannot ask questions of the gods; I cannot see them and talk to them. I feel the spirit of Ma'at within me, but I do not know where it comes from. Is it from my heart? Is it from her? I see the sun every day. Hetephernebti would tell me that I see the god Re, but I see only a great glowing fire.

"My parents, the stories of my childhood, Hetephernebti – everyone and everything – they all teach me that there are gods. In the end, Brian, I cannot explain everything.

"If Sobek did not sweat to create the river Iteru, then where did it come from? It is possible that the story of Sobek is not true, but something must be true. The river is here. I see it, thanks to you, I was part of it. So, we can say it came from a strange land up there," she pointed upstream where the river disappeared into the horizon. "But eventually, we have to say where it started."

Brian nodded. "I understand. I mean, the river comes from rain that falls on mountains deep in Africa. But where did the rain come from. Yeah, I know. You can take it back far enough, but eventually, even if you go back to the Big Bang, you have to stop explaining and start believing something."

Suddenly, Tama began to lightly pound her fists against Brian's chest, softly but rapidly. "You know where the river comes from? And what is Africa and this other big bag thing?" she asked, laughter interrupting her words.

Brian rolled closer and held her so she couldn't hit him. He laughed quietly as he pulled her close.

"It's not fair," she said. "You are so much stronger and you know so much more."

He kissed her forehead and lifted her chin gently to kiss her mouth.

"My head has facts in it, but I'm just starting to understand," he said.

"**W**hy does Djefi want to kill me?" Brian asked two days later as they walked along the road after resting and replenishing their supplies in Sohag.

"I don't know," Tama answered.

"But you have an idea," he said, knowing that Tama would never let a puzzle stay unsolved.

"He sent you into the desert with Siamun who left you there with an injured man. But you returned, carrying the man on your back. Then you stopped a crocodile from taking a little girl," Tama said.

"This raised you in the eyes of the people who live at To-She. Djefi could not permit that."

"Why?"

Tama thought for a moment, looking for words that they shared that would explain Djefi.

"Waja-Hur is loved. He speaks the truth. He has been high priest for Thoth for many, many years. Now many people regard him as Thoth. Sometimes I think he does, too. He always speaks what he believes Thoth would say. Perhaps he is Thoth at those times. He is always true to Thoth, to the god's devotion to balance.

"Hetephernebti is loved also. She doesn't speak as if she were Re. Instead she praises him. She gives him all credit for life and love. She reflects the love she feels from Re. She is always true to Re, always living and speaking in his spirit. The people see this, they see the way she loves and worships Re.

"I serve Ma'at, both the goddess and the idea. I do it because I love the goddess and everything she represents: truth, justice, and the rightness of all things. They are the base on which the Two Lands rests. Every man and woman must follow them, beer brewers, bakers, and scribes, even King Djoser.

"Djefi is First Prophet of the god Sobek. But there are stories about him. I do not know if he truly serves Sobek or if he tries to make Sobek serve him. He says the words he wants Sobek to say, not the words Sobek wants him to say. It is hard to explain, Brian. But the people see this, they hear him, they understand that. Djefi is not stupid. He understands also. So he makes the people fear him. He says it is because Sobek is fearful, but it is because Djefi does not have the love of the people."

Brian stopped walking. The donkey took a few more steps before reaching the end of the tether. It shook its head and snorted.

"I understand," Brian said. "He thought I was coming between him and the people."

Tama nodded her head. "Yes, that is part of it. But people are willing to follow a leader, even if they do not love the leader. They want the order a leader brings. So even if you have come between Djefi and the people at To-She, they would always follow him. What Djefi hates, the reason he wants to kill you, is that you make him see himself through your eyes. You do not see him the way he wants to view himself. You reveal a truth about him that he cannot bear to see.

"He cannot live with that, Brian."

They walked in silence for a few minutes.

Tama laid a hand on Brian's arm.

"We will be in Waset in a few more days," she said.

"I know."

"Djefi will be there."

MA'AT DISTURBED

Waset is a true city, Djefi thought, as his boat slid smoothly toward the riverbank where dozens of other boats were moored. All along the waterfront there was activity – small reed fishing boats coming and going, flat barges being pushed away from shore, others being loaded or unloaded.

He looked along the harbor for the king's boat, but there was nothing there approaching the size of the king's gilded vessel. As his boat slowed beside the wooden wharf, Djefi saw Kanakht's boat tied to a post near him. Bobbing beside it was a larger boat decorated with paintings of lotus plants, its furled sail trimmed in deep blue. Djefi guessed that it belonged to Prince Teti.

The conveniently injured Prince Teti, Djefi thought, as the other two boats in his small convoy followed him to the water's edge.

Although Djefi was eager to meet with Kanakht and find out what news the vizier had, he was more eager to take on supplies and continue his trip to Kom Ombo. His new temple was six more days' journey upriver. He hadn't heard from Siamun since he had sent him to Kom Ombo to accelerate construction of the temple. The lack of communication hadn't surprised Djefi. Siamun didn't write and he didn't trust scribes, so he would have had no way to send a message except with a courier, and Djefi knew that there was no one Siamun would entrust with a message.

A guard was waiting on the riverbank, standing beside a sedan chair and six carriers.

After Djefi was helped from his boat, the guard greeted him: "Kanakht, administrator of the great mansion, royal chancellor of the Two Lands, sends his greetings, First Prophet of Sobek."

This is how a man of prominence welcomes another of his rank, Djefi thought with a self-important smile. *This is how it should be.*

"Please come with us, First Prophet. Kanakht has prepared a table to welcome you to Waset."

Djefi nodded, his face as impassive as he imagined the guard would expect from a man of his rank. He waddled to the sedan and then, turning his back to it, looked sideways impatiently, waiting for the carriers to take his hands and lower him to the seat. He heard a grunt from the guard and two of the carriers hurried to assist Djefi.

He settled back into the cushions and breathed deeply, sighing at the luxury of it all and anticipating the meal Kanakht would have prepared for him. Then they would discuss how they would shape the future of the Two Lands.

"Tell me about Diane," Tama said. "She is why you are traveling to Waset, yes?"

They were resting under a tree along the bank of the river directly across from Waset. No flat-bottomed barges were on the west bank, so Tama had sent a boatman across the river to retain one so they could board the donkey and take it with them into the capital.

"You are lovers?" she asked as Brian tried to find the words to explain why he was following Diane. Their relationship didn't seem so clear to him anymore.

He flushed at her question, then seeing the openness in her face, he reminded himself that Tama viewed the physical side of a relationship in more casual terms than women from his time. He remembered Pahket and her offer to touch him when she gave him a massage.

Tama and he had made love, or had sex, *that is a better description*, he thought, every night. She was energetic, completely uninhibited and playfully curious. He had never laughed so much as when they had sex, or afterward as they held each other.

Sex with Diane had been exciting, but sometimes filled with an almost grim determination, an act to complete so they could say that they had. He worried if she was comfortable, if she was enjoying it, if she really wanted to be with him or if she was just trying to please him. He had been with other women and usually felt that their attitudes had been the same. If he closed his eyes while he was with one of them, he could have been with any of them.

Tama had been a completely different experience. She played with the rhythm and intensity of their lovemaking, sometimes teasing and playful, sometimes grunting and wild, sometimes quiet and languid, but always centered on the moment. He never wondered if she was enjoying the act, and so his attention was focused on the feeling and pleasure it brought.

Brian realized that Tama was waiting for him to reply, giving him time to gather his thoughts.

"Yes," he answered. "We were lovers. She is fragile. No, that isn't exactly right." He sighed and tried to think of Diane in the new way he had come to view people, applying what Tama had taught him.

"I have known Diane for three years. We went to college together, that's a kind of school," he explained. "Her daddy picked the school for her. She said he made a lot of decisions for her, so when she got to school she was going to make her own decisions. That's what she told me later, after we got to know each other. It was something that mattered to her.

"But then she got a boyfriend. He was a big guy, like me. Her daddy's a big guy, too, now that I think about it. So, she got this boyfriend and she let him make all the decisions, where they went to eat, what concerts they went to, who their friends were. Just everything. She said she realized that so she broke up with him."

"And you were different?" Tama asked.

Brian shrugged. "I guess. Except lately she quit talking to me. I mean, this trip was her idea. But then on the way here, we had a fight. She said I didn't care about anything because I never said what I wanted to do. She said she could have picked a trip to Death Valley or Antarctica and I would have gone along just to please her."

"Would you?" Tama asked, putting aside her other questions – what was this Death Valley and Antarctica?

Brian smiled. "Sure. I did want to please her. And I'd go anywhere. I like to find new things." He pulled out a blade of grass, tossed it into the still air and watched it flutter back to earth. "Everything gets so complicated. That's why I like sports. You have rules, you know what you're supposed to do, after it's over, you shake hands and say 'good game.' " He lay back and stared up at the sky.

Tama leaned on her elbow and looked down at Brian. "I understand. Sometimes I wonder if that is why people love the gods or the king. They like rules. The rules supply order – ma'at. If you have to decide about everything every day, you would never get anything done. So you have rules, or sometimes just customs. You eat food at this time, you bathe at this time, and you put on your kohl just so.

"How could you live if every day you had to discover all of this anew? What if you had to decide about the sun every day? It is better to say it is Re and to learn the stories about him. The same with Isis and Osiris, Thoth, Nut, all the gods.

"So Diane wants order in her life. She wants ma'at, yes? Her father was her order, then this other boyfriend. Then she decided to create the order from within. That is a hard thing to do, Brian. I believe it is the right thing to do, but it can be very hard. So now Diane finds herself removed from the order of her world and she turns to you for that order, but she is angry because you do not supply it and she is angrier because the disorder makes her feel weak."

Brian looked up at the sky and realized that there were no clouds floating there, nothing to make shapes of with his imagination.

"So, am I supposed to supply this order for her?" he asked.

"I don't know," Tama answered.

"I know that I am different from other people. For myself, each morning I exercise, you've seen me, and then I sit quietly. I try to let ma'at settle in me. If I think about it, then it isn't there. No, it's always there, just out of reach. So I don't reach for it and then ma'at comes to me.

"I learned that exercise because I am in service to Ma'at. I know that most people do not welcome ma'at that way; they haven't been taught or they do not take the time. I don't know how they follow ma'at. Some lucky people seem to live within ma'at without effort. You are that way most of the time. Truly.

"I have seen women at the loom, their hands and minds focused on their task. Bakers, acrobats and dancers, musicians, children at play, fishermen, almost everyone has those moments when they are doing what they love to do, when they are at peace, when they are living within ma'at.

"If Diane is not living in ma'at, you should try to help her. But she must help herself.

"Each of us thinks we are the most important person, because we are inside ourselves. Does this make sense? We see the world from our eyes and hear it with our ears. I look past the branches and leaves of the trees to the sky and I see the colors I call brown and green and blue. But think, Brian, are they the same colors that you see? We may call them by the same name, but they may look different to you.

"The taste of an onion, the song of a bird, the strum of the harp, the grit of sand. I know what they feel like and taste like and sound like to me. But I cannot know what they are to you. So how can I truly know your thoughts or feel your fears?

"I can listen to you and comfort you, but only you can overcome your fears, only you can bring yourself into balance with ma'at.

"When you find Diane, you can listen to her and help her with her fears, but she must enter ma'at herself."

She watched him as he looked at the sky, his face composed and rested, but his eyes sad.

"Our boat is here," she said, sitting up. "Come, you must meet Hetephernebti."

He waited in a small room near the chambers used by Hetephernebti. A window opened onto a garden, bringing a scent of blossoms and water into the room. Brian leaned against the window and thought about Diane.

There were no malls here, no restaurants nor movie theaters, so he wondered what she was doing. The Diane he knew shopped and complained and never seemed satisfied. The one Tama described was empty and searching for meaning and balance. He saw now that they were two views of the same woman, the same actions.

He wondered if being removed from the distractions of life would help her look within herself, if the idleness here would force her to confront the emptiness of her life.

It was late afternoon and the angle of the sun, or Re, he thought, was casting long shadows from the palm trees in the garden. The shadows, falling across smaller trees and shrubs, were broken, their straight geometric lines bending over arching leaves and skipping from plant to plant.

There were splashes of colored blossoms amid the green leaves and the sandy garden floor. Small dun-colored birds darted from tree to tree, finches, he thought. The birds made him think of orioles and then his thoughts turned to baseball.

He realized that during the two-week trip with Tama he hadn't thought about his old world except to contrast it with the world he was in now. And those comparisons had not been favorable for his old world.

There was so much to do and see in his world – amusement parks, zoos, baseball and football games, television and movies, restaurants, plays, concerts, NASCAR races – that he had once found fulfilling, but now he viewed it all as a distraction.

My god, he thought, I even watched golf and bass fishing for entertainment.

And now I'm watching plants and birds. He chuckled at himself. It wasn't what he was watching or doing, he knew, it was the way he viewed it and how it affected him. When he had watched a sporting event or listened to a band, his mind was pulled and overwhelmed by the action and sound. Here in the quiet room by a garden, his mind was open and calm.

He heard voices in the hallway, one of them curiously high-pitched. At first he thought it was a woman's voice, but then he recognized it as Djefi's.

A flush of anger swept through him overwhelming the contentment he had felt. He crossed the room, looking to confront the priest.

He was halfway across the room when he saw Djefi' fat form waddle past the doorway. He lengthened his stride, unconsciously tightening his hands into fists, his mind turning into a screen of white noise. He was unsure what he would do when he reached Djefi, all he felt was the anger – at being abandoned in the desert; at being assaulted at Khmunu; at the resulting death of the attacker, his blood streaming from his neck onto the dark street.

Suddenly a smaller form darted into the room in front of him, moving toward him quickly.

"No, Brian. Not now, not here," Tama said in a forced whisper, placing both hands on his chest and gently pushing him away from the doorway.

She felt the exaggerated rise and fall of his chest, the heat of anger on his skin.

He allowed himself to be stopped.

Out in the hallway, Djefi paused at the soft sound that came from the doorway behind him. He turned his head to look there, decided that his curiosity wasn't worth the effort and continued his plodding passage away from Hetephernebti's chambers.

The words from Hetephernebti were fresh in his mind. He wanted to turn them over and study them, contrast them with what Kanakht had told him earlier. And he needed to find a bathroom and settle himself on the cold limestone seat. His bowels had been in disarray since he had gotten word that Nimaasted had failed to dispose of the outlander Brian.

Despite the excellent meal and honey-flavored beer – he must get the recipe for his brewers – his visit with Kanakht yesterday had been unsettling. The old vizier was worried about this and that: a gift of land to the temple of Khnum would make the royal guard more alert ... the outlander Tim had gained favor with King Djoser, so much favor that he'd been given a new name and had been asked to accompany King Djoser on his trip to Abu ... Prince Teti was not seriously injured and one of his guards was suspected of trying to kill him, but now another guard was also suspected ... Ma'at had disappeared at the same time Brian had escaped.

Well, she'd reappeared. She had been sitting beside Hetephernebti just now. Never uttering a word, just smiling and watching him. He should have asked her about Brian, but he couldn't think of a way to raise the topic.

If she is here, does that mean the outlander is here too?

Now Hetephernebti was hinting that there were rumors of a plot against King Djoser and asking him if he knew anything. In his head he heard her voice, so smooth and taunting. He stopped at the intersection of two hallways. Which way would lead to a toilet? From the rumbling in his gut he didn't have much time.

Tama stood in front of Brian, her hands flat against his heaving chest, watching him closely. There was anger in his face she had not seen before, his eyes staring off in the distance. She knew that his mind was elsewhere, stalking Djefi, no doubt.

"You are a wanted man here, Brian."

His eyes finally moved from the doorway and she felt the chest muscles under her hands swell up as he took a deep breath.

"Kanakht received word from Nimaasted that you killed a man in Khmunu. It is Kanakht's duty to capture you if he sees you. Then you would be returned to Khmunu where Nimaasted would decide your guilt and your punishment."

"I didn't kill him," Brian answered. "You know that."

She nodded in agreement as he backed away. "I believe you, Brian. But that doesn't matter. Kanakht is vizier to King Djoser. If he decides that you are to be sent to Khmunu and given to Nimaasted for justice, then that is what will happen."

Brian looked down at the stone floor. The peace and contentment he had felt a few minutes ago while looking into the garden was gone. He realized that whatever new understanding he thought he had about himself was shallow. He had gone from tranquility to rage in the time it took him to take three steps.

Breathing deeply, he tried to re-center his emotions, to see the reality of where he was, not his hopes. Djefi, Kanakht and Nimaasted were his enemies now. Whether they were right, whatever their motives, they would try to stop him and punish him.

Tama was his friend and although she said it didn't matter if she believed he was innocent, it mattered to him. Not just because he cared for her, but also because she was a woman of importance; she had friends. There must be a network of people who would believe her and help him.

And Tim is out there somewhere, he thought.

She watched as he calmed himself, bringing himself back to this room, this now, this reality and away from his anger and thoughts of violence.

"Hetephernebti wants to meet with you, Brian. She was with Tim and she has news about Diane."

She reached for his hand and, taking it, led him down the hallway to Hetephernebti's chambers.

Hetephernebti sat at the head of a table full of food.

She was sipping wine when they arrived, pausing by the doorway until she nodded and waved them forward. "Sit here," she said to Brian, touching the wooden back of the chair on her left.

Brian hesitated by the chair, his eyes moving from the table to the open doorway.

"Now, we will have a pleasant meal," Hetephernebti said, "and exchange news as civilized people do. I would have invited Djefi to join us, but he made it clear that he had already eaten and needed to attend to other matters. Which," she turned to Brian, "I understand is convenient since he wants to kill you."

She wiped her mouth with a linen cloth and smiled.

"Brian, please be seated. I have posted a guard by the door. No one will be allowed to enter, except Kanakht, of course. One does not bar the vizier. But, we will have plenty of notice if he approaches. There is a doorway just behind you. If Kanakht decides to join us, you can wait in the room beyond that doorway. It is my private chamber.

"Now, enjoy the meal. The goose is delicious, the bread is still warm from the ovens and the wine is tart. Sit, sit!"

Seeing Tama nod, Brian sat and began to eat. His mouth was full of wine when Hetephernebti spoke again.

"So tell me about this man Kanakht says you killed."

Brian choked and covered his mouth with his hand as he coughed.

"Hetephernebti is as direct as Re's golden rays, Brian," Tama said, watching Brian as he recovered his poise. "The light of Re uncovers truth. You can trust her. Tell her your story."

Hetephernebti let him talk without interruption.

"Do you know Tim?" she asked after he had brought her up to date.

"Not really. I talked to him at To-She and then I expected to meet him at Khmunu, but he wasn't there. I hoped to meet him here."

"Why do you seek him?"

"Because he said he can help us get back home. Diane and me."

"You cannot get home without him?"

Brian shrugged. "I don't know. I'm not sure how we got here," he said with a sad smile.

Hetephernebti rested the palms of her hands on the table and stared off in the distance. Then she turned to Brian. "I believe you, Brian. I think that you, and Diane and Imhotep, which is what we call Tim now, were sent here by the gods. It is not an accident that you are here at the very time so much is happening."

She motioned to the food and the wine. "Eat and enjoy. I will tell you my story now, or rather the story of the Two Lands."

"The Two Lands are as old as time, but they were not always united. King Narmer was the first to rule over the Two Lands, or so we are told. That was in a time beyond reckoning. My earliest memory is of my father, King Kha-sekhemwy. I did not know his father, King Sekhemib, only the stories about him.

"When my brother became king, he took Netjerikhet as his Horus name. His name means 'Divine of Body.' He announced that he had been welcomed by Re and Horus and all the hundred gods as one of them."

She paused for a moment, her eyes moving from Brian to her hands, which were resting on her lap.

"The Two Lands," she continued, her voice even and calm, "is a rich, large land. There is room for Apis, Hathor, beautiful Isis, Tefnut, the eye of Re, Osiris, Sobek, Thoth, Ma'at and Seth. So, there is room for another god – my brother."

She looked up at Brian. "How many gods are in your land?" she asked.

"One," he said.

"One?"

"Yes, there are different ways to worship him, different religions, but just one god."

"What is his name?"

Brian had never heard another name for God, except in movies where Muslims called him "Allah." He thought there was another special name that Jews used, but he couldn't remember it. "Mostly we just call him God," he answered.

She looked at him in disbelief.

"No, wait," Brian said. "He has a son. At least some people think so. His name is Jesus."

"So you have two gods."

That made him pause. "No, just one. I'm pretty sure."

Hetephernebti arched her eyebrows. "You have a god and he has a son, but the son is not a god?"

"Yeah, that doesn't sound right," Brian admitted. "Wait, I remember something from church. We used to say 'God, the father, God, the son, and God, the Holy Spirit.' "

"So, three gods," Hetephernebti said.

Brian was puzzled. He had said the words when he was young and his mother had taken him to church, but he had never made an effort to understand them. "No, I'm sorry. They're all one god. I don't understand it either. But I'm sure that's the way it is."

Hetephernebti nodded. "I'm sorry, Brian, I wandered from my story.

"Because my brother has declared himself a god, it has made some people think that the house of the gods can be rearranged. Djefi believes that if my brother can declare himself a god, then it might be possible for Djefi to declare Sobek as the chief of all gods. A few others, the followers of Amun and those of Aten to name just two, are beginning to have the same thoughts. However, Djefi is a special case.

"Kanakht …" she turned to Tama, "Has he met Kanakht?"

Tama shook her head.

"Kanakht was at To-She for the festival. You did not meet him then?" Hetephernebti asked.

"No," Brian said. "Djefi kept me secluded. I only met Tim because he found me."

"Yes," Hetephernebti said. "I had forgotten. That seems so long ago already. Well, Kanakht was vizier to my father and he remains vizier now for my brother. He is disturbed by the changes King Djoser has made.

And he is growing old. He believes that he has served the Two Lands well and now it is time for the Two Lands to serve him. So he plots to take the throne."

She turned and rested a hand on Tama's arm. "I have not told you this, little sister. Things have happened while you were on your journey. I have no evidence, but I am sure of what I say.

"Kanakht has incited Djefi with idea that if King Djoser is overthrown then Sobek, if he plays a part in this, will be regarded as the chief god of the Two Lands."

Tama interrupted. "And King Djoser knows of all this?"

Hetephernebti nodded.

"He knows of it, but he does not know how widespread Kanakht's plot is, who else is involved. And so he waits and watches."

She paused and reached for her wine cup.

"What about Diane?" Brian asked.

Hetephernebti set down her cup and leaned forward on her elbows. "She is here in Waset, traveling with Djefi and Yunet. I have not seen her, only heard that she is here."

"Is she in danger?" Brian asked.

Hetephernebti met his eyes. "I do not know, Brian. I think Yunet protects her. And I believe that Djefi wants to keep her secure so he can use her to bargain with my brother if something goes wrong with the plot. He also may think that she has powers.

"Do not shake your head, Brian. Imhotep has healed Meryt of the wasting disease. I saw it myself. He has saved Prince Teti's arm. You have carried a man from a certain death in the desert and saved a little girl from the crocodile's jaws. Yes, I know the stories. I was at To-She when you returned from the desert. I heard what the people said. So if you and Imhotep have powers, why shouldn't Diane?

"I know that you say you are not gods. You might believe that. But I do not. I have seen the miracles that Imhotep has worked. You have twice saved people and once escaped death yourself."

"Where is Diane?" Brian asked, shutting out her arguments that he was more than a man.

Hetephernebti glanced at Tama and then answered Brian. "She travels with Djefi, but he has several boats. He stopped here to get food to continue his trip to Kom Ombo. One of the boats left shortly after he arrived. I do not know if Diane was on that one. I only know that she has not come into Waset."

Brian looked at the window and saw that it had grown dark outside.

"Tama," he said, "help me find Diane."

Djefi didn't feel as well as he hoped he would after emptying himself at the palace.

There was more than heavy food weighing on him. If Tama was here in Waset, then Brian was probably here as well. They had disappeared from Khmunu at the same time, so it was likely they had left together.

They must have walked, Djefi concluded, shaking his head in amazement at the idea.

He had dawdled on his way upriver, stopping to rest on land every night, spending time in villages, watching to see if any boats passed him. But there had been no sign of Brian on the river. Eventually he had given up the watch. It was Nimaasted's job, he had concluded. Kanakht had entrusted the priest to dispose of Brian.

It is his failure, not mine.

But now Tama was here in Waset. It didn't mean that Brian was here, but it showed that someone could have traveled here from Khmunu without being seen on the river.

He directed the carriers to take him to Kanakht's home. Even though it was late, he wanted to talk with the vizier again, to hear his soothing words.

And he will have wine to help settle my stomach, Djefi thought, settling back on his cushions and groaning at his discomfort.

Kanakht didn't know how long he had been sitting, staring across the room toward a window. The light outside had disappeared and servants had come in and lit torches in his chamber.

He had started to think about King Djoser and Tim – he refused to think of him as Imhotep – trying to find a way to turn the king's sudden attraction to the outlander into an advantage. Then his mind had drifted to Tim and the little he knew of the other two intruders.

They had arrived in Kemet near the tomb he was having built in Saqqara. His eternal house. He would be there soon. He would rest from this life, the embalmers would respectfully prepare his body and then he would be carried to his tomb. And then he would awaken, young and alive. His heart would be weighed and found to be filled with truth. He would rise on the back of a falcon, rising higher and higher to the eternally green fields of Khert-Neter.

He would be able to eat what he wanted and drink when he liked. His wife and children, all gone before him, would be there, waiting for him, honoring him.

He sighed and smiled a sad smile.

There is a better life waiting for me, he thought.

Not so very long ago he would have scorned someone who was eager to pass on to Khert-Neter.

What happened? When did this change take place? When did I become a tired old man?

Through his unfocused eyes he saw movement at the doorway.

He nodded his head, giving the servant permission to approach.

"First Prophet Djefi wishes to see you, Lord Kanakht."

Kanakht stifled a sigh and nodded.

"Take him to the table and tell someone to prepare some food. I'm sure he will be hungry."

The servant bowed and withdrew.

Kanakht stood, his hip stiff from sitting so long. He steadied himself a moment and then squared his shoulders and turned to go meet Djefi. He disliked the fat priest, but he needed his hunger and ambition.

As he walked toward the doorway, Kanakht realized that his step had lightened.

He looked forward to saying the words, finding the hunger and fear in Djefi's soul and using it to guide the priest to do his bidding. He thought of Makare and how easily he had swayed him.

Once I am king, he thought, these longings for Khert-Neter will pass. I will have Khert-Neter here in the Two Lands.

It was dark by the riverfront. A few torches were lit near loaded barges as watchmen guarded the cargo, but the damp night air seemed to smother the light just a few feet from the yellow flames.

Tama led the way, slipping through the shadows toward the water. Brian walked behind her, watching her protectively and scanning the area in front of them as they approached the river.

Hetephernebti had offered to send men with them, but Tama had argued that the Priestess of Re could not help someone who was sought by the vizier. She said that no one knew Brian was in Waset and so there was little danger unless Djefi had guards posted at his boats. They could easily spot them and avoid them, she said.

As they neared Djefi's boats, it was clear that no watch was being kept. There were no torches, and the sound of scattered snoring came from the boats' decks.

Tama took Brian's hand. "We will walk along the river as lovers sometimes do. It is late, but not so late for those who seek to be alone."

They emerged from the shadows and walked along the riverbank, leaning into each other. There was no movement from Djefi's boats.

"Djefi won't be staying on the boat," Brian said. "On the trip from To-She to Khmunu he went ashore every night."

They stopped near the first boat. Tama turned her back to the river and put her arms around Brian, turning him so that he was facing the boat. He hugged her, looking at the boat as he did. There were sleeping forms on the deck, but none with Diane's shape.

The second boat was even quieter, with only three sleeping forms on the deck.

As they approached the third boat, they realized that it was not one of Djefi's, but a smaller craft that stank of goose droppings.

"There were three, I'm sure," Brian said. "Djefi was on one, I was on one and Diane was on another."

"Can you tell which one is missing?"

"No," he said, "I wasn't paying attention to the boat. I would know the boatmen, though."

He looked at the two boats. The first had an awning over the stern. He remembered that was where Djefi sat to stay out of the sun. The second boat was a little smaller and there was no awning.

He walked closer to the boat, peering through the darkness, trying to see if he recognized any of the boatmen. It was too dark to see their faces clearly. He felt Tama pull on his arm.

"It doesn't matter," she whispered. "If she and Yunet are not on the deck and if Hetephernebti is right that they didn't come into town, then they must be on the boat that isn't here."

He nodded agreement and followed her away from the water's edge.

They walked back into Waset, keeping away from the main streets on their way to the palace.

"Where would she have gone?" he asked.

"Djefi said he was going to Kom Ombo. He is building a new temple to Sobek there. He would want to keep her near him, so I think she would be headed there."

"Why would he have sent her away?" Brian asked.

Tama thought for a few minutes as they walked on in silence.

"He probably sent word for them to leave when he saw me here. I didn't think of that. He might have guessed that we are traveling together."

After a few more steps, Brian asked, "Where is Kom Ombo?"

At first light Brian began walking south toward Kom Ombo.

Tama had given him the donkey and the long striped robes of a Nubian to wear as a disguise. She told him that she could not go with him because she had to return to Khmunu for the ceremony that would help persuade the gods to bring moisture to the Two Lands.

"Djefi will be going to Khmunu also," she had told Brian. "The way should be clear at Kom Ombo to see Diane."

As she stood at the edge of town watching him walk away, leading the small donkey, Tama felt a presence at her side.

"Why did you tell him everything?" she asked Hetephernebti.

Hetephernebti caressed Tama's head. "If Brian is a god, then he already knew what I was saying. If the gods sent him, then either they would tell him or they were acting through me to tell him. And, little sister, if he is only a man, an outlander as you say, then he will leave the Two Lands and his knowledge will not matter."

Tama turned to her friend, a worried look on her face. "But, Hetephernebti, what if he is just a man who now believes that he is a god? What if he acts against Kanakht and Djefi thinking he cannot be harmed because he is a god? What then?"

Hetephernebti gazed at Brian, who was now just a small, distant form moving across the sands of Kemet.

"Then, Tama, that is what the gods want."

AT ABU

Dear Addy, Tim wrote and stopped. He stuck the pencil behind his ear and stared at the journal page. The morning light lay across the empty, ivory-colored paper, highlighting the granular texture of the sketchpad.

Looking up, Tim saw the wooden deck of the boat, narrowing as it approached the stern. The cedar planking was smooth from a combination of age and steady use. Beyond, out of sight from his low perspective, the sluggish water of the river pushed its way north, the opposite direction King Djoser's boat was traveling.

From his seated position, Tim could see the west bank, where there seemed to be fewer and fewer trees as they got closer to Abu and the first cataract, the spot where the river narrowed as it crashed through rocks, and where Prince Teti had fallen.

King Djoser was at the prow of the ship talking with Sekhmire, commander of the house guard. Sekhmire was the only guard on the king's boat. The others followed in smaller boats, making up the rest of the small armada that carried King Djoser through his land.

Yesterday they had passed Kom Ombo, a small gathering of mud huts on the east side of the river. On the opposite bank a new temple was rising from a sandstone plateau that overlooked a bend in the river.

"The new Temple of Sobek," King Djoser had said, nodding at the stone pillars as they passed. "It will be dedicated a few days after the river floods." He had kept his eyes on the nearly completed temple, but Tim knew the comment was directed at him.

Whatever happened now, Tim knew his future was linked with King Djoser's and, more immediately, with the depth of the river.

Meryt sat beside him, a light linen cloth over her head to shelter her from the sun. She was almost fully recovered from her illness. Her humor and inquisitiveness had returned, along with her energy, but exposure to the heat of the sun still tired her.

Tim touched her hand, bringing a squeeze in response. Then he turned his attention back to the journal.

We are just a few days from Abu, which marks the southern border of Kemet. There is a temple there to the ram-headed god they call Khnum. Before I left Cairo, when I was waiting in Diane and Brian's room, I read the history of the Step Pyramid and King Djoser. According to the book, the famine ended after seven years when King Djoser made a sacrifice to Khnum and gave some land to the temple in Abu.

I'm traveling with the king, his personal bodyguard, and with Meryt. She's beside me now, watching me write, keeping me company. I started to tell you about her before.

She has brought color and life back to me. I used to get angry when I heard someone laugh. How could they be happy after what had happened? But now I look forward to her laughter.

I know that I was withdrawing from everything. You know, I actually quit shaking hands with people. I didn't want to touch anyone if I couldn't touch you. I know I was indulging myself by dwelling on my loss and pain. I wanted to never feel happy again. I think I was trying to prove the depth of my love, but I was also angry.

Maybe it's something in the air here. Seriously, when I arrived here, I remember feeling different. It started as soon as I stepped out of the tomb. The air, the light, the colors, everything felt different. I remember drawing in a deep breath of air...

He put the pencil back behind his ear and stretched out his hand to touch Meryt's leg. She was sitting cross-legged, her hands resting on her lap, her head cocked slightly, watching Tim and looking beyond at the riverbank. He laid his hand on her smooth thigh and traced circles with his fingers across her soft skin.

Placing her hand on top of his, she lightly rubbed the back of his hand, feeling the skin drawn tight across the bones that led to his fingers.

He closed his eyes and focused his attention on his hand, feeling and being touched. He knew she was doing the same, making this small point of contact a bridge between them.

"Look over there," Meryt said quietly.

He looked up to see her pointing past the riverbank to distant sand dunes, shaped by the wind into pyramid shapes. "I've never seen anything like that before," she said. "I wonder if it's soft like sand, or hard. Could you run up their side, oh, and roll down?" Her voice was excited, filled with the wonder that Tim saw in all her actions.

It struck him that there were no pyramids here in this ancient time. If he really were Imhotep, THE Imhotep, then he would be the man remembered for directing the construction of the first pyramid. The hills off in the distance were the shape of the true pyramids, the ones that would come later. The inspiration for those tombs, he realized now, came from nature, from these hills in southern Kemet.

He looked from the sliding river bank and the distant hills to Meryt, her face so alive and animated, her skin, even in the shadows beneath the linen scarf, so luminous and beautiful.

Then he glanced down at the journal, the dry, dark strokes against the page – a bloodless attempt to grab life and hold onto it, to pin it down like a collection of dead butterflies. Elegant lines, heart-breaking delicacy and beauty, but no life. All past, no present. And no future.

He raised his hand from her lap and grabbed the corner of the page on which he was writing. Gripping the journal spine firmly, he pulled the page toward him, listening to the ripping sound as it tore free.

He rocked forward and stood up. He slid his journal back into the backpack, but carried the torn page to the center of the boat where a small fire was kept burning, watchfully tended so it didn't spread to the wooden ship. He touched the shoulder of the boatman who was sitting by the small fire. When he looked up Tim gave him the loose paper and nodded toward the fire.

There is so much to do, Tim thought, as he walked back to Meryt. I'm living and there is so much to do. Later, when I've stopped creating, stopped living, there will be time to remember.

Bata was a captive, but he was on an island in a land where there really was no place to hide. And so he roamed free, working on the temple grounds at Abu, waiting for King Djoser to arrive and decide his fate.

Three years ago he had become a member of Prince Teti's guard, joining two other men, none of them older than twenty-five, who traveled with the prince, trained with him, ate with him and hunted with him.

It was a good life. They traveled with Prince Teti up and down the river, standing guard by him during ceremonies; competing with him in races, and wrestling, and throwing spears; visiting the hundred temples along the river, and the thousand girls who longed to be close to the prince.

They had stood together along the riverbank, relieving themselves, contesting who could create the highest arc. They had emptied skins of wine and jars of beer, passing out on the floor and waking up wrenching out their guts, laughing at each other's misery. They had been together with women, comparing their endurance and size.

They were friends, although they never forgot that Prince Teti was of royal blood.

They knew that as Prince Teti grew older and assumed more royal duties this time of wildness and adventure would end. They would grow old together, recalling their youth and laughing at the memories.

But now, now they were still young and wild, strong and fast.

Bata had no idea why he was being punished. They had been in the river, Prince Teti high on a rock when suddenly he fell, silently, arms unmoving. Bata could see it clearly, remembering it happening slowly, implacably. He had run toward the spot in the river where the prince was falling, but got there too late to catch him.

Fortunately, the river was deeper there. The prince's arm hit a rock, Bata could hear the sickening snap as the bone broke, but Prince Teti's head and the rest of his body landed in open water. Bata had run to Prince Teti and raised his face from the water, careful to avoid the mangled arm.

Before he could even shout for help, Nesi had appeared, splashing from behind the boulder from which Prince Teti had fallen. Bata had looked to Nesi for help, but suddenly his friend was yelling, calling out that Bata was trying to kill Teti.

How could such a thing happen?

And so Bata waited at Abu, waited for King Djoser to judge him. Waited and wondered why Nesi had accused him.

He was cutting papyrus stalks along the water's edge when he saw Sekhmire coming toward him, accompanied by a tall, thin man who wore a pleated white kilt and a wide, beaded necklace. When he got closer, Bata recognized the necklace as menat, sign of a healer.

Tossing another stalk on the growing pile on the river bank, Bata straightened up and stepped out of the soft mud. In his right hand he held a wide knife used to hack at the fibrous stems.

Sekhmire ignored the weapon.

"Bata," he said, his voice friendlier than Bata expected. "This is Imhotep, adviser to King Djoser. He wants to talk to you."

"Hello, Bata," Imhotep said, his accent strangely flat, the words said slowly and distinctly as if he paid great attention to each sound.

Bata nodded. "Yes, lord," he said, guessing at the proper greeting from the menat around Imhotep's neck. He wondered where Kanakht was, wasn't he the king's adviser? Or did the king have several advisers. Bata shrugged away the questions and asked Imhotep, "What can I tell you?"

Imhotep motioned toward a nearby tree. "Come to the shade," he said.

Seating himself cross-legged beneath the tree, Imhotep motioned for Bata to sit with him. Sekhmire stood, leaning against the tree, listening and watching.

"Tell me about Prince Teti's accident: the speed of the water, the wind, the sounds, where everyone stood, the color of the stones, what you talked about before the accident. Start when all of you were together on the shore and then tell me everything that happened," Imhotep said.

As Bata told the story, Imhotep interrupted to clarify unclear statements, to have Bata explain again how deep the water was, how much flotsam was in the water, what color the rocks were. His idea was to have Bata relate every detail, especially those that did not matter so that only the truth would fit the weave of the story.

With Imhotep asking questions about everything, Bata gave up trying to guess what was important. He closed his eyes and saw the day again, felt the cold water around his ankles and then his knees. He remembered Teti falling limply and silently toward the water, and he told Imhotep everything.

"**E**ither Prince Teti fell asleep while he was standing on top of that boulder or Nesi threw a rock at him and knocked him unconscious," Tim told Meryt later that day.

"That's what you thought when you examined him at Waset," she said.

Tim nodded and bent down to pick up a stone along the river's bank. He bounced it in his hand a few times, and then threw it out into the river. He picked up another and threw it again, harder and farther.

"What is wrong?" Meryt asked him.

He turned to her, his mouth pulled into a frown, his eyes angry. "I don't have proof," he said. "I can't accuse Nesi of trying to kill Prince Teti without proof. I know he did it. I'm positive. But I can't prove it."

Meryt looked confused.

"I don't understand, Tim. Why would you have to prove it? If you know he did, then that is enough. King Djoser will believe you."

Tim stopped walking and looked at her. "That's true," he said. He thought about what that meant. Because Hetephernebti had taken an interest in him, because he had successfully reduced the swelling of Prince Teti's arm leading King Djoser to add him to his court, Tim's, or rather Imhotep's word carried the weight of authority.

If he accused someone, they would be guilty. If he defended them, then they were innocent. Was justice here simply a matter of which person was more important? Was influence the coin of truth?

He thought of the world he had left behind with local, state and federal police; with district judges, county courts, state courts and federal courts; with courts for criminal cases and others for civil cases; lawyers who specialized in drunk driving cases, in suing other people, in criminal defense, in bankruptcy suits.

It was a huge system with so many layers, so many checks and balances – appeals, sequestered juries, rules of evidence, written records, highly trained professionals to handle every aspect.

Yet when he thought of cases that he knew about, none of them seemed to lead to justice: a famous football player walks away from a double murder charge despite blood stains and everything but a confession, a basketball player rapes a girl and his lawyers frightened her away from testifying, a mentally disabled boy is tricked into admitting a murder he didn't commit so police can close a case, businessmen steal life savings of their employees and never go to jail, a politician runs over a man and kills him, lies about it and spends less time in jail than a shoplifter.

The rich could afford the best lawyers and so they could do what they pleased without fear of punishment. A poor man who stole a thousand dollars with a gun would go to prison for twenty years. A wealthy man who stole millions through fraud would delay and exhaust the court system while living like a king.

A leader could send an army against another country, send a thousand soldiers to their deaths without fear of being made to answer. Another could steal his country's wealth and live a life beyond dreams while his subjects lived in squalor, and still be honored because of his self-awarded titles and stolen wealth.

Justice has always been a tool of the wealthy and powerful, he thought. The Crusades, the Inquisition, the European conquest of North and South America – the victors wrote the history of large events, why would I think it was different for the small, daily confrontations.

Is this system less just?

If I lie to King Djoser and he discovers the lie, I will be punished because he can no longer trust me. His advisers are close to him and he must trust them. Because he depends on those around him, even if no law applies to him, he must be faithful to them and expect loyalty in return.

'To live outside the law, you must be honest,' he thought, recalling a line from a Bob Dylan song.

With a start, Tim realized that he was still walking along the riverbank, but now the water was flowing the other direction, he must have walked around the end of the island and was heading up the other side. He looked around to get his bearings and saw Meryt kneeling by the water's edge. Her small, bare back was to him, the sun lying across the water backlit her, creating a glowing aura.

She felt him watching her and stood, turning to him and smiling. Her hands were filled with wet stones.

She walked to him, her thin arms and legs looking too long for her, her hipbones jutting out from her flat stomach, her breasts small and tight on her bare chest.

The change from his dark musings about injustice to her innocent beauty was breathtaking. He felt a warmth swell from his chest, almost like a blush, but filled with joy instead of embarrassment or guilt.

He felt like laughing, like singing. All the sounds and colors and fragrances of the world suddenly seemed exactly right, precisely as they should be and he felt as if every cell in his body, every nerve, every muscle and fiber was attuned to the beauty of the world and that beauty was centered on the coltish girl who was walking toward him, with her muddy feet, dripping wet hands and flashing brown eyes.

"Some of these stones are so smooth and others are jagged. They look the same color and they are speckled the same. Why would they be so different?" she asked, looking at the stones in her hands.

His throat was so swollen with desire he could hardly speak.

She looked up and saw his eyes taking her in, saw the smile playing at his mouth.

"I thought you were thinking about Bata and Nesi and Prince Teti," she said.

Tim reached for her, his hands caressing her shoulders and back, gently pulling her toward him. She dropped the stones and wrapped her arms around him. Tilting his head down to hers, he kissed her, softly brushing against her cheeks, moving toward her lips.

She turned her face toward his and returned his kiss. After a minute, he broke away and turned to look inland. There was nothing but rocks and sand at this end of the island. He felt her arm wrapped around his waist pull on him, urging him to turn the other way. When he did, he saw only the river.

He felt her fingers playing with the tie of his kilt and then it fell free. She took his hand and smiling up at him, she said, "Come on." She pulled him toward the water, picking up speed as he joined her until they were running across the river's beach.

They splashed into the water, feeling the soft riverbed beneath them. She led him into the water until it was waist deep, then she stopped and turned to him. Bending down she washed away the grit that was on her hands from gathering stones. Cupping her hands, she raised some of the water to his chest and splashed it on him, then rubbed her hands across his wet skin, feeling the firm muscle beneath and the hard line of his sternum.

Tim leaned forward and kissed her, running his hands down her side and then lifting her. She understood what he wanted to do and let the water support her, wrapping her legs around his waist as he raised her and then slowly lowered her.

Joined together they stood unmoving, feeling the water lap against them, feeling their skin on each other, the sun on their backs, the light breeze that followed the river's current brushing against them.

Meryt cupped her hands behind Tim's neck and leaned away from him, arching her back. Her eyes closed, she focused her attention on the sensation of being one with him.

Feeling her energy, Tim saw how immersed she was in the moment. White sunlight danced on the river's ripples. The air gathered and held the light, shimmering with urgency. The colors of the sand, the water, the sky, Meryt's skin, her eyes, the soft underside of her throat all grew richer and purer. He heard the distant cry of a hawk and suddenly sensed himself expanding outside his physical body, his spirit pushing through and soaring and growing, encompassing both of them, spreading across the river and the land, up through the dry desert air and into the sky itself.

He had a glimpse of the timeless procession of the sun across the sky, an endless march of kings and commoners across the unchanging land of Kemet and he felt again that rightness of being here, of being here now, of being here with Meryt.

Afterward, spent and barely able to walk, but energized and filled with the wonder of the pleasure they had given each other, Tim spread his white kilt on the muddy river bank for her, thinking of Sir Walter Raleigh's grand gesture.

"No," she said, laughing. "I want to feel the earth against my skin, not a dead cloth."

He remembered the first time he had seen her, spreading the river's mud over her body. He asked her about it. "I thought you were disguising yourself to go hunting or something," he said. They sat naked together on the ground, their bodies wet and glistening from the river.

He turned to face her and traced the soft line of her shoulder, down her chest and to the tip of her breast, watching the nipple grow hard. With the side of his thumb, he brushed lightly against her skin feeling the warmth, the smoothness and the vibrant thrill of their skin meeting.

"That feels good," she said, leaning back and offering herself to him without shame.

He laid the flat of his hand against her stomach and caressed her belly across her hip and the side of her thigh.

"I was covering myself in mud," she said in a dreamy voice.

"Why?" His hand crossed her knee and drifted along the inner side of her thigh, feeling the warmth there.

"To let it dry in the sun," she said, the words staggered and breathy. "I like to feel it tighten as it dries, feel it change as if the sun is making it come alive."

His hand moved higher, brushing against the softness where he had entered her.

She leaned back on her elbows and sighed.

He traced a line across her waist to her chest and neck.

"You are beautiful," he said.

She smiled and opened her eyes. "I think you see beauty everywhere, Imhotep."

"Is that how you think of me?" he asked, "As Imhotep now?" His fingers lingered on her lips, and then began to slowly move across her cheek and down her neck.

"Yes," she said.

He followed the delicate lines of her collarbone to her breastbone and down the line between her breasts.

"Yes," she said again, "I think of you as Imhotep."

His thumb caressed the arc of the ribs just above the softness of her belly.

"Tim is too small a name for you now."

Across the side of her waist, pausing on the defining shape of her hip, following the line down and across her thigh.

"Imhotep is the right name for you." She lay back completely, as he kissed her neck and began to follow the path of his fingers with his lips and tongue.

Side-by-side they lay on their backs, touching hands, looking up at the cloudless sky.

There is a true difference here, Imhotep thought. Not just in the land, although that is different. The world is so much younger, the air has been breathed less, not yet channeled through the fire of coal furnaces, steam engines and cars, not yet scarred with the millions of anguished screams from wars not yet waged, not torn by the shrieks of jet engines, rockets, missiles, bombs, and bullets.

Will the colors fade in years to come, or do I just see them differently now? Is the air sweeter, the sun brighter, the water softer?

My mind is less cluttered, with fewer decisions, less worry about the day-to-day concerns that seemed to fill it before. With less mental clutter, do I see and hear more clearly? Is my mind less separated from my body?

He felt Meryt prop herself up on her elbow and look down at him.

The back of her hand swept lightly against his cheek, brushing against the stubble of his beard. She rubbed his chest, across his stomach and then held him, tugging gently. "Do you ever touch yourself like this?" she asked, squeezing him.

He nodded. "Yes," he answered, surprised that he was not embarrassed by her question.

She bent down and kissed him once. "So do I. But it is different when you touch me. Is it because I don't know what you will do next? Is it because your skin and touch are different from others? Or is it because I want you to touch me and so I think it feels different?"

Surprisingly he felt himself begin to stir under her touch.

"Touch me like my brother," she commanded him.

Tim squinted up at her. He remembered reading that some of the kings of ancient Egypt married their sisters, or at least called their wives 'little sister.' He didn't know if it was a term of endearment or if royal incest was normal.

"Here," she said, presenting him with the bottom of one of her feet. "Tickle me, like my brother used to when we were little and fighting."

When he didn't move, she said, "I want to see if your touch is the same as his. Tickle me."

He rolled over and grabbed her ankle with one hand and began to tickle the bottom of her foot with the other. She kicked her leg, but he held on as she laughed and rolled, trying to get away.

"Stop," she said.

"Was it the same?" he asked, laughing with her.

"I don't know," she said, gasping for air. "I think it was. But look!" She grabbed her own ankle and tickled her foot. "Nothing! If another tickles me, I cannot control the feeling. If I tickle myself, nothing. If I touch myself here," she put her hand on her groin, "it can feel good if I want it to, but at other times, nothing. It depends on what I want. But here," she stretched her foot in the air, "Here, I have no control. I cannot tickle myself. Here I can, there I can't."

"Are you the same way? We must investigate," she said, laughing as she lunged for him and they began to roll across the beach.

IMHOTEP AND DJOSER

When they returned to the temple complex, Meryt said she needed to send a message to Hetephernebti at Waset, to let her know what they had learned about the attack on Prince Teti.

"What can she do?" Tim asked.

"She can ask King Djoser to appoint someone she trusts to guard Prince Teti, maybe my brother, Meryptah. He is a member of the House Guard and he is someone Hetephernebti knows.

"And she needs to know what happened," she said. "Nesi wouldn't have just attacked Prince Teti. Someone must have ordered him to do it. There had to be some kind of reward promised. Hetephernebti is going to the festival of Thoth at Khmunu. Kanakht will be there, as will priests from throughout the Two Lands. Whoever ordered Nesi to attack the prince will probably be there."

Meryt shrugged. "I don't know how Hetephernebti uses her knowledge, but she knows, more than anyone, what is happening in Kemet. She has friends all along the river and others, like me, who tell her what we see and hear. Sometimes she sends people out to different towns and festivals. I know that she writes many letters to her brother and gets many messages from him.

"That was how I found you. She heard from someone in Ineb-Hedj that a god had appeared there. She sent three of us to find you."

"You were sent to find me? But I saw you, that morning by the river. I found you."

Meryt nodded. "Yes, you found me, but I was looking for you. I knew who you were when you waded across the river, remember? You raised your kilt to keep it dry but you were wearing something underneath. I knew you were the stranger then."

"You were watching me at the festival. It wasn't an accident that you were waiting in the tunnel, was it?" he asked.

She nodded again. "Yes, I was watching you. I didn't know you would come into the tunnel, but I was watching you. I saw you find the path that Hetephernebti uses to cross from the island and I saw you try to talk to Diane before Yunet woke up. When she grabbed at you, I gasped and almost turned to run for the guards."

"The guards?"

"Yes, I would have had them arrest you for Hetephernebti. Just to save you from Djefi. But then you escaped and I was able to lead you to safety."

For a second Tim wondered if what had passed between them since had been at Hetephernebti's direction, but he quickly discarded that notion and felt embarrassed that he had even considered it. Meryt had never been anything but open and honest with him. He knew she was intelligent and certainly knew much more about ancient Egypt and how things worked here. He trusted her. He trusted that she was exactly what she seemed.

"You said that Hetephernebti sent three people looking for me. What if one of the others had found me?"

Meryt laughed. "They didn't, Imhotep. You found me and now here we are.

"When I was younger," she stopped and looked up at Tim earnestly, "I know that you think I am still very young. But when I was younger, I worried about everything. Was I walking the right way to be a priestess of Re? Did I say the right things, with the right tone of voice? I tried so hard to be what I thought Re and Hetephernebti wanted me to be.

"Hetephernebti saw this. She is wise, Imhotep, so very understanding. She told me to stop trying. She said Re loved me the way I am, with my eye to the side, with my peasant accent, with my skinny legs, with my curiosity about everything. She said that in a way, with his warm rays, Re was worshiping me just as I should worship him. And that the best way I could worship him was to be me. The gods had shaped me this way. Why should I be unhappy with what the gods had done?

"When I went looking for you, I was ready to find you, or to not find you. I was not in a contest with the others. And, look, you found me. Did Hetephernebti send three of us looking for you so that you would find only me?" She laughed again. "I love Hetephernebti and I think she is so very wise, but she does not see the future."

"So you think the gods intended for us to be together?" Tim asked.

A small frown took shape on her lips and she shook her head. "I am not so important that the gods plan my days. I honor the gods, Re above all, but I think I am on my own. Of course Hetephernebti helps me, she is wonderful, but I think my happiness and life are my own, not owed to or owned by any gods. If I step into the river and a crocodile eats me, it is because I chose a foolish action. If I fall in love with a man and he beats me, then I have chosen a bad man.

"And when I do something foolish, it is up to me to fix it. My friends can help me but this is my life.

"When I saw you I thought you were beautiful, but I did not know you. Then when Hetephernebti asked me to stay with you and teach you, I got to know you and I liked you. Then when I was ill and you saved my life, I thought that I loved you, but I was afraid that my feelings were being influenced by what you had done. So I watched and waited to see how you felt and how I truly felt. If you had not wanted me, then I would have accepted that, Imhotep. Not because it was what the gods wanted, but because it was that way."

Tim shook his head. "Here I thought you were just a mindless creature who smears herself with mud," he teased.

"Tama speaks of that," she said. "Not that I smear myself with mud, but about being mindless. I don't understand exactly what she means, but I know she means it in a good way. She says that our minds cloud our thinking. You know, when you tickled me and I couldn't tickle myself. That has to be my mind. I know that my skin feels it the same way. It has to. But my mind decides that one touch should make me laugh and another should not. So sometimes I think I should not trust my mind, but should trust my heart instead.

"Tama teaches that there is a deeper way to see things, where the mind is used, but something else helps you to see and understand. Hetephernebti teaches acceptance and love, but her mind is constantly occupied. She thinks about the people of Iunu, about her brother, the king, about the Two Lands. She and Tama are very much alike in many ways, but I think they are very different, too."

She stopped and put her hand to her mouth. "I am sorry. I talk too much. It is my heart, Imhotep. It is full to bursting because of what we have done and it is singing."

Tim smiled, his thoughts filled with admiration for Meryt. She was so young, but she had so much to teach him. "My heart is singing, too, Meryt. Now, go send your message to Hetephernebti. I must go see King Djoser and tell him what I've learned."

King Djoser, Sekhmire and Imhotep left early in the morning to survey the lands on the east bank of the river near the temple of Khnum.

Meryt stayed at the temple to work in the bakery.

"I miss making bread, grinding the flour, working the dough with my hands. Go," she had told Imhotep.

Three days had passed since Meryt had sent a letter to Hetephernebti. King Djoser also had sent a message north to his sister at Waset after hearing Imhotep's theory of what had happened to Prince Teti in the river.

Bata had been told that he would stay at Abu with them until King Djoser traveled north to Kom Ombo.

Sekhmire and King Djoser rowed the small boat across the water, the king enjoying the physical activity, pulling hard and challenging the younger soldier to keep up with him. Imhotep watched, wondering if Sekhmire was trying as hard as he could or if he was allowing King Djoser to move the boat in a slow curl.

When they reached the bank, King Djoser jumped out first to pull the reed boat up on the bank. Sekhmire and Imhotep splashed into the water and waded onshore.

King Djoser's skin was glistening with perspiration, but his breathing was steady and even. He held out the palms of his hands for Imhotep to see. "Look," he commanded. "These are the hands of a soldier. They can row a boat without tearing or blistering, throw a spear, swing a sword. But they get no use now. I sit, I listen, I send messages."

He clapped his hands together.

"Now, Imhotep, let us look at the land that you want me to give to the great ram-headed Khnum."

Turning, he led the way inland.

They explored more the next day and the day after that. Imhotep drew maps as they walked, identifying fields and boundaries, labeling huts that they saw, asking the residents their names and the names of their fathers and fathers before them.

"Isn't this recorded anywhere?" Imhotep asked King Djoser toward the end of the third day. "Doesn't the governor of the nome have records?"

King Djoser tossed his head back and laughed. Sekhmire smiled, but kept quiet. King Djoser clapped Imhotep on the back. "You are a strange man, Imhotep. So smart, and so innocent. Or are you making a joke, pointing out something I should know, but haven't seen?"

Imhotep shook his head. "I am sorry, King Djoser, I only thought ..."

"Yes," King Djoser said. "Of course, the governor has records. I am sure he would show them to me, what choice would he have? But those records and maps would be different from the ones we are making. His maps would show that he owns more than he does. Or he might have other maps for my tax collectors that show that he owns much less than he has. Don't frown, Imhotep. I would do the same.

"So, I could look at his maps and say this and this will go to the temple of Khnum. I would have to trust his maps to show the fields and the homes, wonder if they are good land or not, worry if I was taking land away from a poor farmer.

"Or, and this is what we will do with the maps you are making, I could show him my choice of the land, based on what I have seen. He will know that I have walked the land myself and that I would know that the maps he will show me are not truthful.

"To avoid losing face, he will never show me his maps. Instead he will accept that my maps are accurate, which they are. He will see the wisdom of my decision and realize that giving up the land he claims to own will be less trouble than arguing over a claim he cannot prove because he would have to show me maps he has hidden from my tax collectors.

"He will act generously, I will accept his generosity as my due. I am king after all. We both will act our parts with honor and the god Khnum will benefit. And the river will flood."

He looked hard at Imhotep. "Or so I am told," he added.

That night King Djoser called Imhotep to his chambers.

The maps Imhotep had drawn over the past three days were spread out on a table, held in place with rocks. King Djoser was standing at the table, leaning forward, his eyes on the maps. Imhotep went to the table and stood opposite King Djoser, waiting quietly until the king raised his eyes. The playfulness that Imhotep saw there so often was missing now.

"This offering must be generous, but I must not take too much land from the governor. There is a balance to maintain. You understand?" King Djoser asked.

Imhotep nodded. There was fertile land near the river, but some of it was rocky, its fields interrupted by large boulders dropped there eons ago by the river. At other spots, the riverbank rose sharply, the arable land on a steep slope fit only for trees. Still other areas were flat, they flooded easily and then held the rich silt deposits.

"This is what I have decided," King Djoser said. He pointed to tracts of land with a silver knife. "This, this, this and this I will give to Khnum," he said.

Looking at the map, Imhotep pictured the land in his mind and remembered the words of the Famine Stele he had read about that night so long ago at the Mena House.

According to the engraving on the stele, King Djoser had given land on both sides of the river from the water as far as the distant mountain ranges, including all the settlements on those lands. King Djoser had also given the temple the right to take a tenth of the gold, ivory, wood and minerals that came into Kemet from Nubia, and the hunters and fishermen in the lands given to the temple were required to give a tenth of their fish and game to the temple.

The offering King Djoser was suggesting was far, far less.

"It is a generous offering to Khnum. It is what you said I should do," King Djoser said. "The river will rise."

Imhotep stared at the table, unable to raise his eyes to King Djoser, unsure what to say. Was the stele wrong, was his memory flawed? He had hoped that King Djoser would have suggested making the same offering described on the stele.

Once he had gotten over the shock of being named Imhotep, he had felt that it was right, that somehow his passage through time was necessary, that if he hadn't followed Brian and Diane something fundamental would have been changed.

When he thought about it too much, his brain curled up in the fetal position and surrendered.

But now he worried that if King Djoser didn't make the offering history recorded that some other fundamental shift would happen and the future that had unfurled to his time would be changed. For better or worse – he had no way of knowing – he suddenly felt the weight of the unborn lives, all waiting for their chance to live.

One of them was Addy. One of them was him.

The future had to follow the path it had followed or else he wouldn't be here.

Although the thought made sense as it crossed his mind, it became elusive and slippery when he tried to examine it. Still it left him with a hollow, aching fear. King Djoser had to make the right offering.

And Imhotep knew that only he could make it happen.

"Speak, Imhotep."

He looked up at King Djoser who was leaning on the table with one hand, his other hand playing with the engraved handle of the knife he had used as a pointer.

"King Djoser," Imhotep said slowly, trying to organize his thoughts. "The river will rise only if Khnum is satisfied. The water comes from beyond Nubia, many days' journey south through a forest so thick with trees that you must cut your way through. That land is the land of Khnum.

"He is a god, King Djoser. A gift that would satisfy a man, a governor or a priest is a small thing to a god. All of the Two Lands is yours. All of the Two Lands is dry, the river has not risen for seven years. You must be more than generous to Khnum. You are not only making an offering to the god, you are acting to save the Two Lands."

King Djoser crossed his arms.

"What would you have me offer Khnum?" King Djoser asked softly.

As Imhotep looked at the maps, the feeling of belonging that had swept through him as he tended to Prince Teti, and the fullness of spirit that had came over him when he had been with Meryt returned to him, filling him with the moment and the possibilities it held, showing him the pathways that opened up from this pivotal instant.

Giving in to the impulse that swept through him now, he stepped to the table and brushed the maps to the floor.

He stood straight and, looking at King Djoser, recited the words he remembered from the stele.

"King Djoser, you must give to Khnum the lands from the river to the mountains of dawn on the east side of the river and as far as the mountains of dusk on the west side. All the land, all the wealth, all the settlements, all the farmers, from the island south as far as an oxen can plow in twelve days."

King Djoser moved with incredible speed, driving the blade of the silver knife deep into the table.

"You do not know what you ask," he said, his voice seething.

"And more, King Djoser," Imhotep said, hearing – as if from a distance – his voice level and calm. "Give to Khnum a tenth of the riches that flow from Nubia through here and into the Two Lands. A tenth of the game and the fishes, of all the wealth found within the offering."

"Who are you," King Djoser asked, "to demand such an offering?"

"Not for me, King Djoser. For Khnum. For the waters of the River Iteru. For the life of the Two Lands. Only a great offering such as this will satisfy Khnum."

King Djoser wrenched the knife from the table. He flipped it into the air and caught it as he paced, walking the length of the table and then turning back.

"If I refuse," he said to himself, "and the river does not rise, then the Two Lands will cry out for justice and the gods will know my greed has betrayed Kemet. If I refuse and the river does rise, then the Two Lands will be blessed, but the gods will still know of my avarice."

He turned to Imhotep. "Words are powerful, Imhotep. Have you met Tama, the priestess of Ma'at? She believes that words unleash all action.

"You have said the words. But it is I who must give them life."

He brought his arm back and in a quick motion brought it forward again, throwing the knife across the room. Spinning silently through the swaying light of the torches, the silver knife seemed to blink in and out of existence as it cut through the air toward a carved wooden pillar.

With a heavy thud it struck the pillar and embedded itself deep in the wood.

"I must give your words life," King Djoser repeated, "or kill them."

Imhotep bowed his head and waited.

"Repeat these words to no one, Imhotep. We will talk tomorrow."

King Djoser sent for Imhotep late the following afternoon.

The anger that had been visible the night before was gone now, replaced by the serenity Imhotep had come to expect from the king.

"Let us walk, Imhotep," King Djoser said. He led him out of the temple toward the river. They walked in silence, heading toward the western edge of the island.

"Meryt is recovering from her illness?" King Djoser asked.

Imhotep was surprised to hear the king asking about Meryt. "Yes, King Djoser. She is better every day."

"Is she carrying your child yet?"

Imhotep stopped short.

"No, no, I haven't heard any rumors," King Djoser said with a wry smile. "It is just that she is of age and it would not be unexpected."

They walked on in silence until they reached the island's edge. The sun had turned almost a blood red as it lowered itself toward the western desert. The ragged peaks of the distant mountains were silhouetted by the red glow.

"Are you a god as some have said?" King Djoser asked.

Imhotep shook his head. "I am just a man. I have come from a distant place and I bring knowledge that others here do not have. But I am a man."

"Do you believe that I am a god?" King Djoser asked.

"I am not sure I understand what that means here," Imhotep answered.

"Are gods different in your land?" King Djoser asked.

"I don't think we have any gods," Imhotep answered.

"What is a god?" King Djoser said, turning back to face the river. "I understand you have seen Djefi and were at To-She for The Cutting Out of Sobek's Tongue. Djefi keeps a crocodile that represents the god Sobek. Is the crocodile a god? At times he is a vessel for the god's ka, his spirit. But the rest of the time, Imhotep, I think he is just a crocodile.

"What about Re? So distant, so painful to look at. Eternal, unchanging, giver of life. Hetephernebti has no doubts that the fiery circle is the great god Re, and my sister is a very smart woman, Imhotep. Very wise.

"There is a difference, I think between the embodiment of the god and the spirit of the god. Am I a god? I cannot crush a rock with my hand or bring a dead person back to life. But I believe that my spirit is a god's spirit. I truly believe that, Imhotep. I believe that Kemet deserves nothing less than a god as ruler. I am the ruler. When I die, whoever takes the throne will be filled with the godlike spirit that rules Kemet, the very ka that lives inside me.

"I can make mistakes. This body is a man's, after all. But the ka, the essence of what I am, that, Imhotep, is godlike. It must be."

They stood by the riverbank, listening to the water slowly pass.

"And so I will give this gift to Khnum. I will give it gladly and freely. Khnum is my father, creator of the Two Lands and I am giving to him what is already his. If this pleases him and he brings the water, then all will be well."

He looked at Imhotep, his face just inches away from his adviser.

"And all will be well, will it not, Imhotep?"

King Djoser announced the gift and the additional expansion of the Temple of Khnum and then settled in on the island, refusing to leave until the waters began to rise.

Imhotep, as much a captive now as Bata, waited with the king and his guard. To keep the young soldiers from boredom, Sekhmire sent a hunting party into the western desert. The boatmen were allowed to go to their homes on leave, but were ordered to return within a month or sooner if the waters began to rise.

The days settled into a routine of exploring the island, swimming in the river and waiting for the water to rise. As much as he enjoyed the time with Meryt and the luxury of the leisure, Imhotep remained on edge, worried if he remembered the translation of the stele correctly, wondering if history correctly recorded that the famine ended after seven years and fearful of what King Djoser's reaction would be if the flood was meager again.

His concern only increased one morning when Sekhmire arrived after breakfast and asked him to walk with him.

Imhotep had quickly learned that 'going for a walk' meant important matters needed to be discussed away from others' ears. He had also learned that small talk in ancient Egypt never started with the weather. It didn't rain, there was no change in temperature; there was nothing to talk about. The only change was in the level of the river. Until recently, that had never been a concern because it always rose and fell at the same time each year.

Instead, conversation often opened with questions about one's family: parents, children, and spouses, whatever was at hand.

"Meryt looks well," Sekhmire said as they started down the gentle incline from the temple to the river.

"Thank you," Imhotep answered. "She is well. And your son and wife? Is there news?"

Sekhmire smiled a smile of genuine pleasure. "Siptah got into a fight with a neighbor boy who is two years older. Siptah has a black eye, but the other boy ran home crying to his mother. He shouldn't fight, but if he does, I am happy that he won. His mother will punish him, of course. Gently, I hope."

"He will be a soldier?"

Sekhmire nodded, but his eyes were distant. "I always thought my sons would be soldiers. There is honor there and Kemet needs strong hands. I was chosen for the guard of the king. Now I command it, and there is no higher honor. But I wonder sometimes what lies beyond our borders, beyond the cataracts.

"When King Djoser said that the temple, my father's temple, would receive a tenth of all the wealth that comes from Nubia and beyond, I began to wonder what Nubia would look like. King Djoser told me that you said there is a land beyond Nubia where there are so many trees that you have to cut a path through them.

"Is that true?"

Imhotep nodded. "Kemet is a beautiful land and the river is life itself. The land that I come from has small mountains that are covered with trees and grass. It has higher mountains, so high that the tops are cold and covered with ice. There are valleys so deep that it takes a full day to climb out of one. There are fields of grain, so wide and long that it takes days to cross them."

"Is there gold?" Sekhmire asked.

"Not as much as here, or in Nubia."

Sekhmire squatted by the river and picked up some gravel. He played with the small pebbles, pouring them from one hand to another. Imhotep sat beside him, waiting for him to come to his point.

"They say you see the future," Sekhmire finally said. He turned to look at Imhotep.

"Some of it," Imhotep answered. "I know more about what will happen five thousand years from now than what will happen tomorrow."

"How?"

"The country I come from is five thousand years in the future. I don't know how it happened that I am here and I am not certain how I can get back. Or that I want to go back."

Sekhmire looked down at the stones in his hand. "What you say is hard to understand. It has never happened before. Some people would say it has not happened now. Some people would say that you are from a land that we do not know and that you tell us things because your king wants to take control of the Two Lands."

Imhotep nodded his head at what Sekhmire said.

"That would make more sense. But it isn't true. What have I done, Sekhmire? I have tried to help Prince Teti, I have told King Djoser what I know. I am telling you the truth now, even though it sounds impossible."

Sekhmire weighed his words. "Why did you tell King Djoser to make such a huge gift to the Temple of Khnum?

"You know that it is my father's temple. Do you think you can buy my allegiance to King Djoser this way?" He said the words quietly, but Imhotep heard an underlying anger in his voice.

When he had recited the words of the stele to King Djoser, Imhotep hadn't known that Sekhmire's father was priest of the temple here. When he learned of the relationship, he knew Sekhmire would be suspicious. He knew he had to persuade the guard's leader that he was sincere.

"How long has the temple stood here?" Imhotep asked. "Longer than our lives, longer than your father's life, longer than King Djoser's life will be. The gift is to the temple, to Khnum. The temple will hold the land when memories can no longer recall you and me."

"Yes," Sekhmire said, "but we are here now and this gift will help my father now. Now, when threats are building around the king, now when even his closest adviser is plotting against him, now when the people of Kemet are worried and angry, now when the king needs his guards more than ever."

Sekhmire stood and wiped his hands on his kilt.

"I cannot be bribed, Imhotep. I do not think King Djoser would attempt it, but you are an outlander. I do not know you. I think you have planted ideas in the king's mind. If you can do that to the king, then I do not believe you should be trusted."

Imhotep stood beside Sekhmire and crossed his arms. He looked out across the river and saw a bird dive into the water and come up with a fish wriggling in its beak. The water level, he saw, was the same as the day before and the day before that.

"Yes, I was an outlander," Imhotep said. "But my spirit has become one with Kemet.

"Sekhmire, I know that trust isn't bought with words," Imhotep said. "I agree with you. I understand that you don't know me, and you have no reason to trust me. So watch what I do, listen to what I say and then decide. I had no feelings about the Two Lands before I came here, but I have grown to love it, even as much as you do.

"As far as buying your loyalty ... I think we all follow our hearts. I don't think your heart is filled with gold. But if you do follow the shine of gold, then your loyalty can't be bought, only rented. And then only until someone else has more money to pay. I don't think you and I are like that."

AT THE TEMPLE OF SOBEK

Standing on the east bank of the river, Brian stared at the tall pillars that rose from a bluff on the other side of the slow-moving water. The setting sun turned the tapering pillars of the temple of Kom Ombo into shadows, their edges painted in blood.

He didn't see anyone moving on the plateau, but Tama said that Diane would be there and that Djefi would not; the priest would be heading north, back to Khmunu.

But Siamun was there.

Brian walked closer to the water's edge, looking for a boatman or one of the small reed boats he had been eager to try. He found one pulled up on the riverbank almost directly across the river from the temple.

He noted where it was and then returned to the road to get his donkey. Once night fell, he would tether the donkey to a tree, cross the river in the reed boat and find Diane. If she was willing to come with him, then they would re-cross the river, get the donkey and head back to Waset where he would hide with Tama while waiting for Tim.

If Diane refused to go with him, then he would leave, knowing that it was her decision to stay here.

Either way he would be free: Free to see what life would be like here with Tama or free to find Tim and return to his time. He wasn't sure what he would do, but he couldn't abandon Diane alone in this ancient, alien land without offering her one last chance to leave with him.

He needed to be sure she understood what the decision to stay meant and that she was making it freely.

He was only a few feet from shore when he tipped over the reed boat and splashed heavily into the water. When he resurfaced, he saw the boat bobbing beside him. He pulled himself back onto it and lay flat on his stomach using his hands to paddle across the weak current, trying hard not to think about crocodiles.

A few minutes later, sighing with relief that he hadn't been attacked by crocodiles, Brian pulled the boat up on the western bank a short distance from some other boats that were tied to wooden posts. A dirt pathway led up the side of the steep cliff.

He shook himself, spraying water from his hands and arms. Listening for a moment, he heard nothing. The river behind him was silent. No frogs, no night birds, not even the empty rustle of the reeds along the bank disturbed the quiet.

Looking back across the river at the town, he saw a few fluttering lights from carried torches, but no sounds floated across the river.

Ahead of him, the path disappeared into the darkness as it rose along the side of the cliff.

Stone steps were cut into the cliff near the top of the pathway. When Brian reached them he hesitated and listened again. There was no sound of footsteps or voices. As his head cleared the top of the final step, he saw the flat plateau, paved in stone with large unfinished pillars off to his left and several small stone buildings across the stone courtyard.

Near the biggest pillars, a large circular hole was cut into the stone floor.

Brian took the last few steps and hurriedly crossed the open plaza to the pillars, stepping behind one to hide.

A gently sloping ramp led down into the circular hole, which was swallowed by the darkness. As Brian stood over it he felt a light air pull on his ankles, drawing toward the opening.

Stepping around the hole, he walked to the first stone building.

The temple was obviously still being built. He saw now that there were small mud buildings out beyond the stone paving, shelter for the workers. The stone buildings would be the apartments for the priests who would live here once the temple was completed. Now they were the obvious place for Diane and Yunet to be living.

He paused by the first building and listened. After a moment he almost started to laugh at himself. He felt like a secret agent. *Bond, James Bond,* he thought.

Tama and Hetephernebti had frightened him with stories about Djefi and he knew first hand that Siamun was mean, but really, he wondered, what was he afraid of? There were no guns here, no ninjas in black outfits with gleaming, curved swords. He imagined that the worse that would happen would be that Siamun would find him and mouth off. He really was more afraid of Diane and what she would say.

As he stepped inside the first building, an unnoticed shadow moved behind him.

It was darker inside. As he waited for his eyes to adjust he realized that he smelled perfume. Soon he could see two forms lying under a thin blanket on a low bed. Even in the dim light, he recognized the size and shape of Diane's body. He walked to the bed and knelt by her.

It took him a moment to realize what looked so strange about her: her head was not shaved. He had grown used to seeing shaved heads on everyone except young boys who wore a short ponytail pulled off one side of the head. At formal gatherings the women wore long, black wigs, but most of the time their heads were bare.

He softly brushed Diane's hair and whispered her name.

He glanced at Yunet, her back was turned to them, her breathing deep and regular. He remembered how she had walked up to them so long ago when they had first arrived at To-She after the long trek across the desert. She had been so exotically beautiful. But then she had ignored him and hidden away with Diane while he was left to wander To-She and worry.

He gripped Diane's shoulder and shook her gently, saying her name louder. She had always been a deep sleeper, hard to wake, even in the morning with the smell of brewing coffee.

She stirred and shrugged her shoulder away from him. He leaned closer and putting his mouth close to her ear, he whispered her name again.

"Diane, it's me, Brian. Wake up. We have to talk."

Her eyes fluttered open and then closed again.

"Brian," she said in her sleep.

He shook her again. "Come on, babe, wake up."

Her eyes opened again, blinking and unfocused. Then she saw him and sat up. Her face, so calm and relaxed in her sleep, took on an angry edge as soon as she saw him. He felt his heart sink.

"How are you?" he asked. "I've been looking for you, following you, ever since we got separated at Khmunu. Are you all right?"

She looked puzzled, then her face returned to its angry mask.

"We didn't get separated. You went off with that Ma'at woman. You left the boat at night and told Djefi you were staying there. You abandoned me, you son of a bitch."

Brian didn't know what to say. He had gone off to look for Tama, but he hadn't meant to abandon Diane.

"No, that's not true. I mean, I did leave the boat, but it was a trick. Djefi tried to have me killed, Diane. A man came on the boat and said I was supposed to go to the town, and then three men followed me and attacked me. I was lucky to get away."

"Supposed to go into town?" she said.

"OK, I was going to meet Tama, but, Diane, let's not fight. I came here to help you."

She folded her arms and stared at him, waiting. But listening. He felt a glimmer of hope.

"I met Tim." Seeing her confusion, he said, "Oh, you don't know about him. OK, this guy named Tim followed us here. He thinks he can help us get back to our time. Do you want to come with me?"

"Back to our time?"

"Yes, look, I know it sounds unreal, but Tim says we're five thousand years in the past. Think about it. We haven't seen any televisions, my cell phone doesn't work, there aren't any airplanes flying overhead.

"We're in ancient Egypt. This isn't some Disneyland resort. This is the real thing. It's crazy and it doesn't make sense. But it's true. There isn't any law here, no malls, no doctors, no way to get back to our homes. Hell, America won't be discovered for thousands of years.

"This is real. It's serious. We don't belong here."

He ran out of breath and watched her in the dim light, waiting for her response.

With a small shake of her head, she said, "No, Brian. You think I don't belong here." She gathered strength as the words came, whispered but riding an edge of anger.

"First off, I don't believe you. I think that you ran off to that woman and now you're finished with her and you think you can come back and snap your fingers and I'll go with you.

"You left me in the desert when we were with Bakr. Then you left me at Khmunu. Now you're done playing and I'm supposed to just leave with you because now, all of a sudden, it's too dangerous here?"

Brian thought he heard something outside. He cocked his head to look at the doorway. The darkness, the strange feel of the temple, Diane's harsh words, together they made his skin creep.

"I know where we are, Brian, I'm not stupid. I mean, I don't know, like, what year it is, they don't number them like we do. I know it's different here."

He shook his head. "No, it's not just different. It's dangerous. They look at life differently here. You might think you understand, Diane, but believe me, you don't."

"Like you're the expert all of a sudden."

He sighed. Nothing was going right. "I'm sorry, Diane. Look, I'm not going to tell you what to do ..."

"That's right, you're not."

"... but if you want to leave, I'll help you. And you might think I'm exaggerating, but I can't stay here, in this temple, any longer. We need to leave before it gets light, before anyone finds us. If they catch us they won't let us go."

"What do you mean, 'us'? Yunet and I do what we want. You're not rescuing me, Brian. She already rescued me. From you. You dragged me here, ignored me and then abandoned me for that Ma'at woman. I don't know what you think you're doing, but you are definitely not saving me."

Her voice had grown louder and Yunet stirred beside her.

"OK, OK," Brian said. "I'm sorry. I know you've been through a lot. If we leave now, we can go back home. Do you want to come with me?

Don't you miss your family and friends? Movies, shopping, restaurants?" He tried to think of other things that she liked and would miss.

He looked at her, not sure what to expect.

"Look, Brian, every time I depend on someone else I get let down. I know that, I'm not stupid. It starts out being about me, but then as soon as they get what they want – me – it changes. Everybody expects me to be something – a good daughter, a perky cheerleader, the polite little sorority girl. Even when we have sex – even you – it's do this, touch this, how's this feel, move here. You know it's true.

"Yunet is different. OK? She knows what it's like. She gives me space, lets me decide what I want to do. And you know what, Brian? If I mess up and do something wrong, or choose something different than she wants, it's OK with her. For the first time in my life I can be me without worrying about pleasing somebody else.

"Do you know how many times she's made me feel guilty because I didn't want to have sex? Zero. Zip. Do you know how many times she told me she loved me and then expected me to go have sex with her because I'm supposed to be grateful? Huh? How about never? Do you know how many times she's treated me like a person with a brain, not just a pair of tits and an ass? All the time."

Brian reached out to touch her shoulder, but Diane jerked back.

"Nobody touches me anymore unless I want them to."

"Diane, I wasn't ... Look, I'm sorry if I was a jerk. I'm sorry if people expected you to be something you weren't. I've changed a lot too in the past couple of weeks. Tama has taught me how to see things differently."

"That's great, Brian," Diane said sarcastically. "Really great. I'm very happy for you. For you and Tama, is it? But it's a little late. You know what I think? I think you see me with somebody else, see I'm happy and you feel like 'How can she be happy without me?' and you come sneaking in here trying to ruin it. Or, no, you know what? You see me with a woman and you start thinking threesome."

"No, Diane." He shook his head and stood up. "Look, babe, you're probably right, right about all of this. A couple weeks ago I probably would have thought, oh boy, two women, they can't resist me.

"But can we just not make this about you and me? Do you want to go back? I'll help you get there and once you're there you can do whatever you want. I promise."

"I can do whatever I want now," she answered.

"You sure?"

"I'm happy, Brian," she said, and for the first time he heard a note of satisfaction in her voice.

He shrugged and started to reach down to tousle her hair. "Sorry," he said, catching himself.

"Well, I'll see you around, I guess," he said.

"Are you going back?" she asked.

"I don't know." He leaned down and kissed the top of her head. "Goodbye, Diane."

He turned and walked out of the hut. He stepped clear of the building and sniffed. There was a sour smell in the air. He shook his head as it triggered a memory. It came to him – it was a locker room smell, the smell of unwashed perspiration.

He started to turn toward the source of the smell as Siamun swung his club. Brian caught a glimpse of movement, but before he could raise his arm, the club hit the back of his head and he fell into the darkness.

Brian's shoulder hurt as much as his head ached. His arms were twisted tightly behind him, his hands tied together and tethered to what felt like a wooden stake. His mouth was gagged with a dirty strip of linen and he had no idea where he was.

It was dark. The air was dank. He could hear someone snoring lightly, but couldn't see who it was. The last thing he remembered was the feeling of guilt he felt as he turned away from Diane and walked out of the hut she shared with Yunet. He closed his eyes as a wave of nausea hit him. He started to sweat as he realized that if he threw up while he was gagged it could go back down his windpipe and kill him.

He hung his head and tried to calm his breathing, but every breath made his shoulder ache. He remembered stepping out of the hut and sensing, no smelling someone behind him. He remembered turning and seeing a shadow cutting through the air at his head.

Siamun!

He took a slow, deep breath, trying to hold his shoulder still while his chest filled. He recognized the smell now; it was the same sweaty stench that had hung like a cloud outside her hut. He looked at the sleeping man and realized his vision was blurry.

Damn it! Clubbed on the head, a shoulder that might be broken, gagged and hands tied, and Siamun waiting for me.

He thought about Tama, hoping he could find calmness there. She knew he was heading this way. But she was turning north, going to Khmunu for a festival. She had told him that it would be dangerous, but he thought he was like Indiana Jones or something: He'd just sneak into the secret temple and rescue the beautiful woman.

Where is Tim? Who is going to help me?

No one, he thought. OK, so what do I do?

A foot kicked Brian awake. Looking up he saw Siamun.

"You don't get any food today," Siamun said. "If you're alive tomorrow, then maybe some." He laughed. "But then, you're a god, right? You don't need food."

Brian sat in the hut, his back and legs cramping, his stomach growling in anger and his head and shoulder aching. His mouth got drier and drier. He saw light outside the hut, even saw people moving off in the distance, but no one came into the hut.

Evening fell and then the shadowy haze turned dark. Brian nodded off to sleep several times, awaking when his head lolled to the side and pulled on his injured shoulder. He woke one more time as Siamun and two men came into the hut. Siamun carried a torch; each of the men had a short length of rope.

One man knelt on each side of him. They each tied one end of the rope they were carrying to Brian's wrists. Then one of them reached behind and untied him from the post.

Siamun left the hut and waited outside as the men helped Brian to his feet and then pulled him from the hut. They kept as far away from him as the ropes would let them, keeping the lines taut. Siamun led the way across the temple compound toward a solitary stone chair.

As he walked, Brian tried to flex his legs and hips to loosen the joints so he could run. He casually pulled on the ropes, trying to gauge how firmly they were being held.

At the chair, the men turned him so he could sit in it. He realized that they would have to untie his hands if they wanted him to sit.

Siamun leaned closer, bringing the torch up to illuminate Brian's face.

"If you try to escape, then Sobek gets dead meat," he said.

He reached behind Brian and cut the ties around his wrists. Brian pulled his arms quickly. The man on his left held the rope tightly, but the other's grasp wasn't as firm. Brian's arm came free, his fist moved quickly at Siamun's head and he felt a satisfying crack as the blow landed. Siamun staggered back, but caught himself before falling over.

Brian stepped quickly toward the man on his left, the motion making the rope slack. He pulled up his left hand and suddenly felt a jerk as the other man regained the rope and pulled Brian's right arm back.

Siamun sprang from his crouch and drove a fist into Brian's stomach.

"Hold him, hold him!" he shouted.

Brian kicked at Siamun, but he was off balance and the kick had no speed to it. Siamun danced away from it and swung his fist again at Brian while the two men jerked hard on the ropes around Brian's arms. The motion pulled Brian back into the seat and Siamun's punch missed him.

As Brian fell into the seat, his injured shoulder slammed against the back of the stone chair and he screamed in pain. The two men held the ropes tight as Siamun circled the chair, one hand rubbing the side of his face where Brian's punch had landed.

"You stupid bastard," he cursed as he came close to the man who had relaxed his grip on the rope. He reached out suddenly and slapped the man, his hand cracking loudly across the man's face. "Hold the rope, hold the rope," he said. "If he gets loose, if he touches me again, I swear you'll be in that chair next."

Brian felt his arm jerk as the man pulled hard on the rope. As the arm was yanked back, Brian's shoulder twisted and another bolt of pain shot through him.

Siamun took the rope from the man's hands.

"Tie his feet," he ordered.

After Brian's feet were tied, the men pulled the ropes around the back of the chair and tied them together there, pulling his arms tight.

Once Siamun was sure Brian was secured, he leaned close to his face.

Brian saw with hollow satisfaction that Siamun's face had already started to swell where he had hit him.

"Tonight will be the start. If Sobek is hungry enough, it will be the end, one that I will enjoy watching as a true god devours you alive," Siamun sneered.

One of the men disappeared for a moment and then came back into the circle of yellow light cast by the torch. He was carrying a basket filled with dead fish.

"Start by the well," Siamun ordered. "Lay a trail to the chair."

The man put a dead fish at the top of the circular opening in the courtyard. He lined up the rest of the fish in a row that stopped by Brian's feet.

"Have a good night," Siamun said. He reached out and slapped Brian hard across his face, turned and walked away.

It was quiet in the courtyard. The moon and stars gave enough light that Brian could distinguish between open space and the pillars of the rising temple. He could see where the low wall around the complex ended. Far off to the east he thought he could see a darker ragged line where the tops of the trees interrupted the horizon.

His head ached, his shoulder was on fire and he tasted blood on the linen cloth that gagged him. He didn't know if he had bitten himself somehow or if Siamun's farewell slap had broken the skin. His stomach was empty and he had to piss.

He tried to think of Tama and the nights they had spent together during the trip from Khmunu. He thought about baseball games he had played. He thought about the early part of his relationship with Diane.

When he felt calmer, he began to assess his situation, trying to think of what was really happening, not what his fears were projecting.

Just then he saw a shadowy movement from the well, something large and dark was moving within the blackness. There was a heavy scratching sound. The movement came again, narrow but heavy. Then another movement and he saw that it was a huge crocodile, its head tilted up as it swallowed a fish.

It shook its knobby head and turned toward him. Its right forefoot was raised a few inches off the ground as it began to pivot. Then it saw him. The huge head stopped moving and its leg remained off the ground as it froze. The grotesque angle and the beast's rigid pose cut through Brian. As he watched in horror, the crocodile slowly put its foot down and pushed itself forward, another step closer to him.

Brian began to scream through his gag.

THE TRAINING OF SOBEK

Samut arrived in the village of Kom Ombo two days after Brian was taken captive in the temple across the river.

No one in the village had seen Brian, although a farmer at the northern end of town told Tama's messenger that he had found a donkey two days earlier and another farmer said his reed boat had drifted away the same night.

An old woman who had trouble sleeping told Samut that she heard unhappy spirits moaning in the night air that floated along the river. But she also heard Khepri speak in the scratchy sound of scurrying scarabs and Mehen whispered to her whenever she saw a snake uncoil and slither away.

Samut went to each house in the small village, telling the same story. He told the villagers that he had been sent by Hetephernebti, priestess of Re, and Tama, priestess of Ma'at, in search of a stranger.

"You would know him. He is tall and fair skinned. He speaks our tongue, but not very well. If you find him, give him shelter. Re and Ma'at will bless you."

When he was shown the donkey the farmer had found, Samut recognized it as the one Tama had given Brian. He thanked the farmer for taking care of it and told him to keep the animal as a gift from Ma'at.

"But I would have you do me a favor," Samut added.

With the farmer's help, Samut was able to find a messenger to carry a letter north to Hetephernebti at Waset. Samut told the priestess that although no one had seen Brian, he believed that Brian had crossed the river to the Temple of Sobek. He promised to wait at Kom Ombo until Brian returned. Then he would take him to the village of Edfu, a short distance north of Kom Ombo where they would wait for Tama or Hetephernebti.

By the fourth day Brian had given up hope.

He was weak from hunger, and the nightly fear from being exposed to the crocodile had drained his spirit. He no longer struggled when they dragged him to the stone chair, where he expected to bleed to death as the crocodile ate him alive.

His worst enemy was his imagination.

He pictured the crocodile chewing on his legs. He saw himself kicking at it, his legs reduced to a shinbone with bloody scraps of skin hanging from the torn flesh. He imagined the pain and the screams and he prayed that he would lose consciousness quickly.

But each night, although the crocodile had grown braver, Brian had not been killed. And each morning, before dawn, Siamun and his guards untied Brian and led him stumbling on stiff legs back to Siamun's hut where he was bound and tethered to a post. Each afternoon the gag was removed and he was given warm, dirty water, which he lapped at hungrily.

He dozed through the day, dreaming of his college friends, of playing baseball, of Tama. The awkward angle of his tied arms, the pain in his shoulder, which had changed from a sharp pang to a throbbing ache, kept him from ever forgetting where he was, even in those brief dreams.

At times he daydreamed of somehow wrestling free of the ropes and attacking Siamun, but as the days wore on, he knew he wouldn't have the strength to fight him even if he did break free.

On the second night, exhausted from straining against the ropes, he had fallen asleep in the stone chair. The crocodile had eaten fish after fish, following the trail that led to Brian. It had brushed its snout against his shin, almost as if it were taunting him. Then it had walked away, exploring the confines of the courtyard, which was bordered by a short wall.

When Brian woke, he was disoriented but the ropes on his arms and the hard stone against his bare skin brought his fear rushing back, bringing with it an adrenaline surge.

Looking around, he couldn't see the crocodile, and he wondered if it had returned down the wide ramp to its well.

He pushed his toes hard against the stone paving and felt the chair move. His legs were tied to the legs of the stone chair, but when he slid as far forward on the chair as the ropes around his arms would let him, he was able to wiggle his legs a little lower.

He pushed again and felt the front legs of the chair rise. He let the chair fall forward. Then he pushed again, rocking his chest and head backward at the same time. The chair rocked back farther and then fell forward with a dull thud.

The chair was stone, but so was the pavement. If he could rock the chair over, the arms of the chair could shatter and his hands would be free.

He almost smiled.

Calming his breathing, he closed his eyes and focused his energy. He relaxed his shoulders and hands, leaned forward, pressed his toes against the stone and pushed hard, flinging himself backward. The chair tilted, farther this time. It fell forward heavily and Brian pushed back again, trying to create a rhythm to his movement.

On the fifth try, the chair tilted farther and he slammed his shoulders backward desperately, ignoring the pain. The chair tottered on its back legs and then began to fall backward. Brian cocked his head forward trying to brace himself so his head wouldn't slam against the back of the stone chair.

It seemed to fall in slow motion. He saw the stars slide by, he felt the air brush against him as he fell and then suddenly he was on the ground. There was a loud thud, but no shattering sound. The arms of the stone chair were intact; he was still tied and unable to move.

He lay on the courtyard, staring at the uncaring stars. He felt moisture on his cheek and realized that he was crying. He gave in to his fear when he saw the dark shape of the lumbering crocodile emerge from the well and pause as it saw him on the ground.

Diane learned about Brian a week after he had been captured.

Siamun appeared at the doorway of the room she and Yunet shared. And said, "Come."

Yunet took Diane's hand and they followed Siamun across the temple grounds, behind the main temple building to a small collection of huts.

Siamun motioned for them to enter one of the huts that stood apart from the others.

"Oh my god," Diane cried when she saw Brian. He was propped sitting against the wall, one eye red and swollen, his arms tied behind his back. He looked as if he had lost twenty pounds and aged fifteen years.

He looked up at her, barely conscious. "Hey, babe," he whispered.

She started to rush to him, but Siamun moved between them.

"Get out of my way, you animal," she said and pushed against him. Siamun grunted and pushed back, shoving her against Yunet, who stood unmoving in the doorway.

"What is he saying?" Siamun demanded.

"Let him go, right now!" Diane ordered.

Siamun spit on the ground near her feet. "He says the same thing over and over. What does it mean?" he asked.

Turning to Yunet, Diane said, "Please, make him let Brian go. This isn't right."

Yunet looked at her sadly. "Djefi has said you are to remain safe. But he has ordered Brian killed. There is nothing I can do. I am sorry."

"Killed? What do you mean? He can't just order someone killed. How long have you known about this? Why didn't you tell me?"

Yunet started to speak, but Siamun grabbed Diane's arm and spun her around to face him.

"Answer me!" he shouted. "He says the same words, over and over. What do they mean?"

Diane shrugged away from his touch. Siamun scowled and stepped quickly to Yunet. He grabbed her throat and put his knife at Yunet's eye. "Tell me what he says," he demanded, looking at Diane.

"What does he say? I'll tell you what it means."

Siamun glared at Brian. "Say the words!" he commanded.

"Go to hell," Brian said hoarsely.

Siamun turned back to Diane. "Those sounds. What do they mean?"

Yunet held her head tensely, her eyes wide with anger, her fists clenched. She watched Diane and waited. Siamun dug the point of his knife into her cheek, just below her right eye.

He turned to Diane. "Another scar, for my wife?" he said.

"It's a curse," Diane said quickly. "He is cursing you."

"I know that. But what does the curse mean?" He pressed the knife harder and a drop of blood rolled down the blade from the cut he made under Yunet's eye.

Diane tried to think of a curse that would belittle Siamun, show him that she wasn't afraid. She knew men and she knew the kind of pride a bully like Siamun would have.

"I don't know your words for the curse," Diane said, "but it means that you aren't man enough to make a child. That you can't get hard."

Yunet gasped and jerked away from Siamun, but she was too slow. He pulled the knife viciously across Yunet's face.

"Bitch," he seethed. "What have you said? There will be a day when Djefi doesn't care about you and then, Yunet, then I will finish it."

He put his open hand against her face and pushed her out of the hut.

Whirling at Diane he grabbed her arm and pushed her outside. Then he turned to Brian.

Outside Diane heard Siamun shout at Brian, she heard a wet thud as Siamun kicked Brian and she heard Brian's weak response, "Go to hell."

The scream that startled Diane from her sleep ended in a gargled moan. She sat up in her bed and swung her legs over the side to get up.

"Don't go," Yunet said, grabbing her arm.

Diane pulled away from her.

"I thought he had escaped at Khmunu. Please believe me," Yunet said.

Diane stood, refusing to answer her.

"There is nothing we can do. You don't understand Djefi or Siamun. Believe me," Yunet said.

"I'm not going to sit here while he's being killed."

"I thought you hated him."

"Are you coming with me?" Not waiting for an answer, Diane turned and headed for the door. She looked around the room for a weapon, but didn't see anything she could use to fight Siamun.

Then I'll use my hands, she thought, stepping into the night.

She saw three men standing near the center of the courtyard by the stone chair.

She hurried across, recognizing Siamun among the group. A clay pot was at his feet, red coals glowing within it. One of the men was holding a thin, rod, whose tip was glowing red-hot.

"What are you doing? Stop it," she shouted, breaking into a run.

Siamun turned to her, his face twisted into a grin, his eyes bright with excitement. As he turned, she saw Brian, tied to the stone chair, blood dripping from his mouth. Siamun laughed and held out his hand. His fingers, dark with blood, held something thick, floppy and bloody pinched between them.

She stopped as she looked in horror from the bloody flesh to Siamun's happy face and then to Brian, his head slumped, his chest heaving and his mouth held strangely open. The smell of burnt flesh hung in the air.

She heard Yunet's soft footsteps behind her, but couldn't tear her eyes away from the gruesome scene in front of her. Suddenly a shadow moved close to the courtyard floor. Siamun and the others stepped back from it. Brian, his head lolling against his chest, didn't register the movement.

The shadow stepped into the dim light of the torches and Diane saw that it was a huge crocodile.

The other two men backed away as Siamun extended his arm.

"Here, Sobek," he called. "Have a taste of what awaits you."

The crocodile tilted its head back and opened its long jaws to catch the flesh Siamun tossed to it.

Diane was petrified, unable to move. She felt Yunet come up and put an arm around her shoulders, turning her away from the men.

"What is happening? This is a nightmare," Diane said numbly.

"There is nothing we can do," Yunet said. "I am sorry."

Diane started to cry as Yunet led her back to their room.

"I don't understand," she said. "What did they do? Why?"

"Siamun has done this before. It is what he is known for. It is because he is cruel."

"What?" Diane asked, not sure if she wanted to know.

"He has cut out Brian's tongue."

Watching from the doorway of her small hut on the far side of the courtyard, Pahket saw Diane collapse and fall to the ground.

Pahket had learned about Brian's capture the morning after it happened. Every night she watched from her hut as he was led across the empty courtyard to the stone chair. Every night she watched the men tie him in place and leave him there. She had seen him tip over the chair, she had seen the crocodile sniff at him and then walk back to its dark well.

And she had seen the guard Siamun left behind, standing by a pillar, keeping watch.

Although she was petrified of Siamun and his guards, she swore to herself that if Brian survived this night, she would somehow find a way to save him.

After Siamun had cut out his tongue, the other men had held a red-hot iron to the stump to cauterize it. The pain from the knife had been nearly overwhelming. The pain of the iron, the taste of his own burning flesh and the sure knowledge that he was going to die had released Brian.

As his body slumped, exhausted and brutally abused, his consciousness seemed to rise. The smell of burning flesh was with him, but he was somewhere else, high above them, looking down, seeing everything through a haze.

So this is death, he thought.

He felt the throbbing pain in his mouth, but his mind was on Tama. He heard her voice, felt her skin and saw her quick, sure smile. He saw her face, her eyes, and her mouth, and then he saw only darkness.

"Take him to the hut," Siamun said. "Let Sobek get hungrier. Tomorrow night we will rub him with fish oil and leave no other food out for the crocodile."

He laughed and walked away. The two guards untied Brian and carried him, his legs dragging behind him as they crossed the courtyard.

Pahket ducked back into her hut as they went by. She saw that their faces were drawn; they didn't share Siamun's enthusiasm for torture.

Diane drank her courage from a clay pot the next day, alternating between tears of sorrow and tears of rage. She started drinking beer at breakfast and continued until she passed out.

"You can't just decide to have someone killed. You don't just cut out someone's tongue. You can't just tie them up and leave them for a crocodile to eat. That just doesn't happen," she mumbled, her words awash with anger and alcohol.

But despite her anger and worry, Diane knew that there was nothing she could do.

She had allowed herself to use her anger at Brian as an excuse: an excuse to ignore him, an excuse to experiment with Yunet, an excuse to pretend that this was all some sort of exotic adventure, that it wasn't real.

She knew that all of her life she had allowed others to make her decisions. She had learned to manipulate men, and women, too. But in the end, she had let others decide, so that she was never to blame. If a restaurant was bad, it wasn't her fault, her date had picked it. If a concert sucked, it wasn't her fault.

There was always someone else to blame.

And now Brian, poor, sweet Brian, is paying the price, she thought. I could have stayed with him at To-She. I could have insisted we go to the Caribbean for a trip instead of this god-forsaken, barbaric land.

Could have, should have.

Cursing her weakness, she finished another pot of beer and passed out as night crept into the temple grounds.

Brian didn't know why he was still alive.

He thought he had died last night. All day as he sat hunched in pain, quivering with the sharp pangs that came in wave after wave over his face, his mouth and his shoulder. He wished he were dead.

And then he remembered Siamun.

If there were any way he could be free, even for a moment, he would find a way to kill Siamun. He thought of Tim, traveling with the king, of Tama and Hetephernebti. *If I can get free and find them, then something will be done,* he thought. *No, if I get free, I'll kill him myself.*

But when he tried to picture himself with his hands around Siamun's throat, he realized that he barely had the strength to raise his arms. He needed to escape, to recover and then …

He closed his eyes and tried to picture Tama.

Then it was night and they came to take him again to the stone chair.

Pahket watched his struggle to walk across the courtyard.

They tied him in the chair, cut the head from a dead fish and smeared in on his legs and lap and then left. Siamun returned to his hut, one of the guards following after him. The second guard walked to a pillar and leaned against it, his eyes on Brian.

She didn't know how long it would take for the crocodile to come out of the well, so as soon as Siamun entered his hut, she walked out into the courtyard.

The guard straightened up as he saw her.

"Go back to your bed, Pahket, you shouldn't be here."

"Why?" she asked, looking over at Brian.

"It's dangerous," the guard said.

"I saw what happened last night," she said. "He doesn't look too dangerous." Pahket nodded toward Brian.

The guard shook his head. "No, he's not dangerous. It's Sobek. He's loose. You're not safe out here."

She drew closer to him.

"I'm safe if I'm with you," she said, stopping and then turning her back to him, pretending she was looking at Brian. She knew that the guard would be looking at her, wondering if he should take her, if she would cry out or if she came here because she wanted him.

Pahket knew that some women were attracted to danger and power. She hoped the guard would think she was one of them.

Soon she felt his hand on her bare shoulder, felt it slide down her back and squeeze her hard.

"Maybe I'm not safe with you," she said without looking at him.

"Maybe you don't want to be safe," he said, turning her around.

She allowed him to take her, urging him to last longer, to be stronger and rougher.

He was gasping from the exertion when he finished and then he fell heavily on her, exhausted and satisfied.

She slipped out from under him and sat leaning against the pillar, waiting for him to stir, prepared to coax him into more sex if necessary. When he began to snore, she hurried to Brian. He was awake, watching her. His eyes were clearer than she expected.

"Ahket," he said, her name sounding strange from his injured mouth.

She untied him, glancing over her shoulder toward the guard and at the dark well. Releasing the last knot, Pahket helped Brian to his feet.

"Iamun," he said, looking across the courtyard at the hut.

"No, Brian. You haven't the strength. He'll kill you."

Brian knew she was right; he could barely stand.

She led him to the outer edge of the courtyard, to the path that led to the river. Pahket had planned to just set him free, but she saw now that he was too weak to escape on his own. Draping one of his wasted arms over her shoulders, she helped him down the path. When they reached the river, she lowered him to the ground and then pushed one of the small reed boats into the river.

She helped him stagger to the boat and, using the buoyancy of the water, pushed him onto the small boat. Crawling on beside him, she straddled the narrow boat with her legs and began to paddle across the river.

THOTH UNBALANCED

Djefi imagined himself sitting on the throne of the Two Lands.

The walls of the palace would be covered with paintings of himself among the gods. Sobek, standing upright, his fierce crocodile snout held open to display his ferocious teeth, would be foremost among them.

Fear and strength would be the foundation of Kemet once Djefi was on the throne. The armies would no longer just patrol its borders. They would storm into the land of cedar and gold and precious spices; they would seize gems and silver. They would return to the Two Lands with wealth and with slaves, the just rewards for a land as strong as Kemet!

The generals would come to him, followed by slaves carrying the wealth of their land. Kemet would be powerful and feared.

By the light of a hundred flickering torches, a banquet would be spread before Djefi. The finest beers and wines, platters of roasted oxen and geese, fish and lamb would be set for him. He could almost smell the aromas and almost taste the perfectly seasoned foods, enough to make Sobek regrow his tongue!

Servants would wait on him, holding his wine cup, feeding him figs and wiping his lips for him.

Yes, he would sit upon the throne of the Two Lands and upon his lap would sit a young boy, a beautiful innocent thing. He would stroke the soft skin of the young boy's shoulders unbent by work, not yet dried and toughened by sun, so soft and smooth. And the boy would nestle against him and touch him, reminding him of his own lost childhood.

Djefi unconsciously emitted a soft sigh.

The carriers reached the door of Waja-Hur's room and carefully lowered the sedan chair to the ground. Two of them came to Djefi and helped him from the low seat, hearing his bowels loudly belching as he stood up, a sound they had come to expect from him. They averted their eyes from the other carriers, who would be making faces at the noise and odor.

Oblivious to it all, Djefi held a satisfied smile on his face as he waddled through the doorway of Waja-Hur's room to meet again with Kanakht and the aging priest.

He was pleased to see three chairs in the room.

Waja-Hur stood by one of them, his hands twitching slightly as they rested on its straight wooden back. Kanakht, his posture formal and erect as always, stood beside his old friend, talking softly. They both turned as Djefi's shadow led him into the small room.

"You've been here before, haven't you?" Waja-Hur asked.

Kanakht came around from behind the chair, his arms spread wide in welcome. "Djefi, how goes the progress on your temple? And the training of Sobek?" he added softly as he hugged Djefi in greeting.

Djefi allowed the awkward embrace and then sat in one of the chairs.

He nodded in appreciation as a servant appeared with a jar of beer. After taking a long drink he looked up at Kanakht.

"The temple will be ready, as will Sobek." He took another long drink and, seeing no linen cloths, wiped his mouth on his arm. "The beer is good, Waja-Hur, or Kanakht," he added when he saw the confusion on Waja-Hur's face.

Kanakht stepped in smoothly.

"Waja-Hur is focusing his attention elsewhere, Djefi. But he will attend the dedication of your temple at Kom Ombo and he remains as convinced as ever that the Two Lands are not in balance."

He patted Waja-Hur softly on the back, "Isn't that so, old friend?" Waja-Hur looked up at him, seemingly startled to see him.

"Kanakht," he said as if recognizing him for the first time.

"I was just telling First Prophet Djefi about your concerns. That the Two Lands must be brought back into balance," Kanakht prompted.

Waja-Hur nodded fiercely.

"Just as each man's spirit must be balanced, so must the Two Lands." His voice came alive. "It was always so. It always will be so. There is a time for work and a time for rest. We must honor the gods and we must honor the land, and even ourselves. Balance! We must strive and we must know our place. The gods have given us the land, the sun, the water, the strength, the knowledge. When all are in harmony, then Kemet thrives."

The old man paused as if out of breath, then he gulped in more air. Little white flecks of spittle clung to his lower lip. He looked around the room confused and grew silent.

Turning to Djefi, Kanakht said, "Tell me about Sobek."

Disconcerted by the old man's ramblings, Djefi took a moment to gather his thoughts.

"At the dedication, there will be one chair for the king. Everyone else will stand. Sobek will be led from his lair, guided by two acolytes, each of them holding a leash. If a leash should break, or if one of the boys should stumble and drop one, then Sobek will be free to do what he pleases." Djefi arched his eyebrows knowingly and sipped from his beer.

"And what will Sobek do, Djefi?"

"He will attack whoever is sitting in the chair, of course. He will show his fierce displeasure with the king. He may tear off his leg; he may drag him screaming into his lair, he may devour him on the spot. He will do …"

Kanakht interrupted him. "How do we know he will do that?"

Djefi showed his annoyance at the question. He was no longer the minor priest from a hidden oasis that he had been when Kanakht first recruited him. Now he had been to Waset, he had seen the fruits of power, he had ordered a new temple to be built and it was being built – his word was iron!

Once Sobek attacks King Djoser, once the pathway to the throne is open, although Kanakht may think he will walk that path, Siamun and I will have something to say about that, Djefi thought.

He put his annoyance aside and decided to give Kanakht a glimpse of who really held the power.

"Do you know that your man Nimaasted failed to deal with the outlander named Brian?"

Kanakht nodded. "I know. This Brian was aided by someone – someone from one of your boats," he said, turning the weakness back to Djefi.

"No," Djefi answered quickly. "By another outlander! This Imhotep who is now by the king's side – in your place – he is the one. But Brian was foolish enough to go to Kom Ombo, to the temple I am building. There he was caught. He is the one who sits on the king's chair, teaching Sobek, offering himself to the great god so that Sobek will have a hunger for whoever sits in that chair!"

For a moment Kanakht imagined the terror Brian must be going through, then he steeled himself and put the feeling aside. What was one man's life compared to the greater good his sacrifice would bring to the Two Lands?

He nodded at Djefi. "Excellent!" he said. "You have found a way to solve your problem and at the same time create a powerful force. You have gifts I did not see before."

Djefi emptied his beer and motioned for the servant to refill his cup. He belched loudly and smiled at the hearty sound.

As Kanakht turned away to hide his own smile, a shadow darkened the doorway. He looked up to see Hetephernebti standing there, Tama by her side, looking like a small, younger version of the priestess of Re.

"Greetings, dear Hetephernebti, greetings Tama," Kanakht said, wondering if the women had been lingering outside the doorway long.

As she always seemed to, Hetephernebti anticipated his question.

"I told your guards that there was shade and food to be had in the courtyard, Kanakht. What need to guard us in the temple of Thoth? Only outlanders need to have fear here in Khmunu."

Djefi looked into his cup of beer. He didn't like Hetephernebti, liked her even less since her haughty attitude weeks ago when his party had been attacked by the outlander now called Imhotep.

Once your brother is gone, I'll put you in your proper place, he thought.

Kanakht shook his head. "I'm sorry, dear Hetephernebti, but I think you have heard rumors. It is the outlanders who bring fear to Khmunu. One of them attacked and killed a temple acolyte a few weeks ago. A man named Brian. I'm sure you have heard of it."

He turned to Tama. "You were here. I'm sure that you've heard of this Brian."

Tama stepped into the crowded hut. "Yes, I've heard of him. In fact, I have talked with him. He says that Nimaasted and three others attacked him. I believe him."

"He is an outlaw, Tama. He is dangerous. Or should I say, that he was dangerous?"

Djefi chuckled and broke wind loudly. "I don't think danger is one of his attributes any more," he said in his squeaky voice.

Tama and Hetephernebti waited for him to continue, but it was Kanakht who spoke.

"He was captured at Kom Ombo. Djefi is holding him for me until after the ceremony here. Then I'll journey to Kom Ombo; I'm heading there for the dedication of Sobek's new temple. Once there I'll dispense justice to this outlander."

"Be careful of the 'justice' you administer, vizier," Tama said. "A final justice waits for us all. Keep your heart light."

"Thank you, Tama. Advice is always welcome, especially on matters of ma'at. But, I believe that sometimes strong measures must be taken when the balance is disturbed. I think the gods understand."

Tama was about to answer when she saw Waja-Hur begin to sway. She hurried to him and, putting her arms around him, steadied him.

"Little father," she said, leading him around to the front of the chair and helping him to sit. She knelt by him and looked up at his aged face. "Waja-Hur, have you eaten today?"

He looked at her, his eyes watery and confused.

Hetephernebti left the hut quickly. "I'll find him food," she said over her shoulder.

Kanakht knelt beside Tama at Waja-Hur's side.

"You know that Waja-Hur believes as we do, Tama," he said quietly. "There is an unbalance in the land. I know that you and Hetephernebti are good friends. I am her friend, too. And yours. But she is blinded by love for her brother. He is not a god. You know it in your heart.

"King Djoser's actions offend the gods," Kanakht continued. "The result is famine, unrest, unhappiness. Change is coming, Tama. Brian disappeared when you did. We both know it was not coincidence. Now he has been caught and he will be punished.

"I do not think that Brian and this pretender, who Djoser has chosen to name Imhotep, arrived here at this time by accident. The gods are testing Kemet. They are showing us how unbalanced the Two Lands have become.

"I am not a priest, Tama, but I am vizier. The Two Lands are my heart and I will preserve them. No matter what it takes. Be sure of that. Change is coming. Be careful where you stand. You are with us, Tama, or you are against us."

The young priestess kept her eyes on her friend Waja-Hur. His eyes were unfocused, his breathing shallow. A sheen of sweat had appeared on his skin.

"I don't know what you see through your eyes, Kanakht. I have walked the Two Lands. The people are hungry, yes, that is true. But they are hungry for food, not power. They want to fill their bellies, not their ..." She turned to him now.

He expected to see anger in her eyes, or fear. Instead he saw confidence and honesty.

"You are older than I and more experienced," Tama said. "But please listen to me, Kanakht. I do not seek power, I do not want rewards. I am Ma'at. I seek the truth.

"This is truly the Two Lands, but in a different way. There are those, like you and me, who live a life of ease. I do not sew or cook. Your hands have not seen hard work in the years I have known you. We do not work the land, we do not bake the bread or brew the beer, yet our bellies are never empty and our skin is always oiled.

"No wait, hear me out," she said as he scowled and started to speak.

"We are needed. I am not suggesting that we are not. Without your guidance, our granaries would never be filled or maintained, our borders would not be secure. Djefi, Waja-Hur, Hetephernebti and I, the gods we represent give the land order and give the people a framework in which to live their lives.

"But, Kanakht, without the other half of the Two Lands, without the farmers and the bakers and the pressers of oil and the butchers and the fishermen, without them, you and I would be hungry. We would die. We may think that they need us, but we need them more.

"This change you say is coming, it may be no more than changing kohl, no more than fresh linens. What means so much to us may be meaningless to the people who fill the Two Lands.

"They follow King Djoser now. They followed his father before him and they will follow Prince Teti once he becomes king. But what they really follow is their bellies and their hearts. When they awake each day they answer to their own needs, their hungers, their aches, and their desires. It matters not to them who sits on the throne of the Two Lands."

Kanakht leaned closer to her, his face drawn tight with anger.

"You think the people have no will?" he asked. "You think the army is only strong arms and willing backs? Ask King Djoser, ask Hetephernebti. You live in your world of truth and ideals, Tama. The world I live in is colored with half-truths, with ambition, with unrealized dreams and desires. The people in my world, Tama, in the real world, they want more than a full belly. And they see that King Djoser cannot give them even that."

Tama looked at Waja-Hur, his face pale, his eyes distant, his breathing more regular now, but still shallow.

"Kanakht," she said, gathering her thoughts, "What you say is true. I know that. But it is only part of our world. I search for truth, the truth that lies beneath all. The world you live in, with King Djoser, with the generals, with the governors of the nomes is a small, small part of the Two Lands.

"I agree that part of the Two Lands is filled with ambition and a hunger that would devour all of Kemet. And that is why Waja-Hur's words, as old as they are, are true. The balance must be maintained. I don't believe the people of the Two Lands would rise up against King Djoser, or against whoever sits on the throne, but if disorder is sown, if the balance is struck down, then it is possible that more than one person will seek to restore it.

"If the disorder is too great, the people may choose to follow a different leader than the one you would put on the throne."

Suddenly Djefi spoke, his voice high pitched, but held in control.

"Ah, but they will follow a king the gods put on the throne," he said smugly.

Tama and Kanakht turned to look at the fat priest, whose presence they had forgotten.

He was leaning forward in his chair, his robe straining against rolls of fat, his small eyes intense and bright.

"So much talk," he said. "At To-She we do not talk so much. We act. Come to Kom Ombo, Tama. You will see your precious 'truth' in action."

He leaned back in his chair and looked toward the doorway. Snapping his fingers, he called, "More beer, boy, more beer."

The young boy who was standing by the doorway picked up the jar of beer and using both hands, carried it to Djefi and carefully poured more beer into the priest's cup. As he turned, Hetephernebti entered the hut carrying a round loaf of bread.

She was followed by Nimaasted.

Seeing Waja-Hur, the young priest pushed past Hetephernebti and rushed to Waja-Hur's side. He bent down and cupped Waja-Hur's face in his hands.

"Little father," he said, leaning close to him. He moved his hand down Waja-Hur's neck to feel the weak pulse there. Waja-Hur rolled his eyes toward Nimaasted and opened his mouth to speak, but no words came out.

Nimaasted put an arm under Waja-Hur's legs and easily lifted the small man. He headed toward the door.

"Please," he said over his shoulder, "Come with me, Tama. Go to my room. There is a sack by the altar, it has amulets in it. I will take Waja-Hur to Akhenre, he has treated him before. Bring the amulets to him."

Tama turned to Hetephernebti before she left. "Waja-Hur has grown weaker since I last saw him. His ka is preparing to leave his body. Akhenre is a good doctor and will help him, but I'm not sure what more can be done," Tama said.

"Go, little sister," Hetephernebti answered.

Kanakht and Hetephernebti stood silently for a moment, looking absently out the doorway. Djefi sipped noisily at his beer.

"You and Tama have been talking," Kanakht said.

Hetephernebti didn't answer.

"I advised Tama to be careful," Kanakht continued. "She is a smart woman. I hope she sees the wisdom of my advice."

Hetephernebti turned to him now. She glanced at Djefi who sat unmoving on his chair, his eyes fixed on them.

"I know that you are planning to kill my brother," she said. Djefi coughed at her openness, but Kanakht merely smiled at her.

"And I thought Tama was the direct one. You have always been more discreet, Hetephernebti. Much like your brother," Kanakht said.

"Be careful what you plan," she said. "If I know of your intentions, you can be sure my brother knows."

Kanakht looked away from her, out the door into the fading light.

He nodded. "In some few ways King Djoser has been a good king, Hetephernebti. But he has reached too far. We both know it. I think that in some way he welcomes the idea of being tested. He allows it to see if the gods are truly with him, if he truly is one of them. I think he will accept what the gods decide. You would be wise to accept it, too."

Hetephernebti raised her chin as she looked at Kanakht.

"I will fight for my brother," she said.

"Then you will lose," he answered.

THE EYE OF RE

In the days before the Two Lands were united, when the gods still walked along the river banks and made their life in Kemet, Tefnut, also called 'She-of-Moisture,' argued with her father, the god Re. Of what, no one remembers.

Tefnut changed herself into a murderous lion and fled south to Nubia, leaving behind her father and all the other gods.

Now Tefnut was also known as "The Eye of Re" and "Lady of the Flame," but most importantly the goddess was "She-of-Moisture." When she fled Kemet she took with her the green waters of the oases and the clear waters from the wells and the slow-moving water from the canals and irrigation ditches and all the water from the River Iteru.

And Kemet became dry. Drier than the skin of a camel's knee, drier than scales of a sloughed snakeskin, drier than a farmer's throat after a day of cutting dusty stalks of wheat.

Kemet sank into chaos, and even Re, in time, felt the loss of his daughter. He called Shu, god of air, filled with divine knowledge; and Thoth, god of scribes, master of words, recorder of knowledge; and he sent them to Nubia to find his angry daughter and to persuade her to return.

Thoth and Shu disguised themselves as baboons, sacred to the god Thoth, and began their journey. They passed beyond the Two Lands, beyond the first cataract, the second and the third, and on into the land of Nubia. Then beyond Nubia to Begum where they found Tefnut.

The goddess was happy as a lion. She was free to roam the desert, to kill what she pleased. Thoth told her about the sadness that had spread throughout Egypt. She shrugged her tawny shoulders and growled in disinterest. Thoth told her about the pain of the people of Kemet and she yawned. He told her that her father wept and she paced and flicked her tail, eager to return to the hunt.

Thoth told her stories about the Two Lands, stories of pain and of joy, stories of great hunts and feasts, stories of the gods and goddesses. And she listened. Thoth used his words, he sang his stories, he made the sounds and the empty spaces between the sounds into a net and eventually Tefnut's interest was snared and she agreed to come home.

Tama and Hetephernebti stood together at the fringe of the crowd as Waja-Hur, with Nimaasted holding his arm, triumphantly led Tefnut's homecoming procession through the courtyard.

Screeching baboons, representing the two gods, knuckle-walked beside Waja-Hur, casting anxious glances over their shoulders at a desert lion that followed them, kept at bay by twin acolytes holding golden leashes.

A train of musicians, dancers and acrobats accompanied them, surrounding six Nubians who carried a sedan chair on which the statue of a lion-headed woman was carried.

"I pray that the moisture does return," Hetephernebti said, as much to herself as to Tama. "I watch daily for the ibises," she said, referring to the flocks of birds that flew north to Kemet each year just before the flooding waters arrived.

Tama took Hetephernebti's hand. "I watch for them, also."

Hetephernebti turned to her friend. She brought her eyes up slowly and looked at the younger priestess.

"The time may come, Tama, when we must do more than watch and pray. It may be here now."

Tama smiled sadly.

"It is not just my brother," Hetephernebti said. She led Tama away from the crowd so they could talk privately.

"Djoser can take care of Kanakht. If not, then he doesn't deserve to sit on the throne. The schemes of Kanakht do not concern me. No, don't look at me that way, Tama. I love Djoser, he is my brother. But I do question what he has done. He is no god. I know that. You know that. I cannot argue that with Kanakht.

"My worry is with Djefi. Not just him, but others like him. I know they are watching and wondering and waiting, like a pack of jackals. They each believe in their god. And not just in their god, but that their god is the most important of all the gods.

"We all do, I admit," Hetephernebti said.

"But we must content ourselves with the family of gods. I believe Re guides us best, you follow Ma'at, Waja-Hur follows Thoth. Each represents a different truth, a different aspect of the ma'at that guides us all, even the gods themselves. If Djefi is allowed to elevate Sobek, if the viciousness of that mean-spirited man is given free rein, then the spirit of Kemet will change.

"I will not allow it," she said, biting the words out angrily.

Tama had never seen this side of her friend.

"Hetephernebti," she said. "We must trust the gods. Who are we to try to work our small wills over the gods? Do you not trust in Re?"

"I trust Re to be Re, yes," Hetephernebti said. "But I do not expect Re to raise a cup to my lips when I am thirsty or to wash away my sweat when

I am hot. No, I do for myself. We all do. Re is Re. I must act on what I believe is his desire. I cannot believe that he would want Sobek to rise above all gods. Never! I will do everything I can to help Re and to stop Djefi."

Tama was quiet, observing and thinking.

"Dear sister," she finally said. "I do not like Djefi either. But think, he is doing what he believes Sobek wants him to do. He is acting just as you say you will act, trying to interpret Re's desire and make it happen here in Kemet. If you act against Djefi, how are you different from him?"

Hetephernebti looked at Tama, her face composed, reflecting the confidence she felt.

"Because, Tama," Hetephernebti said, "I am right and he is wrong. Sobek is an evil god, a destroyer. Re is a loving god, he nurtures Kemet. I will help my brother because Kanakht is an ambitious, grasping man and if he succeeds, then Djefi succeeds and I can not allow that to happen. Never."

Tama was about to answer when Hetephernebti raised her hand.

A man approached them, stopping short and waiting for Hetephernebti to signal him closer. She nodded permission and as he walked toward them, he said, "I bring a message from Samut. He said that the man you sent him to find is with him at Edfu. They wait for you there."

"Brian?" Tama said to Hetephernebti.

"Yes. He must have escaped from the temple at Kom Ombo," Hetephernebti answered.

Tama's eyes filled with tears of relief. "I am going to him."

HERALDS OF THE FLOOD

Prince Teti's arm was withered and pale, his face was tense and worried.

Hesire had removed the last wrappings of the cast and was gently probing the prince's forearm.

"No, it doesn't hurt. Yes, I can feel it. Hesire, what is wrong with my arm? Look at it!"

"I am, Prince Teti, I am. What about this? Does this hurt?" Hesire moved his grip lower to the spot where the bone had protruded through the skin. A dark jagged line marked where the skin had been torn.

"It's all skinny and my hand feels weak," Prince Teti said as he clenched and unclenched his fist. "I have no strength. How can I hold a spear?"

Hesire turned Prince Teti's arm over. He pinched the narrow forearm. *Yes, it is more withered than I have ever seen*, he thought. But the bone felt properly aligned. There was a small bump where the break had been, but the bone was solid and Prince Teti didn't pull away or grimace when Hesire ran his fingers over it.

The cast Imhotep had created had done its job. To be sure, Rudamon had done the hard part – setting the original break. Hesire made a mental note to praise the young priest in front of King Djoser.

"Your arm is healed, Prince Teti," Hesire said, releasing the arm.

"How can you say that?" Prince Teti asked. "Do you see it? It looks like a little girl's arm. Something is wrong." He looked in disgust at the healed arm.

"Prince Teti, you've seen newly born donkeys, haven't you?"

Prince Teti nodded his head suspiciously.

"They can barely stand. Their legs are weak. But in a few days they can run and soon they can carry a pack," Hesire said with a smile.

"I am not a donkey. You do not compare a prince of Kemet to a donkey," Prince Teti said, straightening his back.

Hesire sighed. The boy had grown so much. He remembered squatting by the boy's mother as she sat on the birth chair pushing the boy into the world. Looking back, Hesire thought, Prince Teti had always seemed aware of his status. He hadn't cried so much as demanded the nursemaid's milk. He had been imperious all his short life.

Perhaps he is the son of a god, Hesire thought.

"I am sorry, Prince Teti. What I meant to show was that the donkey's legs are weak because they have not been used while it is curled up inside its mother. Your arm has not been used while it has been in this cast. Once you exercise it, it will regain its strength." He bent down to his basket and pulled out an object Imhotep had sent from Abu. It was a small bag of sand, the grains sewn in a white linen pouch embroidered with a vulture with its wings spread.

"Here," he said as he handed the fist-sized bag to Prince Teti. "Imhotep said you are to use this, squeeze it with your right hand. It will strengthen your hand and your arm."

Prince Teti took the bag and squeezed it with his weak hand. Then he took it in his uninjured arm and squeezed it. "Will it make this arm stronger, too?" he asked.

"Yes," Hesire answered, happy to see Prince Teti's enthusiasm.

"Good." Prince Teti took it back in his weak hand and began to squeeze it. "How long?"

"A few weeks," Hesire said.

"Weeks!"

Hesire stifled a smile at the look of dismay on Prince Teti's face. He tried to remember when a week had seemed like a long time. He was sure that it had, but now the days flowed together so quickly that it seemed only yesterday, not six weeks ago that he had first met the strange Imhotep.

"It is not such a long time," Hesire said.

"I was planning a hunting trip," Prince Teti said. He tossed the sand ball into the air and caught it with his freshly healed hand. A smile lit up his face as he gripped the bag tightly.

"I'll work harder," he said. "I'll be ready."

Hesire allowed himself a chuckle. "I'm sure you will, Prince Teti. You are truly amazing."

Prince Teti nodded in unabashed agreement. "Where is Imhotep? Is he still with my father at Abu?"

"Yes," Hesire answered. "King Djoser refuses to leave Abu until the waters appear."

Prince Teti tossed and caught the ball again, the action mimicking his father's habit of tossing and catching an unsheathed knife. "Then I shall go to Abu to wait for the flood with my father."

Imhotep and King Djoser hadn't spoken a word to each other for nearly half an hour. The only sound in the king's chambers was the dry clack of the Senet sticks landing on the wooden table.

King Djoser gathered the four sticks and rolled them from his hand. Imhotep watched in bewilderment as they all landed with their black-painted side up. King Djoser reached across for the green cone, his last piece on the game board. He tapped the piece triumphantly against each of the six squares that led to the end of the board.

"Another?" he asked.

"How do you do that?" Imhotep asked, more to himself than to the king. He picked up the flat sticks and rolled them. Three landed with their black side up, the fourth showed its white side, the worst roll. He scooped them up and rolled again. All four landed showing black.

"Sure, now I roll it," Imhotep said in mock exasperation.

King Djoser laughed.

"Hetephernebti said she thought you might be a god. Apparently she never saw you play Senet," King Djoser said.

Imhotep realized that he was scowling over losing another game. Looking up from the beautifully painted game board he saw King Djoser smiling and watching him.

He started to laugh. "There are many ways I could prove to Hetephernebti that I am not a god," he said. He reached for the sticks again. He shook them loosely in his hand and tossed them on the table again. Two white faces showed this time.

King Djoser scooped them up, rubbed them with his thumb and gently rolled them from his hand. They flashed black and white, tumbled against the Senet board and landed with only the black faces showing.

King Djoser smiled broadly.

"I've always been lucky at Senet. I used to think hard about the number I needed. Now," he shrugged, "I just know that I will get what I need." He slid open the drawer at the end of the raised board and carefully put the sticks away.

Imhotep picked up the playing pieces and added them to the drawer.

This was how their meetings began – a few games of Senet, which King Djoser always won, then the casual turn of the conversation to the topic King Djoser wanted to discuss.

"When I slept last night, Imhotep, I had a dream. Sleep is a strange thing when you think about it. Our bodies lie inert, but our spirits, ah, they fly. Don't they? Some nights I dream of battles, some nights I dream of other conquests. Last night I dreamed that Khnum himself stood before me. Even as the god spoke, part of my mind said, 'This is the dream Imhotep foretold.'

"And it was, Imhotep. It was."

Imhotep felt a chill run up his spine as he heard the king talk. He had a brief disconnected moment as he wondered if his memory of history was being proven correct or if his suggestion to King Djoser that he would have this dream was creating history.

In another time he knew that he would have been paralyzed into inaction by this circular thought. Now he had adopted Meryt's acceptance of life. If this was what happened, then it was happening. He would seize the moment, revel in it and live it as fully as he could.

King Djoser had continued to talk while Imhotep was lost in thought. His serene voice was tinged with amazement. "Khnum stood before me and he said he would put his arms around me, steady my body. He would safeguard my limbs. It was the most pleasant and comforting feeling."

King Djoser turned to Imhotep.

"Do you have your papers, royal scribe?"

Imhotep opened his journal.

"The god's words were so clear to me. I want you to record them while they still sing in my memory. Here is what Khnum said.

"He said, 'I am master of creation. I have created myself; the great ocean which came into being in past times, according to whose pleasure the River Iteru rises. For I am the master who makes, I am he who makes himself exalted in Nun, who first came forth, Hapi who hurries at will; fashioner of everybody, guide of each man to their hour. I am Tenen, father of Gods, the great Shou living on the shore. The two caves are in a trench below me. It is up to me to let loose the well. I know the Iteru, urge him to the field, I urge him, life appears in every nose.'

"And he said, 'I will make the river swell for you, without there being a year of lack and exhaustion in the whole land, so the plants will flourish, bending under their fruit.'

"I heard those very words, Imhotep. When I awoke, my heart was decided and at ease. I knew that my gift was pleasing to Khnum.

"Tomorrow Prince Teti will arrive. We will celebrate his return to health and I will make the sacrifice. Khnum will be pleased and harmony will return to the Two Lands."

The Temple of Khnum filled only a small part of the northern tip of the island of Abu. The temple courtyard, enclosed by a low stone wall, was filled with fruit trees and flowering plants, a fitting display for Khnum who also was the god of fertile soil.

The grounds of the temple and the cleared area around it had become crowded with tents as guests arrived for the dedication of the gift King Djoser was bestowing on the temple.

High priest Sennufer was sharing his chambers with his son Sekhmire, his wife, Sati, and their son, Siptah, who had joined the commander at Abu for the ceremony.

Recognizing that the seven-year famine was the most dangerous threat the Two Lands faced, King Djoser had abandoned Waset, his administrative center, until the river rose and the threat was gone.

He had even delayed his visit to the army beyond the second cataract. No military threat could do as much harm to Kemet as another year without a heavy harvest.

No ceremonies for other gods mattered to the king until this god, who controlled the rise of the river, was satisfied and showed his satisfaction by bringing the rush of silt-laden waters from beyond Nubia.

And so King Djoser had chosen to stay at Abu.

He met daily with Sennufer. He prayed to Khnum and made offerings. He had brought in a court scribe from Asuan, just across the river, to officially record the huge offering he was making to Khnum. Stone workers had been ordered to carve a stone stele commemorating the offering.

Prince Teti had arrived, the rest of King Djoser's personal guard had been called back from their leaves, the boatmen had returned with them.

Ptahhotep, an elderly wrinkled man who had outlived all of his sons, was governor of the southernmost nome, which also was called Abu. Arriving on the island to watch King Djoser give away so much of his province, Ptahhotep had wisely chosen to embrace the king's idea, offering his own scribes to help with the paperwork.

All was ready. The flood season of Ahket was at hand.

Sekhmire wore a solemn face when he greeted King Djoser in the king's chambers before the temple dedication.

King Djoser saw the change in the commander's demeanor and raised an eyebrow in question. Before he could say anything, Sekhmire dropped to one knee and bowed his head.

"I know there is no need for this, King Djoser, I have pledged loyalty to you before. But I want to swear again before all the gods that I will protect you with my arms, with my heart, with my eyes and mind, with my very spirit."

He looked up earnestly at King Djoser. "This is not because of the gift of land to the temple or because my father is high priest. My father taught me to be humble before the gods, to value my friends and family and to serve the Two Lands. During our weeks here I have seen all of this in your actions. You are king of the Two Lands. Thousands of men serve in your armies. All of the land and the water, the fishes and the game, the fields of wheat and the stands of papyrus are yours. And still you humble yourself before the gods and make offerings to them.

"I swear to serve and protect you, King Djoser, Lord of the Two Lands."

King Djoser laid a hand on Sekhmire's shoulder, urging him to his feet. Once he was standing, King Djoser embraced him, holding him as he had dreamed the god Khnum held him.

When they moved apart, King Djoser saw tears in Sekhmire's eyes. He clapped his hands on the commander's broad shoulders and smiled at him.

"We will serve the Two Lands together, Sekhmire. The people will thrive and the gods will smile on us."

Sekhmire nodded, unable to speak.

King Djoser clapped Sekhmire's shoulders one more time. "Now, off to the temple. We must not keep Khnum waiting. Or your father," he added with a wink.

"**H**ere is some water," Imhotep said.

Meryt shook her head wearily.

"You must have something," he pleaded.

"No," she said weakly. "I will just throw it up if I drink it."

"Some bread?" he asked.

"No," she said, laying her head on her arm. She was lying on the floor at the back of the room they shared on the temple grounds. Her head was just inches away from a half-open stone water drain.

Imhotep knelt beside her, worried that she was having a relapse, that somehow, through his carelessness, she had caught dysentery again. He caressed her head, feeling the dampness on her skin. She smiled up at him. "It will pass," she said. "It did yesterday and the day before."

He looked down at her small form, so slight and fragile.

"It will pass," she repeated. "Go prepare yourself for the ceremony."

As he stood, he heard a sound behind him. Turning he saw Sekhmire's wife, Sati, standing in the doorway. A look of concern filled her face when she saw Meryt lying on the floor.

"She is ill," Imhotep said.

"Sati," Meryt said, pushing herself up to a sitting position. "Thank you for coming. I forgot." She turned to Imhotep. "Sati came by to help me prepare for the ceremony. I don't think I can go," she said, looking back at the short, plump woman.

"What is wrong, little Meryt," Sati said, coming to her side.

Imhotep bent down to help Meryt to her feet. She leaned back against the cool stone wall and waved him away. "I'll stay here," she said with a small smile. "Please, go prepare yourself for the ceremony."

"She has been vomiting," Imhotep said, not moving. "Every morning for three days now. She cannot even drink water."

Ignoring her own clean linen robe, Sati sat on the floor beside Meryt and took her hand.

"Does your stomach feel uneasy, as if a snake were coiled in there?" she asked.

Meryt gulped hard and nodded.

Sati chuckled. "I'm sorry," she said. "That was stupid for me to say." She rubbed the back of Meryt's hand calmly. "But it passes and you feel better as the day wears on?"

Meryt nodded, happy to hear that Sati was aware of such an illness.

"When you feel better, in the afternoons, then eat as much as you can. And drink. A little unfermented wine will stay down. You will need the extra food," she said, smiling happily.

She reached over and rubbed Meryt's belly softly. "There is life in there, Meryt. The feeling you have is that life taking hold. It is good. In a few weeks the illness will pass as the life inside grows stronger."

She stood up and brushed the dust from her robe.

"King Djoser told Sekhmire this would happen," she said. "He'll be very happy. He said you two are very much in love. Well, he said you were seen demonstrating that love in every flat and quiet place on the island."

She laughed. "I remember those days with Sekhmire."

'Should we tell King Djoser?" Imhotep blurted out, shocked by the news and unable to think clearly.

Meryt and Sati looked at Imhotep in confusion.

"Remember, Sati," Meryt said softly, happy to hear Sati confirm her hopes, "Imhotep is not from the Two Lands."

Sati nodded. "I had forgotten." She turned to Imhotep. "Why would we not tell everyone that there is a life growing within? It is the most wonderful news one can ever tell."

Imhotep shrugged, trying to come to grips with the news that he was going to be a father. "In my land we usually wait for a few months."

"Until the belly starts to swell?" Sati asked. "So then everyone knows that you have kept a great secret from them? Why would you do that?"

He looked down at the floor. "In case something happened."

"You mean if she loses the baby?" Sati asked.

Imhotep flushed. He felt they should not talk so openly in front of Meryt. In fact, he thought angrily, his emotions swirling, Sati should not even talk this way to him.

Meryt, who knew his moods, saw the misunderstanding on his face.

"It is our way, Imhotep," she said. "Sati is right." She patted her belly, looking down at it happily. "This is joy. I want to share it. If I lose it, then we will start a new one. The baby's ka will live on." She reached up for Sati's hand. "I feel better now."

Imhotep turned to fetch some bread.

"Not yet, Imhotep. No food yet. After the ceremony I will try to eat."

Sati hugged her. "In a few weeks you will glow. The life within will double your joy. I am so happy for you. But now," she smiled, "You look terrible. Sit down on this stool and I will help with your makeup."

Imhotep stood aside, his trembling hands clasped behind his back.

It was early afternoon. Imhotep was amazed at the number of people who had arrived at Abu. The courtyard was filled with families forming an outer circle around a stone altar.

Birds sang in the trees and a light breeze from the river carried the scent of blossoms from the garden, the fragrance mingling with the acrid aroma of incense burning from stands placed throughout the courtyard.

Imhotep stood near the center, behind King Djoser and Sennufer, wearing the brilliant, white robe Sennufer had provided. The menat hung heavily around his neck, the pendant itself resting on his back between his shoulder blades. Meryt stood by his side. She wore a long dark wig and a robe that covered her from shoulders to her ankles. Around her neck she wore a leather necklace, which held a golden orb representing Re.

King Djoser had made the formal presentation of the land to Khnum, Sennufer had accepted it in the god's name and promised his blessing on the Two Lands and on the god's immortal brother, King Djoser.

They had sung hymns to Khnum, the ram-headed god represented by a golden statue that stood on the altar. Now Sennufer raised his hands and the crowd directly in front of him parted as he began chanting a prayer.

"Hail to thee, O Iteru! Who manifests thyself over this land, and comes to give life to Egypt!

"Come and prosper!

"Come and prosper!

"O Iteru, come and prosper!"

Imhotep saw a figure make its way through the opening in the crowd. He wasn't sure if it was a man or a woman. The person was covered with blue paint and wore a short, pointed beard, but pendulous breasts hung from his chest. He wore a crown of lotus blossoms and in his right hand he carried a vase painted with pictures of stalks of papyrus.

"O you who make men to live through his flocks and his flocks through his orchards!

"Come and prosper!

"O Iteru, come and prosper!" Sennufer chanted.

"It is Hapi, god of the river," Meryt whispered.

The blue-painted god stopped before Sennufer and King Djoser. King Djoser held out his open hands and Hapi poured water from the decorated vase onto the king's hands. Then he knelt and poured more water onto King Djoser's feet.

"I bring you water, Netjerikhet Djoser," Hapi sang as he poured the water. "I bring you prosperity, Divine of Body.

"I will cause the river to rise above its banks and spread across the fields. I will carry the black earth to Kemet. The Two Lands will be inundated. The river will be filled with fishes and the land will sing.

"I bring you water, Divine of Body.

"I bring you prosperity, Netjerikhet Djoser."

The god rose, his vase emptied of water, and stood before the king. As King Djoser raised his hands in blessing, Meryt squeezed Imhotep's hand. It was a gentle squeeze, a simple reminder that she was there, with him, that they were sharing this time and place, that their skin was not really a separation but rather one more way for them to make contact with each other. It was a physical extension of their emotions, an echo of the powerful encounter between their souls.

The gentle touch triggered a rush of emotion as Imhotep thought of the new life that was growing within Meryt. He inhaled the aroma of incense intertwining with the tang of the orchard blossoms. The flutter of birds in the fruit trees provided a whispering counterpoint to King Djoser's rhythmic chanting. The heavy Egyptian sun bore down on Imhotep, lapping at his eyelids and pressing against his shoulders.

As the priests joined in the prayer King Djoser was leading, the susurrant murmuring swirled around Imhotep. He thought of his past and future, of his parents and Addy. He thought of the evening he had stood alone peering into the dark chamber of the Step Pyramid and the vision he had that night of the royal burial amid wavering torch light.

He wondered if this was another dream now, a grand, powerful vision. Would he awake alone by the tunnel that sloped under the pyramid? He closed his eyes, pressing them hard, blocking out his thoughts and his hopes, his fears and his dreams.

He felt the sun on his face, heard the murmur of the prayers, felt Meryt's warm hand in his. Now he heard another sound, a distant empty sound and beneath that a weak vibrating sound, almost like the baaing of sheep, except that it came from the sky.

There was a loud, excited rustle in the crowd. The sound from the sky grew louder and it was as Imhotep, not as Tim, that he opened his eyes beneath the ancient Egyptian sky and saw that it was filled with thousands of white birds. Approaching from the south, they followed the river into The Two Lands, their tremulous cawing sound filling the air.

"Ibises!" Meryt said, squeezing his hand and pointing into the air with her other hand. "I have never seen so many."

Everyone looked to the sky; some held a shielding hand to their eyes. King Djoser and Sennufer stood side by side, their faces turned upward.

"I don't understand," Imhotep said to Meryt.

"They arrive each year before the flood," she explained. "But never so many." She shook her head in wonder. "Never so many."

The feast began under a sky still darkened by the flocks of ibises; their cawing so loud that the harp player could not be heard.

Meryt was careful to eat only bread and to drink only unfermented wine. As she sat quietly with Imhotep, King Djoser approached, followed by Prince Teti and the guard Bata.

King Djoser leaned down and kissed Meryt softly on each cheek. "I have heard the good news," he said, smiling at her as he straightened. Meryt blushed at the attention. "I wish you a healthy child. With Imhotep by your side, I am sure all will be well."

"Thank you," she said quietly.

Although he waited until his father was finished, Prince Teti couldn't stop himself from bouncing up and down on the balls of his feet. It was the first he had seen Imhotep since the cast had been removed from his arm.

Imhotep was surprised to see Bata by the prince's side, smiling and watching the prince protectively. He was even more surprised to see the rest of the prince's bodyguards standing nearby, including Nesi whom Imhotep suspected of trying to kill the prince.

"Lord Imhotep," Prince Teti said. "Thank you for the gift."

Imhotep looked puzzled.

"The linen-covered ball of sand," Prince Teti reminded him. "I have used it every day. Look!"

He reached out with his healed arm and grabbed Imhotep's forearm. He squeezed, increasing the pressure until Imhotep winced.

Prince Teti released Imhotep's arm, ignoring the white marks that he left there. "A week ago," he said, "I could barely squeeze it a hundred times before I tired. Now," he laughed, "I had to have three more made as replacements because I have crushed them."

Imhotep massaged his forearm. "A good patient is the best medicine," he said. "You healed yourself Prince Teti. I only helped. As did Rudamon and Hesire. Hello, Bata." Imhotep nodded to the young guard, who returned his nod with a bright smile.

"Lord Imhotep," Prince Teti said, a formal edge to his voice. "As a reward for your aid, I have asked my father to place Bata at your service."

"Bata?" Imhotep said, unsure what the prince meant.

"Yes," Prince Teti said.

"I don't understand," Imhotep said.

Meryt said, "He means Bata will travel with us and protect us."

"I have a guard?" Imhotep said.

"A companion, Lord Imhotep," Bata said. "I am your companion."

King Djoser rejoined them, followed by Sekhmire.

"Imhotep!" the king said.

Imhotep looked up, startled at the loudness of the king's voice. He saw that King Djoser was laughing silently.

"I had to shout," King Djoser said. Imhotep had never seen him so happy and so relaxed. "They are making so much noise." He pointed up at the sky where another huge flock of birds was crossing over the island.

The king took Imhotep's arm and led him away from the others.

"You were right," he said when they were alone. "Sennufer has never seen a passage of birds this large. Neither has Ptahhotep and he is nearly as old as Waja-Hur. They foretell a flood that will fill the land. The famine is surely over!"

He looked at the sky, then out across the water to the east bank. The riverbank was lined with villagers and farmers, all of them watching the great migration. He knew that they would equate the arrival of the ibises to the offering he had made to Khnum. Word would spread along the river, faster than the birds themselves.

As he looked across the river, he saw a reed boat leave the far bank. The man who sat on it was paddling fast, aiming at the temple. Imhotep saw where King Djoser was looking and watched with him as the man approached the island.

"Today, Imhotep, we will enjoy this ceremony. We will drink until we see the gods," King Djoser said.

The reed boat reached the island's narrow beach. King Djoser and Imhotep lost sight of the man when he left the boat and ran toward the temple entrance.

"Do you know who he is?" Imhotep asked.

King Djoser shook his head. "No. There are many officials here. He is probably a messenger seeking one of them."

King Djoser turned his attention to Imhotep.

"You left your notebook – is that the word you use? – when you were in my chambers yesterday. There are drawings in it. Yes, yes, of course I looked through it, Imhotep. You guard it as if your very ka were within.

"One drawing was a tower of stone blocks. Your foot was in the drawing. Do you remember it? What was it?"

Imhotep thought of the drawing. He remembered sitting against the low stone wall in Saqqara, sketching the Step Pyramid, watching Brian and Diane cross the sandy courtyard toward him.

He started to answer King Djoser when he saw Sennufer hurrying toward them leading the stranger from the boat. King Djoser turned to meet them, expecting Sennufer to address him.

"Excuse me, King Djoser, Lord Imhotep. This man has just arrived from Edfu. He said he has a message for the stranger called Tim from a man called Brian."

BRIAN REBORN

The first time Brian woke he saw only blackness.

His mouth felt strange and the air smelled of his own sour sweat. When he tried to call out for help, he remembered what was different about his mouth. The nights tied to the stone chair came rushing back at him and his mind revolted, deciding it had been a nightmare. Then he pressed the nub of his tongue against his gums, knew it wasn't a dream and passed out.

The next time he woke it was in response to a cool dampness on his forehead. He opened his eyes and saw a blurry form silhouetted against a bright light that pushed in from the doorway beyond.

"Brian," said a soft, female voice.

"Am I dead?" he asked in English, the words thick and clumsy.

"Brian," she repeated. "We are in Edfu."

He nodded and fell back to darkness.

Pahket was holding a bowl of soup by him when he awoke the third time, blinking awake and sitting up suddenly, frightening Pahket so that she slopped some of the warm soup from the wooden bowl.

Wild-eyed and terrified, he scanned the interior of the small hut, his frightened eyes finally finding his untied wrists and legs.

Pahket waited silently, afraid to disturb him as he got his bearings.

"Pahkeh," he said finally. He gingerly put his hand to his mouth, slowly exploring inside with his fingers. He felt his eyes start to tear up, and then wiped them dry with the back of his wrist.

She watched him with sad eyes.

"I have some soup and some bread," she said.

He reached for the bowl and began to eat, grimacing each time he tried to move food around with his lost tongue. "Where am I," he asked in Egyptian, the words a slur of open sounds.

"I'm sorry, Brian. I don't understand. Let me tell you what has happened. Shake your head if something doesn't make sense."

She told him about their escape from the temple of Sobek and how she had left him hidden among bushes on the east side of the river bank and walked to a farmer's hut where she had learned that a messenger from the Temple of Ma'at was looking for Brian.

The farmer had led her to the hut where Samut was staying. Borrowing the farmer's donkey, they returned to Brian, pushed him up on the animal and then struck out across the fields toward the village of Edfu, she and Samut walking on either side to steady him.

Clear of the village, they had looked back to see a cluster of torches bobbing across the river from the temple as Siamun led a search party to find Brian. Turning their backs, they walked as quickly as they could through the black night.

Now they were waiting for Tama in Edfu, a small village two days' walk downriver from Kom Ombo.

"How long?" he tried to say.

She shook her head. He tapped his wrist to indicate a wristwatch and then realized that the gesture was meaningless to her. He set the empty soup bowl on the dirt floor and drew a circle with lines coming out of it to represent the sun. Then he rubbed it out and drew it again. He looked up at Pahket and shrugged.

"We left the temple at night. Three more nights have passed since then. You have been sleeping, Brian. We did not know if you would awake and we could not send for a physician because we were afraid Siamun would find out."

Brian nodded to show he understood. Strangely, although his tongue ached and he felt exhausted, his spirits were good. Pahket had saved him and Tama would soon arrive to help him. Although his arms felt ridiculously weak and he wasn't sure he had the strength to stand, he was alive! Now he needed to regain his strength because he planned to revisit the Temple of Sobek. This time he would be looking for Siamun. This time he would be ready.

He picked up the empty bowl and patted his stomach.

"More?" she asked.

He nodded. He held on to the bowl when she tried to take it. She looked up at him, puzzled. "Pahkeh," he said. "Hank ou, ou aved my ife."

She didn't understand what he tried to say, but she understood his smile and touch. She leaned forward and kissed his forehead.

"Rest," she said. "I will be right back."

Samut was nervous.

He didn't know if Siamun was still looking for Brian. If Siamun did find them hiding here in Edfu, there was nothing Samut could do. Brian was a criminal and it would be within Siamun's right, acting for Priest Djefi, to take Brian back to Kom Ombo, back to the Temple of Sobek.

Samut had wanted to keep moving, to get as far from Kom Ombo as possible, but Brian had been too weak. What good would it have done to bring Brian's dead body to Tama?

So they had stopped in Edfu and he had sent a message to Tama. He would either see her in a few more days or get a message from her. Until then they would hide and hope.

He had left Pahket and Brian in a hut past the edge of town beside a dried up irrigation ditch that ran through a small grove of willow trees. A farmer who lived near there had promised to supply them with food for a few days in return for the donkey.

During the day, Samut stayed at the southern edge of town near the roadway where he could watch for Siamun. Each night he went back to the small hut to check on Brian and Pahket.

Until Tama arrived, or until Brian got strong enough to travel, there was little Samut could do except wait, watch, and worry.

The hut that had seemed so protective, almost womb-like, was too small now. He needed to get outside. He wanted to run, do some push-ups, get his muscles working and strong again.

Pahket had explained to him that they were only a short distance from Kom Ombo and Siamun. Samut had told her that Kanakht had declared Brian an outlaw, so that anyone who saw him was supposed to restrain him and notify Kanakht.

When Brian had nodded in understanding, she was happy to see anger instead of resignation in his eyes.

"We can go out at dusk or early in the morning before travelers are moving on the road," she said. "Samut is keeping watch. If Siamun approaches, Samut will warn us and we will flee. So, you see, we are safe. But we must be careful."

On the second day of his new life, Brian walked along the canal with Pahket. The stump of his tongue throbbed but the only alternative to enduring the pain was to drink himself to a stupor.

He refused to do that; he was in training.

On the third day he felt strong enough to jog. Each step jolted the severed nerves in his tongue, but each step also brought him closer to regaining his strength. He clenched his teeth, fought past the pain and thought about Siamun. He saw his face, smelled his breath, and heard his raspy voice.

Part of his mind told him that if he allowed Siamun to become an obsession then he was losing his freedom and entering into Siamun's dark world. But he believed he could control it; use the anger and hatred to push himself harder. Once he felt strong again, then he would distance himself from his hatred. But until then he would stare into the past, pound against the sand along the irrigation canal and do his push-ups and sit-ups with the vision of his hands around Siamun's neck clear and strong in his imagination.

A fter breakfast one morning, Brian picked up a stick and began to draw in the sand. He had given up trying to talk; the language here had too many harsh, clicking sounds that required a tongue.

He drew a girl with wavy hair, and a larger man beside her. Then he drew a smaller man. Pahket sat on the sand beside him.

He pointed to the girl and said "Iane."

Pahket nodded. "Diane."

He pointed to the large man and then patted his chest. Then he pointed to the third man and said "im." He looked at her, anxious to see if she understood.

"Tim," she repeated. "Samut told me about him. All I had heard before are rumors. You want to know about him?"

Brian nodded.

"He is now called Imhotep and he travels with King Djoser. Samut said that Imhotep healed Prince Teti. That is King Djoser's son. So the king has made Imhotep an adviser, one of the few people he truly trusts. They are at Abu, a temple that sits on an island near the first cataract. That's a place in the river where there are a lot of rocks. I've never been there.

"The king is waiting there until the floods come. Don't look worried, Brian, the floods are good. The river comes over the bank and covers the fields. Then it goes back down and leaves behind the soil that the farmers need."

She leaned against him playfully.

"I had forgotten that you are a stranger in the Two Lands. Everything I know is new to you. Remember at To-She when we took long walks and I taught you the words of our language. It was so peaceful and," she looked away from him as she remembered, "and nothing bad had happened."

Suddenly she started to cry. "I'm sorry that he hurt you, Brian. It was so terrible. I saw them tie you to the chair every night and I was afraid to help. And then I heard your screams and, I'm sorry."

She turned to leave, but he reached for her and, putting his arm around her shoulders, he pulled her close. She wrapped her arms around him and laid her head against his chest. He felt her warm tears on his skin as she cried.

Lost in his own pain, he hadn't thought about her. She had risked her life to save him, rebelling against a lifetime of obedience to rescue a stranger. He thought about her bravery and about his own loss. They were both changed forever, but she had chosen the change.

He laid his head against hers and held her close, feeling her small body quiver as she cried.

The day after his morning jog, after he was able to make her understand that he wanted to write a letter to Imhotep, Pahket brought him a sheet of papyrus, a brush and ink.

He wasn't used to writing letters and after just a few moments he realized how painstakingly slow it was going to be to paint English words with a brush. He would have to be brief.

"Djefi kill king. Croc attack man in chair. Kom Ombo temple. I look for you."

Some of the letters were smeared and the small letter "o's" had filled in, but the note was readable.

He shook his head in disappointment. There was so much more to say. He hoped he would be able to speak English better than Egyptian. Tim would be able to understand him and then he could explain everything.

He touched the ink lightly. Looking in dismay at the smudge that was left behind, he sighed and laid the papyrus aside, waiting for the ink to dry.

"For im," he said to Pahket.

She had watched him labor over the short note, complimenting him on his talent. He knew from his conversations with Tama that writing was an unusual skill here. He had wondered about putting the note in some kind of code and then laughed at himself: There were only three people in this world who could read English.

"When Samut returns tonight I will ask him to send it to Imhotep," she said.

He ran again that evening, breaking into a sprint at times. It was good to feel his chest heaving, the air rushing in and out of his lungs. His legs were recovering their strength. He had regained some of the weight he had lost, but his ribs were visible and the small bones in the back of his hand were no longer hidden beneath thickening flesh.

The cut edge of his tongue was healing, a crusty scab had formed and then scaled away from it. The sharp pain and constant throbbing had given way to phantom twitches and occasional aches.

Each evening he assessed himself, measuring his progress and deciding what he could add to his workout.

Pahket was always with him, her presence sometimes reminding him of when he and Diane had first arrived at To-She and everything had seemed mysterious and fun. She was more somber since the evening when she had cried, and he caught her watching him at times, searching his expression for signs of disapproval.

He had tried to let her know that being afraid of Siamun was not something that should cause her shame, but he knew that she understood very little of what he tried to say. He smiled at her, laughed at her when she flopped on the sand while trying to do push-ups, and he held her when they slept.

She was shyer now than she had been at To-She and he didn't understand why until he remembered her expression at Khmunu after they had watched the ceremony and he had seen Tama for the first time. He knew that Pahket had had a crush on him and he realized now how he had hurt her with his open desire for Tama.

And still she had braved Siamun's men and saved him.

That night as they held each other, he rubbed her back, his hands exploring her skin and feeling the life beneath it. She moaned softly and moved closer to him, but kept her hands curled against his chest.

He kissed her forehead and lifting her chin, kissed her mouth gently.

She returned the kiss and then pulled away.

"When you left that night at Khmunu and didn't come back, Djefi said that you had gone to Tama. Is that true?"

He started to shake his head, then stopped. He had been tricked into leaving the boat and then ambushed. But he had left the boat thinking that Tama wanted to see him. He didn't know how to explain that without words, but then he realized that the truth – the view that Tama would have – was that, yes, he had gone to Tama.

He looked at Pahket, her eyes locked on his, and he nodded.

"Later we heard that you killed a man ..."

He shook his head angrily before she could finish the question.

"I believe you," she said. "After you left the boat, until you arrived at the Temple of Sobek. What did you do? How did you survive?"

"Ama and me," he used his fingers to show people walking. He tried to say Waset, but it came out as "Waheh." He sighed and then used his fingers to show Tama and himself separating. "Me, Kom Ombo," he said.

Pahket shook her head. "She should not have let you go to Kom Ombo alone. It was too dangerous."

Brian nodded. He made a fist and patted his chest to show that it was his decision.

"You couldn't know, Brian. This isn't your land. She should not have let you go. I wouldn't have."

She had propped herself up on an elbow. Resting her head against her raised shoulder, she looked at Brian and asked, "Do you love her?"

He didn't know how to answer. When he had been with Tama and they had first made love he was sure that he would fall in love with her. Then he learned that she didn't expect or want a commitment from him. The sensation of touch, the thrill of the motion, and excitement of the moment were reasons enough for her.

The release from expectations had hit him like a rock shattering a stained-glass window. He had seen everything in a fresh way, uncolored by social conventions or religious rules or family traditions. And he had fallen in love with Tama, or rather the idea of Tama and everything she was and wasn't. The physical Tama remained a joyful celebration, whether she was walking beside him, splashing water on him, wrestling playfully or riding him in a sweaty flush.

Yes, he decided, he loved her. He loved her like the sun and the wind on his face, like the power in his muscles, like the dreams of his childhood, like the rush of anticipation and the exhilaration of success. She was a natural force, so real and unassuming. Too strong to be owned or contained, he thought.

He loved her as she was, not as a possible possession.

And suddenly he realized that that was her gift to him, this understanding of love and acceptance and unselfishness.

He started to laugh. Yes, he loved Tama. And he loved Diane, not because she looked good walking beside him, not because of her father's money, not because she dressed right or felt good, but because she was a bundle of imperfect human impulses and desires, just as he was. He loved her and he wanted her to be happy, by herself or with Yunet or with another man. It didn't matter.

He looked at Pahket, her eyes confused at his laughter, but eager to give way to his joy.

He brushed his fingertips across her cheek and watched as her face opened into a smile that matched his own.

He started to speak and then thought that the words, especially coming from his mangled tongue, would simply confuse and get in the way. He and Tama had talked about how words conceal reality. Now, without his tongue, he was free of that illusion. He shook his head at the thought that somehow, all that he had been through at the Temple of Sobek had actually been good for him.

He had been through a fire of pain and was cleansed.

"Are you all right?" Pahket asked.

He realized that he had tears in his eyes, but they were from happiness.

Samut led Tama to the hut in the early evening light as shadows lengthened across the bottom of the irrigation canal.

"There's no one here," she said, emerging from the darkened hut.

Samut looked around in panic.

"They were here. I promise you," he said.

"Samut, everything is in order. Two people have been sleeping here; the sand has held their shape. One is large, the other small. There is a smoldering fire near the door. They have probably gone for a walk."

She turned and looked along the irrigation canal.

"See," she said, pointing. "There is a pathway worn along the canal."

He started to walk toward it. "I will get them," he said.

"No, Samut. Stay with me. While they are out you can tell me everything that has happened. You said Brian is well, but you looked away from me when you said it. I'll see him soon, so there is no need to spare me. Tell me what you know."

He took a deep breath and began to talk.

"Twenty-eight, twenty-nine, thirty!" Pahket counted loudly. She stopped pacing and turned to look at Brian. Breathing heavily and drenched in sweat, he was waiting, bent over with his hands on his knees.

"On your mawrk, geg seh, go," she said, mimicking the English sounds he had taught her. She clapped her hands when she said 'go' and Brian began to sprint, breathing deeply though his nose and exhaling through his mouth. His bare feet dug into the sand, pushing hard as he ran.

She had counted to eleven but not yet twelve when he pulled past her.

"Your best ever," she cheered as he slowed to a stop.

He smiled widely as he sucked in the cool evening air.

"Enough?" she asked.

He nodded again and waited for her to catch up to him. She reached to hug him, but he moved away, holding his nose.

She playfully slapped at him. "Do you know how bad you smelled when we first got here? I put up with that, I can put up with this."

He shook his head, but waited for her with a smile. She hugged him and then backed away, pretending to be disgusted. "I was wrong. You are worse than an onion-eating camel in heat."

She squealed in laughter and ran away as he tried to grab her.

He ran after her. She was fast, but he could have caught her. Instead he stayed on her heels, growling and waving his arms whenever she turned her head to look at him.

They saw the second person waiting at the hut at the same time, and came to a quick stop.

"I'm sure the first is Samut," Pahket said. "The other is slim. I think it is a woman. It could be Tama," she said, a note of sadness creeping into her voice.

Brian took her hand and squeezed it as they started to walk.

Tama came down the pathway to greet them. She saw immediately that Brian was diminished. His chest was less full and his legs were leaner, the muscles hard ropes beneath the dark skin. He was turned a little sideways, as if protecting the girl.

Pahket's head was slightly lowered, but her eyes were alert and ready.

They stopped as Tama reached them.

Tama came closer and opened her arms to them both. She pulled Brian close and held Pahket at the same time. With their heads close together, she said softly, but clearly so they both could hear, "I am so relieved that you are well, Brian. I only heard that you were taken by Djefi the day before the messenger arrived to say that you had escaped."

She raised herself on her toes and kissed his cheek.

"Pahket," she continued. "Samut told me what you did. You have the bravest heart of anyone I have met."

She brushed her fingers across Pahket's face and then kissed her cheek. "May Ma'at bless you always," she added.

She stepped back, taking their hands in hers.

"You are a beautiful woman, Pahket. I am glad you are with us. I want to hear your story." She turned to Brian. "I heard about your tongue, Brian." She shook her head. "That is not our way. I am sorry. But look at you. You were laughing and running. Your spirit is as strong as ever. As is your aroma," she added with a smile.

"Come, Pahket, it is dark enough. Let's take him to the river so he can wash himself. Then you must tell me about the Temple of Sobek."

She dropped Brian's hand, but held onto Pahket's. Turning toward the river, she said, "I only met Djefi once, at Khmunu, so I don't know him, Pahket. What can you tell me?"

As they walked to the river the women talked, but Brian saw how Tama glanced at him, her look serene and accepting, but her eyes assessing and measuring. He knew that she realized that Pahket would feel threatened by her arrival and was making her comfortable. And he knew she was giving him time and space to adjust to her return.

He moved up beside her and took her free hand. She squeezed his hand and he felt a wave of confidence and love sweep through him.

Somehow, everything would be all right.

DJEFI AT KOM OMBO

The river began to stretch its fingers up the sloping bank.

Ripples of current brushed against dry, exposed pebbles, coloring them with moisture, covering them and then finally dislodging them. Stands of papyrus reeds began to sway as the current gained strength, and soon they began to tilt, bending north toward the distant mouth of the river. Light reed boats, tied off and left floating in the water, bobbed and strained against their moorings, twisting to turn their untethered ends away from the river's gathering force.

Floating crocodiles unconsciously turned to face the water flow, flicking their tails to stay in place. Others dove and, swimming to the bottom of the river, found that the bed had become invisible, covered by a swirl of murky water carrying so much silt that it pelted against them. Rising again, they swam to the banks and climbed out of the water.

The wind, dragged along by the invisible friction of water current, gathered strength and pushed upward, shaking the willow trees and the giant fronds of the palms that lined the river.

Had Djefi not been shaking from rage, he would have felt the difference as the river began to awake in the Two Lands. The boatmen had felt the change as they rowed toward the bank at the Temple of Sobek. The guards who leaned down to help the fat priest step from the boat onto the dry land, felt the change in the wind.

But no one spoke about it to Djefi. The seething fury that froze his face into a mask stilled their tongues.

He wanted to hurt someone, to pass the pain he felt onto someone else. He had started to beat the messenger who had brought him the news of Brian's escape, but the boat had begun to rock and he was afraid he would lose his footing. So he had the man thrown overboard. But that wasn't enough. That didn't begin to take the edge off his anger.

He shook free of the guards once he was on land. The one to his right didn't let go quickly enough, so Djefi pushed a hand against the man's unsuspecting face. Caught off balance, the guard stepped backward into the water, lost his balance and fell.

The muted laughter from the boatmen didn't satisfy him. Djefi wanted tears and cries of pain.

If only Siamun hadn't already fed the guard to the crocodile, that would have been something to savor. Well, he thought, there are other guards.

He started to lose his breath halfway up the steep walkway.

There should be steps cut here, he thought. How will King Djoser, how will Waja-Hur ever get up here? So much to attend to!

He gasped for air, felt his bowels break in a long, rumbling fart, and plunged on ahead.

Siamun better have a seat and beer waiting for me, he thought.

Djefi headed for the stone chair at the center of the courtyard. The guards walked a few steps behind him. The guard who had been pushed into the water looked around for the crocodile praying that the beast would charge from its dark well and attack the fat priest.

Siamun was standing by the chair. To Djefi's eye, Siamun looked leaner and at the same time larger. He looked as if he was carved from the same stone as the chair. The muscles of his arms and chest seemed to strain against his skin, which looked mottled in the dusky night air, almost as if he was covered in bruises.

His face, however, was lined. He looked much older than his thirty years. The ragged flap of skin that had grown over where his ear used to be looked like a baby's fist against the side of his head. His smile stopped at his mouth; his eyes were narrow and dead. His teeth, never clean, looked almost black and another was missing.

Suddenly Djefi quivered, thinking of what Yunet must have put up with during her marriage to Siamun.

"This is where King Djoser dies," Siamun said proudly, patting the stone chair.

Djefi's eyes widened. What if the guards heard? What if a rumor escaped the temple?

Siamun saw his look. "Do you think they would say anything?" he gestured toward the guards. Djefi looked at them, they all had their eyes on the ground, not daring to confront Siamun.

"They saw what happened to Naqada," he said, referring to the guard who had allowed Brian to escape. "His screams lasted three days. After Sobek tore off his right leg, we bound his stump and tied him back on the chair the next night. The last night, we didn't tie him because both his legs were gone." Siamun laughed. "He tried to drag himself away. Sobek took him into the well. He wasn't hungry for almost a week. But now, he is ready again."

"You used the oil King Djoser uses? With the same aroma?" Djefi asked. He had given Siamun specific instructions. He wanted the crocodile trained to attack the right person.

Siamun ignored his question. "He will attack whoever sits in this chair. I just wish he had learned it quicker. We should have kept him hungrier."

Djefi looked at him hard.

"If he fails, if something goes wrong, Siamun, then King Djoser will have his revenge. On all of us."

Siamun leaned close. Djefi steeled himself not to pull back from the man's ferocious breath. "Are you losing your nerve, Djefi?"

"I don't intend to lose anything," Djefi answered, straining to keep his voice from squeaking. "But you lost something, didn't you?"

Siamun stared at him, his eyelids lowering as he waited.

"Brian! You lost Brian."

Siamun didn't answer.

"Do you know where he is? No, you don't. I don't either. But there are only two possibilities. Either he's dead, in the river and eaten by Sobek's brothers, or he's alive. If he's alive, then that means someone has helped him and is hiding him.

"I heard that Hetephernebti was searching for him," Djefi continued. "You do know that she is the king's sister, don't you? If she has found Brian and if he tells her what he saw here, then we are dead men, Siamun, dead men."

He stopped when he saw Siamun smile and then start to laugh.

"Do you want to die, Siamun? Are you eager to get to Khert-Neter? Is your heart that light?"

Siamun shook his head smiling. "He won't tell anyone anything. I cut out his tongue!" He laughed and turned away from Djefi.

As Djefi watched Siamun saunter toward his hut, he unconsciously wiped his lips with his tongue. He turned to the guards behind him.

"Is this true?"

The guards nodded.

"We saw it, and heard it, First Prophet," one of them answered. "I don't know how this man could have survived. I don't think he is still alive. If he somehow got to Kom Ombo he could not last long. He was weak and dying."

Djefi thought about the agony Brian would have felt, the blood that would have flowed, and he smiled.

But, he worried, what if Siamun is wrong? Siamun thought Brian would die out in the desert, but he had survived. Diane! The other outlander, the one whom King Djoser has taken to calling Imhotep, he tried to talk to Diane during the ceremony at Iunu. She is my lever. As long as I have her, I can use her to bargain with King Djoser if he survives Sobek.

He turned toward the central temple complex where his rooms were waiting, his anger and tiredness forgotten as he made new plans.

In the morning Djefi sent for Yunet and Diane.

Diane looked like a different woman. Her hair was still red, but it was tangled and dirty. Her pale skin was pasty and unhealthy, her eyes were red rimmed and bloodshot. She had lost weight and her breasts, their outlines visible beneath her linen robe, seemed to hang lower.

She had looked like a goddess. Now she was an empty shell.

Yunet looked as tired, but still strong, driven by anger.

"Greetings, little sisters," Djefi said.

Siamun, standing by Djefi's chair, said nothing as the women entered.

"Greetings, First Prophet," Yunet answered.

Diane raised her eyes from the stone floor and stared at Siamun. "Go to hell," she said.

Djefi was puzzled at the foreign words, but when he saw Siamun stiffen, he looked at Yunet for an answer.

"She is angry with Siamun because of what he did to Brian."

Djefi nodded. "Then the news I have for her will not be pleasing." He paused, waiting for a response. When he got none, he continued, "The dedication of the temple is approaching. I think it will be a very confusing time. I have so much to do. I won't have time to be a proper host to Diane. So, I have asked Siamun to take the two of you back to To-She, where you can relax without all this, uh, confusion."

Yunet looked at Djefi, trying to understand what was really happening. They were being banished from the temple, kept away from the priests, priestesses and officials who would be arriving. So Djefi was intent on hiding Diane from everyone. It wasn't because of the way she looks now, Yunet reasoned, because he had made the decision before he saw her.

She didn't understand why.

"Yes, First Prophet," she said. "We would be happy to return to To-She. But I'm sure you have important tasks here for Siamun. We could travel alone. Or with one of the boatmen."

"Of course, you could. But his work here is done and he is ready to return to To-She. Aren't you, Siamun?"

The guard grunted a sound that could have been 'yes.'

So Siamun is being banished, also, Yunet thought. *Or he is being sent to guard Diane, to keep her from escaping.* Suddenly she was gripped with fear that Siamun had been told to take Diane away from the temple and to kill her. Then she shook free of the thought. If he wanted to kill her she would have been placed in the stone chair days ago.

"As you wish, First Prophet," Yunet said, bowing her head. *I have no choice,* she thought. *We will go back to To-She and wait.*

There had been no word about Brian or the other stranger, except rumors that he was traveling with the king. At To-She they would be able to see less of Siamun than here in the temple complex. Perhaps Diane would begin to recover, to eat and regain her health.

"Thank you," she added as they withdrew.

"And go to hell," Diane added under her breath.

"**W**hy did you agree?" Diane asked. "Why'd you kiss his fat ass," she added in English, knowing that, while Yunet wouldn't understand the words, she would understand the tone.

Yunet stroked Diane's shoulder. She hated what had happened to her since she had seen Brian's tongue cut out. It was hard, Yunet understood that. But it was not something that could be changed.

If Diane wants revenge on Siamun, then she must stay strong, not sulk and go hungry, Yunet thought. She understood that the country Diane came from was different, but that did her no good now. She was here.

"If we go to To-She, then we'll be away from this spot, from these memories," Yunet said soothingly. "We can get away from this heat and all this sand and rock. Remember the orchards and the gardens, Diane? It will be like it was when you first arrived. Once this temple is dedicated, everything will return to normal."

Diane spoke without emotion, as she had since that night. "I don't want normal. I want Siamun dead."

Yunet put her hand over Diane's mouth.

"You must never say that," she warned her. "I know you are angry. I know you are hurt. But if he hears what you are thinking, he will hurt you. I know."

Diane jerked her head away.

"You know. You know," Diane mocked her. She switched to English. "You don't know shit. If Brian ever gets Siamun alone, he'll rip his head off. Brian is still alive, I know it. So yeah, I'll go to To-She if it gets Siamun away from here so Brian has a chance to get better. Then he'll come looking for Siamun. Brian found us here; he'll find us in To-She. And this time, I'll be ready." She picked up a vase and threw it against the wall. "This time I won't let him down."

Yunet let her rant, listening to the anger spill from her. She knew the feeling of pain and helplessness and how it could build inside until a balance was tipped, until the heart became so full that it had to explode.

Now was not the time for soothing, she knew. That would come later. But would Diane be able to contain herself on the long trip back to To-She or would she try to strike out at Siamun then? That would be disastrous.

She thought she knew this redheaded goddess-child, but now she wasn't sure.

When Diane and Brian had arrived at To-She after their trek across the desert with Bakr, Yunet had seen immediately that Diane was angry with Brian. When they had fought that evening, Yunet had instinctively moved to comfort Diane. She knew what it was like to fear a man.

She had feared Siamun during their marriage, but she had known that her half-brother Djefi would always protect her. Then one night during a drunken argument Siamun had told her the truth about the night Djefi had saved her.

As she listened to the horrible story, the trust and love she had had for Djefi had turned into a dread, deeper and more consuming than any fear she had of Siamun.

Two years before Yunet was born, her mother, Sitra, lost her first husband when he was killed hunting hippos in the delta. She had one child by him, a boy named Djefi who was eight years old by the time the widow Sitra caught the eye of Sesostris, who was visiting Iunu for the Festival of Re in His Barge.

Sesostris took Sitra and her boy to his home in To-She where he was a priest in the service of Sobek. A year later, after Yunet was born, Sesostris was elevated to First Prophet. With that came a change.

Sesostris spent more and more time at the temple, which suited Sitra because she wanted nothing more than to play with her little girl, to teach her to spin and sew and cook. Yunet was a quick learner and she showed signs of becoming a strong and beautiful woman.

The boy Djefi had become withdrawn when his father died. Now as his mother showered her attention on his sister, he desperately reached out to his stepfather for attention.

Sesostris moved Djefi to the temple where he roomed with another young acolyte named Siamun. The boys became friends, sweeping the temple hallways together, daring each other to race past sleeping crocodiles in the temple garden, peeking around doorways at the priests when they had secret meetings.

One evening, when Siamun left with his father for a hunting trip into the desert mountains, Djefi found himself alone in the temple.

After his chores, he went to the temple garden as it was growing dark. It was a dangerous place to be. The crocodiles roamed the garden freely. The darkness made it impossible to see them at a distance, and they moved so fast that if they chose to attack, Djefi would never be able to avoid them.

Djefi entered quietly and slowly, giving his eyes a chance to adjust to the darkness. After a few minutes it seemed to him as if the stars had become more bright. He could see the leaves of the palm trees as a blacker black, their knife edges sharply defined in the cooling air. The roughed-skinned tree trunks formed beautiful abstract patterns of sharp angles of black-hewed brown. The ridges on the back of a crocodile that was lying immobile just a few steps away seemed to glisten.

He was sure that if he waited Sobek would rise from the pond, his fierce crocodile head atop a man's body. He would walk godlike across the grounds and speak to Djefi, tell him about the mysteries of Khert-Neter, about the power of being a god, about the love that flowed from the family of gods, and about the paradise Djefi's dead father now enjoyed.

Djefi was standing on the cusp of a hidden world. The air itself about the pond grew lighter. It was expanding, coming toward him and he knew that when it reached him he would be transported to a higher realm. He would understand and know. He would see his father again.

He was glad Siamun was not here. He would never have understood and his brutishness would have broken the spell.

The light was closer now and Djefi could feel the hairs on his arms and his neck rise to attention. A chill came over him. He closed his eyes, his face turned upward, eager for illumination.

But instead of the booming voice of the god, he heard a low moan, a guttural cry that turned into a series of grunts. He knew that sound. He and Siamun had followed it before, watching in the shadows as one of the women who came at night to the temple lay on her back beneath a priest.

He opened his eyes to see, as he feared, that the spell had been broken by the grunting sound. Instead of a magical garden ready to divulge secrets, he saw only shadows and veiled corners. Instead of incense, he smelled decay and waste.

He turned back to the temple and started down the hallway toward his room. Suddenly a woman ran from one of the rooms, blood dripping from between her legs. One hand was over her mouth; the other was lodged between her legs. She ran past him, crying loudly.

Djefi looked back to the room she had left. His stepfather Sesostris was standing in the doorway. He was holding a whip in his right hand, the handle of it dripping with blood.

He was quivering in anger. "Get back here, whore!" he shouted. "I am First Prophet of Sobek and you will do whatever I say!"

Suddenly his eyes found Djefi who was cowering against the wall.

"What are you doing here?" he shouted.

Djefi shook his head, his eyes on the whip. Sesostris saw what Djefi was looking at. He saw the fear on the boy's face. He nodded as if making a decision. He let the rolled whip thong fall to the stone floor. To Djefi it looked like a silent snake uncoiling from his stepfather's hand.

He wanted to run, but fear overcame his legs and he suddenly sat on the cold stone floor. Sesostris advanced slowly, his wrist flicking the whip handle, making the thong slither across the stones.

Every night Siamun was away, Sesostris found Djefi and dragged him through the temple to his room. The first night Djefi had screamed in pain, but he saw that it only gave Sesostris more pleasure and the boy knew that no one would come to his aid.

He had feared the pain of the whip, but instead Djefi discovered that his stepfather had other plans for him. The priest had grown inured to the pleasures of a woman and had decided when he saw young Djefi that the boy offered a new world of pleasure and pain to explore.

Djefi endured silently, not admitting to Siamun when he returned, how his stepfather was abusing him. But he listened with intense attention when Siamun described the hunt and how he had driven a spear into the shaking side of a desert gazelle.

For almost a year, Djefi suffered.

Siamun saw the change in his friend, but to his eyes it was a change for the better. Djefi was more sullen, angrier, and ready to lash out and hurt smaller people. To Siamun's eyes, his friend was becoming a man.

But as Djefi grew meaner, he also grew fat. He ate huge helpings at meals and drank his belly full of beer whenever he could. He became derelict in his duties at the temple.

By his thirteenth year, Djefi had become a different person. His legs were so fat they rubbed together when he walked. Fat hung from his sides over his hips, his breasts were larger than a wetnurse's. His throat was hidden behind three folds of flesh. His physical transformation was matched by the changes within.

He had never realized the enlightenment that had been at his fingertips that night in the garden. But he had come to his own understanding: Sobek had dangled paradise in front of him for a moment and then allowed it to be taken away. Sobek was a cruel god.

The lessons of that night and the endless nights with his stepfather were well learned: Life was cruelty and one had to take what one wanted before someone else did.

Djefi decided he would be First Prophet. Then he would interpret Sobek's teachings and the people would learn to obey his word.

He told Siamun his dream and Siamun, aware of the changes within his only friend, knew better than to laugh. He knew that although Djefi looked like a fat fool, within he was capable of as much cruelty as Sobek.

As he became grotesque, his stepfather tired of abusing him. Left alone at last, Djefi told Siamun about his stepfather and together they plotted ways for him to get his revenge.

When Yunet turned five years old, Djefi saw a chance. He made sure his stepfather overheard him talking to Siamun about Yunet, praising her untouched, smooth skin and innocent beauty. Finally, Sesostris told Djefi to bring his little sister to the temple one night. Siamun looked at his friend, wondering what reaction the order would bring. He didn't expect to see the secret smile that stole into Djefi's eyes.

As the boys walked to fetch Yunet, Djefi told Siamun his plan.

He had picked a spot in the enclosed garden where four trees formed a large square. A rope was tied around the trunk of each tree. They would bring Yunet back and take her to the garden and tell her that Sesostris wanted to see her.

Then they would tell Sesostris that Yunet had run into the garden to get away from them and that they were afraid to go in there because of the crocodiles. That would inflame and enrage the priest. They would follow Sesostris to the garden, overpower him and bind his arms and legs to the separate trees.

The plan worked as Djefi hoped.

When the boys followed the angry priest into the garden, Siamun ducked forward and slashed at the back of Sesostris' ankle with a chipped stone knife he had stolen from his father. The slash cut his tendon and Sesostris grabbed at his injured leg and fell.

Djefi carried a fist-sized rock. He fell on his stepfather now, his weight knocking the man's breath out of him, and began to smash the rock against Sesostris' head. He did it calmly, waiting between each blow to see if the man had lost consciousness. Djefi wanted him helpless, not dead.

Once Sesostris was unconscious, Djefi and Siamun dragged him to the trees and ropes.

While Siamun tied Sesostris, Djefi talked to his little sister. "He was going to do mean things to you, little sister."

"What things?" she asked, her eyes wide as she watched Siamun wrap ropes around Sesostris' arms.

"I'll tell you when you are bigger. I promise. Just remember, tonight I saved you. I will always save you." He hugged her and felt her warm, sisterly hug in return.

"You must not tell anyone, Yunet. Or I will get in trouble. Now, Siamun and I will punish Sesostris and then we will send him away from To-She forever so he can never harm you. When you hear that he is gone, you must act surprised. Can you do that?"

She nodded her head solemnly. She watched fascinated as Siamun gagged the priest. "Will you hurt him?" she asked.

"We will be as kind to him as he has been to us," Djefi answered.

"He was never kind to me. Was he ever kind to you?" Yunet asked.

"Go now, little sister. Remember to be surprised."

After she had gone, Djefi checked the bindings and the gag.

"Thank you, Siamun," he said, his eyes looking hungrily at his helpless stepfather, tied face-down on the garden's moist soil. He turned and walked to one of the trees and retrieved a spear he had hidden there.

Siamun watched him and then lifted a hand to show his nicked stone knife. He knelt beside Sesostris and raised his hand to stab him.

"No," Djefi said, his voice squeaking.

Siamun stayed his hand and looked up. "We mean to kill him, don't we? After what we have done we have no choice."

Djefi nodded. "Yes, but much slower. And he must be awake." He kicked Sesostris in the ribs and listened to him gasp as he woke.

"Do you mean to stab him with the spear? That will be quicker than my knife," Siamun argued.

Djefi shook his head.

Raising the spear with both hands, he brought it down sharply on his knee, breaking the shaft. He examined the two broken ends. He kept the one whose end was most splintered and rough. Then kneeling beside his stepfather's face he said, "Wake up, Sesostris. Remember the nights you took me and I cried and begged you to stop. Remember my tears and screams?" He showed him the splintered end of the spear. "Tonight it is your turn to scream."

Sesostris raised his head and tried to shout through the gag. He strained at the ropes and tried to twist away.

Djefi walked around to stand between Sesostris's spread-eagled legs. With the ragged spear tip he flicked up the short kilt the priest wore. Then he nestled the broken spear end between his stepfather's parted legs and shoved the broken spear into him.

They had to tear off Sesostris' kilt and add that to the gag as his screams grew in intensity. And still he was too loud, or so it seemed to their guilty ears. "Siamun, do something," Djefi said at last, his arms growing weary from the repeated thrusting.

His eyes aglow with an otherworldly light, Siamun squatted beside Sesostris' head. "Remember the ceremony, Sesostris?" he asked, tearing at the cloth gag.

Sesostris gasped for air as the gag came free. He started to speak, but Siamun jammed the other end of the broken shaft sideways into his open mouth, forcing his jaws open. "Hold this," he told Djefi.

Then he reached into Sesostris' mouth and grabbed his tongue. He pulled it out as far as he could and then with a quick slice of his knife, he cut it off. As Sesostris gagged on the sudden pain and blood, Siamun held the severed tongue above Sesostris' eyes.

"The Cutting Out of Sobek's Tongue," he said, mimicking Sesostris' voice. Then he laughed and tossed the tongue across the courtyard.

The smell of blood brought the crocodiles to life.

Siamun's eyes had danced with light as he recounted the story all those years later, and Yunet had understood for the first time his fear-tinged respect for Djefi.

Although she and Djefi shared a mother, that offered no real security. He had used her once, a five-year-old girl as bait in his trap. What protection would Diane, an outlander, offer? None.

They would obey Djefi, get as far from his plans at Kom Ombo as they could. Diane would have time to heal. All they had to do was to avoid angering Siamun. That was never easy, she knew. He always seemed to be on the verge of erupting into violence.

She would be careful not to upset him during the trip back to To-She.

GATHERING AT KOM OMBO

The river looked like a lake, a wide, black, moving, churning lake.

Imhotep leaned against the side of the boat staring at the bowed tops of willow trees, their whip-like limbs floating on the water. The taller date palm trees stood straight, straining to keep their green branches just above the water.

It seemed strange to see the river flooding when there had been no rain. But Imhotep knew that there had been torrents of rain farther south, beyond Nubia and beyond Kush. The pelting rain had swept across the decaying leaves and the rich loamy soil of the rain forests, washing it into the river, which was surging now below the boat.

Meryt was sitting at his feet. It was morning and she had just finished heaving her breakfast over the side of the boat. She had pushed Imhotep away when her stomach first started to quiver.

"Aren't you tired of watching me be sick?" she had snapped at him. "There's nothing you can do."

He had shrugged. "I can be here."

"I think I can manage ..." she had started to say and then she had to lean over the side of the boat. He stood beside her, rubbing her back until she was finished. Then she had slumped by his feet.

He was worried about the duration of the morning sickness, but Sekhmire's wife had assured them that it varied from woman to woman and even from pregnancy to pregnancy. "You will be fine," Sati had told Meryt before they had left Abu for the short journey to Kom Ombo and the dedication of the new temple to Sobek.

"Take naps and remember to keep eating small meals, little sister. Lots of them." Then she had turned to Imhotep. "If you are like my Sekhmire you'll enjoy one of the changes. She'll grow larger," she had held her cupped hands in front of her breasts when she said this.

Imhotep had blushed. He had gotten used to their comfort with nudity; it fit his artist's view of the world. But he wasn't sure he would ever get used to their casual sexuality.

"But they will be tender, so be gentle." Sati had teased him, enjoying his discomfort. He was such a strange man. King Djoser and her Sekhmire thought he really was a god, a god of medicine, a god who could see into the future.

But to her he seemed like a little boy when it came to some things. He did seem to truly care for Meryt, so she welcomed him into their lives. Still, it was fun to tease him.

"He is always gentle," Meryt had said.

"So, are you ready for the trip?" Imhotep had asked, trying to change the subject.

"That's good," Sati had said to Meryt, ignoring Imhotep's comment. "But sometimes …" she had smiled and raised her eyebrows. "But after the sickness passes, and it will, Meryt, I promise, then you can go back to behaving like new lovers."

Imhotep had tried to interrupt, but Sati hadn't slowed down.

"When your belly starts to swell, then try either riding him or let him come to you from behind."

"I'm sure you have some packing to finish," Imhotep had said. "I know we do."

"No, we have everything ready," Meryt had said innocently.

Sati had embraced Meryt and whispered in her ear. "He's a sweet man. Break him in gently." Meryt had giggled as Sati let her go.

Imhotep had stepped to Sati and opened his arms to embrace her. She had moved inside his arms to hug him. "She is a treasure," she had whispered to him. "I know you'll treat her like one." She had squeezed him and backed away.

"Sekhmire will journey with King Djoser on his boat. Siptah and I will be traveling with some of the other families. You are welcome to travel with us, Meryt, but I'm sure Imhotep will not let you out of his sight."

Meryt had smiled at her. She had become such a good friend, one she never would have met if Hetephernebti hadn't instructed her to travel with Imhotep when he had first arrived in The Two Lands. *How strange the way lives become intertwined,* she had thought.

"Yes, Imhotep has asked King Djoser if I could travel on the royal boat with them. I'm sure the king will enjoy having a sick woman with him," she had said wryly.

"Did you hear what he did?" Sati had said quietly, looking around the small room as if someone could be eavesdropping. "You know that Inetkawes has stayed at Waset, so King Djoser has been without a woman the whole time he has been here."

She had glanced around conspiratorially. "The king loves Inetkawes very much. She is a beautiful wife, a perfect manager of the royal household. But she is not here.

"So," she had lowered her voice even more, forcing Meryt and Imhotep to lean close to her, "after the dedication of the land and all those birds flew over, the king was in a mood to celebrate."

She paused as if remembering. "I have never seen so many birds. At first I was frightened, but they were a good omen, and what a sight. They kept coming and coming. I'm sure it is an omen that the flood will be the best in memory. My brother will be worried, he just married last year. They live so close to the river. He's young and doesn't remember a real flood. We all warned him, but he wouldn't listen to anyone. Now their house will be washed away. But they will be fine; my parents will take them in. They have a darling little girl, just three years old, but so smart.

"They live near Edfu, so I'll be able to stop and visit with them on the way back to Waset. I won't be stopping at Kom Ombo for the temple dedication," she had said, moving on from her original thread of conversation.

"Sekhmire said that King Djoser has ordered all the wives and children to stay away from the ceremony. That is so unusual. Sekhmire was very secretive about that." She had paused and looked suddenly at Imhotep as if expecting him to explain.

When she had seen that he wasn't going to answer, she had continued. "So I'll be going on to Waset from here after stopping at Edfu, little sister. Sekhmire said because the river is rising so much and moving so fast, that I will be home in less than a week. You'll visit when you arrive back at Waset?" she had asked.

Meryt and Imhotep had both nodded, amused smiles on their faces.

"I know, I know," Sati had said. "I talk too much. It's just hard to say goodbye even if it is just for a few weeks. Sekhmire has been very quiet about Kom Ombo and the temple dedication." She had paused and looked at Imhotep again.

Sati had sighed at his silence.

"You men!" she had said with mock anger. "Well, farewell, Meryt. You'll be feeling better soon." She had turned suddenly, as if forcing herself to leave, and walked out of their room without a backward glance.

Imhotep had still been looking at the suddenly empty doorway when Meryt had asked, "What about Kom Ombo?"

I never used to get tired. Now I take naps in the morning and the afternoon. Sometimes it seems as if the sun has just come up and suddenly it is going down. Someone brings me a meal and I set it aside to do something, and then when I look again the meal is eaten and I have onion on my breath.

How do these things happen?

Ah, there is a chair. I can rest just for a moment and then Kanakht will come back. Kanakht was here, I'm sure. Wherever here is.

Waja-Hur walked slowly across the stone-paved courtyard toward the solitary chair. He was almost there when he heard hurried footsteps behind him.

"Wait, Waja-Hur, wait." It was Kanakht's voice.

Waja-Hur turned slowly. Kanakht was hurrying across the courtyard; a fat priest was standing a little way beyond him, looking across the plaza at Waja-Hur. He looked familiar to Waja-Hur.

Kanakht was waving to Waja-Hur, calling the old priest to him. Waja-Hur looked around bewildered and then changed direction to walk back toward his friend. Kanakht stopped and waited for Waja-Hur, his eyes darting behind the priest to watch for movement.

They reached the edge of the courtyard where a low wall defined the perimeter. Waja-Hur nodded. He remembered now. He had stepped over this wall earlier. He had been standing here with Kanakht and the priest. They had been talking about the famine.

Yes, yes, he remembered now. This is the Temple of Sobek. A new one! Tomorrow there will be a dedication. Kanakht and this fat man had asked me to say something. But what was it?

He looked questioningly at Kanakht. "I have forgotten," he said. "I am sorry."

Kanakht reached over and touched his shoulder softly. "No matter, old friend. You have forgotten more than I will ever know and still you know more than I will ever know. Come, let us find some shade for you."

He led Waja-Hur toward a doorway into the temple.

Djefi followed, his face set in anger.

"How can we trust him to say anything? How can he grant legitimacy to this if he doesn't even know what is happening?"

Waja-Hur turned to Djefi.

"You have a small voice for such a large man." Kanakht said.

"Djefi," Kanakht continued before the fat priest could respond. "Waja-Hur is revered above all other priests throughout the Two Lands. We need his blessing. When Sobek shows his displeasure with the king, Waja-Hur will pronounce the god's action as proof that a change is needed to restore the balance to the Two Lands."

Djefi nodded, his chins shaking and bouncing.

"We've been over this, Kanakht. I understand. What I'm saying is how can we depend on him," he nodded his head toward Waja-Hur's bony back, "to remember to say anything."

Kanakht winked at Djefi.

"He doesn't need to say anything. He just needs to be here. When this is over, Djefi, we will spread the story of what happened. We will say that Waja-Hur gave his blessing. He needs to be here so that it could be true. Once I am on the throne, no one will dispute my memory."

He wanted to cry in frustration.

As far as he could tell there were only two other people on the entire planet who could read English. One of them was just two miles away, but she was across the river being guarded by a homicidal maniac. Brian had no idea where the other one was. He thought he had sent a message to him, but he hadn't heard anything back.

He could answer Tama's questions with nods and shakes of his head, but he had been unable to explain that they were training a crocodile to eat King Djoser.

After several tries he had drawn a crocodile well enough that Tama had figured out what it was. He had pretended to eat, so she got that word. But he was stuck on king. Apparently they didn't wear pointy round crowns here and they didn't have any drawings of King Djoser – maybe at one of the temples – but not here in this hut on the edge of Kom Ombo.

He glanced outside. It was getting dark. Soon he could go for his evening run and burn off his frustration.

When Tama had arrived he had been excited, both to see her and because he hoped that she would be able to understand him. He couldn't pronounce the harsh sounding Egyptian words at all without his tongue. He could come close to a lot of English words, but not close enough. She tried to guess what he was saying, but they had given up after two days.

Once Tim arrived, Brian would be able to write out his story and tell Tim what Siamun was planning. Until then he would build his strength for the day when he saw Siamun again.

His ka had never felt this light. His spirit had expanded beyond him and was lifting him. He glanced down at his feet to see if they were still touching the smooth wood of the ship's deck. He chuckled to himself.

The river was rising, the famine would end. His godfather Khnum had brought the waters as he had promised in his dream. The man-god Imhotep had shown him the drawings of his pyramid tomb and explained its size. Can you build it? Djoser had asked him. It was built, so it will be built, Imhotep had answered with a shrug.

Such a strange way to state it.

At first Djoser had thought Imhotep tangled up the language when he said some things, but now he believed that Imhotep truly looked at things from far in the future. Imhotep had said that he had lived five thousand years from now and that he 'remembered' some things that hadn't happened yet. He 'remembered' that the famine would end after the offering to Khnum. He 'remembered' that Djoser would not be killed at Kom Ombo. He 'remembered' that this giant pyramid would be built.

Is Imhotep a god or a madman? Djoser smiled to himself. The people of the Two Lands might wonder the same thing about me.

He leaned back against the rail at the stern of his ship. The current alone was moving the boat so rapidly that he felt a strong breeze on his face. The rowers were by their stations along the sides of the boat, but they were resting, putting the long handled oars in the water only to adjust the boat's course, not to power it.

He saw them talking among themselves, marveling over the power of the river. Sometimes he caught them looking at him, a touch of awe on their faces. They believed that his sacrifice had brought the fast-moving flood.

Tonight they would reach Kom Ombo. He would visit with his sister Hetephernebti, be re-united with Inetkawes – he smiled at the memory of his celebration with the three sisters brought to Abu after the temple dedication, he still had the strength of a king – and prepare for the confrontation he expected at the Temple of Sobek.

The words in the message Imhotep had received were burned in his memory. But even the idea of being attacked by a crocodile didn't lower his spirits. Imhotep had assured him that he would not be harmed.

He saw Imhotep and his young bride at the prow of the ship. She was standing now, her morning sickness over, and Imhotep was standing beside her, his arm casually draped over her small shoulders, pulling her close. He was looking at the passing land, turning to lightly kiss Meryt's forehead and smile down at her.

Djoser wondered what the world looked like through Imhotep's eyes, if he saw the same desert, same eternal sky, if he felt the same intensity of the sunshine, smelled the life in the river below them.

The living air that surrounded him seemed to lift King Djoser even higher. He stepped away from the railing and Djoser, "The Wise," Horus Netjerierkhet, "Divine of Body," King of the Two Lands, the "Golden Falcon" opened his arms, turned his face to the burning fire in the sky that was the god Re and began to sing a hymn of thanksgiving.

Tama watched Brian and Pahket talk for a moment before he leaned down and kissed Pahket, turned and ran off into the night. Pahket kept her eyes on Brian until he disappeared into the darkness, then she turned and saw Tama watching her.

Tama left the doorway of the hut and walked across the still warm desert sand to Pahket.

Their conversation the night Tama had first arrived had been uncomfortable. Pahket had been worried that Tama would try to take Brian away from her again, as Pahket thought she had done at Khmunu so many weeks ago.

Tama had seen Pahket's cold distance, but didn't understand it. During their flight from Khmunu to Waset, Brian hadn't told her about Pahket, except to mention her as the servant girl at To-She who had cared for him. Tama understood that Pahket would be worried about punishment from Djefi, and she knew that Pahket was among strangers, away from everyone and everything she had known all her life.

But it wasn't until she had seen the way Pahket looked at Brian when she thought no one was watching that Tama understood why Pahket had rescued him. And later, when Brian had tried so hard to talk to Tama, she had noticed Pahket's concern. At first Tama had thought Pahket was worried about what Brian might say about Djefi, but this morning she awoke with an understanding. Pahket was jealous of her.

There is no need for that, Tama thought.

If Brian wanted to be with Pahket, then Tama would give them her blessing and wish them well with an open, unburdened heart. One did not try to control and direct one's own heart! How foolish to try to steer another person's love.

But I am lucky, Tama thought. I have lived my life with truth and acceptance. Pahket has lived at To-She fearing Sobek and controlled by Djefi. The accident of our birth can control our life if we let it; we spend our life struggling against the invisible bonds of prejudice and ignorance and custom and habit. But all we have to do is recognize them and they drop away.

Now Tama saw Pahket's expression harden as she approached. Tama wanted to hold her and comfort her. Pahket had been so brave to rescue Brian and it was clear that she loved him.

She should feel happiness, not worry, Tama thought.

Pahket looked up at her, frightened and defiant.

Tama reached out and took Pahket's hand. She felt it hang limp and cold in her grasp.

"Little sister," Tama said. She stepped closer and, dropping Pahket's hand, she put her arms around her and hugged her. "We should talk."

"We both want the same thing." She felt Pahket stiffen slightly. "We want Brian to be happy. I can see that you love him and I see that your love has saved him and makes him happy. That is good. There should be no coldness between us."

She released Pahket and stepped back to watch her face. She glanced over Pahket's shoulder into the darkness.

"He will be gone for some time. Come, we can talk."

Diane saw a flash of brown and suddenly Yunet's hand slapped her hard across her cheek.

She put her hand to her face and glared at Yunet, who glared back at her, her own anger bubbling over. Diane heard an ugly, barking laugh from Siamun who was standing a few feet away, watching them.

"Do you want to die? Are you that stupid?" Yunet screamed at her.

Diane shook from the anger and humiliation she felt.

"Fahk yu," Siamun said, imitating the words Diane had spat at him as he walked past her a moment ago.

"Faahhk yuuuu," he shouted, laughing at her.

"Don't you ever touch me again," she commanded Yunet.

Yunet slapped her again, a quick, stinging slap. Diane turned her head from the blow and kept looking away from Yunet. Walking away from Yunet, Diane started to cry. There was nowhere to go on the small boat, no way to escape from Siamun and Yunet.

Siamun watched a moment longer and then, sensing that the excitement was over, walked to the stern of the boat to piss over the side.

Diane felt Yunet approach her.

"Diane," she whispered. "That was for Siamun's sake. I'm sorry. I would never hurt you, but I had to hit you, otherwise Siamun would have. I saw his face." She hesitantly reached out and touched Diane's shoulder. "I know him, dear one. I know how he would enjoy giving you pain."

Diane bent down, lowering herself to the deck of the boat. Curling against the side of the boat she covered her face and cried. Everything had gone wrong. She couldn't remember the last time anything had been right.

This trip she and Brian had planned was supposed to be an escape from the day-to-day existence that had become meaningless, from the mindless shopping, work, sex, laundry, television, movies, eating, cleaning, more cleaning – the zombie-like life that she knew was waiting for her after college.

She cried into her hands, the warm tears on her skin the only reality she could believe in. Whenever she tried to grasp the real world, it always seemed to elude her.

She had been what everyone wanted – a baton twirler and cheerleader for her mother, field hockey player for her daddy, prom princess for everyone, compliant backseat date for her boyfriends. She handed in her homework on time, she dotted her 'i's with a little heart, she wore the right clothes and said the right things.

She had gone to the college her parents chose, she had joined the sorority her friends had joined and taken the popular classes. But there had been minutes, then hours and later days when she had grown depressed, wondering where this was leading. She knew there was a life waiting for her, a wonderful life with a wonderful man doing wonderful things, but she didn't understand how this would happen.

She had never had to decide anything, the choices had always seemed so clear and easy, and everyone had told her so.

She had awakened one afternoon following a party her sorority had held with its brother fraternity and, after she had thrown up, she had looked at the house: the sleepers with their mouths open, their clothes in disarray, the nearly empty bowls of chips and pretzels, the oily chunks of cheese, the fallen beer bottles and half-filled plastic glasses. She smelled the stale, spilled beer, the sour air filled with the farts and belches of the drunken sleepers, the sweet edge of a dissipating cloud of marijuana.

A swirl of dust motes had hung in the air in front of her, dancing in the hazy slant of the afternoon sun squeezing through the slats of a window blind. Watching them float, she had reached out slowly, trying hard to not disturb their slow, whirling orbit. She had known she would feel nothing. She had known she was acting this out for herself, trying to imbue the moment with meaning.

Suddenly, she had imagined seeing herself from a distance: a hungover slut standing in the middle of a leftover party, her hair limp and skanky, hoping to find enlightenment in some drifting skin cells sloughed off when a drunk scratched his head in his sleep.

She had felt her lower lip tremble and had known that part of her mind was staging the quiver, trying to elicit sympathy from herself.

She had showered, packed her clothes and left the school, determined to make her life her own.

She had met Brian and they began to live together. But soon the newness and excitement of 'real life' had dulled and she began fear that this was all there would be. She wondered if an affair would awaken her, if a new job would give her life meaning, if a baby was the answer. Then one night she stumbled across a television show about the pyramids. They seemed so permanent and long lasting. *Whoever built them knew the answers*, she had thought.

Now she was in that distant past and the people here were savages.

No, she thought, that isn't true.

Yunet had been kind and understanding. When Diane had first met her, after the horrifying trek across the desert, Yunet seemed to be everything Diane was seeking. She was the answer to questions Diane hadn't known enough to ask, the touchstone who would open a mystical doorway for Diane.

She felt the rough timber of the boat on her bare skin and the tingling echo of the slap against her cheek. She remembered the feeling of superiority she had felt when she had ignored Brian at Kom Ombo and then the horrible shock of seeing him helpless and tortured by Siamun.

Slowly her eyes focused on the grain of the wood, the random lines and widths. Within she felt a hardening, a real resolve, not the pretentious resolve she had felt in the sorority house.

Never, never again would she allow events to control her. Never again would she simply react.

This is my life, damn it, my life. I'll listen and watch and think. Then I'll decide what to do. If I screw up, I screw up, she thought. No more acting.

Even as she made her decision, she realized that she had been ignoring Yunet's soft voice. Yunet was explaining something, telling a story.

"And so there were no children," Yunet was saying.

"I was sad, I wanted children. But for Siamun it was something much worse. I don't know if he cared about children. I think now that he didn't. But he wanted to prove he was a man. It was important to him."

She stroked Diane's face lovingly, overjoyed to see that she didn't flinch or withdraw.

"He began to drink more and more. The other guards mocked him, offering to come to our house and help him plow. He got into fights with them, terrible, violent fights. Djefi was First Prophet by then. He made Siamun commander of the guards. It forced the other men to stop mocking him and it ended the fights.

"But he remained angry with me, Diane. He thought I was somehow emptying his seed from my womb. Our sex turned more and more violent. Then one night he began to choke me even as he was in me. I cried and struggled to free myself. Light begin to fade from my eyes and then my hand found a knife. I slashed at him, unable to see what I was doing."

She leaned closer and talked more softly. "I would have killed him, Diane. I wish I had. The knife sliced off his ear. He screamed, as much at my audacity as at the pain. He took the knife from me and then pinned me down, sitting on my chest, using his legs to hold down my arms.

"I shouted and spat at him. He laughed. His warm blood ran down the side of his face and dripped onto me. He held my head down with one hand and with the other he sliced at my face. 'I want you no more,' he said. 'And no one will ever want you when I am finished.'"

Yunet sighed and looked off into the distance, remembering the night. "My screams had awakened our neighbors. They knew there was nothing they could do against Siamun, but they ran to the temple and brought Djefi. By the time he got there my uncles had arrived and they had pulled Siamun off me, but not before he had given me this." She ran a finger along the deep scar on her cheek.

"Since then we have lived in a cold truce. He mocks me at every turn; I try to stay out of his way. But believe me, dear one, if Siamun thought for a moment that Djefi no longer protected me, he would kill me as brutally and savagely as he could. I don't know what protection Djefi has extended to you, but we must be careful.

"We must not anger him. Do you understand?"

Diane nodded.

"Do you forgive me?" Yunet asked.

Brian was gone, perhaps dead, although Diane refused to believe that. There were no police here, no one to turn to for help. If she was going to survive she knew she needed Yunet. She reached up a tear-streaked arm and pulled Yunet close, hugging her.

PREPARATION

Brian pulled his eye back from the small spyhole and shrugged.

Pahket looked through it next and then pulled back and shook her head. "I don't see him either," she said. "Wait here, I'll be right back."

She slipped out of the small alcove along the back wall of the courtyard where King Djoser was holding a feast to celebrate the beginning of the flood. Brian watched her walk along the wall for a moment and then turned his eye back to the spyhole.

He was hiding from the others, waiting for a chance to meet with Tim, or Imhotep as Tama and the others insisted on calling him now. Tama and Hetephernebti were helping him to hide; officially Brian was still an outlaw.

He had spotted Djefi at the feast, and it was obvious which one was King Djoser, but Brian couldn't figure out which one was Imhotep. The men all had their heads shaved and were dressed in tight, pleated kilts, except Djefi, who wore a long robe that failed to hide his fat stomach.

And except for Djefi, they all looked the same color and size. Brian remembered that Imhotep was short by modern standards, so he fit right in with this crowd. They all had green kohl painted around their eyes, and most wore bracelets and necklaces. One guy had his on backward; a big pendant that looked like a keyhole was hanging down his back between his shoulder blades.

Brian looked at him harder. *Shit, it's Tim, I mean Imhotep,* he realized with a start.

With a young girl by his side, Imhotep was standing a few feet away from the king. He was talking with Hetephernebti, his face serious and intense. Brian shook his head. Tim had definitely gone native. If Brian hadn't seen him before, he wouldn't have been able to pick him out as someone who hadn't been raised in ancient Egypt.

Brain looked down at himself. He was wearing only a short kilt. His skin had been turned dark by the Egyptian sun and his head also was shaved. However, his unusual size and fast-growing beard, made him stand out from the natives.

He saw Pahket at the edge of the courtyard trying to catch Tama's eye. Tama, wearing the robes of a priestess of Ma'at, along with a long dark wig, and bracelets and necklaces, looked totally different from the woman with whom he had spent several weeks walking south from Khmunu.

Seeing Pahket, Tama excused herself from a conversation with another priestess and an older man wearing a simple white robe. She walked around a line of long tables and took Pahket's hand, kissing her on the cheek in greeting.

The two women had become close friends, Tama acting as the older sister Pahket never had. Watching them, Brian realized how much he had been changed in the four months since his arrival in this ancient land.

He used to undress women with his eyes, imagining the swell of their breasts, the size and color of the aureoles around their nipples, the small curve of their stomach. Now, with most of the women either naked, except for a belt, or dressed in transparent robes, he found that he looked more closely at their faces and, more importantly, at who they were.

He still admired their nude beauty, but being surrounded by it, he discovered he had stopped obsessing about it.

Tama had helped, teaching him so much on their trip. He had fallen in love with her, with her beauty, her spirit, her intelligence, her understanding. He knew that she still would welcome him as a lover, but he also knew that she would never make the kind of commitment to him that he wanted.

Their journey had been a sojourn into a different world for each of them. She had been visiting the land outside her temple world, immersing herself in the reality of the Two Lands that lay outside the pillars and sacred ponds of Khmunu. He had been running from Diane's unexpected rejection and the attack orchestrated by Djefi.

He wasn't sure what she had found in him, except answers to her never-ending curiosity, but he knew that she had opened his eyes to a new view of the world around him and the people in it. And he saw now that although Tama loved him, it was in her fiercely honest and open way. He was not hers and she would never be his. The ideas of possession and jealousy had been expelled from her world.

Although he admired her idea, he wanted a feeling of completeness that he knew he would never feel with her.

Pahket offered it. In her uncomplicated way she was as much a facet of the truth as Tama was. Tama was a powerful light, a sun burning too brightly to look into for more than a moment. Pahket was a warm, comforting fire, nourishing and strong.

Although he felt a tinge of disappointment that his decision to be with Pahket meant that he would not hold Tama in his arms again, he understood, at last, that he didn't need Tama as a lover.

As a friend she offered him a different satisfaction. He knew he would never get anything except an honest opinion from her; she was incapable of anything less. She was his touchstone, a genuine measure of reality.

He returned to the spyhole.

Pahket and Tama were standing near Imhotep now, waiting for him to notice them. When he did, he and Hetephernebti went to them and then led them away from the center of the courtyard. Brian saw that King Djoser had noticed them, as did the older man who stood beside his throne.

Brian shook his head in annoyance. He had seen that man before. It had to be either at To-She or Khmunu. He looked at the man again and then closed his eyes, but he couldn't place him.

Imhotep held a finger to his mouth, signaling Brian to not speak. Silently he took Brian by the arm, leading him away from the wall, down a passageway and into an open garden. Pahket waited by the garden entrance as Imhotep and Brian walked to a bench beneath a willow tree.

"Jesus, Brian, I am sorry to hear what happened to you. Tama and Pahket told me."

Brian almost cried in joy at the sound of English. He opened his mouth to talk, but stopped when Imhotep held up his hand.

"Wait, I have to get back in there before Kanakht wonders where I went. Here's what is going on. The king is having a feast to celebrate the beginning of the flood season. That's extremely important, the flood that is. So I have to be at this feast. But I know we have to talk. Shit. Can you talk? Are you able?"

"A wihel. Ought ery ell."

Imhotep put his hand on Brian's arm. "I'm so sorry, Brian. This Siamun, that's his name, right? He'll be punished. I can promise that. Look, after this feast we'll meet. I'll send someone to bring you to my chambers where we'll be safe. I have a notebook. You can write everything out.

"I really have to go." He turned and took a step away, then he stopped and looked back at Brian. "We'll get this sorted out, Brian. I promise. I have the king's ear. We'll get you and Diane back home."

At Abu, King Djoser had worn a nemes, a blue and gold-striped cloth that covered his shaved scalp and hung down to his shoulders. But tonight he wore the pschent, the double crown of the Two Lands, a tall red outer crown that symbolized his rule over Lower Kemet, with the tapering white crown of Upper Kemet fitted inside the red shell and held in place by an outer coil.

Although clean-shaven like every other Egyptian, for the feast he wore a long, straight-edged goatee. In his right hand he carried the hook-handled heqa scepter made of polished orange quartz and decorated with wide gold bands.

He wore a knee-length pleated kilt, bleached blazing white by the sun. White sandals rested under his feet. A wide pectoral necklace fanned across his bare chest, its colorful beads forming the image of a vulture with widespread wings.

Green kohl covered his upper eyelids; delicate black lines had been drawn to replace his plucked eyebrows, the lines extending from the corners of his eyes to the side of his face. Against his protests, his wife Inetkawes had insisted that a light red paint be applied to his lips.

In truth, his protests had been weak. When he looked in the silver mirror his attendants held for him he saw himself as others saw him – a man so handsome he was beautiful. His wide cheekbones and broad forehead gave his beauty an underlying strength. His eyes, highlighted by the makeup, showed depth, intelligence, and understanding. It was hard to not smile at the face that stared back at him so serenely, so godlike.

He sat on his golden throne beside his beautiful wife, Inetkawes, her face still glowing from the exertion of their vigorous lovemaking before the feast. King Djoser smiled at her and enjoyed her provocative, knowing eyes as she looked back at him. She was not a shy, retiring little princess. She was a strong woman with a powerful ka.

King Djoser didn't give any thought to whether or not she knew of his sexual celebration at Abu after the river began to rise. He assumed she would know and understand. He was after all, King of the Two Lands, a Mighty Bull.

As if reading his mind, her fingers tightened on his and she leaned her perfumed head closer. "I know what you are thinking, Netjer," she said, using her pet name for him, playing on its meaning of 'god.' She leaned closer and said in a throaty whisper, "Mighty Bull, indeed. After this feast we will see who is mighty."

He squeezed her fingers in return.

He felt a stirring of the peaceful ecstasy that had come over him earlier on his boat. The river was rising; his son was restored to health. All along the river the people of the Two Lands had come out to watch him pass on his journey from Abu to Kom Ombo. Some stood silently, others sang prayers of thanksgiving.

His new adviser, Imhotep, had explained his ideas for a grand tomb, an eternal house worthy of a god. Made of huge stone blocks, the tomb would rise from a giant square mastaba base, each new layer smaller than the one below it as the form rose skyward.

Once the flood receded, the planting would begin and soon the river would be a ribbon of blue between lush green fields of flax and barley and wheat. The harvest would follow, surely a bountiful one, and then, after the celebrations, he would order work to begin on the tomb. In his mind's eye he saw quarrymen cutting the stone, barges taking the blocks to Saqqara, and the building of his eternal house beginning.

But first, the dedication of the new temple of Sobek. His smile turned cold as he thought of what Imhotep had told him about Djefi's plans. The strange adviser said moments ago that he would have more information later tonight. They would complete their plans then.

Two harp players entered the room followed by a line of young dancing girls. King Djoser turned his attention to them, his mind closed to the worries of tomorrow and to the plans of the future. It was his special talent: He focused on what was before him, bringing all of his attention to whatever lay there, whether it be a drawing of a tomb, the sweaty, writhing body of Inetkawes or the shimmering landscape of the country he loved.

Excused from guard duty for the night, Makare met with his brother Nesi to go over their plans for tomorrow. Kanakht had explained Djefi's plan to attack the king with a crocodile.

"It will be a diversion, and a reason to explain what happened. Remember, when I am on the throne, my version of what happened at Kom Ombo will be the only story. So, listen to me now. The crocodile will attack, or it will not. It doesn't matter, as long as it becomes free and a diversion is created. People will be moving, there will be confusion. You will strike the king and Prince Teti. Afterward Waja-Hur will declare balance restored. He will ask me to take the throne.

"You," he had looked at Makare, "will replace Sekhmire, who may be wounded during the attack, or even killed." He had reached out and placed a hand on each of the young men's shoulders. "Together, we will restore glory to Kemet. We will lead the armies south into Nubia and east through Sinai."

He had paused and looked knowingly at the two brothers.

"I am old. My time here grows shorter each day. Once I have restored Kemet on the path of Ma'at, then I will retire, Makare and Nesi. My work will be done. The Two Lands will need strong, young leaders."

Makare and Nesi had exchanged hopeful looks.

Now, on the eve of the attack, they were drinking and building their courage.

"I will take the king," Makare said for the fifth time, tilting up the empty clay beer pot.

Nesi nodded his head. "Yes, yes. I know. I'll be standing right behind Teti. This time, I won't depend on the river or the rocks." He fingered the handle of his knife.

"Beer! More beer!" Makare shouted. A servant girl appeared in the doorway of the hut carrying a jar. She poured beer into Makare's pot and then into Nesi's.

As she straightened, Nesi grabbed her wrist. "Do you have a friend, or a sister?"

She nodded, knowing what he wanted.

"Go get her. She's not too old, is she?"

The girl shook her head, stifling a smile. The two men were barely past their childhood themselves.

"Well, go get her," Nesi shouted. "Tomorrow my brother and I will shake this world. Tonight it's your turn," he said, grabbing his crotch and shaking it at her.

Brian and Pahket had gone.

Imhotep sat with his notebook, rereading what Brian had written. They had had to resharpen his last, nubby pencil three times. There was less than an inch of it left and only a single page of clean notebook paper. After that, Imhotep would turn to papyrus and inks.

He had felt a strange disconnect as he watched Brian write and listened to his futile attempts to talk. He knew it had only been a few months since he had leaned against the wall at the ruins of Saqqara and watched Brian saunter through the sand following the fat tour guide. The man who had sat beside him writing about crocodiles and torture and a plot to kill the king of Kemet was a totally different man than the one who had winked at him from behind his sunglasses.

He felt the pull of the menat around his neck and realized that he hadn't removed the heavy necklace. As he took it off he saw Meryt watching him, waiting for him to explain what he had learned. She had waited patiently during the last two hours as he had spoken only English, asking Brian questions and trying to learn everything he could about the plot.

"There is so much to tell," he said to her. "Let's go find King Djoser and that way I will only have to tell it once."

Meryt nodded and came to him.

"He said very bad things," she said. "I watched your face."

Imhotep picked up his notebook, leaned to kiss Meryt's forehead and put his arm around her still tiny waist. "Yes, Meryt. I have never heard things like this before." They moved toward the doorway. "I don't understand how people can be like this."

They walked silently through the dimly lit passageways toward King Djoser's rooms. A guard stopped them outside the king's chambers.

"I am Imhotep. King Djoser is expecting me," Imhotep said.

The guard nodded and clapped his hands softly. Two other guards came out of the shadows.

For a moment Imhotep was frightened. Had Kanakht and Djefi already struck? Was the king overthrown, already dead?

"This is Imhotep," the first guard said. "Take him to Sekhmire. King Djoser said he would want to see him."

From beyond the doorway, there came a sharp, high-pitched cry of pleasure. "Yes, my mighty bull, yes!"

Meryt tittered.

"The king said you should go to see Sekhmire," the guard said, his face betraying nothing.

"I can wait," Imhotep said. "It is very important."

The guard shook his head. "You would wait a very long time. But it does not matter. King Djoser said you should talk with Sekhmire. He is waiting for you by the river."

Imhotep nodded and turned to follow the guards.

Meryt leaned close to Imhotep and whispered, "King Djoser doesn't seem worried."

Sekhmire was waiting with Meryptah and Bata.

"You know that you cannot expect help from any of the other guards with Prince Teti," he told Meryptah.

The young man nodded. "Hetephernebti told me that I should be friendly with all of them, but to watch them also."

"Especially Nesi," Bata said, spitting on the ground after saying the guard's name.

"Why is he with the guard if he can't be trusted?" Meryptah asked.

Sekhmire thought before answering. He wasn't sure how much of King Djoser's thinking he should reveal.

"Look," he said finally. "If you are hunting and you approach a watering hole and see a deer. You don't run up and start shouting. You'd scare it away. And there might be others there. No, you watch them and see how many there are and then you strike them all at once."

"I never went deer hunting," Meryptah said.

"He's not talking about deer," Bata said.

"I know," Meryptah shrugged. "I'm just saying I never went hunting."

Sekhmire put his arm around Meryptah's shoulders. *He's so young,* Sekhmire thought, and immediately realized that he himself wasn't so young anymore.

"These men are planning to kill the king and the prince," Sekhmire said. "I agree that it would be easier if we just took them now, but it is important that we let them try." He saw that both men were confused.

"If you know this, just take them," Bata said.

Sekhmire shook his head.

"No. The attack must be allowed and then stopped. That way King Djoser demonstrates his power in public. He shows that it is folly to attack him. It discourages others."

"But what if there are more than Nesi and his brother? What if Makare has others?" Bata asked.

Sekhmire smiled. "Then we will stop them, too, and uncover a nest of vipers. More glory to King Djoser."

Bata shook his head. "No, I mean what if he has a lot of others."

Sekhmire pointed upriver where dark shadows could be seen moving toward them. Bata and Meryptah strained to see the shapes.

"The king's company," Sekhmire said. "They have been recalled from the border and they will be at the ceremony tomorrow. Don't worry, Bata, Meryptah, we will not be alone."

The young guards watched as the boats carrying the elite soldiers silently sailed toward Kom Ombo.

THE HUNGER OF SOBEK

Deep in the well at the Temple of Sobek, the god floated in the rising water, his eyes and nostrils just above the surface.

He inhaled the scent of fish and algae carried on the surface of the water, and a stronger earthy smell that lay atop the other scents. Other smells tumbled down from the circle of daylight at the top of the ramp: roasted geese and oxen, the sour smell of beer, acrid aromas of incense. He breathed in the air, testing it and tasting it.

Intertwined with the other aromas was a sweet fragrance, one that sent a signal through his reptilian brain, triggering desire and hunger. It was the smell that he had come to associate with a feast of living flesh.

He drank in a deep draught of air and bellowed, his tail waving snake-like in the water behind him. He hadn't been fed in a week and his hunger was a gnawing ache. He sniffed again at the air and felt the strand of perfumed oil grow stronger.

He was beast and he did not think, he did not anticipate, he did not plan. But his hunger and the recognition of a smell that led to food triggered his energy and he lurched out of the water toward the light only to be stopped by two ropes looped around his neck and secured in iron rings in the wall.

He swung his head, trying to catch the ropes and roared his frustration.

King Djoser had just crossed the courtyard, passing near the well that led to Sobek's lair. He was stepping across the low retaining wall when Sobek roared, the beast's cry echoing up from the stone passageway that led to his watery den.

Hesitating as the sound vibrated across the courtyard, it seemed to King Djoser that the cry was aimed at him.

He stepped across far side of the low wall and followed Djefi into the outer temple.

Guarded by Sekhmire and a handful of the house guards, the king was accompanied by Imhotep and Kanakht. Prince Teti and his escort, including Bata and Nesi, had gone to the beer jars in the shade of the small forest of stone columns that formed a covered courtyard. A group of other priests and priestesses from throughout the Two Lands followed the king on his tour of the new temple.

Although King Djoser had cautioned her not to come, Hetephernebti had insisted on attending the ceremony. She and Ma'at were escorted by Samut and a tall Nubian hidden beneath a colorful robe and hood despite the hot sun.

Imhotep had insisted that Meryt stay across the river with Pahket. He walked beside King Djoser, his right hand closed around and hiding a small, black cylinder he had taken from his backpack.

Djefi was sweating as he led the tour through the brightly painted temple. They paused by the narrow doorway that led to the inner sanctum. The chamber was dark, illuminated only by a narrow shaft of light from a single window high on the back wall. A boy was waiting by the doorway with a small lamp.

As the king stopped at the doorway, Djefi motioned for the boy to take the lamp into the room. The light from the lamp seemed to explode as it reflected from the polished gold walls of the small chamber.

In the center of the room, a gleaming pedestal supported a gold-plated boat. Two long, polished cedar poles ran through leather thongs on the side of the boat so that it could be carried. At the center of the boat was a flat platform on which a statue of Sobek stood. The god was shown as a man wearing a short kilt, one leg stepping forward. His head was the head of a crocodile, his mouth slightly open to show his teeth. His arms were held straight at his side. One hand held a small flail, the other a short, hook-handled scepter.

There was an audible gasp from some of the priests as they recognized the royal symbols of power in the god's hands. They looked at King Djoser to see what his reaction would be at seeing the symbols that marked his power being held in the god's hands.

King Djoser stepped to the small statue and gently touched its polished surface. He ran his fingers across the ridges of teeth and swept his thumb along its chest.

"It is beautiful, First Prophet Djefi. Simply beautiful," he said in a reverent voice. "I see you have given it the royal scepter and flail. So you envision Sobek as a guardian of the king. How wise. We welcome another protector. Mehen and his hooded serpents, Selket and her scorpions and even Shu and Amun will welcome Sobek to their ranks. As Horus, I welcome Sobek's might and protection."

He stroked the golden figure again, a serene smile on his face. He turned to the assemblage behind him; saw their faces – some amazed at his reaction, the older priests frowning, whether at his acceptance or his identification as the god Horus, King Djoser didn't know.

Or care.

He knew what lay ahead. Imhotep had told him. Suddenly he was eager to move on, to put an end to the intrigue. He clapped his hands sharply.

"Let us see Sobek now, let me view this new guardian of the Two Lands. Have you managed to tame this wild, raging spirit, First Prophet? I think not. You may think you have, but gods sometimes hold surprises."

He turned and swept from the room, heading to the courtyard and the stone chair that sat in its center.

Kanakht couldn't believe that Djefi had had the audacity to fashion a statue of the god holding the symbols of royal power. What, if anything, did the fat idiot have in his mind?

The moment of decision was here. Everything was in place: Kanakht's assassins were primed; the gathering would witness Sobek's rebuke of Djoser. All Kanakht had to do was allow events to unfold. As soon as the king and Teti were dead, he would assume command and order Sekhmire to immediately execute the assassins Nesi and Makare. Djefi, too! The loose ends would be eliminated and suspicion averted from him.

Blood would fill the courtyard. It would be a fitting dedication for a temple to a bloodthirsty god!

They emerged from the temple and Kanakht was shocked to see that the king's elite company, soldiers personally selected and nurtured by Djoser himself, had arrived and taken up a position ringing the courtyard.

Suddenly Kanakht had a premonition that it was he, not the king, who was about to die. The king's company shouldn't be here. They were not expected. King Djoser must have recalled them secretly, which could only mean that he knew about the plot.

A wave of fear swept through Kanakht at the sight of the hard, loyal soldiers. The sky grew black, his vision collapsed to a single bright point of light and he felt himself stumble. Strong arms caught him and a comforting voice penetrated his darkness.

"Here, old friend," King Djoser said under his breath so that only Kanakht could hear. "Stay strong just a little longer." Then the king raised his voice so that all could hear.

"Make way," he said loudly. "Here, Kanakht, sit and rest. I can stand for the ceremony."

Kanakht stumbled across the courtyard supported by the king himself. He sank into a chair and as his head cleared, he realized with a horrible thrill that he, not King Djoser, was sitting in the stone chair at the center of the courtyard.

Djefi saw Kanakht sit in the chair where King Djoser was supposed to sit, where he had to sit! He felt his bowels churn and then a new thought pushed its way forward. This was wonderful, perfect! Sobek would attack Kanakht and kill him while the vizier's secret assassins attacked the king and Prince Teti.

There would be no one left to implicate him in the plot except Waja-Hur, who couldn't even remember his name. All Djefi needed to do was allow the attack to unfold, and then remind everyone that the king himself had designated Sobek as a protector of the king. And Sobek had protected the king by attacking the evil Kanakht, that's what he would say.

It would be unfortunate that Kanakht's assassins had been successful, but Sobek had punished the traitor Kanakht. *Yes, yes,* Djefi thought excitedly. *Sobek will increase in standing, I will gain power and I will sit beside whoever claims the empty throne. Then, once things have settled down, who knows? Sobek may decide it is time for me to occupy the throne.*

He could hardly stop smiling as he walked to a low table filled with food offerings for Sobek. He reached the table, stopped and turned to face the assemblage.

Imhotep watched Kanakht stagger to the chair. He had seen the vizier's face blanch when they emerged from the temple and Kanakht had seen the king's company arrayed around the courtyard. Imhotep thought for a minute that Kanakht had suffered a stroke. Perhaps he had. He was sitting immobile in the chair, his face drained of color, his hands gripping the stone arms.

Kanakht's reaction to the presence of the soldiers and his petrified posture in the chair confirmed King Djoser's suspicions that Kanakht had been the leader of the plot. His heart swelled in gratitude to the gods for revealing all.

From the shadow of his hooded robe, the Nubian guard grimaced at the sight of the stone chair.

Tama looked at the other priests, at the shimmering air rising from the stone courtyard. She saw the fear on Kanakht's face, the jubilation on the king's, the fierce determination on Imhotep's, and the secret smile playing at Djefi's mouth. She looked into the dark opening of the well that led to Sobek's lair and had a vision of truth and order emerging from the darkness. She smelled the sweet, heavy smell of blood and saw it washing away the disorder. And she shivered.

Makare led Waja-Hur to the gathering, his frail body moving with an awkward stiffness that reflected the confusion of his mind. The old man saw the offering table of food and the fat priest who looked so familiar. He saw the crowd gathered in an arc that followed the circular courtyard.

Above them the sky was a deep and endless blue. The water, just visible beyond the high rise of the plateau, was a churning, roiling brown. Waja-Hur saw a flock of pigeons moving north, following the river. They suddenly swirled to their left as a circling hawk dove into them, its claws striking and then clutching one of the birds.

He wondered if it was an omen, or just another isolated moment in the long life of the Two Lands. The world had seemed so clear to him when he was younger, rights and wrongs so easy to distinguish. There had been no confusion, no indecision.

Now he knew he was drifting away, his mind and ka making ready for the journey to Khert-Neter. At a time when everyone saw everything filled with meaning, he saw the hawk's attack as simply an act of nature: a predator striking, a helpless pigeon dying. He wondered if this new clarity was truth, or just a pale vision of the world seen through a mind that grew increasingly cloudy.

Makare placed Waja-Hur near the center of the crowd, just a few feet from his old friend Kanakht, the only familiar face among the group. Waja-Hur saw that Kanakht's face was strained and tight.

Something is wrong, Waja-Hur thought.

Waja-Hur was about to speak to his old friend when the fat priest began to talk and gesture toward the opening that led beneath the courtyard. A brutish bellow came from the opening, as if in response to the priest's words. Waja-Hur cringed at the roar and then suddenly realized where he was and remembered what was about to happen. He jerked around to look at Makare and saw the soldier's hand move slowly toward his knife, his eyes on the king who was standing on the other side of the chair.

Almost everyone turned their attention to the mouth of the well where the crocodile's claws could be heard scraping against the stone ramp. Makare stared at King Djoser, measuring the number of steps it would take to reach him, imagining how he would push past the adviser Imhotep, slip behind Sekhmire and bury his knife in the king's back.

He would twist it and then quickly withdraw it in case he needed to fend off Sekhmire.

He glanced at his brother and saw that Nesi was inching closer to Prince Teti. Then he noticed that Bata was watching his brother also, shadowing Nesi as he approached the prince. There was nothing Makare could do except expect his brother to complete his mission.

The Nubian guard edged through the crowd also, slipping closer to Makare and King Djoser.

Sekhmire felt the crowd shifting behind him and tried to relax, to keep the tension he felt out of his body so he could move and respond quickly.

There was a murmur of appreciation as the crocodile emerged into the courtyard. It was huge, worthy of representing Sobek. The ridges on its back glistened in the light, its huge angular head rotated slowly as it looked over the crowd. Then it seemed to freeze as it looked at Kanakht in the stone chair.

The two acolytes who were holding Sobek in check reached the spots where they were instructed to let go of the ropes tied to Sobek's head. The crowd's eyes were on the beast so no one noticed the boys.

Sobek seemed to crouch low against the stone and then suddenly he raised himself high on his legs and ran toward the stone chair.

Kanakht screamed in terror and tried to stand, but Sekhmire, who had moved behind him pressed down on his shoulders, holding him in place. Kanakht kicked at Sobek, but the crocodile's hunger drove him past the old man's foot.

In a blur its mouth opened and then snapped shut with a loud crunch. The crocodile twisted onto its left side and rolled away from the chair ripping Kanakht's lower left leg off.

As Kanakht screamed, the crowd scattered, turning away from the crocodile and running toward the path that led down from the temple.

With the crowd providing cover, Nesi closed in on Prince Teti and brought his arm back to drive his knife into the prince's back. Someone caught his arm. He turned to see Meryptah gripping his arm. Before he could wrench it free, he felt a pain in his own back and heard Bata's grunt as his knife drove into Nesi's side.

Makare moved more quickly.

He pushed past Waja-Hur and, as Sekhmire released Kanakht's shoulders, Makare slammed his elbow against the back of Sekhmire's head. The guard commander, caught off balance, fell forward against the back of the stone chair, his ribs cracking hard against the rock.

Makare moved on, two steps away from King Djoser.

Somehow, Imhotep had slipped between them. Annoyed, Makare raised his unarmed hand to swat the little man away, but Imhotep stepped to the side and raised his own hand.

"Stop!" Imhotep shouted and clenched his raised fist awkwardly.

King Djoser turned toward the sound and saw Makare's upraised hand, the knife's edge gleaming. As if in slow motion, he saw Sekhmire straighten up from the stone chair, one hand holding his chest, the other pulling his own knife free from his kilt belt.

King Djoser heard a sound like the hiss of a snake coming from Imhotep's hand and suddenly Makare's free hand went to his face and he stumbled.

Imhotep drove his shoulder against Makare, pushing him out into the center of the courtyard.

Sekhmire jumped toward Makare, his knife ready.

With one hand, Makare wiped his tear-streaked face. With his other hand he desperately threw his knife at the king.

However, the huge Nubian had moved between Imhotep and King Djoser. Seeing Makare bring his arm back to throw his knife, the Nubian grabbed the king by his shoulders and, clutching him tightly, he twisted, using his own body to shield the king.

Makare's knife buried itself in the Nubian's back.

Sekhmire caught Makare as he turned to run away. The assassin, his eyes tearing from the pepper spray Imhotep had sprayed on his face, blindly swung a fist at the commander. Sekhmire ducked under it, pushed his knife into Makare's stomach and ripped his belly open. Makare clutched at his stomach, trying to keep his guts inside, but the slippery coils fell to the ground.

Makare fell to the stone courtyard. Lying on his side, he pulled at his intestines, trying to bring them back to his body. Sensing movement, he looked up and screamed. Sobek had dropped Kanakht's leg from his mouth and was scuttling toward him, his cold eyes focused on Makare's bloody intestines. Sekhmire stepped back from the fallen assassin as the crocodile reached Makare and began to chew on his open stomach.

"He is the third stranger from my land," Imhotep told King Djoser.

Brian, hidden within the Nubian robe, was standing between two of the king's guards. They were restraining him and supporting him. The back of his robe was red with blood that oozed out from Makare's knife that was still embedded there.

"He saved your life, King Djoser. The knife in his back was thrown at you by Makare."

King Djoser nodded curtly and the guards released their grip on Brian, then caught him again as he began to fall.

"Let me help him" Hesire said, rushing to Brian. The king's physician motioned for the guards to carry Brian to the shade.

Makare lay dead in the center of the courtyard in a pool of viscera and blood. The crocodile was feeding on him, ignoring the few people who hadn't run away from the temple.

Men from the king's company placed themselves between the crocodile and King Djoser, their short spears held ready.

Kanakht lay beside the stone chair, his hands clenched around the stump of his left leg. Imhotep tore a strip from his kilt and, kneeling by Kanakht, tied a tourniquet around the bloody stump, using the small pepper spray canister to twist the bandage tighter.

As the bleeding stopped, King Djoser knelt by Imhotep's side.

"Will he live?" the king asked.

"If he hasn't lost too much blood."

Kanakht moaned and his eyes fluttered.

"Leave us," King Djoser ordered Imhotep.

The king leaned close to Kanakht's head.

"I have served Kemet all my life," Kanakht said, his eyes unfocused. "I thought I was serving it now," he said.

"Who else?" King Djoser asked.

"Only Djefi and Waja-Hur," Kanakht said. "It is the truth. I make my heart light."

"No others?"

"None."

King Djoser began to untwist the bandage. "You have no need to make your heart light, old friend," he said.

Kanakht's eyes found the king's face. "I am not going to die?"

King Djoser finished unwrapping the leg. A blood began to seep from the wound. He massaged Kanakht's thigh roughly and the blood began to flow more heavily.

"No, old friend," King Djoser said. "You are going to die. But you will never come before Ma'at. I will feed your body to Sobek, piece by piece, as you were ready to do to mine. You will die today, Kanakht, and your ka will have no home."

The old man's eyes closed before King Djoser finished speaking. He gave a small shudder and stopped breathing.

"Is he dead?" Djefi asked, his wide shadow falling on Kanakht.

King Djoser wiped the blood from his hands on Kanakht's white robe. Then he stood and looked at Djefi.

The fat priest looked down at Kanakht, then past him to the stone ramp where Sobek was dragging the remains of Makare's body down to his lair leaving behind a wide bloody trail on the white stones.

"He protected you, did you see that, King Djoser? The great Sobek knew there was evil in Kanakht's heart and he attacked him. I saw it all."

King Djoser heard murmuring behind him. He turned and saw the priests and priestesses who had run away returning now, curious to see what had happened.

He motioned to one of his guards to hand him his short spear. He held it firmly in his hand and stared at Djefi. King Djoser waited until the crowd had gathered closer to him.

"This is what happens to those who oppose the throne. This is what will ever happen to traitors. I am Horus. I am He Who is Above. I am Horus on the Horizon. I am his Left Eye and his Right Eye. I trample my enemies beneath my feet," King Djoser proclaimed.

He stared at Djefi, and then he took two steps to stand over Kanakht's body. Putting his right foot on Kanakht's face, he drove the spear into the dead man's chest.

He pulled the spear out and held it over his head, the red tip dripping blood on the temple stones.

"I am Horus, son of Isis and Osiris. I have contended with Seth, I have taken the throne that was my father's. My name is in the mouths of men, I am the substance of the Two Lands."

"Life, prosperity, health!" the gathering answered him as he shook the bloodied spear over his head.

Now another voice was heard, one that had been muted so long that only the oldest of the crowd could remember it.

Waja-Hur, his frail body seeming to shed its years, stood upright beside King Djoser.

"I am Thoth, the judge of right and truth in the great company of gods," he said, his voice booming across the courtyard with a power he had not felt in years. "Hear this judgment. I find no wickedness in the heart of Horus, he has not wasted the offerings which have been made in the temples; he has not committed any evil act; and he has not set his mouth in motion with words of evil."

"Life, prosperity, health!" they answered.

King Djoser brought the spear down and laid it on the ground beside Kanakht's body. "Take him to the well of Sobek," he ordered the guards.

BANISHMENT OF DJEFI

"**I** would have killed Djefi," Prince Teti said that night.

Imhotep looked at King Djoser to see his reaction. The king lifted a roasted leg of goose to his mouth and pulled at it with his teeth.

"He deserved it twice. The statue was an insult and you know he trained that crocodile to attack you. The gods saved you from sitting in that chair, otherwise, it would have been you instead of Kanakht," Prince Teti said.

King Djoser looked across the table at Imhotep, who was suddenly very busy studying a piece of bread. When Imhotep had told King Djoser and Sekhmire what he had learned from Brian about Djefi's plans, the king had decided that the three of them would tell no one else. He would let it seem as if the gods had favored him. If Kanakht had not taken ill – *perhaps the gods did save me*, King Djoser mused – the king would have feigned a sore back and asked Kanakht to sit in the chair in his place.

"Yes, the gods intervened," King Djoser said finally. "And yes, Djefi is guilty of treason. And yes, Teti, he will be punished. Do you know why I did not order him executed today?"

He smiled to himself, as Teti remained silent. It was good to see that Teti had learned that there was a time for listening.

"You are young and strong, Teti," King Djoser said.

"You can teach a donkey by beating it, but it is hard work and you will never be able to trust it. But if you train it by rewarding it with food, then you have spared it and yourself pain and it will be more trustworthy. You can lead men by making them fear you. They will fight for you and obey you. But if they love you, then they will die for you.

"When I saw the statue Djefi had made, I decided to embrace it. He wanted a confrontation, which he knew he could not win unless something happened to me. Which, of course, he expected. So, I embraced the statue and welcomed Sobek as my protector, not an equal, but a protector. This eliminated the intended insult and, as you saw, proved to be true. Sobek did protect me. The other priests saw that I was not threatened by Djefi's offense. I was above it, bigger than Djefi, bigger than Sobek.

"That will raise me in their eyes."

"But the attack, father," Teti said.

"When I saw the statue I knew Djefi was part of the plot."

"You knew? Did you know about the crocodile?" Teti asked eagerly.

King Djoser saw the excitement in his son's eyes. He smiled in return. "Yes, Teti," he said.

"How?"

King Djoser looked off in the distance. Should he bring Teti into his confidence or keep him at arm's length a little longer? Would the boy be suspicious that his father was treating him like a child?

"Do you think that I am what I say I am, the living Horus?" King Djoser asked.

"Yes," Teti answered without hesitation.

"You are sure?" King Djoser asked.

Teti nodded his head with certainty. "Yes, father. I am certain. If you are a god, then I am the son of a god, someday to be a god myself."

Imhotep stopped eating and held his breath, waiting to see King Djoser's reaction.

King Djoser threw his head back and laughed, openly and loudly. He leaned forward and clapped his son on the back. "The answer I would have given," he said, still laughing.

Teti beamed at his father's open show of affection.

"Sometimes, Teti, I know things, things I have no reason to know. This is the truth. Last week when we were sailing downriver, I was happy that the land would be replenished, I was filled with joy that my offering to Khnum had been accepted. I felt as if my body could no longer contain my spirit and it seemed to soar above and beyond me. I saw all the Two Lands, the river, the fields, the people, the temples, the markets, the brewing houses and bakeries, I saw the fishermen on the river and the fish and crocodiles and snakes and hippos beneath it. I saw the desert and the mountains, the hawks and vultures and songbirds that fly above it and the lions and deer that live below them.

"My heart was lighter than the air and I knew that I was blessed and the gods would embrace me and protect me.

"So when I learned about the plans Djefi and Kanakht had made I was unafraid."

Teti nodded. "Did you know about Nesi also?"

King Djoser's face lost its humor. "Yes, Teti. That was why Bata and Meryptah were there. They were watching him, protecting you."

"I could have protected myself if I had known," Teti said softly.

"I know," King Djoser agreed, extending a hand to grip his son's arm. "But you know that I would not allow anyone to harm you. I needed you to act unconcerned so that I could learn who all the plotters were. I asked no more of you than I did of myself." He leaned toward Teti as he saw questions hanging behind his eyes.

"I am a god, Teti. Make no mistake about it. I knew that I would not be harmed. I knew that you would not be harmed. You may think I was taking a chance, putting you at risk. But I tell you, as Horus, as the Eye of Re himself, I had no doubts."

Father and son looked into each other's eyes for several heartbeats and then Teti bowed his head.

King Djoser watched him, looking for signs of rebellion, a hint of sulking, but it seemed that Teti was digesting the information, not questioning it.

"What will happen to Djefi now?" he asked, turning the conversation to the future.

King Djoser took a long drink of wine.

"This is very good," he said to Imhotep.

"I like the wine, King Djoser, but your beer makers are fantastic. I have never had better beer." Imhotep looked down at his small belly. "It is easy to drink too much of it."

"I sent him back to To-She, Teti," King Djoser said turning back to his son. "He protested that he had no part in Kanakht's plans and that Sobek had saved me, not attacked me. I answered that the temple had been desecrated by the spilling of blood and could not be used for three years. He can return then to try again to dedicate it."

"Then what is his punishment?" Prince Teti asked.

"Death. But not here in front of everyone. I want Sobek to be a protector, not an adversary. I would not have the god lose face by killing his First Prophet. No, Djefi will return to To-She, thinking and planning for his return to power. I will continue my journey down river, following the flood and celebrating with the people.

"Teti, you will take half the king's company with you, under your command, to Ineb-Hedj and wait there for me. When I arrive we will go together to To-She. We will visit Djefi and take him on a hunting trip to the western mountains where we will tether him to a stake and use him as bait for desert lions, as he wished to use me for the crocodile."

They were quiet for a moment, and then Imhotep spoke. "What if he tries to flee?"

Father and son looked at Imhotep as if he had just suggested a hippopotamus might grow wings.

"Where would he go?" King Djoser asked. "There is only Kemet. There is a desert to the east and to the west. The sea lies to the north and hostile Nubia to the south, along with my army. I control the River Iteru."

Imhotep nodded in agreement, but he thought of one way out of Kemet that King Djoser didn't know about – the unfinished tomb at Saqqara. It was where he would flee if he were Djefi.

Waja-Hur knew he was going to die.

He looked across the length of the boat and saw the fat priest sitting under his awning, eating and drinking, always eating and drinking. He looked to Waja-Hur like a petulant little boy, withdrawn from his friends, turning inward and finding only an empty shell that he forever tried to fill.

There was madness about him.

Waja-Hur had seen Djefi's face when the crocodile was eating the living entrails of Makare. His eyes had been wide and gleaming, his lips moving softly. He had almost quivered with excitement, like some animal in heat.

The old man sighed softly, the air rattling through his small, withering chest. He lifted his eyes across the rising level of the river to the green trees that lined the banks.

Such a soothing color. The color of Khert-Neter.

He turned to the fat priest, almost started to walk toward him to ask about Kanakht: Why wasn't he on the boat, where was his old friend? Then, like a desert mirage shimmering into focus, a memory returned of Kanakht writhing in a pool of blood, a huge crocodile standing beside him with a bloody stump of flesh protruding from its snout.

Waja-Hur cried out in fear, his hands gripped the boat railing. Was it a memory or a premonition? There was a scent of incense, a smell of sweat and fear with the memory, a clue Waja-Hur recognized now that this was a memory, not a vision. So Kanakht was dead. As the words ran through his mind, he recognized that they had been there before. Tagging along behind them was guilt: He had done something wrong. Fear lingered there, too, and it took the shape of the fat priest.

Brian was sitting up and his color had already begun to return.

It was three days since the assassination attempt. Hesire had tended the knife wound which had hit high enough to miss Brian's kidneys, glancing off the back of his rib cage, cracking a rib, but missing his lungs.

"Ipy," Imhotep said in English. "King Djoser insists on calling you Ipy. So, how are you, Ipy?"

"Ipy?" Brian shook his head.

"Ipy is a strong goddess, she is magical protection. It is an honor, Brian. She is a hippopotamus, strong, powerful," said Pahket, who was sitting beside him. She leaned her head against Brian's shoulder.

Brian started to laugh, then groaned suddenly as the movement tugged at his wound.

Imhotep and Pahket looked at him strangely.

He spoke to Imhotep in English. "Ell him my mahical ame ih Oode."

"Oode?" Imhotep repeated.

Brian rolled his eyes. "Ig ebowki. Remember?" He cocked his head.

Tim shook his head. Brian was amazing. He had been tortured, almost fed to a crocodile, knifed in the back and still his spirits remained high. He hugged Brian. "Dude, you are something else," he told him in English.

Brian nodded his head excitedly and pointed to Imhotep. "Yeah, yeah, Oode!"

Imhotep laughed now. "Got it, you want the king to call you Dude."

Brian beamed.

What Djefi wanted to do was wrap his hands around the old man's throat and choke him until he turned blue.

Djefi emptied his cup of beer and stared out across the water. In another two weeks they would be at Khmunu and he would put Waja-Hur ashore. He couldn't be trusted. The old man had lost his mind. Three times in six days he'd asked Djefi where Kanakht was, why wasn't he on the boat with them.

"He's crocodile shit by now. Stinking turds sinking to the muck at the bottom of the river," Djefi had told the old man the last time he'd asked. The old priest had looked at him like he didn't understand and then suddenly his eyes had misted over and tears ran down his cheeks.

Too late for that, Djefi had thought.

He couldn't believe that Waja-Hur had walked up beside King Djoser and pronounced him pure of heart, like he really was the god Thoth and not some raggedy old man who had lived too long, his body an empty shell, his mind gone.

Djefi stared across the water, but he saw nothing.

He had been banished to To-She. The king hadn't used those words, but that was what had happened. It was only a matter of time now. In a few weeks, a few months – what did it matter to the king? – someone would come to To-She and they would kill him. Djefi knew it. It's what he would do; it's what any man of power would do.

There was no place to run and he knew that he couldn't hope to fight the king.

I have Siamun, the king has an army.

He threw his beer cup over the side of the boat and watched it bob and tilt along the surface. He saw himself as the cup, floating along, driven by the currents. His face set in grim concentration.

In his heart he knew that he was lost. He had clung to the hope that having Diane in his possession would somehow give him bargaining power with the king. But after seeing the king drive his spear through the body of his vizier, after seeing the blood lust in the king's eyes, Djefi knew that Diane wouldn't make a difference.

He couldn't barter, he couldn't fight. His only chance was to flee.

But where?

Suddenly he thought of Diane again. Not her beauty, not her relationship with Brian or Imhotep. No! She was a stranger. She had come from some mysterious land that no one had ever heard of before.

That's where he could flee. He only needed to persuade her to tell him how to get there.

They put ashore at dusk, the fading light casting long shadows in front of them on the shore at Khmunu. No one, not even Nimaasted was there to greet them.

After his boatmen secured the boat, Djefi sent them into town to get a sedan. Until King Djoser sent an assassin, he was still First Prophet of Sobek and he would not walk when he could be carried.

While Djefi was waiting, Waja-Hur decided to leave the boat. Djefi called after him, ordering him to stay on the boat. The old man ignored him and walked up the bank toward the town.

Djefi clenched his hands and thought of the pleasure he would have shortly.

THOTH DEPARTS

They found Waja-Hur's body crumpled on the floor of his hut.

Nimaasted helped to carry the small body to a boat to be taken across the river to the place of purification. There he bathed Waja-Hur's body in a solution of natron, sanctifying it and preparing it for mummification.

The chief embalmer took charge of Waja-Hur's body then, wearing a jackal mask as he removed the priest's brain, coated his face with resin and carefully repacked the cranial cavity with linen rags soaked with resin.

The internal organs, except the heart, were removed to be embalmed separately and placed in canopic jars. Waja-Hur's empty body was stuffed with more resin-soaked linen and gently set down in a trough where it was covered with natron crystals to dehydrate for forty days.

When Tama and Hetephernebti arrived, Waja-Hur's body had been in the care of the embalmers for almost a week.

"What happened?" Tama asked Nimaasted.

"He was old, Tama," Nimaasted said, his love for the old man thickening his voice. "He was eager to leave Kemet for Khert-Neter."

Tama closed her eyes. She was suspicious of the timing of Waja-Hur's death, but she heard the pain in Nimaasted's voice.

"I'm sorry, Nimaasted," she said. "I know you loved him as a father. He was a special man, truly dedicated to Thoth and to the Two Lands." She waited a few moments to separate the questions she wanted to ask from her condolences.

"What I meant to ask, Nimaasted, was how did he pass?"

"I don't know. He returned from Kom Ombo in the evening. I was not expecting him so soon." Nimaasted looked at her, his face drawn and worried. "I've had no news, Tama, but there are rumors reaching us that something horrible happened at the dedication."

"You've had no messages from the king?" she asked.

He shook his head.

"Just rumors. They say the king was attacked but turned himself into Sobek and ate his attacker. They say Waja-Hur regained his youth and spoke with the voice of a god, cleansing Kemet and returning the Two

Lands to ma'at. They say the king's new adviser killed a man by pointing his hand at him. They say Makare was trying to kill King Djoser.

"Is this true?"

Hetephernebti, who had been silent until now, put a hand on Nimaasted's shoulder.

"The voice of the gods is in these stories, Nimaasted. I was at Kom Ombo. I saw," she said. "King Djoser did not turn into Sobek, but Sobek did devour the man who plotted against the king. It was Kanakht. And Waja-Hur was truly visited by Thoth. Of that I am sure. His face and voice became that of a young man, a man possessed by a terrible strength. He looked in King Djoser's heart and saw the truth that is there. He pronounced him a god and proclaimed that Kemet had been restored to ma'at.

"The truth is in the river, Nimaasted. Do you see how it has risen? King Djoser made an offering to Khnum to show his love of his father. And now Khnum has unleashed a mighty flood."

It was true. Nimaasted had never seen the waters rise as they were now. He heard the passion in Hetephernebti's voice, saw the belief in her eyes.

"Nimaasted," Tama said. "Did you see Waja-Hur after he arrived? Did you see him with Djefi?"

"I don't understand."

"Waja-Hur was traveling with Djefi. They must have arrived together."

Nimaasted nodded. "Yes. Djefi came to me the night before we found Waja-Hur. He said the trip had exhausted Waja-Hur and that he had gone to his room to sleep. Djefi said we should let Waja-Hur rest, that it been his habit to sleep until late in the day while on the boat.

"He has been tired, Tama. And lately he has kept unusual hours, sleeping during the day and walking the streets at night. You saw that. So we waited until after noon before checking on him. He was on the floor, his ka free."

Tama took Nimaasted in her arms and hugged the young priest.

"I'm sorry, Nimaasted. But, as you say, his ka is free and he will soon walk the green fields of Khert-Neter, young and strong again."

Brian had mixed feelings as Khmunu came into view along the river.

He was no longer an outlaw, and he was traveling with Imhotep who wore the menat as a sign of his royal office as adviser to the king. Tama and Hetephernebti had traveled ahead of them, so Nimaasted and Waja-Hur would know that he was no longer a hunted man.

Still, the town was where everything had changed for him.

He had been attacked by strangers and saved by a boatman. He had hidden from a search party and been rescued by Tama. He had fled the village in disguise and then found himself during the journey with Tama. He had loved and been loved.

He, Imhotep and Bata were traveling with Pahket and Meryt. They were a few days behind Hetephernebti and Tama, having waited at Kom Ombo for Hesire to be satisfied that Brian's wound was healing properly.

They planned to stop to get provisions and news. After three weeks on the boat with the men, Meryt and Pahket were eager to be among women.

"**E**ffi killed him," Brian said, nodding his head with certainty.

Imhotep nodded agreement. "Probably, Brian, but I don't know how we would prove it."

They were standing in Waja-Hur's room with Tama who had told them that no one had seen Waja-Hur alive after he had arrived with Djefi.

"Nimaasted said they found him here the next day," she said, pointing to the dirt floor by the bed. "He said it looked like Waja-Hur had gotten up and started to walk to the doorway when he collapsed."

They looked at the dirt floor, each picturing Waja-Hur there. Suddenly Brian took a long step that brought him to the low bed by the wall. "Ook," he said, pointing to the bed and the neatly folded sheet at the foot of it.

"Yes?" Tama said.

Brian mimed folding a sheet. Then he pointed again at the bed.

"You're right," Imhotep said. "The sheet is neatly folded. Waja-Hur didn't sleep here."

Tama shook her head. "We don't know that. It is possible someone cleaned the room and folded the sheet."

"Can we ask?" Imhotep asked Tama.

"Cahn we ee is bahee?" Brian asked.

Tama looked at Imhotep for a translation. Instead, Imhotep looked at Brian. "How would that help? If Djefi killed him with a knife, they would have noticed. And the body will be different. They are mummifying it. I don't know what we'd gain."

Brian shrugged. "I wah hinking. Ow ould he ill im?"

Imhotep squinted, trying to understand Brian's mangled English. During the trip downriver, Imhotep had learned to understand much of what Brian said, but Brian was excited now and hard to understand.

Brian sighed deeply and suddenly reached out and took Imhotep by the neck, as if strangling him. Imhotep stifled his reaction to jerk away and let Brian demonstrate his point. He felt a pressure on his windpipe, which Brian released as soon as Imhotep winced.

"Oones, ooken oones," Brian said pointing to his throat.

Imhotep got it. "Right, broken bones. We should be able to tell that." He looked at Brian in amazement. "How did you think of that?"

"EV," Brian answered. He pretended to use a remote control.

"Got, it, television," Imhotep said.

Tama had followed part of Imhotep's English, but Brian's gibberish made no sense to her. "I don't understand," she said.

"If Djefi killed Waja-Hur like this," Imhotep put his hands around his own throat because he didn't know the Egyptian word for strangle, "then the bones here might be broken. Can we see his body?"

Nimaasted was resistant until Hetephernebti intervened.

"He is King Djoser's adviser, Nimaasted. You were not at Kom Ombo when he stepped in front of Makare and saved King Djoser's life by merely pointing his hand at the assassin. And you see the royal menat he wears.

"If he wants to see Waja-Hur's body, you must let him."

The priest led Imhotep, Brian and Tama across the river to the tent where Waja-Hur's body was drying in the natron trough.

It was the first time Brian had seen Nimaasted since the night Nimaasted had lured him to the ambush and pulled a knife on him. Tama had explained to Brian that Kanakht had ordered the attack and Nimaasted was bound to obey the vizier's orders.

Brian understood, and having seen Kanakht attacked by the crocodile, he no longer felt the need for revenge. But he found himself disliking the young priest despite Nimaasted's apologies.

Inside the tent, Nimaasted knelt by the trough and lovingly brushed the salt crystals from Waja-Hur's face. The natron had begun to tighten and darken the body's skin, which looked delicate and paper-thin.

Imhotep knelt beside Nimaasted and unfolded a Swiss Army pocketknife. As he reached slowly toward Waja-Hur's throat, Nimaasted grabbed his arm to stop him. Imhotep glanced at him angrily, and Brian quickly clamped a rough hand on Nimaasted's shoulder.

"Nimaasted," Tama said quietly. "We are in search of the truth here. Release him or I will ask Brian to take you outside."

His arm free, Imhotep brought the shining blade closer to Waja-Hur's throat, glancing at the dead man's face, half expecting him to open his mouth in protest. Swallowing hard, Imhotep reached in with his other hand and brushed away the crystals from Waja-Hur's neck.

"Ook," Brain said as the neck became visible.

The natron had started to absorb the fluids from Waja-Hur's skin leaving behind dark circles where blood had formed bruises.

Imhotep folded up his knife and reached in with both hands, placing his fingertips on the bruises. As he placed his fingers on the bruise marks, his hands wrapped around Waja-Hur's neck as if he were strangling him.

Tama and Brian stared silently. Nimaasted gasped and shouted for Imhotep to stop.

Tama understood first. "No, Nimaasted, he isn't desecrating the body. Imhotep, please move your hands. See, Nimaasted? The bruises on Waja-Hur's neck are exactly where they would be if they had been made by someone's fingers squeezing there. Waja-Hur was strangled, Nimaasted. Someone killed him."

"It wasn't someone," Imhotep said. "It was Djefi."

Tama shook her head. "We do not know that."

"Waja-Hur's bed was not slept in, we saw the folded sheet. Yet Djefi told Nimaasted not to disturb Waja-Hur because he was sleeping. Djefi was lying," Imhotep said. "He must have taken him to his room and killed him there. Then he told Nimaasted not to disturb Waja-Hur so he had time to leave Khmunu."

"I agree that it makes sense, Imhotep," Tama said. "I'm just saying that we don't know that it is true."

"Iane," Brian said.

Imhotep looked at him sharply. "That's right, she's at To-She." He turned to Tama. "Brian and I are leaving for To-She, as soon as possible."

"No," she said. "If Djefi has done this, then he has gone mad."

"He knows I am the king's vizier now. He will not harm us."

"No, Imhotep, think. If he has gone mad, he will not care who you are. Wait here. We will send word to King Djoser and he will send men to go with you."

Brian grabbed Imhotep's arm. "We muh help her," he said.

Imhotep looked at Brian. He remembered the swaggering jock who had walked across the sand at Saqqara. Now he saw a man who had been tortured and almost killed, yet he was ready to place himself in danger for someone else.

And he thought about Djefi. He was desperate or deranged enough to kill another priest. He would know that there was no place for him to hide or to escape the king's revenge unless he found the passage through the unfinished tomb to the land he, Brian, and Diane had come from.

In his heart Imhotep knew that Djefi would look for the passageway, and he knew Djefi would do anything to force Diane to help him.

"Let's find Bata," he told Brian in English. He turned to Tama. "We must go. I will leave Meryt in your protection."

"An Paheh," Brian added.

Prince Teti's three boats arrived two days later.

He expected to find Imhotep and the others resting at Khmunu, but instead he learned that Waja-Hur had been murdered and that Imhotep had headed north to To-She determined to rescue Diane himself. He sent a message to the king, dispatching pigeons to different towns, unsure where King Djoser would be.

Then he and the soldiers who were traveling with him returned to their boats and headed north to Ineb-Hedj to await the king's orders.

FLIGHT FROM TO-SHE

Bakr slid his tongue across the edges of his top teeth, stopping when he came to the gap. Gently he probed the space with the tip of his tongue. The raw edges of the gum were swollen and sore.

The teeth had been gone three days and the pain was getting worse.

Hearing footsteps approach from his right, Bakr pressed back against the mud wall and waited, alert and ready.

The footsteps grew closer and, recognizing them, Bakr relaxed. It was Abana bringing the evening meal to Yunet and Diane.

She gave him a quick smile and then averted her eyes as she entered the hut where the women were being kept. Bakr looked after her, wondering why she hadn't stopped and then he heard the heavier footsteps.

Siamun's face was the same scowling mask of anger he had worn since returning to To-She with the women a month ago.

"Where are they?" he asked, barely breaking his stride.

"Inside," Bakr answered quickly, nodding toward the doorway. "Abana just took them food."

Siamun brushed past him and looked inside.

Bakr heard Yunet shout at Siamun to leave them alone. He heard a heavy slap and Abana ran past him crying and holding her cheek. Bakr wanted to follow her and comfort her, but he knew it would only make Siamun angry and then someone would suffer.

He felt the empty space in his gum once more.

He had been sitting by the fire, eating with the others, Siamun squatting beside him. The men had been talking about a hunt, trading stories, laughing. Bakr had been quiet, thinking about his sister Pahket.

She had gone to Kom Ombo with the others, but hadn't returned.

Something bad had happened at Kom Ombo. He knew that. The few men who had been there and returned with Siamun didn't talk about it. They were like Siamun, rough, angry and unfeeling, but strangely quiet about Kom Ombo.

Naqada hadn't returned either. From the look in the eyes of the men it was clear something horrible had happened to Naqada.

Siamun had been as quiet as Bakr, simply staring into the fire, watching the dance of the flames; lost in whatever world he lived in.

Gathering his courage, Bakr softly asked, "What happened to Pahket?" He spoke quietly so the others wouldn't hear.

Siamun's hand had moved too fast for Bakr to react. He had grabbed a rock by the edge of the fire and smashed it into Bakr's mouth, breaking off two teeth and splitting open his lip.

"You ask too many questions," Siamun had said.

Djefi returned late at night.

He went to Siamun's hut, but found him asleep, broken beer jars lying on the ground around him. After kicking him twice without waking him, Djefi lumbered away, headed for Yunet and Diane.

Bakr, who was guarding the women, heard Djefi's heavy breathing as he approached.

He ducked into the hut and whispered a warning to Neswy, Yunet's crippled uncle, who had sneaked in to talk with her. Neswy hobbled out and got around the side of the dwelling as Djefi came up the path.

"Greetings, First Prophet," Bakr said.

Djefi was startled. "What are you doing here?" he asked.

"I am guarding Yunet and Diane. At Siamun's orders."

"Guarding? Why? Has something happened?"

"No, First Prophet. When Siamun returned, he ordered Yunet and Diane to be watched."

Djefi looked at the ground and shook his head. "Go home, Bakr. The women do not need to be guarded here at To-She. The time for that was at, oh, never mind. I will speak to Siamun in the morning."

He waited for Bakr to disappear into the darkness, then he turned and entered the hut.

The women were standing against the far wall of the first room. A low doorway led to their sleeping chambers.

"Greetings, brother," Yunet said, relief in her voice. "We thought you were Siamun."

Djefi wondered what had happened to make Yunet so afraid of Siamun, and how he could use it to get their help.

Yunet motioned to a chair and offered Djefi food and beer.

"We haven't much, Siamun has not allowed us to leave or to cook here. We only have what is brought to us."

Djefi waved his hand in dismissal as he sat.

"Have you heard what happened at Kom Ombo?" he asked.

Yunet shook her head.

"Kanakht tried to assassinate King Djoser!" he said, his voice rising higher as he pretended to be offended. "It was horrible, Yunet. Fortunately, Sobek intervened and attacked Kanakht, saving King Djoser."

"Was he sitting in the chair? The one Siamun tied Brian to every night?" Diane spat.

Djefi blinked slowly and looked at Diane. Ever since he and Siamun had killed his stepfather, no one had ever talked to him with that tone of voice, not until this strange red-haired woman and her friend had emerged from Kanakht's unfinished tomb.

He glanced at Yunet and saw her face was strained with worry.

"I have been traveling," Djefi said.

"I don't know what Siamun was doing at Kom Ombo," he said. "If you remember, I sent him away when I arrived there."

"You didn't know," Diane said in English. "Siamun doesn't fart unless you tell him to. You knew what he was doing."

Djefi looked from Diane to Yunet. "What did she say?" he asked.

"I do not know, brother. I haven't learned her language."

"I said I remember. I will always remember what Siamun did," Diane said, speaking in Egyptian.

Djefi shifted his weight and tried to keep his face impassive. He needed the information this woman had. Djefi would try to persuade Diane to help him. If that failed, there was always Siamun.

He turned back to Yunet. "Because the attack took place at Sobek's temple, King Djoser is angry with me. With Sobek."

"Angry? But you said Sobek saved the king."

"Yes. But King Djoser was frightened, too frightened to think clearly. He associated the attack with the temple, even though Kanakht confessed before he died. He whispered something to the king with his dying breath. I think he implicated me."

"Why would he do that?" Yunet asked.

Djefi sighed. It was so hard to make up lies, so much easier to just take what he wanted. He looked at Diane, saw defiance in her eyes, and began to lose his temper.

"It doesn't matter, Yunet. What matters is that I am in disfavor. All of us are in disfavor."

"Because you plotted to kill the king," she said.

"Because Kanakht plotted," Djefi said, his voice rising. "You were not there, you don't know."

Yunet didn't answer.

Djefi took a moment to compose himself, but he felt his blood rushing.

"I want her," he nodded toward Diane, "to take us to her country, away from Djoser and his fears."

Yunet shook her head. "She doesn't know how she got here. I've talked to her. Her friend brought her."

Djefi stared at her. "She doesn't know? How can she not know?"

Yunet shrugged.

Djefi remembered the coldness in King Djoser's eyes as he untied the cloth around Kanakht's leg and forced blood from the ragged stump. He closed his eyes and saw the blood lust in the king's face as he drove his spear into Kanakht's body.

"I must leave Kemet, Yunet," he said simply. He turned his face toward. "Where did you come from?" he asked.

"America," she said.

"Where is it? How do we get there?"

Diane shook her head. After what Djefi had ordered done to Brian there was no way she would help him.

Seeing the defiance in Diane's eyes, Djefi stood and shouted, "She knows!" He stepped toward her. "She knows how to get there."

Yunet slipped between them.

"No, Djefi. She doesn't know. She is angry because of what Siamun did to Brian. That's what you see. She does not know."

She stopped and put her hands against his fat shoulders, but Djefi leaned into her and pushed her aside.

Diane slid away, moving toward the low table by the other wall.

Djefi turned to follow her, but Yunet moved in between again.

"Out of my way. She knows and she will tell me," Djefi shouted. He pushed at Yunet, shoving her away. Stumbling back, she fell against the wall with a groan, but quickly pushed herself away and grabbed Djefi's arm.

He whirled on her with surprising speed and slapped her face with his free hand. Blood flew from her mouth, but she didn't let go of his arm.

"Run, Diane," she said.

Djefi slapped her again, harder, jerking her head to the side. He moved his hands down to her throat.

"Shut up," he said as he started to choke her.

Remembering how she had stood by unmoving when Brian was being tortured by Siamun, Diane took two long steps and jumped on Djefi's back, digging her fingers into his eyes.

He swayed from the weight shift and began to fall backward, letting go of Yunet. As he lost his balance and began to topple, Diane slid free. He fell heavily to the hard-packed dirt floor, landing on his back with a loud grunt as the air rushed out of him. His head snapped back with a thud and he stopped moving.

There was no sound except for Yunet's raspy gasps and Diane's heavy breathing. Yunet stared at Djefi's inert form.

"Is he dead?" she asked, rubbing her throat and moving toward him.

Diane ignored Djefi. "Are you OK?' she asked Yunet.

Yunet ducked her head as she swallowed. "Yes," she said.

Kneeling by Djefi, she placed a hand flat on his chest and felt it moving. "He breathes," she said. His head lolled to the side and he groaned. Hearing a noise from the doorway, Yunet looked up to see Neswy standing there, his eyes wide as he looked at Djefi on the floor.

"Did you kill him? I hope so," he said. He glanced over his shoulder and then entered the hut.

Yunet shook her heard. "No, he is breathing and he moaned."

Neswy looked from Djefi to Yunet. "You know you must leave, don't you?" he asked.

Yunet bit her lower lip and nodded.

Djefi's head started to move as he began to wake. Neswy untied his kilt and gripping the hem with his teeth he tore a strip of linen from it. Quickly he dropped beside Djefi and wrapped the cloth around Djefi's head, gagging him. He nodded at the torn kilt as he worked on the gag. "Tear more strips," he said.

They blindfolded Djefi and rolled him onto his side so they could tie his arms behind his back. Then they tied his feet together.

"You must leave, now," Neswy whispered to Yunet and Diane. "Siamun is asleep so you have a few hours. I don't know where you should go, but get as far from To-She as you can. Perhaps you can flee to Iunu and seek refuge with Hetephernebti at the Temple of Re."

Yunet looked around the hut. She grabbed a sack and began to fill it with bread.

"I have a water skin," Neswy said. "I will fill it and meet you at the edge of town." He took a last look at Djefi, bending down to test the strength of the linen ties. "Hurry," he said as he left the hut.

Siamun awoke early and went to the canal to wash. He was standing in the water, shaking his head dry when Bakr arrived at canal bank, a frightened look on his face.

"Come quick, Siamun. Djefi has been attacked."

Siamun splashed his way to land and followed Bakr. They ran through the village to the hut where Yunet and Diane had been held.

"What happened?" Siamun shouted as they ran.

"I went to Yunet's hut this morning and found First Prophet Djefi there. He returned late last night and sent me away so he could speak with

Yunet alone. This morning, the women are gone and I found First Prophet Djefi tied and gagged. I freed him and he sent me to get you."

They found Djefi sitting on a stool in the hut, his robe stained with sweat, the stench of human waste filling the small chamber. Djefi glared at them, daring them to comment.

"Find them," he said to Siamun. "I don't care what you do with Yunet, but bring the red-haired woman back to me alive."

"Unharmed?" Siamun asked, his eyes glowing.

Djefi snorted in disgust.

"You want her, don't you? How can you think of that now?" He shook his head. "Have her, I don't care. But bring her back to me alive AND able to talk.

"No," he said as he thought of the day Diane and Brian had arrived in the Two Lands, "take them to Saqqara, to the tomb of Kanakht."

SIAMUN IN PURSUIT

The sun seemed to linger on the western horizon as if Re were resisting his nightly trip through Khert-Neter. In the fading light Diane and Yunet shook the sand from the linen cloth they had used as a tent, preparing to roll it up so they could resume their trek.

Following Neswy's instructions they had walked through the night and early morning. He had urged them to travel only at night to save their water and their strength. He said they should hide during the daylight under the dun-colored square of linen he had given them.

Yunet had wanted to take camels to make the trip quicker, but Neswy had pointed out that Siamun would travel faster and they would be more visible sitting high on a camel.

"I would go with you, Yunet," he had said, tears welling in his eyes. "But I am of little use anymore." He looked down at his leg. Brian had saved his life when he carried him out of the desert, but his broken leg had not healed correctly.

"I can only give you my knowledge.

"You cannot travel by boat because it will be too easy for Siamun to find you. There is no place to hide on the water. You cannot travel across the desert because you would lose your way and die. I am sorry, Yunet," he said as she protested, "but it is true.

"But there is a way."

He had led them out from under the trees and pointed to the sky. "See, there," he had said pointing to the horizon. "Hold your hand like this." He had turned his right hand sideways, with the fingers aligned with the horizon. "Stretch out your arm and lay your thumb along the horizon. Yes, like that. Now, just above your hand there is a bright star, brighter than the others. Do you see it? Yes? Now, turn your hand so the heel is at the horizon and the bright star is along the side of your small finger. Look, Yunet, look at the top of your fingertips. See the bright star there? It is the brightest star in the sky. It marks the east.

"When you leave here, follow the canal toward the river until it begins to be light. Then you must move into the desert. Walk into the desert until you can no longer see the trees. Then walk some more. Take the cloth and stretch it out. Scatter sand over it and then crawl underneath it.

"It will give you shade and it will hide you.

"When it grows dark, walk back to the canal. Always keep the water to your right. Take time to bathe and drink. It will give you strength. Walk until the sky begins to grow light, then head back into the desert to hide. I know this will seem slow, but you must be careful. Djefi will send Siamun after you and there is no better hunter.

"If you lose your way and cannot get back to the water, then follow that bright star. It will lead you east to the river. Once there, you follow the river's flow. It will take you north to Ineb-Hedj. Remember, you must hide during the day, as far from the canal and the river as you can. They will look for you along the water."

He had hugged her.

"This will pass, Yunet. Someday you will be able to return to To-She. This evil that Djefi and Siamun have brought will not last."

The first night they had run on nervous energy, their ears attuned to every sound in the darkness, each of them lost in her own thoughts.

For Yunet, the world had shifted, the eternal landscape of the Two Lands changed forever. She had been born into a world where order – ma'at – was the foundation of life.

The rhythm of life was immutable.

Each day Re appeared in the cloudless eastern skies and each night he entered Khert-Neter, knowing he would be guided through the darkness and reborn. In the proper season Khnum unleashed the great river to bring life to the land. Khonsu, the wanderer, passed across the sky each night, gliding through the darkness that was the god Kuk.

In the Two Lands that lay between the sky goddess Nut and her brother Geb, the earth god, each step of life had been taken before, by ancestors and by the gods themselves. Deadly quarrels, illicit couplings and strange births, dismemberment and loving salvation – all had taken place among the gods. Their examples guided each man and woman in their daily life.

When one drank and danced it was as Hathor, Lady of the West, the great cow-headed goddess of love and fertility, had done since the beginning of time. Bes, strange little dwarf with a lion's mane, aided in childbirth. Everyone kept magical amulets, the ankh of life, the sa – magical papyrus scrolls to protect against the desert sun.

What she and Diane had done – assaulting the First Prophet of Sobek and fleeing from their homes in the dead of night – these had never been done. Never should be done.

Yunet knew that they had disturbed ma'at. She wondered what price they would pay.

Diane was euphoric.

A lifetime of doing what was expected – of accepting her fate with unspoken resentment – was over. She felt an exhilaration and lightness that she wanted to hold onto forever.

She knew that she had snapped when she had seen Brian tied to the stone chair with Siamun standing beside him holding Brian's bloody tongue. She had sunk into depression, her world black and bleak. She would have drunk herself to death, but there had been only beer and wine and her stomach could not hold enough to kill her.

She had heard Yunet's pleadings, she had lain stone cold within her embrace, but Diane had withdrawn to a silent world. It had been death.

The trip downriver away from the bleak stone and desert of Kom Ombo had revived her. The movement of all the life around her – the power of the re-energized river, the sight of the birds darting from tree to tree along the river bank, the swaying reeds, the splash of fish jumping from the water, the calls of hawks as they soared through the sky – slowly it had washed away the self-pity and dejection.

She was certain that Brian was still alive. She knew she would see him again and somehow things would be made right.

No one would ever stand in her way again.

Siamun was thrumming with energy.

He didn't know about Waja-Hur's death, and he was unaware that King Djoser and his sister Hetephernebti both wanted Djefi removed, the king for political reasons, his sister because she feared the rise of the cult of Sobek. But it wouldn't have mattered.

He was preparing for a hunt, one that would end with Yunet and Diane in his power, to do whatever he wanted.

He gathered water bags and dried strips of oxen, said a quick prayer to Sobek and to Anhur, god of war and hunting, ordered his men to keep Djefi safe and tethered three camels together. He would ride one until it was exhausted, then switch to a fresh one.

Instinctively he headed into the desert toward Ineb-Hedj. Once he was moving he began to think, trying to put himself in Yunet's mind, just as he would try to anticipate what an antelope would do if he were stalking it.

She would not have gone into the red western desert. There was nothing there but sand, heat and death. If she crossed the canal and went south she would be heading toward Khmunu where Waja-Hur and Nimaasted would stop them. If she was able to cross the river and continue eastward there was only more desert and beyond that the sea known as Great Green.

Her only hope was to reach Iunu and the Temple of Re. And that was an uncertain hope. While Hetephernebti might give her sanctuary, she also might turn her over to Djefi. Hetephernebti was, after all, a priestess, just as Djefi was a priest. Ma'at would be maintained.

Atop a plodding camel, Siamun headed northeast through the desert, his eyes darkened with wide swaths of kohl, his spirits high as he thought of what he would do once he caught the women.

Unconsciously he fingered the side of his head and the knobby growth where his ear had been sliced away by Yunet. He would have his revenge at last. He would hear her cry for death, beg for an end to the pain.

And he would take the red-haired bitch who thought she was a goddess. He had seen the way she looked at him on the boat, the anger in her eyes. She would know real anger as he rode her, driving himself into her, taking his pleasure as he gave her pain.

He dug his fingers deep into the matted hair at the camel's neck and studied the desert for signs of movement.

He had ridden across the desert to Saqqara, almost reaching the high plateau without finding them. Waiting through the night on the outskirts of Ineb-Hedj, Siamun wondered where they could have gone.

If they had trekked across the desert toward Ineb-Hedj he would have found them, unless they had become so disoriented that they had walked more than a day's journey in the wrong direction. He didn't think they had enough of a head start to get that far out of sight by mistake.

Neswy! The old man helped them, Siamun realized. Yunet is strong and brave, but she knows nothing about hunting or traveling, except as a passenger on Djefi's boats. But Neswy does, and there was no one else she could have turned to after attacking Djefi.

Neswy would have told them to stay along the canal and then the river. They would have no chance of losing their way and they would have water to drink. And he would have told them to travel only at night.

He decided in an instant. Abandoning two of the camels, Siamun took the tether of the third camel, which would serve as a pack animal, and began to follow the river south from Ineb-Hedj, confident that he would find them.

Yunet and Diane were talking again, the tension of the flight abrading the anger Diane had been silently nursing.

They had reached the river and were heading north, following its flow toward Ineb-Hedj, beginning to believe that they had escaped.

"If I had died at his hands it would have been worth it to see his fat face when you jumped on his back and began to claw at his eyes," Yunet said as they washed the sand from their bodies. They were knee-deep in the river, preparing for the night's walk. Yunet's dark skin made her almost invisible in the fading light; Diane's fair skin seemed to glow.

"You don't know what you've done, do you?" Yunet continued when Diane didn't answer. "I don't know the way you live in your country, but here there is an order – we call it ma'at – that we do not disturb. When you attacked Djefi, you didn't just disturb it, you ripped it apart."

"You sound like you regret it," Diane said.

Yunet shook her head. "No, I don't think so. Yes, a little. It makes me wonder what else can happen. It is very unsettling."

"And being choked to death would have been better?" Diane asked.

"No. But the world seems different to me now. If the rules, the way of life are not what I thought they are, what I was raised to believe, then I don't know what they are."

"Maybe there aren't any rules," Diane said.

They climbed out of the river and gathered up their water skin, the diminishing sack of food and the linen tent.

Hefting the food sack, Yunet said, "Now that we have reached the river, we should start seeing small settlements. We'll be able to get some food then."

Diane nodded as they turned together and began to follow the river's flow north.

They walked in silence, listening to the water and the occasional small movement in the underbrush. When they had begun walking at night, Diane had been terrified at every small sound, expecting lions or crocodiles to pounce on her after every rustle of a leaf. Now she had grown to love the night, with its cooler air, the hint of moisture along the river and the blazing night sky, filled with more stars than she had ever imagined.

Yunet was good company, too. She didn't press Diane to talk and she didn't fill the air with idle chatter.

Diane looked at her now as Yunet walked slightly ahead, feeling her way along the path as the darkness grew heavier. She watched as Yunet studied the ground, pushing at bushes with a sturdy walking stick she had picked up a few days ago.

Yunet's confidence and beauty made her seem so much larger and older than she really was, but looking at her now, Diane saw that Yunet was not much older than she was.

And she abandoned everyone she knew, dismissed a lifetime of habits and training to help me, Diane thought.

"Yunet," she called. She watched as Yunet stopped and turned to look back at her, her expression focused and anxious.

"No," Diane said, smiling, "I'm not hurt. I just want to thank you."

Yunet shook her head, not understanding.

"For everything." Diane sighed heavily. "I've been a bitch," she said in English. She looked around in the darkness and saw a clearing off to the side of the path. She stepped slowly to Yunet and took her hand.

Yunet grasped her hand in return.

Diane leaned closer to kiss her. Yunet returned her kiss and, dropping the food bag, put her arms around Diane to pull her close.

After a moment Diane pulled back and rested her cheek against Yunet's shoulder. She ran her fingertips down Yunet's back and flattened her hand against her curves.

"Diane," Yunet said. "I want you very much. But we cannot take the time for this. We are not safe yet." She hugged her close.

"I know," Diane answered. "It's just that you have done so much for me. Before now, I mean, when I first got here. You didn't tell me do anything; you were so patient and understanding. I've been selfish in every way. I was angry with Brian and so I expected you to make it up. I know that sounds stupid."

Yunet brushed Diane's hair with her hand and kissed the top of her head softly.

"Anyhow," Diane continued. "I feel different about Brian now. I know that I still care for him, but it's like I want to make sure he's safe before I can say goodbye to him. I don't know what will happen with you and me, but I want you to know how wonderful you've been to me. I've been so lucky to have you as a friend, and as a lover."

She tilted her head back and kissed Yunet again, her eyes closed, her entire being focused on the warmth and tenderness where they touched. When she opened her eyes, she gasped. Siamun's leering face had materialized over Yunet's shoulder.

He killed Yunet quicker than he wanted to.

She fought more fiercely than he expected and Diane even tried to fight him. He knocked Diane away with a sweep of his arm, but when the momentum of the blow twisted him away from Yunet, she squirmed out of his grasp and grabbed a rock.

They circled each other warily, Yunet calling out to Diane to run. Siamun watched Yunet intently, waiting for an opening. When he saw it, he swung in low, dropping to his knee as he swiped his knife at her ankle. Instead of backing away as he expected her to, Yunet stepped closer.

She swung the rock hard at his head, clipping just the back of it as he ducked toward her legs. He saw fiery lights in his head as he rolled forward, his momentum knocking Yunet down. He scrambled to get on top of her, but was knocked sideways as Diane kicked him in the ribs.

Rolling with the kick, he came to his knees as Yunet rushed him, swinging her thick walking stick at him. He rocked back on his heels and launched himself at her, trying to get inside her swing. As he moved, Diane tossed a handful of dirt in his face. Blinded, he felt the walking stick slam against his shoulder.

He screamed in anger and, twisting his arm around, grabbed Yunet's stick. He pulled it violently toward himself with one hand. With his other hand he thrust his knife toward where he thought Yunet would be.

Yunet was gripping the stick with both hands, realizing it was her only hope. When Siamun jerked on it, it pulled her toward him so quickly she wasn't able to dodge the knife that came at her at the same time.

The knife caught her under the rib cage, driving upward under the bones, its sharp tip cutting through her lungs and slicing into her heart.

She fell against Siamun, her hot blood pumping out onto his outstretched arm. She was dead before she landed.

Diane had emptied the food sack and gripping each end, she twisted it around Siamun's neck, trying to strangle him. She heard him laugh as he jerked his head forward, the movement slamming her against his back as he reached up to grab her arms. She felt the slippery blood on his hands and realized what it was. A cold wave of terror replaced her anger.

She landed heavily on her back as Siamun came to his feet.

Now there was a burning pain along her cheek and a sharp, bruising ache between her legs. She stretched her legs and felt the sticky pull of drying blood on her inner thighs.

Slowly, Diane opened her eyes. She was lying on her stomach in a small clearing. She could hear the river rushing past behind her. She reached up to her face and felt the open gash where Siamun had cut her. From her other pains she knew that he had raped her after he had knocked her out.

She tried to breathe deeply, to slow the fear that was making her entire body quiver. In the back of her mind she was surprised to still be alive. She thought of Yunet and in her memory she saw again the ugly, chipped knife drive into Yunet's stomach, she saw the surprised look on Yunet's face and then the sudden slacking of the muscles as her heart stopped.

After Siamun had overpowered Diane, he had ripped away her kilt to rape her. She had fought as hard as she could, twisting and trying to get a knee between his legs.

Eventually he had clamped both her wrists in one hand and stretched them over her head. Then he had put the knife against her face and threatened to cut her if she continued to fight. In a flash she remembered

Brian's battered body on the stone chair and she had known that Siamun would show her no mercy.

"Go to hell," she had answered and had spit in his face.

She had screamed as the knife cut her, but her legs had stayed clamped together. As he had fought to pry her legs open, she had pulled a hand free and clawed at him, raking open his face. She remembered his hand drawing back and then rushing toward her. Then all was blackness.

Now she raised her head and felt it suddenly jerk backward as Siamun pulled on a rope he had tied around her neck.

She reached up and grabbed at the rope, but Siamun pulled it tighter.

"Come on," he said. "We have someone to meet."

As they came up the wadi, Diane felt an overwhelming sense of déjà vu. When they rounded the last turn and she saw the opening of the tomb that she and Brian had walked out of a few months ago, her knees buckled and she fell to the sand.

Siamun swung his leg around the camel's neck and slid down to the ground. He stooped over to pick up the rope that hung from Diane's neck. He was tempted to pull it and drag her across the sand by her neck.

The three-day journey had been exhausting. He had never believed that a woman could be so stubborn and so willing to die. He had beaten her, cut her and threatened her, but she refused to surrender. He had taken her as she lay unconscious after a beating, but it was less satisfying than using his own hand.

She continued to try to escape, even though there was nowhere for her to go and no chance of her getting away from him. The first few times he had knocked her down, but then he had to wait until she was able to walk again. Eventually he had tied her up and draped her over the camel, but even there she fought and twisted until she had fallen from the beast.

It would have been so much easier to kill her.

Siamun saw movement near the entrance of the tomb. He pulled his knife from his belt as he saw a person emerge from the dark opening.

It was Bakr.

He came toward Siamun, his eyes moving from back and forth between him and Diane.

"Where is Djefi?" Siamun asked.

"He is in Ineb-Hedj. I am to get him when you arrive." He looked at Diane, his face filled with pity. He started to ask Siamun what he had done to her and where Yunet was, but his tongue brushed against the opening where his teeth had been and he held his questions.

"I'll get Djefi. He asked that you wait here."

Siamun shrugged and tugged on the rope, heading for the dark shade of the tomb.

RETURN TO INEB-HEDJ

Because it did not lie along the river, To-She had fewer visitors than Ineb-Hedj, Waset, Khmunu and most other villages in the Two Lands.

Still, rumors did drift along the canal to the oasis.

The guards who had been at Kom Ombo with Siamun had been unusually quiet about what had happened there, but wild rumors arose, fed by their silence. When Djefi returned, an air of desperation followed him into To-She.

Bakr and his other most trusted guards left with Djefi the morning Bakr had found him tied up in Yunet's hut. They left quickly, taking to boats and pushing hard against the growing current that came up the canal.

They left behind rumors of the debacle of the dedication. Neswy heard whispers of torture and of Siamun's re-enactment of the cutting out of Sobek's tongue. He knew better than to believe everything he heard, but he also knew that there usually was a kernel of truth in the tales.

He leaned against a palm tree at the edge of the village and looked down the pathway that Yunet and Diane had taken. He had been overjoyed to see Siamun head into the desert, but he knew that even the Two Lands were not vast enough to hide Yunet from Siamun forever.

If there was a whiff of truth to the rumors, then it was possible that Djefi was in disfavor with King Djoser. Neswy didn't know anyone associated with the royal family; the only two people he knew who had actually spoken with the king were Djefi and Yunet.

Still, Yunet was out there and Siamun was on her trail. Neswy hadn't gone with the women because he would have slowed them. But his staying at To-She would be no help. So he shouldered a small sack of food and followed after Yunet, headed for the great highway of the River Iteru.

In a few days he could smell the change in the air that followed the stronger flowing river, and his spirits had grown lighter. He had seen no signs of violence along the path and so he believed that Yunet and Diane had traveled this far without harm.

Ineb-Hedj lay several more days north along the river. There was a good chance the women would reach it safely. From there they could follow more frequently used trails that would lead them north to the delta and Iunu where Hetephernebti lived.

He sat on the riverbank to ease his aching leg, resting for a few minutes before trying to walk a little farther before daylight left.

He saw movement upriver. Two boats were heading south, their sails raised as the wind pushed them against the current. A third boat was near them, but its sails were down, so he knew that it was following the river, heading north.

Neswy watched the third boat grow larger as it approached. It began to veer cross current toward the canal opening.

Unsure exactly what he would say, Neswy stood and waved his arms at the boat.

There were two men rowing it, a third stood by the stern holding the tiller. He must have seen Neswy because the boat began to curve toward him. Neswy didn't recognize the man at the tiller. The rowers had their backs to him as they bent over the oars, but Neswy's heart leaped as he saw the broad shoulders of the one man. He smiled to himself. He would recognize those shoulders anywhere; he had clung to them for three days.

He waved his arms quicker and shouted the man's name, "Brian!"

"So they were going to Iunu to find Hetephernebti?" Imhotep asked.

"Yunet said they would ask her for sanctuary."

Imhotep shook his head. Hetephernebti was the king's sister and high priestess of Re, but she did not keep armed men at her temple. Her strength and influence came from her integrity and willpower. Would that be enough to protect Diane and Yunet from Djefi? Waja-Hur's reputation and holiness hadn't protected him.

If the women get that far, if they are able to elude Siamun, he thought.

Although he had never met Siamun, from what Brian had told him, Siamun was a brutal, murderous thug.

Neswy seemed confident that the women had gotten a good start on their escape from To-She because Siamun had gone into the desert while the women followed the water. But he was just as sure that as each day passed it was more likely that Siamun would turn his search to the river and eventually find them.

"Can you protect them if we find them first?" he asked.

Imhotep nodded. "The king has given me authority. I will place the women under my protection."

Neswy looked at Imhotep, Bata, and Brian. Bata carried a knife with a soldier's practiced ease, and he seemed confident. Neswy knew that Brian was strong and brave. But neither of them had seen Siamun since his return from Kom Ombo. He was no longer human. It would take more than these three to protect Yunet and Diane from Siamun.

"Are there others?" Neswy asked.

Imhotep understood what he was asking. Why did Imhotep think his authority would be any stronger than Hetephernebti's?

This land was so different. On the one hand, the king's word was law. On the other, if there was no fist, then the word was meaningless. He carried the king's word, its presence shown in the menat he wore around his neck. But he lacked the king's fist. Would Djefi and Siamun obey him knowing that the king's might was behind him, or would they kill him, feed his body to the crocodiles and deny that they had ever seen him?

He turned to Bata. "Who is governor of this nome?"

Bata shook his head. "Prince Teti only came through here once, to hunt in the delta. We didn't visit with anyone."

"I know a family there," Imhotep thought out loud.

"When we get to Ineb-Hedj, we'll go to the home of Paneb, the tomb artist. I know where he lives and he will know who we can find in the city to help us."

He turned to look downriver, eager to see the white walls of the city.

Djefi was shocked at how battered Diane was, but in his heart he wasn't surprised. When he had turned Siamun loose on the women, he had known there would be violence; he had suspected that Yunet would not survive.

Now he hoped Diane had enough spirit left to care about living.

But she refused to answer his questions, even as Siamun yanked her head back, gripping her dirty red hair in one fist and placing his knife against her white throat.

Instead, she stared back at him defiantly, her eyes aflame with hate.

Although she refused to answer his questions – and Djefi was beginning to wonder if she really didn't know how she got here – he wasn't ready to discard her.

If she didn't hold the secret to escaping Kemet, then perhaps she could be used to pry it from Imhotep. He put her in Bakr's care. "Keep her alive, but do not let her escape," he ordered him.

Bakr reached for Diane's arm to help her walk, but she twisted away from his touch, falling in the process. As she sat on the ground, Bakr removed the rope from her neck and tossed it aside. He leaned close to her and whispered, "Stay alive, Diane. I will try to help you."

If she heard him, she gave no sign. But she allowed him to help her to her feet. Bakr led her to a small shelter – four poles and a palm branch roof – that provided a little shade. He helped her sit and then ran for a water skin.

Djefi motioned for one of the guards to bring a stool and follow him into the tomb.

Just inside the tomb entrance, Djefi sat and peered down the dark passageway. The paintings on the walls were more complete than they had been the first time he visited the tomb. Then the walls had been covered only with gray sketches. He couldn't see the length of the hallway because the light faded, leaving the far end shrouded in darkness.

There is a great secret hidden here, he thought.

Somehow Brian, Diane, and Imhotep had emerged from this tomb. There had to be another doorway, an exit somewhere down the tunnel.

He was fairly certain that the three strangers were not gods. Diane had been beaten and was near death. During the time she had been with him he had seen no sign that she was anything other than a woman like any other. Until now. Threatened with death and after three days with Siamun, she still had the strength to ignore his threats.

Brian had been left to die in the desert, Djefi had assassins sent after him, he had his tongue cut out, and Siamun had tried to feed him to a crocodile. *His tongue cut out, like the god Sobek.* Djefi's skin began to crawl as he thought about Brian and Diane. After what they had been through, they still were not dead. They were still defiant.

Are they gods after all?

Djefi shook his head. This line of thought was taking him nowhere.

He peered down the dark hallway. Somehow it led to another land, a strange land far from Kemet, far from King Djoser. Did a false door open into this other world? Would a magic enchantment open it? Was there a secret lever to pull?

Paneb, the tomb artist! He had been here when the strangers arrived. He would know the inside of the tomb and its secrets better than anyone.

"Siamun!" he shouted. "Go into Ineb-Hedj and bring me the artist. His name is Paneb. And bring his helper. I don't know his name. He's a young boy. And Siamun," he added, "don't harm them. I want to give them a chance to help me first."

As they disembarked from their boat, Brian grabbed Imhotep's arm. "Effie's bow," he said, pointing to a decorated boat that bobbed in the water near them.

Neswy saw what they were looking at and gasped. "Djefi's boat," he said, not knowing that he was repeating what Brian had said.

Imhotep frowned. "He was banished to To-She. He is supposed to stay there until King Djoser visits him. That was clear."

He pulled Brian aside and spoke softly in English. "There is only one thing here that can interest Djefi – the tomb we all came through. That's where he's heading. If he's left To-She despite the king's command to stay there it's because he's planning to run away and there's no place in this land, in this time where he can hide from King Djoser. I don't know what Diane told him, but he must think that there's some way for him to get away.

"What does Diane know, what can she tell him?"

Imhotep didn't wait for Brian to answer. "I don't want Djefi to escape. No, that's not right. I mean I don't want him to find that secret panel and get into the tomb where we passed through. Because if he does find the passage, then people from our time might find their way here. Can you imagine what that would mean? Our time and world are messed up with greed and violence …" he paused when Brian scowled.

"Yes, it's violent here, too. But imagine Siamun with a machine gun or Djefi with an air force?"

"This," he opened his arms to indicate the world they were in, "is so innocent and clean. If people from our time find it, who knows? Do the Americans storm in here and set up democracy so that five thousand years from now they'll have a foothold in the Mideast? Do radical Muslims come in and somehow prevent the rise of Christianity? No matter what happened, it would pollute time."

Brian looked at him puzzled.

"Yeah, I've been thinking about this a lot. You know King Djoser has named me Imhotep. You know who he was? He built the Step Pyramid. There isn't anybody here named Imhotep. So, I must be him. And it feels right. I mean, I really think I am Imhotep. I belong here."

He stared down the river as he collected his thoughts.

"The point is if people could travel back and forth from our time to ancient Egypt, then evidence of it would have shown up. So, however we got here, and I have an idea about that, it just happened for the first time. I think we have to make sure it doesn't happen again.

"So we have to keep Djefi from getting to our time because once he's there the people in the modern world won't stop until they figure out how he got there from ancient Egypt."

He saw that Brian was staring at him in confusion.

"Yeah, I'm rambling and maybe all I really want is to keep this for myself. I mean, to lose myself here." He sighed. "I don't know. What do you think?"

"I whan kill iamun and effie. Anh hep Iane."

Imhotep turned to Bata.

"We'll go to Paneb's house and then see who we can get to help us, who will act in the king's name."

Paneb was trying to decide if there was enough light left in the day to go to the tomb.

Taki had been ill this morning.

Last night her brother had brought them the hindquarters of an ibex he had killed. They had roasted it and after their guests had gone, Taki had said that she didn't feel well.

She had gargled with a garlic mixture and gone to bed, but Paneb had heard her get up several times during the night.

"Should I get the doctor?" he had asked her in the early morning after she had returned from the courtyard where she had thrown up again.

"Not yet," she had answered weakly. "I think the meat was bad. It will pass."

"I don't know, beloved. I ate it and I am well."

"You would eat anything. Your belly never gets sick," she had moaned as she lay down. "You could do something," she had added softly. "I have an amulet. It is by the loom, I think. It is small and wrapped with a red string."

"I'll get it," he had said.

Now it was midafternoon. Taki seemed better and Paneb was restless. The painting was going well and he was eager to complete the hallway and begin work on the other rooms in the tomb.

Standing in the doorway of his home, he looked through the courtyard toward the dusty street where he saw a savage-looking man standing by the outer gate. He was hard muscled and dirty, the expression on his face was angry. When he turned to look into the courtyard, Paneb saw that the man's one ear was mangled.

The stranger stepped into the courtyard.

"Are you Paneb, the tomb artist?" he shouted.

Paneb nodded.

"Djefi, First Prophet of Sobek, commands you to come to Kanakht's tomb. Now."

Paneb saw movement out of the corner of his eye. Ahmes, who had been on the roof practicing his drawing, was coming down the outside stairs to see what the shouting was about.

"Is he your helper?" the man called.

Paneb nodded, puzzled why the coarse man had been sent to fetch him, rather than a court official.

"Bring him, too. Djefi said so."

"Who is it?" Taki asked.

"I don't know," Paneb answered quietly. Turning, he called out to the man, "Let me gather my tools and I'll be right there."

The man shook his head. "You don't need them. He said to just bring you and your helper."

Paneb knew this day would come.

When the gods first had arrived and Djefi had taken them, threatening to feed Ahmes to Sobek if Paneb revealed the existence of the new gods, Paneb had known Djefi would return. He had known the fat priest would want more, he was a man of boundless appetite.

Tim had stayed and worked with Paneb for a few days, asking questions about the artwork and the meanings behind the symbols. He had been a quick student, hampered only by his inability to speak Egyptian. But in a few days that had improved.

Although he tried to hide it, Tim had been especially interested in one of the false doors. Paneb hadn't revealed that he noticed Tim's interest, but after Paneb had returned from the Festival of Re in His Barge, he had studied the false door closely.

The invocation above the door panel was different. Paneb had shaken his head, trying to remember if the priest who drew them had said anything about them being different.

As he studied the hieroglyphs, the light entering the tomb from the brass reflecting disks shifted and a thin echo of light flashed away from something above the lintel. Reaching up, Paneb had pried away a tiny smooth stick that had been wedged in a crack between the stones. With a thrill, Paneb guessed that the gods had passed through this doorway and marked it with the smooth stick.

He had looked more closely at the false doorway's inscription. He was sure it looked different than in previous tombs he had painted. He would ask the priest when he returned. Until then he would leave these inscriptions unpainted.

Now Paneb stood before Djefi outside the tomb, trying to control his fear. Across the sandy clearing, Ahmes stood uncomfortably beside the man who had brought them to the tomb. The man's hand was resting on the back of Ahmes' neck. From the way his stepson was squirming, Paneb knew the man was gripping Ahmes' neck tightly.

"Paneb," Djefi said, "you remember the last time we spoke. The two strangers emerged from the tomb."

"Yes, First Prophet," he answered.

"Excellent. And then a third came out."

"Yes, First Prophet."

"They came from another land."

"Yes, First Prophet."

"Show me how they got here."

Paneb pointed to the tomb entrance. "Through there," he said. He spun around when he heard a sudden smacking sound and a yelp. Ahmes was holding the side of his face. The man beside him was smirking.

"I was here when they walked out of the tomb, Paneb," Djefi said, his squeaky voice rising as he became impatient. "I want to know how they got into the tomb." He snapped his fingers in front of Paneb's face to draw his attention away from Ahmes and Siamun.

"Don't hurt him," Paneb pleaded. "He hasn't done anything."

Djefi nodded at Siamun who hit Ahmes again, harder this time.

"You don't understand, do you? I ask the questions. I give the orders," Djefi told Paneb.

Paneb was not used to being treated this way. He was chief artist of the necropolis, and he had never treated the men who worked for him with such arrogance and disrespect.

"I will answer your questions," he told Djefi. "But please, First Prophet, do not hurt my son."

"Then answer better. How did they arrive here in the Two Lands?"

Paneb turned to the tomb entrance. "I will show you what I know," he said. He glanced over his shoulder at Ahmes as he entered the tomb.

Together Paneb and Djefi walked down the hallway, the light failing as they went farther. Paneb stopped in front of the false door. "I believe they came through here," he said, pointing to a false door in the tomb wall.

"How?" Djefi asked.

Paneb shook his head. "I do not know, First Prophet."

Djefi studied Paneb. There was something the man wasn't saying. He was sure. "You know something," he said. He turned and walked toward the tomb entrance.

"Wait!" Paneb shouted.

Djefi turned and waddled back to him, coming so close, the artist could smell the stink of the priest's own fear.

"Do not waste my time, Paneb. If you hold your son's life dear, you will not waste my time."

Paneb gulped and nodded. "I am sorry, First Prophet. I truly do not know how they came through this tomb," he said, and then added quickly as Djefi's eyes grew small, "but I will tell you everything I know and perhaps you can understand what I do not.

"When the last god came through ..."

"They are not gods!" Djefi interrupted.

"Yes, First Prophet. When the last one came through, he stayed with me a few days. He also is an artist. I showed him the drawings and the plans for the tomb. He had a book with a very smooth papyrus that he used to make his drawings. They were wonderful, so life-like that they seemed to float over the pages. There was one ..."

He stopped as Djefi snapped his fingers in front of his face. "I don't care about his drawings," he said. "Tell me about this door."

"Yes, First Prophet. Understand that I am chief artist, not a priest. I am responsible for the paintings, the sky, and the representations of the gods. Sobek, for example. A priest trained at the temple of Thoth, by, oh, I can't remember his name, the very old priest."

Djefi felt a chill, as if Waja-Hur's ka had entered the tomb with them. He snapped his fingers at the artist again. "The door, the door," he said.

"Yes, First Prophet," Paneb said nervously. He was trying to tell the priest everything he knew, to show that he was cooperating, that there was no reason to hurt Ahmes.

"The paintings on the false door show Hathor welcoming Kanakht into Khert-Neter. I drew those," he said, pointing to the paintings that were barely visible this deep in the dark tomb. "The old priest drew the hieroglyphs on the lintel above it." He pointed to the symbols. "I was to paint them black, following his outlines. I thought that they were somehow incorrect so did not paint them immediately. They were not yet painted when the three gods, I mean three strangers, came through. If they indeed came through here."

Djefi was so exasperated his voice came out as a tiny squeak. "That is all you can tell me? They were not painted? That gives me no help!"

Paneb almost touched the fat priest, trying to stop him from turning. Djefi looked at the man's outstretched hand in distaste. Paneb quickly withdrew it and bowed his head. "No, First Prophet. What I mean to tell you is that they have been changed.

"I have painted other tombs and I have never seen the inscription drawn the way it was here. I pointed it out to the old priest when he came to check on the progress, before I painted them, of course. He shook his head and said he didn't know how those symbols came to be on the wall. Even though he had drawn them himself! I swear. He rubbed them out and drew in the proper symbols – the ones that are on the wall now."

Djefi studied the symbols closely. He had never learned to read them, that was the job of scribes.

There is a secret here, he thought. Some powerful incantation, some magic that made this false door real and allowed it to open to a different world.

He needed to get to that world, to escape this one where the king was bound to kill him.

"What did the other inscription say?" Djefi asked.

"I do not know, First Prophet. I only paint over the lines the priest draws. I noticed that they looked different and were in a different order, but I didn't know their meaning."

Djefi wanted to pound his fists against the wall. He was so close. His escape was just on the other side of this stone wall. He knew it. Only a few inches of stone stood between his certain death and freedom.

He had to get through it.

"Do you remember what the symbols looked like? Can you paint them over these?"

Paneb nodded. "I can try. I have sketches of all the symbols at my home. I keep them so I can compare them to what is drawn on the tombs. Sometimes the priests get sloppy in the drawing, a hand turned so instead of this way. A head at the wrong tilt. These are little things, but they are important. They are the symbols of eternal life and they ..." He stopped as Djefi snapped his fingers at his face again.

"Siamun will take you back to your home. Get the drawings and return here. You will re-create the inscriptions for me."

"Ahmes?"

"He will stay here, Paneb. It will help you to focus on your work if you know Ahmes is under my protection."

AT THE TOMB OF KANAKHT

Imhotep ran through the small courtyard to Taki, who looked pale and worried. "Is something wrong?" he asked.

He felt a wave of relief as she shook her head. "No, Lord Tim," she said, addressing him as she had so many months ago when he was a guest in her home.

Imhotep embraced her and then held her at arm's length. "You look troubled," he said. "Are the girls healthy? Has little Hapu been playing with scorpions again?" he asked with a smile.

As she shook her head, Imhotep saw her eyes stray past him to look at Brian and Bata.

"I'm sorry," he said. "These are my friends. Brian is one of my countrymen and Bata is a friend I've made here."

Taki hugged each of them and then offered them food.

"No, Taki, not now, thank you. I've brought Brian here to show him the tomb where I met your husband. Is Paneb here?" Imhotep asked.

"He is out at the site. He and Ahmes. A man came by unexpectedly and told him First Prophet Djefi was there and needed to see him." She looked out at the courtyard gate as she spoke and missed Imhotep's frown.

"He was rude," she said, a frown forcing its way onto her usually happy face. "He stood at the gate over there and just shouted for Paneb to come with him. What has happened to manners? And he looked so rough."

"Rough?" Imhotep said.

She squinted as she remembered. "He was dirty, but perhaps it was only because he was working. But there was something about his face."

"His ear?" Imhotep prompted.

"Iamun," Brian said, moving closer to them.

Imhotep nodded. "Did the man say his name?" he asked Taki. "Did he call himself Siamun?"

"Siamun?" Taki repeated, shaking her head. "I … I don't remember hearing his name. Who is Siamun?"

"I haven't met him, but I know who he is," Imhotep said, trying to keep the concern from his voice. He didn't want to worry Taki. "When did they leave?" he asked.

"It was just after noon. I was ill last night and Paneb stayed with me this morning. He was eager to go to the tomb, but he stayed until he was sure I was feeling better. Then this man came by, so they left."

Imhotep looked at the sky. The sun was midway to the western horizon; there were no more than four hours of daylight left.

"Brian," he said, "what do you think? We can be there in less than an hour. If Siamun is there, it's possible he caught up with Diane and Yunet and they will be there, too." He left unspoken his fears that Siamun could have found them and killed them.

"We ood oh," he said, nodding his head toward the street.

Bata shook his head. "We should get help. If Djefi is here, then he has decided to live outside the law. Your word as vizier will carry no weight."

"Lord Tim, what has happened?" Taki asked, picking up on the concern in their voices. "Who are Diane and Yunet and this Siamun? Are Paneb and Ahmes in danger?"

Imhotep shook his head. "I don't think so," he told her. "Siamun is trying to find Diane, she came here with Brian. Did Siamun say anything about a woman?"

Taki started to answer and then pointed toward the gate that opened between the head-high walls that surrounded the courtyard. "We can ask him," she said. "There they are now."

They turned to look toward the gate. Brian recognized Paneb as the man who had been with his son outside the tomb so long ago. He also recognized the man who was standing just behind him.

"Iamun!" he shouted and began to run across the courtyard.

Siamun was shocked to see Brian, alive and looking leaner and stronger than before. He had a brief thought of staying and finally killing him, but then he saw Bata draw his knife and join the chase with Brian.

Turning, Siamun ran back down the street as Brian reached the gate.

Paneb grabbed at Brian as he pushed past him, trying to stop him. "No, stop, they have Ahmes," he said.

Brian jerked away from him, his mind filled only with catching Siamun. When he looked back up the street, he saw Siamun turn onto a side path. He rushed after him. Bata pushed through the gate a second later and raced after Brian.

Worried that Ahmes would be in danger if Siamun were hurt, Paneb turned to join in the chase. Before he could begin to run, he felt a hand grip his arm.

"Paneb," Imhotep said. "You will just endanger yourself if you chase them. Tell me what Djefi is doing at the tomb."

Paneb looked at Imhotep. He had changed so much from the young man who had emerged from the tomb, uncertain where he was, drowning in an unnamed sorrow, dressed in strange clothes and unable to speak the language of the Two Lands.

Now he spoke with confidence and authority, he was wearing a beautiful linen kilt, its hem embroidered with the spread wings of a vulture, divine protector of the king. A wide beaded strand wrapped around his neck. With wonder, Paneb recognized it as a menat.

Imhotep saw the confusion in his friend's eyes.

"We have a lot to talk about, Paneb." He touched his fingers to the beaded strands of the menat. "Life has been very good to me here," he said with a smile. Then he looked past Paneb to watch Bata turn down the alley where Siamun and Brian had run. He knew that he couldn't catch them and that he wouldn't be able to stop Brian from trying to kill Siamun even if he did reach them in time. After what Brian had suffered at Siamun's hands, he wasn't sure he would try to stop him.

He looked back at Paneb and gave him a tight smile.

"You said something about Ahmes?"

After hearing what had happened at the tomb, Imhotep said, "I speak with King Djoser's authority, Paneb. Take me to the governor's home and I will ask him for help. Then we can go to the tomb. Don't worry," he said, resting a hand on Paneb's arm. "Ahmes will be safe."

Paneb nodded agreement, although he knew he wouldn't relax until they had secured help from the governor. He hugged Taki good-bye and led Imhotep through the town toward the governor's home, which overlooked the river.

They walked quickly, not noticing the man who was watching them from the shadows of the alley beside Paneb's house. As they crossed the dirt street, Siamun, who had doubled back after eluding Brian and Bata, stepped out of the shadows. He jogged into a parallel alleyway and ran to get ahead of them.

Brian stood at the edge of the village, staring down the path that led into the desert. He heard Bata's heavy breathing as the guard joined him.

He knew it was useless to try to talk to Bata. No one but Imhotep understood his slurred English. He waited until Bata caught his breath, then he pointed into the desert and shrugged.

"He was going this way, I know," Bata said. He scanned the area around them. The village's intrusion into the desert ended here with a few huts tucked under a scattering of scrubby trees. There were no towering palm trees and no tethered animals or pens of geese.

396

"We've lost him. He must be hiding someplace back in the village, waiting for us to leave," Bata said.

Brian shook his head. He knelt in the sand and made a furrow, then walked his fingers through it.

"Yes, of course," Bata said. "The desert here isn't flat. If the path ahead leads into a wadi, then Siamun could be there out of sight." He looked at Brian. "We should wait for Imhotep. Then we can go to the governor and get more help."

Worried about the danger Diane could be facing, Brian shook his head. He patted his chest and pointed into the desert, his face set with determination. He touched Bata's chest and pointed back to town.

Bata had been ordered to guard Imhotep, not Brian. He looked at the giant man and nodded.

"I will look for Imhotep and find help from the governor, as we had planned. You should come with me, but I know you won't." He squeezed Brian's tight bicep. "Be careful in the desert."

Brian nodded, but he was thinking that it was Siamun who would need to be careful.

Bata hadn't jogged far when he heard Imhotep's voice.

He stopped and ducked between two buildings as he realized that Imhotep should not be coming this way, toward the desert. Imhotep had planned to ask Paneb to take him to the governor and seek help. It was impossible for him to have gone to the governor's small palace by the river and returned this far already.

Then Bata heard a strange man's voice say "Shut up."

"You should listen to me, Siamun," Imhotep said. "The king knows Djefi was part of the plot, he's just letting him live to draw out the other conspirators. If you go with me to the governor, then I can ..."

"I said, 'Shut up!' " Siamun growled. He slapped the back of Imhotep's head.

Imhotep kept his composure. "You don't know what you're doing, Siamun. I can help you. Turn around, take us to the governor."

There was another slap.

They walked past Bata's hiding place. He saw that Siamun had tied ropes around Imhotep's and Paneb's necks and was walking close behind them, holding the ropes in one hand. His other hand held a knife pressed against Imhotep's back.

Bata knew that if he tried to surprise him, Siamun would simply pull on the ropes and as Imhotep fell back to relieve the pressure, Siamun could stab him. There would be no way for Bata to stop it. Even if he were able to throw his knife, it wouldn't guarantee Imhotep's safety.

He waited until they walked past him, then he took to the street and ran as fast as he could toward the river where he would find the governor and ask for help.

Prince Teti stepped on shore and stretched. He turned and watched as the other two boats came to a stop and the king's guards disembarked, the men swinging their arms and twisting their aching backs.

After learning about Waja-Hur's murder at Khmunu, Prince Teti had continued downriver, putting in at each town to see if King Djoser had sent any change of orders. When there had been no word at Tehna, the men had bent harder at the oars, pulling with the current, racing each other as they flew down the river. There was no word at Medum nor at Tarchan, so they had pulled even harder, racing for Ineb-Hedj, where the king surely would have sent a message.

While there had been no news from the king, neither had there been word of Imhotep.

Because Hetephernebti and Tama said Imhotep was heading for To-She to find Diane, Prince Teti had debated making a side trip there to make sure Imhotep was safe. But his father's orders were to go to Ineb-Hedj, so Prince Teti's three-boat fleet had sailed past the canal without pause.

Now they had reached Ineb-Hedj, capital of Men-Nefer, gateway to the delta.

When they had left Khmunu they were three days behind Imhotep. Prince Teti looked over at his men, sore and tired, but young and strong. They had rowed without break, churning the river's water so hard the boat seemed to skim above it. Prince Teti wouldn't have been surprised if they had passed Imhotep on the river.

Looking at the other boats in the harbor, he spotting one decorated with a golden disk, the emblem of Re. It looked like the boat Hetephernebti had given Imhotep, which meant that Imhotep had come here instead of going to To-She.

Prince Teti smiled; it would be good to see the strange physician who had captured his father's trust. He was so open, yet so mysterious.

The men had finished stretching and kicking their legs and were gathering their weapons from the boats, when Prince Teti saw a familiar figure running along the waterfront.

"That's Bata," he heard Meryptah say.

"Go catch him," Prince Teti told him. "Find out where Imhotep is."

As Meryptah ran off, Prince Teti turned to his men. "Follow Meryptah. I want to find out where Imhotep is and then go see the governor."

"Is there a tavern along the way?" one of the men said.

"Forget a tavern," another answered. "I want a woman."

"You want a bath."

Prince Teti listened to their banter, wishing he could join in. This was his first real command and he felt more distant from these men than from his personal bodyguard. These were older, more seasoned men. He knew that if he began to joke with them, their view of him would begin to change and he would become one of them and not their leader.

And so he listened and tried not to smile.

Pleasant memories tugged at his mind as Imhotep walked through the familiar wadi toward Saqqara. He had traveled this pathway every day with Paneb and Ahmes, when he was first learning about their world.

He was a different person now, walking in a land that he felt was his, although now there was a noose around his neck and a knife at his back.

They passed through the narrow throat of the wadi and emerged into the clearing by the tomb entrance.

Four of Djefi's guards were standing to one side, near the palm branch canopy where Paneb and Ahmes had eaten their lunches. Imhotep saw that the men were gathered around someone who was sitting in the sand. Drawing closer he caught a glimpse of dirty, red hair, and realized that it was Diane.

As he turned to start toward her, Siamun yanked on the rope around his neck and nodded toward the tomb entrance. Djefi was sitting just inside the tomb.

"First Prophet," Imhotep called. "King Djoser banished you to To-She, not Saqqara."

Siamun yanked on the rope again, almost pulling Imhotep off his feet.

"You forget where you are, Tim," Djefi called from the shadows. "Look around you. Do you see King Djoser? No. Do you see your precious Hetephernebti? No. Are you in a position to give orders? No, I don't think so.

"I am First Prophet of the god Sobek, not some peasant who will take orders from you, or from the king, for that matter."

He looked at Paneb. "Where are the drawings?"

"We chased Siamun away from Paneb's house before he could get them," Imhotep said. "Now, we should just turn around and go to the governor's house. If you surrender …" Siamun yanked on the rope again, choking Imhotep before he could finish speaking.

"Bring him over here," Djefi shouted at Siamun.

"Paneb said you were very interested in one of the false doors in the tomb," Djefi said to Imhotep. "He said you are an artist."

Imhotep waited, feeling the rope tight around his neck.

Djefi stood and held out his hand. "Give me the rope," he said to Siamun. "Show me the door you came through," he ordered Imhotep. "And tell me how to open it."

He yanked on the rope and Imhotep stumbled after him into the tomb.

With the sun moving lower on the horizon it was nearly too dark to see inside the tomb.

"A minute, Djefi," Imhotep said. "We need Paneb to shine light in here."

He turned back to the entrance, feeling Djefi move to his side. The tension on the rope around his neck decreased as the priest came close.

He knew that if he turned quickly and grabbed at the rope he could free himself. Looking out into the clearing he saw the four soldiers guarding Paneb, Ahmes and Diane. Siamun was pacing by them.

His shoulders sagged as Imhotep realized that even if he was able to pull from Djefi there was no way he could rescue the others. "Paneb," he called. "Can you and Ahmes set up the reflectors?"

After Djefi nodded approval to them, Paneb and Ahmes went to the sand bank and each picked up one of the large polished brass disks that they used to bounce sunlight into the tomb. Paneb handled his easily, but Ahmes still struggled to lift the two-foot wide circle of metal. The reflecting surface was slightly concave to focus the light. The edges of the disks had grown thin and sharp from repeated polishing.

Father and son glanced at the sun and then Paneb pointed to a spot near the northern wall of the wadi. After Ahmes was positioned there, Paneb walked to the tomb entrance and quickly arranged his disk to angle the light from Ahme's disk into the tomb hallway.

As Imhotep turned to go back into the tomb he saw someone move along the top of the wadi. By the size of the person, he thought it was Brian, but he had caught only a glimpse.

Siamun hadn't bragged about killing Brian and Bata, so Imhotep hoped that they were out there somewhere.

Imhotep gasped with surprise when he saw the interior of the tomb.

The walls were fully painted now, the colors vibrant and alive even in the dim light. Along one side of the wall a procession of servants brought food to Kanakht, who was seated in a banquet chair. Three of them were butchering a spotted ox that was lying on its back, while a fourth carried one of its severed forelegs. Others carried woven baskets filled with fruit and grain. Platters of fish and jars of beer and wine were carried toward Kanakht. Still other servants led small deer, captured in the desert.

On the left wall were scenes of Kanakht enjoying himself hunting. In one he was standing on a small reed boat, a throwing stick raised as the boat nudged into a stand of reeds from which geese were flying.

Imhotep wondered how Paneb had drawn Kanakht so accurately. He knew the vizier had been busy traveling in the months before his death at Kom Ombo. He hadn't come to visit the tomb to pose, yet the images Paneb had drawn definitely were of Kanakht, a much younger Kanakht, full of life and energy. Imhotep thought that Paneb had done a wonderful job of capturing Kanakht's features in the flat style of the time and making the vizier look young.

A tug on the rope around his neck brought Imhotep up short. In his amazement at Paneb's work he had forgotten about Djefi.

"Yes, it's all very nice," Djefi said. "But Kanakht won't be enjoying it, will he? Now, show me the doorway to your land."

He pulled on the short rope, leading Imhotep down the hallway.

Imhotep had no idea what he could do. If he opened the panel and let Djefi through and returned to the clearing without him, there would be no one to stop Siamun and his men from killing all of them. If he refused to help him, then Djefi would have them all killed.

When the panel opened – if it opened – he might be able to squeeze through it ahead of Djefi, race through the tomb to the spiral stairs and call for help. Then he pictured the sleepy, unarmed guards at the tomb and he knew they would be no match for Siamun's ruthlessness.

"I was here when Diane and Brian came out of the tomb. I saw them with my own eyes. I know there is a pathway from here to your land," Djefi was saying as they walked.

"Diane does not know where it is or what secrets you use to open it. Paneb believes there was a enchantment contained in the hieroglyphs. You came through here alone, unlike Diane. So I know that you understand."

"I will try," Imhotep answered.

Djefi followed, watching him closely, holding the rope in his hand. He didn't think Imhotep would try to attack him; he had a reputation as a healer, not a fighter. Still, Djefi had seen Imhotep stop a man simply by raising his hand, and so Djefi gripped his knife, ready to protect himself if Imhotep turned on him.

Imhotep remembered turning to his right after he came through the panel, but was that after he had turned and pushed the panel shut? He couldn't remember.

But he did remember marking the entrance with the toothpick from his Swiss Army knife. He wished he had the knife with him now, but it was in his backpack, which he had left behind at Khmunu when he had left there in a rush. His small spray bottle of pepper spray was there, too.

When it felt like he had walked far enough into the tomb, he turned back to see how distant the entrance was. Looking back at the wall, he reached above the lintel, feeling for the toothpick.

There was nothing there.

He stepped back and studied the drawings, but he couldn't remember what had been sketched there before. The hieroglyphs at the top looked almost the same as he remembered, but not quite.

He checked the next panel, and then the one beside that. Still no toothpick. He realized he had begun to sweat. He turned to the other wall and felt along the top of the panel of the false door there and then another panel and another.

Djefi started to say something, but suddenly the light disappeared, leaving them in darkness, and they heard Diane scream.

Brian had watched Siamun marching Imhotep and Paneb through the wadi, but he knew that Imhotep would be hurt or killed if he attacked then. Careful to keep himself out of sight, he had crawled along the top of the sandbank that rose from the clearing at the tomb's entrance.

Peering over the crest of the sand now, he saw Diane's battered face, the scratches on her arms and the rope burns on her neck. He felt adrenaline surge through him, but he tamped it down, waiting for the right moment.

There were four guards. He recognized one of them as Bakr. Brian thought that if Bakr stopped the other guards from attacking him, then he would have a chance against Siamun.

A chance was all he wanted.

He lay back away from the edge and listened and waited. Suddenly hearing Djefi's squeaky voice, Brian jerked his head up to peek over the ridge; he hadn't noticed Djefi in the shadows of the tomb.

Are there other guards with Djefi?

Rolling back to the edge he looked down and watched Imhotep enter the tomb. Siamun pushed Paneb toward the small shelter, where Diane and a boy were being guarded. Then he walked to the edge of the wadi across from Brian and turned his back to piss.

Now!

Brian vaulted over the edge and landed soundlessly on the soft sand. Ahmes saw him and gasped. The guard nearest to Ahmes looked up and saw Brian as he recovered his balance and began to run across the sand.

Shouting a warning to Siamun, the guard threw his short spear at Brian.

Brian saw the throw and stutter-stepped to avoid the spear, but the hesitation gave Siamun time to turn. He saw Brian charging toward him, his movement off balance from dodging the spear.

In one practiced motion, Siamun ducked and pulled his knife.

Twisting his body, Brian dropped to his side and slid toward Siamun as if going into second base.

Siamun rose from his crouch, preparing to jump over Brian, but Brian dug his lead heel in. He let his momentum bring him to his feet and suddenly he was face to face with Siamun.

Quickly Brian twisted his right shoulder forward and slammed an elbow at Siamun's head. He felt it connect with a satisfying jolt and Siamun fell back against the wall of sand. Brian danced backward, took a quick glance at the other guards and then turned back to see that Siamun was still conscious and had held on to his knife.

The Egyptian pushed himself away from the wall, shaking his head to clear it. Blood trickled from his mouth.

Siamun and Brian began to circle each other warily. Out of the corner of his eye, Brian saw two of the guards move away from the palm shelter to get behind him. He heard Diane plead with Bakr to help Brian.

"If you help him, you will die next," Siamun said to Bakr without looking over at him.

Siamun made occasional feints with his knife as he and Brian continued to circle each other.

Brian knew he couldn't continue this; sooner or later the other guards would intervene. He felt them closing behind him, waiting for Siamun to signal them to charge.

As Brian twitched his head to find the other guards Siamun took a step toward him, tossing the knife to his other hand as he lunged and swiping with it as Brian dodged. Brian heard Diane shout a warning as the two guards charged from behind. Brian twisted away from them, but he lost his balance as his feet tangled with the shaft of a spear one of them had poked at him. He fell and Siamun leaped on him, driving a knee into Brian's stomach.

Brian felt Siamun's rough hand grab his throat and the tip of his knife press against his stomach. He tried to roll away, but Siamun's grip tightened on his throat and he felt the knife begin to cut into his skin.

Looking to his left, Brian saw that one of the guards who had been circling behind him had gone to stand beside Paneb, the other was standing by Ahmes who was only a few feet away, his eyes wide with fear. Across the clearing he saw Bakr and another guard watching over Diane who had pushed herself up into a crouch.

Diane felt a hand push down on her shoulder as she raised herself to her feet. Looking, she saw the strange guard restraining her. Then Bakr reached over and pulled the man's arm away.

He nodded to Diane.

Paneb's stone mallet was resting in the sand by Diane's feet. She grabbed its handle and charged across the sand, dragging the heavy hammer with both hands.

Focused on Brian, Siamun laughed.

"I tried to kill you twice before. This time, I will cut your body into pieces as Seth did to Osiris. But there will be no gathering of your parts. This will be a final death."

Brian saw Diane moving out of the corner of his eye, but he kept his face turned toward Siamun so Siamun wouldn't look toward Diane. He felt the tip of the knife pushing into his stomach.

"Go oo hell!" he shouted at Siamun and then he arched his back, pushing his stomach toward the blade, drawing it into his own stomach to lock it there.

With a desperate effort Brian brought his hand up to hit the inside of Siamun's arm that held his throat. He whipped his head forward hard at the same time. His forehead slammed against Siamun's nose and Brian heard a satisfying crunch. Siamun's blood began to gush from his broken nose and fall on Brian's chest.

Through the sharp, surprising pain, Siamun heard Diane scream as she swung the hammer with a two-handed tennis backhand.

As Siamun turned his bloody face toward the scream, Diane swung the hammer forward, turning her shoulders and keeping her eyes on his face. Siamun tried to roll away, but Brian held the Egyptian's arms in a death grip.

Siamun's eyes grew large with fear as the stone hammer drove through the air in front of him. Bones cracked as the hammer smashed into Siamun's face, driving his broken nose deep into his skull and splattering teeth down his throat and across the clearing.

His lifeless body jerked away from the blow and fell from Brian, landing heavily in the sand.

The two men who had been guarding Ahmes and Paneb rushed toward Diane, but Bakr shouted at them to stop. Looking at him, they saw him point to the rim of the sand bank where Prince Teti and his soldiers were gathering in formation.

The rope slipped from Djefi's hand as Imhotep ran to the tomb entrance. He stopped there in shock at what he saw in the clearing.

Siamun's body, his face crushed into his skull, lay on the sand in a seeping puddle of blood. Brian was lying nearby, a pool of blood gathering under his belly where the hilt of Siamun's knife wobbled in the air. Diane knelt beside him weeping. Two of the guards stood near her, the others stood with Ahmes under the canopy. No one was speaking.

Sensing other people, Imhotep looked up at the rim of the clearing to see Prince Teti and his men. He was about to shout to them when he felt a knife prick against his side and the rope drew tight around his neck.

"Tell Prince Teti that you and I must return to the tomb," Djefi said to Imhotep, pressing the knife against him.

"He doesn't have to speak, Djefi. I have young ears. I can hear you. Release him now," Prince Teti called.

"So you can kill me?" Djefi squeaked. He turned Imhotep toward Prince Teti, using him as a shield. With his back turned, Djefi didn't see Brian begin to drag himself across the sand, his eyes full of pain, but focused on the sharp-edged reflecting disk that Ahmes had dropped.

The men who were at the tomb that day would boast about what they had witnessed, telling the story in the hushed voice one uses when talking about the gods.

They would say that they saw the god Ipy, magical protector of the Two Lands, slain and lifeless, a knife stuck in his gut. Yet he brought himself back to life. Moving slowly as a shadow, the god crawled behind the evil priest Djefi and with a sweep of his mighty arm, hurled the sun at the priest. The sun sliced into the priest's fat back and then flew away, returning to the sky.

And as the evil priest fell to the sand, unable to control his now lifeless legs, the god Ipy uttered a long, howling roar and collapsed, his great ka leaving his lifeless body for the green fields of Khert-Neter.

Imhotep felt a sudden yank on the rope around his neck. He fell backward and landed on Djefi who was surprised to find himself abruptly lying on his side in the sand. Twisting away from the fat priest, Imhotep saw a brass reflecting disk roll through the sand leaving a trail of blood.

He looked at Djefi and saw a red gash across the priest's back where the sharp edge of the disk had cut into him, severing his spinal cord.

"I can't feel my legs. How can that be?" Djefi asked himself.

Ignoring him, Imhotep rushed over to Brian who had fallen face forward in the sand after throwing the reflecting disk.

"Jush ike a fribbee," Brian whispered.

Diane crawled over to him. "Brian," she said, caressing his face softly.

"Bye, babe," he said softly.

"No," she cried. "This isn't fair!" She pressed her face against his and held him close as he exhaled a long, slow breath.

"Do something," she said to Imhotep.

He laid his hand on Brian's neck. There was no pulse.

"I'm sorry, Diane," he said.

Bakr came across the clearing and knelt beside her. "He truly was a god," he said reverently.

Diane wanted to kill Djefi herself, but Imhotep intervened.

"Don't do this, Diane," he said to her in English. "Djefi can't harm anyone now."

She stood over the fat priest, then she spit on him and turned away.

Prince Teti and his men scrambled down the loose bank of the wadi to join them.

"What do you want us to do with him?" Prince Teti asked Imhotep.

Imhotep shook his head. "That is up to you, Prince Teti. I want nothing of him."

Prince Teti turned to the two guards who had helped Siamun. "Take Djefi and Siamun's body into the desert. Two days' journey. Once you are there, tie Siamun's body to Djefi's back. Leave him there to crawl home."

"I am First Prophet of Sobek," Djefi said. "You cannot treat me like a common criminal."

Prince Teti smiled.

"You are right, First Prophet." He looked at the guards. "Leave a water bag with him."

As the men dragged a screaming Djefi away, Prince Teti said to Diane, "We will give Brian this tomb."

She looked at him uncomprehendingly.

"He means Brian will be buried here, in this tomb, Diane," Imhotep explained in English. "It is a great honor."

She stared at him. "Then how do I get back? I want to leave this place. Forever."

Imhotep shook his head.

"I don't know, Diane. I thought I found the panel we came through, but it looks different now. I had marked it with a toothpick, but the toothpick is gone, so I don't know for sure which false door we used. You might not be able to return."

INTO THE TOMB OF IPY

After Prince Teti ordered Brian's body carried to the mortuary temple to be embalmed, he went with Imhotep to Paneb's home.

"I am sorry your friend was killed," Prince Teti told Diane as they walked through the town's dark streets. "Although I did not know him, I heard that he was a brave man."

She nodded an acknowledgment, but stared off silently into the distance. Walking beside her, Imhotep saw the effort she was going through not to cry. She had already told them how she and Yunet had been captured by Siamun and what had happened afterward.

He thought of all she had lost and the pain she had suffered. He thought of the love he had found with Meryt and the child she was carrying, the honors he had received from King Djoser and the certainty he felt that this was where, and when, he belonged.

The passage through the tomb had brought him home.

It had led her to hell.

When they reached Paneb's house, Imhotep took Diane aside to talk with her while Paneb and Ahmes were reunited with Taki.

The air around them soon filled with the smell of roasting goose as Taki, her mother and sister began to prepare a meal. Prince Teti, seeing Taki's intent to feed him and his company, sent three of his men to find a bakery and brewery. Another was dispatched to the governor's house with a message to be sent to King Djoser.

Noticing Imhotep trying to find a private place to talk, Paneb took him to the stairs that led to the roof. As Imhotep and Diane climbed them, he recalled his first nights in this ancient land, how the air had smelled fresh and clean, how the sand had seemed whiter and newer.

Despite the deaths at the tomb, he still was willing to trade the random violence, poverty and material greed of his time for the rigors and hardships of life here.

He knew Diane wouldn't feel the same way.

She had seen only the brutal side of the Two Lands. While what she had experienced was horrifying, Imhotep thought it was individual violence, an aberration from normal behavior. The violence and uncaring from his time had become an epidemic.

None of this would matter if they couldn't figure out how to return her to her time.

He led her to a low stool along the edge of the roof beneath the dark fronds of a palm tree, a spot he had sat at so long ago to avoid the sun.

"You don't know how to get back," she said, making it a statement, not a question.

"Not exactly. Well, no," he conceded.

Her arms were crossed in front of her bare chest, a sense of modesty returning as they spoke in English.

"Wait here," he said. He walked across the roof and jogged down the steps. "Dedi," he called when he saw Paneb's oldest daughter in the courtyard pouring beer for the soldiers. "Could you give me a robe for my friend?"

Dedi gave him a questioning look, but went into the house and returned with a linen robe.

Imhotep gave it to Diane and then turned his back as she put it on.

"I don't want to stay here," she said quietly.

"I know," he nodded. "If I were you I wouldn't either. I'm so sorry about everything. These people," he gestured toward the courtyard, "they are the most giving, helpful, gentle people. But," he hurried on, "there is a raw violence here, and a different view of death. I know that. I'm not saying this is paradise.

"I think it's because they don't live as long as we do and they don't get as attached to things, cars, books, whatever. They don't want to die and I'm sure they are afraid of it, but they see it every day. They don't have hospitals, so they care for their ill as best they can at home and then that's where they die.

"It might be better, I mean, it's natural. Everyone dies. We shouldn't fear it. Animals don't." He knew he was rambling. He stopped when he saw the expression on her face.

"I know. You don't want to stay here. I'm not trying to talk you into it. I'm just sorry that you ran into Djefi and Siamun instead of Hetephernebti and Tama and Meryt."

She drew a deep breath and shuddered.

"I just want to go home," she repeated, her voice dissolving into sobs.

Kneeling by her, Imhotep said, "I'm not sure how, Diane. Tell me about you and Brian, how did you get through?"

She looked off into the distance, remembering. "We went into that tomb with that guide. I don't even remember his name."

Imhotep nodded. "I saw you. I was sitting near the Step Pyramid sketching." He shook his head. "I told this to Brian. I forgot that I haven't talked to you. Well, at least that you remember."

She looked at him in confusion.

"I saw you at the festival in Iunu a week or so after I arrived here. Everyone was drinking and that night I came across the canal to where you were, but you were pretty wasted.

"Anyhow," he continued, "I saw you and Brian go down into the tomb with the guide, then the guide came up by himself all confused. That got me curious. I ended up sneaking into your room at the Mena House and then looking for you in the tomb. I was scared that the guide had mugged you or something and left you down there."

She sighed. "That was forever ago."

"Yeah," he agreed. "When I got into the tomb, I found this tunnel. I had to crawl through a broken wall to get to it. Then I saw handprints on the wall. I pushed where they were and the wall swung away."

She nodded. "That's what happened with us. Brian was just playing around. We sneaked through that opening to hide from the guide. Brian was always playing tricks like that. Then our flashlight died. He was feeling along the back wall to try and find an exit. The wall just opened up."

"When you got through, did you look at the wall, see what was marked on it?" Imhotep asked.

She shook her head.

"No, we just followed the light and ended up out in the desert. We had no idea anything weird had happened."

Imhotep remembered his own sensations when he had emerged from the tomb and the hawk had flown overhead, cawing loudly.

"How did it happen?" she asked.

"The ancient Egyptians," he nodded toward the courtyard, "spend a lot of time thinking about and planning for the next life.

"Did you ever hear of the Book of the Dead? Well, it's not a bunch of scary hexes or curses; it's more like a manual for priests. It has magical spells they're supposed to say to help the dead pass into the next life, the Field of Reeds. Some of those spells, they're more like prayers really, would be written on the tomb walls. That way the dead person didn't have to memorize them. Some of the spells are really praises to different gods and or prayers asking for their help. The Book of the Dead also has the words a priest is supposed to say at different times during the burial ceremony.

"So, anyhow," he said, "I think that the priest who wrote the spells over the false door where we came through made a mistake in the wording and it turned the false door into a doorway to our time."

He waited for her to object.

"Look," she said finally, "I really don't know how we got here. I just want to get out. Take me back there tomorrow and we'll push the door back open and I'll leave."

"It doesn't open anymore. I tried with Djefi. The inscriptions are different now," Imhotep said.

"So put them back the way they were," she said.

"I don't know what they were. Neither does Paneb. I asked him," he said.

"So who does? Find the guy who put them up there, find the guy who changed them."

Imhotep shook his head.

"They were drawn by the Priest of Thoth. His name was Waja-Hur and he was very old, Diane, I mean really old, especially for this time. Later when he inspected the tomb, he saw the mistake and wiped it out and drew the correct hieroglyphs."

"So get him. Aren't you like a commander or something?"

"I can't. Djefi killed him."

They sat together in silence, each looking out at the distant desert. Diane was filled with despair. She was determined to not let events or other people shape her life any longer and now, finally free of Djefi and Siamun, she was still under their thumb.

Imhotep had mixed feelings. He was sorry that Diane couldn't go home, but he was relieved that no one else would wander through the passage into ancient Egypt.

Taki's head appeared over the roof line as she climbed the stairs bringing them food. Ahmes was walking behind her, carrying a jar of beer and two cups.

Imhotep rose quickly and went to help Taki with the platter of food.

"Thank you," he said, taking the tray from her.

She glanced at Diane, but Imhotep stopped her from walking over to Diane. "Please, Taki, give us a few more minutes."

Ahmes had gone to Diane and, setting the two cups on the roof, poured beer for them. He set the jar of beer down and turned to follow his mother back down the stairs. He took two steps down and then, turning back toward the roof, he ran up the steps and crossed to Imhotep.

"Yes, Ahmes," Imhotep said.

The boy looked up at Imhotep, his eyes bright and excited. Reaching into the lock of hair that was gathered at the side of his head, he pulled out a shiny, plastic toothpick. "Is this yours, Lord Tim? I found it in the tomb when we came back from the Festival of Re."

Imhotep took the toothpick from the boy. He understood now why he couldn't find it earlier. But it didn't matter anymore, the inscriptions over the marked panel had been changed. It was just another painted wall.

Unless ...

Imhotep dropped to his knees before the boy and grabbed his shoulders excitedly. "Ahmes," he asked, "do you remember the inscriptions that were on that panel?"

"No," Ahmes answered, shaking his head. "There were too many to remember. But I copied them down."

The next day Imhotep, Paneb and Ahmes looked at the drawings.

"He is always copying the drawings," Paneb said, examining the sheet of papyrus. "His hand is getting surer. See, the lines are drawn without hesitation." He turned to Imhotep. "His early lines waver. They were without confidence. But look, now," he sounded like any proud parent.

Diane leaned over Imhotep's shoulder. "Do you know what they mean? Can you read them? Are these the right ones?"

"No, I haven't learned to read them. I will, though. I don't know if these are the right ones or not," Imhotep said.

"Should we get someone who can read them?" she asked. "Just to make sure they'll work."

Imhotep shook his head and answered in English. "I don't want anyone to know about these. I'll have Paneb paint these over the panel. We'll get you back to your time and then I'll change them back to the way they were. Then we'll destroy these," he said, nodding to the papyrus. "I don't want anyone like Djefi finding a way to get to your time or one of our modern day Djefis finding a way back here."

They left at dawn the next morning, walking quietly past Prince Teti and his soldiers who were sleeping off the beer from the night before.

"I don't know if Waja-Hur said any incantations as he drew the signs," Paneb told Imhotep as they reached the wadi.

Imhotep nodded. "I know, Paneb. This might not work. But we have to try now. King Djoser will be here in a few days and I want to have this finished and the papyrus burned before he arrives. No one must know about this. Once Brian is entombed, and the door is sealed, I'll feel better. But these," he clutched the drawings, "must be destroyed."

After Ahmes and Paneb set up the reflecting mirrors, Imhotep and Paneb went inside. They agreed on which panel had been changed and Paneb began to cover the new hieroglyphs and replace them with the ones Ahmes had drawn.

Imhotep went outside to wait with Diane who was sitting in the shade of the palm shelter, trying hard to not think about what she had seen in the clearing the day before.

"I keep wondering how things would have been different if I hadn't been angry with him that first night at To-She. Or if I had insisted that he come with us to Iunu. You could have talked with him then, we could have left with you and gone back to our time then," she said.

Imhotep thought back to the night Addy had gotten a phone call and drove away into the night. What if he had gone with her? What if her friend had been at a different restaurant? And as much as it hurt to think the thoughts, if Addy hadn't been killed he wouldn't have followed Diane and Brian here and he never would have met Meryt. The life that was growing inside her would never have been created.

"I think Brian changed here, Diane," Imhotep said. "He seemed different after he escaped from Kom Ombo. As awful as it sounds, I think he lived more in the time he was here than he would have if he hadn't encountered this land."

"He wouldn't be dead," she said.

"You don't know. He could have been hit by a bus, or eaten a bad meal. I mean, people die these strange, meaningless deaths all the time. Just random shit," he said angrily. Then he caught himself. "I'm sorry," he said. "It's just that we never know.

"We're all going to die, everyone knows that, but back in our time we keep ourselves so busy, so occupied with cell phones and texting, television shows, movies, parties, bars, nightclubs, fancy restaurants, sixty-hour-a-week jobs, shopping, buying clothes and furniture and jewelry, working to save up for a car, a house, a second house, a beach house. Here people have time to live, really live. I've done more, I mean drawing, making friends, doing things that really matter, than I did my entire life before.

"This is life stripped down to what matters, without the distractions," Imhotep said.

"You can do that back in our time," Diane said.

He shook his head. "I don't think so. Maybe if you're the Dalai Lama, but not ordinary people. I don't see how."

Diane shrugged and looked at the tomb entrance.

"I think you can. I think it's just a matter of deciding what you really are going to do and then doing it," she said, determination in her voice.

"I hope you're right," Imhotep said, getting to his feet. "It looks like Paneb's finished. Let's go."

Paneb and Ahmes waited outside the tomb under the palm canopy.

"Is Lord Tim leaving, too?" Ahmes asked.

Paneb shook his head. "His name is Imhotep now, Ahmes. King Djoser gave the name to him. And no, I don't think he is leaving. But with the gods, you never know."

Diane and Imhotep held hands as they walked down the tomb hallway.

"What should I do when I get there? I mean about Brian."

"I guess just say he's missing."

"Yeah. Shit, this is weird. His body is going to be in this tomb, isn't it? I mean when they find this tomb, his mummy will be in it, right?"

Imhotep shrugged. "I guess. There wasn't much information about the tomb in the guide books in your room."

"Who was this tomb being built for?" she asked, trying to keep her mind from worrying.

"It was for Kanakht, the king's vizier. But he betrayed the king and lost the right to eternal life."

She shook her head. "I still can't believe Brian is gone," she said.

She started to cry.

Imhotep squeezed her hand.

"We're here," he said, pointing to the freshly painted symbols above the door. "I'm sorry, Diane, but we have to do this now. We can't leave this doorway open for long. What if some other tourist is in the tomb?"

She nodded and wiped her eyes.

"Are you sure you want to leave?" he asked.

"Are you sure you want to stay?" she answered.

They turned to the panel and Imhotep raised his hands and placed them gently against the door. He looked at the wall and then over at Diane. Then he leaned into the wall, pressing hard.

He stepped back as the stone started to swing open.

They stood by the opening, feeling the stale air from the long closed tomb drift through the gap in the wall toward them. There was no sound nor light following the air from the tomb.

"It'll be morning, just like here, but five thousand years later. Here are three wooden matches that I brought with me. They're all I have left. They should last long enough for you to get back to the staircase. As soon as you're through, I'm going to paint over these symbols, so you won't be able to turn back."

She took the matches. "Wait until I have one of them lit and get through the hole in the other wall."

Imhotep nodded. "Goodbye Diane. I hope things go well for you."

She turned and stepped through the door. He watched as she struck the match against the stone wall, found her way to the break in the facing wall and stepped through.

He saw the light dim as the match burned out and then flare again as she lit the second match. Pushing shut the wall, he bent down for a brush. He hesitated for just a moment, listening through the wall.

Then he began to paint over the hieroglyphs.

EPILOGUE

The outlander renamed Ipy was buried in the unfinished tomb that was to be Kanakht's resting place.

King Djoser honored Ipy by attending the funeral, which his sister Hetephernebti conducted.

Tama, priestess to the goddess Ma'at, pronounced Ipy's heart truthful and light, assuring its owner passage to Khert-Neter. It was the first time anyone had seen the priestess cry during the ceremony of the weighing of the heart. A young wbt-priestess named Pahket assisted her.

Modern archaeologists who discovered the tomb could offer no explanation for the unusually large size of the sarcophagus.

King Djoser ruled for almost thirty years. The Stele of Sehel Island records his anguish over the seven-year famine and his success in persuading the god Khnum to unleash the waters of the river.

He was entombed in the Step Pyramid, the precursor of the more famous pyramids later built at Giza. His fame was overshadowed in later years by that of his famous adviser, Imhotep.

Imhotep directed the building of the Step Pyramid, and served King Djoser as adviser, official scribe, and personal physician. The ancient Egyptians regarded him so highly that he came to be viewed as a god himself.

His tomb has not been found.

IT'S HISTORY

Although this is a work of fiction, the ancient Egyptian world is depicted as accurately as the passage of five thousand years (and my limited knowledge) allows.

There is a Tomb of Kanakht at Saqqara. I was in it. Like Tim, I tripped, fell and rolled into the recessed hold of the sarcophagus.

There is a temple at Kom Ombo. It includes a chamber in which are stored the mummified remains of crocodiles, which were worshiped as the god Sobek. I saw them, too.

The hymn sung to Re by Hetephernebti is a translation of a prayer to the god from the time of King Djoser. (The ruler was called king, not pharaoh, in the Third Dynasty.)

Hetephernebti was either a wife or sister, or both, to King Djoser. I chose to make her a sister.

King Djoser did declare himself a god, and there was a devastating seven-year drought. Its history is recorded in the Famine Stele found near Aswan. The offerings King Djoser made to the god Khnum and his dream are recorded on the stele.

And Imhotep, Djoser's adviser and physician, was the architect of the Step Pyramid, the precursor to the more famous pyramids at Giza.

IMHOTEP

THE BURIED PYRAMID

Following is an excerpt from "The Buried Pyramid," the second novel in the tetralogy about the famous ancient architect Imhotep

THE BURIED PYRAMID

A novel by Jerry Dubs

HETEPHERNEBTI AND THE ONION

Alone in the walled garden behind her father's palace, thirteen-year-old Hetephernebti was determined to discover if she was ready to bear children.

Holding it by its grassy stem Hetephernebti dangled a small spring onion close to her face and sniffed. She rubbed her fingers over the small bulb making sure there was no dirt on it. With a fingernail she scraped off the hair-like roots at the bottom of the bulb and then she examined the pale green translucent root as if she would be able to see into its heart and understand the mystery of its power.

She shook her head. She didn't understand how it would work, but all the older girls told her that what she was about to do was necessary if she wanted to marry. With an ease that came from months of practice, she closed her eyes and conjured a picture of herself holding an infant to her breasts. She could feel the warmth of the baby's breath on her breast. She could feel his, yes, it would be a boy, weight on her arms and she could hear the soft whistle of his breath as he slept in her arms.

She opened her eyes from her dream and sighed.

She needed to be a mother.

Cupping her free hand over her mouth Hetephernebti exhaled. Her breath smelled fresh and clear, perhaps a little yeasty from bread she had eaten earlier. She shrugged and, opening her legs, she slowly slid the small onion bulb inside herself. Clamping her legs together to keep the onion within she picked up a small green faience figurine of Taweret, goddess of childbirth and fertility who took the form of a pregnant river hippopotamus with the tail of a crocodile. As Hetephernebti caressed the large snout of the goddess she realized that she had forgotten to ask how long she needed to keep the onion inside her.

If she were truly old enough to bear a child, then the fragrance of the onion would pass upward through her stomach and soon fill her mouth with its pungent aroma. If the gates to her womb were not yet open, well, she would try again next month.

She ran her hands over her body. Her breasts were small, barely formed, but she was sure that they would swell with milk if she were to have a child. Her concern was her hips. They were narrow, not the wide girdle of her mother, and even she grimaced in pain as she sat astride the birthing blocks. Hetephernebti didn't understand how a baby could pass through her own narrow channel.

She caressed the pregnant belly of the icon. The gods would provide.

Just then she heard the shouts of her younger brother. "Nebti! Nebti!"

She crossed her legs to hide the grassy stem that protruded from her.

"Yes, Djoser, I'm over here," she called.

Her eleven-year-old brother appeared from behind a cluster of young date palm trees. Unlike Hetephernebti who wore only a gold-threaded belt, Djoser was wearing a pleated kilt. His head was shorn except for a short sidelock.

"I'm going with father to Sinai! I'm going to have my own company, the Lion Company!" he shouted as he ran to her.

"That's wonderful," she said, standing to hug her little brother. Ever since he was old enough to pretend a stick was a spear, Djoser had played at being soldier. He was shorter than his older sister, but broad-shouldered, his ropy muscles growing stronger every day.

"I know," he agreed. "The Lion Company is from Sais, down in the delta. All the men are fishermen and hunters of hippos, so they have strong arms." He pulled his right arm back as if he were holding a spear. He threw the imaginary spear and grunted. "Like that," he said, laughing.

He stopped and pointed between her legs.

"What's that?"

Hetephernebti leaned toward him. She put her hands on either side of his head and held his face still. "Smell my breath," she said, exhaling.

Realizing that she was testing her fertility, Djoser pulled away. "Onions! You reek of onions!" he said and then he started to laugh.

She cupped her hand in front of her mouth and exhaled. Her breath was sweet as freshly baked bread. She frowned; there was not a hint of onion.

Djoser saw her disappointment and stopped laughing.

"I'm sorry, Nebti," he said solemnly. "I'm sure you'll have many, many children."

He started to smile, "You'll have so many children they'll have their own company in the army and I'll lead them." He backed away from her. "They'll be the Onion Company," he said as he turned to run through the garden.

Hetephernebti couldn't pretend to be angry with her little brother; they were more than siblings. They confided their dreams to each other, they confessed their fears and they wondered aloud about the many things they didn't understand.

Djoser often came into her room at night and told her stories about his training at the barracks near the palace.

He would relay rumors from other towns, always filling in the gaps in the stories with his own ideas of what had really happened, who had actually fought someone and who had boasted of things they would be too afraid to do.

As she lay on her bed listening to her little brother, Hetephernebti marveled not so much at his ability to remember all the details of each story but rather his understanding of why some of the boys lied and why others didn't. He intuitively grasped their characters, their weaknesses, and their desires.

She knew other boys his age feared not only Djoser's strength but also his position as prince of the Two Lands, but she thought that their fears were misplaced. It was his understanding and intelligence that were his true weapons.

Suddenly, she remembered the onion.

She checked her breath once more, shrugged at its stubborn sweetness and tugged the onion free. She started to toss it behind a young fig tree and then stopped. It wasn't the onion's fault. She found a clear spot in the garden and scooped a small hole in the ground. She put the onion bulb in the hole and brushed dirt over it. She straightened the straggly green leaves only to watch them sag again.

Sighing, she stood and clapped the dirt from her hands.

Her time would come.

She knew that the royal blood of the Two Lands passed through women. Her father, Kha-sekhemwy, was king, but it was because he had married Hetephernebti's mother, Menathap.

Hetephernebti paused at that thought.

Suddenly it didn't make sense to her that her mother would know who to marry, that she would be able to pick which of her suitors should become king. She wondered if instead the strongest man decided to become king and then he married a woman with royal blood to make himself legitimate.

She sat again.

What did that mean? Who would she marry?

There was Djoser, of course. He was Menathap's and Kha-sekhemwy's son and the prince of Kemet. It was natural that he would become king.

But what of Nebka? He was also Kha-sekhemwy's son, from a wife he had before he became king and took Menathap as his chief wife. Nebka was much older than Djoser, almost thirty years old. If something should happen to Kha-sekhemwy before Djoser was old enough to take the throne, then Nebka might be king even though he was not truly of royal blood.

She thought of him. He was taller than Djoser, but not as athletic. He spent his time in shadowy, lamp-lit rooms with scribes talking about …

Hetephernebti realized she had no idea exactly what her half-brother did. He never traveled with Kha-sekhemwy on military expeditions. He didn't wear the leopard skin of a priest. He wasn't married. He didn't hunt or fish. He didn't lead expeditions to Punt or Sinai.

I don't even know him, Hetephernebti thought. He might be king and I might become his wife and he is my father's son and I don't know him.

She walked over to the bare patch of ground where she had planted the disappointing onion. Saying a quick prayer to Renenutet, goddess of harvest, Hetephernebti squatted over the onion and watered it. Then, standing, she turned toward the palace.

Somewhere in there Nebka was doing whatever he did.

She would find out what that was.

THE TERRACES OF TURQUOISE

A month later on a distant mountain range King Kha-sekhemwy poured a handful of turquoise gems from his right hand to his left. Unpolished and rough, just pulled from the sandstone beneath the rocky ground, the stones were more brown than blue-green.

King Kha-sekhemwy motioned for Djoser to come closer.

"Cup your hands," he told his son. He poured the stones into Djoser's hands.

"What do you think, son? Worth dragging our ships across Deshret and sailing them across the Great Green? Worth marching through the red dust and climbing those jagged boulders to these hard, dark caves?"

They were standing in the shade of a small mud-brick hut near the cave entrance to one of more than a dozen mines at the Terraces of Turquoise, the richest gemstone deposit in Mafkat, the Land of Turquoise.

A month earlier, a few days before Hetephernebti tested her fertility, King Kha-sekhemwy had begun assembling his army of four thousand men, calling on the governors of each nome of the Two Lands to send men to Waset.

They had come from the delta region, racing upriver to beat the floods that would soon wash down the length of the River Iteru. Others had floated down the river from Abu. Some of the men were farmers whose lands would be flooded for the next three months; others were sons of bakers, weavers, fishermen or merchants; some were members of the standing militia from each nome; and others, mingled among them, a platoon within each company, were Nubian archers, tall, black mercenaries from the land beyond the first cataract.

In Waset their first job was to reassemble the wooden sledges kept to carry the flat-bottomed cedar fleet across the eastern desert to the banks of the Great Green, the sea that divided the Two Lands from Sinai, an empty land of deserts and red rock mountains.

Provisioned by merchants who grumbled about the king's demand for discounted prices but who were happy to find a voracious buyer for their bread and meat and grain, the army marched into the red desert they called Deshret, singing and taunting each other as they dragged the sand-bound fleet eastward. But as the green trees, brown water, and dark soil of Kemet disappeared from sight, and as the sledges seemed to grab at the sand as they slid over it, the taunting and singing were replaced by grunts and calls for water.

Leaner and with freshly callused hands and aching backs and legs, the army reached the shores of the Great Green. Across the narrow sea loomed the mountains of Mafkat. Far to the south was the land of Punt, source of gold and incense.

As the army launched itself into the Great Green, a small contingent of men watched from the shore, left behind to guard the sledges. They loudly cheered and silently laughed as the rest of the army, many of the men nervous about crossing the sea, bent to the oars and began to row to the east.

After two days, with a new set of muscles burning and aching, they beached their ships at Ras Abu-Rudeis, a small outpost set in front of distant, reddish mountains. Here King Kha-sekhemwy left another platoon of men to guard the beached fleet. The rest of the army, including Djoser's Lion Company, marched toward the eastern mountains. At the foot of the mountain range the army entered Wadi Martella, one of the many ancient, dried riverbeds that wound through the mountains.

A week of trekking, with pain finding a new collection of muscles, took them deep within the mountain range to the caves where the turquoise stones that decorated the royal jewelry and that provided the rich blues of the tomb paintings and the dyes for the royal linens were mined.

Now, standing before one of the caves, Djoser contemplated the dirty stones while behind him the army erected tents, began cook fires and took turns filling goat skins with water from a stream that trickled down from the mountain top.

King Kha-sekhemwy studied Djoser as the boy rubbed his thumbs across the turquoise gemstones.

"I talked with Sabef while we were marching here," Djoser said slowly.

"Sabef?"

"He is the leader of the Nubian archers in my company. He showed me how he works flint to create a sharp arrow head."

King Kha-sekhemwy raised an eyebrow. He had had little interaction with his youngest son until two years ago when the boy turned nine years old and was ready to begin military training.

Menathap had told him that Djoser was not an ordinary boy. King Kha-sekhemwy had smiled at her words, assuming them to be nothing more than the proud boast of a proud mother. She had seen his smile and shook her head at him, her eyes filled with knowledge that he didn't share.

"Yes, he is my son, our son, but I am not speaking as his mother, Hemwy," she had said. "There is a presence about him. He is an old soul, his Ba is not that of a child. The look of his eyes when he studies something, the care in his choice of words, his patience and his measured response to surprises, he has a wisdom beyond his years. It is almost … " she had hesitated until Kha-sekhemwy had nodded for her to continue, "I sometimes wonder if one of our ancestors, perhaps Narmer or Menes, has decided to return to the Two Lands."

King Kha-sekhemwy waited now for Djoser to explain himself.

"When Sabef began working the flint it was dull and useless, as these stones are now," Djoser said, raising his turquoise-laden hands. "But when Sabef was finished he had given the flint an edge so sharp that it drew blood when he pulled it across his thumb."

"So the turquoise is like the flint?" King Kha-sekhemwy said.

Djoser smiled. "Yes, father." He looked up to his father's broad face and met his eyes.

King Kha-sekhemwy had to stop himself from looking away from his son's penetrating gaze. After a moment Djoser smiled and slowly blinked his eyes, tacitly conceding his father's superior position.

"I think, King Kha-sekhemwy, Powerful One, Lord of Kemet, my beloved father, that stones, trees, earth, water, even men, especially men, are like that. They might seem to have little worth, but if they are worked and polished they become valuable."

King Kha-sekhemwy opened a linen bag and motioned for Djoser to pour the gems into it.

"A good lesson, Djoser," he said, beaming at his son. He tied the bag shut and turned to give it to an attendant. As he presented his vulnerable back to his son, King Kha-sekhemwy had a sudden thrill of fear.

Yes, the boy was only eleven years old. But he had not merely kept up with the men in the Lion Company in the long march across the red desert, he had led them, even taking his turn pulling the sledges. When they camped he was tireless, making sure the men had food and water before he attended to himself. Before he retired each night he always presented himself to Harkhuf, his battalion commander, to review his orders for the next day.

Rumors of his endurance and his strength - he could shoot an arrow nearly as far as the strongest Nubian archer and he could throw a spear farther than most of the men he commanded - had quickly reached King Kha-sekhemwy, which meant, the king knew, that everyone in the army had heard the rumors and soon the rumors would grow into legends.

Before long, King Kha-sekhemwy thought, my son will want to sit on the throne of the Two Lands. How many others, he wondered, have already had the same thought?

King Kha-sekhemwy and Djoser peered over the ridge of a small sand dune. Behind them ten men from the first platoon of Djoser's Lion Company quietly shuffled along the base of the shifting sand.

The hunting party had left the day before, winding their way down twisting mountain passes to the endless desert east of the mountain range. King Kha-sekhemwy had left the army behind under the command of General Babaef, who led the Upper Division of the army. Babaef had the unexciting job of overseeing repairs to the mines, taking inventory of the turquoise treasure and clearing fallen boulders from the trails connecting the mines.

Meanwhile, the king would enjoy a hunt.

But the king had left in a bad mood.

Babaef, a thin, humorless man, with his own small army of aides and scribes, insisted that everything be done properly. It was a good quality in an administrator, but an irritant when Babaef turned that same unwavering attention to the king, which is what happened when Babaef had insisted on knowing where the king was going.

King Kha-sekhemwy, silently bridling under Babaef's attention, had pointed east and said he would be over there. Babaef had shaken his head, barely perceptibly, but enough to let the king know that his answer wasn't sufficient. Then he had produced a clean piece of linen and sketched a rough map of the mountain passes. He handed the charcoal stick to King Kha-sekhemwy and asked him to mark the pathways he planned to take.

Whichever path I want, the king wanted to say, but faced with Babaef's implacable insistence and surrounded by the general's lieutenants, King Kha-sekhemwy knew his general would lose face if he refused his request. So, feeling like a schoolboy, he had solemnly marked a trail on the map and then commended Babaef for his excellent planning.

At the first fork in the wadi, King Kha-sekhemwy had chosen the opposite path from the one he had marked on the map. Then, looking over his shoulder, he thought he saw movement behind him. He shook his head; Babaef had anticipated the king's contrariness and had sent a spy to map his actual route.

It would feel good to drive my spear into the side of a gazelle, King Kha-sekhemwy had thought.

Now, with warm sand pooling around his ankles as he stood on the slope of a small dune, King Kha-sekhemwy could see a small herd of gesa, straight-horned gazelles, gathered around a pool in one of the streams that ran along the edge of the mountains.

Sabef, the Nubian archer, waited just behind the king and prince. He carried his own bow, a weapon nearly as long as the Nubian himself made of two curved antelope horns joined at the center with a shaft of ebony wood.

Pointing off to his right with his bow, Sabef grunted.

King Kha-sekhemwy nodded.

"Do you see them, Djoser?" he asked.

Djoser had seen the small billow of sandy dust and the straight lines of the gazelles' horns when they had first mounted the ridge, but he had waited for his father to point them out.

"Yes, King Kha-sekhemwy," he said, speaking formally while Sabef was near enough to hear. "Do you think there will be lions also?"

"Perhaps," King Kha-sekhemwy said. "More likely foxes, maybe even one of the spotted cats. But the gesa are better eating."

Eyes closed, the king slowly turned his wide face to catch a sense of the direction of the wind. Behind them Sabef gathered a handful of sand and let it slide from his fist watching to see where the air took the dust from the sand.

King Kha-sekhemwy sensed the motion behind him. He turned to Sabef and pointed off to their right. "Yes?" he asked. Sabef, his skin so black that his eyes and teeth seemed to float in a living shadow, nodded agreement. The wind was coming from the north, toward them from the gesa.

"Over this way," King Kha-sekhemwy said to the men below them on the sandy ridge. He motioned to his left.

"We'll stay below the ridge line as long as we can, moving downwind of the gesa," he told Djoser as they slid down the dune.

"Sabef and I could go in the other direction," Djoser suggested. "I know that our scent could alarm them, but we could move more slowly than you, staying off wind from the gesa. Then when you signal, we could let them see us."

King Kha-sekhemwy considered the question for a moment, then he nodded agreement. It was a small request and it would give Djoser a sense of independence. If it worked, the gazelles would move away from Djoser and into the spears of the king's hunting party.

"Yes, Djoser," he said. "Move slowly. When you have circled around them, approach the crest of the dune but do not cross it. I will signal when my men are in place." Then he extended his right arm, his hand sideways and open. Surprised by the offer, Djoser hesitated and then he reached forward and clasped his hand around his father's forearm, feeling King Kha-sekhemwy's strong grip on his forearm in return.

"Thank you, father," he said, tears suddenly threatening to fill his eyes.

"Good hunting," King Kha-sekhemwy said, breaking off the embrace and silently moving down the dune.

The king's hunting party killed three of the fast-sprinting gazelles. They carried the slain animals back to the small watering hole where the gesa had first been spotted. One of the hunters had directed the digging of a roasting pit where the gutted animals were laid after a bed of coals had been fired and banked.

While the meat roasted, the soldiers, filled with energy after the successful hunt, raced each other and wrestled before cooling off in the shallow pool surrounded by date palms. King Kha-sekhemwy watched the contests from the shade, but Djoser, brimming with energy had joined the soldiers.

In his wrestling match he surprised one stocky soldier with his speed and his understanding of leverage and body joint locks. He quickly brought the larger man to the ground but the stronger and heavier man eventually gained the advantage, holding Djoser's squirming shoulders against the sand.

Afterward, instead of sulking at his defeat, Djoser threw an arm around the winner's shoulders and asked him to teach him how he had been able to gain the advantage when they were on the ground.

In an archery contest Djoser was as accurate as the Nubians but his bow, a smaller bow made of sycamore, didn't generate the power to send an arrow through the small copper target that was pinned against a palm tree trunk.

After watching Sabef bury arrow after arrow in the heart of the target, Djoser asked to try the antelope-horn bow. His arms weren't long enough to draw the string as fully as the Nubian could and so his arrows, lacking speed, still bounced off the metal target.

"I need a smaller bow," Djoser said.

"Or longer arms, my prince," Sabef told him.

"Then I would look like one of Thoth's baboons," Djoser said with a laugh.

King Kha-sekhemwy watched, wondering if Djoser would imitate one of the knuckle-walking monkeys, but to the king's relief, Djoser's innate dignity drew the line at monkey imitations.

As the contests wound down, Djoser suggested one more game: throwing sticks.

Similar in shape to boomerangs, but smaller and more rounded, throwing sticks were used to hunt ducks in the marshlands of the delta. Although they were used in combat, they were more of a distraction than a weapon, something to draw a fighter's attention away from a spear thrust or the swing of a wooden club.

The men balanced a severed antelope head on a rock and then tried to hit it with their throwing sticks. It was soon apparent that Djoser was incredibly accurate and the contest evolved into Djoser trying to hit the antelope head from greater and greater distances while the men cheered each success.

Once he had reached the limit of his arm, Djoser started trying to hit the antelope head while he was running. After one throw, one of the hunters picked up Djoser's throwing stick and softly threw it back toward him. Instead of waiting for it to land, Djoser ran forward and snatched it from the air. Soon a game of catch developed and after a short while the men were left with bruised arms from missed catches and humbled egos from watching Djoser's speed and reflexes.

"Next you'll be catching spears and arrows," King Kha-sekhemwy told him as they settled to eat the roasted antelope.

Instead of laughing, Djoser stopped tearing at the meat and looked at his father.

"Has anyone done that?" Djoser asked. "I think it would be possible, at least with spears. I think arrows would be too fast and their shafts aren't long enough." He darted out his right hand and pretended to grab a flying arrow. "No, father, I don't think I could catch arrows."

He went back to pulling at the meat. Holding a chunk of it, he tore off a bite with his teeth. After he swallowed, he said, "I might give spears a try."

"I would suggest blunt ones at first," King Kha-sekhemwy said with a grin.

"Thrown by children," Djoser added with a laugh. Then he said quietly, "Thank you, father. Thank you for bringing me with you."

King Kha-sekhemwy smiled back and said, "We're near one of Hathor's temples."

"Hathor, here?" Djoser asked.

King Kha-sekhemwy nodded. He pointed back into the mountain range. "Here she is called Lady of Turquoise. There is a temple up that wadi, a day's walk."

"Are we going there?"

King Kha-sekhemwy shook his head.

"No, I am staying here at the edge of the mountains where there is water and game. I'll have plenty of mountain climbing when we go back to the mines."

Djoser nodded assent.

"You can go," King Kha-sekhemwy said.

Djoser looked up eagerly. Like his sister, he was fascinated by the gods, always eager to learn more, to wander the temples, to touch the sacred statues, to stare at the painted scenes of the gods' lives, to listen to the priests tell the stories.

"Yes, I mean it," King Kha-sekhemwy said. "Take your archer with you. There isn't much there, however, Djoser. It is very small, hardly decorated and no one lives there. But the miners go there to ask Hathor for guidance. There are Sleeping Chambers where the miners receive visions of where to search for gemstones."

The king smiled. "It must work, we've seen the gems. Spend the night there, perhaps you'll dream of riches."

King Kha-sekhemwy stood and stretched his arms above his head.

Releasing a satisfied sigh, he pointed along the base of the mountain ridge. "I'll take the hunting party up that way," King Kha-sekhemwy said. "I'd like to kill one of the spotted cats. The pelt would make a beautiful robe for your mother.

"It might take you a full day to reach the temple, another to return. So, we'll meet here in three days."

With water-filled goatskins and dangling shoulder pouches packed with leftover meat, Djoser and Sabef left at dawn. Before they left, King Kha-sekhemwy gave Djoser a small packet of incense. "An offering to Hathor," he said. The he added wryly, "Never approach a temple with empty hands."

Djoser and Sabef turned their backs to the rising sun and began to climb the rock-strewn wadi. The mountain wasn't steep, but the pathway was never clear. The faint trail often disappeared beneath boulders that they were forced to climb and then search for traces of the path farther up the mountainside.

They climbed steadily for two hours and then, as the morning sun began to burn down on them they found shade beside a large, jagged overhang and drank some water and flexed their cramping legs.

Looking down across the desert that stretched away from the base of the mountain Djoser saw choppy waves of sand. Unlike the smooth desert on the western side of the River Iteru, this one was scraggy and littered with sharp rock outcroppings and tufts of high, dry grass.

Although last night's campsite was marked by ripples of sand, like a rumpled bed linen, and a trace of darker color, ashes from the campfires, King Kha-sekhemwy and the hunting party were no longer in sight. Djoser shielded his eyes from the rising sun and looked south, but there was no sign of movement. The king had been in a hurry.

Leaning against the mountain, Djoser breathed deeply and smiled. All his life he had been surrounded and protected. There were always adults with him … teachers, military instructors, his mother, palace guards. Now, except for Sabef, he was alone. There was no one to tell him where to go, what to say or what to do.

He wished Hetephernebti could experience this. She, of all the people he knew, would appreciate the solitude.

He looked at Sabef to see if he was feeling the same thrill of being alone. The Nubian was crouched, his hands idly playing with loose pebbles. His eyes were on the northern horizon, his lips turned into a small frown.

"Sabef, what is it?" Djoser asked.

The Nubian shook his head.

"Do you see something? A lion or one of father's spotted cats? Desert-dwellers?"

Sabef rose to his feet and pointed to the north, back up the curve of the plateau that the hunting party had followed earlier.

"I don't know. I thought I saw a change in the air."

"A whirlwind?" Djoser asked, swirling a finger like a cyclone.

Sabef shook his head. "No, the way the air danced above the rocks seemed to change."

"What does that mean? Is it a sign?" Djoser asked. Although he was not a tracker, he knew that more experienced men could read ripples in the water, the change of a bird's flight, the widening of a camel's eye.

"I think it was a lizard taking a piss on a hot rock." He watched Djoser's face for a smile and then started to laugh when he saw that Djoser wasn't offended by the joke.

As Djoser turned to continue the climb, Sabef paused and took another studied look at the edge of the plateau; the change in the air could have been a campfire being smothered. Someone was following the hunting party.

Another two hours brought them to a series of steps cut into a steeper passage. A shallow, loose stone wall followed the path here. Beyond the wall, the mountain simply stopped, falling away to a rock-strewn valley.

At the top of the cut steps, the path wound to their right following a curve of the mountain where a small ledge had been widened. There was no protection here, just a straight drop from the narrow path.

Walking in front, Sabef took pains to keep his eyes away from the abyss, but Djoser paused, peering into the emptiness and imagining what it would feel like to be a hawk soaring through the blue space between Nut, the sky goddess, and Geb, her earthly husband. He looked at the crumpled mountain below him and the low-lying plateau off to the north.

For a moment he thought he saw movement, a group of darker specks against the brown earth. Then his attention was drawn to the sound of cascading stones and a loud grunt from Sabef.

Turning, Djoser saw Sabef's muscled back and legs and at his feet, a gaping hole where a piece of the mountain had crumbled way leaving a gap in the trail. Sabef was on the other side of the breach, leaning against the mountain and breathing heavily.

The path was narrow here and the mountainside sloped more steeply toward the precipice. Whoever had cut the trail hadn't widened the base enough and now a small section of it was gone.

"I was almost a bird, my prince, when I need to be a goat," Sabef said. He reached a hand across the opening to Djoser.

To reach across to Djoser, Sabef had to stand as close as possible to the gap in the trail. His position left no place for Djoser to step. Djoser shook his head and motioned for the Nubian to back away. Then, without hesitation, Djoser jumped across the opening. He felt the air support him as if the hand of Osiris, son of Nut and Geb, lord of the afterlife, was shielding him from harm.

And as he floated above the abyss Djoser had a sudden premonition that something evil was stalking him but that he would be protected.

The temple was a disappointingly small cave with a pair of stone stele the height of a man by the entrance.

Djoser and Sabef peered into the darkness and then walked past it, looking for something grander. But they were atop a high plateau now, the flat cap of the mountain and there were no structures in sight.

They walked about the plateau, enjoying the view of the reddish-brown mountains that stepped away from them, sharp and steep as crocodile teeth. Off to the south and westward toward the Great Green Sea the mountain range continued beyond their vision, hidden at the far horizon by a haze of heat.

Eastward they could see the desert spreading out, the brown sand turning bluish gray far in the distance until it merged with the sky, Geb and Nut united.

They walked back to the cave entrance and found a stone bowl on a ledge just inside the opening. Djoser filled the bowl with some of the incense his father had given him and then lit it. A tendril of white smoke rose from the bowl and streamed into the cave.

"There is an opening inside," Sabef said, "pulling the smoke to it."

"The Sleeping Chamber?" Djoser said as he sat at the cave opening and drank from the goatskin. He passed the bag to Sabef. The Nubian took the bag and drank deeply.

"Are there mountains like this in Nubia?" Djoser asked Sabef.

"We call it Ta-Seti," Sabef said, passing the water back to Djoser.

He picked up his antelope bow and shook it. "Ta-Seti means Land of The Bow. It is much like Kemet. There is the river and that is all. Beyond it only sand. Small hills, but no mountains like this."

Djoser had heard old soldiers, men in their thirties, talking about the land of Punt where the sky was obscured by overhanging trees so no one wore kohl to protect their eyes and where the air was so full of moisture that no oil was needed for the skin.

Someday, Djoser thought, I'll lead an expedition there.

But now he was here, atop a barren mountain and a simple cave dedicated to Hathor.

He jumped to his feet and stepped into the cave. With his back to the light, he waited for his eyes to adjust to the darkness. In a few moments he saw that the entrance room led to an opening as wide as two men. A faint gray light came from the passage. He walked toward it.

The passage opened into a larger chamber with smoother walls that had obviously been worked. There were paintings of Hathor, her twin horned-headdress supporting the red orb of the sun. Unlike the few paintings Djoser had seen on urns in temples in Waset, here Hathor's eyes were larger and rounder. Her chin receded creating a short snout, making her face look cow-like. He wondered if the difference was because of the artist's unpracticed hand, or if he intended to give the goddess more of an animal form.

Again his thoughts went to his sister and her curiosity about all the gods. He wondered if she had had any luck with the onion. *And what happens when she does? Will she marry King Kha-sekhemwy who already has a chief wife and three minor wives? Will she marry me? Or Nebka, our half-brother? Or someone I don't know?*

The questions tugged at him for a moment and then Djoser shook his head lightly. They were questions that couldn't be answered and so he would put them aside.

"This must be the Sleeping Chamber," Sabef said from beyond the larger central room.

Djoser followed Sabef's voice to a circular chamber with niches cut into the wall, spaced out around the entire room. Rough hides hung from the wall and when Sabef lifted one to examine it, light poured through behind it. He raised the hide higher and they saw a rough-cut opening in the cave wall that admitted sunlight.

The additional light showed white ashes in the niches.

Pointing to the ashes, Djoser asked, "Incense?"

"Our holy men do this," Sabef said, looking around the dark chamber. "They enclose themselves in darkness and burn seeds from a plant we call sikran. Then the gods come to them and speak through them."

He nodded respectfully at the wall niches. "Very holy."

"Do they see the future?" Djoser asked.

"Yes, the future. They see who will be your wife, they see how to cure someone, they see why the gods are angry and what to do about it. They can see who will be king," Sabef said.

"Do you have this sikran?" Djoser asked.

Sabef shook his head. "I am not a shaman." He held his bow and smiled at Djoser. "This tells me my future. If I shoot true, I live." He tossed his head back and laughed.

"Don't you want to know your future?" Djoser asked him.

"No!" Sabef said without hesitation. "If I see something bad, then I will worry. If I see something good, then I will stop working and wait for it. It might not come, then I will worry if I have done something wrong and the gods are angry with me. For me, my prince, it is better to know where my next step will fall. That is enough."

Djoser nodded understanding, but he said softly, "I would like to see beyond that. I would like to talk with the gods." *Or be a god,* he thought.

AUTHOR'S NOTE

I extend a huge thank-you to the hundreds of readers who have posted reviews of Imhotep. It is humbling and thrilling to read your comments.

This edition of Imhotep has been thoroughly edited and corrected (most recently in December, 2016) to eliminate the grammatical errors or misspellings some readers found. And, on re-reading the novel after a few years, I decided that the harsh and profane language used by some of the characters was unnecessary. It has been removed. The f-bomb has been defused.

One reviewer pointed out that camels were not used in Egypt at the time my story takes place. He is right. I tried to make everything historically accurate – names, the size of communities, foods, which gods were in ascent, festivals, dress, weapons, and so on. I did not check on those darn camels. Mea culpa.

In response to requests from readers I have extended Imhotep's story.

"The Buried Pyramid," which is both a prequel and a sequel to this story, is available for the Kindle through Amazon. The first two chapters of it are appended to the end of "Imhotep."

"The Forest of Myrrh" is the third novel in the series. Its narrative continues the story told in "The Buried Pyramid." It is also available on Amazon for the Kindle reader.

The fourth, and final, novel about Imhotep, "The Field of Reeds," was published in August, 2015.

Reluctant to leave the Two Lands, and curious about what might have happened after the events described at the end of "The Field of Reeds," I decided to write a sequel to the Imhotep series. Published in December of 2016, the novel is called "Suti and the Broken Staff." I hope you take a look at it.

Cheers!
Jerry Dubs, December 12, 2016

ABOUT THE AUTHOR

A journalist for more than 30 years, Jerry Dubs won numerous awards for reporting and for graphic design. He and his wife are vagabonds who wander the southeast searching for warm weather and well-kept tennis courts.

He can be contacted at jerrydubs@imhotepliterary.com

Printed in Great Britain
by Amazon

37267709R00253